JAMES LEE BURKE
Three Great Novels

James Lee Burke
Three Great Novels

Dixie City Jam
Burning Angel
Purple Cane Road

ORION

Dixie City Jam Copyright © 1994 James Lee Burke
Burning Angel Copyright © 1995 James Lee Burke
Purple Cane Road Copyright © 2000 James Lee Burke

This omnibus edition first published in Great Britain in 2002 by Orion,
an imprint of the Orion Publishing Group Ltd.

A CIP catalogue record for this book is available
from the British Library.

ISBN 0 75285 352 X (hardback)
ISBN 0 75285 353 8 (trade paperback)

Typeset by Deltatype Ltd, Birkenhead, Merseyside

Printed in Great Britain by Clays Ltd, St Ives plc

The Orion Publishing Group Ltd
Orion House
5 Upper Saint Martin's Lane
London, WC2H 9EA

Contents

Dixie City Jam

for Porteus and Alice Burke

1

Not many people believe this, but in the early months of 1942 Nazi submarines used to lie in wait at the mouth of the Mississippi for the tankers that sailed without naval escort from the oil refineries at Baton Rouge into the Gulf of Mexico.

It was a shooting gallery. Because of wartime censorship the newspapers and radio carried no accounts of the American ships sunk off the Louisiana coast, but just after sunset people could see the oil fires burning on the southern horizon, like a quickening orange smudge low in the winter sky.

As a little boy in New Iberia, I heard shrimpers talk about the burned, oil-coated bodies of four merchant sailors who had been found floating like lumps of coal in an island of kelp, their sightless eyes and poached faces strung with jellyfish.

I had nightmares for many years about Nazis, who I imagined as pinch-faced, slit-eyed creatures who lived beneath the waves, not far from my home, and who would eventually impose a diabolical design upon the earth.

While scuba diving in college, on a calm, windless day, I accidentally found one of those submarines in sixty feet of water, resting at an angle on its keel, the deck rails and forward gun gray and fuzzy with seaweed, a chain of tiny bubbles rising from the stern.

My heart was tripping against my rib cage, the blood vessels tightening in my head, but I refused to be undone by my childhood fears, and I swam down to the twisted remains of the periscope until I could see the swastika and ship's numbers painted on the side of the conning tower.

I took my bowie knife from the scabbard on my side, and, like the primitive warrior who must touch the body of a slain enemy, I tapped with the butt of the knife on the conning tower's rim.

Then one of the strangest occurrences of my life took place.

I felt a bone-numbing coldness in the water, where there had been none before; then a sound, a vibration, like a wire cable snapping, rang through the entire length of the submarine. The conning tower began to right itself in the current, the metal plates on the hull grating on the sand, and clouds of silt and trapped oil rose from under the keel. I watched in horror as the submarine seemed to poise itself just above the gulf's floor, streamers of moss fanning back from the tower like tattered battle flags, then dip its bow downward into the darkness and slide over the edge of the continental shelf, my bowie knife toppling onto the rising stern, while sand sharks spun like minnows in the wake of its screws.

I discovered later that there was no mystery about the U-boat. It had been caught recharging its batteries on the surface, shelled by a U.S. Navy destroyer, then blown out of the water by depth charges, its spine broken; since that time it had scudded and bounced with the currents up and down the floor of the gulf along the Louisiana coast.

But sometimes in a dark moment I wondered about the crew that had gone down in a scream of sirens and whistles and torrents of water bursting through the ruptured plates or cascading down the tower that no one could close in time. Did they claw one another off the ladders? Were they willing to blind or maim or kill one another just to breathe air for a few more seconds? Did they regret embracing the scheme that would make the lights go out all over the world?

Or were they still sailing beneath the waves, their skins pickled in salt, their uniforms nests for moray eels, their plan to turn the earth into a place of concertina wire and guard towers still on track, as certain in prospect as the phosphorescent and boiling wake of a torpedo streaking toward a distant ship silhouetted against an autumnal moon?

It had been a strange day out on the salt. The wind was hot and sere out of the south, and in the swells you could see the shiny backs of stingrays and the bluish pink air sacs of jellyfish, which meant a storm was probably kicking them in toward shore; then the barometer dropped, the wind died, and the sun looked like a white flame trapped inside the dead water.

It rained for only about five minutes, large, flat drops that struck the water like lead shot, then the sky was clear and hot again and the sweat and humidity ran off your skin like snakes. Far to the south I could see the storm become stationary. Gray clouds were anchored low on the horizon, and right where they met the water there was a white line of surf and an occasional fork of lightning, like silver threads trembling inside the clouds.

While Batist, the black man who worked for me, put out the lines for gafftop catfish, I slipped on my air tanks, flippers, and mask and went over the side, following the anchor rope down through the cone of translucent green light, down to a level of water that was suddenly cold and moving and gray with silt, spinning with yellow blades of seaweed, perhaps alive with sand sharks that could whisk past you with such energy and force that you felt you had been struck by an invisible hand.

The anchor rope was taut and hard when I touched it. Above me I could see the silhouette of my boat's hull wobbling against the light, the bow dipping into the chop against the pull of the anchor. I blew my mask clear and went down ten more feet along the rope, into a barrel of darkness, of swirling silt that had been blackened with oil, into sounds that shouldn't have been there – metal knocking against itself, like a ball peen hammer bouncing idly off an anvil, steel plates grinding across hard-packed sand, perhaps wire cables lifting in the current and lighting on twisted spars.

I gave it up and headed for the surface, rising once more into water bladed with sunlight, into the predictable world of wind and salt spray blowing against the mask, of gulls and pelicans gliding overhead, of Batist straining with both hands against a stingray he had foul-hooked through the stomach.

I pulled off my tanks and rubbed my head and face dry with a towel. Batist was stripped to the waist, his back knotted with muscle, his cannonball head popping with sweat as he got the gaff into the stingray and lifted it over the gunwale. The gaff had gone all the way through one of the ray's leathery wings. Batist flopped it on its back, shook the gaff loose, then knelt on one knee and sawed the treble hook out of its stomach. He wiped the blood off his knife, looked at the bent prongs on his hook, then flung the ray overboard with both hands.

'How far down was you, Dave?' he said.

'Thirty or forty feet maybe.'

'Ain't smart. They's a lot of trash down there. They's even trees, yeah, you know that? They float all the way down the Miss'sippi. Some big as your house.'

'I suspect you're right.'

'Well?' He put a cigar in the corner of his mouth.

'What?'

'You found that sub down there?'

'I heard some metal banging around, but I don't know what it is. It's too murky to see anything.'

'Maybe it's a wrecked oil rig down there. You t'ink of that? Maybe you gonna get tangled up in it, lose your life, Dave, all 'cause that Hippo fellow wavin' ten t'ousand dollars around. He want that sub, let him get his fat butt out here and look for it.'

'Okay, Batist.'

'It don't do no good to be rich in the graveyard, no.'

'I'm getting your drift. I really appreciate it.'

'You ax me my opinion.'

'How about we catch some fish?'

'That's what I been tryin' to do. Except somebody been swimmin' around under my line.'

Hippo Bimstine was a mover in the state Democratic party and probably owned half of the drugstores in New Orleans. His girth was elephantine, his bejeweled, pudgy fingers and yellow-and-black checkered sports coats legendary. On any given afternoon you could see him in the Pearl on St Charles, eating anywhere from five to eight dozen oysters on the half shell, washing them down with pitchers of beer, his thick neck powdered with talcum, a purple rose in his lapel, his jowls freshly shaved and glowing with health, his eyes squinting almost completely shut when he smiled. Years ago I had told him the story about the wreck of the German U-boat I had discovered on a calm summer day when I was in college. Last week a friend of Hippo's, a charter skipper out of Cocodrie, said his sonar had pinged a huge metal object just south of Grand Isle. Hippo remembered the story about the sunken sub, called me in New Iberia, and said he would pay a ten-thousand-dollar finder's fee if I could locate the sub and he could salvage it.

'What are you going to do with a World War II U-boat, Hippo?' I said.

'Are you kidding? You ever see this Geraldo guy on TV? He had millions of people watching him dig into a basement wall under a Chicago hotel where Al Capone used to live. He had everybody believing there was a car, dead bodies, gold bars, machine guns, all kinds of bullshit, buried in this underground vault. The show went on for three hours. It was so boring you had to keep slapping yourself awake. You know what he found? A big pile of wet sand and some old bottles. He also almost punched a hole in the retaining wall that keeps Lake Michigan out of the city of Chicago.

'You know what I could do with a sub full of drowned Nazis? Use your imagination, Dave.'

But I had struck out. And it was just as well. Hippo's projects were usually as grandiose and thespian as his epicurean consumption of seafood in the Pearl, and if you became involved with him for very long, you began to realize that perhaps you had not successfully avoided the role of court jester in this life after all.

Batist and I caught and gutted over a dozen gafftop, ripped out the stingers and peeled the skin with pliers, fileted the meat in long, pink strips, and laid them out in rows on the crushed ice in the cooler. Then we ate the po'-boy sandwiches we'd made with fried oysters, mayonnaise, *sauce piquant*, sliced tomatoes, and onions and wrapped in waxed paper that morning; then we headed back toward the coast as the afternoon cooled and the wind began to blow out of the west, smelling of distant rain and speckled trout spawning and beached shellfish and lines of seaweed drying where the tide had receded from the sand.

As the late red sun seemed to collapse and melt into a single burning ember on the horizon, you could see the neon glow of New Orleans gradually replace the daylight and spread across the darkening sky. The clouds were black-green and low over the city, dancing with veins of lightning, roiling from Barataria all the way out to Lake Pontchartrain, and you knew that in a short while torrents of rain would blow through the streets, thrash the palm trees on the esplanades, overrun the gutters in the Quarter, fill the tunnel of oak trees on St Charles with a gray mist through which the old iron, green-painted streetcars would make their way along the tracks like emissaries from the year 1910.

New Orleans was a wonderful place to be on a late evening in August.

That's what I thought, anyway, until I called Hippo Bimstine to tell him that he'd have to hire somebody else to dive the wrecks of Nazi submarines.

'Where are you?' he said.

'We're having supper at Mandina's, out on Canal.'

'You still tight with Clete Purcel?'

'Sure.'

'You know where Calucci's Bar is by St Charles and Carrollton?'

'Yeah, it's across from your house, isn't it?'

'That's right. So right now I'm looking out my window at a shitstorm in the making. I'm talking about they got a SWAT team out there. Can you believe that? A fucking SWAT team in the middle of my neighborhood. I think they could use a diplomat out there, before the meat loaf ends up on the wallpaper, you get my meaning?'

'No.'

'The salt water still in your ears, Dave?'

'Look, Hippo—'

'It's Clete Purcel. He went apeshit in Calucci's and ran one guy all the way through the glass window. The guy's still lying in the flower bed. They say Purcel's got two or three others in there on their knees. If he don't come out, there's a supervising plainclothes in front says they're gonna smoke him. I got fucking Beirut, Lebanon, in my front yard.'

'Who's the supervising officer?'

'A guy named Baxter. Yeah, Nate Baxter. He used to be in Vice in the First District. You remember a plainclothes by that name? . . . Hey, Dave, you there?'

2

Calucci's Bar had been fashioned out of an old white frame house, with tin awnings on the windows, in an old residential neighborhood at the end of St Charles by the Mississippi levee. The rain looked like purple and green and pink sleet in the neon glow from the bar, and on the far side of the levee you could see mist rising off the river and hear horns blowing on a tug-boat.

The street in front of the bar was filled with a half dozen emergency vehicles, their revolving lights reflecting off the shrubs and wet cement and the palm trees on the esplanade. When Batist and I parked my pickup truck by the curb I saw Nate Baxter in the midst of it all, rainwater sluicing off his hat, his two-tone shoes and gray golf slacks splattered from passing cars. His neatly trimmed reddish beard was glazed with wet light, his badge and chrome-plated revolver clipped on his belt, his body hard and muscular with middle age and his daily workouts at the New Orleans Athletic Club.

A flat-chested black woman plainclothes, with skinny arms and a mouthful of gold teeth, was arguing with him. She wore a rumpled brown blouse that hung out of her dark blue slacks, makeup that had streaked in the rain, and loafers without socks. Nate Baxter tried to turn away from her, but she moved with him, her hands on her thin hips, her mouth opening and closing in the rain.

'I'm talking to you, Lieutenant,' she said. 'It's my opinion we have a situation that's gotten out of hand here. The response is not proportionate to the situation. Not in my opinion, sir. If you persist, I plan to file my own report. Are you hearing me, sir?'

'Do whatever you feel like, Sergeant. But please go do it somewhere else,' Baxter said.

'I'm responding to the call. I resent your talking to me like that, too,' she said.

'All right, I'll put it a little more clearly. You're a nuisance and a pain in the ass. You want to make a civil rights case out of that, be my guest. In the meantime, get out of here. That's an order.'

A uniformed white cop laughed in the background.

Baxter's eyes narrowed under the brim of his hat when he saw me.

'What are you doing, Nate?' I said.

He ignored me and began talking to a cop in a bullet-proof vest and a bill cap turned backwards on his head.

'What are you trying to do to Clete Purcel?' I said.

'Stay behind the tape, Robicheaux,' he said.

'I can talk him out of there.'

'You're out of your jurisdiction.'

Even in the rain his breath was heated and stale.

'Nobody needs to get hurt here, Nate,' I said.

'Purcel dealt the play, not me. You know what? I think he's been looking for this moment all his life.'

'Have you called him on the phone?'

'That's a good idea, isn't it? I'd really like to do that. Except he tore it out of the wall and wrapped it around a guy's throat. Then he rammed the guy through the front window.'

'The Calucci brothers are mobbed up. It's some kind of personal beef between them and Clete, you know it is. You don't call out a SWAT team on barroom bullshit.'

'We've got a vigilante loose in New Orleans, too. I think Purcel's a perfect suspect.'

I could feel my palms open and close at my sides. Baxter was talking again to the cop in the vest, pointing at a high area on the levee.

'You're not going to get away with this,' I said.

'End of conversation, Robicheaux.'

'Clete stuck your head in a toilet bowl in a bar on Decatur,' I said. 'You didn't report it because he knew you were taking freebies from street hookers in the Quarter. That's what all this is about, Nate.'

Four white cops, as well as the black woman, were staring at us now. The skin around Nate Baxter's right eye was pinched like a marksman's when he sights along a rifle barrel. He started to speak, but I didn't give him the chance.

I held my Iberia Parish Sheriff's Department badge high above my head and walked toward the front door of the bar.

Clete had dropped the venetian blinds over all the windows and was leaning on the bar counter, one foot on the rail, drinking Mexican rum from a shot glass and sucking on a salted lime. He wore his powder blue porkpie hat slanted on the front of his head, his pants hanging two inches below his navel. His round, pink face was smiling and happy, his green eyes lighted with an alcoholic shine. Through one eyebrow and across the bridge of his nose was a scar, as thick as a bicycle patch, perforated with stitch holes, where he had been bashed with a pipe when he was a kid in the Irish Channel. As always, his tropical print shirt looked like it was about to split on his massive shoulders.

The bar was empty. Rain was blowing through the broken front window and dripping off the venetian blinds.

'What's happenin', Streak?' he said.

'Are you losing your mind?'

9

'Harsh words, noble mon. Lighten up.'

'That's Nate Baxter out there. He'd like to paint the woodwork with both of us.'

'That's why I didn't go out there. Some of those other guys don't like P.I.'s, either.' He looked at his watch and tapped on the crystal with his fingernail. 'You want a Dr Pepper?'

'I want us both to walk out of here. We're going to throw your piece in front of us, too.'

'What's the hurry? Have a Dr Pepper. I'll put some cherries and ice in it.'

'Clete—'

'I told you, everything's copacetic. Now, disengage, noble mon. Nobody rattles the old Bobbsey Twins from Homicide.' He took a hit from the shot glass, sucked on his sliced lime, and smiled at me.

'It's time to boogie, partner,' I said.

He looked again at his watch.

'Give it five more minutes,' he said, and smiled again.

He started to refill his glass from a large, square, brown bottle that he held in his hand. I placed my palm lightly on his arm.

'Look, let me give you the big picture, noble mon,' he said. 'I'm involved with a lady friend these days. She's a nice person, she never hurt anybody, she's intelligent, she goes part-time to the Ju-Co, she also strips in a T&A joint on Bourbon owned by the Calucci brothers. We're talking about Max and Bobo here, Dave, you remember them, the two guys we ran in once for pulling a fingernail off a girl's hand with a pair of pliers? Before I met Martina, my lady friend, she borrowed two grand off the Caluccis to pay for her grandmother's hospitalization. So when she didn't make the vig yesterday, Max, the bucket of shit I put through the window glass, called her in this morning and said it was time for her to start working out of the back of a taxicab.'

He took off his porkpie hat, combed his sandy hair straight back on his head, clipped the comb in his shirt pocket, and put his hat back on.

'The Caluccis aren't going to make a beef, Dave, at least not a legal one. They get along in police stations like shit does in an ice cream parlor,' he said. He filled his shot glass, knocked it back, and winked at me.

'Where's the other one – Bobo?'

He glanced at his watch again, then looked across the counter, past a small kitchen, toward the massive wood door of a walk-in meat locker.

'He's probably wrapping himself in freezer foil right now,' he said. 'At least that's what I'd do.'

'Are you kidding?'

'I didn't put him in there. He locked himself in. What am I supposed to do about it? He's got an iron bar or something set behind the door. I say live and let live.'

I went to the locker and tried to open it. The handle was chrome and cold in my hand. The door moved an inch, then clanked against something metal and wouldn't move farther.

'Bobo?' I said.

'What?' a voice said through the crack.

'This is Dave Robicheaux. I'm a sheriff's detective. It's over. Come on out. Nobody's going to hurt you.'

'I never heard of you.'

'I used to be in Homicide in the First District.'

'Oh yeah, you were dick-brain's partner out there. What are you doing here? He call you up for some laughs?'

'Here's the agenda, Bobo. Let me run it by you and get your reactions. I'm holding a forty-five automatic in my hand. If you refuse to open the door, I'll probably have to shoot a few holes through the lock and the hinges. Do you feel comfortable with that?'

It was silent a moment.

'Where is he?' the voice said.

'He's not a player anymore. Take my word for it.'

'You keep that animal away from me. He's a fucking menace. They ought to put his brain in a jar out at the medical school.'

'You got my word, Bobo.'

I heard an iron bar rattle to the floor, then Bobo pushed the door open with one foot from where he sat huddled in the corner, a rug wrapped around his shoulders, his hair and nostrils white with frost, clouds of freezer steam rising from his body into the sides of beef that were suspended from hooks over his head. His small, close-set black eyes went up and down my body.

'You ain't got a gun. You sonofabitch. You lied,' He said.

'Let's take a walk,' I said, lifting him up by one arm. 'Don't worry about Clete. He's just going to finish his drink and follow us outside. Believe it or not, there're cops out there who were willing to drop one of their own kind, just to protect you. Makes you proud to be a taxpayer, I bet.'

'Get your hand off my arm,' he said when we reached the door.

Batist and I stayed overnight in a guesthouse on Prytania, one block from St Charles. The sky was red at sunrise, the air thick with the angry cries of blue jays in the hot shade outside the French doors. Nate Baxter had held Clete for disturbing the peace, but the Caluccis never showed up in the morning to file assault charges, and Clete was kicked loose without even going to arraignment.

Batist and I had beignets and café au lait in the Café du Monde across from Jackson Square. The wind was warm off the river behind us, the sun bright on the banana and myrtle trees inside the square, and water sprinklers ticked along the black piked fences that bordered the grass and separated it from the sidewalk artists and the rows of shops under the old iron colonnades. I left Batist in the café and walked through the square, past St Louis Cathedral, where street musicians were already setting up in the shade, and up St Ann toward Clete's private investigator's office.

Morning was always the best time to walk in the Quarter. The streets were still deep in shadow, and the water from the previous night's rain leaked from the wood shutters down the pastel sides of the buildings, and you could smell coffee and fresh-baked bread in the small grocery stores and the dank, cool odor of wild spearmint and old brick in the passageways. Every scrolled-iron balcony along the street seemed overgrown with a tangle of potted roses, bougainvillea, azaleas, and flaming hibiscus, and the moment could be so perfect that you felt you had stepped inside an Utrillo painting.

But it wasn't all a poem. There was another reality there, too: the smell of urine in doorways, left nightly by the homeless and the psychotic, and the broken fragments of tiny ten-dollar cocaine vials that glinted in the gutters like rats' teeth.

The biscuit-colored stucco walls inside Clete's office were decorated with bullfight posters, leather wine bags, *banderillas* that he had brought back from his vacation in Mexico City. Through the back window I could see the small flagstone patio where he kept his dumbbells and the exercise bench that he used unsuccessfully every day to keep his weight and blood pressure down. Next to it was a dry stone well impacted with dirt and untrimmed banana trees.

He sat behind his desk in his Budweiser shorts, a yellow tank top, and porkpie hat. His blue-black .38 police special hung in a nylon holster from a coatrack in the corner. He pried the cap off a bottle of Dixie beer with his pocketknife, let the foam boil over the neck onto the rug, kicked off his flip-flops, and put his bare feet on top of the desk.

'You trying to leave the dock early today?' I said.

'Hey, I was in the tank all night. You ought to check that scene out, mon. Two-thirds of the people in there are honest-to-God crazoids. I'm talking about guys eating their grits with their hands. It's fucking pitiful.'

He pushed at a scrap of memo paper by his telephone.

'I was a little bothered by something Nate Baxter said last night,' I said.

'Oh yeah?'

'This vigilante stuff. He thinks you might be the man.'

He drank out of his beer and smiled at me, his eyes filled with a merry light.

'You think I might actually have that kind of potential?' he said.

'People have said worse things about both of us.'

'*The Lone Ranger* was a radio show, mon. I don't believe there's any vigilante. I think we're talking about massive wishful thinking. These hits are just business as usual in the city. We've got a murder rate as high as Washington, D.C.'s now.'

'Five or six of them have been blacks in the projects.'

'They were all dealers.'

'That's the point,' I said.

'Dave, I've run down bond jumpers in both the Iberville and Desire projects. Life in there is about as important as water breaking out the bottom of a paper bag. The city's going to hell, mon. That's the way it is. If somebody's out there taking names in a serious way, I say more power to them. But I don't think that's the case, and anyway it's not me.'

He took a long drink from the beer. The inside of the bottle was filled with amber light. Moisture slid down the neck over the green-and-gold label.

'I'm sorry. You want me to send out for a Dr Pepper or some coffee?' he asked.

'No, I've got to be going. I had to bring my boat up from New Iberia for some work. It'll be ready about noon.'

He picked up the slip of memo paper by his phone and rubbed it between thumb and forefinger.

'I ought to save you a headache and throw this away,' he said. But he flipped it across the desk blotter at me.

'What is it?'

'That black broad, the sergeant who was in front of Calucci's, called this morning. She didn't know how else to get ahold of you. My advice is that you pitch that telephone number in the trash and go back to New Iberia. Forget New Orleans. The whole place is just waiting for a hydrogen bomb.'

'What's the deal?'

'She's a hard-nosed black broad named Lucinda Bergeron from the projects who doesn't take dog shit from white male cops. That's the deal.'

'So?'

'Last night she evidently got in Nate Baxter's face. So today he's trying to kick a two-by-four up her ass. He wrote her up for insubordination. He says she cussed him out. She says she's innocent and you can back her up.'

'She didn't cuss him out while I was there. In fact, she really kept her Kool-Aid.'

'Don't get sucked in, mon. Messing with Baxter is like putting your hand in a spittoon.'

I picked up the slip of paper and put it in my pocket.

'What do I know?' he said.

I called the dock from the guesthouse and was told that the mechanic had gone home sick and my boat would not be ready until the next day. Then I called the number on the slip of paper, which turned out to be Garden District police headquarters, and was told that Lucinda Bergeron was not in. I left my name and the telephone number of the guesthouse.

Batist was sitting on the side of his bed, his big, callused, scar-flecked hands in his lap, staring out the French doors, his face full of thought.

'What's troubling you, partner?' I asked.

'That nigger out yonder in the lot.'

'That what?'

'You heard me.'

'What'd he do?'

'While you was still sleepin', I got up early and went down to the dining room for coffee. He was eatin' in there, talkin' loud with his mout' full of food, puttin' his hand on that young white girl's back each time she po'ed his coffee. Pretendin' like it's innocent, like he just a nice man don't have no bad t'oughts on his mind, no.'

'Maybe it's their business, Batist.'

'That kind of trashy nigger make it hard on the rest of us, Dave.'

He walked to the French doors, continued to stare out at the parking lot, peeled the cellophane off a cigar, and wadded the cellophane up slowly in his palm.

'He leanin' up against your truck,' he said.

'Let it go.'

'He need somebody to go upside his head.'

I knew better than to argue with Batist, and I didn't say anything more. He took off his short-sleeve blue denim shirt, hung it on the bedpost, and lathered his face with soap in front of the bathroom mirror. The muscles in his shoulders and back looked like rocks inside a leather bag. He began shaving with a pearl-handled straight-edge razor, drawing the blade cleanly down each of his jaws and under his chin.

I had known him since I was a child, when he used to fur-trap with my father on Marsh Island. He couldn't read or write, not even his own name, and had difficulty recognizing numbers and dialing a telephone. He had never been outside the state of Louisiana, had voted for the first time in 1968, and knew nothing of national or world events. But he was one of the most honest and decent men I've known, and absolutely fearless and unflinching in an adversarial situation (my adopted daughter, Alafair, never quite got over the time she saw him reach into a flooded pirogue, pinch a three-foot moccasin behind the head, and fling it indifferently across the bayou).

He walked back to the French doors, blotting a cut on his chin with a towel, the razor still in his hand. Then he folded the razor, dropped it in the back pocket of his denims, and began buttoning on his shirt.

'What are you doing, Batist?'

'Take a look out yonder.'

A tall, thin mulatto with skin the color of a new penny was talking to a half dozen black kids by my truck. He wore striped brown pants, with a braided black belt, and a lavender short-sleeve shirt with a white tie. He grinned and jiggled, and his hands moved in the air while he talked, as though a song were working inside him.

'A man like that just like a movie star to them raggedy kids, Dave.'

'At some point they'll learn he isn't.'

'It won't be no he'p then. He's a dope dealer or a pimp, don't be tellin' me he ain't. He'll use up them young boys' lives just so he can have money for a nice car, take womens out to the racetrack, put dope up his nose . . . Hey, you t'ink I'm wrong? Come see.'

The mulatto man rubbed one kid on his head, the way a baseball coach might, then hooked two fingers inside the kid's belt, drew the kid close to him, and stuffed something small inside his pants. Then he cupped his hand around the nape of another kid's neck, his face beaming with goodwill and play, and shoved something down inside his pants, too.

'I be right back,' Batist said.

'Leave this guy alone, Batist. I'll call the locals and they'll send somebody out.'

'Yeah, in t'ree hours they will.'

'This isn't our pond, partner.'

14

'Yeah? How come you run across town last night to get mixed up with Purcel and them dagos?'

He picked up his dry cigar from the ashtray, put it deep in his jaw, and went out the door.

Oh boy, I thought.

Batist walked from the guesthouse through the shade of the mulberry tree to the edge of the parking lot. The mulatto man was leaning against the headlight of my truck, entertaining his audience by one-handedly rolling a half-dollar across the backs of his fingers. He propped one shined shoe behind him on the truck bumper and gingerly squeezed his scrotum. I don't know what he said to Batist. It may have been a patronizing remark or perhaps even a pleasant greeting; he was smiling when he said it. But I don't think he expected the response he got.

The flat of Batist's right hand, which could curve around a brick and shale the corners off it, seemed to explode against the side of the man's head. His face went out of round with the blow, and the blood drained from his cheeks; his jaw hung open, and his eyes were suddenly small and round, shrunken in his head like a pig's. Then Batist hit him with his open hand again, harder, this time on the side of the mouth, so that the bottom lip broke against the teeth.

Batist waved his hands in the midst of the black kids like someone shooing chickens out of a brooder house. They ran in all directions while the mulatto man held the back of his wrist against his mouth, one palm turned outward in a placating gesture.

Batist pointed his finger into the man's face and walked toward him silently, as though he were leveling a lance at him. The man broke and ran through the parking lot toward a cottage on the opposite side of the street. Batist ground a tiny glass vial into the cement with the heel of his boot, then walked past a group of stunned tourists who had just emerged from the guesthouse dining room; his perspiring face was turned away in embarrassment.

I called my wife, Bootsie, in New Iberia and told her that I would be at least another day in New Orleans, then I tried calling Lucinda Bergeron again at Garden District headquarters. She was still out, so I decided to drive over there, file a statement, and be done with the matter. I didn't know that I would end up talking to Sergeant Benjamin Motley, who used to be in Vice when I was a homicide lieutenant in the First District.

He was a rotund, powerful black man, whose clothes always smelled of cigar smoke, with a thick black mustache and glistening fire-hydrant neck, who had little sympathy for the plight of his own people. One time a black wino in a holding cell had ridiculed Motley, calling him the white man's hired 'knee-grow,' and Motley had sprayed the man from head to foot with a can of Mace. Earlier in his law-enforcement career he had been the subject of a wrongful death investigation, when, as a bailiff, he had escorted seven prisoners from the drunk tank on a wrist chain to morning arraignment and a fire in the courthouse basement had blown the circuits and stalled the elevator between floors. Motley had gotten out through the trap-door in the top of the elevator; the seven men on the chain had died of asphyxiation.

His office was glassed in and spacious, and several merit and civic citations were framed on the walls. Outside was a squad room filled with uniformed cops doing their paperwork at their desks. Motley leaned back in his swivel chair, one shoe propped on his waste-basket, and ate a half-peeled candy bar while I finished writing out in longhand what little I could report about the exchange between Nate Baxter and Lucinda Bergeron.

I signed my name at the bottom of the form and handed it to him. His eyes went up and down the page while he brushed at his chin with one knuckle.

'What are you doing in New Orleans, anyway, Robicheaux? I thought you were a plainclothes in Iberia Parish,' he said.

'I'm on leave for a while.'

'You couldn't stay out of New Orleans?'

'You need anything else, Motley?'

'Not a thing. Use your time any way you want to.'

'What's that mean?'

'You think this is going to bail that broad out?' He shook the page between his fingers.

'I don't know. But she didn't cuss out Nate Baxter while I was there. In fact, in my opinion, it was Baxter who was out of line.'

'Baxter got you suspended without pay when he was in Internal Affairs. You even punched him out in a squad room at First District. You should have written this on toilet paper and put it in the john.'

'You haven't lost your touch, Motley.'

He chewed on the corner of his lip and rolled his eyes sideways.

'Look through the glass,' he said. 'Count the white officers in the squad room, then count the black officers. When you get done doing that, count the female officers in the room. Then count the black female officers. Is the picture coming clear for you?'

'Do they give her a lot of heat?'

'You didn't hear it from me.'

I looked at his face and didn't speak. He wiped the chocolate off his fingers with the candy wrapper and threw the wrapper into the wastebasket.

'Dog shit in her desk drawer, a dildo Scotch-taped to a jar of Vaseline in her mailbox, phony phone messages from David Duke's campaign headquarters, that kind of stuff,' he said. 'She seems like a stand-up broad, but they'll probably run her off eventually.'

'It sounds like she could use some friends,' I said, and got up to go.

'You mean the brothers? Like me?'

I shrugged.

'Last hired, first fired,' he said. 'That's the way it is, my man. It doesn't change because you wear tampons. And let's be clear, the only reason you're involved in this is because of your buddy Purcel. So go pull on your own pud, Robicheaux.'

*

That evening Batist and I walked over to St Charles and took the streetcar up to Canal, then walked into the Quarter and ate at the Acme on Iberville. It was crowded and warm inside and smelled of flat beer and the piles of empty oyster shells in the drain bins. We heard thunder out over the river, then it started to rain and we walked in the lee of the buildings back to Canal and caught the streetcar out on the neutral ground.

As we clattered down the tracks around Lee Circle, past the equestrian statue of Robert Lee, St Charles Avenue opened up into a long green-black corridor of moss-hung oak trees, swirling with mist, touched with the red afterglow of the sun. The inside of the streetcar was cool and dry and brightly lit, the windows flecked with rain, and the world felt like a grand and beautiful place to be.

Back at the guesthouse we watched a movie on television while the rain and wind shook the mulberry tree outside the French doors. I paid no attention to the sirens that I heard on the avenue, nor to the emergency lights that beat angrily against the darkness on the far side of the parking lot. We were picking up my boat in the morning, and with luck we would be somewhere south of Terrebonne Bay by noon, on our way back to New Iberia, our baited jigs bouncing in the trough behind us.

Sheets of lightning were trembling against the sky, and I lay down on the pillow with my arm across my eyes. Batist began undressing for bed, then walked to the French doors to close the curtain.

'Hey, Dave, they's a ambulance and a bunch of po-licemens over at that cottage where that nigger run to,' he said.

'I'm hitting the sack, partner. Clete's right. Leave New Orleans to its own problems.'

'They carryin' somebody out of there.'

'Tell me about it in the morning. Good night.'

He didn't answer, and I felt myself drifting on the edges of sleep and the sound of the rain blowing against the windows; then I heard him click off the lamp switch.

It must have been an hour later that we were awakened by the knock on the door. No, that's wrong; it wasn't a knock; it was an incessant beating, with the base of the fist, the kind of ugly, penetrating sound sent by someone whose violation of your sleep and privacy is only a minimal indicator of his larger purpose.

I walked to the door in my skivvies, turned the dead bolt, and opened the door two inches.

'Take off the night chain, Robicheaux.'

'What do you want, Nate?'

'What's this look like?' He held a warrant up in front of me. His chrome-plated .357 Magnum hung from his right hand. The skin of his face was tight with fatigue and muted anger, beaded with rainwater. Three uniformed white cops stood behind him.

'For what? That beef at Calucci's Bar?' I said.

'You never disappoint me. Tell me stink and shit don't go hand in hand.'

'Why don't you try making sense, Nate?'

'We just hauled away a carved-up boon from across the street. Guess who knocked him around in front of a half dozen witnesses today? It's great having you back in town, Robicheaux. It's just like old times.'

He pulled his handcuffs from his belt and let them swing loosely from his index finger like a watch fob. Behind me, Batist sat on the edge of his bed, his big hands splayed on his naked thighs, his eyes focused on a sad and ancient racial knowledge that only he seemed able to see.

3

There are those who, for political reasons, enjoy talking about country club jails. But any jail anywhere is a bad place to be. Anyone who thinks otherwise has never been in one.

Imagine an environment where the lights never go off and you defecate in full view of others on a toilet seat streaked with other people's urine, where you never quite fall asleep, where you are surrounded by the sounds of clanging iron, irrational voices resonating down stone corridors, a count-man or irritated turnkey whanging his baton off steel bars, or the muffled and tormented cries of an eighteen-year-old fish being gang-raped behind a shower wall.

Perhaps even a worse characteristic of jail is the denial of any identity you might have had before you stepped inside a piece of geography where time can sometimes be measured in five-minute increments that seem borne right out of Dante's ninth ring. Here you quickly learn that the personal violation of your *self* is considered as insignificant and ongoing an occurrence as routine body cavity searches, as the spraying of your genitals for crab lice, or as a wolf telling the server in the chow line to spit in your food, until you no longer think of yourself as an exception to the rules of jailhouse romance.

Batist spent the night in the tank and wasn't booked until the next morning. I sat on a wood chair in a waiting area next to a squad room and a row of glassed-in offices, one of which was Nate Baxter's. Through a doorway at the back of the squad room I could see the holding tank where Batist was still being held, though he had already been fingerprinted and photographed.

I had been waiting an hour and a half to see Nate Baxter. Then Sergeant Lucinda Bergeron walked past me, in navy blue slacks, a starched white short-sleeve shirt, and a lacquered black gunbelt with a leather pouch for handcuffs. She carried a clipboard in her hand, and if she noticed me, her face didn't show it.

'Excuse me, Sergeant,' I said.

She stopped and looked at me but said nothing. Her eyes were turquoise and elongated, like an Oriental's, and her cheekbones were rouged high up on her face.

'Could I talk with you a minute?' I asked.

'What is it?'

'I'm Dave Robicheaux. You left a message for me with Cletus Purcel.'

'Yes?'

'I came in and filed a report with Sergeant Motley yesterday.'

She looked at me, her face as still and expressionless as a picture painted upon the air.

'I was at Calucci's Bar,' I said. 'You asked me to come in and file a statement.'

'I understood you. What can I help you with?' she said.

'I have a friend back there in the tank. The black man, Batist Perry. He's already been booked.'

'What do you want from me?'

'How about getting him moved into a holding cell?'

'You'll have to talk to the officer in charge.'

'That's what I've been trying to do. For an hour and a half.'

'I can't help you. I'm sorry.'

She walked away to her desk, which was located in the squad room, among the uniformed officers, rather than in an enclosed office. Ten minutes later Baxter stepped out of his office door, studying some papers in his hand, then glanced in my direction and beckoned to me with one finger.

While I sat down across from him, he tipped his cigarette ashes in an ashtray and continued to concentrate on the papers on his desk blotter. He looked rested and fresh, in a sky blue sports coat and a crinkling shirt that was the color of tin.

'You're really charging Batist with murder?' I said.

'That decision comes down from the prosecutor's office, Robicheaux. You know that.'

'The man's never been in trouble. Not in his whole life. Not even for a misdemeanor. What's the matter with you?'

'Well, he's in trouble now. In a big way.' He leaned forward and tipped his ashes into his ashtray, cocking his eyebrows at me.

'I don't think you have a case, Nate. I think this is all smoke.'

'His prints are on the door at the crime scene.'

'That's impossible.'

'Tell that to our fingerprint man. Does this look like smoke to you?' He removed a half dozen eight-by-ten glossy black-and-white photographs from his desk drawer and dropped them in front of me. 'You ever see that much blood at a crime scene? Check out the chest wound. Has your friend ever been into voodoo?'

'You're using a homicide investigation to settle an old score, Nate. Don't tell me you're not.'

'Is the light in here bad? That must be the problem. The killer sawed the guy's heart out. That wasn't enough for him, either. He stuffed purple roses into the heart cavity.'

'What's your point?'

'Your friend wears a dime on a string around his ankle,' Baxter said. 'He carries a shriveled alligator's foot in his pocket. He had bones in his suitcase. The murder has all the characteristics of a ritual killing. If you were in my place, who would be your first suspect? Is there any chance it might be a superstitious backwater black guy who had already assaulted and threatened the victim the same day of the homicide and then left his prints at the crime scene? No, don't tell me. Just go think about it somewhere and drop me a card sometime.'

'I want to see him.'

'Be my guest. Please. By the way, I saw the black broad blow you off. In case you want to get more involved with her, I hear she's starting up a charm school. Take it easy, Robicheaux. You never surprise me,' he said.

But while I had been talking with Nate Baxter, Batist had already been locked to a wrist chain and taken to morning arraignment. By the time I got to the courtroom the public defender, who did not look to be over twenty-five, was trying to prevail upon the judge to set a reasonable bail. He was methodical, even eloquent, in his argument and obviously sincere. He pointed out that Batist had no arrest record and had been employed for years at a boat-rental dock run by a law officer in Iberia Parish, that he had lived his entire life in one small community and was not apt to leave it.

But Judge James T. Flowers was a choleric white-knuckle alcoholic who stayed dry without a program by channeling his inner misery into the lives of others. His procedures and sentences kept a half dozen ACLU attorneys occupied year round.

He looked at the clock and waited for the public defender to finish, then said, 'Hell's hot, my young friend. Perhaps it's time some of your clients learned that. Bail is set at fifty thousand dollars. Next case.'

An hour later Sergeant Motley arranged for me to see Batist in an interrogation room. The walls were a smudged white and windowless, and the air smelled like refrigerated cigarette smoke and cigar butts. Batist sat across from me at the wood table and kept rubbing his hands on top of each other. The scars on them looked like tiny pink worms. His face was unshaved and puffy with fatigue, his eyes arterial red in the corners with broken blood veins.

'What's gonna happen, Dave?'

'I'm going to call a bondsman first, then we'll see about a lawyer. We just have to do it a step at a time.'

'Dave, that judge said fifty t'ousand dollars.'

'I'm going to get you out, partner. You just have to trust me.'

'What for they doin' this? What they get out of it? I never had no truck with the law. I ain't even seen these people befo'.'

'A bad cop out there is carrying a grudge over some things that happened a long time ago. Eventually somebody in the prosecutor's office will probably figure that out. But in the meantime we have a problem, Batist. They say your fingerprints were on the door of that cottage across the street.'

I looked into his face. He dropped his eyes to the table and opened and closed his hands. His knuckles looked as round and hard against the skin as ball bearings.

'Tell me,' I said.

'After you was gone, after I bust that man's lip, I seen them kids t'rew the window, hangin' round his cottage do' again. When I call the po-lice, they ax me what he done. I say he sellin' dope to children, that's what he done. They ax me I seen it, I seen him take money from somebody, I seen somebody lighting up a crack pipe or somet'ing. I say no I ain't seen it, you got to see a coon climb in a tree to know coons climb in trees?

'So I kept watchin' out the window at that nigger's do'. After a while he come out with two womens, I'm talkin' about the kind been workin' somebody's crib, and they got in the car with them kids and drove round the block. When they come back them kids was fallin' down in the grass. I call the po-lice again, and they ax what crime I seen. I say I ain't seen no crime, long as it's all right in New Orleans for a pimp and his whores to get children high on dope.

'This was a white po-liceman I was talkin' to. So he put a black man on the phone, like nobody but another black man could make sense out of what I was sayin'. This black po-liceman tole me to come down and make a repote, he gonna check it out. I tole him check out that nigger after I put my boot up his skinny ass.'

'You went over there?'

'For just a minute, that's all. He wasn't home. I never gone inside. Maybe he went out the back do'. Why you look like that, Dave?'

I rested my chin on my fist and tried not to let him read my face.

'Dave?'

'I'm going to call a bondsman now. In the meantime, don't talk about this stuff with anyone. Not with the cops, not with any of those guys in the lockup. There're guys in here who'll trade off their own time and lie about you on the witness stand.'

'What you mean?'

'They'll try to learn something about you, enough to give evidence against you. They cut deals with the prosecutor.'

'They can do that?' he said 'Get out of jail by sendin' somebody else to Angola?'

'I'm afraid it's a way of life, podna.'

The turnkey opened the door and touched Batist on the shoulder. Batist stared silently at me a moment, then rose from his chair and walked out of the room toward a yellow elevator, with a wiremesh and barred door, which would take him upstairs into a lockdown area. The palms of his hands left tiny horsetails of perspiration on the tabletop.

It was going to cost a lot, far beyond anything I could afford right now. I had thirty-two hundred dollars in a money market account, most of which was set aside for the quarterly tax payments on my boat-rental and bait business, four hundred thirty-eight dollars in an account that I used for operating expenses at the dock, and one hundred thirteen dollars in my personal checking account.

I went back to the guesthouse and called every bondsman I knew in New Orleans. The best deal I could get was a one-week deferment on the payment of the fifty-thousand-dollar bail fee. I told the bondsman I would meet him at the jail in a half hour.

I couldn't even begin to think about the cost of hiring a decent defense attorney for a murder trial.

Welcome to the other side of the equation in the American criminal justice system.

Our room was still in disarray after being tossed by Nate Baxter and his people. Batist's cardboard suitcase had been dumped on the bed, and half of his clothes were on the floor. I picked them up, refolded them, and began replacing them in the suitcase. Underneath one of his crumpled shirts was the skull of what had once been an enormous catfish. The texture of the bone was old, a shiny gray, mottled with spots the color of tea, polished smooth with rags.

I remembered when Batist had caught this same mud cat three years ago, on a scalding summer's day out on the Atchafalaya, with a throw line and a treble hook thick with nutria guts. The catfish must have weighed thirty-five pounds, and when Batist wrapped the throw line around his forearm, the cord cut into his veins like a tourniquet, and he had to use a club across the fish's spine to get it over the gunwale. After he had driven an ice pick into its brain and pinned it flat on the deck, skinned it and cut it into steaks, he sawed the head loose from the skeleton and buried it in an anthill under a log. The ants boiled on the impacted meat and ate the bone and eye sockets clean, and now when you held up the skull vertically, it looked like a crucified man from the front. When you reversed it, it resembled an ecclesiastical, robed figure giving his benediction to the devout. If you shook it in your hand, you could hear pieces of bone clattering inside. Batist said those were the thirty pieces of silver that Judas had taken to betray Christ.

It had nothing to do with voodoo. It had everything to do with Acadian Catholicism.

Before I left the guesthouse for the jail, I called up Hippo Bimstine at one of his drugstores.

'How bad you want that Nazi sub, Hippo?' I asked.

'It's not the highest priority on my list.'

'How about twenty-five grand finder's fee?'

'Jesus Christ, Dave, you were yawning in my face the other day.'

'What do you say, partner.'

'There's something wrong here.'

'Oh?'

'You found it, didn't you?'

I didn't answer.

'You found it but it's not in the same place now?' he said.

'You're a wealthy man, Hippo. You want the sub or not?'

'Hey, you think that's right?' he asked. 'I tell you where it's at, you find it and up the fee on me? That's like you?'

'Maybe you can get somebody cheaper. You know some guys who want to go down in the dark on a lot of iron and twisted cables?'

'Put my schlong in a vise, why don't you?'

'I've got to run. What do you say?'

'Fifteen.'

'Nope.'

'Hey, New Orleans is recessed. I'm bleeding here. You know what it cost me to get rid of – when he was about to be our next governor? Now my friends are running a Roto-Rooter up my hole.'

(Hippo had spent a fortune destroying the political career of an ex-Klansman who had run for both the governor's office and the U.S. Senate. My favorite quote of Hippo's had appeared in *Time* magazine, during the gubernatorial campaign; he said of the ex-Klansman, '– doesn't like us Jews now. Check out how he feels after I get finished with him.')

'I won't charge expenses,' I said.

'I'm dying here. Hemorrhaging on the floor. I'm serious. Nobody believes me. Dave, you take food stamps?'

Hippo, you're a jewel, I thought.

Batist and I picked up my boat and left the dock at three the next morning. The breeze was up, peppered with light rain, and you could smell the salt spray breaking over the bow. The water was as dark as burgundy, the chop on the edge of the swells electric with moonlight, the wetlands to the north green and gray and metamorphic with mist. To the southeast I could see gas flares burning on some offshore rigs; then the wind dropped and the sky turned the color of bone and I could see a red glow spreading out of the water into the clouds.

It was completely light when I cut the engine and drifted above the spot where I had dove down into darkness and the sounds of grinding metal three days earlier. Batist stood on the bow, feeding the anchor rope out through his palms, until it hit bottom and went slack; then he tied it off on a cleat.

The water was smoky green, the swells full of skittering bait fish, the air hazy with humidity. I had fashioned a viewer box from reinforced window glass inset in a waterproofed wood crate, and I lowered it over the side by the handles and pressed it beneath the surface. Pockets of air swam across the glass, then flattened and disappeared, and suddenly in the yellow-green light I could see schools of small speckled trout, like darting silver ribbons, drumfish, as round and flat as skillets, a half dozen stingrays, their wings undulating as smoothly as if they were gliding on currents of warm air, and down below, where the light seemed to be gathered into a vortex of silt, the torpedo shapes of sand sharks, who bolted and twisted in erratic circles for no apparent reason.

Batist peered downward through the viewer box over my shoulder. Then I felt his eyes studying me while I strapped on my tanks and weight belt.

'This don't make me feel good, Dave,' he said.

'Don't worry about it, partner.'

'I don't want to see you lunch for them sharks, no.'

'Those are sand sharks, Batist. They're harmless.'

'Tell me that out yonder's harmless.' He pointed past the cabin to the southwest.

It was a water spout that had dropped out of a thunderhead and was moving like an enormous spinning cone of light and water toward the coast. If it made landfall, which it probably would not, it would fill suddenly with mud, rotted vegetation, and uprooted trees, and become as black as a midwestern tornado coursing through a freshly plowed field.

'Keep your eye on it and kick the engine over if it turns,' I said.

'Just look up from down there, you see gasoline and life jackets and a bunch of bo'rds floatin' round, see me swimmin' toward Grand Isle, that means it ain't bothered to tell me it was fixin' to turn.'

I went over the side, swam to the anchor rope, and began pulling myself downward hand over hand. I felt myself sliding through three different layers of temperature, each one cooler than the last; then just as a school of sea perch swept past me, almost clattering against my mask, I could feel a uniform level of coldness penetrate my body from the crown of my head down to the soles of my feet. Clouds of gray silt seemed to be blowing along the gulf's floor as they would in a windstorm. The pressure against my eardrums began to grow in intensity; it made a faint tremolo sound, like wire stretching before it breaks. Then I heard iron ring against iron, and a groan like a great weight shifting against impacted sand.

I held the anchor rope with one hand and floated motionlessly in the current. Then I saw it. For just a moment.

It was pointed at an upward angle on a slope, buried in a sand-bar almost to its decks, molded softly with silt. But there was no mistaking the long, rounded, sharklike shape. It was a submarine, and I could make out the battered steel flanges that protruded above the captain's bridge on the conning tower, and I knew that if I scraped the moss and layers of mud and shellfish from the tower's plates I would see the vestiges of the swastika that I had seen on the same conning tower over three decades ago.

Then I saw it tilt slightly to one side, saw dirty strings of oil or silt or engine fuel rise near the forward torpedo tubes, and I realized that years ago air must have been trapped somewhere in a compartment, perhaps where a group of terrified sailors spun a wheel on a hatch and pretended to themselves that their friends outside, whose skulls were being snapped like eggshell, would have chosen the same alternative.

I felt a heavy surge in the current from out in the dark, beyond the continental shelf. The water clouded and the submarine disappeared. I thought I heard thunder booming, then the anchor rope vibrated in my palm, and when I looked up I could see the exhaust pipes on my boat boiling the waterline at the stern.

When I came to the surface the chop smacked hard against my mask, and the swells were dented with rain circles. Batist came outside the cabin and pointed toward the southeast. I pushed my mask up on my head and looked behind me; three more water spouts had dropped out of the sky and were churning across the surface of the water, and farther to the south you could see thunderclouds as thick as oil smoke on the horizon.

I climbed up the ladder, pulled off my gear, tied the end of a spool of clothesline through a chunk of pig iron that had once been a window sash, and fed the line over the gunwale until the weight bit into the bottom. Then I sawed off the line at the spool and strung it through the handles of three sealed Clorox bottles that I used as float markers. The rain was cold and dancing in a green haze on the swells now, the air heavy with the smell of ozone and nests of dead bait fish in the waves. Just as I started to fling the Clorox bottles overboard, I heard the blades of a helicopter thropping low over the water behind me.

It passed us, flattening and wrinkling the water below the downdraft, and I saw the solitary passenger, a blond man in pilot's sunglasses, turn in his seat and stare back at me. Then the helicopter circled and hovered no more than forty yards to the south of us.

'What they doin'?' Batist said.

'I don't know.'

'Let's get goin', Dave. We don't need to be stayin' out here no longer with them spouts.'

'You got it, partner,' I said.

Then the helicopter gained altitude, perhaps to five hundred feet directly above us, high enough for them to see the coastline and to take a good fix on our position.

I left the Clorox marker bottles on the deck and pulled the sash weight back up from the bottom. We could return to this same area and probably find the sub again with my sonar, or 'fish finder,' which was an electronic marvel that could outline any protrusion on the gulf's floor. But the sky in the south was completely black now, with veins of lightning trembling on the horizon, and I had a feeling that the Nazi silent service down below was about to set sail again.

4

We lived south of New Iberia, on an oak-lined dirt road next to the bayou, in a house that my father had built of notched and pegged cypress during the Depression. The side and front yards were matted with a thick layer of black leaves and stayed in deep shade from the pecan and oak trees that covered the eaves of the house. From the gallery, which had a rusted tin roof, you could look down the slope and across the dirt road to my boat-rental dock and bait shop. On the far side of the bayou was a heavy border of willow trees, and beyond the willows a marsh filled with moss-strung dead cypress, whose tops would become as pink as newly opened roses when the sun broke through the mist in the early morning.

I slept late the morning after we brought the boat back from New Orleans. Then I fixed coffee and hot milk and a bowl of Grape-Nuts and blackberries, and took it all out on a tray to the redwood picnic table under the mimosa tree in the backyard. Later, Bootsie came outside through the screen door with a glass of iced tea, her face fresh and cool in the breeze across the lawn. She wore a sleeveless white blouse and pink shorts, and her thick, honey-colored hair, which she had brushed in swirls and pinned up on her head, was burned gold on the tips from the sun.

'Did you see the phone messages from a police sergeant on the blackboard?' she asked.

'Yeah, thanks.'

'What does she want?'

'I don't know. I haven't called her back.'

'She seemed pretty anxious to talk to you.'

'Her name's Lucinda Bergeron. I think she probably has problems with her conscience.'

'What?'

'I tried to help her on an insubordination beef. When I asked her to do a favor for Batist, she more or less indicated I could drop dead.'

'Maybe it's just a misunderstanding.'

'I don't think so. Where's Alafair?'

'She's down at the dock with Batist.' She drank from her iced tea and gazed at the duck pond at the foot of our property. She shook the ice in the bottom of the glass and looked at it. Then she said, 'Dave, are we going to pay for his lawyer?'

'It's either that or let him take his chances with a court-appointed attorney. If he's lucky, he'll get a good one. If not, he can end up in Angola.'

She touched at her hairline with her fingers and tried to keep her face empty of expression.

'How much is it going to cost?' she said.

'Ten to twenty grand. Maybe a lot more.'

She widened her eyes and took a breath, and I could see a small white discoloration, the size of a dime, in each of her cheeks.

'Dave, we'll go into debt for years,' she said.

'I don't know what to do about it. Nate Baxter targeted Batist because he couldn't get at me or Clete. It's not Batist's fault.'

The breeze blew through the mimosa, and the shade looked like lace rippling across her face. I saw her try to hide the anger that was gathering in her eyes.

'There's nothing for it, Boots. The man didn't do anything to deserve this. We have to help him.'

'All this started with Clete Purcel. He enjoys it. It's a way of life with him. When are you going to learn that, Dave?'

Then she walked into the house and let the screen slam behind her.

I hosed down some boats at the dock, cleaned off the telephone-spool tables after the lunch crowd had left, then finally gave in and used the phone in the bait shop to return Lucinda Bergeron's call. I was told she had gone home sick for the day, and I didn't bother to leave my name. Then I called three criminal attorneys in Lafayette and two in New Orleans. Their fees ran from eighty to one hundred and fifty dollars an hour, with no guarantees of anything.

'You all right, Dave?' Alafair said. She sat on a tall stool behind the cash register, her Houston Astros cap on sideways, her red tennis shoes swinging above the floor. Her skin was dark brown, her Indian black hair filled with lights like a raven's wing.

'Everything's copacetic, little guy,' I said. Through the screened windows the sun looked like a wobbling yellow flame on the bayou. I wiped the perspiration off my face with a damp counter towel and threw the towel in a corner.

'You worried about money or something?'

'It's just a temporary thing. Let's have a fried pie, Alf.'

'Batist is in some kind of trouble, Dave?'

'A little bit. But we'll get him out of it.'

I winked at her, but the cloud didn't go out of her face. It had been seven years since I had pulled her from the submerged wreck of an airplane carrying illegal refugees from El Salvador. She had forgotten her own language (although she could understand most words in Cajun French without having been taught them), and she no longer had nightmares about the day the soldiers came to her village and created an object lesson with machetes and a pregnant woman in front of the medical clinic; but when she sensed difficulty or discord of any kind in our home, her brown eyes would immediately become troubled and focus on some dark concern inside herself, as though she were about to witness the re-creation of a terrible image that had been waiting patiently to come aborning again.

'You have to trust me when I tell you not to worry about things, Squanto,' I said.

Then she surprised me.

'Dave, do you think you should be calling me all those baby names? I'm twelve years old.'

'I'm sorry, Alf.'

'It's all right. Some people just might not understand. They might think it's dumb or that you're treating me like a little kid or something.'

'Well, I won't do it anymore. How's that?'

'Don't worry about it. I just thought I ought to tell you.'

'Okay, Alf. Thanks for letting me know.'

She punched around on the keys of the cash register while blowing her breath up into her bangs. Then I saw her eyes go past me and focus somewhere out on the dock.

'Dave, there's a black woman out there with a gas can. Dave, she's got a pistol in her back pocket.'

I turned and looked out into the shade of the canvas awning that covered the dock. It was Lucinda Bergeron, in a pair of faded Levi's that barely clung to her thin hips, Adidas tennis shoes, and a white, sweat-streaked T-shirt with the purple-and-gold head of Mike the Tiger on it. She wore her badge clipped on her beltless waistband; a chrome snub-nosed revolver in an abbreviated leather holster protruded from her back pocket.

Her face was filmed and gray, and she wiped at her eyes with one sleeve before she came through the screen door.

'Are you okay?' I said.

'May I use your rest room?' she said.

'Sure, it's right behind the coolers,' I said, and pointed toward the rear of the shop.

A moment later I heard the toilet flush and water running, then she came back out, breathing through her mouth, a crumpled wet paper towel in one hand.

'Do you sell mouthwash or mints?' she said.

I put a roll of Life Savers on top of the counter. Then I opened up a can of Coca-Cola and set it in front of her.

'It settles the stomach,' I said.

'I've got to get something straight with you.'

'How's that?'

She drank out of the Coke can. Her face looked dusty and wan, her eyes barely able to concentrate.

'You think I'm chickenshit,' she said.

'You were in a tough spot.'

'But you still think I'm chickenshit, don't you?'

29

'I know you're not feeling well, but I'd appreciate it if you didn't use profanity in front of my daughter.'

'Excuse me. Did you have a reason for not returning my phone calls?'

'When I called back, you were already gone. Look, Sergeant, I appreciate your coming down here, particularly when you're sick. But you don't owe me anything.'

'You've decided that?'

I let out my breath. 'What can I say? It's not my intention to have an argument with you.'

'You sell gas? I ran out down the road. My gauge is broken.' She clanked the gasoline can on the counter.

'Yeah, I've got a pump for the boats at the end of the dock.'

'Your friend, the black man, Batist Perry, they're sticking it to him. Nate Baxter held some information back from you.'

'Alafair, how about telling Bootsie we'll go to Mulate's for supper tonight?'

She made an exasperated face, climbed down from the stool, unhitched Tripod, her three-legged pet raccoon, from his chain by the door, and went up the dock toward the house with Tripod looking back at me over her shoulder.

'The murdered man had his heart cut out,' Lucinda Bergeron said. 'But so did three other homicide victims in the last four months. Even one who was pitched off a roof. He didn't tell you that, did he?'

'No, he didn't.'

'The press doesn't know about it, either. The city's trying to sit on it so they don't scare all the tourists out of town. Baxter thinks it's Satanists. Your friend just happened to stumble into the middle of the investigation.'

'Satanists?'

'You don't buy it?'

'It seems they always turn out to be meltdowns who end up on right-wing religious shows. Maybe it's just coincidence.'

'If I were you, I'd start proving my friend was nowhere near New Orleans when those other homicides were committed. I've got to sit down. I think I'm going to be sick again.'

I came around from behind the counter and walked her to a chair and table. Her back felt like iron under my hands. She took her revolver out of her back pocket, clunked it on the table, and leaned forward with her forearms propped on her thighs. Her hair was thick and white on the ends, her neck oily with sweat. Two white fishermen whom I didn't know started through the door, then turned and went back outside.

'I'll be right with y'all,' I called through the screen.

'Like hell you will,' I heard one of them say as they walked back toward their cars.

'I'll drive you back to New Orleans. I think maybe you've got a bad case of stomach flu,' I said to Lucinda.

'Just fill my gas can for me. I'll be all right in a little bit.' She took a crumpled five-dollar bill from her Levi's and put it on the tabletop.

'I have to go back for my truck, anyway. It's at a dock down by Barataria Bay. Let's don't argue about it.'

But she wasn't capable of arguing about anything. Her breath was rife with bile, her elongated turquoise eyes rheumy and listless, the back of her white T-shirt glued against her black skin. When I patted her on the shoulder, I could feel the bone like coat hanger wire against the cloth. I could only guess at what it had been like for her at the NOPD training academy when a peckerwood drill instructor decided to turn up the butane.

I carried the gas can down to her Toyota, got it started, filled the tank up at the dock, and drove her to New Orleans. She lived right off Magazine in a one-story white frame house with a green roof, a small yard, and a gallery that was hung with potted plants and overgrown with purple trumpet vine. Around the corner, on Magazine, was a two-story bar with a colonnade and neon Dixie beer signs in the windows; you could hear the jukebox roaring through the open front door.

'I should drive you out to the boatyard,' she said.

'I can take a cab.'

She saw my eyes look up and down her street and linger on the intersection.

'You know this neighborhood?'

'Sure. I worked it when I was a patrolman. Years ago that bar on the corner was a hot-pillow joint.'

'I know. My auntie used to hook there. It's a shooting gallery now,' she said, and walked inside to call me a cab.

Way to go, Robicheaux, I thought.

It was late evening after I picked up my truck down in Barataria and drove back into the city. I called Clete at his apartment in the Quarter.

'Hey, noble mon,' he said. 'I called you at your house this afternoon.'

'What's up?'

'Oh, it probably doesn't amount to much. What are you doing back in the Big Sleazy, mon?'

'I need some help on these vigilante killings. I'm not going to get it from NOPD.'

'Lose this vigilante stuff, Dave. It's a shuck, believe me.'

'Have you heard about some guys having their hearts cut out?'

He laughed. 'That's a new one. Where'd you get that?' he said.

'Lucinda Bergeron.'

'You've been out of Homicide too long, Streak. When they cancel them out, it's for money, sex, or power. This vampire or ghoul bullshit is out of comic books. Hey, I got another revelation for you. I think that Bergeron broad has got a few frayed wires in her head. Did she tell you she went up to Angola to watch a guy fry?'

'No.'

'It probably just slipped her mind. Most of your normals like to watch a guy ride the bolt once in a while.'

'Why'd you call the house?'

31

'I'm hearing this weird story about you and a Nazi submarine.'

'From where?'

'Look, Martina's over here. I promised to take her to this blues joint up on Napoleon. Join us, then we'll get some étouffée at Monroe's. You've got to do it, mon, it's not up for discussion. Then I'll fill you in on how you've become a subject of conversation with Tommy Blue Eyes.'

'Tommy Lonighan?'

'You got it, Tommy Bobalouba himself, the only mick I ever met who says his own kind are niggers turned inside out.'

'The Tommy Lonighan I remember drowned a guy with a fire hose, Clete.'

'So who's perfect? Let me give you directions up on Napoleon. By the way, Bootsie seemed a little remote when I called. Did I spit in the soup or something?'

The nightclub up on Napoleon was crowded, the noise deafening, and I couldn't see Clete at any of the tables. Then I realized that an exceptional event had just taken place up on the bandstand. The Fat Man, the most famous rhythm and blues musician ever produced by New Orleans, had pulled up in front in his pink Cadillac limo, and like a messiah returning to his followers, his sequined white coat and coal black skin almost glowing with an electric purple sheen, had walked straight through the parting crowd to the piano, grinning and nodding, his walrus face beaming with goodwill and an innocent self-satisfaction, and had started hammering out 'When the Saints Go Marching In.'

The place went wild.

Then I realized that another event was taking place simultaneously on the dance floor, one that probably not even New Orleans was prepared for – Clete Purcel and his girlfriend doing the dirty boogie.

While the Fat Man's ringed, sausage fingers danced up and down on the piano keys and the saxophones and trumpets blared behind him, Clete was bopping in the middle of the hardwood floor, his porkpie hat slanted forward on his head, his face pointed between his girlfriend's breasts, his buttocks swinging like an elephant's; then a moment later his shoulders were erect while he bumped and ground his loins, his belly jiggling, his balled fists churning the air, his face turned sideways as though he were in the midst of orgasm.

His girlfriend was over six feet tall and wore a flowered sundress that fit her tanned body like sealskin. She waved bandannas in each hand as though she were on a runway, kicking her waxed calves at an angle behind her, lifting her chin into the air while her eyelids drifted shut and she rotated her tongue slowly around her lips. Then she let her mouth hang open in a feigned pout, pushed her reddish brown hair over the top of her head with both hands, flipped it back into place with an erotic challenge in her eyes, and rubbed a stretched bandanna back and forth across her rump while she oscillated her hips.

At first the other dancers pulled back in awe or shock or perhaps even in respect; then they began to leave the dance floor two at a time and finally in large numbers after Clete backed with his full weight into another dancer and sent him careening into a drink waiter.

The Fat Man finished, wiped his sweating face at the microphone with an immaculate white handkerchief, and thanked the crowd for their ongoing roar of applause. I followed Clete and his girl to their table, which was covered with newspaper, beer bottles, and dirty paper plates that had contained potatoes French-fried in chicken fat. Clete's face was bright and happy with alcohol, and the seams of his Hawaiian shirt were split at both shoulders.

'Martina, this is the guy I've been telling you about,' he said. 'My ole bust-'em or smoke-'em podjo.'

'How about giving that stuff a break, Clete?' I said.

'I'm very pleased to meet you,' she said.

Her face was pretty in a rough way, her skin coarse and grained under the makeup as though she had worked outdoors in sun and wind rather than on a burlesque stage.

'Clete's told me about how highly educated you are and so well read and all,' she said.

'He exaggerates sometimes.'

'No, he doesn't,' she said. 'He's very genuine and sincere and he feels very deeply for you.'

'I see,' I said.

'He has a gentle side to his nature that few people know about. The people in my herbalist and nude therapy group think he's wonderful.'

Out of the corner of my eye I saw Clete study the dancers out on the floor as though he had never seen them before.

'He says you're trying to find the vigilante. I think it's disgusting that somebody's out there murdering colored people in the projects and nobody does anything about it.'

'Clete doesn't seem to give it much credence.'

'Look, mon, let me tell you where this vigilante stuff came from. There's a citizens committee here, a bunch of right-wing douche bags who haven't figured out what their genitalia is for, so they spend all their time jacking up local politicians and judges about crime in the streets, dope in the projects, on and on and on, except nobody wants to pay more taxes to hire more cops or build more jails. So what they're really saying is let's either give the blacks a lot more rubbers or do a little less to stop the spread of sickle-cell.'

Martina had taken a pocket dictionary from her purse. She read aloud from it: '"Credence – belief, mental acceptance or credit." That's an interesting word. It's related to "credibility," isn't it?'

Clete widened his eyes and looked at her as though he were awakening from sleep. Then somebody on the opposite side of the dance floor caught his attention.

'Dave, a guy's coming over to our table,' he said. 'He just wants to talk a minute. Okay? I told him you wouldn't mind. He's not a bad guy. Maybe you might even be interested in what he's got to say. It doesn't hurt to listen to a guy, right?'

Through the layers of drifting cigarette smoke my eyes focused on a man with two women at a table. His solid physique reminded me of an upended hogshead; even at a distance his other features – his florid, potato face, his eyes that were as blue as ice, his meringue hair – were unmistakable.

'You shouldn't have done this, partner,' I said to Clete.

'I provide security at two of his clubs. What am I supposed to say to him, "Drop dead, Tommy. My buddy Dave thinks you're spit on the sidewalk, get off the planet, sonofabitch"?'

'He's not just an eccentric local character. He was up on a murder beef. What's the matter with you?'

'The guy he did with the fire hose was beating up old people in the Irish Channel with an iron pipe. Yeah, big loss. Everybody was real upset when they heard he'd finally caught the bus.'

'Fire hose?' Martina said, and made a puzzled face.

There was nothing for it, though. The man with the red face and the eyes that were like flawless blue marbles was walking toward our table.

Clete mashed out his cigarette in a paper plate.

'Play it like you want, Dave,' he said. 'You think Tommy Bobalouba's any more a geek than Hippo Bimstine, tell him to ship out.'

'What about Hippo?' I said.

'Nothing. What do I know? I thought I might bring you a little extra gelt. You're too much, Streak.'

Tommy Lonighan hooked two fingers under an empty chair at an adjacent table without asking permission of the people sitting there, swung it in front of him, and sat down. He wore a long-sleeve pink shirt with French cuffs and red stone cuff links, but the lapels were ironed back to expose the mat of white hair on his chest, and the hair on his stubby, muscular forearms grew out on his wrists like wire. He had the small mouth of the Irish, with downturned corners, and a hard, round chin with a cleft in it.

'What d'you say, Lieutenant?' he said, and extended his hand. When I took it, it was as square and rough-edged as a piece of lumber.

'Not much, Mr Lonighan. How are you this evening?' I said.

'"Mr Lonighan," he says. I look like a "mister" to you these days?' he said. The accent was Irish Channel blue-collar, which is often mistaken for a Brooklyn accent, primarily because large sections of New Orleans were settled by Irish and Italian immigrants in the 1890s. He smiled, but the clear light in his eyes never changed, never revealed what he might or might not be thinking.

'What's up?' I said.

'Boy, you fucking cut straight to it, don't you?'

'How about it on the language, Tommy?' Clete said.

'Sorry, I spend all day with prizefighters down at my gym,' he said, glancing sideways at Martina. 'So how much is Blimp-stine offering you to find this sub?'

'Who?' I said.

'Hippo Bimstine, the beached whale of south Louisiana. Who you think I'm talking about?'

'How do you know Hippo's offering me anything?'

'It's a small town. Times are hard. Somebody's always willing to pass on a little information,' he said, and put a long French fry between his lips, sucking it deep into his mouth with a smile in his eyes.

'You're right, there's a Nazi sub out there someplace. But I don't know where. Not now, anyway. For all I know, it's drifted all the way to the Yucatán. The alluvial fan of the Mississippi probably works it in a wide circle.'

He set his palm on my forearm and looked me steadily in the eyes. There were thin gray scars in his eyebrows, a nest of pulsating veins in one temple that had not been there a moment ago.

'Why is it I don't believe you?' he said.

'What's your implication, Tommy?' I said.

'It's "Tommy" now. I like it, Dave. I don't "imply" anything. That's not my way.' But his hand did not leave my forearm.

Martina read from her pocket dictionary: '"Alluvial fan – the deposit of a stream where it issues from a gorge upon an open plain." The Mississippi isn't a stream, is it?'

Lonighan stared at her.

'I'm not sure why either you or Hippo are interested in some World War II junk, but my interest is fading fast, Tommy,' I said.

'That's too bad. Because both Hippo and me are going into the casino business. I'm talking about riverboats here, legalized gambling that can make this city rich, and I'm not about to let that glutinous sheeny set up a tourist exhibit on the river that takes maybe half my business.'

'Then tell it to Hippo,' I said, and pulled my arm out from under his hand.

'*What?*' he said. 'You got your nose up in the air about something? I come to your table, you act like somebody's flushing a crapper in your face? You don't like me touching your skin?'

'Take it easy, Tommy. Dave didn't mean anything,' Clete said.

'The fuck he didn't.' Then he said it again: 'The *fuck* he didn't.'

'I'd appreciate your leaving our table,' I said.

He started to speak, but Martina beat him to it.

'I happen to be part Jewish, Mr Lonighan,' she said, her face serene and cool, her gaze focused benignly on him as though she were addressing an abstraction rather than an enraged man at her elbow. 'You're a dumb mick who's embarrassing everybody at the table. It's not your fault, though. You probably come from a dysfunctional home full of ignorant people like yourself. But you should join a therapy group so you can understand the origin of your rude manners.'

The crow's-feet around Lonighan's eyes were white with anger and disbelief. I looked at Martina in amazement and admiration.

5

I slept on Clete's couch that night, and in the morning I called Nate Baxter at his office and asked about the other homicides that involved mutilation.

Nate had never been a good liar.

'Mutilation? How do you think most homicides are committed? By beating the person to death with dandelions?'

'You know what I'm talking about.'

'Yeah, I do. You got to somebody under my supervision.'

'Your office is a sieve, Nate.'

'No, there's only one broad I smell in this. Nothing racial meant. Stay out of the investigation, Robicheaux. You blew your career in New Orleans because you were a lush. You won't change that by sticking your nose up that broad's cheeks.'

He hung up.

I got back home just before lunch. The air was already hot and breathless and dense with humidity, and I put on my tennis shoes and running shorts, jogged three miles along the dirt road by the bayou, then did three sets of arm curls, dead lifts, and military presses with my barbells in the backyard. My chest was singing with blood when I turned on the cold water in the shower.

I didn't hear Bootsie open the bathroom door.

'Do you have a second?'

'Sure,' I said, and twisted the shower handle off.

'I acted badly. I'm sorry,' she said.

'About what?'

'About Batist. About the money. I worry about it sometimes. Too much, I guess.'

'What if I had a wife who didn't?'

I eased the water back on, then through the frosted glass I saw her undressing in muted silhouette. She opened the door, stepped inside with me, and slipped her arms around my neck, her face uplifted, her eyes closed against the spray of the shower over my shoulders.

I held her against me and kissed her hair. Her body was covered with tan, the tops of her breasts powdered with freckles. Her skin was smooth and warm and seemed to radiate health and well-being through my palms, the way a rose petal does to the tips of your fingers, but the reality was otherwise. Lupus, the red wolf, lived in her blood and waited only for a slip in her medication to resume feeding on her organs and connective tissue. And if the wolf was not loosed by an imbalance in the combinations of medicine that she took, another even more insidious enemy was – temporary psychosis that was like an excursion onto an airless piece of moonscape where only she lived.

She was supposed to avoid the sun, too. But I had long since given up trying to take her out of the garden or force her back into the shade of the cabin when we were out on the salt. I had come to feel, as many people do when they live with a stricken wife or husband, that the tyranny of love can be as destructive as that of disease.

We made love in the bedroom, our bodies still damp and cool from the shower, while the window fan drew the breeze across the sheets. She moved her stomach in a circular motion on top of me, her arms propped against the mattress; then I saw her eyes close and her face become soft and remote. Her thighs tensed, and she bent forward suddenly, her mouth opening, and I felt her heat spread across my loins just as something crested and burst inside me like water edging over a dam and cascading in a white arc through a dark streambed.

She was one of those rare people for whom making love did not end with a particular act. She lay beside me and touched the white patch in my hair, my mustache, the rubbery scar high up on my chest from a .38 round, the spray of lead gray welts along my right thigh where a bouncing Betty had painted me with light on a night trail outside a pitiful Third World village stinking of duck shit and unburied water buffalo.

Then I felt her hand rest in the center of my chest.

'Dave, there was a man outside this morning,' she said.

'Which man?'

'He was out by the road, looking through the trees at the gallery. When I opened the screen, he walked back down the road.'

'What did he look like?'

'I couldn't see his face. He had on a blue shirt and a hat.'

'Maybe he was just lost.'

'Our number and name are on the mailbox by the road. Why would he be looking up at the gallery?'

'I'll ask Batist if he saw anyone unusual hanging around the front.'

She got up from the bed and began dressing by the back window. The curtains, which had the texture of gauze and were printed with tiny pink flowers, ruffled across the arch of her back as she stepped into her panties.

'Why are you looking at me like that?' she said.

'Because without exaggeration I can say that you're one of the most beautiful women on earth.'

When she smiled her eyes closed and opened in a way that made my heart drop.

Later, I went down to the dock to help Batist clean up the tables after the lunch crowd had left. Parked by the boat ramp, pinging with heat, was a flatbed truck with huge cone-shaped loudspeakers welded all over the cab's roof. On the doors, hand-painted in a flowing calligraphy, were the words *Rev. Oswald Flat Ministries.*

I remembered the name from years ago when he had broadcast his faith-healing show from Station XERF, one of the most powerful radio transmitters in the Western Hemisphere, located across the Rio Grande from Del Rio, in old Mexico so that the renters of its airtime were not governed by FCC restrictions. Sandwiched between ads for tulip bulbs, bat guano, baby chicks, aphrodisiacs, and memberships in every society from the Invisible Empire to the Black Muslims, were sermons by Brother Oswald, as he was called, that were ranting, breathless pieces of Appalachian eloquence. Sometimes he would become virtually hysterical, gasping as though he had emphysema, then he would snort air through his nostrils and begin another fifteen-minute roller-coaster monologue that would build with such roaring, unstoppable intensity that the technicians would end his sermon for him by superimposing a prerecorded ad.

He and his wife, a woman in a print cotton dress with rings of fat under her chin, were eating barbecue at the only table in the bait shop when I opened the screen door. It must have been ninety degrees in the shop, even with the window fans on, but Oswald Flat wore a long-sleeve denim work shirt buttoned at the wrists and a cork sun helmet that leaked sweat out of the band down the sides of his head. His eyes were pale behind his rimless glasses, the color of water flowing over gravel, liquid-looking in the heat, the back of his neck and hands burned the deep hue of chewing tobacco.

'That's Dave yonder,' Batist said to him from behind the counter, seemingly relieved. He picked up a can of soda pop and went outside to drink it at one of the telephone-spool tables under the awning that shaded the dock.

Flat's eyes went up and down my body. His wife began eating a Moon Pie, chewing with her mouth open while she stared idly out the window at the bayou.

'Looks like you're a hard man to grab holt of,' he said.

'Not really. I was up at the house.'

'Don't like to bother a man in his home.'

'What could I do for you, sir?'

'I belong to the Citizens Committee for a Better New Orleans.

I make no apology for hit. The town's a commode. But I don't like what got done to your colored boy.'

'*Boy?*'

His southern mountain accent grated like piano wire drawn through a hole punched in a tin can. He took a toothpick from his shirt pocket, worked it into a back tooth, and measured me again with his bemused, pale eyes.

'You one of them kind gets his nose up in the air about words he don't like?' he said.

'Batist is older than I am, Reverend. People hereabouts don't call him a boy.'

'He probably ain't gonna get much older if you don't take the beeswax out of your ears. There's something bad going on out yonder. I don't like hit.' He waved his hand vaguely at the eastern horizon.

'You mean the vigilante?'

'Maybe. Maybe something a whole lot bigger than that.'

'I don't follow you.'

'Things falling apart at the center. I think it's got to do with the Antichrist.'

'The Antichrist?'

'You got woodpecker holes in your head or something?'

'I'm sorry, but I have no idea what you're talking about.'

'There's signs and such, the way birds fly around in a dead sky right before a storm. You had a president with the numbers in his name.' He puffed out both his cheeks. 'I can tell you're thinking, son. I can smell the wood burning.'

'What numbers?'

'Ronald Wilson Reagan. Six-six-six. The Book of Revelation says hit, you'll know him by the numbers in his name. I think that time's on us.'

'Could I get y'all anything else?'

'Does somebody have to hit you upside the head with a two-by-four to get your attention?' he said.

'Stop talking to the man like that, Os,' his wife said, opening another Moon Pie, her gaze fixed indolently on the willows bending in the breeze.

'That colored fellow out yonder's innocent,' he said to me. 'These murders, I don't care if hit's dope dealers being killed or not, they ain't done by somebody on the side of justice. People can pretend that's the case, but hit ain't so. And that bothers me profoundly. God's honest truth, son. That's all I come here to tell you.'

'Do you know something about the murders, Reverend?'

'You'll be the first to hear about hit when I do.' His face was dilated and discolored in the heat, as though it had been slowly poached in warm water.

After he and his wife drove away in their flatbed truck, the exact nature of their mission still a mystery to me, I called up to the house.

'Hey, Boots, I'm going to Lafayette to talk to a lawyer, then I have to pick up some ice for the coolers,' I said. 'By the way, that man in the blue shirt you saw ... I think he was just in the shop. He's a fundamentalist radio preacher. I guess he's trying to do a good deed of some kind.'

'Why was he staring up at the house?'

'You've got me. He's probably just one of those guys who left his grits on the stove too long. Anyway, he seems harmless enough.'

If I had only mentioned his name or the fact that he was with his wife, or that he was elderly, or that he was a southern mountain transplant. Any one of those things would have made all the difference.

6

She had just changed into a pair of shorts and sandals to work in the garden when he knocked on the front screen door. He wore a blue cotton short-sleeve shirt and a Panama hat with a flowered band around the crown. His physique was massive, without a teaspoon of fat on it, his neck like a tree stump with thick roots at the base that wedged into his wide shoulders. His neatly creased slacks hung loosely on his tapered waist and flat stomach.

But his green eyes were shy, and they crinkled when he smiled. He carried a paper sack under his right arm.

'I wasn't able to give this to your husband, but perhaps I can give it to you,' he said.

'He'll be home a little later, if you want to come back.'

'I'm sorry, I forgot to introduce myself. My name's Will Buchalter. Actually this is for you and the little girl.'

'I'm not quite sure I understand.'

'It's a gift. Some candy.' He slipped the box, which was wrapped in ribbon and satin paper, partially out of the sack.

'That's very nice of you, I'm sure, but it might be better if you drop back by when Dave's here.'

'I didn't mean to cause an inconvenience. I'm a little bit inept sometimes.'

'No, I didn't mean that you were—'

'Could I have a glass of water, please?' He took off his hat. His fine blond hair was damp in the heat.

Her eyes went past his shoulder to the dock, where she could see Batist washing fish fillets in a bloody pan.

'Or I can just walk down to the bait shop,' he said.

'No, no, come in. I'll get you one,' she said, and opened the screen for him. 'Dave said he was talking to you earlier about something?'

He nodded, his eyes crinkling again, filling with light, focusing on nothing. When she returned from the kitchen, he was sitting on the couch, examining two seventy-eight rpm records that he had removed from the metal racks where I kept my historical jazz collection.

'Oh,' she said. 'Those are quite rare. They have to be handled very carefully.'

'Yes, I know,' he said. 'This is Benny Goodman's nineteen thirty-three band. But there's dust along the rim. You see, the open end of the jacket should always be turned toward the back of the shelf.' He slipped his large hand inside one of the paper jackets and slid out the record.

'Please, you shouldn't do that.'

'Don't worry. I have a big collection of my own,' he said. 'Watch my hands. See, I don't touch the grooves. Fingerprints can mar a record in the same way they cause rust on gun blueing.'

He rubbed the record's rim softly with a piece of Kleenex, then carefully inserted it back in the paper jacket. He looked up into Bootsie's face.

'I'm sorry. I shouldn't have handled them,' he said, twisting sideways and replacing both records on the rack. 'But a shudder goes through me when I see dust on a beautiful old record. You have some wonderful ones in your collection. I'd give anything to have those Bix Beiderbeckes and Bunk Johnsons in mine.'

'Dave's collected them since he was in high school. That's why I'm a little nervous if somebody picks them up.' She handed him the glass of water and remained standing.

'Well, I won't take any more of your time. I just wanted to leave this little gift and introduce myself.' He took a small sip from the water glass and placed the box of candy on the arm of the couch. 'Before I go, could I show you something? It'd mean a lot to me.'

The hair on his forearms looked golden and soft, like down, in the shaft of sunlight that fell through the side window. He removed a silver leather-bound scrapbook from the paper bag and rested it in his lap.

'It'll only take a minute,' he said.

'I'm a little behind in my work today.'

'Please. Then I won't bother y'all any more.'

'Well, for just a minute,' she said.

She sat down next to him, her legs crossed, her hands folded on her knee.

'I know that Mr Bimstine has talked to Dave, but unfortunately he's sometimes not a truthful man,' he said.

'Bimstine?'

'Yes, Hippo Bimstine. Sometimes he has a way of concealing what he's really up to. I'm afraid it might just be another racial characteristic with him and some of his friends.'

'I'm not making the connection. I'm not sure of what you're doing here, either.'

He patted his palms lightly on the silver leather of the scrapbook.

'I don't want to say something that's offensive to anyone,' he said. 'But Mr Bimstine lies about the causes he serves. I doubt that he's told your husband he raises money for Israel.'

'You had better come back later and talk to Dave about this.'

'You're misunderstanding me. I didn't come here to criticize Mr Bimstine. I just wanted to show you how a hoax can be created.' His thumb peeled back several stiff pages of the scrapbook to one that contained two clipped-out newspaper photographs of men in striped prison uniforms and caps, staring out at the camera from behind barbed wire. Their faces were gaunt and unshaved, their eyes luminous with hunger and fear. 'These are supposed to be Jews in a German extermination camp in nineteen forty-four. But look, Mrs Robicheaux.' He flipped to the next page. 'Here are the same photographs as they appeared in a Polish newspaper in nineteen thirty-one. These were Polish convicts, not German political prisoners. This is all part of a hoax that was perpetrated by British Intelligence. . . . I'm sorry. Have I upset you about something?'

'I mistook you for someone else,' she said rising to her feet. 'I have to go somewhere now.'

'Where?'

'That's not your . . . Please go now.'

He rose to his feet. His face looked down into hers, only inches away. For the first time she noticed that there were blackheads, like a spray of pepper, at the corners of his eyes.

'I only wanted to help,' he said. 'To bring you and your husband some information that you didn't have before. You invited me in.'

'I thought you were someone else,' she repeated. 'It's not your fault. But I want you to leave.'

'I'd like to help you, if you'd let me.'

'I'm going out the door now. If you don't leave, I'll call—'

'Who? That black man washing fish? I think you're very tense. You don't need to stay that way, Mrs Robicheaux. Believe me.'

'Please get out of my way.'

He rested both of his hands on her shoulders and searched in her eyes as a lover might. 'How does this feel?' he asked, then tightened his fingers on her muscles and inched them down her back and sides, widening his knees slightly, flexing his loins.

'You get away from me. You disgusting—' she said, his breath, the astringent reek of his deodorant washing over her.

'I wouldn't hurt you in any way. You're a lovely woman, but your husband is working for Jews. Hush, hush, now, I just want to give you something to remember our little moment by.'

His arms encircled her waist, locking hand-on-wrist in the small of her back, tightening until she thought her rib cage would snap. He bent her backwards, smothering her body with his, then pushed his tongue deep inside her mouth. He held her a long moment, and as he did, he clenched her left kidney with one hand, like a machinist's vise fastening on a green walnut, and squeezed until yellow and red patterns danced behind her eyes and she felt urine running from her shorts.

She sat cross-legged and weeping against the wall, her face buried in her hands as he started his red convertible in the drive, tuned his radio, and backed out into the dirt road, the dappled sunlight spangling on the waxed finish of his car.

7

There was no record of a Will Buchalter with the New Iberia city police or the sheriff's department or with the state police in Baton Rouge. No parish or city agency in New Orleans had a record of him, either, nor did the National Crime Information Center in Washington, D.C. Nor could Bootsie identify him from any of the mug shots at the Iberia Parish sheriff's office.

Our fingerprint man lifted almost perfect sets of prints from the water glass used by the man who called himself Will Buchalter, from the record jackets he'd touched, and from the box of candy he'd left behind. But without a suspect in custody or corresponding prints on file, they were virtually worthless.

There was another problem, too, one that many victims of a sexual assault discover. Sexual crimes, as they are defined by our legal system, often fall into arbitrary categories that have nothing to do with the actual degree of physical pain, humiliation, and emotional injury perpetrated on the victim. At best we would probably only be able to charge the man who called himself Will Buchalter with misdemeanor battery, committed under circumstances that would probably make a venal defense lawyer lick his teeth.

I called Hippo Bimstine early the next morning, then drove to New Orleans and met him at his house in the Carrollton district by the levee. He sat in a stuffed red velvet chair by the front window, which reached from the floor to the ceiling, and kept fooling with a cellophane-wrapped cigar that was the diameter of a twenty-five-cent piece. His hair was wet and freshly combed, parted as neatly as a ruled line down the center of his head. His lower stomach bulged like a pillow under his slacks. Hanging on the wall above the mantel was a gilt-framed photograph of Hippo and his wife and their nine children, all of whom resembled him.

'How about sitting down, Dave?' he said. 'I don't feel too comfortable with a guy who acts like he was shot out of a cannon five minutes ago.'

'He knew you.'

'So do a lot of people. That doesn't mean I know them.'

'Who is he, Hippo?'

'A guy who obviously doesn't like Jews. What else can I tell you?'

'You'd better stop jerking me around.'

'How about a Dr Pepper or something to eat? Look, you think I rat-fuck

43

my friends? That's what you're telling me, I set you up for some lowlife to come in your house and molest your wife?'

'He said you were raising money for Israel.'

'Then he's full of shit. I'm an American businessman. The big word there is *American*. I care about this city, I care about this nation. You bring me that Nazi fuck and I'll clip him for you.'

'How do you know he's a Nazi?'

'I took a wild guess.'

'What's in that sub?'

'Seawater and dead krauts. Jesus Christ, how do I know what's in there? Like I've been down in German submarines?' He looked at me a long moment, started to unwrap his cigar, then dropped it on the coffee table and stared out the window at a solitary moss-strung oak in his front yard. 'I'm sorry what this guy did to your wife. I don't know who he is, though. But maybe there're more of these kinds of guys around than you want to believe, Dave. Come on in back.'

I followed him deep into his house, which had been built in the 1870s, with oak floors, spiral staircases, high ceilings, and enormous windows that were domed at the top with stained glass. Then we crossed his tree-shaded, brick-walled backyard, past a swimming pool in which islands of dead oak leaves floated on the chemical green surface, to a small white stucco office with a blue tile roof that was almost completely encased by banana trees. He used a key on a ring to unlock the door.

The furniture inside was stacked with boxes of documents and files, the corkboards on the walls layered with thumbtacked sheets of paper, newspaper clippings, yellowed photographs with curled edges, computer printouts of people's names, telephone numbers, home and business addresses. The room was almost frigid from the air-conditioning unit in the window.

I stared at an eight-by-ten photograph in the middle of a cork-board. In it a group of children, perhaps between the ages of five and eight, had rolled up their coat sleeves from their right forearms to show the serial numbers that had been tattooed across their skin.

'Those kids look like they're part of a hoax, Dave?' he said.

'What's going on, partner?'

He didn't answer. He sat down at his desk, his massive buttocks splaying across the chair, his huge head sinking into his shoulders like a pumpkin, and clicked on his computer and viewing screen. I watched him type the name 'Buchalter' on the keyboard, then enter it into the computer. A second later a file leaped into the blue viewing screen. Hippo tapped on a key that rolled the screen like film being pulled through a projector while his eyes narrowed and studied each entry.

'Take a look,' he said. 'I've got a half dozen Buchalters here, but none of them seem to be your man. These guys are too old or they're in jail or dead.'

'What is all this?'

'I belong to a group of people who have a network. We keep tabs on the guys who'd like to see more ovens and searchlights and guard towers in the world – the Klan, the American Nazi party, the Aryan Nation, skinheads out on the coast, a bunch of buttwipes called Christian Identity at Hayden Lake, Idaho. They don't just spit Red Man anymore, Dave. They're organized, they all know each other, they've got one agenda – they'd like to make bars of soap out of people they disagree with. Not just Jews. People like you'd qualify, too.'

'Try another spelling,' I said.

'No, I think we've got the right spelling, just the wrong generation. I'll give you a history lesson. Look at this.' He tapped the key again that rolled the screen, then stopped at the name *Buchalter, Jon Matthew.* 'You ever hear of the American-German Bund?'

'Yeah, it was a fascist movement back in the nineteen thirties. They held rallies in Madison Square Garden.'

'That's right. And an offshoot of the Bund was a group called the Silver Shirts. One of their founders was this guy Jon Matthew Buchalter. He went to federal prison for treason and got out in nineteen fifty-six, just in time to die of liver cancer.'

'Okay?'

'He was from Grand Isle.'

'So maybe the guy who came to my house is related to him?'

He clicked off his computer and turned to face me in his chair. His head sank into his neck, and his jowls swelled out like the bottom of a deflated basketball. 'I've got no answers for you,' he said. 'Sometimes I wonder if I haven't gone around the bend. How many people keep a rat's nest of evil like this in their backyard?'

I looked into his eyes.

'I don't want to offend you, Hippo, but I don't think you've squared with me. Is there something about this submarine you haven't told me?'

'Hey, time for a flash, Dave. You told *me* about the sub, remember? You bargained with *me* about the finder's fee. You think I got secrets, I live in a private world? You bet your oysters I do. The bars on my house windows, the electronic security system, the rent-a-cops I pay to watch my kids, you think I got all that because I'm worried a bunch of coloreds from Magazine are gonna walk off with my lawn furniture? You're living in the New Jerusalem, Dave. It's the year zero; it's us against them. We either make it or we don't.'

'I'm not sure I get what you're saying, Hippo. I'm not sure I want to, either. It sounds a little messianic.'

His face was flushed, his collar wilted like damp tissue paper around his thick neck.

'Go on back to the worm business, Dave,' he said. 'That guy comes around your house again, do the earth a favor, screw a gun barrel in his mouth and blow his fucking head off. Leave me alone now, will you? I don't feel too good. I got blood pressure could blow gaskets out of a truck engine.'

He wiped at his mouth with his hand. His lips were purple in the refrigerated gloom of his office. He stared at a collection of thumbtacked news articles and photographs on his corkboard as though his eyes could penetrate the black-and-white grain of the paper, as though perhaps he himself had been pulled inside a photograph, into a world of freight cars grinding slowly to a stop by a barbed-wire gate that yawned open like a hungry mouth, while dogs barked in the eye-watering glare of searchlights and files of the newly arrived moved in silhouette toward buildings with conical chimneys that disappeared into their own smoke.

Or was I making a complexity out of a histrionic and disingenuous fat man whose self-manufactured drama had accidentally brought a stray misanthrope out of the woodwork?

It was hard to buy into the notion that somehow World War II was still playing at the Bijou in New Orleans, Louisiana.

I left him in his office and walked outside into the light. The heat was like a match flame against my skin.

'It sounds deeply weird,' Clete said, biting into his po'-boy sandwich at a small grocery store up by Audubon Park, where the owner kept tables for working people to eat their lunch. 'But maybe we're just living in weird times. It's not like the old days.'

'You believe this American Bund stuff?'

'No, it's the way people think nowadays that bothers me. Like this vigilante gig and this Citizens Committee for a Better New Orleans. You knew Bimstine and Tommy Lonighan are both on it?'

'No. When did Lonighan become a Rotarian?'

'Law-and-order and well-run vice can get along real good together. Conventioneers looking for a blow job don't like getting rolled or ripped off by Murphy artists. Did you know that Lucinda Bergeron is NOPD's liaison person with the Committee?'

He chewed his food slowly, watching my face. Outside, the wind was blowing and denting the canopy of spreading oaks along St Charles.

'Then this preacher whose head glows in the dark shows up at your dock and tells you he's part of the same bunch. You starting to see some patterns here, noble mon?' he said.

'I don't know what any of that has to do with the guy who hurt Bootsie.'

'Maybe it doesn't.' He watched the streetcar roll down the track on the neutral ground and stop on the corner. It was loaded with Japanese businessmen. In spite of the temperature they all wore dark blue suits, ties, and long-sleeve shirts. 'If I were a worrying man, you know what would worry me most? It's not the crack and the black punks in the projects. It's a feeling I've got about the normals, it's like they wouldn't mind trying it a different way for a while.'

'What do you mean?'

'Maybe I'm wrong, but if tomorrow morning I woke up and read in *The Times-Picayune* that an election had just been held and it was now legal to run the lowlifes through tree shredders, you know, the kind the park guys use to grind oak limbs into wood chips, it wouldn't be a big surprise.'

'Did you ever hear of anybody in the city who fits the description of this guy Buchalter?'

'Nope. I've got a theory, though; at least it's something we can check out.

He's an out-of-towner. He went to your house to shake up your cookie bag. Right? There doesn't seem to be any obvious connection between our man and any particular local bucket of shit we might have had trouble with. Right? What does all that suggest to you, Streak?'

'One of the resident wise guys using out-of-town talent to send a message.'

'And whose Johnson did we just jerk on? It can't hurt to have a talk with Tommy Bobalouba again, can it?'

'I thought he was part of your meal ticket.'

'Not anymore. I don't like the way he acted in front of Martina. You take an Irish street prick out of the Channel, put him in an eight-hundred-thou house by Lake Pontchartrain, and you've got an Irish street prick in an eight-hundred-thou house by Lake Pontchartrain. How about we have a little party?'

'I'm on leave, and I'm out of my jurisdiction.'

'Who cares? If the guy's clean, it's no big deal. If he's not, fuck that procedural stuff. We scramble his eggs.'

The cashier cut his eyes toward us, then turned the floor fan so that our conversation was blown out the open door, away from the other customers.

'Let me call home first,' I said.

'No argument?'

I shrugged my shoulders. He watched my face.

'How much sleep did you get last night?' he asked.

'Enough.'

'You could fool me.'

'You want to go out to Lonighan's or not?'

There was a pause in his eyes, a fine bead of light. He made a round button with his lips and scratched at his cheek with one fingernail.

Lonighan lived a short distance from the yacht club in an imitation Tudor mansion that had been built by a New Orleans beer baron during the 1920s. The grounds were surrounded by a high brick wall, at the front of which was a piked security gate, with heavy clumps of banana trees on each side of it, and a winding driveway that led past a screened-in pool and clay tennis courts that were scattered with leaves. We parked my truck, and Clete pushed the button on the speaker box by the gate.

'Who is it?' a voice said through the box.

'Clete Purcel. Is Tommy home?'

'He's over at his gym. You want to come back later or leave a message?'

'Who are all those people in the pool?'

'Some guests. Just leave a message, Clete. I'll give it to him.'

'When'll he be home?'

'He comes, he goes, what do I know? Just leave a fucking message, will you?'

'Here's the message, Art. I don't like talking to a box.'

'I'm sorry, I'll be down. Hey, Clete, I'm just the hired help, all right?'

A moment later the man named Art walked down the drive with a pair of hedge clippers in his hand. He was bare-chested and sweaty and wore grass-stained white shorts and sandals that flopped on his feet.

'Open up,' Clete said.

'You're putting me in a bad place, man. Why'd you have to get Tommy upset?'

'I didn't do anything to Tommy.'

'Tell that to him. Christ, Clete, you know what kind of guy he is. How you think he feels when a broad tells him off in public?'

'You gonna open up?'

'No.'

'You're starting to piss me off, Art.'

'What can I say? Wait in your truck, I'll send you guys out some drinks and sandwiches. Give me a break, all right?'

He walked back toward the house. The swimmers were leaving the screened-in pool for a shady area in the trees, set with lawn chairs, a drinks table, and a smoking barbecue pit. The skin flexed around the corners of Clete's eyes.

'You still got your binoculars?' he asked.

'In the glove compartment.'

He went to the truck and returned to the gate. He focused my pair of World War II Japanese field glasses through the steel bars and studied the people in the shade.

'Check it out, mon,' he said, handing me the glasses.

One woman lay on a reclining chair with a newspaper over her face. A second, older, heavyset and big-breasted, her skin tanned almost the color of mahogany, stood on the lawn with her feet spread wide, touching each toe with a cross-handed motion, her ash blond hair cascading back and forth across her shoulders. A third woman, with dyed red hair, who could not have been over twenty or twenty-one, was bent forward over a pocket mirror, a short soda straw held to one nostril, the other nostril pinched shut with a forefinger. Seated on each side of her was a thick-bodied, sun-browned, middle-aged man with a neon bikini wrapped wetly around the genitals, the back and chest streaked with wisps of black and gray hair. The face of one man was flecked with fine patterns of scab tissue, as though he had walked through a reddish brown skein of cobweb.

'When did Tommy Blue Eyes hook up with the Caluccis?' Clete said. 'They always hated each other.'

'Business is business.'

'Yeah, but the micks always looked down on the greaseballs. They didn't socialize with them.' He took the glasses out of my hand and looked again through the bars. 'If you think Bobo and Max are geeks, check out the cat flopping steaks on the grill.'

A man who must have been six and one half feet tall had come out of the side entrance to the house with a tray of meat. He had a flat Indian face, a cheerless mouth, and wide-set, muddy eyes that didn't squint or blink in the smoke rising from the pit. His hair was jet black and freshly barbered and looked like a close-cropped wig glued on brownish red stone.

'All the guy needs are electrodes inset in his temples,' Clete said.

'I don't think this is going anywhere,' I said. 'I probably should head back to New Iberia.'

His green eyes roamed over my face. 'You don't think Bootsie can handle it?' he asked.

'How do I know, Clete? He humiliated her, he put his tongue in her mouth, he left bruises on her kidney like he'd taken a pair of pliers to her.'

He nodded and didn't speak for a moment. Then he said, 'That blonde doing the aerobics is Tommy's regular punch when his old lady's out of town. No, she's more than that, he got a real Jones for her. Believe me, Tommy and that clunk of radiator hose he's got for a schlong aren't far away. Dave, look at me. You got my word, I'm going to dig this guy Buchalter out of the woodwork. If you're not around, I'll give you a Polaroid, then you can burn it.'

He continued to stare into my face, then he said, 'You're troubling me, noble mon.'

'What's the problem?'

'You look wired to the eyes, that's the problem.'

'So what?'

'You have a way of throwing major monkey shit through the window fan, that's what.'

'*I* do?'

'Go down to the corner and call Bootsie. Then we'll give it another hour. If Tommy's not back by then, we'll hang it up.'

We waited in the truck for another hour, but Tommy Lonighan didn't return. The metal of my dashboard burned my hands when I touched it, and the air smelled of salt and dead water beetles in the rain gutters. I started the engine.

'Wait a minute. They're coming out. Let's not waste an opportunity, mon,' Clete said.

The electronic piked gate opened automatically, and the Calucci brothers, in a light blue Cadillac convertible, with the two younger women in the backseat, drove out of the shade into the sunlight. I started to block their exit with the truck, but it was unnecessary. Max Calucci, the driver, and one of the women in back were arguing furiously. Max stepped hard on the brakes, jolting everyone in the car forward, turned in his leather seat, and began jabbing his finger at the woman. The woman, the one who had been doing lines through a soda straw earlier, climbed out of the backseat in her shorts and spiked heels, raking a long, paint-curling scratch down the side of the Cadillac.

Max got out of the car and struck the woman full across the mouth with the flat of his hand. He hit her so hard that a barrette flew from her lacquered red hair. Then he slapped her across the ear. She pressed her palms into her face and began to weep.

None of them saw us until we had walked to within five feet of their car.

'Better ease up, Max. People might start to think you abuse women,' Clete said.

'What are *you* doing here?' Max said. He was bald down through the center of his head, and drops of sweat the size of BB's glistened in his thick, dark eyebrows. Up close, the scabs on his face and neck looked like curlicues of reddish brown, fine-linked chain.

'Art didn't let you know we were out here?' Clete said. 'That's why you didn't invite us in?'

'You blindsided me the other night, Purcel. It's not over between us. You better haul your fat ass out of here,' Max said.

'Y'all know a dude by the name of Will Buchalter? Streak here'd really like to talk to him,' Clete said.

'No, I don't know him. Now get out of here—' He stopped and raised his finger in the face of the woman with the dyed red hair. 'And *you*, get back in the car. You're gonna polish that scratch out if you have to do it with your twat. Did you hear me, move! You don't open that mouth again, either, unless I want to put something in it.'

He clamped his hand on the back of her neck, squeezed, and twisted her toward the car while tears ran from her eyes.

The shovel lay propped among some rosebushes against the brick wall. It had a long, work-worn wood handle with a wide, round-backed blade. Max Calucci did not see me pick it up. Nor did he see me swing it with both hands, from deep behind me, as I would a baseball bat, until he heard the blade ripping through the air. By then it was too late. The metal whanged off his elbow and thudded into his rib cage, bending him double, and I saw his mouth drop open and a level of pain leap into his eyes that he could not quite find words to express.

Then I reversed the shovel in my hands and swung the blade up into his face, as you would butt-stroke an adversary with a pugil stick. I saw him tumble backwards on the grass, his knees drawn up in front of him, his face bloodless with shock, his mouth a scarlet circle of disbelief. I heard feet running down the drive, Bobo Calucci blowing the car horn with both hands in desperation, then Clete was standing in front of me, pressing me back with his palms, his armpits drenched with perspiration, the strap of his nylon shoulder holster biting into one nipple.

'For Christ's sakes, back off, Dave, you're gonna kill the guy,' he was saying. 'You hear me? Let it slide, Streak. He's not the guy we care about.'

Then his big hands dropped to the handle of the shovel and twisted it from my grasp, his Irish pie-plate face two inches from mine, his eyes filled with pity and an undisguised and fearful love.

8

That night, as I lay next to Bootsie in our bed, I did not tell her about the incident with the Calucci brothers. Even though I had been in Alcoholics Anonymous a number of years, and to one degree or another had been through the twelve steps of recovery and had tried to incorporate them into my life, I had never achieved a great degree of self-knowledge, other than the fact that I was a drunk; nor had I ever been able to explain my behavior and the way I thought, or didn't think, to normal people.

I always wanted to believe that those moments of rage, which affected me almost like an alcoholic blackout, were due to a legitimate cause, that I or someone close to me had been seriously wronged, that the object of my anger and adrenaline had not swum coincidentally into my ken.

But I had known too many cops who thought the same way. Somehow there was always an available justification for the Taser dart, the jet of Mace straight into the eyes, the steel baton whipped across the shinbones or the backs of the thighs.

The temptation is to blame the job, the stressed-out adversarial daily routine that can begin like a rupturing peptic ulcer, the judges and parole boards who recycle psychopaths back on the street faster than you can shut their files. But sometimes in an honest moment an unpleasant conclusion works its way through all the rhetoric of the self-apologist, namely, that you are drawn to this world in the same way that some people are fascinated by the protean shape and texture of fire, to the extent that they need to slide their hands through its caress.

I remember an old-time gunbull at Angola who had spent forty-seven years of his life shepherding convicts under a double-barreled twelve-gauge out on the Mississippi levee. During that time he had killed four men and wounded a half dozen others. His liver had been eaten away with cirrhosis; the right side of his chest was caved in from the surgical removal of a cancerous lung. To my knowledge, he had no relatives with whom he kept contact, no women in his life except a prostitute in Opelousas. I asked him how he had come to be a career gunbull.

He thought about it a moment, then dipped the end of his cigar in his whiskey glass and put it in his mouth.

'It was me or them, I reckon,' he said.

'Beg your pardon?'

'I figured the kind of man I was, one way or another I was gonna be jailing. Better to do it up there on the horse than down there with a bunch of niggers chopping in the cane.'

I didn't tell Bootsie about the Caluccis, nor did I say anything to her about the smell of bourbon that she brought to bed with her that night. I fell asleep with my hand on her back. At about one in the morning I felt her weight leave the mattress. I heard her walk barefooted into the kitchen, open a cabinet without turning on the light, then clink a bottle against a glass. A moment later she was in the bathroom, brushing her teeth.

She seldom drank and had little physical tolerance for alcohol. The following morning she stayed in the shower for almost fifteen minutes, then ate an aspirin with her coffee and talked brightly at the breakfast table for a long time, until finally her face became wan and she put her forehead down on her palm.

I walked around behind her chair and rubbed her neck and shoulders.

'Sometimes it's hard to accept this, Boots, but there's no reason to feel shame when we're overcome by superior physical force,' I said. 'No more than a person should be ashamed of contracting the flu or being undone by the attack of a wild animal.'

'I keep smelling his odor and feeling his tongue in my mouth,' she said. 'I feel somehow that I allowed him to do it.'

'It's what all victims feel. We open our doors to the wrong person, then we think that somehow our expression of trust means we're weak and complicit. You didn't do anything wrong, Boots. You mustn't think that way anymore.'

But that kind of advice, under those kinds of circumstances, is similar to telling a person who has been stricken with a cerebral disease to rise from his sickbed and walk.

I turned off the grits on the stove, washed and put away our coffee cups and saucers, and took Bootsie to a restaurant on the Vermilion River in Lafayette for brunch. When I went to the men's room, she called the waiter back to the table and ordered a vodka collins. After we had eaten, we walked out on the deck that overlooked the water and watched some kids waterskiing. The sun was white and straight up in the sky, the air laced with the smell of diesel smoke from the trucks passing over the concrete bridge. Down below in the muddy current, a dead snow egret floated among an island of twigs and torn camellia leaves. The egret's wing had been broken, and above one eye was the coppery glint of an embedded BB in the feathers.

'Oh,' Bootsie said, and let out her breath. Then she turned away from the deck railing and said, 'Maybe we should go now, Dave. I'm going to listen to you and stay out of the sun. I've been terribly careless about it, I know. It's wrong to make other people worry about you, isn't it? I am not going to allow myself to be a careless person anymore, I promise.'

Her eyes were as bright and intent as if she were putting together a syllogism that in one way or another would solve a particular problem for all time. She walked back through the restaurant and out the front without waiting for me.

When we got home the phone was ringing in the kitchen. Bootsie went into the bedroom, turned on the window fan, and lay down on the bed with her arm across her eyes.

'Hello,' I said into the telephone receiver.

'This Mr Robicheaux?'

'Yes.'

'How come you ain't he'ped my mama?'

'Excuse me?'

'She he'ped you, ain't she? How come you ain't he'ped her?'

'Who is this?'

'Zoot Bergeron.' But the tone of voice had become less aggressive and certain. 'My mama said Mr Baxter's gonna get her fired if he can.'

'You're Lucinda's son?'

'Yes, suh.' Then he tried to deepen his voice. 'Yeah, that's right.'

'How old are you, podna?'

'Seventeen. I'm seventeen years old.' In the background I could hear echoes, like people shouting at each other in a public hall, and slapping sounds like leather hitting against leather.

'Does your mother know you're making this call?' I said.

'She tole you some stuff and you tole it back to Mr Baxter. That ain't right she got to be in trouble 'cause you went and tole what you wasn't supposed to.'

Oh boy, I thought, *the business about the other homicide victims being mutilated.*

'I'll talk to your mother about it,' I said.

I could almost hear his breath click in his throat.

'That won't do no good. I can tell you who them vigilantes are. Then you and my mama can arrest them.'

'Oh? Why don't you just tell her?'

''Cause she don't believe me.'

'I see.'

'You coming down here?' he said.

'Where would that be?'

'The gym. Mr Lonighan's Sport Center. You know where that's at?'

'What are you doing around Tommy Lonighan, partner?'

'I box here and I sweep up in the evening. You coming?'

'I'll think about it.'

I heard somebody begin to do a *rat-a-tat-tat* on a timing bag.

'You gonna tell her I called?'

'What's your name again?'

'Zoot.'

'That's a nifty name, Zoot. No, I'm not going to tell your mama that you called. But you listen to what I tell you, now. Don't be telling other people you know anything about vigilantes. Particularly around that gym. Okay?'

'Yes, suh. I mean, I got it. I'll be expecting you though. A deal's a deal, right? We got us a deal, ain't that right?'

'Wait a minute . . .'

53

'My mama said you was a nice man, said for me not to be blaming her trouble with Mr Baxter on you. She's right, ain't she? I be here this evening, I be here early in the morning.'

He hung up before I could answer.

At three that same afternoon I received a call from the lawyer I had retained to represent Batist. He was the most successful criminal attorney in Lafayette. My five-minute conversation with him was another lesson in how the laws of finance apply to our legal system. The lawyer had confronted the prosecutor's office in New Orleans with the information given me by Lucinda Bergeron about the other murders; he also told them he could present a half dozen depositions to the effect that Batist was nowhere around New Orleans when they were committed. He also mentioned the possibility of civil suit against the city of New Orleans.

The homicide charge against Batist was to be dropped by tomorrow morning.

'That's it?' I said.

'That's it.'

'Did they bother to explain why he was ever charged in the first place?'

'They make mistakes like anybody else.'

'It sounds like they're pretty good at self-absolution.'

'I think we've done pretty well today.'

'How much do I owe you, Mr Guidry?'

'There're no fees beyond what we originally agreed upon,' he said.

'You're telling me six thousand dollars for making some phone calls?'

'There was some investigative work involved as well.'

'Six thousand dollars without even going to trial?'

'I thought you'd be pleased to hear your friend was out of trouble.'

I was. I was also down eleven thousand dollars in attorney and bondsman's fees, which I would have to pay in monthly installments or with borrowed money.

That evening I took Bootsie and Alafair to a movie in New Iberia. It was raining when we got home, and the air smelled like fish left on the warm planks of a dock and wet trees and moldy pecan husks. Then, just when we were going to bed, Clete called from New Orleans and told me a strange story that had been passed on to him by a friend of his in the Coast Guard.

Two days ago, at sunset, out on the salt south of Cocodrie, a Coast Guard cutter had spotted a twenty-two-foot cabin cruiser anchored in the swells, the bow bouncing against the incoming tide. All week the cutter had been looking for a mother ship, perhaps a Panamanian tanker, that had been dumping air-sealed bales of reefer, with floating marker bottles, overboard for smaller, high-powered boats to fish out of the water and run through the bayous and canals to overland transporters who waited on high ground up in the wetlands.

There were two men in wet suits on board the cabin cruiser. They were lowering a cluster of underwater lights on a cable over the side when they saw the cutter approaching them. The Coast Guard skipper was sure he had found a pickup boat.

He lost any doubt when the men on the cabin cruiser pulled the cluster of lights clattering back over the rail, sawed loose the anchor rope with a bowie knife, and hit it full-bore for the coastline and shallower water, where there was a chance the cutter would go aground on a sandbar.

But when they made their turn the late sun must have been directly in their eyes. Or perhaps in their attempt at flight they simply did not care that they had left a diver overboard, a man in a wet suit, with air tanks, whose head was shaved as bald as a skinned onion. He popped through a swell at exactly the spot his friends had cut the anchor rope. He probably had no explanation for the fact that the rope had suddenly gone slack in his hands and the gulf's placid surface had churned to life with the cabin cruiser's screws and the dirty roar of exhaust pipes at the waterline.

Then through the humidity inside his mask, through the green chop against the glass, he must have realized that his worst fears as a diver – losing his electric light deep in the bowels of a sunken ship or perhaps being pulled down into a bottomless canyon by a mouthful of hooked teeth that snapped his bones as easily as sticks – were never legitimate fears at all, that the most terrible moment of his life was now being precipitated by his companions, for no reason that he could understand, in a way that made his screams, his waving arms, his last-second attempt to dive deep below the surface the impotent and futile gestures of a nightmare.

The cabin cruiser must have been hitting thirty-five knots when it plowed over him and the screws razored his body and left him floating like a rubber-wrapped tangle of mismatched parts in the boat's wake.

'Why were the guys on the boat running?' I said to Clete.

'They'd stolen it. Well, not exactly. It's owned by some millionaire yachtsman in Baltimore, but this alcoholic skipper keeps it for him in Biloxi. So the drunk thought he'd make a few bucks by renting it to these three guys. But at the last minute the three guys decided they didn't need to pay him the money after all, so instead they just stomped the shit out of him. They told him if he made a beef about it they'd catch him later and kick one of his own whiskey bottles up his ass.'

'Who were the guys?'

'The two in custody are just a couple of Biloxi beach farts who've been in and out of Parchman on nickel-and-dime B&E's. But dig this, the guy who got run through the propeller had some beautiful Nazi artwork on both arms – swastikas and SS lightning bolts.'

'So do most cons in the Aryan Brotherhood,' I said.

'But here's the kicker, mon. This guy was not homegrown. The Coast Guard found his passport on the cabin cruiser. He was from Berlin.'

'Do the guys in custody say what they were after?'

'They were hired by the German guy, but they claim the German guy wouldn't tell them what was down there. They thought maybe it was a scuttled boat with a lot of dope on it. Here's the real laugh, though. The Coast Guard says there's no boat down at that spot. What the beach farts and the skinhead probably saw on their sonar was an oil rig that sank there in a hurricane about twenty years ago.'

'Thanks for the information, Clete.'

'You want to talk to the guys in custody?'

'Maybe.'

'I'd do it soon. The rummy in Biloxi isn't filing charges, and the kraut's death is going down as accidental. I don't guess anybody's going to lose sleep over a skinhead getting turned into potted meat out on the salt.'

'Thanks again, Clete.'

'You think they were after that sub?'

'Who knows?'

'Hippo Bimstine does. I want in on this, mon. When Streak operates in the Big Sleazy, he needs his old podjo to cover his back. Am I right?'

'Right. Good night, Cletus.'

I heard him pop the cap on a bottle and pour it into a glass.

'Bless my soul, I love that old-time rock 'n' roll, when the Bobbsey Twins from Homicide made their puds shrivel up and hide,' he said.

My palms felt stiff with fatigue, hard to fold closed, and my eyes burned as though there were sand behind the lids. Clete was still talking, rattling fresh ice into his glass, when I said good night a final time and eased the receiver down into the telephone cradle.

Tommy Lonighan's Sport Center was located on the edge of downtown New Orleans, in a late-nineteenth-century two-story brick building that had originally been a firehouse, then an automotive dealership in the 1920s, and finally a training gym for club boxers who fought for five dollars a fight during the Depression.

The interior smelled of sweat and leather and moldy towels; the canary yellow paint on the walls was blistered and peeling above the old iron radiators; the buckled and broken spaces in the original oak flooring had been patched over with plywood and linoleum. The bodybuilding equipment was all out of another era – dumbbells and weight-lifting benches, curling bars, even a washtub of bricks hung on a cable for pull downs. The canvas on the four rings had been turned almost black from scuff marks, body and hair grease, and kicked-over spit buckets.

But it was still the most famous boxing gym in New Orleans, and probably more Golden Gloves champions had come out of it than out of any other boxing center in the South. In the sunlight that poured down through the high windows, black, Latin, Vietnamese kids and a few whites sparred in headgear and kidney guards, clanked barbells up and down on a wide rubber pad, skipped rope with the grace of tap dancers, and turned timing bags into flying, leathery blurs.

A small, elderly white man, with a thick ear and a flat, toylike face, who was pulling the laces out of a box full of old gloves, pointed out Zoot to me.

'That tall kid about to break his nose on the timing bag,' he said. 'While you're over there, tell him he ain't carried the trash out to the Dumpster yet.'

The boy had his mother's elongated turquoise eyes and clear, light-brown skin. But he was unnaturally tall for his age, over six feet, and as slim and narrow-shouldered as if his skin had been stretched on wire. The elastic top of his trunks was sopping with the sweat that streamed in rivulets down his hairless chest. Each time his fist missed the timing bag, he would glance nervously a few feet away at another kid who had turned *his* timing bag into an explosion of sound and movement. Then Zoot would smash the bag with a right cross, snapping it back on the chain, try to connect with a left, miss, swing again with his right, and miss again.

'Try not to hit harder with one hand than the other,' I said. 'You have to create a kind of circular momentum.'

'A what?'

Great choice of words, I told myself.

'You called my house yesterday,' I said.

'You Mr Robicheaux?'

'Yes.'

'Oh, yeah, well – I be with you in a minute, okay? They waiting for me over at the ring. I'm gonna go three with that white boy putting on his kidney guard.'

'You said you had some pretty important things to tell me, Zoot.'

His eyes flicked sideways, then came back on my face again.

'I gotta go my three. This ain't an easy place to talk, you know what I mean?'

'Yeah, I guess so.' I looked at the white kid who was climbing up in the corner of one of the rings. His skin had the alabaster iridescence of someone who seldom went out in the sunlight, but his stomach, which was tattooed with a red-and-green dragon, was a washboard, and the muscles in his arms looked like pieces of pig iron. 'Who is he?' I asked.

'Ummm, he fights in Miami and Houston a lot.'

'He's a pro?'

'Yes, suh.'

'You sure you want to do this, partner?'

He licked his lips and tried to hide the shine of fear in his eyes.

'He's a good guy. He's been up against some big names. He don't do this for just anybody,' Zoot said. 'I'll be right back. You ain't got to watch if you don't want. There's a Coca-Cola machine back in the dressing room.'

'I'll just take a seat over here.'

'Yes, suh. I'll be right back.'

I don't think I ever saw anyone box quite as badly as Zoot. Either he would hold both gloves in front of his face so that he was unable to see his opponent or he would drop his guard suddenly and float his face up like a balloon, right into a rain of blows. His stance was wrong-footed, he led with his right hand, he used his left like a flipper, he took shot after shot in the mouth and eyes because he didn't know how to tuck in his chin and raise his shoulder against a right cross.

Fortunately the white kid went easy on him, except in the third round when Zoot swung at the white kid's head coming out of a clench. The white kid stepped inside Zoot's long reach and hooked a hard chop into his nose.

Zoot went down on his butt in the middle of the canvas, his long legs splayed out in front of him, his mouthpiece lying wet in his lap, his eyes glazed as though someone had popped a flashbulb in his face.

Twenty minutes later he came out of the dressing room in his street clothes, combing his wet hair along the sides of his head. His nose had stopped bleeding, but his left eye had started to discolor and puff shut at the corner. We walked across the street to a café that sold pizza by the slice and sat at a table in back under a rotating electric fan.

'Have you been boxing long?' I said.

'Since school let out.'

'You trying for the Golden Gloves?'

'I just do it for fun. I don't think about the Gloves or any of that stuff.'

'Let me make a suggestion, Zoot. Keep your left shoulder up and don't lead with your right unless you go in for a body attack. Then get under the other guy's guard and hook him hard in the rib cage, right under the heart.'

He fed a long slice of pizza into his mouth and looked at me while he chewed.

'You been a fighter?' he said.

'A little bit, in high school.'

'You think maybe I could try for the Gloves?'

'I guess that'd be up to you.'

He smiled and lowered his eyes.

'You don't think I'm too good, do you?' he said.

'You just went three rounds against a pro. That's not bad.'

'I know what you're really thinking, though. You ain't got to make me feel good. Like I say, I do it for fun.' He touched at the corner of his puffed eye with one fingernail.

'You said you were going to tell me something about the vigilante murders,' I said.

'It's gang bangers. They fighting over who's gonna deal tar in the projects. Tar's real big again, Mr Robicheaux. Lot of people don't want to mess with crack anymore.'

'How do you know it's the gangs, Zoot?'

'I get around. I got friends in the projects – the St Thomas, the Iberville, the Desire. They all say there ain't no vigilante.'

'Is there a particular murder you have information about?'

He thought for a moment. 'Yeah, last spring,' he said. 'A dealer got thrown off the roof across from our school. The gang bangers said he was working the wrong neighborhood.'

He watched my face expectantly.

'Are there any names you want to give me?' I said.

'I'm just telling you what my friends say. I ain't got no names.'

'You come from a good home, Zoot. You think you should be hanging around gang bangers?'

'I got the friends I want. People don't tell me who I hang with.'

'I see. Well, thanks for the information.' I stood up to leave.'

'Ain't you gonna he'p out?'

'I'm afraid I don't have a lot to work with here.'

'Mr Robicheaux, my mama's gonna lose her job.'

I sat back down. 'Where's your dad?'

His eyes became unfocused, then he looked over at the jukebox as though he had just noticed it.

'I ain't got one. Why you ax that?' he said.

'No reason. Your mother's a tough lady. Stop worrying about her.'

'Easy for you to say. You ain't there when she come home, always telling me—'

'Telling you what?'

'I ain't nothing but a big drink of water, I gotta be a *man*, I gotta stop slouching around like somebody pulled my backbone outta my skin.' He rolled up a paper napkin in his palm and dropped it in his plate. 'It ain't her fault. They get on her case where she works, then she just *got* to get on mine. But I'm tired of it.'

For the first time I noticed how long and narrow his hands were. Even his nails were long, almost like a girl's.

'You feel like putting your trunks back on?' I said.

'What for?'

'Take a walk with me to the drugstore, then we'll head back to the gym and talk about clocks and bombsights.'

'What?'

'Come on, I'm over the hill. You'll dump me on my butt, Zoot.'

We went into the drugstore on the corner, and I bought a rubber ball, just a little smaller than the palm of my hand, and dropped it in the pocket of my slacks. Then we crossed the street to the gym, and Zoot put on his trunks again and met me in an alcove with padded mats on the floor and a huge ventilator fan bolted into the wire-mesh windows. I hung my shirt on a rack of dumbbells and slipped on a pair of sixteen-ounce gloves that were almost as big as couch pillows.

Advice is always cheap, and the cheapest kind is the sort we offer people who have to enter dangerous situations for which they are seriously unprepared or ill-equipped. I probably knew a hundred one-liners that a cut-man or a trainer had told me in the corner of a Golden Gloves ring while he worked my mouthpiece from my teeth and squeezed a sponge into my eyes ('Swallow your blood, kid. Don't never let him see you're hurt . . . He butts you again in the clench, thumb him in the eye . . . He's telegraphing. When he drops his right shoulder, click off his light').

But very few people appreciate the amount of courage that it takes to stand toe-to-toe with a superior opponent who systematically goes about breaking the cartilage in your nose, splitting your eyebrows against the bone, and turning your mouth into something that looks like a torn tomato, while the audience stands on chairs and roars its approval of your pain and humiliation.

'Let's try to keep two simple concepts in mind,' I said. 'Move in a circle with the clock. You got that? Circle him till he thinks you're a shark. Always to the left, just like you're moving with the clock.'

'All right . . .' He started circling with me, his gym shoes shuffling on the canvas pad, the skin around his temples taut with expectation, his eyes watching my fists.

'Then you look him right in the eye. Except in your mind you're seeing his face in a bombsight . . . Don't look at my hands, look at my face. His face is right in the crosshairs, you understand me, because you know it's just a matter of time till you bust him open with your left, maybe make him duck and come up without his guard, and then pull the trigger and bust him with your right.'

He circled and squinted at me above his gloves with his puffed left eye.

'Hit me,' I said.

His jabs were like spastic jerks, ill-timed, fearful, almost pathetic.

'I said hit me, Zoot!'

His left came out and socked into my gloves.

'Hit *me*, not the glove,' I said. 'You're starting to piss me off.'

'What?'

'I said you're pissing me off. Do you have some problem with your hearing?' I could see the verbal injury in his eyes. I flipped a left jab at his head and drove my right straight into his guard. Then I did it again. His head snapped back with the weight of the blow, then he caught his balance and hunched his shoulders again. I saw him lower his right slightly and a glint form in one eye like a rifleman peering down iron sights.

His left missed me and scraped past my ear, but he had forced me to duck sideways, and when he unloaded his right he snapped his shoulder into it, the sweat leaping off his face, and caught me squarely across the jaw.

I lowered my gloves and grinned at him.

'That one was a beaut,' I said, and started pulling off my gloves.

'You quitting?'

'I told you, I'm over the hill for it. Besides, I have to get back to New Iberia.'

'Go three with me.'

I reached in my slacks, took out the rubber ball I had bought at the drugstore, and tossed it to him.

'Squeeze that in each hand five hundred times a day. Do *that*, and keep working on that right cross, and you'll be able to tear off your opponent's head and spit in it, Zoot.'

When I walked toward the exit, I looked back and saw him shadowboxing in front of the ventilator fan, his right hand working the rubber ball, his head ducking and weaving in front of the spinning fan blades. Advice might be cheap, but there is nothing facile about the faith of those to whom we give it. I wished Zoot lots of luck. He was probably going to need a pile of it.

9

I was almost out the front door of the gym when Tommy Lonighan came out of his office and shook my hand like a greeter at a casino. His muscular thighs bulged out of a pair of cut-off gray sweat trunks. His light blue eyes and pink face were radiant with goodwill.

'I saw you working out with Zoot,' he said.

'He's a good kid. I hope he does all right here, Tommy.'

'I'm a bad influence?'

'He shouldn't be going up against pros.'

'He got in the ring with that white kid, the one with the dragon tattooed on his belly?'

'Yes.'

'No kidding? That's not bad for a kid whose mother was probably knocked up by a marshmallow.'

'You know how to say it, Tommy.'

'Step into my office,' he answered, smiling. 'I want to talk.'

'I'm on my way out of town.'

'I'll buy you a beer. You want a pastrami sandwich? I got your pastrami sandwich. Forget about the other night. I had too much to drink. Come on, don't be a hard-ass.'

'What's on your mind?'

'On *my* mind? Somebody hurts your wife, and the next thing I know you're beating up people in my fucking driveway. Hey, it's all right. The Caluccis are scum. I just want to talk.'

I went inside his glassed-in office and sat down in front of his desk. The walls were covered with old prizefight posters and newspaper clippings about fighters that Lonighan had owned or managed. Above a shelf filled with boxing trophies was an autographed photograph of President Reagan, with two crossed American flags tucked behind the frame.

'How did you know about my wife, Tommy?' I said.

'Because Clete Purcel's been all over town, threatening to jam a chain saw up the butt of anybody with information who doesn't pass it on.' He took a long-necked bottle of beer out of a cooler by his feet, wiped off the ice, set the cap on the edge of his desk, and popped it off with the heel of his hand. He offered it to me.

'No, thanks.'

He poured it into a schooner, took a deep drink, and wiped the corners of his mouth with the back of his wrist.

'Let me cut to it, Tommy,' I said. 'You're right, a man came to our house and harmed my wife. It was right after you tried to discourage me from working for Hippo Bimstine.'

'I got a hard time believing this, Dave. You think that's how I operate, I got to send degenerates around to hurt the wives of people I respect?'

'You tell me.' I looked directly into his eyes. The cast in them reminded me of light trapped inside blue water. They remained locked on mine, as though wheels were turning over in his brain. Then he looked out the window with a self-amused expression on his face and picked up a sandwich from a paper plate in front of him.

'Is there a private joke you want to share with me, Tommy?'

'Dave, you insulted me at your table, in front of people, then you beat the shit out of a guy with a shovel in my driveway. Then you come to my place of business and tell me I'm sending perverts over to New Iberia to bother your family. What did I do to deserve this? I offered you a fucking business situation. You don't see the humor in that?'

'I remember a line a journalist for *The Picayune* used about you once, Tommy. I never forgot it.'

'Yeah?'

'You're a mean man in a knife fight.'

'Oh yeah, I always liked that one.' He leaned forward on his elbows. His curly white hair hung across his forehead. 'I want that fucking sub. Anything the mockie's paying you, I'll double.'

'See you around, Tommy.'

'I don't get you. You act like I got jock odor or something. But it doesn't bother you to do business with a fanatic who gets people fired from their jobs.'

'I don't follow you.'

'Your buddy, bubble butt . . . *Bimstine*, Dave. He belongs to the Jewish Defense Organization. They don't like somebody, they rat-fuck him where he works.'

'I wouldn't know. I don't like the way you talk about him, though.'

'Excuse me?'

'You take cheap shots, Tommy.'

'Like maybe I'm un-American, an anti-Semite or something?'

'Read it like you want.'

'I was sixteen years old at Heartbreak Ridge. I love this country. You saying I don't—' He stopped and smiled. 'You and me might have to forget we're mature people.'

'You don't know anybody named Will Buchalter?'

'This the guy hurt your wife?'

I didn't answer and stared straight into his face. He set his sandwich on his plate, removed a wisp of lettuce from his lip, then took a sip of beer from his schooner and brought his eyes back to mine.

'What can I say? I'm fighting with cancer of the prostate,' he said. 'You want to know what's on my mind? Dying. You know what else is on my mind? Dying broke. I don't know any guy named Buchalter.'

'I'm sorry to hear about your health problem, Tommy.'

'Save it. That sweaty pile of gorilla shit you call a friend is trying to break me. We get casino gambling in New Orleans, he's gonna own it all. I got to take a piss. Which I do with my eyes closed because half the time there's blood in the bowl. You want a beer, they're in the cooler.'

He opened a small closet that had a toilet inside and, without closing the door, began urinating loudly into the water while he flexed his knees and passed gas like it was a visceral art form.

How do you read a man like Tommy Lonighan?

Heartbreak Ridge, Irish bigotry, right-wing patriotism, morbidity that he used like a weapon, speech and mood patterns that had the volatility of tinfoil baking in a microwave.

The day a person like Lonighan makes sense to you is probably the day you should seriously reexamine your relationship to the rest of the human gene pool.

And on that note I waved good-bye and left before he had finished shaking himself and thumbing his gray sweat trunks back over his genitalia.

I stopped by Clete's office on St Ann to see if he had found out anything about the man who called himself Will Buchalter.

'If the guy's local, he's low-profile,' Clete said. 'Like below street level. I think I talked to every dirtbag and right-wing crazoid in town. Have you ever been to any of these survivalist shops? I think we ought to round up some of their clientele while there's still time.'

He started to take a cigarette out of a pack on his desk; instead, he put a mint on his tongue and smiled at me with his eyes.

'How about hookers?' I said.

'The ones I know say he doesn't sound like any of their johns. I don't think he's from around here, Streak. A guy like this earns people's attention.'

'Thanks for trying, Clete.'

'Hang on. You've got two messages,' he said, taking his feet off his desk and looking at two memo slips by his telephone. 'That black sergeant, Ben Motley, you remember him, he always had his fly unzipped when he was in Vice, he wants you to call him about some dude who electrocuted himself in custody last night—'

'What?'

'Hang on, mon. I got a similar message from this character Reverend Oswald Flat. Isn't that the guy who was out at your bait shop? He's got a voice like somebody twanging on a bobby pin.'

'That's the guy.'

'Well, he called Bootsie and she told him to call here. NOPD picked up some wild man in the Garden District, can you dig this, a forty-year-old guy with tattoos on his head, wearing black leather in August. The autopsy showed he'd been shooting up with speed and paint thinner. How about that for a new combo?'

'What's the connection?'

'He had a silenced .22 Ruger automatic on him and Hippo Bimstine's address in his pocket. We'd better go talk to Motley and this guy with a mouthful of collard greens.'

'*We?*'

'Let's be serious a minute, Dave. I think you're fucking with some very bad guys. I don't know who they are, why they're interested in this submarine, or what the connections are between this citizens committee and dope dealers in the projects having their hearts cut out. But I'll bet my ass politics doesn't have diddle-shit to do with it.'

'I think this time it might.'

'Anyway, I'm backing your action, Jackson, whether you like it or not.' He leaned back in his swivel chair, grinned, and drummed on his stomach with his knuckles like a zoo creature at play.

I called Motley and told him that Clete and I would meet him at his office.

'You don't need to bring Purcel,' he said.

'Yeah, I do.'

'Suit yourself. I remember now, you always did drink down.'

'Thanks, Motley.'

Then I called the Reverend Oswald Flat and asked what I could do for him.

'Hit's about this man killed hisself in custody,' he said.

'Why would you call me?'

'Because you cain't seem to keep your tallywhacker out of the hay baler.'

'I beg your pardon?'

'You disturb me. I think there's people fixing to do you some harm, but you have a way of not hearing me. Is there a cinder block up there between your ears?'

'Reverend, I'd appreciate it if you'd—'

'All right, son, I'll try not to offend you anymore. Now, get your nose out of the air and listen to me a minute. I do counseling with prisoners. I bring 'em my Faith Made Easy tapes. I tried to counsel this crazy man they brought in there with tattoos on his head and a stink you'd have to carry on the end of a dung fork—' He stopped, as though his words had outpaced his thoughts.

'What is it?' I said.

'Hit wasn't a good moment. No, sir, hit surely wasn't. I looked into his eyes, and if that man had a soul, I believe demons had already claimed hit.'

'He was shooting up with speed and paint thinner, Reverend.'

'That may be. Your kind always got a scientific explanation. Anyway, I taped what he said. I want you to hear hit.'

I asked him to meet Clete and me down at Motley's office. He said he'd be there, but he didn't reply when I said good-bye and started to hang up.

'Is there something else?' I said.

64

'No, not really. Maybe like you say, he was just a man who filled his veins with chemicals. I just never had a fellow, not even the worst of them, claw at my eyes and spit in my face before.'

Oswald Flat was wearing a rain-spotted seersucker suit, a clip-on bow tie, white athletic socks with black shoes, and his cork sun helmet when he came through the squad room at district headquarters and sat on a wood bench next to me and Clete. He carried a small black plastic tape recorder in his hand. He blew out his breath and wiped his rimless glasses on his coat sleeve.

At the other end of the room we could see Motley through the glass of Nate Baxter's office. Motley was standing; he and Baxter were arguing.

'You want to hear hit?' Oswald Flat said, resting the recorder on his thigh. The side of his face wrinkled, as though he were reluctant to go ahead with his own purpose.

'That'd be fine, Reverend,' I said.

When he pushed the play button I could hear all the noises that are endemic to jailhouses everywhere: steel doors clanging, radios blaring, a water bucket being scraped along a concrete floor, cacophonous and sometimes deranged voices echoing through long corridors. Then I heard the man's voice – like words being released from an emotional knot, the syntax incoherent, the rage and hateful obsession like a quivering, heated wire.

'You got mud people coming out of your sewer grates, you got—' he was saying when Motley came out of Baxter's office and Oswald Flat clicked off the recorder.

'Movie time,' Motley said, scratching at the side of his mustache.

'What's Nate Baxter on the rag about?' Clete said.

'What do you think, Purcel? He's just real glad to see you guys down here again,' Motley said.

'Get him transferred back to Vice. At least he could get laid once in a while,' Clete said. He looked at the expression on my face. 'You think I'm kidding? The transvestites in the Quarter really dug the guy.'

The four of us went inside Motley's office. He closed the door behind us and inserted a videocassette into a VCR unit.

'The guy's name was Jack Pelley,' Motley said. 'He had a dishonorable discharge from the Crotch for rolling queers in San Diego, priors in New Orleans for statutory rape and possession of child pornography. One federal beef for possession of stolen explosives. From what we can tell, he became an addict in the joint, muled tar for both the Aryan Brotherhood and the Mexican Mafia while he was inside, then jumped his parole about three years ago.'

'How'd he get picked up?' I said.

'He locked himself in a filling station rest room on Carrollton and wouldn't let anybody else in. When the owner opened the door, Pelley had his leathers down over his knees and was shooting into his thigh with a spike made out of an eyedropper. The Ruger was sitting on top of the toilet tank.'

'How far away was he from Hippo Bimstine's house?' I said.

'About two blocks,' Motley said. 'His pockets were full of rainbows, blues, purple hearts, leapers, you name it. I think somebody gave him the whole candy store to fuck up Bimstine's day.' He glanced at Oswald Flat. 'Sorry, Reverend.'

'Get on with hit,' Flat said.

Motley dropped the blinds on his office glass, turned off the overhead light, and started the VCR.

'The arresting officers put him in the tank,' Motley said. 'In five minutes half the guys in there were yelling through the bars at the booking room officer to move him to a holding cell. The guy had five-alarm gorilla armpit odor. Anyway, we messed up. We should have transferred him to a psychiatric unit.'

The film, made without sound by a security camera, was in black and white and of low grade, the images stark in their contrast, like those in booking room photography. But the tortured travail of a driven man, flailing above a self-created abyss, was clearly obvious. Like those of most speed addicts, his body was wasted, the skin of his face drawn back tightly over the bone, the eyes sunken into skeletal sockets. His head looked like it had been razor-shaved and the hair had grown out in a thin gray patina, the color of rat's fur, below a wide bald area. Beginning at the crown of his skull, right across the pate, was a tattoo of a sword, flanged by lightning bolts.

He paced about maniacally, urinated all over the toilet stool, banged with his fists on the bars, whipped at the walls with his leather jacket, then began slamming the iron bunk up and down on its suspension chains.

'This is where we blew it big-time,' Motley said. 'That cell should have been shook down when the last guy went out of it.'

The man in custody, Jack Pelley, raised the bunk one final time and crashed it down on its chains, then stared down at a piece of electrical cord that had fallen out on the concrete floor. He picked it up in both hands, stared at it, then began idly picking at the tape and wire coil that were wrapped on the end of it.

'What do you call them things?' Flat said.

'A stinger,' Motley said. He paused the VCR. 'It's like a home-made hot plate. Except our man here has got other plans for it. You sure you want to watch this, Reverend?'

'You got something on that tape worse than Saipan?' Flat answered.

Motley took a Baby Ruth out of his desk drawer, started the film again, sat on the corner of his desk, and peeled the wrapper off his candy bar while he watched the television screen.

Jack Pelley splashed water from the toilet bowl onto the cement floor of the cell, peeled off his leather trousers, flattened his skinny buttocks into the middle of the puddle, inserted the stinger's coil into his mouth, sank one hand into the toilet, then calmly fitted the other end of the stinger into a wall socket.

His head snapped back once, as though he had just mainlined a hot shot; his eyes widened, one arm trembled slightly inside the toilet bowl; his lips seemed to curl back momentarily from his clenched teeth, then his jaw fell open like that of someone experiencing an unexpected moment of ecstasy.

Then he slumped against the stool, his head on his chest, as though he had tired of a wearisome journey and had simply gone to sleep.

'The ME said the shock shouldn't have killed him by itself,' Motley said. 'But he'd probably hyped eight or nine times in the twenty-four hours before he got busted. The ME said his heart looked like a muskmelon.'

'Have you got any registration on the Ruger?' I asked.

'The serial numbers are burned off,' Motley said.

'Sounds like the greaseballs,' Clete said.

'The greaseballs don't send speed freaks on a hit,' Motley said.

'How about ties to the AB?' I said.

'Maybe. But these guys don't have much organization outside the joint. Most of them are more worried about their cock than politics, anyway,' Motley said. 'Reverend, why don't you go ahead and play your tape?'

Flat snapped the play button down on his recorder, then set the recorder on the desktop. Once again, I heard the heated voice of Jack Pelley, like a disembodied hiss rising with gathering intensity out of the din of jailhouse noise.

'You got mud people coming out of your sewer grates, you got 'em eating dogs out of the city parks, fucking like minks in the projects, queers spreading AIDS in the blood banks, you think I'm kidding, you ever heard of Queer Nation, it ain't an accident half of them got kike names, how about that mud person over there in New Iberia thinks he's gonna deliver up the gift to a Jew, you think we come this far to let that happen, the sword ain't gonna allow it, no way, motherfucker, tell the screw to send down some toilet paper, they didn't leave none when they fed me, hey, you put that on that tape, what the fuck you think you doing, man—'

The recording ended with a brittle, clattering sound.

'That's when he knocked hit out of my hand,' Flat said. 'I never saw a man in so much torment.'

'Run it again,' Clete said.

We listened once more. I saw Clete put a breath mint on his tongue, then crack it between his molars and stare thoughtfully into space. When the tape ended he smiled in order to hide whatever thought had been in his eyes.

'How's it feel to be a mud person, Streak?' he said.

'We talked to the feds and a couple of snitches in the AB about any group that might call itself "The Sword." They never heard of it,' Motley said.

'Who's "we"?' I said.

'Me.'

'Baxter's blowing it off?' I said.

'What do I know?' Motley said.

Clete, Oswald Flat, and I walked out into the squad room. Clete and Flat went ahead of me. I stepped back into Motley's office.

'I appreciate what you've done, Motley,' I said.

'Tell me straight, Robicheaux, what's "the gift" this guy was talking about?'

'I don't have the slightest idea.'

'Somebody thinks you do.'

'Maybe he was talking about somebody else.'

'Yeah, probably the archbishop. A thought you might take with you – if they're using meltdowns like Jack Pelley, you can bet they've got a shit pile of them in reserve. Purcel's a cracker, but sometimes he's got his point of view, you know what I mean?'

'Not really.'

'People tend to fuck with him only once. There's never any paperwork around later, either.'

'Bad advice from a cop, Motley.'

'I got a flash for you, Robicheaux. I made a copy of the preacher's tape and gave it to Baxter. Ten minutes later I saw him erase it and throw it in the trash.'

He bit down on his Baby Ruth and stared at me reflectively.

10

Outside, I shook hands with Oswald Flat and thanked him for his help, then I drove Clete back toward his office in the French Quarter. It was raining, and the thick canopy of oaks over St Charles looked gray in the blowing mist. The streetcar rattled past us on the neutral ground, its windows down to let in the cool air.

'You were a little quiet in there,' I said.

'Why argue with Motley? I think he pissed his brains out his pecker on beer and hookers a long time ago.'

'What are you saying?'

'Come on, Dave. Have you ever seen a hit done with a silenced twenty-two that wasn't a mob contract? It's their trademark – one round in the back of the head, one through the temples, one in the mouth.'

'They use pros, not guys like this Pelley character.'

'It's Pelley that convinces me even more that I'm right. Think about it. Where's a brain-fried hype like that going to come up with a silenced Ruger, one with burned serial numbers?'

'You're thinking about Lonighan?'

'Maybe. Or maybe Lonighan *and* the greaseballs. Look, Dave, you stomped the shit out of Max Calucci in front of his chippies. Max is a special kind of guy. When he was up at Angola he found out his punk was getting it on with another con. The kid begged all over the joint to go into lockdown. Nobody'd listen to him. A couple of days later somebody broke off a shank made from window glass in his throat.'

'They don't hit cops, Clete.'

'But what if it's not a regular contract? What if Max and Bobo Calucci just pointed the meltdown in your direction and gave him the Ruger, or had somebody give it to him? Nobody's going to make it for a greaseball hit, right? Motley didn't.'

'You've got more reason to worry about the Caluccis than I do.'

We drove out of the tunnel of oaks on St Charles into Lee Circle. Clete took off his porkpie hat and readjusted it on his brow.

'You're wrong there, noble mon,' he said. 'I was never big on rules. They know that.'

I looked at him.

'But you are. They know that, too,' he said. 'They feel a whole lot safer when they go up against guys who play by the rules.'

'Stay away from them, Clete.'

'You've been out of New Orleans too long, Dave. All the old understandings are gone. It's an open city, like Miami, anybody's fuck. There's only one way to operate in New Orleans today – you keep reminding the other side they're one breath away from being grease spots in the cement.'

It was raining much harder now, and people were turning on their car lights. I looked at Clete's hulking profile in silhouette against the rain. His face was cheerless, his green eyes staring straight ahead, his mouth a tight seam.

After I dropped him at his office, I made one final stop in New Orleans – at Hippo Bimstine's house, down by the Mississippi levee. The rain had almost quit, and he was in his backyard, dipping leaves out of his swimming pool with a long pole. He wore wraparound black sunglasses, plaid Bermuda shorts, and a Hawaiian shirt printed with brown-skinned girls dancing in grass skirts. The fatty rings in his neck were bright with sweat.

'Yeah, that colored cop Motley told me all about it,' he said. 'This tattooed guy sounds like some kind of zomboid, though. I don't think we're talking the first team here.'

'I had to learn a hard lesson a long time ago, Hippo. The guy who blows out your candle is the one who's at your throat before you ever expect it.'

'A guy with a sword tattooed on his head, shooting dope in his crotch with an eyedropper? Dave, give me a break. I got serious enemies. I don't lose sleep over guys who get arrested in filling station rest rooms.'

'You have a very copacetic attitude, Hippo.'

'You're trying to insult me? That's what we're doing here?'

'I don't think you want me asking you hard questions.'

He set down the pole on a stone bench, removed his sunglasses, and wiped his face on his sleeve. The air was hot and muggy, and raindrops dripped from the trees into the pool.

'I got no secrets. Everybody in New Orleans knows my politics,' he said.

'What's the Jewish Defense Organization?'

'It's the network I belong to. There's no mystery here. We got a project called Operation Klan Kick. We find out who these cocksuckers are, where they work, and we make some phone calls. You got a problem with that, Dave?'

'Do you know why this guy Pelley might talk about "a gift" or a group called The Sword?'

'What are you talking about *gift* and *sword*? Listen, you know why Tommy Lonighan wants that sub? Because I bother him. Everything I do bothers him. You know why I bother him? Because he's got a guilty conscience, like a big, black tumor always eating on his brain.'

'Over what?'

'He killed my little brother.'

'He did what?'

'He didn't bother to tell you that, huh? We grew up across the street from each other in the Channel. We were all playing in a homemade cart, you know, made out of crates and planks with some roller skates nailed on the bottom. Tommy wheeled my little brother out from behind a car right into an ice truck. To this day, that sonofabitch has never said he was sorry.'

'I didn't know that, Hippo.'

'Maybe there's some other stuff you don't know, either, Dave. Come in my office.'

'What for?'

'Because you don't like the way me and my friends do business. Because you think these shitheads should have their day in court. Indulge me, blow five minutes of your day.'

We went inside the stucco cottage he used as an office. He began clattering through a box of videocassette tapes. He took one out and read the taped label on it.

'Some friends of mine got this off a bunch of guys who were watching it for entertainment,' he said. 'In a cinder-block house, up in a piney woods, just north of Pascagoula. When my friends got finished with them, they weren't interested in watching old newsreels anymore. So they really didn't mind giving up their cassette.'

'Who are your friends?'

'Some guys who could be great baseball players, you know what I mean? Terrific guys with a bat.'

'You think it's a victory to become like the other side?'

'Dave, you're a laugh a minute. That's why I like you. You already ate lunch, didn't you? Because this film seems to fuck up people's appetite for some reason.'

He started the tape in the VCR under his television set. The video was composed of a series of newsreels, Nazi propaganda footage, and still photographs spliced together in a collage that was almost like watching distilled evil: the profiles of Jews being superimposed upon those of rats, Heinrich Himmler reviewing concentration camp inmates in striped uniforms behind barbed wire, columns of children with bundles, their faces distorted with terror, marching between rows of black-helmeted SS; and finally a scene that was the most cruel I had ever seen on film – nude Polish women, deep in a forest, their arms gathered over their breasts and pubic hair, lining up to be shot in the back of the neck and flung into an open trench.

'On your worst day in Vietnam, you ever see anything like that, Dave?'

'No.'

'It's back. On an international level. You don't buy it, do you?'

'Maybe. But it doesn't change anything with us, Hippo. I think my family and I are swimming into somebody else's field of fire. I think you're responsible, too.'

He looked down at his hands, which were folded between his thighs. He looked at them a long time.

'Hippo?'

His sleek, football-shaped face was morose when he looked back up at me.

'Who can plan how things turn out?' he said. 'What I do or don't do no longer matters. There're people, I'm talking about cretins like that pervert at your house, who believe you can find that sub. It's what they *believe* that counts, Dave.'

'Why's it important to them?'

'Why does a tumblebug like to roll in shit?'

'Cut the Little Orphan Annie routine, Hippo. I'm getting tired of it.'

'They like shrines.'

'Not good enough.'

'I don't want you killed. Forget about the sub. I'll find it on my own or I won't. Don't come around here anymore. I'm going to put out the word that you're a waste of time, you couldn't find your butt with both hands. Maybe they'll believe it.'

'It's too late for contrition, Hippo. This guy Buchalter has left my wife a memory that she'll never quite get rid of.'

'You can put out a hit in this town for five hundred bucks. Did you know that, Dave? For a hundred, you can have a guy remodeled with a ball peen hammer and Polaroids left for you in a bar on Claiborne. You want a phone number? Or you want to keep hanging your ass out in the breeze and blaming me for your troubles?'

'I didn't know you and Tommy Bobalouba grew up together, Hippo. It explains a lot.'

'No kidding?'

'No kidding.'

'Sounds real clever.'

'Not really. You're both full of shit.'

'I wish I had a wit like that,' he said, then held up the videocassette in his hand. 'Then I could explain how there're people can watch stuff like this for fun in my own country and nobody cares. Hey, Dave, if they ever fire up the ovens again, I'll probably be one of the first bars of soap off the conveyor belt. But you and your kind won't be far behind. You don't mind letting yourself out, do you?'

I drove back toward New Iberia, through Baton Rouge, across the wide yellow sweep of the Mississippi into the western sun and the Atchafalaya marsh. I noticed a wallet stuck down in the crack of the passenger's seat. It was Clete's and must have slipped out of his back pocket before I dropped him off at his office. When I got off I-10 at Breaux Bridge I stopped at a convenience store and called him on a pay phone, then headed down the back road through St Martinville, past the old French church and the spreading oaks on Bayou Teche where Evangeline and her lover are buried, and through the cooling afternoon and waving fields of green sugarcane into New Iberia.

I pulled into the dirt drive and parked under the oaks at the foot of my property. The house was deep in shadow, my neighbor's cane field and the woods that bordered it silhouetted against a blazing sunset. Bootsie's car was parked by the side of the house, the trunk open and sacked groceries still inside. The front rooms of the house were dark, the rose-print curtains fluttering in the windows, but the light was on in the kitchen. Batist was out on the dock, pushing pools of rainwater out of the folds in the awning with a broom handle.

'You need any help closing up?' I called.

'Ain't much bidness this afternoon. The rain brung in everybody early,' he said.

'Is Alafair down there?'

'She gone to the show wit' some ot'er children.'

I waved at him and walked up the slope toward my house, lifted two sacks of groceries out of Bootsie's car trunk, and walked around to the back door. Fireflies had started to light in the trees, and the dome of lavender sky overhead reverberated with the drone of cicadas. The house was still; no sound came from the radio on the kitchen windowsill, which Bootsie almost always listened to while she fixed supper.

I hefted the grocery sacks in my arms, opened the back screen with my shoe, and let it slam behind me. The wood planks of the back porch were littered with pet bowls and dry cat food. Through the doorway all the surfaces in the kitchen looked bright and clean, but I could smell okra burning and hear water hissing through a kettle top and scorching in the fire.

'Bootsie?' I said.

Out front, the tin roof on the gallery pinged in the cooling air.

'Bootsie?' I said again, hitching the sacks up against my chest.

I walked into the kitchen and started to set the sacks on the drain board; I saw her sitting at the breakfast table, motionless, her posture rigid, her eyes straight ahead, one hand resting on top of the other.

'Bootsie, what's wrong?' I said.

Then I saw the film of perspiration on her brow and upper lip, the flutter in her throat, the rise and fall of her breasts. Her mouth opened stiffly, and her eyes broke and fastened on mine; they were charged with a light I had never seen in them before.

'Get out, Dave. Run! Please!' she said, her voice seeming to crack and rise from a great depth at the same time.

But it was too late. The blond man with a neck like a tree stump, with hands that had the power of vise grips, stepped out of the hallway into the light. He wore a Panama hat with a flowered band tilted on his head and a boyish, lopsided smile. His pleated white slacks, tropical shirt printed with green and yellow parrots, and shined, tasseled loafers gave him the appearance of a health enthusiast you might see on a morning television show, perhaps with a beach at his back. In the shadow of his hat brim you could hardly see the spray of blackheads that fanned back from his eyes like cat's whiskers.

'Come on in, Dave. I'm glad you're here. We weren't sure when you'd be back. We're going to work this thing out. Hey, I was listening to your records. I love them,' he said.

Behind him, seated on a chair turned backwards in the hallway, was a small man with defective eyes and a head shaped like a tomato. There was even a furrow in his scalp, with a twist of hair in it, like the indentation and stem of a tomato freshly torn from the vine. In his hands was a military-issue crossbow, the kind sometimes used in special operations, with a steel-flanged arrow mounted on the bowstring. The small man's elbows were propped on the back of the chair, and his eyes, which were crossed, one locking intermittently by the bridge of his nose, were sighted in their peculiar way along the arrow's shaft at the side of Bootsie's face.

11

They had drawn the blinds on the windows now, and the small man with crossed eyes was drinking from a bottle of milk at the breakfast table and spitting pistachio shells into a paper bag. After he had locked my wrists behind me with the handcuffs he'd found on my dresser he bound Bootsie's forearms to her chair with electrician's tape, then crisscrossed it through her breasts and wrapped it around the back of the chair. The man named Buchalter watched with a small .25 caliber Beretta in the palm of his hand, a torn smile like that of Will Rogers at the corner of his mouth.

'You remember me?' he said.

'No.'

'You saw me in the helicopter. Out on the gulf,' he said.

'This is of no value to you, or your cause, or whatever it is you're after,' I said. 'You've got the wrong people.'

He pulled up a chair and sat between me and Bootsie. He pushed his hat back on his head. A strand of fine blond hair fell in his eyes.

'Are you mad at me? Because of what I did to Mrs Robicheaux?' he said.

I stared at his face, his unblinking, inquisitive eyes, and didn't answer. I could feel the handcuffs biting into my wrists, cutting off the blood, swelling the veins.

'We don't know why you've come here. You have nothing to gain by being here. Don't you understand that?' Bootsie said.

'I wouldn't say that. There're always possibilities in every situation. That's what I like to believe, anyway,' he said, and reached out, touched my cheek with his hand, and let his glance rove lazily over my face.

I saw tears well in Bootsie's eyes.

'Try to hear this, Buchalter,' I said. 'I'm a police officer. I work with people who'll square this one way or another. No matter what happens here tonight, they'll find you and blow up your shit, I guarantee it.'

He made shushing noises with his lips, and again his hand reached up and touched my face and brushed gingerly around the corners of my mouth. I could feel the grain of his skin against mine and smell an odor on it like hair oil and the inside of a leather glove.

'You take your hands off him, you degenerate, you vile animal—' Bootsie said. Her eyes were hot and receded, her face as gray as cardboard.

Buchalter nodded to the small man with crossed eyes. He spat a pistachio shell into the paper sack, then walked behind Bootsie's chair and wound the electrician's tape across her mouth, wrapping it around and around the thick swirls of her hair at the back of her head, tightening it across her mouth each time he made a revolution. She leaned forward and gagged on her tongue.

I could feel my heart thundering against my rib cage, hear the blood roaring in my ears like wind in a seashell.

'I don't know where the sub is,' I said. 'I'd tell you if I did. I don't even known why you guys want it. Why would I keep the information from you?'

'Because you work for Jews, my friend,' he said. 'Because I think you lie.'

'It's got air trapped in the hull. It floats right above the gulf's floor. It probably drifts in a pattern with the Gulf Stream,' I said. 'Hire some salvage people who understand those things. New Orleans and Miami are full of them.'

'But evidently you've found it twice. That means you know something other people don't.'

'There may be more than one sub down there,' I said. 'The Navy nailed three or four of them during nineteen forty-two. Maybe I saw two different subs.'

He took a nautical chart from his pocket, unfolded it, and spread it flat on the table in front of me. It showed the Louisiana coast, all its bays and soundings, and the northern gradations of the gulf. He stood behind my chair and fitted his huge hands over my shoulders, inserted his thumbs in the back of my neck.

'Our business can end here tonight in a couple of ways,' he said. 'I believe you understand me.'

'After you know where the sub is, you'll just go away?'

'Why not?' he said. His fingers tightened on my shoulder tendons.

'Because you're in over your head.'

He lowered his mouth to my ear. 'It isn't a time to be clever, Dave,' he said. 'You want me to make you trace the drift pattern with your nose?'

I tried to lean forward, away from the steady beat of his breath on my skin. Then he cupped one hand under my chin, the other on the back of my neck, like a man about to do a trick shot with a basketball.

'Would you like me to snap it?' he said. 'I can turn your body into a slug's from the neck down. I'm not exaggerating, Dave. I've done it twice before. Ask Chuck there.'

Think, think, think.

I tried to avoid swallowing, tried to keep my voice empty of fear. I closed and opened my eyes, and blinked the sweat out of them. Bootsie's hair had fallen in her face; the black tape that cut across her mouth was slick with saliva, and her eyes were red and liquid with terror at what she was about to witness.

'There're two things that aren't going to happen here tonight, Buchalter,' I said. 'I'm not going to give you information I don't have, and nobody here is going to kiss your butt. You're a piece of shit. Nothing you can do here will ever change that fact.'

He was quiet a moment. I felt his fingers move, but they were uncertain now, the pressure against my chin and neck temporarily in abeyance.

'You want to say that again?' he asked.

'Guys like you are cruel because you got fucked up in toilet training. That's how it works. Go to a psychologist and check it out. It's better than living with skid marks in your underwear.'

The man with crossed eyes started to laugh, then looked at Buchalter's face.

Buchalter was breathing heavily now. His hands were moist with perspiration, poised on my chin and neck. But the indecision, the physical pause, was still there, the means of resolving the insult not quite yet in place.

Then the man with crossed eyes turned in his chair and stared at the side window, whose blinds were drawn. He raised one hand in the air.

'Will, there's somebody outside,' he said.

Buchalter's hands slid away from me. He took the Beretta from his pocket while the man called Chuck peeked out the side of the blinds.

'It's a delivery guy,' he said.

'What do you mean "a delivery guy"?' Buchalter said.

'A fucking delivery guy. With a clipboard and a flashlight. He's coming to the back door.'

'Let him give you what he's got, then get rid of him.'

'Me?'

'Yes, you.'

The man called Chuck went out on the back porch, beyond my angle of vision. Buchalter rested one hand on my shoulder and placed the barrel of the Beretta behind my ear.

'UPS. I got a box for Dave Robicheaux. I guess your doorbell's broke,' a voice said out in the darkness.

I saw Bootsie's eyes fasten on mine.

'Put it on the gallery,' Chuck said.

'It's COD.'

'How much?'

'Eight fifty.'

'Wait a minute.'

The man named Chuck came back into the kitchen, his face filled with consternation.

'I ain't got any money, Will,' he said.

'Here,' Buchalter said, and handed him a twenty-dollar bill.

'What if I got to sign for it?'

'Just scribble on the board. Now, get out there and do it.'

Chuck went back out on the porch. I could see his shadow moving about under the bug-crusted light.

'All right, thanks a lot,' I heard him say. 'Just set it on the gallery. I'll carry it in later.'

'I'll bring it around. It's no trouble.'

'No, man. You don't need to do that.'

'It's going to rain. We're responsible for water damage.'

Chuck came back into the kitchen, the skin around one eye twitching with anxiety.

'Calm down,' Buchalter said. 'Go out front and help the man. Just keep him away from the back.'

'I'm cool, I'm cool.'

'I can see that, all right.'

'I don't need you on my case, Will. This one gets fucked up, I'm going down on a habitual.'

'It's better you not talk anymore, Chuck.'

'You don't get it. I been down four times. I don't need this kind of shit in my life. Now there's this fucking weird guy for UPS. I'm telling you, I don't need this kind of shit, man. I ain't up for it.'

'You're under a strain, Chuck. Wait a minute, what do you mean "weird guy"?'

'He looks like an ape with a UPS cap on its head. Wearing fucking Budweiser shorts. You don't call that weird?'

Buchalter's hand pinched at his mouth. I could feel the heat from his body, smell the mixture of sweat and deodorant secreting under his arms.

'Go out the front door, Chuck,' he said. 'You talk to the man out front. You keep him there. That's your assignment. You understand me?'

'Why me? I don't like this, Will. You want to 'front the guy, you 'front the fucking guy.' Then the skin of Chuck's face drew tight against the bone, stretching his eyebrows like penciled grease marks.

'The sonofabitch is coming around the side again,' he said.

'I'll handle it. You keep these two quiet,' Buchalter said.

'You wouldn't listen to me, man. Now it's turning to shit. I can feel it.'

'Shut up, Chuck. If it goes sour, you make sure Mr and Mrs Robicheaux catch the bus,' Buchalter said. 'If he doesn't work for us, he doesn't work for the Jews, either.'

'You want to clip a cop? With our prints all over the place? Are you out of your goddamn mind?'

Buchalter raised his fingers for the cross-eyed man to be silent, then dropped the Beretta into his pants pocket and walked out onto the back porch, with a smile at the corner of his mouth that looked like an elongated keyhole.

Chuck picked up his crossbow and leveled it at my throat. His hands looked round and white and small against the bow's dark metal surfaces. He breathed loudly through his nose and shook a fly out of his face. Large, solitary drops of rain began hitting in the trees outside.

I heard Buchalter open the screen door out on the porch.

'Okay? Is that everything now?' he said.

'I need you to sign.'

'All right.'

'You got a pen? Mine must have fallen off my clipboard.'

'No, I don't. And I'm rather busy right now.'

'Maybe it's in my pocket—'

'Now listen, my friend—'

78

'Hands on your head, down on your knees, motherfucker! Do it! Now! Don't think about it!'

I heard the weight of two large bodies crash against the wood slats and rake across the tangle of garden tools on the porch; then Buchalter and Clete Purcel fell into the kitchen, and Clete's blue-black .38 revolver skittered across the linoleum.

Buchalter got to his feet first, his flat buttocks pinched together, the change jangling in his slacks, his triangular back rigid with muscle, and drove his right fist into the center of Clete's face. Clete's head snapped sideways with the force of the blow, blood whipping from his nose across his cheek. But he grabbed Buchalter around the legs, locked his wrists behind Buchalter's thighs, and smashed him against the doorjamb.

'Chuck!' Buchalter yelled out, as he tried to get his hand into his pants pocket.

But Chuck had taken his crossbow and gone through the hallway and out the front door like a shot.

Buchalter began swinging both his fists into the top of Clete's head. He wore a large Mexican ring on his right hand, one with a raised, knurled design on it, and each time he swung his right fist down, he twisted the ring with the blow, and I could see gashes bursting like tiny purple flowers in Clete's scalp.

But Clete Purcel was not one who gave up or went down easily. With rivulets of blood draining out of his hair into his eyes, he reached behind him, grasped a three-pronged dirt tiller by the wood handle, and jerked the sharpened tines upward into Buchalter's scrotum.

Buchalter's face went white, his mouth opening wide with a roar that seemed to rise like a rupturing bubble from the bottom of his viscera, as though bone and linkage were being sawed apart inside him. He stumbled sideways, lifting his knees into Clete's face, and crashed through the screen door into the backyard. Then I heard his feet running into the darkness.

Clete pulled himself up by the doorknob and walked like a drunk man into the kitchen, soaked a dish towel under the faucet, and pressed it to the top of his head. He kept widening his eyes and breathing hard through his mouth. His knees were barked, and one sock was pulled down over his ankle.

'Pick up your piece,' I said.

He wiped at his nose and eyes with the towel, then leaned over heavily, holding the towel to his scalp, and closed his hand around his .38.

'The handcuff key is on the dresser in the bedroom,' I said.

He went into the bedroom, came back with the key, and began unlocking the handcuffs. I could feel water dripping out of his hair onto my neck. The handcuffs clattered to the floor. My hands were purple, bloated with lack of circulation, the skin dead to the touch. I opened my pocketknife, cut through the electrician's tape at the back of Bootsie's head, eased it out of her mouth, then began sawing loose the tape on her arms.

'Oh God, Dave,' she said. Her breath came in gasps, as though she had been held underwater for a long time and her lungs were aching for air. 'Oh Lord, God. Oh God, he was going—'

'It's over,' I said.

'He was going to cripple you. He was going to deliberately cripple you,' she said, then squeezed her eyes shut against the tears that coursed down her cheeks. I held her face against my chest and kissed the top of her head. I could smell the heat in her hair.

'Your phone's dead. They must have cut it outside,' Clete said.

'Give me your piece,' I said.

'Where's yours?'

'In the glove compartment of the truck.'

'Man, I can't see straight. That guy's got fists like chunks of concrete.'

'Take Boots down to the bait shop and call the sheriff's office from there,' I said.

'Where are you going, Dave?' Bootsie said, her eyes clearing with a new sense of alarm.

'They probably parked their car farther up the road,' I said.

'No,' she said. 'Let somebody else handle it this time.'

'He's a fanatic and a psychopath, Boots. If we don't nail him now, he'll be back.'

I looked away from the expression on her face. I started out the door with the revolver in my hand.

'Hey, Dave—' Clete said.

He followed me onto the back porch.

'Forget the rules on this one,' he said. 'You get the chance, close this cocksucker's file.'

'Tell the sheriff to call the bridge tender and have him raise the drawbridge,' I said.

'Listen to me—' he began, his face stretching with impatience. Then he stopped and lowered his voice. 'This kind of guy sits in a jail cell and thinks for a long time about things to do to people. Don't live with regret later, Streak. Buchalter is as bad as they get.' He pointed a finger at my face, then wiped a smear of blood off his nose on his wrist.

The moon had risen in the east from behind a bank of black clouds, and a steady, warm rain was dancing on the duck pond at the foot of my property and clicking on the tall stalks of sugarcane in my neighbor's field. When I had returned from New Orleans I hadn't seen any vehicles parked on the dirt road by the bayou, and I guessed that Buchalter and the man with crossed eyes had driven past my house, parked on the far side of it, and cut back through a pecan orchard by the four corners, over a wooded knoll, and through my neighbor's cane field.

Beyond the duck pond, right by the remnant of my collapsed barn, I saw two fresh sets of footprints glistening in the mud, leading through the barbed-wire fence into the field. I lifted up the top strand of barbed wire and stepped into the cane. It grew so thick that the earth was still dry inside the rows. The sound of the rain on the leaves was like marbles striking dry sheets of newspaper. I saw a bolt of lightning splinter the sky and pop in the woods, and when the thunder echoed off the trees, my neighbor's cattle began lowing in terror at the bottom of the coulee.

There was no wind inside the cane, and the air was heated and alive with insects. Ahead, I could see a winding pattern, like a faint serpentine tunnel, through the rows where somebody had either wedged the stalks sideways or cracked them at the base with his shoe. I knelt in the row and listened. At first I heard only the sound of the rain clicking on the leaves overhead, then there was a voice, one man calling out to another, just as lightning burst in a white tree all over the southern horizon and thunder rumbled across the fields.

They must have gotten all the way to the wooded knoll, almost to the pecan orchard and the four corners down the bayou road, I thought. I stepped back outside the sugarcane and began running toward the far side of the field, toward the elevated grove of oak trees whose leaves were flickering with a silver light in the wind off the marsh.

Long ago Clete Purcel had made his separate peace with the system of rules that govern the justifiable taking of human life. I never questioned the validity of Clete's moral vision, no more than I would have questioned his loyalty and courage and his selfless devotion to me during the worst periods in my life. In truth, I often envied the clarity of line that he used to distinguish between right and wrong. I had also harbored fears since I first became a street patrolman in New Orleans that I would one day wrongly exercise the power of life and death over an individual, through accident or perhaps fearful impetuosity or maybe even by self-righteous design.

But Buchalter was not an ordinary player. Most of the psychological mutants with whom a police officer comes in contact daily are bumbling, ineffectual losers who sneak through life on side streets and who often seek out authority and self-validation through their adversarial relationship with police and parole officers, since in normal society they possess about the same worth as discarded banana peels.

Psychopaths like Ted Bundy and Gary Gilmore have a way of committing their crimes in states which practice capital punishment. Then they turn their trials and executions into televised theater of world-class proportions.

The Will Buchalters have no such plan for themselves. They don't leave paperwork behind; they stay out of the computer. When they do get nailed, they make bond and terrify witnesses into perjuring themselves; they convince psychologists that they have multiple personalities that cannot be simultaneously put on trial; their fall partners either do their time or are murdered in custody. No one is ever sure of how many people they actually kill.

Will Buchalter belonged to that special group of people who live in our nightmares.

I could still smell his odor; it was like animal musk, like lotions that were at war with his glands, like someone who has just had sex. I could still feel the grain and oil of his skin on mine.

I pressed my hand tighter around the butt of the .38. The hand-worn walnut grips felt smooth and hard against my palm.

As I neared the end of the cane field I heard a strand of fence wire twang against a post, heard someone curse, as though he were in pain or had fallen to the ground. I swung wide of the field to broaden my angle of vision; then I saw two silhouettes against the veiled moon – one man on his buttocks, holding his ankle, the other man bent over him, trying to lift him up, and I remembered the old fence that my neighbor had crushed flat with his tractor so his livestock could drink at the coulee.

They saw me, too. Before I could squat into a shooting position and yell at them to put their hands on their heads, a small-caliber pistol popped in the darkness, then popped again, just like a firecracker. I ran for the lee of the sugarcane, out of their line of vision, and squatted close into the stalks away from the moon's glow, which streaked the rain with a light like quicksilver.

I heard someone burrow into the cane, thrash through several rows, then stop.

Were there one or two men inside the field now? I couldn't tell. There was no sound except the rain hitting on the leaves over my head.

I worked my way down a furrow, deeper into the cane. I could smell something dead in the trapped air, a coon or possum, an odor like that of a rat that has crawled inside a wall and died. My eyes stung with salt, and the dirt cut into my knuckles and knees like pieces of flint. I saw a wood rabbit bolt across the rows, stop and look at me, his ears flattened on his head, then begin running again in a zigzag pattern. He crashed loudly through the edge of the cane and was gone.

Not twenty feet from me a man rose from his knees in the midst of the cane, his body almost totally obscured by the thickly spaced stalks and long festoons of leaves around him. He tried to ease quietly through the rows to the far side of the field, which opened onto a flat space and the wooded knoll and the pecan orchard.

I pulled my shirt up and wiped my face on it, then aimed as best I could at the man's slowly moving silhouette. I cocked the hammer on the .38 and brought the sight just below an imaginary line that traversed his shoulder blades.

Now! I thought.

'Throw your weapon away! Down on your face with your hands out in front of you!' I yelled.

But he wanted another season to run.

He tore through the sugarcane, flailing his arms at the stalks, stumbling across the rows. I was crouched on one knee when I began shooting. I believe the first shot went high, because I heard a distant sound in a tree, like a rock skipping off of bark and falling through limbs. And he kept plowing forward through the cane, trying to hack an opening with his left hand, shielding a weapon with his right.

But the second shot went home. I know it did; I heard the impact, like a cleated shoe connecting with a football, heard the wind go out of his lungs as he was driven forward through the cane.

But he was still standing, with a metallic object in his right hand, its flat surfaces blue with moonlight, and he was turning on one foot toward me, just as a scarecrow might if it had been spun in a violent wind.

Clete had loaded only five rounds in the cylinder and had set the hammer on an empty chamber. I let off all three remaining rounds as fast as I could pull the trigger. Sparks and fine splinters of lead flew from the sides of the cylinder into the darkness.

His left arm flipped sideways, as if jerked by a wire, his stomach buckled, then his chin snapped back on his shoulder as if he had been struck by an invisible club.

The hammer snapped dryly on the empty sixth chamber. Then something happened that I didn't understand. As he crumpled sideways to the earth, breaking the stalks of cane down around him, he yelled out in pain for the first time.

I walked across the rows to where he lay on his back, his crossed eyes opening and closing with shock. He kept trying to expel a bloody clot from his mouth with the tip of his tongue. My last round had hit him in the chin and exited just above the jawbone. His left arm was twisted in the sleeve like a piece of discarded rope. He had taken another round in the side, with no exit wound that I could see, and blood was leaking out of his shirt into the dirt. Then I saw his right hand quivering uncontrollably above the feathered shaft of the aluminum arrow that had discharged from his crossbow when he fell. The flanged point had sliced down into the thigh and emerged gleaming and red through the kneecap.

I knelt beside him, loosened his belt, and brushed the dirt out of his eyes with my fingers.

'Where's Buchalter?' I said.

He swallowed with a clicking sound and tried to speak, but his tongue stuck to the roof of his mouth. I turned his head with my hands so his mouth could drain.

'Where did Buchalter go, Chuck?' I said. 'Don't try to protect this guy. He deserted you.'

'I don't know,' he said. His voice was weak and devoid of all defense. 'Get the arrow out.'

'I can't do it. You might hemorrhage. I'm going to call an ambulance.'

His crossed eyes tried to focus on mine. They were luminous and black with pain and fear. His tongue came out of his mouth and went back in again.

'What is it?' I said.

'I need a priest. I ain't gonna make it.'

'We'll get you one.'

'You gotta listen, man . . .'

'Say it.'

'I didn't have nothing against y'all. I done it for the money.'

'For the money?' I said as much to myself as to him.

'Tell your old lady I'm sorry. It wasn't personal. Oh God, I ain't gonna make it.'

'Give me Buchalter, Chuck.'

But his eyes had already focused inward on a vision whose intensity and dimension probably only he could appreciate. In the distance I heard someone start a high-powered automobile engine and roar southward, away from the drawbridge, down the bayou road in the rain.

12

The next morning I went down to the sheriff's office and got my badge back.

Chuck, whose full name was Charles Arthur Sitwell, made it through the night and was in the intensive care unit at Iberia General, his body wired to machines, an oxygen tube taped to his nose, an IV needle inserted in a swollen vein inside his right forearm. The lower half of his face was swathed in bandages and plaster, with only a small hole, the size of a quarter, for his mouth. I pulled a chair close to his bed while Clete stood behind me.

'Did Father Melancon visit you, Chuck?' I said.

He didn't answer. His eyelids were blue and had a metallic shine to them.

'Didn't a priest come see you?' I asked.

He blinked his eyes.

'Look, partner, if you got on the square with the Man Upstairs, why not get on the square with us?' I said.

Still, he didn't answer.

'You've been down four times, Chuck,' I said. 'Your jacket shows you were always a solid con. But Buchalter's not stand-up, Chuck. He's letting you take his fall.'

'You're standing on third base,' Clete said behind me.

I turned in the chair and looked into Clete's face. But Clete only stepped closer to the bed.

'Chuck was in max at Leavenworth, he was a big stripe at Angola. He wants it straight,' he said to me. 'Right, Chuck? Buchalter'll piss on your grave. Don't take the bounce for a guy like that.'

Chuck's defective eyes looked as small as a bird's. They seemed to focus on Clete; then they looked past him at the swinging door to the intensive care unit, which had opened briefly and was now flapping back and forth.

His mouth began moving inside the hole in the bandages. I leaned my ear close to his face. His breath was sour with bile.

'I already told the priest everything. I ain't saying no more,' he whispered. 'Tell everybody that. I ain't saying no more.'

'I don't want to be hard on you, partner, but why not do some good while you have the chance?' I said.

He turned his face away from me on the pillow.

'If that's the way you want it,' I said, and stood up to go. 'If you change your mind, ask for the cop at the door.'

Out in the corridor, Clete put an unlit cigarette in his mouth.

'I never get used to the way these fuckers think. The sonofabitch is on the edge of eternity and he's scared he'll be made for a snitch,' he said, then noticed a Catholic nun with a basket of fruit two feet from him. 'Excuse me, Sister,' he said.

She was dressed in a white skirt and lavender blouse, but she wore a black veil with white edging on her head. Her hair was a reddish gold and was tapered on her neck.

'How is he doing?' she said.

'Who?' I said.

'That poor man who was shot last night,' she said.

'Not very well,' I said.

'Will he live?' she said.

'You never know, I guess,' I said.

'Were you one of the officers who—'

'Yes?'

'I was going to ask if you were one of the officers who arrested him.'

'I'm the officer who shot him, Sister,' I said. But my attempt at directness was short-lived, and involuntarily my eyes broke contact with hers.

'Is he going to die?' she said. Her eyes became clouded in a peculiar way, like dark smoke infused in green glass.

'You should probably ask the doctor that,' I said.

'I see,' she said. Then she smiled politely. 'I'm sorry. I didn't mean to sound rude. I'm Marie Guilbeaux. It's nice meeting you.'

'I'm Dave Robicheaux. This is Clete Purcel. It's nice meeting you, too, Sister,' I said. 'You're not from New Iberia, are you?'

'No, I live in Lafayette.'

'Well, see you around,' I said.

'Yes, good-bye,' she said, and smiled again.

Clete and I walked out into the sunlight and drove back toward my house. It was the beginning of the Labor Day weekend, and the convenience stores were filled with people buying beer and ice and charcoal for barbecues.

'Why didn't the nuns look like that when I was in grade school?' Clete said. 'The ones I remember had faces like boiled hams ... What are you brooding about?'

'Something you said. Why's Chuck Sitwell stonewalling us?'

'He wants to go out a mainline, stand-up con.'

'No, you said it earlier. He's scared. But if he's scared Buchalter will be back to pull his plug, why doesn't he just give him up?'

Clete looked out into the hot glare of the day from under the brim of his porkpie hat and puffed on his cigarette. His face was pink in the heat.

'You're a good guy, Streak, but you don't always think straight about yourself,' he said.

'What's that supposed to mean?'

'You parked four rounds in the guy.'

I looked at him.

'Come on, Dave, be honest,' he said. 'You only stopped popping caps when you ran out of bullets. You were trying to blow him all over that cane field. You don't think the guy knows that? What if he or Buchalter tell you what they had planned for you and Bootsie, Bootsie in particular, maybe even Alafair if she walked in on it? I'd be scared of you, too, mon.'

He glanced sideways at me, then sucked once on his cigarette and flipped it in a spray of sparks against the side of a red stop sign.

The weekend was hot and dry and uneventful. A guard remained on duty twenty-four hours at the door of Charles Arthur Sitwell's hospital room. Sitwell kept his promise; he refused to answer questions about anything.

I got up Tuesday morning at dawn, helped Batist open the bait shop, then walked up the slope through the trees to have breakfast with Bootsie before going to the office. The house was still cool from the attic and window fans that had run all night, and the grass in the backyard was thick with mockingbirds who were feeding on bread crumbs that Bootsie had thrown out the screen door.

'A deputy will be parked out front again today,' I said.

'How long do you plan to keep one here, Dave?' Bootsie said. She sat across from me, her shoulders straight, her fingers resting on the sides of her coffee cup. She had put aside her piece of toast after having eaten only half of it.

'It gives the guy something to do,' I said.

'We can't live the rest of our lives with a deputy parked out front.'

'We won't have to.'

She had just washed her face, but her eyes looked tired, still not quite separated from the sleep that came to her with certainty only at first light.

'I want to buy a gun,' she said.

'That's never been your way.'

'What kind of pistol is best for a woman? I mean size or whatever you call it.'

'A thirty-two, or maybe a thirty-eight or nine millimeter. It depends on what a person wants it for.'

'I want to do that this evening, Dave.'

'All right.'

'Will you show me how to use it?'

'Sure.' I watched her face. Her eyes were flat with unspoken thoughts. 'We'll take the boat down the bayou and pop some tin cans.'

'I think we ought to teach Alafair how to shoot, too,' she said.

I waited a moment before I spoke. 'You can teach kids how to shoot a pistol, Boots, but you can't teach them when to leave it in a drawer and when to take it out. I vote no on this one.'

She gazed out the back screen at the birds feeding in the grass under the mimosa tree.

Then she said, 'Do you think he's coming back?'

'I don't know.'

Her eyes went deep into mine.

'If I get to him first, he'll never have the chance,' I said.

'I didn't mean that,' she said.

'I did.'

I felt her eyes follow me into the hallway. I changed into a pair of seersucker slacks, loafers, a brown sports shirt, and a white knit tie, then went back into the kitchen, leaned over Bootsie's chair, hugged her across the chest, and kissed her hair.

'Boots, real courage is when you put away all thought about your own welfare and worry about the fate of another,' I said. 'That was my wife the other night. A fuckhead like Buchalter can't touch that kind of courage.'

She stroked the side of my face with her fingers without looking up.

The phone rang on the wall above the drain board.

'I hear you're back on the clock,' a voice with a black New Orleans accent said.

'Motley?'

'Do you mind me calling you at your house?'

'No, not at all. How'd you know I was back on duty?'

'We're coordinating with your department on this guy Sitwell. Did you know he and the space-o speed freak who electrocuted himself were cell mates at Angola?'

'No.'

'They were both in a rock 'n' roll band in the Block. So if they did everything else together, maybe they both muled dope for the AB.'

'I already talked to the warden. Sitwell didn't have any politics; there're no racial beefs in his jacket. He was always a loner, a walk-in bank robber and a smash-and-grab jewel thief.'

'I think you should come to New Orleans this morning.'

'What for?'

'There's a shooting gallery up by Terpsichore and Baronne. The main man there is a bucket of shit who goes by the name of Camel Benoit. You know who I'm talking about?'

'He used to pimp down by Magazine sometimes?'

'That's the guy. We've been trying to shut down that place for six months. We bust it, we nail a couple of sixteen-year-olds with their brains running out their noses, a week later Camel's got Mexican tar all up and down Martin Luther King Drive. Except at about five this morning, when everybody was nodding out, some sonofabitch broke the door out of the jamb and pasted people all over the wall with an E-tool.'

'With an *entrenching tool*?'

'You heard me. Sharpened on the edges with a file. After he broke a few heads, he went after our man Camel. I would have bought tickets for that one.'

'What happened?'

'I don't know, we're still finding out.'

'Come on, Motley, you're not making sense.'

'There used to be adult education classes in that building. The guy who busted down the door evidently chased Camel through a bunch of rooms upstairs with a flagstaff. At least that's what we think.'

'I don't understand what you're saying. Where's Camel Benoit?'

He made a whistling sound in exasperation.

'I'm trying to tell you, Robicheaux. We don't know for sure. We think he's inside the wall. Anyway, there's blood seeping through the mortar. You know any mice that are big enough to bleed through a brick wall?'

The two-story building had been the home of a Creole slave trader and cotton dealer in the 1850s. But now the twin brick chimneys were partially collapsed, the iron grillwork on the balconies was torn loose from its fastenings, and the ventilated wood shutters hung at odd angles on the windows. An air compressor for a jackhammer was wheezing and pumping in front of the entrance. I held up my badge for a uniformed patrolman to look at as I threaded my way between two police cars and an ambulance into the entrance of the building.

At the back of a dark corridor covered with spray-can graffiti, a workman in gloves and a hard hat was thudding the jackhammer into the wall while Motley and two white plainclothes watched. Motley was eating an ice cream cone. The floor was powdered with mortar and brick dust. I tried to talk above the noise and gave it up. Motley motioned me into a side room and closed the door behind us. The room was strewn with burnt newspaper, beer cans, wine bottles, ten-dollar coke vials, and discarded rubbers.

'We should have already been through the wall, but it looks like somebody poured cement inside it when the foundation settled,' he said. He brushed a smear of ice cream out of his thick mustache.

'What was this about a flagstaff?'

'A couple of noddies say there was an American flag on a staff in the corner with a bunch of trash. The wild man grabbed it and ran Camel Benoit upstairs with it, then stuffed him through a hole in the wall. For all we know, he's still alive in there.' He took a bite of his ice cream and leaned forward so it wouldn't drip on his tie.

'What have you got on the wild man?'

'Not much. He had on a Halloween mask and wore brown leather gloves.'

'Was he white or black?'

'Nobody seems to remember. It was five in the morning. These guys were on the downside of smoking rock and bazooka and hyping all night.' He used his shoe to nudge a rubber that was curled on top of a piece of burnt newspaper like a flattened gray slug. 'You think these cocksuckers worry about safe sex? They get free rubbers from the family planning clinic and use them to carry brown scag in.'

'Motley, I think you might be a closet Republican.'

'I'm not big on humor this morning, Robicheaux.'

'Why did you want me down here?'

'Because I want to take this guy off the board. Because I'm not feeling a lot of support from Nate Baxter, or from anybody else, for that matter. If it hasn't occurred to you, nobody's exactly on the rag because a few black dealers are getting taken out.'

'Maybe Camel's operation is being hit on by another dealer.'

'You mean by another *black* dealer, don't you?' He bit into the cone of his ice cream, then flipped it away into a pile of trash. 'Come on, they've quit out there. Let's go see the show.'

'I didn't mean to offend you, partner.'

'Get off of it, Robicheaux. As far as the department is concerned, this is still nigger town. On a scale of priority of one to ten, it rates a minus eight.'

The air in the hallway was now gray with stone dust. Two workmen used crowbars to rake the bricks from the wall and the chunks of concrete inside onto the hallway floor. The gash in the wall looked like a torn mouth that they kept elongating and deepening until it almost reached the floor. One of the workmen paused, pushed his goggles up on his forehead, and leaned into the dark interior.

He brought his head back out and scratched his cheek.

'I can see a guy about three feet to the left. I'm not sure about what else I see, though,' he said.

'Look out,' Motley said, pushed the workman aside, and shined a flashlight into the hole. He pointed the light back into the recess for what seemed a long time. Then he clicked off the light and stood erect. 'Well, he always told everybody he was a war veteran. Maybe Camel'd appreciate a patriotic touch.'

I took the flashlight from Motley's hand and leaned inside the hole. The air was cool and smelled of damp earth, rats and old brick.

The flashlight beam danced over Camel's body, his copper-bright skin, his hair shaved into dagger points and corn-rolled ridges, his dead eye that looked like a frosted blue-white marble. He was wedged in a reclining position between the bricks and a pile of broken cinder blocks. The workmen had entered the wall at the wrong location because Camel's blood had drained down a cement mound into a bowllike depression at the bottom of the wall.

The wound was like none I had ever seen in my years as a homicide detective. Someone had driven the winged, brass-sheathed end of a broken flagstaff through Camel's back, all the way through the heart cavity, until the staff had emerged below the nipple. The remnant of an American flag, long since faded almost colorless and partially burned by vandals, was streaked bright red and glued tightly against the staff by the pressure of the wound.

'Get the rest of the wall down,' Motley said to the workmen. Then he motioned me to follow him up the stairwell to the second floor. We stood on a landing outside a closed door. The building shook with the thudding of the jackhammer. 'What do you think?'

'I don't know,' I said. 'I thought the vigilante specialized in heart removal.'

'So he modified his technique.'

'I thought he usually left flowers behind.'

'Maybe he didn't have time.'

'Did the killer take anything? Money or drugs?'

'He seemed to be too busy breaking heads. At least according to our witnesses.'

'Where are they?'

'Either in the hospital or in a holding cell at the district . . . Except one.'

'Oh?'

'Yeah,' he said. 'You want to check him out?'

He opened the door on a room that was stacked with school desks. Sitting on the floor, under a portable blackboard with holes the size of bowling balls knocked in the slate, was Zoot Bergeron, his knees drawn up before him, his eyes red-rimmed with fatigue. There was a puddle of what looked like urine in the corner.

'He walked in the back door about five minutes after two patrolmen got here,' Motley said. 'Bad luck for Lucinda's boy.'

Zoot looked at me, then dropped his eyes to his tennis shoes. He had made fists of both his hands, with his thumbs tucked inside his palms. Motley kicked him in the sole of the shoe.

'Look at me,' he said.

'Yes, suh,' Zoot said.

'Tell Detective Robicheaux what you told me.'

'I was picking up a friend. That's all. I don't know nothing about what goes on here.'

'Do you think all big people are dumb, Zoot? Do I look like a big, dumb, fat man to you?' Motley asked.

'I ain't said that, Sergeant Motley. My friend ax me to pick him up here and carry him to work.'

'Maybe we ought to take you down to the detox and get you UA-ed,' Motley said. 'You ever been there? You got to watch out for some of those old-time hypes in the shower, though. They'll try to take your cherry.'

'I don't care you UA me or not. I don't care you try to scare me with that kind of talk, either. I ain't used no dope, Sergeant Motley.'

'What do you know about Camel Benoit?' I said.

'Everybody up Magazine know Camel. He's a pimp.'

'He was a drug dealer, too, Zoot,' I said.

He fastened his eyes on his shoes again.

'Do you know who killed him?' I said.

'Sergeant Motley just said it. I wasn't here.'

He locked his hands on his knees, then rested his forehead on the back of his wrist. His eyelashes were as long as a girl's.

'You trying to fuck your mother?' Motley said.

'Suh?' Zoot said, raising his head. His face was the color of dead ash.

'You heard me, fuck your mother. Because that's what you're doing, you stupid little shit.'

Zoot tried to return Motley's stare, but his left eye began to tremble and water.

'Get out of here,' Motley said.

'Suh?'

'You got earplugs on? Get out of here. If I catch you around a crack house again, I'm going to kick your skinny ass all up and down Martin Luther King Drive.'

Zoot got to his feet uncertainly. He flinched when he straightened his back. Motley opened the door and leaned over the stair railing.

'There's a kid coming out. Let him go. He doesn't know anything,' he called to the detectives below. Then he walked back to Zoot and punched him in the breastbone with his forefinger.

'Don't ever give me reason to get mad at you. Do you understand me?' he said.

'Yes, suh. I ain't.'

'You tell anybody I cut you loose, I'll kick your ass anyway.'

'Yes, suh.'

'Get out!'

After Zoot was gone, I looked at Motley. He was lighting a cigar. His whiskers were jet black inside the grain of his cheeks.

'You're all right, Motley.'

'Tell me that five years from now. That kid's going to end up face down on a sidewalk.'

'Why?'

'Because he's like half the black kids in New Orleans. Every day he's got to prove he doesn't have his mama's pink finger up his butt. Come on, I'll buy you a beignet. This place is depressing me.'

I spent the next two hours in the library, or morgue, as it's called, of *The Times-Picayune*. I could find almost nothing on German U-boat activity in the Gulf of Mexico that had been printed during the war years, since all military news was censored from late 1941 until after V-J Day. There was one exception, however: a headline story which ran for three days concerning four Nazi saboteurs who had been apprehended by the FBI south of Baton Rouge in a truck loaded with explosives.

A page one photograph showed them in fedoras and baggy suits, locked to a wrist chain, staring out at the camera with pale, rectangular faces and buckshot eyes. The cutline below said they had planned to blow up the Standard Oil refinery on the banks of the Mississippi at Baton Rouge. The last article in the series dealt with the arrest of an American accomplice, a retired oil man in Grand Isle by the name of Jon Matthew Buchalter, who had been a founder of the American Silver Shirts.

I jumped the microfilm ahead to the year 1956 and found the name of Jon Matthew Buchalter once again. It was in a twenty-inch feature story in the regional section, written with the detached tone one might use in examining an anthropological curiosity, about the oil man who had betrayed his country, flashed a signal one night through the mist at a U-boat south of Grand Isle, and helped bring ashore four men who, had they succeeded in their mission, would have dried up the flow of fuel to American and English forces for at least two weeks.

At the bottom of the page was a 1935 wire-service photograph of Buchalter with Adolf Hitler and Hermann Goering. Buchalter was a barrel-chested, vigorous-looking man, resplendent in white riding breeches, silver shirt, polished Sam Browne belt, black tie, and red-and-black armband. His right hand clasped Hitler's; he was smiling with the confidence of a man who knew that he had stepped into history.

After he was arrested in Grand Isle, a drunken mob of shrimpers tried to break him out of jail. They fled when sheriff's deputies began firing shotguns in the air. They left behind a thirty-foot spool of chain and a five-gallon can of gasoline.

He did his fourteen years of federal time in isolation, despised by both his warders and his fellow prisoners, eating food delivered through a slit by a trusty who in all probability spat in it first.

His wife and children had long ago moved out of state; his property had been confiscated for taxes. He weighed eighty pounds when his liver finally failed and he died in a public ward at Charity Hospital in New Orleans. There was no marker placed on his grave in potter's field other than a stamped tin number pressed into the sod.

I wondered what importance he would give the fact that the old potter's field in Orleans Parish was not segregated, like other cemeteries during that historical period, and that he would sow his teeth and bones among those of Negroes and perhaps even Jews.

Later that afternoon I parked in front of Lucinda Bergeron's house off Magazine. Just as I was turning off the engine, an open Jeep with oversized tires and four black kids inside pulled to the curb in front of me. The rap music playing on the stereo was deafening, like an electronic assault on the sensibilities. Zoot got out of the Jeep and went inside his house, his eyes straight ahead, as though I were not there. The three other boys did leg stretches on the lawn while they waited for him. All three were dressed in an almost paramilitary fashion – baggy black trousers like paratroopers might wear, gold neck chains, Air Jordan tennis shoes, black T-shirts with scrolled white death's-heads on them. Their hair was shaved to the scalp on the sides, with only a coarse, squared pad on the crown of the skull. Zoot came back out the front door and gave each of them a can of Pepsi-Cola.

When they drove away, the rap music from their stereo echoed off housefronts all the way down the street.

'You get an eyeful?' Zoot said.

'You run the PX for these characters?'

'The what?'

'Sergeant Motley's worried about you.'

He looked at me, waiting to see what new kind of trap was being constructed around him.

'He thinks you're going to get cooled out one of these days,' I said.

'Cooled . . . what?'

'He thinks you're cruising for a big fall.'

'Why y'all on my case? I ain't done nothing.'

'Did you tell your mother about what happened this morning?'

93

His eyes flicked sideways toward the house. He sucked in his cheeks and tried not to swallow.

'I remember something a guy told me once,' I said. 'He said it's as dishonorable to let yourself be used as it is to use someone else.'

'What you mean?'

'Your friends impress me as shitheads.'

'I don't care what you say. We stand by each ot'er. They're my friends in all kinds of ways.'

'Zoot, I didn't see one of those guys say thank you when you handed him a soft drink. Who's kidding who, podna?'

I found his mother on her knees in the backyard, spading out a hole for a pot of chrysanthemums. The Saint Augustine grass was thick and spongy underfoot, and the beds along her weathered wood fences were bursting with azaleas, banana trees, elephant ears, flaming hibiscus, and pink and blue hydrangeas. She was barefoot and wore a pair of white shorts and a purple blouse with green flowers on it. Her hair was on her shoulders, and her face was hot with her work. For the first time I saw a prettiness in her. I sat on a wood box next to her and turned on the garden hose and let it sluice into the fresh hole while she fitted the plant in and troweled dirt over the roots.

'How'd you know I was home?' she said.

'Your office told me you're working nights now.'

'What were you talking to Zoot about out there?' she said, without looking up.

'Not too much ... His friends.'

'You don't approve of them?'

'People sure know when they're around.'

'Well, I guess you're glad you don't have to be around them very long, aren't you?'

'A boy can gravitate to certain kids for a reason.'

'Oh?' she said, and rested her rump on her heels. As she looked at me she tilted her head in feigned deference.

'I don't know why you think it's funny. He's a good boy,' I said. 'Why don't you stop treating him like a douche bag?'

She made a sound like she had swallowed bile. 'I can't believe you just said that,' she said.

'Why don't you give the kid some credit? He's got a lot of courage. Did he tell you he went three rounds against a professional fighter who could have turned his brains into mush?'

'Where do you get off telling me how to raise my child?'

'*That's* it, Lucinda. He's not a child.'

Then she made the same sound again, as though she couldn't remove a vile taste from her throat. 'Please spare me this, would you?' she said. 'Go away somewhere, find a nice white neighborhood, find a white lady digging in her garden, and please give her your advice about the correct way to raise children. Can you do that for me, please?'

'We've got another dead dealer, a guy named Camel Benoit down on Terpsichore and Baronne.'

The heat went out of her eyes.

'Did you know him?' I said.

She brushed the dirt off her palms. 'He used to work some girls out of this neighborhood,' she said.

'Somebody drove an American flag through his heart.' I saw the question mark in her face. I told her about the man in gloves and a Halloween mask who had torn up the shooting gallery, about the body in the wall and the force that must have been required to drive the brass-winged staff through the heart cavity. All the while she continued to sit with her rump on her heels and look reflectively at the flower bed in front of her.

'Who's in charge of the investigation?' she said.

'Motley.'

'He'll do his best with it.'

'Somebody else won't?'

'The department has its problems.'

'Is Nate Baxter one of them?' I said.

She smoothed the wet dirt around the base of the chrysanthemum plant with her garden trowel.

'Is there another problem, too?' I asked. 'Like this citizens committee that doesn't seem too upset over a bunch of black lowlifes being canceled out?'

'You think the Citizens Committee for a Better New Orleans is involved with murder?' But her tone did not quite reflect the outrageousness of the idea.

'Some funny people keep showing up on it. Tommy Blue Eyes, Hippo Bimstine . . . you as the liaison person for NOPD. That's a peculiar combo, don't you think?'

'Lots of people want New Orleans to be like it was thirty years ago. For different reasons, maybe.'

'What's your own feeling? You think maybe the times are such that we should just whack out a few of the bad guys? Create our own free-fire zone and make up the rules later?'

'I don't think I like what you're saying.'

'I heard you went up to Angola to watch a man electrocuted.'

'That bothers you?'

'I had to witness an execution once. I had dreams about it for a long time.'

'Let me clarify something for you. I didn't go *once*. I do it in every capital conviction I'm involved with. The people who can't be there, the ones these guys sodomize and mutilate and murder, have worse problems than bad dreams.'

'You're a tough-minded lady.'

'Save the hand job for somebody else.'

I stood up and turned off the hose. The iron handle squeaked in my hand.

'The bad thing about vigilantes is that eventually they're not selective,' I said.

'Is that supposed to mean something to me?'

'I'm going to violate a confidence. If Zoot had walked into that crack house a little earlier this morning, he might have had his head opened up

95

with that E-tool like some of the others. He's not a good listener, either, Lucinda.'

Her lips parted silently. I could not look at the recognition of loss spreading through her face.

It was hot that night, with an angry whalebone moon high above the marsh. The rumble of dry thunder woke me at three in the morning. I found Bootsie in the kitchen, sitting in the dark at the breakfast table, her bare feet in a square of moonlight. Her shoulders were rounded; her breasts sagged inside her nightgown.

'It's the lightning,' she said. 'It was popping out in the marsh. I saw a tree burning.'

I walked her back to the bed and lay beside her. In a little while the rain began ticking in the trees; then it fell harder, drumming on the eaves and the tin roof of the gallery. She fell asleep with her head on my arm and slept through a thunderstorm that broke across the marsh at daybreak and flooded the yard and blew a fine, cool mist through the screens.

At eight o'clock the sheriff called and told me to go directly to Iberia General rather than to the office. Charles Sitwell, our only link to Will Buchalter, would never be accused of ratting out on his friends.

13

The window blinds in Sitwell's hospital room were up, and the walls and the sheets on his bed were bright with sunlight. A nurse was emptying Sitwell's bedpan in the toilet, and the deputy who had stood guard on the door was chewing on a toothpick and staring up at a talk show on a television set whose sound was turned off.

'I can't tell you with any certainty when he died,' the doctor said. 'I'd say it was in the last two or three hours, but that's a guess. Actually, I thought he was going to make it.'

Sitwell's head was tilted back on the pillow. His mouth and eyes were open. A yellow liquid had drained out of the plaster and bandages on his face into the whiskers on his throat.

'You want to guess at what caused his death?' I said.

The doctor was a powerfully built, sandy-haired man, a tanned, habitual golf player, who wore greens and protective plastic bags over his feet.

'Look at his right hand,' he said. 'It's clutching the sheet like he was either afraid of something or he was experiencing a painful spasm of some kind.'

'Yes?'

'That's not unusual in itself, so maybe I'm just too imaginative.'

'You're going to have to be a little more exact for me, Doctor.'

He flipped out his rimless glasses, fitted them on his nose, then bent over Sitwell's body.

'Take at look at this,' he said, rotating Sitwell's chin sideways with his thumb. 'You see that red spot in his whiskers, like a big mosquito bite? Come around in the light. Here, right by the jugular.'

'What about it?'

'Look closely.' He used his thumb to brush back the whiskers. 'The skin's torn above the original puncture. You want to know what I think, or had you rather I stay out of your business?'

'Go ahead, Doc, you're doing just fine.'

'I think maybe somebody shoved a hypodermic needle in his throat.'

I rubbed back Sitwell's whiskers with the tips of my fingers. His blood had already drained to the lowest parts of his body, and his skin was cold and rubbery to the touch. The area right above the puncture looked like it had been ripped with an upward motion, like a wood splinter being torn loose from the grain of the skin.

'If someone did put a needle in him, what do you think it might have been loaded with?' I said.

'Air would do it. A bubble can stop up an artery like a cork in a pipe.'

I turned toward the deputy, who was sitting in a chair now, still staring up at the silent talk show on television. His name was Expidee Chatlin, and he had spent most of his years with the department either as a crossing guard at parish elementary schools or escorting prisoners from the drunk tank to guilty court.

'Were you here all night, Expidee?' I asked.

'Sure, what you t'ink, Dave?' He had narrow shoulders and wide hips, a thin mustache, and stiff, black hair that no amount of grease seemed capable of flattening on his skull.

'Who came in the room during the night?' I asked.

'Hospital people. They's some ot'er kind working here?'

'What kind of hospital people, Expidee?'

'Nurses, doctors, all the reg'lar people they got working here.' He took a fresh toothpick from his shirt pocket and inserted it in the corner of his mouth. His eyes drifted back up to the television set. The doctor went out into the hall. The nurse began untaping the IV needle from Sitwell's arm. I reached up and punched off the television set.

'Did you leave the door at all, Expidee?' I said.

'I got to go to the bat'room sometimes.'

'Why didn't you want to use the one in the room?'

'I didn't want to wake the guy up.'

'Did you go anyplace else?'

He took the toothpick out of his mouth and put it back in his pocket. His hands were cupped on the arms of the chair.

'Being stuck out there on a wooden chair for twelve hours isn't the best kind of assignment, partner,' I said.

'Come on, Dave . . .' His eyes cut sideways at the nurse.

'Ma'am, could you leave us alone a minute?' I said.

She walked out of the room and closed the door behind her.

'What about it, podna?' I said.

He was quiet a moment, then he said, 'About six o'clock I went to the cafeteria and had me some eggs. I ax the nurse up at the counter not to let nobody in the room.'

'How long were you gone?'

'Fifteen minutes, maybe. I just didn't t'ink it was gonna be no big deal.'

'Who was the nurse, Expidee?'

'That one just went out . . . Dave, you gonna put this in my jacket?'

I didn't answer.

'My wife ain't working,' he said. 'I can't get no ot'er job, neither.'

'We've got a dead man on our hands, Expidee.'

'I'm sorry I messed up. What else I'm gonna say?'

There was nothing for it. And I wasn't sure of the cause of death, anyway, or if the deputy's temporary negligence was even a factor.

'If you weren't at the door when you should have been, it was because you went down the hall to use the men's room,' I said.

'T'anks, Dave. I ain't gonna forget it.'

'Don't do something like this again, Expidee.'

'I ain't. I promise. Hey, Dave, you called up the church for that guy?'

'Why do you ask?'

'A man like that try to hurt your family and you call the church for him, that's all right. Yes, suh, that's all right.'

I asked the nurse to come back in. She was in her fifties and had bluish gray hair and a figure like a pigeon's. I asked her if anyone had entered Sitwell's room while Expidee was away from the door.

'I wouldn't know,' she said.

'Did you see anyone?'

'You gentlemen have such an interesting attitude about accountability,' she said. 'Let me see, what exact moment did you have in mind? Do you mean while Expidee was asleep in his chair or wandering the halls?'

'I see. Thank you for your time,' I said.

She flipped the sheet over Chuck Sitwell's face as though she were closing a fly trap, released the blinds, and dropped the room into darkness.

I went to the office and began opening my mail behind my desk. Through the window I could see the fronds on the palm trees by the sidewalk lifting and clattering in the breeze; across the street a black man who sold barbecue lunches was building a fire in an open pit, and the smoke from the green wood spun in the cones of sunlight shining through the oak branches overhead. It wasn't quite yet fall, but the grass was already turning a paler green, the sky a harder, deeper blue, like porcelain, with only a few white clouds on the horizon.

But I couldn't concentrate on either my mail or the beautiful day outside. Regardless whether the autopsy showed that Charles Sitwell had died of complications from gunshot wounds or a hypodermic needle thrust into his throat, Will Buchalter was out there somewhere, with no conduit to him, outside the computer, running free, full-bore, supercharged by his own sexual cruelty.

What was there to go on, I asked myself.

Virtually nothing.

No, music.

He knew something about historical jazz. He even knew how to hold rare seventy-eights and to place them in the record rack with the opening in their dustcovers turned toward the wall.

Could a sadist love music that had its origins in Island hymns and the three-hundred-year spiritual struggle of a race to survive legal and economic servitude?

I doubted it. Cruelty and sentimentality are almost always companion characteristics in an individual but never cruelty and love.

99

Buchalter was one of those whose life was invested in the imposition of control and power over others. Like the self-serving academic who enjoys the possession of an esoteric knowledge for the feeling of superiority it gives him over others, or the pseudojournalist who is drawn to the profession because it allows him access to a world of power and wealth that he secretly envies and fears, the collector such as Buchalter reduces the beauty of butterflies to pinned insects on a mounting board, a daily reminder that creation is always subject to his murderous hand.

The phone on my desk rang.

'Detective Robicheaux?' a woman said.

'Yes?'

'This is Marie Guilbeaux. I hope I'm not bothering you.'

'I'm sorry, who?'

'The nun you met at the hospital. Outside Mr Sitwell's room.'

'Oh yes, how are you, Sister?'

'I wanted to apologize.'

'What for?'

'I heard about Mr Sitwell's death this morning, and I remembered how judgmental I must have sounded the other day. That wasn't my intention, but I wanted to apologize to you anyway.'

'There's no need to. It's good of you to call, though.'

I could hear a hum in the telephone, as though the call was long-distance.

'You've been very nice,' she said.

'Not at all . . . Is there something else on your mind, Sister?'

'No, not really. I think I take myself too seriously sometimes.'

'Well, thanks for calling.'

'I hope to see you again sometime.'

'Me too. Good-bye, Sister.'

'Good-bye.'

The musical community in southern Louisiana is a large and old one. Where do you begin if you want to find a person who's interested in or collects historical jazz?

There was certainly nothing picturesque about the geographic origins of the form. If it was born in one spot, it was Storyville at the turn of the century, a thirty-eight-block red-light district in New Orleans, named for an alderman who wanted to contain all the city's prostitution inside a single neighborhood. *Jazz* meant to fornicate; songs like 'Easy Rider' and 'House of the Rising Sun' were literal dirges about the morphine addiction and suicidal despair of the prostitutes who lived out their lives in the brothels of Perdido Street.

When I walked down Bourbon that evening, not far from Basin, one of the old borders of Storyville, the air was filled with a purple haze, lit with neon, warmly redolent of the smell of beer and whiskey in paper cups, the sky overhead intersected by a solitary pink cloud off Lake Pontchartrain. The street, which was closed to automobile traffic, was congested with people, their faces happy and flushed in the din of rockabilly and Dixieland bands.

Spielers in straw boaters and candy-striped vests were working the trade in front of the strip joints; black kids danced and clattered their clip-on steel taps on the concrete for the tourists; an all-black street band, with tambourines ringing and horns blaring, belted out 'Millersburg' on the corner at Conti; and a half block farther up, in a less hedonistic mood, a group of religious fanatics, with signs containing apocalyptical warnings, tried to buttonhole anyone who would listen to their desperate message.

I talked to an elderly black clarinetist at Preservation Hall, a sax man at the Famous Door who used to work for Marcia Ball, a three-hundred-pound white woman with flaming hair and a sequined dress that sparkled like ice water, who played blues piano in a hole-in-the-wall on Dumaine. None of them knew of a Will Buchalter or a jazz enthusiast or collector who fit his description.

I walked over on Ursulines to a dilapidated book and record store run by two men named Jimmie Ryan and Count Carbonna, who was also known sometimes as Baron Belladonna. Jimmie was a florid, rotund man with a red mustache who looked like a nineteenth-century bartender. But the insides of both his forearms were laced with the flattened veins and gray scar tissue of an old-time addict. Before he had gotten off the needle, he had been known as Jimmie the Dime, because with a phone call he could connect you with any kind of illegal activity in New Orleans.

His business partner, the Count, was another matter. He had blitzed his brain years ago with purple acid, wore a black vampire's cape and slouch hat, and maintained that the soul of Olivia Newton-John lived under the waters of Lake Pontchartrain. His angular body could have been fashioned from wire; his long, narrow head and pinched face looked like they had been slammed in a door. Periodically he shaved off his eyebrows so his brain could absorb more oxygen.

'How do you like being out of the life, Jimmie?' I asked.

As always, my conversation with Jim would prove to be a rare linguistic experience.

'The book business ain't bad stuff to be in these days,' he said. He wore suspenders and a purple-striped long-sleeve shirt with sweat rings under the arms. 'There's a lot of special kinds of readers out there, if you understand what I'm saying, Streak. New Orleans is being overrun by crazoids and people who was probably cloned from dog turds, and the government won't do anything about it. But it's a crazy world out there, and am I my brother's keeper, that's what I'm asking, a buck's a buck, and who am I to judge? So I've got a bin here for your vampire literature, I got your books on ectoplasm, your books on ufology and teleportation, I got your studies on tarot cards and Eckankar, you want to read about your Venusian cannibals living among us, I got your book on that, too.'

'I'm looking for a guy named Will Buchalter, Jimmie. He might be a collector of old jazz records.'

His mustache tilted and the corners of his eyes wrinkled quizzically.

'What's this guy look like?' he asked.

I told him while he rolled a matchstick in his mouth. The Count was cleaning bookshelves with a feather duster, his eyes as intense as obsidian chips in his white face.

'He's got blackheads fanning back from his eyes like cat's whiskers?' Jimmie said.

'Something like that,' I said.

'Maybe I can give him a job here. Hey, is this guy mixed up with this Nazi submarine stuff?'

'How do you know about the sub, Jimmie?'

'The whole fucking town knows about it. I tell you, though, Streak, I wouldn't mess with nobody that was connected with these tin shirts or whatever they used to call these World War II commonists.'

'Wait a minute, Jim. Not everybody knows about the Silver Shirts.'

'I'm Irish, right, so I don't talk about my own people, there's enough others to do that, like you ever hear this one, you put four Irish Catholics together and you always got a fifth, but I got to say you cross a mick with a squarehead, you come up with a pretty unnatural combo, if you're getting my drift, mainly that wearing a star-spangled jockstrap outside your slacks ain't proof you're one-hunnerd-percent American.'

'You've truly lost me, Jimmie.'

'I lived right down the street from his family.'

'*Who?*'

'Tommy Bobalouba. Sometimes you're hard to get things across to, Streak. I mean, like, we got jet planes going by overhead or something?'

'Tommy Lonighan's family was mixed up with Nazis?'

'His mother was from Germany. She was in the, what-do-you-call-'em, the metal shirts. That's why Tommy was always fighting with people. Nobody in the Channel wanted anything to do with his family . . . Hey, Count, we got a customer named Will Buchalter?'

Count Carbonna began humming to himself in a loud, flat, nasal drone.

'Hey, Count, I'm talking here,' Jimmie said. 'Hey, you got stock in the Excedrin company . . . Count, knock off the noise!'

But it was no use. The Count was on a roll, suddenly dusting the records with a manic energy, filling the store with his incessant, grinding drone.

Jimmie looked at me and shrugged his shoulders.

'Listen, Jim, this guy Buchalter is bad news,' I said. 'If he should come in your store, don't let on that you know me, don't try to detain him or drop the dime on him while he's here. Just get ahold of me or Clete Purcel after he leaves.'

'What's this guy done?'

I told him.

'I'm not showing offense here,' he said, 'but I'm a little shocked, you understand what I'm saying, you think a geek like that would be coming into my store. We're talking about the kind of guy hangs in skin shops, beats up on hookers, gets a bone-on hurting people, this ain't Jimmie Ryan just blowing you a lot of gas, Streak, this kind of guy don't like music, he likes to hear somebody scream.'

He leaned on his arms and bit down on his matchstick so that it arched upward into his mustache.

But my conversation with Jimmie was not quite over. A half hour later he called Clete Purcel's apartment, just before I was about to head back to New Iberia.

'I'm glad I got you,' he said. 'Something's wrong here.'

'What's happened?'

'It's the Count. After we close the shop, he always goes upstairs to his room and eats a can of potted meat and watches Pat Robertson on TV. Except tonight he kept droning and humming and walking in circles and cleaning the shelves till the place looked like a dust storm, then for no reason he goes crashing up the stairs and throws everything in a suitcase and flies out the back door with his cape flapping in the breeze.'

'You're saying Buchalter *was* in your store? Maybe when the Count was by himself?'

'You tell me. Hey, when a guy who talks to Olivia Newton-John through the hole in the lavatory is scared out of town by sickos, I'm wondering maybe I should move to Iraq or one of them places where all you got to worry about is your nose falling off from the BO.'

In the morning I got the autopsy report on Charles Sitwell. He didn't die of an air bubble being injected into his bloodstream. The syringe had been loaded with a mixture of water and roach paste.

It was time to talk to Tommy Lonighan about his knowledge of German U-boats and Silver Shirts, preferably in an official situation, in custody, outside of his own environment. I called Ben Motley and asked about the chances of rousting him from his house or gym and bringing him down to an interrogation room.

'On what basis?' he said.

'He's lying about the reasons for his interest in this U-boat.'

'So he didn't want to tell you his mother was a Nazi. It's not the kind of stuff anybody likes to hang on the family tree.'

'It's too much for coincidence, Motley. He's connected with Buchalter. He's got to be.'

'You want me to get a warrant on a guy, in a homicide investigation, because of something his mother did fifty years ago?'

'We just bring him in for questioning. Tommy likes to think of himself as respectable these days. So we step on his cookie bag.'

'I wonder why the words *civil suit* keep floating in front of my eyes. It probably has something to do with my lens prescription.'

'Don't give this guy a free pass. He's dirty, Motley. You know it.'

'Give me a call if you come up with something more. Until then, I don't think it helps to be flogging our rods over the wastebasket.'

'Listen to me, Ben—'

'Get real, Robicheaux. NOPD doesn't roust people, not even Tommy Blue Eyes, when they live on lakefront property. Keep it in your pants, my man.'

I worked late that evening on two other cases, one involving a stabbing in a black nightclub, the other, the possible suffocation of an infant by his foster parents.

The sky was the color of scorched pewter when I drove along the dirt road by the bayou toward my house. The wind was dry blowing across the marsh, and the willows were coated with dust and filled with the red tracings of fireflies. The deputy on guard at the house started his car engine, waved at me as he passed, and disappeared down the long corridor of oak trees.

Bootsie was washing dishes at the sink when I came in. She wore a pair of grass-stained white dungarees and a rumpled yellow blouse that was too small for her and exposed her midsection.

'Where's Alafair?' I said, and kissed her on the cheek. I could smell cigarette smoke in her clothes and hair.

'In the living room. Doing her homework,' she said. She kept her face turned toward the open window when she spoke.

'Where'd you go today?' I said.

'What does it matter?'

'Beg your pardon?'

'What does it matter where we go?'

'I don't understand, Boots.'

'It doesn't matter where we go. He's going to be there.'

'You mean Buchalter?'

'He called.'

'Here? When?'

'This afternoon.'

'Why didn't you call me at the office?'

'And tell you what?'

I put my hands lightly on her shoulders and turned her toward me. She breathed through her nose and kept her face at an angle to me.

'What did he say, Boots?'

'Nothing. I could hear music, like the kind you hear in a supermarket or an elevator. And then a man breathing. His breath going in and out, like he was waiting for something.'

'Maybe it was somebody else, maybe just a crank.'

'He did something else. He scratched a fingernail back and forth on the receiver. The way a cat paws at the door.'

Her mouth parted, and she looked up into my face. Her breath smelled like bourbon-scented orange slices.

'We'll get an unlisted number in the morning,' I said.

'It *was* Buchalter, wasn't it?'

'Maybe. But what we have to remember, Boots, is that when these guys try to scare people with telephone calls, they're running on the rims. They don't have anything else going.'

Her eyes went back and forth, searching inside mine.

'We've got a computer sketch of the guy all over town,' I said. 'I don't think he'll come back.'

'Then who killed the man in the hospital?'

'I don't know.'

'He's out there, Dave. I know he is.'

Her experience with Buchalter had been even worse than mine, and I knew that my words could not take the unrelieved sense of vulnerability out of her face. I held her against me, then walked her into the bedroom, turned on the shower, waited while she got inside the stall, locked the house, then said Alafair's prayers with her. The moon was down, the pecan and oak trees were motionless and black outside the screens, and the only sound I could hear besides the suck of the attic fan was Tripod running up and down on his chain and wire clothesline.

I poured a glass of milk, fixed a ham and onion sandwich, and ate it at the kitchen table. When the phone on the wall rang, I knew who I would be talking to.

His voice sounded as though he were waking from sleep, or as though he had been disturbed during copulation. It was in slow motion, with a *click* to it, deep in his throat, that was both phlegmy and dry at the same time.

'It doesn't have to be bad between us.'

'What doesn't?'

'You, me, your wife. Y'all could be part of us.'

'Buchalter, you've got to understand this. I can't wave a wand over the gulf and bring up a depth-charged sub. I think you're a sick man. But if I get you in my sights, I'm going to take you off at the neck.'

Again, I heard a wet, clicking sound, like his tongue sticking to the insides of his cheeks.

'I like you,' he said.

'You *like* me?'

'Yes. A great deal.'

I waited before I spoke again.

'What do you think is going to happen the next time I see you?' I said.

'Nothing.'

'Nothing?'

'You'll come around to our way. It's a matter of time.'

My palm was squeezed damply on the receiver.

'Listen, every cop in Iberia Parish knows what you look like. They know what you've done, they're not big on procedure. Don't make the mistake of coming back here. I'm telling you this as a favor.'

'We can give you power.'

You're learning nothing. Change the subject.

'I know where you've been in New Orleans,' I said. 'You talked too much about music. You left a trail, Buchalter.'

'I could have hurt you the other night, in ways you can't dream about, but I didn't,' he said. 'Do you want to hear how they reach a point where they beg, what they sound like when they beg?'

'Will you meet with me?'

I heard him drinking from a glass, deeply, swallowing like a man who had walked out of a great, dry heat.

'Because I'm different, you shouldn't treat me as though I'm psychotic.

105

I'm not. Good night,' he said. 'Tell your wife I remember our moment with fondness. She's a beautiful specimen of her gender.'

He hung up the receiver as gently as a man completing a yawn.

My heart was racing inside my chest. My pistol was still clipped to my belt. I unsnapped the holster, slipped the .45 out of the leather, which I had rubbed with saddle soap, and ran my fingers along the coolness of the metal. The balls of my fingers left delicate prints in the thin sheen of oil. I released the magazine from the butt, rubbed my thumb over the brass casing of the top round, pulled the slide back and forth, then shoved the magazine back into the butt. The grips felt hard and stiff inside my hand.

I looked through the window into the dark. I wanted Buchalter to be out there, perhaps parking his car behind a grove of trees, working his way across the fields, confident that this time he could pull it off, could invade my house and life with impunity. And this time—

I put the .45 on the nightstand in our bedroom and undressed in the dark. My own skin felt as dry and hot as a heated lamp shade. Bootsie was still asleep when I moved on top of her, between her legs, without invitation or consent, a rough beast who could have been hewn out of desert stone.

I made love to her as a starving man might. I put my tongue deep in her mouth and tasted the whiskey and candied cherries and sliced oranges deep in her wet recesses. I plummeted into her fecund warmth, I inhaled the alcohol out of her breath, I robbed her of the golden and liquid heat that had been aged in oak and presented mistakenly as a gift to her heart's blood rather than to mine.

14

The early sun looked like a sliver of pink ice, just above the horizon's misty rim, when I stopped my truck at the locked entrance to Tommy Lonighan's driveway. I got out of the truck and pushed the button on the speaker box.

'Who is it?' the voice of the man named Art said.

'Detective Dave Robicheaux. I'm here to see Tommy.'

'He's busy.'

'No, he's not.'

'The last time you were here you were busting up people with a shovel.'

'Yesterday's box score, Art.'

'It's seven o'clock in the fucking morning. How about some slack?'

'Are you going to open up or not? If not, I can come back with a warrant that has your name on it.'

'Is Purcel with you?' ·

'No.'

'You sure?'

'Last chance, Art.'

'Okay, take it easy, I'm buzzing you in. Tommy's out back. I'll tell him you're here. Hey, can you do me a favor?'

'What?'

'It's a nice day. The Indian and me are serving breakfast for Tommy and his guests out on the terrace. Let's keep it a nice day. Okay, man? Shit don't go good with grits and eggs.'

A minute later I parked my truck at the end of Lonighan's drive. The interior of the compound was the architectural and landscaped antithesis of everything in the Irish Channel neighborhood where Tommy had grown up. His imitation Tudor house was surrounded by citrus and pine and oak trees; steam rose from the turquoise surface of his screened-in pool and his coral goldfish ponds; the Saint Augustine grass was thick and wet from soak hoses, shining with dew in the hazy light. Beyond his protective brick walls, I could hear canvas sails flapping and swelling with wind on the lake.

He was behind the house, in an orange bikini swimsuit and a pair of black high-top ring shoes, thudding his taped fists into what looked like a six-foot stack of sandbags. His pale body, which rippled with sweat, was the color and texture of gristle. A tubular, red scar, with tiny pink stitch holes on each side, wound in a serpentine line from his right kidney up to his shoulder blade.

He stopped hitting the bags when he saw me, and wiped his meringue hair and armpits with a towel. His flushed face smiled broadly.

'You're just in time to eat,' he said, pulling the adhesive tape off his hands. 'How about this weather? I think we got ourselves an early fall.' He flipped his towel on top of an azalea bush. His knuckles were round and hard and protruded from his skin as though he were holding a roll of quarters in each hand.

'You work out on sandbags, Tommy?'

'Cement. If you don't bust your hand or jam your wrist on a cement bag, you sure ain't gonna do it on a guy's face. What's up, Dave?'

'I've got a big problem with this guy Buchalter. He can't seem to stay out of my life.'

'If I can help, let me know.' He worked a blue jumper over his head as we walked down a gravel path toward a glass-topped table on his patio, where an ash blond woman in a terry-cloth robe was drinking coffee and reading the paper. 'I don't want a guy like this around, either. He gives the city a bad reputation.'

'I didn't say he was from New Orleans, Tommy.'

'You wouldn't be here unless you thought he was. Sit down and eat. You're too serious. Charlotte, this is Dave Robicheaux.'

She lowered her paper and looked at me with eyes that had the bright, blue tint of colored contact lenses, that were neither rude nor friendly, curious or wary. I suspected that she read news accounts of airline disasters with the same level of interest as the weather report. Her freckled, sun-browned skin had the smooth folds in it of soft tallow.

Her mouth was red and wet when she took it away from the coffee cup and acknowledged me.

'The gentleman who performs so well with a shovel,' she said.

'Sometimes it's better to use visual aids when you're talking to the Calucci brothers,' I said.

'Fucking A,' Tommy said. 'Neither one of those dagos could give himself a hand job without a diagram. But when you got to do business with the oilcans, you got to do business with the oilcans, right?'

'What kind of deals do you have with the Caluccis, Tommy?' I said.

'Are you kidding? Restaurant linen, valet parking, food delivery, carpenters and electricians working on my casino, you deal with the greaseballs or you get a picket line in front of everything you own.'

His house servant came out the back door with a huge, rope-handled wood tray between his hands and began setting silver-topped containers of scrambled eggs, grits, sausage links, bacon, and peeled oranges and grapefruit in front of us. The servant was the same enormous man I had seen on my earlier visit. His Indian face was as expressionless and flat as a cake pan, his brown, skillet-sized hands veined with scar tissue like tiny bits of white string.

'You're staring, Mr Robicheaux,' Charlotte said.

'Excuse me?'

'At Manuel. It's rude to stare at people,' she said.

'He didn't mean anything,' Tommy said. 'Dave's a gentleman. He's got a college degree. In English literature, right, Dave? We're talking fucking class guy here.'

He winked at me as he spread his napkin.

The house servant named Manuel brushed against me when he poured my coffee. I could smell chemical fertilizer and garden dirt in his clothes. He never spoke, but after he went back inside the house, I saw his face look back at me from a kitchen window.

'Dig this,' Tommy said. 'Manny looks like he just got up out of a grave in *Night of the Living Dead*, but actually he's a fruit. He's gonna be in a music video called 'She's a Swinging Stud.' Hey, y'all quit looking at me like that. You think I could make up something like that? They show these kinds of videos in those homo joints on Dauphine.'

'Your mother was in the American-German Bund, Tommy,' I said.

'What?' His face looked as though ice water had been poured on it.

'I guess it's common knowledge in the Channel. That's why you know what's in that sub, isn't it, partner?' I smiled at him.

'You're sitting at my breakfast table . . .' He cleared his throat and tried to regain his words. 'Right here at my table, at my own house, you're making insults about my mother?'

'That's not my intention.'

'Then clean the fucking mashed potatoes out of your mouth.'

The woman named Charlotte put her hand in his lap.

'It's one way or the other, Tommy,' I said.

'What is?'

'You either know something about the sub through your mother, or you've got a serious personal problem with Hippo Bimstine that you're not talking about.'

His tangled, white eyebrows were damp with perspiration against his red face. I saw the woman named Charlotte biting her lip, kneading her hand in his lap.

'What problem you talking about?' he said.

'You want it right down the pipe?'

'Yeah, I do.' But his face looked like stretched rubber, like that of a man about to receive a spear through the breastbone.

'He says you killed his little brother.'

His breath went in and out of his mouth. His eyes looked unfocused, impaired, as though he had been staring at a welder's electric arc. He pinched his nose and breathed hard through his nostrils, rolled his head on his neck.

But it was the woman who spoke.

'You filthy bastard,' she said.

'You want a free shot, Tommy?' I said.

'If I want to take a shot, you won't know what hit you,' he said. But his voice was suddenly hoarse and somehow separate from himself.

'Maybe it was a rough thing to say. But Will Buchalter is doing a number on my wife,' I said. 'It has to stop, Tommy. You understand what I'm saying to you? When you create a free-fire zone, it works both ways. We're not operating on the old rules here.'

'Where you get off talking free-fire zone? I had a Chinese bayonet unzip my insides when you were still fucking your fist.'

'You want one of my Purple Hearts?'

'You're a sonofabitch, Robicheaux,' he said.

'You don't make a convincing victim, Tommy.'

'We were all kids. It was an accident. What's the matter with you, what kind of guy you think I am? Why you doing this?'

'Are you going to help me out?'

'Get off my property.'

'All right,' I said, and stood up to go. Then I saw Zoot Bergeron jogging up the drive in black gym shorts, a red bandanna tied around his forehead. I looked down at Tommy Lonighan.

'I've got a deal for you,' I said. 'You put Buchalter in my custody, you'll probably never see me again. But if he comes back around my house, I'm going to punch your ticket.'

'Yeah?' he said, the rims of his nostrils whitening. 'That's what you're gonna do? You can't bust the right people, you can't protect your own wife, you need somebody to wipe your ass for you, you come around making threats, telling me I killed a child, I'm about to take your fucking head off, Dave, you got that?'

'We'll see who walks out of the smoke, Tommy,' I said, and walked across the sun-spangled, blue-green lawn toward my truck. I didn't look back.

Zoot slowed from his jog, his sleek chest rising and falling, his sweat-soaked gym shorts twisted around his loins.

'What are you doing here, partner?' I asked.

'Mr Tommy give me a job around his yard, let me work out wit' him.'

'You're staying here?'

'I did last night.'

'Why?' He didn't answer, and I said it again, 'Why's that, Zoot?'

'She got a man at the house.' His eyes avoided mine. 'A white man she goes out wit' sometimes. I come over here and Mr Tommy let me stay.'

'I don't want to tell you what to do, Zoot, but I think Tommy Lonighan is a gangster and a racist prick who you ought to avoid like anthrax.'

Then, too late, I saw the alarm in Zoot's eyes as they focused on something behind me.

Tommy Lonighan was moving fast when he hit me between the shoulder blades and drove me into the side of my truck. Before I could turn, he had ripped my .45 loose from my belt holster. He clenched it at an upward angle in front of me, his neck corded with veins, his nostrils flaring, and pulled back the slide, feeding a hollow-point round into the chamber. I could hear the gravel crunch under the soles of his shoes.

'Don't be a dumb guy, Tommy,' I said.

'You think you can punch my buttons, make me ashamed of myself in front of people?'

'Give me the piece, Tommy.'

'You want it? Then you got it, cocksucker.'

He jammed the butt into my palm, but he didn't let go. He wrapped both his hands around mine, tightening his fingers until they were white with bone, and pointed the .45's barrel into his sternum. His blue eyes were round and threaded with light; his breath stank of the pieces of meat wedged in his teeth.

'You talk war record, you talk Purple Hearts, you got the balls for this?' he said.

The hammer was cocked, the safety off, but I was able to keep my fingers frozen outside the trigger housing.

'Step back, Tommy.'

His breath labored in his chest; there was a knot of color like a red rose in his throat.

'I didn't kill no kid back there in the Channel,' he said. 'It was an accident. Everybody knows it but that mockie. He won't let go of it.'

For just a moment the focus in his eyes seemed to turn inward, and his words seemed directed almost at himself rather than at me. I felt the power go out of his grip.

I flipped up the safety on the slide, jerked the .45 loose from his grasp, and whipped the barrel across his nose. He stood flat-footed, his fists balled at his sides, his eyes the same color as the sky, a solitary string of blood dripping from his right nostril. I started to hit him again.

But his face broke, just like a lamp shade being burned in the center by a heat source from within. One eye seemed to knot, as though someone had put a finger in it; his mouth became a crimped, tight line, downturned at the corners, and the flesh in one cheek suddenly filled with wrinkles and began to tremble. He turned and walked into his house, his back straight, his arms dead at his sides, his eyes hidden from view.

I stared openmouthed after him, my weapon hanging loosely from my hand like an object of shame.

15

I had always wanted to believe that I had brought the violence in my life with me when I came back from Vietnam. But one of the most violent moments in my life, or at least the most indefensible, came at the end of my first marriage and not because I was a police officer or a war veteran.

My first wife was a beautiful, dark-haired girl from Martinique who loved thoroughbred horses and racetrack betting as much as I, but she also developed a love for clubhouse society and men who didn't daily mortgage their tomorrows with Beam straight up and a Jax draft on the side.

We were at an afternoon lawn party on Lake Pontchartrain. The sky was storm-streaked, the water out on the lake slate green and capping, the sailboats from the yacht club dipping hard in the swells. I remember standing at the drinks table, next to my wife, while a black waiter in a white butler's jacket was shaking a silver drink mixer. Then my wife's current lover, a geologist from Houston, was next to her, chatting with her, idly stroking the down on her forearm as though I were not there.

I could hear the palm fronds rattling overhead, a jazz combo playing on the terrace, the words of my wife and her lover disappearing like bubbles in the wind. He was an athlete and mountain climber and had the profile and rugged good looks of a gladiator. Then I remember a sound like Popsicle sticks breaking and a wave of red-black color erupting behind my eyes.

When they pulled me off him, he was strangling on his own tongue. .

Later, I pretended that he had deserved it, and that my wife had deserved to be shamed and humiliated in front of her friends. But I was deceiving myself, as was my way in those days when I sincerely believed that I could experience no worse fate in this world than to be deprived of charcoal-filtered whiskey and the amber radiance with which it animated and filled my life. I had simply made my wife and her lover pay for events that had occurred many years earlier.

My father, whose name was Aldous, who was also called Big Al in the oil field, where he worked as a derrick man up on the monkey board, was a huge, dark, grinning Cajun with fists the size of cantaloupes. He loved to fight in bars, sometimes taking on three or four adversaries at once. Oil field roughnecks would break their hands on his head; bouncers would splinter chairs across his back; but no one ever hurt Big Al except my mother, who worked in a laundry with Negro women to support us while he was in the parish jail.

When he went back to Marsh Island for the muskrat season, a man named Mack, a bouree dealer from Morgan City who wore a fedora, zoot slacks, suspenders, French cuffs, and two-tone shoes, began to come by the house and take her for rides in his Ford coupe.

One day in late fall I came home early from school. There was no sound in the house. Then I walked past my parents' bedroom door. My mother was naked, on all fours, pointed toward the head of the bed, and Mack was about to mount her. He had a thin, white face, oiled black hair parted in the center, and a pencil mustache. He looked at me with the momentary interest that he might show a hangnail, then entered my mother.

I sat on a sawhorse in the barn until it was almost dusk. The air was raw, and leaves were blowing across the dirt yard. Then Mack was standing in the barn door, his silhouette etched with the sun's last red light, a bottle of beer in his left hand. I heard him tilt it up and drink from it.

'What you t'ink you seen?' he said.

I looked at my shoes.

'I ax you a question. Don't be pretend you ain't heard me,' he said.

'I didn't see anything.'

'You was where you didn't have no bidness. What we gonna do 'bout that?' He held out his right hand. I thought he was going to place it on my shoulder. Instead, he put the backs of his fingers under my nose. 'You smell that? Me and yo' mama been fuckin', boy. It ain't the first time, neither.'

My eyes were full of water, my face hot and small under his stare.

'You can tell yo' daddy 'bout this if you want, but you gotta tell on her, too.' He drank out of the beer bottle again and waited. 'What's you gonna do, you? Sit there and cry?'

'I'm not going to do anything.'

'That's good,' he said. ''Cause you do, I'm gonna be back.'

Then he was gone, out of the red light, and down the dirt lane to his car. The pecan and oak trees around the house were black-green and coated with dust; the dry coldness of the air felt like a windburn against the skin. I hid when my mother called me from the back porch. Behind the barn, I sat in the weeds and watched our two roosters peck a blind hen to death. They mounted her with their talons, their wings aflutter with triumph, and drove their beaks deep into her pinioned neck. I watched them do it for a long time, until my mother found me and took me back inside the kitchen and, while she fixed our supper, told me that Mack had helped her find a good job as a waitress at a beer garden in Morgan City.

The day after my trouble with Tommy Lonighan, I received a phone call from Clete Purcel at my office.

'I hear you pistol-whipped Tommy Bobalouba,' he said.

'Who told you that?'

'A couple of the Caluccis' lowlifes were talking about it in the Golden Star this morning.'

'Ah, the Caluccis again.'

'That's what I was trying to tell you, mon. They're going across tribal lines.'

'Who were these two guys?'

'Nickel-and-dime gumballs. Were you trying to sweat Tommy about that sub?'

'Yeah, but I didn't get anywhere.'

'Dave, maybe there's another way to get Buchalter out of the woodwork. What if you *can* find that sub again, you mark it, then you tell *The Times-Picayune* and every salvage company in town about it?'

'It's a thought.'

'By the way, congratulations on getting Lonighan's attention. Somebody should have mopped up the floor with that guy a long time ago . . . Why the silence?'

'I shouldn't have hit him.'

'Why not?'

'He's a tormented man. The guy's got a furnace in his head.'

'I'm weeping on my desk, Dave. Oh, that's great, mon. Tommy Lonighan, the tormented man . . .' He was laughing loudly now. 'Did you see the body of the guy Tommy drowned with the fire hose? It looked like the Michelin Man. Tommy shoved the nozzle down the guy's mouth. Tommy the tormented man, oh Dave, that's beautiful . . .'

I went home early that evening, with plans to take Bootsie and Alafair to Mulate's in Breaux Bridge for crawfish. When the deputy who was on guard by the drive saw my truck approaching, he started his engine and headed back toward New Iberia. At the head of the drive, close by the house, was a two-door white Toyota that I didn't recognize.

I walked down to the end of the dock, where Alafair was skipping stones across the water into a cypress stump.

'Want to go eat some crawfish, Alf?' I said.

'I don't care,' she said. Her face was sullen. She whipped another stone across the bayou.

'What's wrong, little guy?'

'I told you I don't like 'little guy' anymore, Dave.'

'All right. Now, what's wrong, Alf?'

'Nothing. Bootsie says she's sick. That's all.'

'"Says" she's sick?'

'She's been in her room all afternoon. With the door shut. She says she's sick. I told you.' She propped one hand against a post and brushed dried fish scales off the planks into the water with her tennis shoe.

'Tell me the rest of it, Alf.'

Her eyes followed a cottonmouth moccasin that was swimming across the bayou into a flooded cane brake.

'She put an empty whiskey bottle in the garbage can out back,' she said. 'She wrapped it up in a paper bag so nobody would see it. Then the sister went and got her some beer.'

'What?'

'There's a sister up there. She went down to the four corners and bought Bootsie a six-pack of beer. Why didn't Bootsie just get it out of the bait shop if she wanted some beer?'

'Let's go find out.'

'I don't want to.'

'You want to go to Mulate's later?'

'No. I don't like the way Bootsie is. I don't like that sister, either. What's she doing here, Dave?'

I rubbed the top of her head and walked up the slope through the deep shade of the trees and the drone of the cicadas. There was no sound or movement in the front of the house, and the door to Bootsie's and my bedroom was closed. I went on through the hallway into the kitchen. Sister Marie Guilbeaux was rinsing glasses and two plates in the sink.

'Oh!' she said, her shoulders twitching suddenly when she heard me behind her. She turned, and her face colored. 'Oh, my heavens, you gave me a start.'

I continued to stare at her.

'Oh, this is embarrassing,' she said. 'I hope you understand what's, why I—'

'I'm afraid I don't.'

'Of course ... you couldn't. I called earlier, but you weren't here.'

'I *was* at my office.'

'I tried there. You had already left.'

'No, I was there until a half hour ago.' I could see a half dozen empty beer cans in the yellow trash basket. 'No one called.'

'*I* did. A man, a dispatcher, took a message.'

'I see. Where's Bootsie, Sister?'

'Asleep. She's not feeling well.' Her face was filled with perplexity. 'I know this looks peculiar.'

'A little.'

'I teach part-time at an elementary school in Lafayette. We're having a program on safety. You were so courteous at the hospital and over the phone I thought you might be willing to visit our class.'

'I'm a little tied up right now.'

'Yes, Bootsie told me.'

'Can you tell me why you bought beer for my wife, Sister?'

Her face was pink. 'Mr Robicheaux, I wandered into somebody's personal situation and I've obviously mishandled it.'

'Just tell me what's happened here, please.'

'Your wife was going to drive to the store for some beer. I didn't think she should be driving. I told her I'd go for her.'

'Why didn't you just get it from the bait shop? We own it.'

'She didn't want me to.'

'I see. Is there anything else I can help you with?'

'No ... I apologize. I don't know what else to say. I'll go now. Please excuse my coming here.'

Then she was out the back door, walking fast toward her car, her green eyes shiny with embarrassment. I caught up with her just as she was opening her car door.

'Sister, there's something going on here you don't understand,' I said. 'My wife has a problem because of some events that occurred at our house. But when a person is drunk or has had too much to drink and wants you to give him more, you don't do it.'

'Then I guess I've learned a lesson today.'

'Come see us again.'

'That's kind of you.' My hand was resting on the windowsill. She placed hers lightly on top of mine and looked directly into my eyes. A shaft of sunlight fell through the tree on her reddish gold hair. I removed my hand from under hers and walked back into the house.

I opened the bedroom door and looked in on Bootsie. The blinds were drawn, and she was sleeping with her clothes on and her head under the pillow. While I fixed supper I tried to concentrate on Alafair's conversation from the table about something that Tripod had done, but my thoughts were like birds clattering about in a cage, and I found myself absently touching the top of my right hand.

You're imagining it, I thought. *It was an innocent gesture. Some of them are just socially inept.*

But my energies were too dissipated to worry about Sister Marie Guilbeaux. I knew that beyond our closed bedroom door, my wife had taken up residence in that special piece of geography where the snakes hang in fat loops from the trees and a tiger with electrified stripes lights your way to his lair.

It rained that night, and through the screen window I could smell the trees and an odor from the marsh like fish spawning. As I fell asleep, I wondered again about the Nazi submarine and Buchalter's obsession with it. When I was a child in Catholic school, we were taught that evil eventually consumes itself, like fire that must destroy its own source. Was the submarine an underwater mausoleum or historical shrine from which Buchalter and his kind believed they could renew and empower their demented and misanthropic vision? Did they hate the present-day world so much that they would seek the company of drowned men who had reveled in setting afire the seas, in machine-gunning clusters of oil-streaked merchant sailors who had bobbed like helpless corks in the swell?

It rained all night. The air in the bedroom was cool and damp, and in my sleep I thought I could smell salt in the wind. I dreamed of black-clad submariners, their white skin layered with deodorant, their unkempt beards like charcoal smeared on their faces. They guided a long, gleaming torpedo into a waiting tube, touching its hard sides like a farewell caress. The torpedo burst from beneath the bow, its propeller spinning, its steel skin rippling with moonlight just below the surface. The men in black dungarees stood motionless in the battery-lighted interior of their ship, their eyes lifted expectantly, their breasts aching with an unspoken and collective wish that

116

made them wet their lips and nudge their groins against the cool, cylindrical side of another torpedo.

The explosion against the hull of the freighter on the horizon, the screech of girders and rent metal, the avalanche of salt water into the hold, the secondary explosion of boilers that blew the bridge into sticks and heated the hatches into searing iron rectangles that would scorch a human hand into a stump, even the final geysering descent beneath the waves and the grinding of the keel against the sand – it all filtered through the darkness outside the sub with the softness of an old Vienna waltz swelling and dissipating in the mist.

It must have been two or three in the morning when I felt the coldness in the room. In my sleep I reached for the bedspread at the foot of the bed and pulled it up over Bootsie and me. I thought wind was blowing through the house, when there should have been none, then I realized that my pillow was damp from the mist that was blowing through the window fan, which was turned off.

I sat up in bed. The doors to both the closet and the bathroom were open, and the night-light in the bathroom had either burned out or been turned off. From the back porch I could hear the screen door puffing open and falling back upon the jamb in the wind. I reached under the bed and picked up the .45.

I didn't have far to go before I knew he had been there. As I walked past the closet I felt water under my bare feet. I turned on every light in the house. The screen was slit on the back porch door, the deadbolt prized out of the jamb on the door to the kitchen.

'What is it, Dave?' Bootsie said, blinking her eyes against the light.

I stared at the floor area in front of the closet. There were two stenciled shoe prints on the boards, surrounded by a ring of water that had dripped off his coat. Then she saw what I was looking at.

'Oh God, I can't take this, Dave,' she said.

'Take it easy. He's gone now.'

'He was here. Watching us sleep.' She sat up and pressed her hands to her stomach. 'I think I'm going to be sick.'

'Use the other bathroom.'

'What?'

'Don't go in our bathroom.'

'Why? Wh—'

'He might have left evidence in there, Boots, that's all.'

When she was gone, I clicked off the light in our bathroom, closed the door, and turned the lock, but not before having to look again at the words that he had lipsticked brightly across the wall: *DAVE, YOU MUST BECOME ONE WITH THE SWORD. I'LL LOVE YOU IN A WAY THAT NO WOMAN CAN, W.B.*

16

The next morning I tried to concentrate on the daily routine at the office. But it was no use. I stared out the window at the rain.

What drove the engines of a man like Will Buchalter?

The conclusion I came to wasn't a pleasant one. He was a sadist, pure and simple, and, like all sadists, he developed erotic fixations about the people and animals he planned to hurt in a methodical way. The pain he imposed upon his victim was intended to humiliate and degrade and was always administered personally, by his hand, only a breath away from the victim's face. As with all of his kind he had found an ideological purpose that justified his perversity, but in reality the cries with which he could fill a room made his back teeth grind softly together while his loins tingled like a swarm of bees.

The phone on my desk rang. It was Lucinda Bergeron.

'Your friend over here is becoming a pain in the ass to a lot of people,' she said.

'Who?'

'Cletus Purcel.'

'What's wrong with Clete?'

'What's right with him?'

'Give it a break, Lucinda.'

'He tried to turn somebody into a human bell clapper. Do you know a character by the name of Dogshit Dolowitz?'

'No Duh Dolowitz, the merry prankster?'

'Yeah, I guess he's called that, too. Your friend crammed a garbage can over his head, then pounded the can all over an alley with a baseball bat.'

'What for?'

'Ask him . . . Wait a minute.' She set the phone down and closed a door. 'Listen, Detective, Nate Baxter would like to put your buddy's ham hocks in a skillet. I'd have a serious talk with him.'

'Is Zoot back home yet?'

'I don't *believe* you. I think you must come from outer space.'

'You're telling me he should be living over at Tommy Lonighan's?'

'I thought I was doing a favor for your friend.'

'I appreciate it.'

I heard her make a sound like she was digesting a thumbtack.

'Take it easy,' I said.

'God, I hate talking to you!' Then she caught her breath and started again. 'Listen, your buddy hasn't been arraigned yet, but my guess is his bond will be around two thousand dollars. You want me to give him a message?'

'No Duh pressed charges?'

'No, Nate Baxter did. Disturbing the peace and resisting arrest. Good-bye, Detective Robicheaux. In all honesty I don't think I'm up to many more conversations with you.'

She hung up the phone.

I called her back.

'Look, I can't take off work just to bail a friend out of the slam. Why'd Clete knock Dolowitz around?'

'It has something to do with the Calucci brothers.'

'What about them?'

'I don't know,' she said, the exasperation rising in her voice. 'Nate Baxter's handling it. What's that tell you, Robicheaux, besides the fact he's got a major hard-on for Purcel?'

'I'm not sure.'

'He's on a pad.'

'For the Calucci brothers?'

'Who else?'

'You can prove that?'

'Who to? Who cares? The city's broke. *That's* what's on people's minds.'

'I'll try to get over there. It's a bad day, though.'

'What's wrong?'

I told her about Buchalter's visit of the night before.

'Why didn't you tell me that?' she said.

'You've got your own problems.'

She paused a moment. 'You saw Zoot over at Tommy Lonighan's?' she said.

'Yeah, for just a few minutes.'

'Did he say—' She let out her breath in the receiver and didn't finish.

'I think you mean a lot to him, Lucinda. I'd bring him back home. I'm sorry if I sound intrusive sometimes.'

I called Bootsie at the house, then signed out of the office. It was still raining when I got to NOPD headquarters in the Garden District. Lucinda Bergeron was out of the office, but Benjamin Motley told me that the Reverend Oswald Flat had gotten Clete released in his custody without having to post bail and they were waiting for me at a café up on St Charles by the Pontchartrain Hotel.

It was a working man's place that served rib-eye steaks, deep-fried catfish, and biscuits with sausage gravy that you could stoke boilers with. It was also the café where the Calucci brothers ate lunch every day.

I parked my truck around the corner, then ran back in the rain under the dripping overhang of the oak trees on St Charles. The inside of the restaurant was warm and crowded and loud. Clete and the preacher were at a checker-cloth-covered table in front. In the center of the table was a solitary, green-stemmed purple rose set in a dime-store glass vase. Between the preacher's feet I could see a worn-edged, black guitar case with the words *The Great Speckled Bird* hand-lettered on the side.

I let my eyes rove over the people at the tables; then I saw Max and Bobo Calucci and a half dozen of their entourage eating at a long table against the back wall, three feet from an old jukebox, whose maroon and orange plastic casing rippled with light.

I sat down with Clete and the preacher.

'You ought to get you an umbrella, son. You look like a hedgehog somebody drowned in a rain barrel,' Oswald Flat said.

'Thank you, Reverend,' I said.

'Sorry to get you down here for no reason, Streak,' Clete said. 'I tried to catch you after Brother Oswald here got me out of the bag, but you were already down the road.' He grinned while he chewed on a bread stick.

'What are you doing beating up on a guy like No Duh Dolowitz?' I said.

'Yeah, I always dug ole No Duh myself,' Clete said, then turned to the preacher. 'You see, this guy No Duh – sometimes they call him Dogshit because that's what he put in some sandwiches once at a Teamsters convention in Miami – he used to be a second-story creep till a night watchman bonged a big dent in his forehead with a ball peen hammer. But instead of turning into a mush brain, he developed a genius for playing pranks. The mob knows talent when it sees it.

'If they want to take over an apartment building or a bunch of duplexes at fire-sale prices, they send in Dolowitz. He pours cement mix down all the drains, puts Limburger cheese in the air vents, tapes bait fish under the furniture, maybe has a landscape service pour a dump truck load of cow manure in the swimming pool. This contractor built some real class condos in Jefferson Parish, then he finds out too late that he doesn't have clear title to the land and that part of it is owned by the Giacano family. So while he's trying to hold off the Giacanos in court, they send in No Duh, who makes keys to all the doors, stops up the toilets, stocks the cabinets with Thunderbird and Boone's Farm, then buses in about twenty winos from skid row and tells them to have a good time. I heard the cleaning crews had to scrape the carpets up with shovels.'

He laughed, pushed his porkpie hat up on his head, and put a cigarette in the corner of his mouth. His hand looked huge on his Zippo lighter. I noticed that his eyes never looked in the Caluccis' direction.

'Why the beef with a guy like that, Clete?' I said.

The humor drained out of his face, and his eyes drifted toward the rear of the restaurant.

'I gave Martina the two grand to pay off the Caluccis. Guess what? They told her that's just the back payment on the vig. She still owes another two large. Last night we came back from the show and there's Dolowitz hiding in the shrubs by the side of Martina's garage. So I ask him what the hell he thinks he's doing there.

'He tells me he lives two blocks away, up by Audubon Park, and he's been walking his dog. I say, "That's funny, I don't see any dog." He says, "No duh, Purcel. Because my dog run away." "Oh, I see. That's why you're in the shrubs," I say. "No duh, my fast-thinking man," he says.

'I say, "I got another problem here, No Duh. People like you don't live by Audubon Park. Not unless the neighborhood has recently been rezoned for meltdowns and toxic waste. If I remember right, you live in a shithole by the Industrial Canal. So why are you hiding here by Martina's garage, and if you give me one more wiseass answer, I'm going to stuff your dented head up the tailpipe of my car."

'So he puts his fingers in the corners of his mouth and stretches out his lips like a jack-o'-lantern. Can you believe this guy? I say, "No Duh, your mother must have defecated you into the world," and I shake him down against the wall, and what do we find, our man's got a bottle of muriatic acid in his pants pocket.'

'I don't get it. Dolowitz isn't an enforcer,' I said.

'I didn't get it, either. Also, dispensation time for dimwits was starting to run out. I go, "What do you think you're doing with this, fuckhead?" Suddenly he's like a guy who just sobered up. He goes, "It's just a prank, Purcel. I don't hurt people." That's when I screwed the trash can down on his head and got a ball bat out of my car and bounced him around the alley. Finally he's yelling inside the can, "I was going to put it in her gas tank! I wasn't going to have nothing to do with the rest of it!"

'You want to know what "the rest of it" was?' Clete mashed out his cigarette in the ashtray. His eyes cut sideways toward the rear of the café. 'Martina goes on shift cocktail-waitressing at a club in Gretna at ten p.m. Dolowitz was going to mess up her car so it'd kill somewhere between her house and work. A guy was going to be following her. You want to hear how No Duh put it? "Max and Bobo Calucci got some kind of geek working for them, not no ordinary button guy, either, Purcel, a guy who can fuck up people real bad, in ways nobody ever thought about."'

Clete propped his elbow on the table and inserted a thumbnail in his teeth.

'You think I was too hard on ole Dogshit?' he said.

'Sir, could you watch your language?' the manager, who had come out from behind the cash register, said quietly.

'Yeah, yeah, yeah,' Clete said, flipping his hand at the air.

'You think it could be Buchalter?' I said.

'Maybe. But I don't know how he'd tie in with the greaseballs back there in the booth.'

'Maybe he's connected with Tommy Lonighan's interest in the Nazi sub, and now Lonighan's mixed up with the Caluccis. Anyway, he was in my house last night,' I said.

'He was *what?*'

'Standing in our closet, watching us while we slept.'

'Jesus Christ, Dave.'

'He cut the back screen, prized out the deadbolt, walked around in the house, and I never heard him.'

Clete sat back in his chair.

'This guy's a new combo, mon,' he said. 'I thought if he ever came back, it'd be to cool you out.'

'You think the real problem is y'all don't have no idea of what you're dealing with?' Oswald Flat said.

We both looked at him. His clip-on bow tie was askew on his denim shirt. His pale eyes looked as big as an owl's behind his glasses.

'You cain't find that fellow 'cause maybe he ain't human,' he said. 'Maybe y'all been dealing with a demon. You ever consider that?'

'I can't say that I have,' I said.

'It's the end of the millennium,' he said.

'Yes?' I said.

'Son, I don't want to be unkind to you. But when the brains was passed out, did you grab a handful of pig flop by mistake?'

He paused to let his statement sink in.

'The prophesy is in Nostradamus. The Beast and his followers are going to be loosed on the earth,' he said. 'Call me a fool. But you're a policeman, and the best you got ain't worth horse pucky on a rock, is hit?'

I looked back at him silently. His short, dun-colored hair was combed neatly and parted almost in the center of his scalp. His washed-out eyes never blinked and seemed wide with a knowledge that was lost on others.

The waiter set plates of deep-fried pork chops, greens, and dirty rice in front of him and Clete.

'You're not going to eat?' Oswald Flat said.

'No, thanks.'

'I offended you?'

'Not at all,' I said.

Clete lowered his fork onto his plate and looked toward the rear of the restaurant again.

'It looks like the Vitalis twins are about to finish their lunch. I don't know if they should slide out of here that easily,' he said.

'Let it go,' I said.

'Trust me.'

'I mean it, Clete. Baxter's got you in his bombsights. Don't play his game.'

'You worry too much, big mon. It's time to check out the jukebox and the ole hippy-dippy from Mississippi, yes indeed, Mr Jimmy Reed. I'll be right back.'

Clete strolled to the rear of the restaurant, past the Caluccis' table, his eyes never registering their presence. He dropped a quarter into the jukebox and punched off 'Big Boss Man,' then began snapping his fingers and slapping his right palm on top of his left fist while he scanned the other titles. The back of his neck looked as thick as a fire hydrant.

The preacher's gaze moved back and forth from Clete to the Caluccis. His false teeth were stiff and white in his mouth.

'He'll be all right, Reverend. Clete just likes to let people know he's in the neighborhood,' I said.

But Oswald Flat didn't answer. There were pools of color in his cheeks, nests of wrinkles at the edges of his eyes.

'You play guitar?' I said.

'I played with Reno and Smiley, I played with Jimmy Martin and the Sunny Mountain Boys. Hit don't get no better than that,' he said. But his eyes were riveted on the Caluccis when he spoke.

Clete sat back down, his green eyes dancing with light, while Jimmy Reed sang in the background.

The Caluccis were watching him now. Clete made a frame of his hands, with his thumbs joined together, tilting the frame back and forth, sighting through it at Max and Bobo, the way a movie director might if he were envisioning a dramatic scene. Then he began pointing his finger at them, grinning, tapping it in time to 'Big Boss Man's' driving rhythm.

'Knock it off, Clete,' I said.

'They need to know they've been ratted out, mon. You never let a shit bag forget he's a shit bag. You got to keep them buttoned down under the sewer grates, big mon.'

'You're both good fellows, but one is as wrongheaded as the other,' Oswald Flat said.

'Excuse me?' Clete said.

'You don't outwit evil. You don't outthink hit, you don't joke with hit, no more than you tease or control fire by sticking your hand in hit.'

'You all right, Reverend?' I said.

'No, I ain't.'

His sun-browned, liver-spotted hands were flat on the table-cloth. His nails looked like hooked tortoiseshell.

'What's the trouble, partner?' I said.

'They took my boy.'

'Who?' Clete said.

'He come back from Vietnam with needle scars on his arm. Wasn't no he'p for hit, either. Federal hospitals, jails, drug programs, he could always get all the dope he needed from them kind yonder. Till he killed hisself with hit.'

The music on the jukebox ended. Clete looked at me and raised his eyebrows. Oswald Flat slipped the purple rose out of the dimestore vase in the center of the table and sliced off the green stem with his thumbnail.

'Hey, hold on, Brother. Where you going?' Clete said.

Oswald Flat walked toward the rear of the restaurant. He moved like a crab, his shoulders slanted to one side, the rose hanging from his right hand. The Caluccis were finishing their coffee and dessert and at first did not pay attention to the man with the clip-on bow tie standing above them.

Then Max stopped talking to a woman with lacquered blond hair next to him and flicked his eyes up at Oswald Flat.

'What?' he said. When Flat made no reply, Max said it again. 'What?'

Then Bobo was looking at the preacher, too.

'Hey, he's talking to you. You got a problem?' he said.

The people at nearby tables had stopped talking now.

'Hey, what's with you? You can't find the men's room or something?' Max said.

The blond woman next to him started to laugh, then looked at Oswald Flat's face and dropped her eyes.

'Y'all think you're different from them colored dope dealers? Y'all think hit cain't happen to you?' the preacher said.

'What? What can happen?' Max said.

'Your skin's white but your heart's black, just like them that's had hit cut out of their chests.'

The restaurant was almost completely silent now. In the kitchen someone stopped scraping a dish into a garbage can.

'Listen, you four-eyed fuck, if Purcel and that cop sent you over here—' Max began.

Oswald flipped the purple rose into Max Calucci's face.

'You're a lost, stupid man,' he said. 'If I was you, I'd drink all the ice water I could while I had opportunity. Hell's hot and it's got damn little shade.'

The Reverend Oswald Flat picked up his guitar case, fitted his cork sun helmet on his head, and walked out the front door into a vortex of rain.

As I crossed the wide, brown sweep of the Mississippi at Baton Rouge and headed across the Atchafalaya Basin toward home, I thought about Oswald Flat's speculation on the elusiveness of Will Buchalter.

It seemed the stuff of an Appalachian tent revival where the reborn dipped their arms into boxes filled with poisonous snakes.

But the preacher's conclusion that we were dealing with a demonic incarnation was neither eccentric nor very original and, as with some other cases I've worked, was as good an explanation about aberrant human behavior as any.

Ten years ago, when Clete and I worked Homicide at NOPD, we investigated a case that even today no one can satisfactorily explain.

A thirty-five-year-old small contractor was hired to build a sun-porch on a home in an old residential neighborhood off Canal. He was well thought of, nice-looking, married only once, attended church weekly with his wife and son, and had never been in trouble of any kind. At least that we knew of.

The family who had contracted him to build the addition on their house were Romanian gypsies who had grown wealthy as slum-lords in the black districts off Magazine. Their late-Victorian home had polished oak floors, ceiling-high windows, small balconies dripping with orange passion vine, a pool, and a game room with a sunken hot tub.

They thought well enough of the contractor to leave him alone with their fifteen- and twelve-year-old daughters.

The father should have been gone for the day, checking out his rental property miles away. Instead, he came home unexpectedly for lunch. Someone waited for him behind the living room door, then fired a .22 Magnum round into his ear. The bullet exited his opposite cheek and embedded in the far wall.

No one heard the shot. Around one in the afternoon neighbors saw the contractor drive away in the father's Buick. Three hours later the mother returned from shopping and found both her daughters drowned in the hot tub. They were bound ankle and wrist with electrician's tape; both had been raped.

The contractor pawned his tools, his watch, and his wedding ring at three different stops between New Orleans and Pensacola, Florida, where he was arrested after a call he made to his wife was traced to a motel there. Clete Purcel and I transported him back to New Orleans from the Pensacola city jail.

He was likable; there was nothing of the con artist about him; he was well-mannered and didn't use profanity; he never complained about riding handcuffed to a D-ring in the backseat.

At his trial he maintained that he'd had a blackout, that he had no memory of the events that took place in the house off Canal, but a sense of terror, with no apparent source, had caused him to flee across I–10 to the Florida panhandle.

Prosecution lawyers, state psychologists, and news reporters came up with every script possible to explain the contractor's behavior: He was a clandestine user of LSD; he had been a marine door gunner in Vietnam; he was badly in debt and teetering on a nervous breakdown. Or, more disturbingly, he had once been seen at a shopping mall with a high school girl from his neighborhood whose strangled and decomposed body was found nude in a swamp north of Lake Pontchartrain. On her ankle was a tattoo of a pentagram.

All the evidence against him was circumstantial. None of his fingerprints were in the game room where the girls died, nor on the electrician's tape that was used to bind them. Also the tape was not the same brand that he always bought from a wholesale outlet. There were no skin particles under the dead girls' fingernails.

He probably would have walked if he could have afforded a better lawyer. But the jury convicted him of second-degree murder, perhaps less out of certainty of his guilt than fear that he was guilty and would kill or rape again if set free.

His friends and family were numb with disbelief. The pastor from his church raised money to begin an appeal of the verdict. His parishioners put together twenty thousand dollars for the conviction of the real killer. Two attorneys from the ACLU took over the contractor's case.

Clete and I went back over the crime scene a dozen times. We must have interviewed a hundred people. We decided that if we couldn't prove this man conclusively guilty, then we would prove him innocent.

We did neither. All we ever determined was that there was a two-year gap in the contractor's younger life during which he had left behind no paperwork or record of any kind, as though he had eased sideways into another dimension. We also concluded, with a reasonable degree of certainty, at least to ourselves, that no else entered or left that house, besides the father, from the time the contractor showed up to work and the time he fled the crime scene in the Buick.

It became the kind of case that eventually you close the file on and hope the right man is in jail. Clete and I were both glad when we heard that the lower court's decision had been overturned and that a new trial date was to be set soon. Maybe someone else could prove or disprove what we could not.

Three days later, a psychotic inmate at Angola, a big stripe, attacked the contractor with a cane knife and severed his spinal cord with one blow across the back of the neck. The body was lying in state at a funeral home in Metairie when the mother and aunts of the murdered girls burst into the room, screaming hysterically like Shakespearean hags, and flung bags of urine on the corpse.

For a long time I had a recurrent dream about the contractor. He awoke in the blackness of his coffin, then realized that tons of earth had been bulldozed and packed down on top of him. He couldn't move his shoulders or twist his body against the hard, sculpted silk contours of the coffin; his screams went no farther than the coffin's lid, which hovered an inch from his mouth.

As time passed and his nails and eyebrows and hair grew long and filled the air cavity around him, and he realized that his death was to be prolonged in ways that no mortal thought imaginable, he began to plan ways that he could burn himself even more deeply, more painfully, into our memory.

He would reveal to the rest of us a secret about his soul that would forever make us think differently about our common origins. With nails that were yellow and sharp as talons he cut his confession into the silk liner above him, his mouth red with gloat as he wounded us once more with a dark knowledge about ourselves.

But those are simply images born of my dreams. Maybe the contractor was innocent. Or maybe in the murder house he began to enact a fantasy, tried to lure one of the girls into a seduction, and found himself involved in a kaleidoscopic nightmare whose consequences filled him with terror and from which he couldn't extricate himself.

I don't know. Ten months on the firing line in Vietnam, twenty years in law enforcement, and a long excursion into a nocturnal world of neon-streaked rain and whiskey-soaked roses have made me no wiser about human nature than I had been at age eighteen.

But Brother Oswald had made another remark that forced me to reexamine a basic syllogism that I had been operating on: 'You think the real problem is y'all don't have no idea of what you're dealing with?'

I had not been able to find any record anywhere on a man named Will Buchalter.

Why? Perhaps because that was not his name.

I had assumed from the beginning that Buchalter was not an alias, that the man who had violated my wife and home was a relative of Jon Matthew Buchalter, a founder of the Silver Shirts. It was a natural assumption to make. Would someone choose the name of Hitler or Mussolini as an alias if he wished to avoid drawing attention to himself?

Maybe the man who called himself Will Buchalter had thrown me a real slider and I had swung on it.

It was time to have a talk with Hippo Bimstine again.

*

But I didn't get the chance. At seven the next morning I went to an A.A. meeting to get some help for Bootsie that I wasn't capable of providing myself, then two minutes after I walked into my office Lucinda Bergeron called from New Orleans.

'Hey, Lucinda. What's up?' I said.

'The East Baton Rouge Parish Sheriff's Department just nailed a mule with a suitcase full of Mexican tar in his trunk. This'll be his fourth time down. He says he'll do anybody he can for some slack.'

'So?'

'The dope drop's in New Orleans. That's why Baton Rouge called us. This guy says the tar's going into the projects.'

'I'm still not with you.'

'He says the Calucci brothers are dealing the tar. It looks like they're making a move on the projects. Anyway, the guy says he can do them.'

'I doubt it.'

'Why?'

'Max and Bobo always have three or four intermediaries between themselves and whatever they're in.'

'I had the impression you thought they were connected with Lonighan and that Lonighan was mixed up with this psychopath who keeps coming around your house.'

'That's right.'

'So do you have a better lead?'

'Not really.'

'Good. I'll meet you at the jail in two hours. Also, I'm a little pissed with you this morning, Mr Robicheaux.'

'Oh?'

'You can't seem to stay out of other people's business.'

'What is it now?'

'I'll tell you when I see you,' she said, and hung up.

Lucinda really knew how to set the hook. All the way across the Atchafalaya Basin, on a beautiful, wind-kissed fall day when I should have been looking at the bays and canals and flooded cypress and willow trees along I-10, I kept wondering what new bagful of spiders she would like to fit over my head.

She met me in the parking lot at the lockup. She wore a pair of white slacks and a purple-flowered blouse, and her hair was brushed out full on her shoulders. She had one hand on her hip and a pout on her face. She looked at the tiny gold watch on her wrist.

'Did you stop for a late breakfast?' she said.

'No, I didn't. I came straight from the office. Get off it, Lucinda.'

'Get *off* it?'

'Yeah, I'm not up to being somebody's pincushion today.'

'My son is back home. He told me you made some inquiries about the company I keep.'

'No, I didn't.'

'He said you seemed to take an interest in the fact that I had a white man at my house.'

'Kids get things turned around. He volunteered that information on his own.'

'Do you think it should be of some concern to you, sir?'

'No. But one troubling thought did occur to me.'

'Yes?'

'Was it Nate Baxter?'

She looked like a wave of nausea had just swept through her system.

'Do you stay up all night thinking of things like this to say to people?' she said.

'I've known him for twenty years. He'll try to coerce a woman in any way he can. If he hasn't done it to you yet, he will later. He's a sonofabitch and you know it.'

'That doesn't mean I'd allow him in my house.'

'Okay, Lucinda, I apologize. But I know what he did to some women in the First District.'

'I'll buy you a cup of coffee later and tell you about Nate Baxter. In the meantime, our man is waiting on us.'

His name was Waylon Rhodes, from Mount Olive, Alabama; he had skin the color of putty, hands dotted with jailhouse art, a narrow, misshapen head, and a wide slit of a mouth, whose lips on one side looked like they had been pressed flat by a hot iron. His premature gray hair was grizzled and brushed back into faint ducktails; his eyes jittered like a speed addict's. Inside his left arm was a long, blue tattoo of a bayonet or perhaps a sword.

Lucinda and I sat across the wood table from him in the interrogation room. He smoked one cigarette after another, crumpling up an empty pack, ripping the cellophane off a fresh one. The backs of his fingers were yellow with nicotine; his breath was like an ashtray.

'There's no reason to be nervous, partner,' I said.

'Y'all want me to do the Caluccis. That ain't reason to be nervous?' he said.

'You don't have to do anybody. Not for us, anyway. Your beef's with the locals,' I said.

'Don't tell me that, man. Y'all got a two-by-four up my ass.'

'Watch your language, please,' I said.

He smoked with his elbow propped on the table, taking one puff after another, like he was hitting on a reefer, sometimes pressing a yellow thumb anxiously against his bottom lip and teeth.

'They're dangerous people, man,' he said. 'They tied a guy down on a table once and cut thirty pounds of meat out of him while he was still alive.'

'Here's the only deal you're getting today,' Lucinda said. 'We can pull the plug on this interview any time you want. You say the word and we're gone. Then you can have visitors from two to four every Sunday afternoon.'

'What she means, Waylon, is we made a special effort to see you. If this is all a waste of time, tell us now.'

He mashed out his cigarette and began clenching one hand on top of the other. *Make him talk about something else*, I thought.

'Where'd you get the tattoo of the sword?' I said.

'It's a bayonet. I was in the Airborne. Hunnerd and first.'

'Your jacket says you were in the Navy and did time at Portsmouth brig.'

'Then it's wrong.'

'What can you give us on Max and Bobo?' Lucinda said.

'They're dealing.'

'They're going to be at the drop?' I said.

'Are you kidding?' he said.

'Then how are you going to do them, Waylon?' I said.

He began to chew on the flattened corner of his mouth. His eyes jittered as if they were being fed by an electrical current.

'A whack's going down. A big one,' he said.

'Yeah?' I said.

'Yeah.'

'Who's getting clipped, Waylon?'

'A couple of guineas were talking in Mobile when I picked up the dope.'

'You're not being helpful, Waylon,' Lucinda said.

'There's nig . . . There's black people mixed up in it. New Orleans is a weird fucking town. What do I know?'

'You'd better know something, partner, or your next jolt's going to be in the decades,' I said.

'They're going to clip some guy that ain't supposed to be clipped. That's what these dagos were saying. That's all I know, man.'

'When you think of something else, give us a call,' I said.

He ran his hand through his grizzled hair. His palm was shiny with sweat.

'I'm sick. I got to go to a hospital,' he said.

'What's the sword on your arm mean?' I said.

He put his face in his hands. 'I ain't saying no more,' he said. 'I'm sick. I got to have some medication.'

'How many times a day do you fix, Waylon?' I said.

'I got it down to three. Look, get me into a hospital and maybe I can he'p y'all a whole lot better.'

'It doesn't work that way, partner,' I said, and slipped my business card under the flat of his arm. 'Give us a call when your memory clears up.'

A half hour later Lucinda and I took coffee and pastry from a bakery downtown and sat on a stone bench in a small green park by the capitol building. It was a blue-gold day, with a breeze off the Mississippi, and the grass in the park looked pale green in the sunlight.

'Why'd you keep asking him about a sword?' Lucinda said.

'I think it's the name or the logo of a group of neo-Nazis or Aryan supremacists of some kind.'

'The tattoo looked like a bayonet to me.'

'Maybe. But he's a speed addict, too, just like the guy who electrocuted himself in y'all's custody. Buchalter called me once during what sounded like the downside of a drug bender. Maybe like Hippo Bimstine says, we're talking about speed-fried Nazi zomboids.'

'You think Waylon Rhodes will give us anybody?'

'He'll try to, when he starts to come apart. But by that time you won't be able to trust anything he tells you.'

'I believe him about the hit. When they lie, they're not vague.'

I took a bite out of my pastry and drank from my paper cup.

'Why the silence?' she asked.

'No reason. What were you going to tell me about Nate Baxter?'

'I don't think he has designs on me, that's all.'

I nodded.

'A white supervisor trying to get into a black female officer's pants doesn't make his kind of racial remarks,' she said.

'You don't have to tell me anything about Nate Baxter, Lucinda.'

'He said Ben Motley got where he is by spitting watermelon seeds and giving whitey a lot of "yas-suhs." He said I'd never have to do that, because I'm smart and I have a nice ass. How do you like that for charm?'

'Nate's a special kind of guy.'

'I don't think so. Not for a black woman, anyway.'

'Don't underestimate him, Lucinda. He raped and sodomized a hooker in the Quarter. Then he ran her out of town before anybody from Internal Affairs could talk to her.'

She stopped eating and looked across the grass at some children running through the camellia bushes. Then she set the pastry down on a napkin in her lap and brushed the powdered sugar off her fingers.

'I was raised by my aunt,' she said. 'She was a prostitute. A white man tried to rape her behind a bar on Calliope. She shot him to death. What do you think about that?'

'Did she go up the road for it?'

'Yes.'

'So even in death he raped her. Drop the dime on Baxter if he gets near you or makes another off-color remark.'

She stood up and walked cooly to a trash can, dropped her paper cup and unfinished pastry in it, and sat back down on the stone bench. Her flowered blouse puffed with air in the breeze.

'Don't try to stonewall me about this contract stuff,' she said. 'Who is it the greaseballs don't clip?'

'Politicians.'

'Who else?'

'Ordinary people who are on the square. Particularly influential ones.'

'Come on, Robicheaux.'

'Would you not call me by my last name, please? It reminds me of the army.'

'Who else?'

'They don't do made guys without the commission's consent.'

'That's it?'

'Cops,' I said.

She looked me evenly in the eyes, biting down softly on the corner of her lip.

That night I dreamed of a desolate coastline that looked like layered white clay. On it was a solitary tree whose curled, dead leaves were frozen against an electrical blue sky. The ocean should have been teeming with fish, but it, like the land, had been stricken, its chemical green depths empty of all life except the crew of a German submarine, who burst to the surface with emergency air tanks on their backs, their bone-hard, white faces bright with oil. They gathered under the tree on the beach, looking over their new estate, and I realised then that they had the jowls and mucus-clotted snouts of animals.

They waited for their leader, who would come, as they had, from the sea, his visage crackling with salt and light, and, like Proteus, forever changing his form to make himself one of us.

A psychologist would smile at the dream and call it a world destruction fantasy, the apocalyptic fear that a drunk such as myself carries around in his unconscious or that you see on the faces of religious fundamentalists at televised revivals.

But when I woke from the dream I sat in the dark and thought about the preacher's words, about things coming apart at the center, about blood-dimmed tides and mackerel-crowded seas that could wrinkle from continent to continent with the reverberating brass gong of the millennium, and I did not sleep again until the trees outside were black and stiff with the coming of the gray dawn.

17

Two days later, at five-thirty on Saturday morning, Bootsie heard a car turn into our driveway. She stood at the window in her nightgown and looked through the curtain.

'It's somebody in a pink Cadillac,' she said.

'Maybe he's just turning around,' I said from the bed. There was mist in the trees outside and a cool smell blowing through the window.

'No, they're just sitting there. Two people.'

'Batist probably hasn't opened the shop yet. I'll go down,' I said.

'Dave—'

'It's all right. Bad guys don't park in your drive at sunrise.'

I dressed in a pair of khakis, old loafers, and a denim shirt, and walked out on the gallery. The light was on in the bait shop. The Cadillac was parked in the shadows under the trees, but I could see two figures in the front seat. The air smelled like flowers and damp earth. I walked across the yard toward the car. To my right I could hear Tripod scratching against the screen on his hutch.

Tommy Bobalouba got out on the driver's side, dressed in striped, dark brown slacks, tasseled loafers, and a form-fitting canary-yellow polo shirt. Across the bridge of his nose was a thick, crusted scab where I had pistol-whipped him. He was smiling. He put his finger to his lips and motioned me away from the automobile.

'Charlotte's sleeping,' he whispered. 'She ain't used to being up this early.'

'What are you doing at my house, Tommy?'

'It's the weekend. Sometimes I like a drive in the country. Maybe I can rent a boat, you can take us out.'

He combed his white hair while he gazed approvingly at the surroundings.

'You didn't come here to square a beef, did you, partner?' I said.

'You got a cup of coffee?'

'We can walk down to the bait shop.'

'The bait shop? What is this, the white trash treatment I get?'

'My wife's not dressed yet.'

'I want a favor from you.'

'Tommy, I'm having a hard time with your presence here.'

'What? I'm a germ?'

'I'm the guy who hit you across the face with a forty-five. Now you're at my house.'

'I don't hold a grudge.'

'Good. Then you won't be offended when I recommend that you give me a call during business hours at the office.'

'You made some remarks at my house. About stuff that's maybe on my conscience. So maybe I'm gonna try to set it right. You don't want to help me, then run it up your hole.'

'I'd appreciate it if you'd watch what you say around my house.'

The door on the passenger's side opened, and the ash blond lady named Charlotte got out and stretched sleepily.

'Oh, Mr Robicheaux, our favorite daytime nightmare,' she said.

'We're gonna have some coffee. Down at his shop,' Tommy said.

'Breakfast among the worms. How could a girl ask for more?' she said.

'His wife ain't up yet,' Tommy said. Then with his back to the woman, he moved his lips silently so I could read the words *Give me some fucking help, man.*

I took a quiet breath and put my hands in my back pockets.

'I apologize for not inviting y'all in,' I said. 'But Batist has some doughnuts and some ham-and-egg sandwiches that I can heat up.'

'Boy, that sounds good. I could go for that,' Tommy said. He hit me hard on the arm with the flat of his hand.

The three of us walked down the slope to the dock. I couldn't begin to explain Tommy Blue Eyes' mercurial behavior. He walked on the balls of his feet, talking incessantly, his shoulders rolling, his eyes flicking from the bayou to the outboards leaving the dock to a flight of black geese dissecting the early sun.

He and the woman named Charlotte sat at a spool table under the canvas awning while I went inside and brought out coffee and doughnuts on a tray.

'Call Hippo for me,' Tommy said.

'What for?'

'Maybe I don't want to be enemies anymore. Maybe we ought to work together.'

'Call him yourself,' I said.

'I get three words out and he hangs up.'

'Write him a letter.'

'What I look like, St Valentine or something?' He glanced at his wristwatch, then shook it close to his ear. 'You got the time?'

'It's ten to six,' I said.

'Look, why should Hippo and me be always cutting a piece out of each other? We're both in the casino business. Hippo's a good businessman, he'd be a good partner, he doesn't steal from people. I want you to tell him I said that.'

'I think you got some damn nerve, Tommy.'

He took his coffee cup away from his mouth and pointed four stiffened fingers into his chest. 'You come out to my house, you give me a lecture on conscience and responsibility, you hit me in the face with a gun, now I get another lecture?'

'Is there anything else you want to tell me? I have some work to do.'

He pushed a knuckle against his teeth, then clamped his hand across my forearm when I attempted to rise. He took it away and made a placating gesture.

'It's not easy for me to talk to Hippo,' he said. I saw his blue eyes fill with a pained, pinched light. 'He just doesn't listen, he sees it one way, it's always been like that, he'd just walk off when I tried to say I was sorry about his little brother. I tried a whole bunch of times.'

'When?'

'When we were growing up.'

'It's between you and him, Tommy. But why don't you say it to him once more, as honestly as you can, then let it go?'

'*He's* not. He sees me on the street, he looks at me like I was butt crust.'

'So long, Tommy. About the other day, I didn't want to hit you. I'm sorry it happened.' I nodded to the woman as I got up to go.

He wiped part of a doughnut off his mouth with his wrist.

'We're gonna rent a boat and some gear, do some fishing,' he said. 'If you're around later, we'll buy you lunch.'

'I'm tied up. Thanks, anyway,' I said, and walked up the dock toward my house just as Alafair was coming down the slope, with Tripod on his chain, to get me for breakfast.

At noontime Batist and I were outside in the cool lee of the bait shop, serving our customers barbecue chickens from our split-barrel pit, when I saw Tommy and the woman named Charlotte coming up the bayou in one of our boat rentals. The engine was out of the water, and Tommy was paddling against the current, his face heated and knotted with frustration as the boat veered from side to side. It had rained hard at midmorning, then had stopped abruptly. The woman's hair and sundress were soaked. She looked disgusted.

A few minutes later they came into the bait shop. Without asking permission the woman went around behind the counter and unrolled a huge wad of paper towels to dry her hair.

'I owe you some money. I ran the motor over a log or something,' Tommy said.

'It's in the overhead,' I said.

He hit on the surface of his watch with his fingers.

'What time is it?' he said.

I pointed at the big electric clock on the wall.

'Twelve-fifteen. Boy, we were out there a long time,' he said. 'A snake ate my fish, too. It came right up to the boat and sucked it off my stringer. Are they supposed to do that?'

'Take an ice chest next time.'

'That's a good idea.' He opened two long-necked beers from the cooler and gave one to the woman, who sat in a chair by a table, rubbing the towels back over her long hair. 'I guess we better hit the road. I didn't know it was already afternoon.'

They went out the screen door, then I saw Tommy stop in the shade, tap one fist on top of another, turn in a circle, then stop again. He looked back through the screen at me and raised his fists momentarily in a boxer's position, as though he wanted to spar. He reminded me of a mental patient spinning about in a bare room.

I walked outside. It was breezy and cool in the shade, and the sun was bright, like yellow needles, on the water.

'What's on your mind, podna?' I said.

He craned a crick out of his neck and pumped his shoulders. The cords in his neck flexed like snakes. Then he shook my hand without speaking. His palm felt like the hide on a roughened baseball.

'You got to understand something, Dave. You mind if I call you Dave?'

'You always have, Tommy.'

'I go by the rules. I don't break rules, not the big ones, anyway. The greaseballs got theirs, cops got 'em, guys like me, micks who've made good from the Channel I'm talking about, we got ours, too. So when somebody breaks the rules, I got no comment. But I don't want to get hurt by it, either. You understand what I'm saying here?'

'No.'

'I never hurt anybody who didn't try to do a Roto-Rooter on me first.'

'A hit's going down that you don't like?'

'I said that? Must be a ventriloquist around here.'

'What's the game, Tommy?'

'No game. I got to do certain things to survive. You hold that against me? But that doesn't mean I wasn't on the square about Hippo. He was once my friend. I ain't trying to job you on that one.'

I watched him walk up the dock toward his car, his head turned sideways into the breeze, the red scab on his nose like an angry flag, his blue eyes hard as a carrion bird's, as though hidden adversaries waited for him on the wind.

I decided that it would take a cryptographer to understand the nuances of Tommy Lonighan.

I walked around the side of the house to the backyard and turned on the soak hose in my vegetable garden. The bamboo and periwinkles along the coulee ruffled in the breeze. Beyond my duck pond, the sugarcane in my neighbor's field flickered with a cool purple and gold light.

Bootsie had gone shopping in New Iberia, and Alafair was fixing sandwiches at the drain board when I walked into the kitchen. From the front of the house I heard the flat, tinny tones of a 1920s jazz orchestra, then the unmistakable bell-like sound of Bunk Johnson's coronet rising out of the mire of C-melody saxophones.

'What's going on, Alf?' I said.

She turned from the counter and looked at me quizzically. I could see the outlines of her training bra under her yellow T-shirt.

'Who put one of my old seventy-eights on the machine?' I said.

'I thought you did,' she said.

The record ended, then the mechanical arm swung back automatically and started again. I walked quickly into the living room. The front door was open, and the curtains were swelling with wind. I opened the screen door and went out on the gallery. The yard and drive were empty and blown with dead leaves. Out on the dirt road black kids on bicycles, with fishing gear propped across their handlebars, were pedaling past the dock. I went back inside, lifted the arm off the record, and turned off the machine. The paper jacket for the record lay on the couch. The record itself was free from any finger smudges; it had been placed on the spindle with professional care.

'Alf, it's all right if you wanted to play the record,' I said in the kitchen. 'But it's important you tell me whether or not you did it.'

'I already told you, Dave.'

'You're sure?'

'You think I'm lying?'

'No, I didn't mean that. How long has it been playing?'

'I don't know. I was outside.'

'Did Bootsie put it on before she left?'

'Bootsie doesn't play your old records, Dave. Nobody does.'

'Bootsie hasn't been herself, Alf.'

She turned back to the counter and began spreading mustard on her sandwich bread, her face empty, the way it always became when she knew something was wrong in the house. Her pink tennis shoes were untied, and her elastic-waisted jeans were stained with grass at the knees from weeding in the garden.

I saw her hand with the butter knife slow, then stop, as a thought worked its way into her face.

'Dave, I heard the front screen slam about fifteen minutes ago. Was that you?'

'I was at the dock, Alf. Maybe it was Bootsie.'

'Bootsie left an hour ago.'

'Maybe she came back for something.'

'She would have said something. Was it that bad man, Dave?'

I picked her up and sat her on top of the drain board, like she was still a small child, and began tying her tennis shoes.

'Was it that bad man?' she said again.

'I don't know, Alf. I truly don't.' My fingers were like a tangle of sticks when I tried to tie the bow on her shoe.

That evening, at dusk, the clouds in the western sky were marbled with orange light, and fireflies spun their wispy red circles in the darkening trees. Bootsie had taken Alafair to the video-rental store in town, and the house was empty and creaking with the cooling of the day. I called Clete at his apartment in the French Quarter.

'Buchalter was here,' I repeated. 'No one else would have put that record on. The guy went in and out of my house in broad daylight and nobody saw him.'

'I don't like what I'm hearing you say, Streak.'

'I don't either.'

'I don't mean that. The Bobbsey Twins from Homicide don't rattle.'

'The guy seems to float on the air, like smoke or something. What am I supposed to say?'

'That's what he wants you to think.'

'Then tell me how he got in and out of my house today?'

'That's part of how he operates. He wants you to feel like you've been molested, like he can reach out and touch you anytime he wants. It's like you don't own your life anymore.'

I could hear my own breath echoing off the receiver.

'My ex's first husband tried to do a mind fuck on her the same way,' he said. 'He hired a P.I. to take zoom-lens pictures of her on the toilet and mail them to her boss, then he got in her bedroom while she was asleep and slashed up all her underwear with a razor ... Hey, lighten up, Dave. Buchalter is flesh and blood. He just hasn't moved across the right pair of iron sights yet.'

'Clete, I've got every cop in Iberia Parish looking for this guy. How—'

'You *think* he was there today. You didn't see him. Listen, big mon, we're going to turn it around on this guy. They all go down, it's just a matter of time ... Are you listening?'

'Yes.'

'Your problem is you think too much.'

'Okay, Clete, I've got your drift.'

'I thought you were calling me about Nate Baxter.'

'Why would I call you about *him*?'

'Nate almost got deep-fried in his own grease early this morning. Evidently he gets it on in Algiers sometimes with this biker broad who used to be his snitch in the First District. But he wakes up this morning, the broad is gone, and the dump she lives in is burning down. Except she's got French doors that are locked across both handles with Nate's handcuffs. He wrapped his head in a wet sheet and curled up in the bathtub or he wouldn't have made it.'

'Where's he now?'

'At Southern Baptist, up on Napoleon. Why?'

'Is he pressing any charges?'

'Not according to the cop who told me about it. I guess getting set on fire just goes with the territory when Nate tries to get laid.'

'Who's the woman?'

'Pearly Blue Ridel, you remember her, she used to work in a couple of the Giacanos' massage parlors, then she got off the spike and hooked up with some born-again bikers or something. Too bad Baxter's still got her by the umbilical cord.'

'Pearly Blue's no killer, Clete. She starts every day with a nervous breakdown.'

'Tell that to Nate.'

'I think it's a hit. A heroin mule in Baton Rouge sheriff's custody told me and Lucinda Bergeron that the Calucci brothers were going to take somebody out, somebody they weren't supposed to touch. Then this morning Tommy Lonighan showed up at my dock and made a point of establishing his whereabouts from six to noon or so.'

'Let them whack each other out. Who cares? If Baxter had caught the bus, half of NOPD would be plastered right now.'

'Would you like Lonighan setting you up for his alibi?'

'Keep it simple, Streak. Buchalter's the target. These other guys are predictable. Your man is not.'

Your man? I thought, after he had hung up. For some reason the possessive pronoun brought back the same sense of visceral revulsion and personal shame and violation that I had felt when Mack, on that raw, late-fall afternoon in the barn, had extended the backs of his fingers to my face and made me an accomplice in the sexual degradation of my mother.

Why?

Because as the object of someone else's perverse sexual obsession, you feel not only that you are alone, and I mean absolutely alone, but that there is something defective in you that either attracts or warrants the bent attentions of your persecutor.

Ask anybody who has ever been there. Even a cop.

I knew Pearly Blue Ridel on another level besides the one that Clete had mentioned over the telephone, but the principles of Alcoholics Anonymous prevented me from acknowledging to an outsider that she was a member of our fellowship.

Bootsie, Alafair, and I went to an early Mass at St Peter's in New Iberia the next morning, then I dropped them off at my cousin Tutta's in town and headed back for New Orleans.

Pearly Blue's A.A. group was not a conventional one. It was made up of low-bottom drunks and outlaw bikers across the river in Algiers, and it was called the Work the Steps or Die, Motherfucker group. Because most of the members rode chopped-down Harleys, often had shaved heads, were covered with outrageous tattoos, and were generally ferocious in their appearance, they couldn't rent a meeting hall anywhere except in a warehouse that adjoined a biker bar where many of them used to get drunk. I parked in the alley behind the warehouse and used the rest room in the back of the bar before I went into the noon meeting.

On the condom machine someone had written in felt pen, *Gee, this gum tastes funny*. Written in the same hand on the dispenser for toilet-seat covers were the words *Puerto Rican Place Mats*.

The A.A. meeting area in the warehouse was gray with cigarette smoke, dense with the smell of sweaty leather, engine grease rubbed into denim, expectorated snuff, and unwashed hair. I stood against the wall by the doorway until Pearly Blue would look at me. She wore Levi's that were too large for her narrow hips, no bra, and a tie-dyed shirt that showed the small bumps she had for breasts. Her hair was colorless, stuck together on the ends, and the circles under her eyes seemed to indicate as much about the hopelessness of her life as about her emotional and physical fatigue. You did not have to be around Pearly Blue long to realize that she was one of those haunted souls who waited with certainty at each dawn for an invisible hand to wrap a cobweb of fear and anxiety around her heart.

My stare was unrelenting, and finally she got up from the table and walked with me out into the alley. She leaned against my truck fender, put a cigarette in her mouth, and lit it with both hands, although there was no wind between the buildings. She huffed the smoke out at an upward angle, her chin pointed away from me.

As with most of her kind, Pearly Blue's toughness was a sad illusion, and her breaking point was always right beneath the skin.

'You want to tell me what happened with Nate Baxter?' I said.

She looked down at the end of the alley, where a clump of untrimmed banana trees grew by a rack of garbage cans and traffic was passing on the street. She took another hit on her cigarette.

'Pearly Blue, as far as I'm concerned, we're still inside the meeting. Which means anything you tell me doesn't go any farther.'

'I went down to the store to buy some eggs to make his breakfast,' she said. She had a peckerwood accent and a peculiar way of moving her lips silently before she spoke. 'He always wants an omelette when he gets up in the morning. When I came back, fire was popping the glass out of all the windows.'

'Who handcuffed the doors together?'

'I don't know. I didn't.' She looked up at the telephone wires, an attempted pout on her mouth, like a put-upon adolescent girl.

'Why are you still hanging around with a guy like Baxter, Pearly Blue?'

'I wrote a couple of bad checks. He said he'll tell my P.O.'

'I see.'

'I wasn't hanging paper. It was just an overdraft. But with the jacket I already got—'

She made a clicking sound with her tongue and tried to look self-possessed and cool, but the color had risen in her throat, and her pulse was fluttering like an injured moth.

'Who torched the place?' I said.

'I don't know, Streak. Everything I owned was burned up. What am I supposed to tell you?' Her eyes were wet now. She opened and closed them and looked emptily at the graffiti-scrolled wall of a garage apartment.

'Were the Calucci brothers behind it?'

'Don't be telling people that. Don't be using my name when you go talking about them kind of people.'

'I won't let you get hurt, Pearly Blue. Just tell me what happened.'

'Some guy called, it was like he knew everything about me, about my kid getting taken away from me, about where I work, about some stuff, you know, not very good stuff, I did at the massage parlour, he said, "Get out of your place by six, have yourself a nice walk, when you come back you won't have to be this guy's fuck no more."'

'You don't know who it was?'

'You think I want to know something like that? You remember what happened to my roommate in the Quarter when she told a vice cop she'd testify against one of the Giacano family? They soaked her in gasoline. They—'

'You're out of it, Pearly Blue. Forget about Baxter, forget about the Calucci brothers. Where are you living now?'

'At my sister's. I just want to go to meetings, work at my job, and get my little boy back. My P.O.'s a hard ass, he hears about the checks, calls from the wise guys, stuff like that, I'm going down again. It's full of bull dykes in there, Streak. I just can't do no more time.'

'You won't, not if I have anything to do with it.'

'Baxter's gonna find me. He's gonna make me ball him again. It's sickening.'

I took a business card out of my wallet, pressed it into her palm, and closed her fingers on it. Her hand was small and moist in mine.

'Believe me when I tell you this,' I said. 'If Nate Baxter ever bothers you again, call me, and he'll wish his parents had taken up celibacy.'

Her face became confused.

'He'll wish his father'd had his equipment sawed off,' I said.

The corner of her mouth wrinkled with a smile, exposing a line of tiny, silver-capped teeth.

Nate Baxter's room was as utilitarian and plain and devoid of cheer as his life. It contained no flowers, greeting cards, clusters of balloons, and certainly no visitors, unless you counted the uniformed cop on duty at the door.

'You don't look too bad, Nate,' I said. Which wasn't true. His face was wan, the reddish gold beard along his jawline was matted with some kind of salve, and stubble had grown out on his cheeks.

He didn't speak; his eyes regarded me carefully.

'I talked with an arson inspector. He said somebody put a fire-bomb under your bed, probably gasoline and paraffin,' I said.

'You're making that your business, along with everything else in Orleans Parish?'

'I've got a special interest in Max and Bobo Calucci. I think you do, too, Nate.'

'What's that mean?'

'You're on a pad.'

'I remember once when you smelled like an unflushed toilet with whiskey poured in it. Maybe that's why IA busted you out of the department. Maybe that's why you can't ever get that hard out of your pants. But I'm not up to trading insults with you. Do me a favor today, go back home.'

He turned his head on the pillow to reach a drinking glass filled with Coca-Cola. I could see a tubular, raw-edged lump behind his right ear.

'I think you tried to up the juice on the Caluccis, Nate. Then they decided to factor you out of the overhead.'

'It's always the same problem with you, Robicheaux. It's not what you don't know, it's what you think you know that makes you a fuckup. No matter where you go, you leave shit prints on the walls.'

'You were asleep, maybe you still had a half a bag on, Pearly Blue went to the store, somebody sapped you across the head, then he really lit up your morning.'

'I was in her apartment because she's still my snitch. You want to give it some other interpretation, nobody's going to be listening. Why? Because you don't work here anymore. For some reason, you can't seem to accept that simple fact.' His hand moved toward the cord and call button that would bring a nurse or the guard at the door.

'You know what denial is, Nate?'

'I breathed a lot of smoke yesterday. I'm not interested in wetbrain vocabulary right now. Every one of you A.A. guys thinks you deserve the Audie Murphy award because you got sober. Here's the news flash on that. The rest of us have been sober all along. It's not a big deal in the normal world.'

'A heroin mule in Baton Rouge custody knew about the hit. So did some greaseballs in Mobile. So did Tommy Lonighan. They're talking about you like you're already off the board.'

'Get out of here before I place you under arrest.' His hand went toward the call button again. I moved it out of his reach.

'You're a bad cop, Nate. Somebody should have clicked off your switch a long time ago.'

I pushed back my seersucker coat and removed my .45 from my belt holster. His eyes were riveted on mine now.

'You're bad not because you're on a pad; you're bad because you don't understand that we're supposed to protect the weak,' I said. 'Instead, when you sense weakness in people, you exploit it, you bully and humiliate them, you've even sodomized and raped them.'

'You've got a terminal case of assholeitis, Robicheaux, but you're not crazy. So get off it.' He tried to keep the conviction in his voice, his eyes from dropping to the pistol in my hand.

'I know an A.A. bunch called the Work the Steps or Die, Motherfucker group. Some of them are bad dudes, guys who've been on Camp J up at Angola. They say you've been hitting on Pearly Blue for a long time. They wanted to do something about it.' I pulled back the slide on the .45 and eased a round from the magazine into the chamber. 'But I told them I'd take care of it.'

'That gun-threat bullshit is an old ruse of yours. You're firing in the well. Get out of my room.'

I sat on the edge of his bed.

'You're right, it is,' I said. 'That's why I was going to shove it down your mouth and let you work toward that conclusion while you swallowed some of your own blood, Nate . . . But there's no need.'

'What are you—'

I released the magazine, ejected the round from the chamber, and dropped it clinking into his drinking glass.

'She found out this week she's HIV positive,' I said. 'I'd get some tests as long as I was already in the hospital. But no matter how you cut it, Nate, Pearly Blue is out of your life. We're clear on that, aren't we?'

His lips looked gray and cracked, the texture of snakeskin that has dried in the sun, and the whites of his eyes were laced with pink blood vessels. The light through the blinds seemed to reflect like a liquid yellow presence in his incredulous glare. I heard his drinking glass crash to the floor and the call button clicking rapidly in his fist as I walked toward the door.

That evening I had to go far down the bayou in a boat to tow back a rental whose engine one of our customers had plowed across a sandbar. It was dark before I finally locked up the bait shop and walked to the house. Bootsie was asleep, but as soon as I entered the bedroom I knew how she had spent the last three hours. Her breathing had filled the room with a thick, sweet odor like flowers soaked overnight in cream sherry.

I sat on the edge of the bed in my skivvies and looked at the smooth white curve of her hip in the moonlight. I rubbed my hand along her rump and thigh; her skin felt heated, flushed, as though she were experiencing an erotic dream, but it was also insensitive to my touch.

I put my fingers in the thick curls of her hair, kissed her back, and felt like a fifty-five-year-old adolescent impotently contending with his own throbbing erection.

I had been saved from my alcoholism by A.A. Why did it have to befall her?

But I already knew the answer. The best way to become a drunk is to live with one.

What are we going to do, Boots? I thought. Bring the dirty boogie full tilt into our lives, then do a pit stop five years down the road and see if the trade-off was worth it?

But somebody else was already working on an answer for me. At 2:00 a.m. I heard the door on my father's old tractor shed, which was always padlocked, knocking against the jamb in the wind, then I heard music, a song that was a generation out-of-date, that seemed to float across wine-dark seas crowded with ships in a time when the lights almost went out all over the world.

I slipped on my khakis and loafers, took my .45 from under the bed, and walked with a flashlight along the edge of the coulee to the shed. I bounced the beam ahead of me on the willows and the weathered gray sides of the shed, the open door that drifted back and forth on two rusty hinges, the hasp and padlock that had been splintered loose from the wood.

Then I clearly heard the words to 'Harbor Lights.'

I clicked off the safety on the .45, flipped back the door with my foot, and shined the light inside the shed. In front of my father's old tractor was a butcher block where we used to dress game. Someone had covered it with white linen that was almost iridescent in the moonlight burning through the spaces in the slats. On the tablecloth was a cassette player, a clean china plate with a blue, long-stemmed rose laid across it, a freshly uncorked bottle of

Jack Daniel's, a glass tumbler filled with four inches of bourbon, and a sweat-beaded uncapped bottle of Dixie beer on the side. A crystal goblet of burgundy that was half empty stood in a shaft of moonlight on the far side of the butcher block. On the rim of the glass was the perfect lipsticked impression of a woman's mouth.

18

Before he had been elected to office, the sheriff had owned a dry-cleaning business and had been president of the local Rotary Club, or perhaps it was the Lions, I don't recall which, but it was one of those businessmen's groups which manage to do a fair amount of civic good in spite of their unprofessed and real objective.

He was watering his window plants with a hand-painted flowered teapot while I told him of my 2:00 a.m. visitor. He had a round, cleft chin, soft cheeks veined with tiny blue and red lines, and a stomach that pouched over his gunbelt, but his posture was always so erect, his shirt tucked in so tightly, that he gave you the impression of a man who was both younger and in better physical condition than he actually was.

But even though the Rotary or Lions Club still held strong claim on the sheriff's soul, he often surprised me with a hard-edged viewpoint that I suspected had its origins in his experience at the Chosin Reservoir during the Korean War, which he refused, under any circumstances, to discuss with anyone.

'Well, you didn't drink any of it. That's what seems most important, if you ask me.'

'Some people might call that a pretty cavalier attitude,' I said.

'It's your call. Write it up, Dave. Bring our fingerprint man in on it. I don't know what else to say.'

He sat down in his swivel chair behind his desk. He pushed at his stomach with his stiffened fingers. Then he had another running start at it.

'Dave, what's it going to sound like when you tell people that somebody, maybe a woman, did a B&E on you so she could cover your butcher block with a tablecloth and set it with burgundy, cold beer, and expensive whiskey?'

'It's Buchalter, Sheriff. Or somebody working with him.'

'What was the motive for his house call last night?'

'He doesn't need one. He's a psychopath.'

'That's no help.' He began picking a series of bent paper clips out of a glass container and throwing them at the waste can. 'Before you came to the department, we had a particularly nasty homicide case.' *Ping.* 'Maybe you remember it. A lowlife degenerate named Jerry Dipple raped and then hanged a four-year-old child.' *Ping.* 'We thought we had him dead bang. His prints were all over the murder scene, there was a torn theater ticket in his shirt pocket from the show where he'd abducted the child, the rope he used was in the bottom of his closet.' *Ping*. 'Guess what? The lamebrain handling the investigation went into Dipple's house and seized the evidence without a warrant. Then when he realized he'd screwed up, he put the evidence back and let his partner find it later.' *Ping*.

'Guess what again? I learned about it and didn't say a thing. But Dipple's lawyer was a smart greasebag from Lafayette, you know him, the same guy who was fronting points for a PCB-incinerator outfit last year, and he found out what the lamebrain and his partner had done.' *Ping*. 'Our case was down the drain and we were about to turn loose a child killer who had done it before and would do it again. Bad day for the good guys, Dave.

'Except six months earlier we had raided a trick pad on the St Martin line. One of the girls had some photographs of our lawyer-friend from Lafayette, I'm talking about real Tijuana specials, you know what I mean? So I invited our friend in and let him have a look. If he wanted to investigate our practices, we'd let some people in the state bar association have a peek at his.' *Ping, ping, ping.*

'Dipple fried. I thought it might bother me. But the night he rode the bolt I took my grandchildren to the movies and then went home and slept like a stone.'

'I don't know if I get your point.'

'I'll be honest with you, I don't know what we're dealing with here. Whatever it is, it's not part of the normal ebb and flow.' He stopped, ran his fingers through his hair, and kneaded the back of his neck. 'Look, I think Buchalter is trying to hit you where you're weakest.'

'Where's that?'

'Booze.'

'A guy like that can't make me drink, Sheriff.'

'I'm not talking about you.' He rubbed one hand on top of the other, then folded them on the desk blotter and looked me in the face. 'This guy's trying to mess up your family and I think he's doing a good job of it.'

'That's not a very cool thing to say, Sheriff.'

'Bootsie almost had a DWI yesterday afternoon.'

I felt something sink in my chest.

'Fortunately the right deputy stopped her and let the other lady drive,' the sheriff said.

The room seemed filled with white sound. I took my sunglasses out of their leather case, then slipped them back in again. I opened my mouth behind my fist to clear my ears and looked out the window. Then I said, 'What other lady?'

'I don't know. Whoever she was with.'

'I'll finish my report now and put it in your box.'

'Don't. The newspaper'll get ahold of it for sure. It's just what this character wants. Walk outside with me.'

It was warm in the parking lot, and the wind was flattening the leaves in the oak grove across the street. The sheriff unlocked the trunk of his car, took out a stiff, blanket-wrapped object, and walked to my truck with it. He laid the object across the seat of my truck and flipped the blanket open.

'Some people might tell you to wire up a shotgun to your back door,' he said. 'The problem is, you'd probably kill an innocent person first or only wound the sonofabitch breaking into your house, then he'd sue you and take your property. You know what this is, don't you?'

'An AR-15, the semiauto model of the M-16.'

'It's got a thirty-round magazine in it. Jerry Dipple's in a prison cemetery and children around here are a lot safer because of it. Nobody cares how the box score gets written, just as long as the right numbers are in it.' He tapped down the lock button on the door with the flat of his fist, closed the door, and looked at his watch. 'Time for coffee and a doughnut, podna,' he said, and laid his arm across my shoulders.

Back in my office I tore my unfinished report in half and dropped it in the wastebasket. There were two ways to think about the sheriff's behavior, neither of which was consoling:

1. *Semper fi,* Mac, you're on your own.

Which was too severe an indictment of the sheriff. But—

2. No application of force or firepower has so far been successful. Since we've concluded that we don't understand what we're dealing with, use more force and firepower.

Yes, that was more like it. It was old and familiar logic. If you feel like a reviled and excoriated white sojourner in a slum area, break the bones of a drunk black motorist with steel batons. If you cannot deal with the indigenous population of a Third World country, turn their rain forests into smoking gray wasteland with napalm and Agent Orange.

But my cynicism was cheap, born out of the same impotence in trying to deal with evil that had caused the sheriff to make me a present of his Colt Industries urban-Americana meatcutter.

My desk was covered with fax sheets from the National Crime Information Center in Washington, D.C., and photocopied files from NOPD that had been sent to me by Ben Motley. The people in those combined pages could have been players in almost any city in the United States. They were uniquely American, ingrained in our economy, constantly threading their way in and out of lives, always floating about on the periphery of our vision. But nothing that we've attempted so far has been successful in dealing with them. In fact, I'm not even sure how to define them.

1. Max and Bobo Calucci: In popular literature their kind are portrayed as twentieth-century Chaucerian buffoons, venial and humorous con men whose greatest moral offense is their mismatched wardrobe, or charismatic representatives of wealthy New York crime families whose palatial compounds are always alive with wedding receptions and garden parties. The familial code of the last group is sawed out of medieval romance, their dalliance with evil of Faustian and tragic proportions.

Maybe they are indeed these things. But the ones I have known, with one or two exceptions, all possessed a single common characteristic that is unforgettable. Their eyes are dead. No, that's not quite correct. There's a light there, like a wet lucifer match flaring behind black glass, but no matter how hard you try to interpret the thought working behind it, you cannot be sure if the person is thinking about taking your life or having his car washed.

I once spent three hours interviewing a celebrity mafioso who lives today in the federal witness protection program. Two-thirds of his stomach had been surgically removed because of ulcers, and his flesh was like wrinkled putty on his bones, his breath rancid from the saliva-soaked cigar that rarely left his mouth. But his recall of his five decades inside the Outfit was encyclopedic. As he endlessly recounted conversations with other members of the mob, the subject was always the same – money: how much had been made from a score, how much had been pieced off to whom, how much laundered, how much delivered in a suitcase for a labor official's life.

Thirty years ago, in the living room of a friend, he had wrapped piano wire around the throat of an informer and pulled until he virtually razored the man's head off his shoulders.

Then I said something that my situation or job did not require.

'The man you killed, he had once been your friend, hadn't he?'

'Yeah, that's right.'

'Did that bother you?'

'It's just one of them things. What're you gonna do?' He shrugged his shoulders and arched his eyebrows as though an impossible situation had been arbitrarily imposed upon him.

Then I posed one more question to him, one that elicited a nonresponse that has always stayed with me.

'You've told the feds everything about your life, Vince. Did you ever feel like indicating to God you regret some of this bullshit, that you'd like it out of your life?'

His eyes cut sideways at me for only a moment. Through the cigar smoke they looked made from splinters of green and black glass, watery, red-rimmed as a lizard's, lighted with an old secret, or perhaps fear, that would never shake loose from his throat.

I clicked off my recorder, said good-bye, and walked out of the room. Later, he told an FBI agent that he never wanted me in his presence again.

2. Tommy Bobalouba: Like Max and Bobo, he operated on the edges of the respectable world and constantly tried to identify himself with an ethnic heritage that somehow was supposed to give his illegal enterprises the mantle of cultural and moral legitimacy. The reality was that Tommy and the Caluccis both represented a mind-numbing level of public vulgarity that sickened and embarrassed most other Irish and Italians in New Orleans.

Tommy had been kicked out of his yacht club for copulating in the swimming pool at 4:00 a.m. with a cocktail waitress. At the Rex Ball during Mardi Gras he told the mayor's wife that his radiation treatments for prostate cancer caused his phallus to glow in the dark. After wheedling an invitation to a dinner for the New Orleans Historical Association, he politely refused the asparagus by saying to the hostess, 'Thank you, anyway, ma'am, but it always makes my urine smell.'

3. We'll call the third player Malcolm, a composite of any number of black male kids raised in New Orleans's welfare projects. Caseworkers and sociologists have written reams on Malcolm. Racist demagogues love Malcolm because he's the means by which they inculcate fear into the electorate. Liberals are far more compassionate and ascribe his problems to his environment. They're probably correct in their assessment. The problem, however, is that Malcolm is dangerous. He's often immensely unlikable, too.

A full-blown crack addict has the future of a lighted candle affixed to the surface of a woodstove. Within a short period of time he will be consumed by the unbanked fires burning inside him or those that lick daily at his skin from the outside. In the meantime he drifts into a world of moral psychosis where shooting a British tourist in the face for her purse or accidentally killing a neighborhood child has the significance of biting off a hangnail.

I knew a kid from New Iberia whose name *was* Malcolm. He had an arm like a black whip and could field a ball in deep center and fire it on one hop into home plate with the mean, flat trajectory of a BB. At age seventeen he moved with his mother into the Desire Project in New Orleans, a complex of welfare apartments where the steady din is unrelieved, like the twenty-four-hour noise in a city prison – toilets flushing, plumbing pipes vibrating in walls, irrational people yelling at each other, radios and television sets blaring behind broken windows. The laws of ordinary society seem the stuff of comic books. Instead, what amounts to the failure of all charity, joy, and decency becomes the surrogate for normalcy: gang rape, child molestation, incest, terrorization of the elderly, beatings and knifings that turn the victims into bloody facsimiles of human beings, fourteen-year-old girls who'll wink at you and proudly say, 'I be sellin' out of my pants, baby,' or perhaps a high school sophomore who clicks his MAC-10 on up to heavy-metal rock 'n' roll and shreds his peers into dog food.

In a year's time Malcolm smoked, hyped, snorted, bonged, dropped, or huffed the whole street dealer's menu – bazooka, Afghan skunk, rock, crank, brown scag, and angel dust. His mother brought him back to New Iberia for a Christmas visit. Malcolm borrowed a car and went to a convenience store for some eggnog. Then he changed his mind and decided he didn't need any eggnog. Instead, he sodomized and executed the eighteen-year-old college girl who ran the night register. He maintained at his trial that he was loaded on speed and angel dust and had no memory of even entering the convenience store. I was a witness at his electrocution, and I'm convinced to this day that even while they strapped and buckled his arms and legs to the oak chair, fitted the leather gag across his mouth, and dropped the black cloth over his face, even up to the moment the electrician closed the circuits and arched a bolt of lightning through his body that cooked his brains and exploded his insides, Malcolm did not believe these people, whom he had never seen before or harmed in any way, would actually take his life for a crime which he believed himself incapable of committing.

That evening I sat at the kitchen table with a nautical chart of the Louisiana coast spread out before me. Through the open bedroom door I heard Bootsie turn on the shower water. Recently she had made a regular habit of taking long showers in the afternoon, washing the cigarette smoke from a lounge out of her hair, holding her face in the spray until her skin was ruddy and the appearance of clarity came back into her eyes. I had not spoken to her yet about the DWI she had almost received the previous day.

I flattened and smoothed the nautical chart with my hand and penciled X's at the locations where I had sighted the German U-boat when I was in college and on my boat with Batist. Then I made a third X where Hippo Bimstine's friend, the charter-boat skipper, had pinged it with his sonar. The three X's were all within two miles of each other, on a rough southwest-northeastwardly drift line that could coincide with the influences of both the tide and the currents of the Mississippi's alluvial fan. If there was a trench along that line, tilting downward with the bevel of the continental shelf, then the movements of the sub had a certain degree of predictability.

But I couldn't concentrate on the chart. I stared out the back window at the tractor shed by the edge of the coulee. The door yawned open, and the late sun's red light shone like streaks of fire through the cracks in the far wall. I called Clete at his apartment in New Orleans and told him about the break-in of last night, the linen-covered butcher block, the offering of bourbon, the crystal goblet half-filled with burgundy and rimmed with lipstick and moonlight.

'So?' he said when I had finished.

'It's not your ordinary B&E, Clete.'

'It's Buchalter or his trained buttwipes, Streak.'

'Why the blue rose on a china plate?'

'To mess up your head.'

'You don't think it has anything to do with the vigilante?'

'Everybody in New Orleans knows the vigilante's MO now. Why should Buchalter be any different?'

'Why a woman's lipstick on the glass?'

'He's probably got a broad working with him. Sometimes they dig leather and swastikas.'

I blew out my breath and looked wanly through the screen at the fireflies lighting in the purple haze above the coulee.

'You got framed once on a murder beef, Dave. But you turned it around on them, with nobody to help you,' Clete said. 'I've got a feeling something else is bothering you besides some guy with rut for brains opening bottles in your tractor shed.'

I could still hear the shower water running in the bathroom.

'Dave?'

'Yes.'

'You want me to come over there?'

'No, that's all right. Thanks for your time, Clete. I'll call you in a couple of days.'

'Before you go, there's something I wanted to mention. It sounds a little zonk, though.'

'*Zonk*?'

'Yeah, deeply strange. Brother Oswald told me he was in the merch when World War II broke out.' He paused a moment. 'Maybe it's just coincidence.'

'Come on, Clete, get the peanut brittle out of your mouth.'

'He says he was a seventeen-year-old seaman on an oil tanker sailing out of New Orleans in nineteen forty-two. Guess what? A pigboat nailed them just south of Grand Isle.'

A solitary drop of perspiration slid down the side of my rib cage. Through the back screen I could see black storm clouds, like thick curds of smoke, twisting from the earth's rim against the molten red ball of setting sun.

'He says while the tanker was burning, the sub came to the surface and rammed and machine-gunned the lifeboats. He was floating around in the waves for a couple of days before a shrimper fished him out . . . It's kind of weird, isn't it, I mean the guy showing up about the same time as Buchalter?'

'Yeah, it is.'

'Probably doesn't mean anything, though, does it? I mean . . . What do you think?'

'Like somebody told me yesterday, I'm firing in the hole on this one, Clete.'

After I hung up I walked into the bedroom. Through the shower door I could see Bootsie rinsing herself under the flow of water. She held her hair behind her neck with both hands and turned in a slow circle, her buttocks brushing against the steamed glass, while the water streamed down her breasts and sides. I wanted to close the curtains and latch the bedroom door, rub her dry with a towel, walk her to our bed, put her nipples in my mouth, kiss her lean, supple stomach, then feel my own quivering energies enter and lose themselves in hers, as though my desperate love could overcome the asp that she had taken to her breast.

Then I heard her open the medicine cabinet and unsnap the cap on a plastic vial. Her face jumped when she saw me in the mirror.

'Oh, Dave, you almost gave me a coronary,' she said. Her hand closed on the vial. I took it from her and read the typed words on the label.

'Where'd you get these, Boots?'

'Dr Bienville,' she said.

'Dr Bienville is a script doctor and should be in prison.'

'It's just a sedative. Don't make a big thing out of it.'

'They're downers. If you drink with them, they can kill you.' I shook the pills into the toilet bowl, then cracked the vial in the palm of my hand and dropped it in the wastebasket. Her eyes were blinking rapidly as she watched me push down the handle on the toilet. She started to speak, but I didn't let her.

'I'm not going to lose you, Boots,' I said, wrapped her terry-cloth robe around her, and walked her to our bed. We sat down on the side of the mattress together, and I blotted her hair with a towel, then laid her back on the pillow. Her face looked pale and fatigued in the gloom. I remained in a sitting position and picked up one of her hands in mine.

'The sheriff told me about your almost getting a DWI,' I said. 'If a person commits himself to an alcoholic life, he or she is going to drive drunk. Then eventually that person gets a DWI or maybe he kills somebody. It's that simple.'

Her eyes started to water; she looked sideways at the window and the curtains that were lifting in the breeze.

'The sheriff's a good guy,' I said. 'He knows we're having problems. He wants to help. Everybody does, Boots. That's why I want you to go to a meeting with me in the morning.'

Her eyes tried to avoid mine. Then she said, 'It's gone that far?'

'An A.A. meeting isn't the worst fate in the world.'

'Do you think I'm an alcoholic?'

'Booze is starting to hurt you. That fact's not going to go away.'

She turned her head sideways on the pillow and rested the back of her wrist on her temple.

'Why did this come into our lives?' she said.

'Because I let Hippo Bimstine take me over the hurdles.'

'It goes deeper than that, though, doesn't it? This man ... Buchalter ... he's evil in a way I don't know how to describe. It's as if he has the power to steal the air out of a room. If I think about him, I can't breathe. It's like I'm drowning.'

'The only power he has is what we allow our fear to give to him.'

But I was falling prey to that old self-serving notion that well-intended rhetoric can remove a stone bruise from the soul.

I pulled the sheet over her and didn't say anything for what seemed a long time. Then I said, to change the subject, 'Who was the woman with you when you got stopped?'

'Sister Marie.'

'Who?'

'Marie Guilbeaux, the nun from Lafayette.'

'What were you doing with *her?*'

'She was bringing some potted chrysanthemums out to the house. Then she saw me coming out of the convenience store, and I asked her to go with me to the drive-in for a beer. She's a nice person, Dave. She felt bad about her last visit here. What's wrong?'

'I don't want her around here anymore.'

'I don't understand your attitude.'

'She keeps showing up at peculiar times.'

'I don't think you should blame Sister Marie for my behavior, Dave.'

'We'll address our own problems, Boots. We don't need anybody else aboard. That's not an unreasonable attitude, is it?'

'I guess not. But she is nice.'

'I'll fix supper now. Why don't you take a short nap?'

'All right,' she said, and touched my forearm. 'I'm sorry about all this. I want to go to a meeting with you. First thing tomorrow morning. I won't break my promise, either.'

'You're the best.'

'You too, kiddo.'

Later, I strung an entire spool of baling wire, six inches off the ground, hung with tin cans, through the oak and pecan trees in the front and side yards, around the back of the house, across the trunk of the chinaberry tree and the back wall of the tractor shed, over the coulee, and back to Tripod's hutch, where I notched it tightly around an oak trunk. Then I put the sheriff's AR-15 on the top shelf of the bedroom closet, my .45 under the mattress, and got under the sheet next to Bootsie. Her body was warm with sleep, her mouth parted on the pillow with her breathing. The muscles in her back and shoulders and the curve of her hip were as smooth as water sliding over stone. Deep inside a troubling dream she began to speak incoherently, and I pressed myself against her, pulled the contours of her body into mine, breathed the strawberry smell of her hair, and, like a bent atavistic creature from an earlier time, his loins caught between desire and fear, waited for the tinkling of cans on a wire or the soft, milky glow of a predictable dawn.

After work the next afternoon, just as I pulled into the drive, I saw Zoot Bergeron sitting on top of a piling at the end of my dock, flipping pea gravel at the water. I parked my truck under the trees and walked back down the slope toward him. He jumped from the piling, straightened his back, and flung the rest of the gravel into the canebrake. His skin was dusty and his pullover sweater stained with food. In the lobe of his left ear was a tiny green stone, like a bright insect, on a gold pin.

'What's happening, Zoot?' I said.

'I need a job. I thought maybe you could put me on here. I done this kind of boat work before. Lot of it.'

'How'd you get here?'

'Rode the bus to New Iberia. Then walked.'

'You walked fifteen miles?'

'That man yonder give me a ride the last two miles.' He pointed up the road to a parked, mud-caked van where a man in coveralls was working under the front end with a wrench. 'I'll work hard for you, Mr Dave. I won't get in no trouble, either.'

'What about school, partner?'

'I ain't going back there. I need to train, get in shape, maybe get on a card. You don't need school for that. Mr Tommy tole me he quit school when he was sixteen.'

'That's part of the reason he's a moral imbecile, Zoot.'

'A wha—'

'What's your mom say about all this?'

He didn't answer.

'Does she know where you are?' I said.

'What she care? She told me this morning I ain't gonna be no better than my daddy. How can I be like my daddy when I never even seen my daddy? I want to join the Marine Corps but she won't sign for me. She say all they'll use me for is cleaning their toilets. She called up the sergeant at the recruiting center and tole him that. That's what she done.'

'Let me be up-front with you, partner. I've got a mess of grief around here right now. I can't help you out, at least not in the way you want me to.'

'Mr Dave—'

'Sorry, Zoot.'

The air was cool, and red and gold leaves tumbled out of the sunlight into the water. He looked down the road at the shadows among the oak trees, as though they held an answer to his situation.

'I'll find you a place to stay tonight, then I'll drive you to the bus depot in the morning,' I said.

I saw the flicker of injury in his face.

'There've been some bad people around my house, Zoot. I don't want you getting mixed up in it,' I said. 'Look, maybe you should give your mom another chance. Maybe she's scared. In her mind, you're all she's got. That makes her possessive and probably a little selfish. But it's not because she doesn't respect you.'

'It don't make what she say right. You ain't got to find a place for me. That fellow yonder's from New Orleans. He say when he get his van fixed, I can ride back wit' him.'

'You want me to call your mom for you?'

'I ain't going back home. Mr Tommy'll he'p me out. Y'all can say what you want about him, he ain't a bad white man. He don't get on my case and run me down, he don't tell me he got a mess of grief and don't got time for his friends.'

'I'm sorry you feel that way.'

'You a cop, Mr Dave.'

'What's that mean?'

'You talk different, you ain't mean like Mr Baxter, you're smart and educated, too, but you a cop, just like my mama. When it come down to it, you ain't gonna go against the rule, you're on the side got the power. Don't tell me it ain't so, neither.'

He walked down the road through the tunnel of oak trees. His tennis shoes and the bottoms of his jeans were gray with dust, and one elbow poked through the sleeve of his sweater. He squatted in a clump of four-o'clocks and watched the man in coveralls work on his van. In the waning afternoon light his black skin seemed lit with an almost purple sheen.

I went in the house, and Bootsie, Alafair, and I had supper at the kitchen table. Later, Alafair and I fed Tripod and put him in his hutch so he wouldn't make noise in the dead leaves during the night, then I checked the baling wire and tin cans that I had strung the day before and locked up the house. Just after Bootsie and Alafair went to bed, someone knocked on the front screen door.

It was Zoot. He was yawning when I opened the door, and his hair was mussed with pieces of leaves under the yellow porch light.

'Can you come he'p the man wit' the van?' he said.

'I thought you didn't want any favors, Zoot.'

'I didn't ax for one. The man did. He got the tire rod fixed. His batt'ry dead, though.'

'Oh, I see, that's different. Zoot, you're becoming a pain in the butt.'

'He tole me to ax. You don't want to he'p, I can walk down to the fo' corners.'

I locked the door behind me, and we got in my truck. Zoot rubbed the sleep out of his face. Then he said, 'I ain't meant to be rude, Mr Dave. I just had a lot of stuff on my mind today. I don't see no answer for it, either.'

'You really want to join the Corps?'

'Sure.'

'Let me talk to your mom about it.'

'You'll do that?'

'Why not, partner?'

We drove down the road toward the parked van. The moon was yellow, veiled with a rain ring, low over the cypress trees in the marsh. A few raindrops began hitting on the bayou's surface. In the headlights I could see the man in coveralls bent down into the van's engine, his back pocket swollen with chrome wrenches. But behind the van's shadow I also saw a parked pickup truck, its lights off.

'It looks like your friend's already found some help,' I said.

'That guy come by earlier but he don't have no cables,' Zoot said.

I left my lights and engine on, got out in the road, and unlocked the lid of the equipment box that was welded to the floor of my truck bed. I looped the jumper cables over my shoulder and walked toward the man in coveralls. His face was as pointed as an ax blade, his jaws covered with a fine silver beard that grew to a point on his chin. His smile was like a wrinkled red line inside his beard.

'Thanks for coming out, Mr Robicheaux,' he said.

'I don't think I know you,' I said.

'You don't. The boy told me your name.'

'I see.' I glanced at his face again in the slanting rain. His eyes were as bright as a pixie's. 'Well, clamp the red cable on your positive terminal and the black on your negative and we'll get you started.' I handed him the ends of the cables and turned to pop my hood. As I did I saw Zoot step backwards toward my truck, his mouth open, his stare suddenly disjointed.

I turned back toward the man in coveralls and saw the Luger in his hand. His smile was wet, his eyes dancing with light.

'That's the way it goes,' he said. 'I wouldn't feel bad about it. It took me a half day and Son of Sambo here to work this scam.'

'What's going on, Mr Dave?' Zoot said.

'Who you working for, podjo?' I said.

'Podjo? I dig it. I heard you were a cute motherfucker,' he said, still smiling, and moved past me to my open truck door, the Luger aimed at my chest, and switched off the ignition and headlights.

'Cut the kid loose. He's not a player,' I said.

'Nits makes lice. Stamp 'em out when you get the chance. That's what some people say.'

'I think you're standing in your own shit, buddy,' I said. 'You pop a cap on this road and you won't get back across the drawbridge.'

But even while I was talking I saw a shadow, a large one, moving from the parked pickup truck, along the side of the van, and I knew that I had not yet confronted my real adversary that night.

A scorched-black bank of thunderclouds over the marsh pulsed and flickered with veins of lightning, and in the white glow through the canopy of trees I saw Will Buchalter step out in front of the van, his Panama hat pushed back on his head, his lopsided Will Rogers grin as affectionate as that of an old friend.

He reached out with his hand to feel my face, just as a blind man might. My head jerked back from the sour smell of his palm.

'I'm sorry to do this to you, Dave, but you don't ride the beef easy,' he said, stepped close to me, his thighs widening, and clamped both his forearms on each side of my neck.

'Yeah, ride the beef, man. Ride that motherfucker down,' the other man said, and began giggling.

Then Buchalter's forearms flexed as tight as iron and squeezed into the sides of my neck like machinery breaking bird bone. I could feel his body trembling with strain, his breath quivering like a feather against my ear, then I felt the arteries to the brain shut down, and my knees buckled as though the tendons had been severed. A wave of nausea and red-black color slid across my eyes, and I was tumbling into a dark, cool place where the rain bounced off the skin as dryly as paper flowers and the distant thunder over the gulf was only the harmless echo of ships' guns that had long since been muted with moss and the lazy, dull drift of sand and time.

19

Pain can be a bucket of gasoline-smelling water hurled into the face, the concrete floor that bites into the knees, the hemp knotted into the wrists behind the squared wood post, the wrenched muscles in the arms, the Nazi flag coming back into focus against a urine yellow cinder-block wall, then once again the gears turning dully on a hand-crank generator, gaining speed now, starting to hum now, whining louder through the metal casing as the current strikes my genitals just like an iron fist, soaring upward into the loins, mashing the kidneys, seizing an area deep in the colon like electric pliers.

I was sure the voice coming out of my mouth was not my own. It was a savage sound, ripped out of the viscera, loud as cymbals clapped on the ears, degrading, eventually weak and plaintive, the descending tremolo like that of an animal with its leg in a steel trap.

A redheaded, crew-cut, porcine man in a black Grateful Dead T-shirt, with white skin, a furrowed neck, and deep-set, lime green eyes, sat forward on a folding chair, pumping his chubby arms furiously on the handles of the generator. Then he stopped and stared at one of his palms.

'I got a blister on me hand,' he said.

'Ease it up, Will. You're gonna lose him again,' the man with the silver beard said.

'It ain't Will's fault. All the sod's got to do is flap 'is fouking 'ole for us,' the man at the generator said.

'Electricity's funny, Will. It settles in a place like water. Maybe it's his heart next,' the man with the beard said.

Will Buchalter was shirtless, booted in hobnails. His upper torso tapered down inside his olive, military-style dungarees like the carved trunk of a hardwood tree. His armpits were shaved and powdered, and, just above his rib cage, there were strips of sinew that wrinkled and fanned back like pieces of knotted cord from the sides of his breasts. He sat with one muscular buttock propped on a battered desk, his legs crossed, his face bemused, lost in thought under the brim of his Panama hat.

'What about it, Dave?' he asked.

My head hung forward, the sweat and water streaming out of my hair.

'Answer the man, you dumb fouk,' the porcine man in the black T-shirt said, and lifted my chin erect with a wood baton. His skin was as white as milk.

'Don't hurt his face again, Freddy,' Buchalter said.

'I say leave off with the technology, Will,' the man called Freddy answered. 'I say consider 'is nails. I could play a lovely tune with 'em.'

Will Buchalter squatted down in front of me and pushed his hat to the back of his head. A bright line of gold hair grew out of his pants into his navel.

'You've got stainless-steel *cojones*, Dave,' he said. 'But you're going through all this pain to prevent us from having what's ours. That makes no sense for anybody.'

He slipped a folded white handkerchief out of his back pocket and blotted my nose and mouth with it. Then he motioned the other two men out of the room. When they opened the door I smelled grease, engine oil, the musty odor of rubber tires.

'Freddy and Hatch aren't the sharpest guys on the block, Dave. But armies and revolutions get built out of what's available,' Buchalter said. His eyes glanced down at my loosened trousers. He picked up one of the generator's wires and sucked wistfully on a canine tooth. 'I promise you you'll walk out of it. We have nothing to gain by hurting you anymore or killing you. Not if you give us what we want.'

A bloody clot dripped off the end of my tongue onto my chin.

'Go ahead, Dave,' he said.

But the words wouldn't come.

'You're worried about the Negro?' he said. 'We'll let him go, too. I promise I won't let Freddy get out of control like that again, either. He's just a little peculiar sometimes. When he was a kid some wogs took a liking to him in the back room of a pub, you know what I mean?'

He placed his palm across my forehead, as though he were gauging my temperature, then pressed my head gently back into the post. His eyes studied mine.

'It's almost light outside,' he said. 'You can have a shower and hot food, you can sleep, you can have China white to get rid of the pain, you can have a man's love, too, Dave.'

He brought his face closer to mine and smiled lopsidedly.

'It's all a matter of personal inclination, Dave. I don't mean to offend,' he said. He looked at the smear of blood and saliva across his squared handkerchief, folded it, and slipped it back into his pocket. Then the light in his eyes refocused, as though he were capturing an elusive thought. 'We're going to take back our cities. We're driving the rodents back into the sewers. It's a new beginning, Dave, a second American Revolution. You can be proud of your race and country again. It's going to be a wonderful era.'

He shifted his weight and settled himself more comfortably on one knee, like a football coach about to address his players. He grinned.

'Come on, admit it, wouldn't you like to get rid of them all, blow them off the streets, chase them back into their holes, paint their whole end of town with roach paste?' he said. He winked and poked one finger playfully in my ribs.

'I apologize, it's a bad time for jokes,' he said. 'Before we go on, though, I need to tell you something. In your house you said some ugly things to me. I was angry at the time, but I realize you were afraid and your only recourse was to try to hurt and manipulate me. But it's all right now. It makes our bond stronger. It's pain that fuses men's souls together. We're brothers-in-arms, Dave, whether you choose to think so or not.'

He got to his feet, went to the desk, and returned with a nautical chart of the Louisiana coast unrolled between his hands. He squatted in front of me again. In the shadow of his hat the spray of blackheads at the corners of his eyes looked like dried scale.

'Dave, the sub we want had the number U-138 on the conning tower. It also had a wreathed sword and a swastika on the tower,' he said. 'Is that the one you found? Can you tell me that much?'

A floor fan vibrated in the silence. I saw him try to suppress the twitch of anger that invaded his face. He put his thumb on a spot south of Grand Isle.

'Is this the last place you saw it?' he asked.

The red, black, and white flag puffed and ruffled against the cinder-block wall in the breeze from the fan.

His hand slipped over the top of my skull like a bowl. I could feel the sweat and water oozing from under his palm.

'You going to be a hard tail on me? Are the Jews and Negroes worth all this?' he said. He slowly oscillated my head, his mouth open, his expression pensive, then wiped his palm on the front of my shirt. 'Do you want me to let Hatch and Freddy play with your hands?'

He waited, then said, rising to his feet, 'Well, let's have one more spin with army surplus, then it's on to Plan B. Freddy and Hatch don't turn out watchmakers, Dave.'

He walked past the corner of my vision and opened the door.

'It's going to be daylight. I need to get 'ome to me mum, Will,' Freddy said.

'He's right. We're spending too much time on these guys,' the man named Hatch said. 'Look at my pants. The burrhead was swallowing the rag I put in his mouth. When I tried to fix it for him, he kicked me. A boon putting his goddamn foot on a white man.'

'We're not here to fight with the cannibals, Hatch,' Buchalter said. 'Dave's voted for another try at electroshock therapy. So let's be busy bees and get this behind us.'

I hear the rotary gears gain momentum, then the current surges into my loins again, vibrating, binding the kidneys, lighting the entrails, but this time the pain knows its channels and territory, offers no surprises, and nestles into familiar pockets like an old friend. The hum becomes the steady thropping of helicopter blades, the vibrations nothing more than the predictable shudder of engine noise through the ship's frame. The foreheads of the wounded men piled around me are painted with Mercurochromed M's to indicate the morphine that laces their hearts and nerve endings; in their clothes is the raw odor of blood and feces. The

158

medic is a sweaty Italian kid from Staten Island; his pot is festooned with rubber spiders, a crucifix, a peace symbol, a bottle of mosquito dope. My cheek touches the slick hardness of his stomach as he props me in his arms and says, 'Say good-bye to Shitsville, Lieutenant. You're going home alive in 'sixty-five. Hey, don't make me tie your hands. It's a mess down there, Loot.'

But I'm not worried about the steel teeth embedded in my side and thighs. My comrades and I are in the arms of God and Morpheus and a nineteen-year-old warrant officer from Galveston, Texas, who flew the dust-off in through a curtain of automatic weapons fire that sounded like ball peen hammers whanging against the fuselage, and now, with the windows pocked and spiderwebbed, the floor yawing, the hot wind sucking through the doors, the squares of flooded rice plain flashing by like mirrors far below, we can see green waves sliding toward us like a wet embrace and a soft pink sun that rises without thunder from the South China Sea.

Oh, fond thoughts. Until I hear the bucket filling again under a cast-iron tap and the water that stinks of gasoline explodes in my face.

'Time I had a go at 'im, Will,' Freddy said.

Then the door opened again, and I could hear leather soles on the concrete floor. The three men's faces were all fixed on someone behind me.

'Give me another hour and we'll have it resolved,' Buchalter said.

''E's a tight-ass fouker,' Freddy said. 'We give him a reg'lar grapefruit down there.'

'It's all getting to be more trouble than it's worth, if you ask me,' Hatch said. 'Maybe we should wipe the slate clean.'

The person behind me lit a cigarette with a lighter. The smoke drifted out on the periphery of my vision.

'You want to call it?' Buchalter said.

'All I ask is ten fouking minutes, one for each finger,' Freddy said. 'It'll come out of 'im loud enough to peel the paint off the stone.'

'I've had a little problem in controlling some people's enthusiasms,' Buchalter said to the person behind me.

'You've got a problem with acting like a bleeding sod sometimes,' Freddy began.

'You're not calling me a sodomist, are you, Freddy?'

'We're doing a piece of work. You shouldn't let your emotions get mixed up in it, Will. That's all I'm trying to get across 'ere,' Freddy said.

I heard the person behind me scrape up a steel ruler that had been lying on a workbench. Then the person touched the crown of my skull with it, idly teased it along my scalp and down the back of my neck.

'I think Dave'll come around,' Buchalter said. 'He just needs to work out some things inside himself first.'

Whoever was behind me bounced the ruler reflectively on my shoulder and pushed a sharp corner into my cheek.

Buchalter kept staring at the person's face, then he said, reading an expression there, 'If that's the way you want it. But I still think Dave can grow.'

I heard the cigarette drop to the floor, a shoe mash it out methodically against the cement; then the door opened and shut again.

Freddy smiled at Hatch. His skin was so white it almost glowed. He shook a pair of pliers loose from a toolbox. Hatch was smiling now, too. They both looked down at me, expectant.

Will Buchalter bit a piece of skin off the ball of his thumb. He crouched down in front of me, removed his Panama hat, and rested it on one knee. His blond hair was as fine as a baby's and grew outward from a bald spot the size of a half-dollar in the center of his scalp. He lifted up my chin gently with the wood baton.

'Last chance. Don't make me turn it over to them,' he said.

I lifted my eyes to his and felt my lips part dryly.

'What is it, Dave? Say it,' Buchalter said.

My lips felt like bruised rubber; the words were clotted with membrane in my throat.

'It's all right, take your time,' Buchalter said. 'You've had a hard night . . . Get him a drink of water.'

A moment later Buchalter held a tin cup gingerly to my lips. The water sluiced over my chin and down my throat; I gagged on my chest.

'Dave, I understand your pain. It's the pain of a soldier and a brave man. Just whisper to me. That's all it takes,' Buchalter said.

Hatch was bent down toward me, too, his hands on his knees, his face elfish and merry. Buchalter leaned his ear toward my mouth, waiting. I could see the oil and grain in his skin, the glistening convolutions inside his ear.

I pushed the words out of my chest, felt my lips moving, my eyes blinking with each syllable.

A paleness like the color of bone came into Buchalter's face. One hobnailed boot scratched against the cement as he rose to his feet.

'What'd 'e say?' Freddy asked.

'He said Will was a cunt,' Hatch answered, his grin scissoring through his beard. He and Freddy rocked on the balls of their feet, hardly able to keep their mirth down inside themselves.

Then Hatch said, 'Sorry, Will. We're just laughing at the guy. He hasn't figured out yet who's on his side.'

'That's right, Will,' Freddy said. ''E's a stupid fouk for sure. Go have breakfast. Me and Hatch'll finish it up here.'

But the insult had passed out of Buchalter's face now. He began pulling on a pair of abbreviated gray leather gloves, the kind a race driver might wear, with holes that allowed the ends of the fingers to extend above the webbing. He dried each of his armpits with a towel, then positioned himself in front of me.

'Stand him up,' he said.

'Maybe that's not a good idea, Will,' Freddy said. 'Unless you've given up. Remember what happened out in Idaho. Like an egg breaking, it was.'

'I say tear up his ticket, Will,' Hatch said. 'He's in with Hippo Bimstine. You're gonna trust what he tells you? Rip his ass.'

Then, as though he had given permission for his own anger to feed and stoke and fan itself, Hatch's hands began to shake, his teeth glittered inside his beard, and he wrenched me under one arm and tried to tug me upward against the wood post, his breath whistling in his nostrils.

'You know what's lower than a Jew?' he said. 'An Aryan who works for one. You think you're stand-up, motherfucker? A punk like you couldn't cut a week on Camp J. See how you like the way Will swings.'

Freddy grabbed my other arm, and they raked me upward against the post like a sack of feed. I could feel splinters biting into my forearms, my ankles twisting sideways with my weight.

'Get your fouking head up,' Freddy said.

'Strap his belt around his neck,' Hatch said.

'Step back, both of you,' Buchalter said.

Strands of hair were glued in my eyes, and a foul odor rose from my lap. I heard Buchalter's boots scrape on the cement as he set himself.

'I'm going to hit you only three times, Dave, then we'll talk again,' Buchalter said. 'If you want to stop before then, you just have to tell me.'

'Your juices are about to fly, Mr Robicheaux,' Freddy said.

Then the three men froze. The Nazi flag rippled along the cinder blocks with pockets of air from the floor fan.

'It's glass breaking,' Freddy said.

'I thought you said the Negro was tucked away,' Buchalter said.

''E was, Will. I locked 'im in the paint closet,' Freddy said.

'The paint closet? It's made of plywood. You retard, there're upholstery knives in there,' Buchalter said.

'Hatch didn't tell me *that*. Nobody told me *that*. You quit reaming me, Will,' Freddy said.

But Buchalter wasn't listening now. He ripped Hatch's Luger from a holster that hung above the workbench and moved quickly toward the door behind the post where I was tied, the muscles in his upper torso knotting like rope. But even before he flung the metal door back against the cinder blocks, I heard more glass breaking, cascading in splintered panes to the cement, as though someone were raking it out of window frames with a crowbar; then an electric burglar alarm went off, one with a horn that built to a crescendo like an air-raid siren, followed by more glass breaking, this time a more congealed, grating sound, like automobile windows pocking and folding out of the molding, while automobile alarms bleated and pealed off the cement and corrugated tin roof.

'He's out the door!' Buchalter said.

'The guy who owns this place uses a security service. They're probably already rolling on that alarm,' Hatch said.

'Y'all had a fucking security service into a place where you meet?' Buchalter said.

'How'd anybody know you'd want to use it for an interrogation? I told you to pop the burrhead last night, anyway.'

'Get out there and stop that noise,' Buchalter said.

'The shit's frying in the fire, it is. Time to say cheery-bye and haul it down the road, Will,' Freddy said.

'Can't you rip a wire out of a mechanism? Do I have to do everything myself?' Buchalter said.

'No, I can drive very nicely by meself, thank you. Since that's me van out there, I'll be toggling to me mum's now. I think you've made a bloody fouking mess of it, Will. I think you'd better get your fouking act together,' Freddy said.

The Luger dripped like a toy from Buchalter's huge hand. The smooth, taut skin of his chest was beaded with pinpoints of sweat; his eyes raced with thought.

Freddy unbolted a door at the far end of the room and stepped out into the gray dawn.

'Fuck it, I'm gone, too, Will,' Hatch said. 'Snap one into this guy's brainpan and clean him out of your head . . . All right, I'm not gonna say anything else. Don't point my own piece at me, man. It ain't my place to tell you what to do.'

Hatch backed away from Buchalter, then paused, chewing on his beard, his eyes trying to measure the psychodrama in Buchalter's face. He unhooked the Nazi flag from the wall and draped it over his arm.

'I'm taking the colors with me,' he said. 'Will, all this stuff tonight don't mean anything. It goes on, man. We're eternal. You know where you can find me and Freddy later. Hey, if you decide to smoke him, lose my piece, okay?'

Then he, too, was gone into the brief slice of gray light between the door and jamb.

Buchalter's thumb moved back and forth along the tip of the Luger's knurled grip. His tongue licked against the back of his teeth; then it made a circle inside his lips. As though he had stepped across a line in his own mind, he slipped the Luger into the top of his trousers and bent his face three inches from mine. He twisted his fingers into my hair and pulled my head back against the post.

'I'm stronger inside than you are, Dave. You can never get away from me, never undo me,' he said. 'I gave Bootsie a gift to remember me by. Now one for you.'

He tilted his head sideways, his eyes closing like a lover's, his mouth approaching mine. The Luger was hard and stiff against his corded stomach. In the next room the burglar and car alarms screamed against the walls and tin roof.

I sucked all the spittle and blood out of my cheeks and spat it full into his face.

His face went white, then snapped and twitched as though he had been slapped. His skin stretched against his skull and made his brow suddenly simian, his eye sockets like buckshot. He wiped a strand of pink spittle on his hand and stared at his palm stupidly.

But he didn't touch me again. He straightened to his full height with a level of hate and cruelty and portent in his eyes that I had never seen in a human being before, then, working his tropical shirt over one arm, snugging the Luger down tight in his belt, one eye fixed on me like a fist, he went out the door into the gray mist. But I believed I had now seen the face that inmates at Bergen-Belsen and Treblinka and Dachau had looked into.

Five minutes later Zoot Bergeron, his face swollen like a bruised plum, sawed loose the rope and leather straps that bound my wrists, and in the wail of the approaching St Mary Parish sheriff's cars, we slammed the door back on its hinges and stumbled out into the wet light, into the glistening kiss of a new dawn, into an industrial-rural landscape of fish-packing houses, junkyards, shrimp boats rocking in their berths, S.P. railway tracks, stacks of crisscrossed ties, a red-painted Salvation Army transient shelter among a clump of blue-green pine trees, oil-blackened sandspits, gulls gliding over the copper-colored roll of the bay, two hoboes running breathlessly over the gravel to catch a passing boxcar, the smells of diesel and salt-water, creosote, fish blood dried on a dock, nets stiff with kelp and dead Portuguese men-of-war, flares burning on offshore rigs, freshly poured tar on natural gas pipe, the hot, clean stench of electrical sparks fountaining from an arc welder's torch.

And in the distance, glowing like a chemical flame in the fog, was Morgan City, filled with palm-dotted skid-row streets, sawdust bars, hot pillow joints, roustabouts, hookers, rounders, bouree gamblers, and midnight ramblers. Zoot helped me stand erect, and I wiped my eyes on my sleeve and looked again at the two hoboes who had belly flopped onto the floor of the boxcar and were now rolling smokes as the freight creaked and wobbled down the old Southern Pacific railroad bed. Their toothless, seamed faces were lifted into the salt breeze with an expression of optimism and promise that made me think that perhaps the spirits of Joe Hill, Woody Guthrie, and Jack Kerouac were still riding those pinging rails. But the scene needed no songwriter or poet to make it real. It was a poem by itself, a softly muted, jaded, heartbreakingly beautiful piece of the country that was forever America and that you knew you could never be without.

20

At home the next day, I sat in the cool shade of the gallery and listened to Clete Purcel talk about his latest encounter with the Calucci brothers. The cane along the bayou's banks looked dry and yellow in the wind, and hawks were gliding high above the marsh against a ceramic blue sky. I had the same peculiar sense of removal that I had experienced after I was wounded seriously in Vietnam. I felt that the world was moving past me at its own pace, with its own design, one that had little to do with me, and that now I was a spectator who listened to interesting stories told by other people.

'You remember how we used to do it when the greaseballs thought they could take us over the hurdles, I mean when they got the mistaken idea they were equal members of the human race and not something that should have run down their mother's leg?' he said. 'We'd show up in the middle of their lawn parties, have their limos towed in, roust them on nickel-and-dime beefs in public, flush their broads out of town, use a snitch to rat-fuck 'em with the Chicago Outfit, hey, you remember the time we blew up Julio Segura's shit in the backseat of his car? They had to wash him out with a hose, what a day that was.'

Clete ripped the tab on a can of beer, drank the foam, and smiled at me. His face was pink with a fresh sunburn, and the corners of his eyes crinkled with white lines.

'So that's what I did, big mon,' he said. 'I started following Max and Bobo all over town. Bars, restaurants, a couple of massage parlors they own, three fuck pads, black slum property, dig this, they've actually got a guy fronting a bail bonds office for them in Metairie, an escort service, a PCB incinerator out on the river. Dave, these two guys get up in the morning and go across Jefferson and Orleans parishes like a disease, it's impressive.

'The problem is, I've got a convertible now, and it's a little hard to be inconspicuous. After a while Max and Bobo are doing big yawns when they see me and I'm starting to feel like part of the scenery while the neighbourhood dogs hose down my tires. So yesterday, when the Caluccis and all their gumballs go to lunch at Mama Lido's, I decide it's time to shift it on up into overdrive and I get a table out on the terrace, three feet behind one of Max's broads.

'It was perfect timing, the ultimate New Orleans lowlife geek-out. Guess who shows up first? Tommy Blue Eyes and his main punch, what's her name, Charlotte, with her ta-tas sticking out of her sundress like a couple of muskmelons, and of course the Caluccis' hired help are winking at each other and squeezing their floppers under the table while Tommy's trying to act big-shit and order Italian dishes like he knows what he's doing, except he sounds like he's got Q-tips shoved up his nose.

'Then Tommy's Indian zombie pulls up in front of the restaurant with Mrs Lonighan in the passenger's seat. Have you ever seen her? Think of a fire hydrant with bow legs. She charges out onto the terrace, her glasses on crooked, spittle flying from her mouth, shouting about Tommy and the punch leaving a used rubber under her bed, and when the maître d' tries to calm her down, she squirts a bottle of seltzer water in his face.

'Naturally, the Caluccis and the other greaseballs and their broads are loving all this. Tommy's face is getting redder and redder, his punch is using a little brush to powder her ta-tas, and the Indian is standing there like a lobotomy case who needs a spear in his hand and a bone in his nose. Then Mrs Lonighan storms out of the place, gets in her car without the Indian, and drives across the curb into a bunch of garbage cans down the street.

'So Tommy tries to blow it all off by talking about how the Jews are taking over legalized gambling in Louisiana. Then he starts telling these anti-Semitic jokes that have got people at the other tables staring with their mouths open, you know, stuff like "This Nazi officer told these Jewish concentration camps inmates, 'I got good news and bad news for you guys. The good news is you're going to Paris. The bad news is you're going as soap.'"'

'Anyway, the greaseballs are roaring at Tommy's jokes, and I'm wondering why I'm letting these guys act like I've used up my potential and I'm not a factor in their day anymore. So I lean over and tap Tommy on the shoulder with a celery stick and say, "Hey, Tommy, too bad you left your peter cheater lying around for Miz Bobalouba to step on. You ought to get you a fuck pad in the Pontalba like Max and Bobo here."

'The whole place goes quiet except for the sound of the Indian slurping up his squids. I'm thinking, *Ah, show time*. Wrong. Bobo calls the maître d' and has me thrown out. Can you dig it? Here's a collection of people that would turn the stomach of a proctologist, but I get eighty-sixed out on the street, right in front of a busload of Japanese tourists who are on their way back from the battleground at Chalmette.

'I'm thinking. What's wrong with this picture? I was humping it outside Chu Lai while Max and Bobo were boosting cars and doing hundred-buck hits for the Giacano family. Plus I look back at the terrace and the maître d' is picking up my silverware and changing the tablecloth like some guy with herpes on his hands had been eating there.

'I look down the street and some guys are taking a break from pouring a concrete foundation for a house. You remember that story you told me about how this mob guy in Panama City got even with his wife for giving a blow job to a judge behind a nightclub?

'The guy in charge of the cement truck is a union deadbeat and a part-time bouncer in the Quarter I went bail for about two years ago. I say, "Mitch, you mind if I drive your truck around the block, play a joke on a friend?" He says, "Yeah, we were just going to have a beer and a shot across the street if somebody'd stand the first round." I say, "Why don't you let me do that, Mitch? I think I have a tab there." He goes, "I was just telling my friends here you're that kind of guy, Purcel."

'I pull the truck right up to Max's Caddy convertible. It's gleaming with a new wax job, the top's down, the dashboard's made of mahogany, the seats are purple leather and soft as warm butter. I get out of the truck, clank that feeder chute over the driver's door, and let 'er rip. Streak, it was beautiful. The cement splatters all over the dashboard and the windows, covers the floors, oozes up over the seats, and hangs in big gray curtains over the doors. Even with the mixer roaring I could hear people yelling and going crazy out on the terrace. In the meantime, the Japanese have piled back off the bus in these navy blue business suits that look like umpire uniforms, laughing and applauding and snapping their Nikons because they think a movie is being made and this is all part of the tour, and while Max and Bobo are trying to fight their way through the crowd, the springs on the Caddy collapse, the tires pop off the rims, the cement breaks out the front windows and crushes the hood down on the engine. You remember that character called "The Heap" in the comic books? That's what the Caddy looked like, two headlights staring out of this big, gray pile of wet cement.'

'Have you lost your mind?' I said.

'What's wrong?'

'You're going to end up in the bag or get your P.I. license pulled. Why do you keep clowning around with these guys? It doesn't get the score changed.'

'They loan-sharked the Caddy out of a builder in Baton Rouge. The last thing Max wants is a police report filed on it. Lighten up, noble mon. You've been around the local Rotary too much.'

Then I saw his eyes look into mine and his expression change. I looked away.

'You really spit in Buchalter's face?' he said.

'It wasn't a verbal moment.'

'I'm proud of you, mon.'

His eyes kept wandering over my face.

'Will you cut it out, Clete?'

'What?'

'Staring at me. I'm all right. Both the guys with Buchalter are fuckups and aren't going to be hard to find. Particularly the cockney. We've got the feds in on it now, too.'

He made tiny prints with the ball of his index finger in the moisture and salt on top of his beer can.

'You think Buchalter's some kind of Nazi superman?' I said. 'He's not. He's a psychotic freak, just like dozens of others we sent up the road.'

'NOPD and the sheriff's office in Lafourche Parish probably haven't gotten hold of your boss yet. But they will.'

'What are you talking about?'

'You're right. Those two were fuckups. That's why they're off the board now.'

The sunlight seemed to harden and grow cold on the garden.

As best as I could reconstruct it, this is how Clete (and later a Lafourche sheriff's deputy) told me the story:

The previous night, out in a wetlands area southwest of New Orleans, a man who had been gigging frogs emerged terrified from the woods, his face whipped by branches and undergrowth, and waved down a parish sheriff's car with his shirt. It had started to rain, and ground fog was blowing out of the trees

'They's a man got some other men tied up on the mudflat. Somebody got to get down there. He's fixin' to—' he said.

'Slow down, podna. It's gonna be all right. He's fixin' to what?' the deputy said.

'He's got one of them lil chain saws. Back yonder, right by the marsh.'

The deputy was young and only eight months with his department. He radioed his dispatcher, then made a U-turn in the middle of the highway and bounced down an abandoned board road that wound through thickly spaced trees and mounds of briar bushes webbed with dead morning glory vines. Sheets of stagnant water and mud splashed across his windshield, and an old road plank splintered under one wheel and *whanged* and clattered against his oil pan. But in the distance, through the blowing mist and the black silhouette of tree trunks, he could see a brilliant white chemical flame burning against the darkness. Then he heard the surge of a chain saw, and a second later, even louder than the erratic, laboring throb and shriek of the saw and the roar of his car engine, the sustained and unrelieved scream of a man that rose into the sky like fingernails scraping on slate.

The deputy snapped a tie-rod and spun out into a tangle of willow and cypress trees fifty yards before the road dead-ended at the marsh. He pulled his twelve-gauge Remington shotgun, sawed off at the pump and loaded with double-ought buckshot, from the clip on the dashboard and began running with it at port arms through the undergrowth.

In a clearing by the swamp's edge, next to a parked pickup truck with a camper shell in the bed, a Coleman lantern hissed on the ground like a phosphorous flare. The deputy could see the shadow of a huge man moving about on the far side of the truck. On the ground, partly obscured by the truck's tires, were the shapes of two prone men, their arms pinioned behind them, their faces bloodless and iridescent in the soft rain and the hissing light of the lantern.

The chain saw was idling on a piece of cardboard now. Then the deputy saw the large man bending over the shapes on the ground, a bouquet of roses scattered about his booted feet, pulling, working at something with his hands. The water and trees in the swamp were black, the shadows in the clearing changing constantly with the frenetic movements of the man, whose hands the deputy now knew were laboring at something tribal and dark, far beyond the moral ken of a youthful law officer, a glimpse into a time before the creation of light in the world, hands as broad as skillets, popping with cartilage, scarlet to the wrist, the fingers wet with the lump of heart muscle that they lifted from a man's chest cavity.

The deputy vomited on a tree, then tried to step into the clearing with his shotgun aimed at the man who had suddenly raised erect, a rain hat tied under his chin, a disjointed and maniacal stare in his eyes.

He wanted to yell *Down on your face, hands on your head,* or any other of the dramatic verbal commands that always reduce television criminals to instant prisoners, but the words hung like pieces of wet newspaper in his throat and died in the heavy air, and he tripped over a tangle of morning glory vines as though he were stumbling about in a dream.

Then the large man was running into the marsh, his legs ripping through islands of lily pads, water splashing to his waist, his shoulders humped, when the deputy let off the first round and sent a shower of sparks out into the dark. At first the deputy thought he had missed, had fired high, and he jacked another shell into the chamber, aimed at the base of the running man's spine, and pulled the trigger. Then he fired twice more and saw the man's shirt jump, heard the slugs *whunk* into his back.

But the running man crashed and tunneled through the flooded cypress and willows and was gone. The deputy's fifth shot peeled away through the trees like marbles rattling down a long wooden chute. He would swear later that he saw a half dozen rents in the shirt of the fleeing man. He would also get off duty that night and get so drunk in a Lockport bar that his own sheriff would have to drive him home.

'The pickup truck was boosted in Lafitte that morning,' Clete said. 'The guy with the silver beard was Jody Hatcher. He was a four-time loser, including one time down as an accessory in the rape of a child. The guy named Freddy is a blank. The feds think he might be a guy who dynamited a synagogue in Portland, but they're not sure . . . Streak, look at the bright side. There're two less of these guys on the planet. I tell you something else. They made a real balloon payment when they checked out. The ME said there was a look frozen in their eyes even he had trouble dealing with.'

Batist was cranking an engine out on the bayou. The wind was wrinkling the water and ruffling the cane in the sunlight.

'None of it makes any sense,' I said.

'It does to me. Buchalter doesn't leave loose ends.'

'Why does he go to the trouble of using the vigilante's MO?'

'Maybe he likes roses. Maybe he has shit for brains.'

'Maybe we're not dealing with Buchalter, either. What's this stuff about the deputy planting double-ought bucks in his back?'

'Maybe the guy doesn't want to admit he was so scared he couldn't hit a billboard with bird shot.'

I stood up to go inside. A pain spread out of my loins into my abdomen.

'You beat Buchalter, Streak. That's all that counts,' Clete said. 'I don't think I could have cut it. I'd have rolled over.'

'No, you wouldn't.'

He crushed his empty beer can in his hand.

'Let me take y'all to supper tonight,' he said.

'That sounds very copacetic,' I said.

'My second day in Vietnam a hard-nosed gunny gave me some advice about fear and memory and all that stuff: "Never think about it before you do it, never think about it after it's over." '

'No kidding?' I said, with the screen half opened.

'I tried,' he answered, and held up his palms and made half-moons of his eyebrows.

21

On Saturday morning, when I walked down to the dock, I noticed a pickup truck with a David Duke sticker parked by the shell boat ramp. Inside the bait shop, Alafair and Batist were working behind the counter and two fishermen were eating chilli dogs with forks and drinking bottled beer at one of the tables. Batist did little more than nod when I said good morning.

'What's wrong with him?' I asked Alafair while we were pulling the canvas awning out on the wires over the spool tables.

'Batist made a mistake with those men's change,' she answered. 'One man said, the one with the big face, he said, "Louisiana's got fifteen percent unemployment, and this place hires something like that to run the cash register." '

I went back through the screen door. The two men, both dressed in the khaki clothes of heavy equipment operators, were sharing a smoked sausage now and drinking their beer. I picked up the cash register receipt from their table, flattened it on the counter, added up the price of the beer and sausage and sales tax, rang open the cash drawer, and placed four one-dollar bills and thirty-six cents in coins on their table.

'This table's closed,' I said, and picked up their beer bottles and the paper shell with the sliced sausage in it.

'What the hell do you think you're doing?' the larger of the two men said. His head looked like granite, and his closely cropped hair was lightly oiled and shaved neatly on his neck.

'You were rude to my employee. I don't want your business.'

'Just hold on a minute, there.'

'End of discussion, gentlemen.'

'Well then ... well ... well then ... Fuck you, then.'

After they were gone, I wiped off their table. Then, before I realized it, Batist had walked down the dock, gotten into his truck, and driven south toward the four corners and his house.

Oh boy.

'Watch the store, Alf. I'll be back in about twenty minutes,' I said.

'Why'd Batist leave?'

'He has his own way of doing things.'

He lived in a rambling, paintless house that had been built on to randomly by three generations of his family. The tin roof was orange with rust, the dirt yard strewn with chicken coops, tractor and car parts. On the sagging gallery were stacks of collapsible crab traps and an old washing machine that he had turned into a barbecue pit. His small farm had once been part of a plantation where Federal and Confederate troops had fought a furious battle during General Banks's invasion of southwestern Louisiana. Through the pines on the far side of the coulee which bordered Batist's property, you could see the broken shell and old brick pillars and chimneys of a burned-out antebellum home that the Federals first looted and then fired as they pushed a retreating contingent of Louisiana's boys in butternut brown northward into New Iberia. Every spring, when Batist cracked apart the matted soil in his truck patch with a singletree plow, minie balls, shards of broken china, and rusted pieces of canister would peel loose from the earth and slide back off the polished point of the share like the contents of a fecund and moldy envelope mailed from the year 1863.

I found him in his backyard, raking leaves onto a compost pile that was enclosed with chicken wire. The dappled sunlight through the oak branches overhead slid back and forth across his body like a network of yellow dimes.

'If you're going to take off early, I'd appreciate your telling me first,' I said.

'When I tole you you gotta t'row people out the shop 'cause of me?'

'Those were low-rent white people, Batist. I don't want them on my dock. That's my choice.'

'If a white man got to look out for a black man, then ain't nothin' changed.'

'This is what you're not understanding, partner. We don't let those kind of people insult Alafair, Bootsie, you, or me. It doesn't have anything to do with your race.'

He stopped work and propped his hands on the wood shaft of the rake. His wash-faded denim shirt was split like cheesecloth in back.

'Who you tellin' this to? Somebody just got off the train from up Nort'?' he said.

'Next time I'll keep my hand out of it. How's that?'

'Get mad if you want. T'rowin' them white men out ain't solvin' nothin'. It's about money, Dave. It's always about money. The white man need the nigger to work cheap. That ain't no mystery to black people. It's white folk don't figure it out, no.'

'I need you to help close up tonight,' I said.

'I'm gonna be there. Hey, you runnin' round in circles lookin' for this man been killin' dope dealers, this man who hurt you so bad the ot'er day, it don't have nothin' to do with no vigilante. When somebody killin' black people, it don't matter if up in a tree, or breakin' in a jail and hangin' a man on a beam, they can say it's 'cause he raped a white woman, or he killed a white man, or he done some ot'er t'ing. But it's over money. It means the black man stay down at the bottom of the pile. The dumbest nigger in Lou'sana know that.'

His eyes lingered indulgently on mine. He squeezed the rake handle, and his callused palm made a soft grating sound like leather rubbing against wood.

Monday morning I returned to work. The first telephone call I received was from Lucinda Bergeron.

'Fart, Barf, and Itch are no help on Will Buchalter,' she said. 'I don't understand it. Is the guy made out of air?'

'He didn't seem like it to me.'

'Then why doesn't he show up in the system?'

'You can't throw an electronic net over every psychopath in the country.'

'Somebody has to know who this guy is. Being around him must be like getting up in the morning and biting into a shit sandwich for breakfast.'

Too much time around squad rooms, Lucinda, I thought.

'How's Zoot doing?' I said.

'He's fine, thank you.'

'What's the problem?'

'He said you thought he should join "the Crotch." That's swinging-dick talk, isn't it? Quite a vocabulary you guys have.'

'How about your own?' I said.

'I'm not the one encouraging a seventeen-year-old boy to drop out of school.'

'He wanted me to talk to you about joining the Corps. He can get a GED there. I don't think it's the worst alternative in the world.'

'He can forget about it.'

'You do him a disservice. Why'd you call, Lucinda?'

Her anger seemed almost to rise from the perforations in the telephone receiver.

'That's a good question. When I figure it out, I'll tell you.' Then she made that sound again, like she had just broken a fingernail. A moment later, she said, 'We're operating a sting out of a motel dump by Ursulines and Claiborne. You want in on it?'

'What for?'

'We're going to roll over some dealers from the Iberville Project.'

'You think they're going to tell you something about the vigilante?'

'They're the bunch most likely to undergo open-heart surgery these days.'

'You think this will lead you back to Buchalter?'

'Who knows? Maybe there's more than one guy killing black dope dealers.'

'Lucinda, listen to me on this one. Buchalter doesn't have any interest in you or Zoot. Don't make it personal. Don't bring this guy into your life.'

'That sounds strange coming from you.'

'Read it any way you want. Zoot and I were lucky. The time to go home is after you hit the daily double.'

'You want in on the sting or not?'

'What's the address?'

I talked with the sheriff, arranged to have a deputy stay at the house until I returned sometime that evening, then signed out of the office and went home to change into street clothes. Bootsie's car was gone, and Alafair was at school. I used the Memo button on our telephone answering machine to leave Bootsie a recorded message. I gave her both Lucinda Bergeron's and Ben Motley's extension numbers, and, in case she couldn't reach me any other way, I left the name and address of the motel off Claiborne where the sting was being set up.

It seemed a simple enough plan.

On the way back down the dirt road, on the other side of the drawbridge, I saw the flatbed truck, with the conical loudspeakers welded on the roof, of the Reverend Oswald Flat, banging in the ruts and coming toward me in a cloud of dust. Crates of machinery or equipment of some kind were boomed down on the truck bed.

Oswald Flat recognized my pickup and clanked to a halt in the middle of the road. His pale eyes, which had the strange, nondescript color of water running over a pebbled streambed, stared at me from behind his large, rimless glasses. His wife sat next to him, eating pork rinds out of a brown bag.

'Where you running off to now?' he said.

'To New Orleans. I'm in a bit of a hurry, too.'

'Yeah, I can tell you're about to spot your drawers over something.'

'Today's not the day for it, Reverend.'

'Oh, I know that. I wouldn't want to hold you back from the next mess you're about to get yourself into. But my conscience requires that I talk to you, whether you like hit or not. Evidently you got the thinking powers of a turnip, son. Now, just stop wee-weeing in your britches a minute and pull onto the side of the road.'

'Os, I told you to stop talking to the man like he's a *mo*-ron,' his wife said, dabbing at the rings of fat under her chin with a handkerchief.

I parked in a wide spot and walked back toward his truck. Through the slats in one of the crates fastened to the flatbed with boomer chains I could see the round brass helmet, with glass windows and wing nuts, and the rubber and canvas folds of an ancient diving suit.

'I hate even to ask what you're doing with that,' I said.

'Bought hit at a shipyard outside Lake Charles – air hoses, compressor, weighted shoes, cutting torch, stuff I don't even know the name of. Now I got to get aholt of a boat.'

'You're going to try to find that sub?'

He smiled and didn't answer.

'Do you know what's in it?' I asked.

'I'd bet on a lot of Nazis ready for a breath of fresh air.'

'I think you're going to get hurt.'

'Hit's something they want. So I'll do everything I can to make sure they don't get hit.'

'Don't do this, sir.'

'I cain't fault you. You mean well. But you still don't get hit. You ain't chasing one man, or even a bunch of men. Hit's something wants to take over the earth and blot out the sun. Hit's evil on a scale the likes of ordinary people cain't imagine.'

His eyes searched in mine like those of a man who would never find words to adequately explain the enigmas that to him had the bright, clear shape of a dream.

'You lost your son to forces you couldn't control, Reverend,' I said. 'I lost my wife Annie in a similar way. I was full of anger, and after a while I came to believe the whole earth was a dark place.'

He was already shaking his head before I could finish.

'I was on a tanker got torpedoed. Right out yonder,' he said, and pointed toward the southern horizon. 'There ain't no way to describe hit for somebody ain't been there. Holding on to the life jacket of a man whose face is burnt off . . . Boilers blowing apart under the water . . . Men crawling around on the hull like ants just before she slips to the bottom . . . Somebody screaming out there inside an island of flaming oil. You don't never want to hear a sound like that, Mr Robicheaux.'

'Sometimes you have to let things go, partner.'

'They got to make people afraid. That's the plan. Make 'em afraid of the coloreds, the dope addicts, the homeless, the homosexuals, hit don't matter. When they got enough people afraid, that's when they'll move.'

'Who?'

'The Book of Revelation says the Beast will come from the sea. In the Bible the sea means politics.'

'I think you're a decent man. But don't go down after that sub with this junk.'

'Just leave things alone . . . Don't be messin' . . . Let the law handle hit . . . You put me in mind of a woodpecker tapping away on a metal light pole.' He pursed his lips and began to whistle, then opened the door to the truck cab and reached behind the seat. 'Tell me what you make of this?'

'An iron rose.'

'Hit was probably tore off a tomb or a gate. But this morning hit was on my front porch. The stem was stuck through the heart on a valentine card.'

It was heavy in my palm, the iron black with age, the edges of the petals thin and serrated with rust.

'Have you given somebody reason to be upset with you?' I said.

'I been working down in the Desire Project for the last week.'

'You know how to pick them.'

'Jesus didn't spend a lot of time with bankers and the fellows at the Chamber of Commerce.'

I placed the iron rose back in his hand.

'Good luck to you, Reverend. Call me if I can help with anything,' I said.

I left him there, a good man out of sync with the world, the era, even the vocabulary of his countrymen. But I doubted if anyone would ever be able to accuse the Reverend Oswald Flat of mediocrity. His kind ended on crosses, forever the excoriated enemies of the obsequious. To him my words of caution bordered on insult and my most reasoned argument had the viability of a moth attempting to mold and shape a flame.

A narcotics sting sounds interesting. It's not. It usually involves what's called rolling over the most marginal players in the street trade – hypes, hookers, and part-time mules, and any of their demented friends and terrified family members who are unlucky enough to get nailed with them. As a rule, the mules, or couriers, are dumb and inept and spend lifetimes seeking out authority figures in the form of probation officers and social workers. In the normal world most of them couldn't make sandwiches without an instruction manual. They are almost always users themselves, dress as though they're color-blind, speak in slow motion, and wonder why cops can easily pick them out of a crowd at a shopping mall.

They scheme and labor on a daily basis at the bottom of the food chain. When they're busted in a sting, their choices are immediate and severe – they either roll over and give up somebody else, or they go straight to jail, sweat out withdrawal over a toilet bowl in a holding cell, then meditate upon their mistakes while hoeing soybeans for several years at Angola.

Shitsville in the street trade is when you're spiking six balloons a day and suddenly you're in custody and the Man can snap his fingers and turn you into a Judas Iscariot or a trembling bowl of Jell-O.

'You telling me you want to ride the beef, Albert?' the plainclothes says to the frightened black man, who sits on the edge of the motel bed, his wrists handcuffed behind him, his thin forearms lined with the infected tracks and gray scar tissue of his addiction.

'If I give you Bobby, he'll fuck me up, man,' Albert answers. 'Cat's got a blade. He did a guy in Houston with it.'

The plainclothes, a heavy, choleric man in a sweaty, long-sleeve white shirt, reaches out and taps Albert sharply on the cheek with his hand.

'Are you stupid, Albert?' he says. 'You're already fucked up. You're taking Bobby's fall. Bobby has kicked a two-by-four up your ass. Look at me, you stupid shit. Bobby told me your old lady whores for lepers. He laughs at both of you behind your back. He's got you copping his joint and you're too fucking dumb to know it.'

'He told you my old—'

'You want to go back to Angola? You want to get turned out again, made into a galboy, that's what you're telling me, Albert? You like those swinging dicks to turn you out? I heard they tore up your insides last time.'

'You gotta he'p me on this. I cain't go down again, man.'

'Get him out of my sight,' the plainclothes says to another cop.

'You gotta keep my name out of it, okay? The cat tole me to meet him in a pizza joint out in Metairie. He's gonna be there in an hour.'

'You got to make him take you to his stash, Albert. That's the only deal you get. Bobby goes down, you walk. Otherwise, your next high is going to be on nutmeg and coffee. Is it true that stuff can give you a hard-on like a chunk of radiator pipe?'

Albert trembles like a dog trying to pass broken glass; Albert vomits in his lap; Albert makes the plainclothes turn away in disgust.

What's it all worth?

You've got me.

The people at the top usually skate. They buy defense attorneys who used to be prosecutors for the U.S. Justice Department. A million-dollar bond is simply factored into the overhead.

Albert goes to jail, or into a diversion program, or into the graveyard. And nobody, except Albert, particularly cares which one, since Albert doesn't even qualify as a footnote.

In an adjoining room Lucinda and I questioned seven individuals – five of them black, two white – about the vigilante. But these were people who long ago had accepted the sleepy embrace of the succubus or incubus that had insinuated itself into their lives through a tied-off, swollen vein. Their concept of mortality did not extend past the next five minutes of their day. They shot up with one another's syringes, used the public health clinic as a temporary means to knock their venereal diseases into remission, looked upon AIDS as just another way of dying, and daily accepted the knowledge that a vengeful supplier could give them a hot shot that would transform their hearts into kettledrums.

Their beef was with the narcs. Their angst was centered on their own metabolism and the fact that they were about to rat out their friends. Why bargain with a couple of homicide investigators who could offer them nothing? They turned to stone.

Then one of those terrible moments happened, the kind that you dream about, that you hope will never occur in your career, that will always somehow be the misfortune of someone else. Later, you'll attribute it to bad judgment, callousness, inhumanity, bad luck, or simple stupidity, like a safety-minded fool righteously padlocking fire exits, but it remains forever as the moment that left you with the mark of Cain.

The plainclothes who had been interrogating Albert decided to tighten and tamp down the dials a little more and whipped Albert repeatedly across his nappy head with a fedora, yelling at him simultaneously, until another cop stopped it and walked him outside for a cigarette. When they came back in, the plainclothes's face was still flushed and his armpits were gray with sweat. The thermostat switch was broken, and the room was hot and dry with the electric heat from the wall panels. The plainclothes ripped off his tie, kneaded the thick folds in the back of his neck, then hung his shoulder holster on the back of a wood chair.

Albert was shirtless, his lap soiled with vomit, his face wringing wet. His shoulders trembled, and his teeth clicked in his mouth. He begged to go to the toilet.

The plainclothes walked him into the bathroom, unlocked one cuff, then snipped it on a water pipe and closed the door.

Albert was strung out, delusional, popping loose seam and joint. His body was foul with its own fluids; his pitiful attempt at integrity had been robbed from him; his new identity was that of snitch and street rat. With luck he'd be out of town before his friend Bobby made bail.

But Albert was jail-wise and had been underestimated.

He feverishly lathered his wrist with soap and pulled his thin hand through the cuff like it was bread dough. The plainclothes stared with disbelief as Albert came through the bathroom door and tore the .38 out of the shoulder holster that hung on the chair back, his hand shaking, his eyes blood-flecked and bulging with fear, sweat streaming down his chest.

The plainclothes's face looked like a large, round, white clock that had run out of time.

'Put it down, Albert!' Lucinda shouted, pointing her nickel-plated .357 Magnum straight out with both hands from the doorway.

The plainclothes's chest was heaving; he clutched at his left breast, and his breath rose from his throat like bubbles bursting from an underwater air hose. Lucinda's feet were spread, her midriff winking above her Clorox-faded Levi's. Albert's eyes were half-dollars, his clenched right hand trembling as though it were painted with electricity.

'You don't want to do this, Albert,' she said, fitted her thumb over the knurled spur of the hammer, and cocked it back. The notched grooves and the cylinder locked into place with a sound like a dry stick snapping. 'We can all walk out of this. You'll go downtown. Nobody'll hurt you. I give you my word. Lower the gun, Albert ... Wait ... Don't do it, don't let those thoughts get in your head ... Albert!'

But it was too late. A facsimile of a man, with the soft bones of a child and muscles like jelly, with lint in his navel and a snake feeding at his heart, was imploding inside and looking for his executioner. He gripped the pistol with both hands, squeezed his eyes shut, turned toward Lucinda, and lowered his head between his extended arms as he tightened his finger inside the trigger housing.

She fired only once. The round caught him in the crown of the skull and knocked him back against the wall as though he had been struck by an automobile.

The air was bitter with the smell of gunpowder, dry heat, and a hint of nicotine and copulation in the bed clothing. My ears were ringing from the explosion, then I saw the plainclothes pointing at the red horsetails on the wallpaper while he giggled and wheezed uncontrollably, his left hand clawing at his collar as though it were a garrote about his neck.

Three hours later, after the paperwork, the questions, the suspension from active duty, the surrender of her weapon to Nate Baxter, I drove her home. Or almost home.

'Stop at the corner,' she said.

'What for?'

'I want a drink.'

'Bad day to feed the dragon,' I said.

'Drop me off and I can walk.'

'Lucinda, this is what happens. Tonight, you'll finally fall asleep. You'll have troubling dreams, but not exactly about the shooting. It's like your soul has a headache and can't allow itself to remember something. Then you'll wake up in the morning, and for a few moments it'll all be gone. Then, boom, it'll wash over you like the sun just died in the sky. But each day it gets better, and eventually you come to understand there's no way it could have worked out differently.'

Her eyes had the unnatural sheen of an exhausted person who just bit into some black speed.

'Are you coming in or not?' she said when I pulled to the curb in front of an old wood-front bar with a colonnade on Magazine.

'I guess not.'

'See you around, sport,' she said as she slammed the door and walked into the bar, the tip of a white handkerchief sticking out of the back pocket of her Levi's, her bare ankles chafing against the tops of her dusty tennis shoes.

Bad situation in which to leave a distraught lady, I thought, and followed her inside.

It was dark and cool inside and smelled of the green sawdust on the floor and a caldron of shrimp the black bartender was boiling on a gas stove behind the counter. I used a pay phone by the empty pool table to call home. It was the second time I had called that afternoon and gotten no answer. I left another message.

Lucinda drank a whiskey sour in two swallows. Her eyes widened, then she let out her breath slowly, almost erotically, and ordered another.

'Join me?' she asked.

'No thanks.'

She drank from the glass.

'How many times has it happened to you?' she said.

'Who cares?'

'I don't know if I can go back out there again.'

'When they deal the play and refuse the alternatives, you shut down their game.'

'How many times did you do it? Can't you answer a simple question?' she said.

'Five.'

'God.'

I felt a constriction, like a fish bone, in my throat.

'Who'd you rather have out there, people who do the best they can or a lot of cops cloned from somebody like Nate Baxter or that blimp in the motel room?'

She finished her drink and motioned to the bartender, who refilled her glass from a chrome shaker fogged with moisture. She flattened her hands on the bar top and stared at the tops of her fingers.

'I busted Albert four years ago,' she said. 'For stealing a can of Vienna sausage out of a Winn-Dixie. He lived in the Iberville Project with his grandmother. He cried when I put him in the holding cell. His P.O. sent him up the road.'

'A lot of people wrote that guy's script, but you weren't one of them, Lucinda. Sometimes we just end up being the punctuation mark,' I said, slid the whiskey glass away from the ends of her fingers, and turned her toward the door and the mauve-colored dusk that was gathering outside in the trees.

I drove her to her house and walked with her up on the gallery. The latticework was thick and dark with trumpet vine, and fireflies were lighting in the shadows. The lightbulb above our heads swarmed with bugs in the cool air. She paused with her keys in her hand.

'Do you want me to call later?' I said.

'I'll be all right.'

'Is Zoot here?'

'He plays basketball tonight.'

'It might be good if you ask somebody to come over.'

Her face looked up into mine. Her mouth was red; her breath was soft with the smell of bourbon.

'I'll call when I get back to New Iberia,' I said.

Her face looked wan, empty, her gaze already starting to focus inward on a memory that would hang in the unconscious like a sleeping bat.

'It's going to be all right,' I said, and placed one hand on her shoulder. I could feel the bone through the cloth of her blouse.

But nothing was going to be all right. She lowered her head and exhaled. Then I realized what she was looking at. On the tip of her tennis shoe was a red curlicue of dried blood.

'Why did it have to be a pathetic and frightened little man like Albert?' she said. She swayed slightly on her feet, and her eyes closed, and I saw the tears squeeze out from under the lashes.

I put my arms around her shoulders and patted her softly on the back. Her forehead was pressed against my chest; I could feel the thickness of her hair against my cheek, the thin and fragile quality of her body inside my arms, the brush of her stomach against my loins. On the neighbor's lawn the iron head of a broken garden sprinkler was rearing erratically with the hose's pressure and dripping water into the grass.

I took the door key from her fingers. It felt stiff and hard in my hand.

'I have to go back home now, Lucinda,' I said. 'Where can we get hold of Zoot?'

Then I turned and saw the car parked at the curb, a two-door white Toyota. The car of Sister Marie Guilbeaux, whose small hands were as white as porcelain and resting patiently on the steering wheel. In the passenger seat sat Bootsie, her face disbelieving, stunned, hurt in a way that no one can mask, as though all the certainties in her life had proved to be as transitory as a photographic negative from one's youth dissolving on top of a hot coal.

22

Bootsie looked straight ahead as we followed I-10 past the sand flats and dead cypress on the northern tip of Lake Pontchartrain. My mind was racing. None of the day's events seemed to have any coherence.

'I left Motley's and Lucinda's extensions on the answering machine, I left the address of the motel. I didn't imagine it,' I said.

'It wasn't there, Dave.'

'Was there a power failure?'

'How would I know if I wasn't home? It wouldn't have affected the recording, anyway.'

'There's something wrong here, Boots.'

'You're right. Sometimes you worry about other people more than you do your own family.'

'That's a rotten thing to say.'

'Goddamn it, he called while you were out of town looking after this Bergeron woman.'

'Buchalter?'

'Who else?'

'How could he? We just changed the number.'

'It was Buchalter. Do you think I could forget that voice? He even talked about what he did to me.'

I turned and looked at her. Her eyes were shiny in the green glow from the dashboard. A semi passed, and the inside of the pickup was loud with the roar of the exhaust.

'What else did he say?'

'That he'd always be with us. Wherever we were. His voice sounded like he had wet sand in his throat. It was obscene.'

'I think he's a hype. He calls when he's loaded.'

'Why does this woman have to drag you into her investigation?'

'It's my investigation, too, Bootsie. But you're right, I shouldn't have gone. We were firing in the well.'

'I just don't understand this commitment you have to others while a psychopath tries to destroy us.'

'Look, something's out of sync here. Don't you see it? How did the nun, what's her name, get involved in this?'

'She dropped by, that's all.'

'Then what happened?'

'Nothing. What do you mean?'

'Come on, think about it. What *happened* after she came by?'

'She used the phone. To call somebody at the hospital, I think.'

'When did Buchalter call?'

'A little later. I tried to get you at your office. That's when the sheriff told me there'd been a shooting. I couldn't just stay at home and wonder what happened to you and wait for Buchalter to call again. Marie and I took Alafair to Batist's, then drove to New Orleans. What else was I supposed to do?'

'Whose idea was it to go to New Orleans?'

'Mine . . . Both of us, I guess . . . She saw my anxiety, she was trying to be a friend.'

'How many nuns do you know who gravitate toward trouble, who are always around when it happens?' I said.

She was looking at me now.

'Did you check the machine when you first came in the house?' I asked.

'No.'

'Our new number is written down by the side of the phone, isn't it?'

'Yes.'

'It's time to check out Sister Guilbeaux, Boots.'

'You think she erased your message and called Buc – That's crazy, Dave. She's a good person.'

'Buchalter's flesh and blood. I think somebody close to us is helping him. How many candidates are there?'

Her eyes became fixed on the tunnel of trees ahead. I could see her chest rising and falling as she touched her fingers to her mouth.

The next morning, in my office, I sorted through all the case notes, crime scene photographs, autopsy reports, computer printouts, voice cassettes, rap sheets, convict prison records, and Xeroxes and faxes from other law-enforcement agencies that had anything to do with the vigilante killings, Tommy Lonighan, the Calucci brothers, and Will Buchalter and his followers.

I also called the office of the Catholic diocese in Lafayette. Both the bishop and his assistant were out. The secretary said one of them would return my call later. She was new to the job and was not sure if she knew a Sister Marie Guilbeaux.

I read every document on my desk twice. The more I read, the more ill-defined and confusing the case became.

Clete Purcel had always been a good cop because he kept the lines simple. I took a yellow legal pad and a felt pen from my desk drawer and tried to do the same. It wasn't easy.

The owner of the car repair shop where Zoot and I had been taken by Buchalter had turned out to be an alcoholic right-wing simpleton who had already fled the state on a bigamy charge. It seemed that anyone who might lead us to Buchalter had a way of disappearing or going off-planet.

Tommy Bobalouba's mother had emigrated from Germany and perhaps had been a member of the Silver Shirts. Tommy wanted to salvage the Nazi U-boat before Hippo Bimstine got to it, and his rhetoric was often anti-Semitic. But in reality Tommy had never had any ideology except making money. He prided himself on his military record and blue-collar patriotism, and didn't seem to have any physical connection with Buchalter.

Why did Buchalter (if indeed it was Buchalter) attempt to ascribe the murder of his followers, the men called Freddy and Hatch, to the vigilante?

Was he involved with the ritualistic killings of black dope dealers in the projects? If not, how many psychological mutants of his potential did New Orleans contain?

Why had Lonighan crossed an old New Orleans ethnic line and gotten mixed up with the Calucci brothers, and did it have anything to do with the vigilante killings?

If you have ever been in psychoanalysis or analytically oriented therapy, you're aware that the exploration of one's own unconscious can be an intriguing pursuit. It is also self-inflating, grandiose, and endless, and often has the same practical value as meditating upon one's genitalia.

The inductive and deductive processes of police work offer the same temptation. You can drown in it. The truth is that most people, with the exception of the psychotic, commit crimes for predictable reasons.

Question: Why steal?

Answer: It's usually easier than working.

Question: Why rape and brutalize? Why rob people of their identity by terrorizing and degrading them at gunpoint, by reducing them to pitiful creatures who will never respect themselves again?

Answer: You don't have to admit that you're a born loser and in all probability were despised inside your mother's womb.

Batist's perception, like Clete's, was not obscured by self-manufactured complexities. He had grown up in Louisiana during the pre-Civil Rights era, and he knew that no one systematically killed people of color for reasons of justice. The vigilante's victims were people whom no one cared about, nickel-and-dime dealers whose presence or absence would never have any appreciable influence on the immense volume of the New Orleans drug trade.

The vigilante, like the plainclothes detective in the motel who was determined to emotionally twist and break Albert on the rack, was selective about his sacrificial offerings, and his purpose had nothing to do with ending the problem they were associated with.

But the preacher had said something on the dirt road by my house that would not go away, that hung on the edge of my consciousness like an impacted tooth that throbs dully in your sleep.

What if, instead of a particular crime, we were dealing with people, or forces, who wished to engineer a situation that would allow political criminality, despotism masked as law and order, to become a way of life?

Was it that hard to envision? The elements to pull it off seemed readily at hand.

Financial insecurity. Lack of faith in traditional government and institutions. Fear and suspicion of minorities, irritability and guilt at the visibility of the homeless and the mentally ill who wandered the streets of every city in the nation, the brooding, angry sense that things were pulling apart at the center, that armed and sadistic gangs could hunt down, rape, brutally beat, and kill the innocent at will. Or, more easily put, the general feeling that it was time to create examples, to wink at the Constitution, and perhaps once again to decorate the streetlamps and trees with strange fruit.

Hitler had to set fire to the Reichstag and place the blame on a Communist student in order to gain power.

The sight of Los Angeles burning, of motorists being torn apart with tire irons on live television, might serve just as well.

I was out of the office three hours that afternoon on a shooting in a black juke joint south of town. The wounded man, who was shot in the thumb, refused to identify the shooter, walked out of the emergency room at Iberia General without being treated, then drove out in the parish with a kerosene-soaked rag wrapped around his hand and tried to run down his common-law wife's brother in the middle of a sugarcane field. The brother refused to press charges. Bottom line: big waste of time.

It rained that afternoon, then the sun came out again and the air was bright and cool and the palm and oak trees along the street had a green-gold cast to them. Just as I was signing out of the office at five, Wally, the dispatcher, whose great bulk made his breath wheeze even when he was seated, looked up from a message that he was writing on a piece of memo paper.

'Oh hi, Dave. I didn't know you were still here,' he said. 'The monsignor called from the bishop's office in Lafayette. His message was—' He squinted at his own handwriting. 'Yes, he knows Sister Guilbeaux and he wants to know is she in any kind of trouble.'

'Did he say anything else?'

'No, not really. He seemed to wonder why the sheriff's office is interested in a nun. What's going on? A big bingo raid coming down?' His round face beamed at his own humor.

'You're up at the hospital sometimes. Did you ever see a nun there with reddish gold hair, about thirty or thirty-five years old?'

'I don't place her. What's the deal, the nuns been rapping the patients on the knuckles?' He smiled again.

'How about giving it a break, Wally?'

Then Wally raised himself from his chair, just far enough to stick his head out the dispatcher's window and look both ways down the hall. His face was ruddy from hypertension, and his shirt pocket bulged with fat, cellophane-wrapped cigars.

'Can I tell you something serious, Dave?' he said. 'All that stuff going on over in New Orleans, leave it alone. It's blacks killing blacks. Ain't we got enough problems here? Let them people clean up their own shit.'

'Thanks for taking the message, Wally.'

'Hey, don't walk out of here mad. People round here care about you, Dave. This Nazi guy been causing all this grief, he gets caught in the right situation, it's gonna get squared, you'd better believe it, yeah. You ain't got no doubt about what I mean, either, podna.'

He peeled the cellophane off a cigar, rolled it wetly in the center of his mouth, and scratched a kitchen match across the bottom of his desk drawer.

That night I couldn't sleep. At one-thirty in the morning I heard the *tink* of a tin can on the baling wire I had strung around the house. I took the AR-15 with the thirty-round magazine from the top of the closet, slid a shell into the chamber, and walked outside with it. It was windy in the trees, and the sky was full of moonlight. There was nobody in the yard or down by the bait shop. Tripod had gotten out of his hutch and was digging in an armadillo's hole by the tractor shed. I picked him up in my arms, refilled his food and water bowls, and put him back inside his hutch. Then I sat down on an upended bucket, under the darkness of an oak tree, the AR-15 propped against the trunk, and waited ten minutes to make sure that the noise I had heard earlier had been caused by Tripod.

The moonlight was the color of pewter on the dead cypress in the marsh. My neighbor had been burning the sugarcane stubble in the field behind my house, and the air was hazy with smoke and dense with a smell like burnt cinnamon. In the quietness of the moment, in the wind that blew through the leaves overhead, in the ruffling of the moonlight on the bayou's surface, and in the perfect black silhouette of my cypress and oak house against the handkerchiefs of flame that twisted and flickered out of the scorched dirt in my neighbor's field, I felt almost as if I had stepped into a discarded film negative from my childhood, in another time, another era.

In the wind I thought I could hear the fiddle and accordion music and the words to '*La Jolie Blonde.*' For some reason I remembered a scene clipped out of the year 1945. It was V-J Day, and my parents had taken me with them to a blue-collar bar with a colonnade and a high sidewalk in front and big, green-painted, collapsible shutters that folded flush with the walls. My mother wore a plum-colored pillbox hat with a white veil pinned up on top, and a purple sundress printed with green and red flowers. My father, Aldous, had just been paid, and he was buying beers for the bar and dancing with my mother, while the jukebox played:

Jolie blonde, gardez donc c'est t'as fait.
Ta m'as quit-té pour t'en aller,
Pour t'en aller avec un autre que moi.

The doors on the bar were all open to let in the cool air after the rain, and the evening shadows and the sun's afterglow had the soft purple-and-gold tone of sugarcane right before the harvest. The streets were filled with people,

184

some of them in uniform, some of them a little drunk, all of them happy because the lights were about to go on again all over the world.

Then my mother picked me up and balanced me on her hip while my father grinned and set his battered fedora on my head. My mother smelled like milk and bath powder, like the mint leaves and bourbon-scented cherries from the bottom of her whiskey glass. It was a happy time, one that I was sure would never end.

But both my parents were dead and so was the world in which I had grown up.

Then another image floated behind my eyes, a fearful and perhaps solipsistic projection of what it might be like if the Will Buchalters of the world were ever allowed to have their way. In my mind's eye I saw a city like New Orleans at nighttime, an avenue like St Charles, except, as in the paintings of Bavarian villages by Adolf Hitler, there were no people. The sky was a black ink wash, the moss-hung oaks along the sidewalks as motionless as stone; the houses had become prisons that radiated fear, and the empty streets were lighted with the obscene hues of sodium lamps that allowed no shadows or places to hide. It was a place where the glands had replaced the heart and the booted and head-shaved lout had been made caretaker of the sun.

The next morning I called the bishop's office again. This time I was told the bishop had gone to Washington and the monsignor was in Opelousas and would not be back until that afternoon. I left my number.

At noon I got a phone call from Tommy Bobalouba.

'I'll treat you to some étouffée,' he said.

'I'm working right now.'

'I drove all the way over here to talk. How about getting your nose out of the air for a little while?'

'The last time you were over here, you set me up as your alibi while somebody tried to clip Nate Baxter.'

'So you lost money? It don't mean I don't respect you.'

'What do you want?'

'I want to *talk*. I got a heavy fucking problem, man. It's something I can't talk to nobody else about. You don't got thirty minutes, then fuck you, Dave.'

'Where are you?' I said.

I drove up to the seafood restaurant on the back road to St Martinville and found him inside, seated on a tall stool at the bar, eating raw oysters from a tray. He had covered each oyster with Tabasco sauce, and sweat was trickling out of his meringue hair. I recognized three of his crew at one of the tables, dour-faced Irish hoods with the mental capabilities of curb buttons, who had always run saloons or upstairs crap games for Tommy or shut down the competition when it tried to establish itself in areas Tommy had staked out for himself.

But Tommy had never used bodyguards and, always desirous of social acceptance by New Orleans's upper classes, did not associate openly with his employees.

'What are you looking at?' he said.

'Your crew seem to be enjoying their meal,' I said.

'I can't bring my boys to your town for a lunch?'

'What's up, partner?'

'I got some personal trouble.' He wiped his mouth with his hand and looked at it.

I waited.

He looked around, closed and opened his eyes, his face flexing like rubber, then stared disjointedly out into space. Then he tried to smile, all in seconds.

'Hey, Dave, you went to Catholic school, you boxed in Golden Gloves,' he said. 'You ever have a mick priest for a coach, guy who'd have all the fighters say a Hail Mary in the dressing room, then tell them to get out there and nail the other guys in the mush?'

'It sounds familiar, Tommy.'

'It was good coming up like that, wasn't it? Them was good days back then.'

'They weren't bad. Are you going to tell me what's on your mind?'

'I tried to get out of this prostate operation. The doc said it might leave me wearing a diaper. So we tried other stuff. Three days ago the doc tells me it's spread. Like a big worm eating its way through my insides. I ain't got to worry about an operation anymore. You understand what I'm saying? It's a funny feeling. It's like you're looking at a clock somebody just snapped the hands off.'

Then I saw it in his face, the grayness and the pinched quality around the mouth, the remoteness in the eyes, the knowledge that he had entered a piece of psychological moonscape on which there was no traveling companion.

'I'm sorry, Tommy,' I said.

He used a folded paper napkin to blot the perspiration around his hairline. He glanced through the big plate glass window at the back of the restaurant. Outside was a small, dark lake, and dead leaves were falling into the water.

'You still go to Mass?' he said.

'Yes.'

'I mean, for real, not just to make your old lady happy or something like that?'

'What can I do for you?'

'Look, if a guy maybe knows about something, maybe about even some people being clipped, people maybe even that's got it coming, but he don't do it himself, like it's out of his hands, you know what I mean, then it ain't on his soul, right?'

I tried to assimilate what he had said, but that was like trying to make ethical or theological sense out of Sanskrit read backwards.

'You want to float that one by me again?' I said.

'Look, I took out one guy in my life, I mean besides Korea. That was the guy I did with the fire hose. This guy was such a bum even the judge said he ought to be dug up again and electrocuted. I don't go around killing people,

Dave. But what if I knew what was going on, maybe like there was other people doing it, and I figure it's their choice, I don't make people do what they got to do, I just hold on to my ass and walk through the smoke, it's a rough fucking town to keep a piece of, the hair ends up on the wallpaper, that's the way it shakes out sometimes, right?'

'I'm a police officer, Tommy. Maybe you'd better give some thought to what you're telling me.'

'I'm standing on third base here. You gonna come to the bone yard to arrest me? What if I made a contribution to the church? Maybe you know a priest don't go through everything with a garden rake. It ain't easy for me to figure all this stuff out, talk about it with people I don't know. I get a headache.'

His knuckles and eyebrows were half-mooned with scar tissue; his blue eyes had a bright sheen like silk. What do you say to an uneducated, confused, superstitious, angry man, with a frightened child inside him, as he tries to plea-bargain his sins and cop to a fine before he catches the bus?

'I can introduce you to a priest, a friend of mine,' I said. 'Just tell him what you told me. I wouldn't get into the area of contributions at that point, though.'

'What? It sound like bribery?'

'You might say that.'

'Oh.'

'Tommy, do you know something about the vigilante killings? Is that what we're talking about here?'

He wiped at the tip of his nose with one knuckle.

'If that's the case, why not come clean on it, get it out of the way?' I said.

His eyes bulged, and he poked me in the chest with his stiffened finger.

'Hey, I don't dime, I don't rat-fuck, you saying I do, Dave, you and me are about to remodel this place.'

'Adios,' I said.

'Hey, don't be like that,' he said, and grabbed my coat. Then he released it and smoothed the cloth with his hand. 'I'm sorry, I got a Coke bottle up my butt. I don't know how to act sometimes. Look, me and the Calucci brothers are quits. They welsh, they lie, they got no class, they'll blindside you and take you off at the neck. You do business with shit bags and greaseballs, you invite a load of grief into your life.

'I can't change what's already happened, I mean, maybe some stuff I'm part responsible for, but maybe I can make up for it a little bit. Your buddy Purcel . . . Hey, I got your attention.'

'What about him?'

'He filled up Max and Bobo's Caddy with cement while about a hundred people were laughing and clapping and grabbing themselves. Even the cops were making jokes about it over their radios.'

'What are you saying, partner?'

'You know how many guys in New Orleans would like to take Purcel down? How many guys he's sent up the road or run through glass windows or stuck their heads in toilet bowls? It's an open contract, fifteen large, Dave, he's anybody's fuck. That ain't all, either. There's a ten large bonus if it's in pieces. You know, with Polaroids or a videocassette.'

He squeezed a lemon slice on an oyster, then lifted the shell and sucked the muscle into his mouth. But instead of swallowing it, he lowered his head, emptied his mouth into a napkin.

'I can't eat no more. I feel sick,' he said. His eyes wandered to the table where the three men from his crew were eating.

'Maybe in New Orleans you're lucky if you get to die from cancer these days,' he said.

'Is there a contract on you, too, Tommy?'

'You're a lot like Purcel. You think the Caluccis are clowns because you busted them up with a shovel and they didn't try to do anything about it. I got news for you, Dave. These guys eat their pain and wait. One time a button guy from the Cardo family was porking Bobo's broad. They waited three years, till everything was forgotten, till the broad had disappeared, till Bobo had a half dozen other bimbos hanging around him, then they asked the button guy out on their boat. They wined and dined him, made fun about the broad, like they were all great buddies and she was just some pork chops they passed around, then they held a gun to the guy's head and made him cut off his own cock.'

He ran his hand through his hair, wiped the perspiration on his shirt, blew out his breath, and ordered a double Scotch straight up. The corners of his mouth looked as gray as fish scale.

By five that afternoon I still had not heard back from the monsignor in Lafayette. Before signing out of the office, I called again.

'His mother's been quite ill. Can he call you at home, Detective Robicheaux? I know he'll want to,' the secretary said.

'Yes, I'd appreciate it if he would,' I said, and gave her our number.

Bootsie and I had planned to go to a seven o'clock A.A. step meeting in town, and I had told her not to prepare supper. On the way home I picked up some po'-boy sandwiches and dirty rice at a take-out place by City Park. As I drove down the dirt road along the bayou, smoke was drifting across the sun from a scorched sugarcane field, and the air smelled like burning leaves and late-blooming flowers. It was raining in the south, and you could see a gray squall line, splintered with lightning, moving inland from the gulf. The wind was already up, straightening the moss in the cypress trees out in the marsh, and most of the fishermen who had been out for saca-lait had turned their boats toward the dock.

The deputy who still guarded the house during the day waved at me and headed for town. I parked in the drive and went inside with the paper sack of po'-boys and dirty rice. The windows were all open, and the curtains were billowing with wind.

'Who's home?' I said.

But the house was quiet. I walked into the kitchen and set the sack of sandwiches on the table. Then I saw the empty sherry bottle and three beer cans half buried in a tangle of wet newspapers and coffee grounds in the plastic trash container. I rubbed my hand in my face, then opened the icebox to get a Dr Pepper, changed my mind for no reason, and slammed the door, rattling everything inside.

The phone rang on the counter.

'Detective Robicheaux?'

'Yes.'

'This is Monsignor DeBlanc. I'm sorry I didn't get back to you earlier. You called about Sister Marie?'

'Yes, Marie Guilbeaux.'

'Right. Is something wrong?'

'I'm not sure, really. I'm working a strange case now . . . Sister Guilbeaux keeps showing up around here at odd times.'

'I'm sorry, I'm confused. What do you mean "showing up"?'

'Just *that*. She seems to take an inordinate interest in things that aren't her affair.'

'You mean she's been in New Iberia recently?'

'Yes.'

'I don't understand. Marie went back home to Napoleonville three months ago. She's had some severe problems with her health.'

I paused a moment. 'What does this lady look like, Monsignor?'

'Good for her age, I guess, but, well, time has its way with all of us.'

'Her age?'

'She's almost seventy years old. How old do you think she is?'

After I hung up I sat at the kitchen table and stared out the back screen at the orange wafer of sun descending into the smoke from the smoldering cane stubble. Why hadn't I seen it? She had been outside the intensive care unit when Clete and I had interviewed Charles Arthur Sitwell, who later was launched into the next world with an injection of water and roach paste. Even Alafair had felt there was something wrong about her, that she was a harbinger of trouble and discord.

I looked again at the empty sherry bottle and cans in the trash. When the bedroom door opened in the hallway I didn't even bother to turn around. There was no point in trying to go to a step meeting tonight. Bootsie's fears and anxieties had obviously sent her into a relapse; maybe tomorrow we'd give it another try. Or maybe I simply had to let go of her for a while, turn her over to my Higher Power, and let her bottom out. How could I demand more of her than had ever been demanded of me? But regardless of what I chose to do, anger would serve no purpose, and would only reinforce her determination to stay drunk.

I smelled the alcohol and the odor of cigarettes even before I felt the warm breath against my cheek, the touch of fingernails in my hair and on my scalp, the soft caress of a woman's breasts against the back of my neck. Then I felt the mouth and tongue in my ear, the tapered hand that slid down my chest toward my loins, and I turned and looked up into the face of the woman who called herself Marie Guilbeaux.

23

'Tough day when they take the scales from your eyes?' she said. Her hand reached out to touch my hair. I pushed it away.

'Where are Bootsie and Alafair?' I said.

'The wifey's passed out. Doesn't she send your daughter off with the black man when she decides to go on the grog?'

I walked into the hall and opened the bedroom door. Bootsie was asleep, half undressed, on top of the sheets, her face twisted into the pillow. The curtains popped in the silence.

The woman who called herself Marie Guilbeaux stood in the center of the kitchen, putting lipstick on in front of her compact mirror. She wore sun-faded jeans, sandals, a beige terry-cloth pullover with a dipping neckline, and a gold chain with a pearl around her throat.

'Did you know the little wife has something of a pill problem?' she said, her eyes still fastened on the mirror.

'Who are you?'

She crimped her lips together in the mirror and clicked the compact closed.

'Want to find out?' she said. She smiled. Her eyes seemed to darken, like charcoal-colored smoke gathering inside green glass. She unsnapped the top of her jeans, exposing the pink edge of her panties, then reached behind her back and unhooked her bra. 'Sit down in the chair, Dave. It's time someone does something nice for you.'

I dumped her purse on the breakfast table. In it were car keys, an empty aspirin tin, a roll of breath mints, a perfume spray bottle, and a doeskin wallet. In the wallet was over six hundred dollars, and a Social Security card and driver's license with the name Marie Guilbeaux on them. The address on the license was in uptown New Orleans, back toward the levee. There were no credit cards.

'Do you like everything to be so hard?' she said, and moved her tongue in a circle inside her lips.

She worked her bra out from under her pullover and laid it over the chair top, then clasped her hands around the back of my neck and pressed her stomach against me. 'I have a feeling the wifey hasn't been treating you right,' she said.

190

'Where's your automobile?'

'Down by the dock.'

'Is anyone with you?'

'No.' She flexed her loins against me.

'I'll tell the wrecker service not to scratch it up,' I said, turning her in a half circle.

'What?'

'The guy we contract to haul cars into the pound is careless sometimes.' I pulled her forearms behind her. Her wrists were narrow and pale, and the undersides were lined with thin green veins. I snipped the handcuffs on each wrist, then stuffed her bra in the back pocket of her jeans.

'The offer's still open. With handcuffs. Think about it, Dave. Ouu,' she said, and made a pout with her mouth. 'You might even like it better than climbing on top of a drunk sow.'

'Try it on our jailer, Marie,' I said. 'He's a three-hundred-pound black homosexual. Maybe you can turn him around.'

The next morning at the department I picked up a cup of coffee and a doughnut by the dispatcher's cage and called Clete at his office in the Quarter. The sun was shining, and there was dew on the grass and trees outside my window. I had called him twice the day before and hadn't gotten an answer.

'The tape on my machine's screwed up. What's happening?' he said.

I told him about my conversation in the restaurant with Tommy Lonighan.

'You sound mad,' he said.

'I am.'

'What's the big deal?'

'I warned you about provoking these guys.'

'Look, Dave, what's "open hit" actually mean? Nothing. It's something these greasebags like to mouth off about while they're stuffing linguine in their faces. A real whack is when they bring in a mechanic, a mainline button man, a full-time sociopath, from Miami or Houston, and this guy *knows* he either leaves meat on the sidewalk or he's the next guy for the cooling board.'

'Clete—'

'Drop it, mon. Max and Bobo are always blowing gas. It's time they both get their snouts stuck in the commode.'

'I just don't believe you. Why don't you go stand in the middle of the streetcar tracks?'

'Okay, big mon, you've warned me. Listen, has Motley called you yet?'

'No.'

'Dig this. Ole Mots stopped thinking about food and cooze and being black long enough to do some real detective work.'

'I think Motley's turned out to be a good guy.'

'That's what I was saying. Is there static on the line or something? Yesterday afternoon he got some chest waders from the fire department, and he and I splashed out into that swamp in Lafourche Parish. It took a while, but we found it.'

'Found what?'

'The armored vest. The guy who cut open the two lowlifes with the chain saw, we found where he got out of the water on a levee not far from Larose. There were depressions in the mud that Sasquatch could have left. Anyway, about two hundred yards back into the swamp he'd dumped the vest by a sandbar. There were a half-dozen pieces of buckshot in the plates.'

'Why would he be wearing a vest?'

He laughed, then took the receiver away from his mouth and laughed again.

'You want to let me in on it?' I asked.

'You're beautiful, Streak. There's a secret that everybody seems to know except my old podjo from the First. You're one of the most violent people I've ever known. Why do you think Buchalter would wear a vest? You've probably got him spotting his Jockeys.'

'Thanks for going out there, Clete.'

'Hold on a minute. There's something else. Maybe it's important, maybe not. There was some stenciling on the cloth. The vest was Toronto PD issue.'

'It's Canadian?'

'Maybe he got it at a surplus store. But it's a thread, right? Anyway, talk with Motley.'

'You remember the nun we saw at the hospital?'

'Yes, she need somebody to pound erasers for her?'

'Not unless you want to visit her in the parish jail.'

Then I told him about all the events involving the woman who called herself Marie Guilbeaux.

'Definitely a weird scam, mon,' he said.

'I'll bet she and Buchalter have their umbilical cords tied together.'

'What are you holding her on?'

'Not much.'

'Don't let them kick her. Give me the address that's on her driver's license.'

I read it to him off the arrest report.

'Salt the shaft if you have to. You know why everybody loves straight shooters? Because they usually lose,' he said.

'See you later, Cletus,' I said, and hung up the phone just as the sheriff tapped on my glass and motioned me toward his office at the other end of the hallway.

He drank from his bottle of ulcer medicine, then leaned back in his swivel chair, bouncing the heels of his hands on the padded arms, and gazed at the potted plants and hand-painted flowered tea-pot on his windowsill. His stomach wedged over his hand-tooled gunbelt like a partly deflated football. He poked at it with his stiffened fingers.

'You never had ulcers, did you?' he said.

'No.'

'I think I'm getting another one. I eat grits and baby food and get up in the morning with barbed wire in my stomach. Why's that?'

'You got me.'

'What are we supposed to do with that gal you locked up last night?'

'We try to keep her there till we find out who she is.'

'She's got no arrest record. Also the charge you've got against her is a joke.'

'Not to me it isn't.'

'At arraignment, what do we tell the judge?'

'The truth.'

'How's this sound? "Your Honor, this lady represented herself as a Catholic nun in order to get the wife of Detective Robicheaux drunk. Because everybody knows that's what nuns do in their spare time."'

I opened and closed my right hand on my thigh. I fixed my gaze on a place about three inches to the side of his face.

'I apologize, I shouldn't have said that,' he said. 'But at best all we've got is a misdemeanor.'

'I think she murdered Charles Sitwell in the hospital.'

'Put her there, in the hospital, in the room, in her nun's veil, around the time of death and we have something. Look, the driver's license and Social Security card are real. She says she never told you or your wife or anybody else she was a nun.'

'You talked to her?'

'I went to the jail early this morning. The jailer's got her in isolation. A couple of the dykes were getting stoked up.'

'They like her?'

'Are you kidding? They were scared shitless. One of them claims your gal threatened to put out a cigarette in her eye.'

'Look, Sheriff, there's no easier ID to get than a driver's license and Social Security. But she had no credit cards. That's because credit bureaus run a check on the applicants. She's dirty, I think she's mixed up with Buchalter, and if we let her walk, we lose the only thread we have.'

'I admit, she puts on quite a performance. If I didn't know better, I'd probably let her baby-sit my grandchildren.'

'What explanation did she give you for being in my house?'

'She says she used to be a part-time librarian and now she's trying to become a freelance magazine writer. According to her, she met Bootsie in a lounge and befriended her because she thought she was a sad lady. She's pretty eloquent, Dave.'

He looked at my face and glanced away.

'Librarian where?' I said.

'She got a little vague.'

'I bet.'

He propped his elbow on the desk blotter and scratched at the hollow of his cheek with a pink fingernail.

'She's got a lawyer from Lafayette. He's already raising hell down at the prosecutor's office,' he said.

'You want to talk to Clete Purcel? He saw her outside Sitwell's hospital room.'

'Great witness, Dave. Purcel's got a rap sheet that few mainline cons have. It looks like something a computer virus printed by mistake.'

'I think he was right.'

'About what?'

'He told me to salt the shaft. He knew how it was going to go down.'

The sheriff stuck his pipe in his leather tobacco pouch and began filling the bowl. He didn't look up.

'I didn't hear you say that,' he said.

'It's one man's point of view.'

He didn't answer. I got up to leave the room.

'The Americans won the Revolution because they learned to fight from the Indians,' he said. 'They shot from behind the trees. I guess it sure beat marching across a field in white bandoliers and silver breastplates.'

'I was never fond of allegory.'

'All I said was I didn't hear Purcel's remark. The woman's purse is in Possessions. Who knows what the lab might find?' He raised his eyebrows.

'We've got to hold her as a murder suspect, Sheriff.'

'It's not going to happen, Dave. You going to the arraignment?'

'You'd better believe it.'

He nodded silently, lit his pipe, and looked out the window.

Back inside my office, I looked again at all the paperwork concerning Will Buchalter. What were the common denominators? What had I missed?

Buchalter was perverse and sadistic and possibly an addict.

He was obviously a psychopath.

His followers were recidivists.

He appeared to be con-wise, talked about 'riding the beef,' but had no criminal record that we could find.

Was he a sodomist, was he depraved, were his followers all addicts? Were they men whom he had turned out (raped) and reduced to a form of psychological slavery? Why not? It went on in every prison in the country.

Except Buchalter had never been up the road.

Maybe Clete had come up with the answer. Maybe we had been looking for Buchalter on the wrong side of the equation. Maybe he was a fireman who set fires. Maybe he was one of us.

I talked with Ben Motley at NOPD. The prints lifted from the armored vest that he and Clete had found in the marsh matched those that Buchalter had left all over my house. But there was no serial number on the fabric.

'I wouldn't spend too much time on it,' he said. 'These paramilitary groups come up with shitloads of this stuff. You know what's still the best way to nail this guy? Find one of his lowlifes, then plug his pud into a light socket.'

Thanks, Mots, I thought.

Then I put in a call to the robbery division of the Toronto Police Department and talked with a lieutenant named Rankin. No, he knew nothing about a stolen armored vest. No, he had no knowledge whether or not the department might have sold off some of its vests; no, he had never heard of a Will Buchalter and, after leaving me on hold for five minutes, he said their computer had no record of a Will Buchalter.

'This man's a Nazi?' he said.

'Among other things.'

'What do you mean?'

'He likes to torture people.'

He cleared his throat.

'About eight or nine years ago I remember a case . . . no, it wasn't a case, really, it was a bad series of events that happened with a detective named Mervain. We had a recruit who bothered Mervain for some reason. He couldn't get this fellow out of his mind. It seems like the fellow was suspected of stealing some guns from us, who knows, maybe it was some vests, too.'

'What was the recruit's name?'

'I'm sorry, I don't remember everything that happened and I don't want to say the wrong thing and mislead you. Let me check with a couple of other people here and call you back.'

'I'd appreciate it very much, sir.'

Arraignment for the nun impersonator was at 11:00 a.m., and my best throw of the dice kept coming back boxcars, deuces, and treys. Clete called collect from a pay phone in Metairie.

'Dead end,' he said. 'Her address is in an apartment building that a wrecking ball went through six months ago.'

'Did you ask around the neighborhood about her?'

'I'm in a phone booth in front of a liquor store that has bullet holes in the windows. There's garbage all over the sidewalk. As I speak I'm looking at a collection of pukes who are looking back at me like I'm an albino ape. Guess what color these pukes are? Guess what color the whole neighborhood is?'

Judge Robert Dautrieve presided over morning court, that strange, ritualistic theater that features morose and repentant drunks who reek of jailhouse funk, welfare cheats, deranged drifters, game poachers, and wife abusers whose frightened wives, with blackened eyes, dragging strings of children, plead for their husbands' release. Almost all of them are on a first-name basis with the bailiffs, jail escorts, bondsmen, prosecutors, and court-assigned attorneys and social workers, who will remain the most important people they'll ever meet. And no matter what occurs on a particular day in morning court, almost all of them will be back.

Judge Dautrieve had silver hair and the profile of a Roman legionnaire. During World War II he had been a recipient of the Congressional Medal of Honor for his valor at Sword Beach, and he had also been a Democratic candidate for governor who had lost miserably, largely due to the fact that he was an honorable man.

The woman who called herself Marie Guilbeaux filed into court on the long wrist chain with the other defendants from the parish jail. Her clothes were rumpled and her face white and puffy from lack of sleep. On the back of her beige pullover was a damp, brown stain, as though she had leaned against a wall where someone had spit tobacco juice. When the jail escort unlocked her wrist from the chain, she straightened her shoulders, tilted her chin up, and brushed her reddish gold hair back over her forehead with her fingers. Her face became a study in composure and serenity, as if it had been transformed inside a movie camera's lens.

I sat three feet behind her, staring at the back of her neck. She turned slowly, as though she could feel my eyes on her skin.

'Tell Buchalter we've got his vest,' I said.

But she looked past me toward the rear of the courtroom, as though she had never visited one before, her gaze innocuous, bemused, perhaps a bit fearful of her plight. To any outside observer, it was obvious that this lady did not belong on a wrist chain, or in a jail, or in a morning court that processed miscreants whose ongoing culpability and failure were as visible on their persons as sackcloth and ashes.

Her lawyer had once been with the U.S. Justice Department. He now represented drug dealers and a PCB incinerator group. His bald head was razor-shaved and waxed, and he had humps of muscle in his shoulders and upper arms like a professional wrestler. His collar and tie always rode high up on his thick neck, which gave him a Humpty-Dumpty appearance.

'Tell Buchalter his prints were all over the vest,' I said to the nun impersonator's back. 'That means he's going down on premeditated double homicide. Nasty stuff, Marie. Lethal injection, the big sleep, that kind of thing.'

She looked straight ahead, her face cool, almost regal, but her lawyer, who was talking to another man at the defense table, glanced up, then walked over to where I sat, his eyes locked on mine.

'What is it that makes you think legal procedure has no application to you?' he said. His body seemed to exude physical power and the clean athletic-club smells of deodorant and aftershave lotion.

'I was just asking your client to pass on a message to one of her associates,' I said. 'He cut open two guys with a chain saw. These were his friends. He's quite a guy.'

'You're harassing this woman, Detective. You're not going to get away with it, either.'

'It's always reassuring to know you're on the other side, Counselor.'

'You, sir, belong in a cage,' he said.

For thirty minutes I watched the judge go through the process of trying to heal cancer with Mercurochrome, his face sometimes paling, his eyes glazing over when a stressed-out defendant would launch into an incoherent soliloquy intended to turn his role into that of victim.

I went out for a drink of water, then took a seat not far from the prosecutor's table. Five minutes before the nun impersonator had to enter her plea, the prosecutor looked at me impatiently, then gathered up a file folder and walked back to where I sat. He was a rail of a man, with a tic in his gray face, who made his daily nest in the high-tension wires. He kept tapping the file folder on my knee.

'This isn't shit. What the hell have y'all been doing?' he said.

'Her address is phony. Does that help?'

'It's shit and you know it. You guys spend your time fucking your fist, then blame us when they walk.'

'How about kicking it down a couple of notches, Newt?'

'You want my job? You tell us we've got the bride of Dracula in the parish jail, but I'm supposed to walk in here with nothing but my dork in my hand. Dautrieve's not in the mood for it, believe me.'

'She had an empty aspirin tin in her purse. I sent it to the lab this morning. Maybe there's a residue that indicates she was in possession.'

'An empty aspirin container? That's the kind of evidence I'm supposed to work with here? Do you live in a plastic bubble?'

'She's hooked up with Nazis. I'd bet my butt on it, Newt.'

'I've got news for you. You are. She's talking about suit. She said you tried to get in her bread when you busted her. That was a smart touch, sticking her bra in her back pocket, Dave. She's also talking about deprivation of civil rights, slander, and sexual assault while in the bag. How's that sound? And in two minutes I get to stand up in front of the court and get buggered by that greasy shit hog she hired. Y'all really fill out my day.'

'Don't let her get out of here, partner.'

'Break my chops.'

Judge Dautrieve was fixing his glasses on his nose and trying to keep the ennui out of his face by the time the woman who called herself Marie Guilbeaux stood before him, her lawyer by her side. He listened attentively to the prosecutor, one finger propped against a silver eyebrow. Then his eyes went from the prosecutor to me and back to the woman.

'This isn't April Fools' Day, is it, gentlemen?' he said.

'Your Honor, we believe this lady to be a serious flight risk,' the prosecutor said. 'She has no ties to the community, we believe she's using an alias, and the address on her driver's license has proved to be a fraudulent one. She's also a potential suspect in a homicide case. We request maximum bail.'

'Your Honor, my client claims she was sexually molested by Detective Robicheaux,' the woman's lawyer said. 'She was humiliated, put in a holding unit with lesbians who tried to assault her, then verbally harassed by Detective Robicheaux in this very courtroom. There's nothing to substantiate the charge against her, except the word of Detective Robicheaux, who himself may face criminal charges.'

The judge suppressed a sigh, took off his glasses, and beckoned with both hands. When no one moved, he said, 'Approach, approach, approach. It's late, gentlemen. The Three Penny Opera here needs to conclude. That means you too, Detective Robicheaux.'

The two attorneys and I stood close to the bench. Judge Dautrieve leaned forward on his forearms and let his eyes rove over our faces.

'Would any of y'all care to explain what we're doing?' he said. 'Is this part of a Hollywood movie? Do I need a membership in the Screen Actors Guild? *What* homicide are you talking about, sir?'

'The ex-convict who was murdered at Iberia General, Your Honor,' the prosecutor said. 'He was part of a neo-Nazi group of some kind. The woman was seen at the hospital in a nun's veil, close by the man's room.'

'Seen by whom? When?' the judge said.

'Detective Robicheaux and others.'

'I don't see the *others*. You didn't answer all my questions, either. Seen when? At the time of death?'

'We're not sure.'

'Not sure? Wonderful,' the judge said.

'That has nothing to do with the charge against her now, anyway,' the defense attorney said.

'It means she has every reason not to come back here,' the prosecutor said.

Then the judge looked me evenly in the eyes.

'What motive would this lady have in coming to your house and telling you she's a nun, when, in fact, she's not?' he said.

'I believe she wanted to do my wife injury, Your Honor,' I said.

'In what fashion?'

I cleared my throat, then pulled at my collar.

'Sir?' he said.

'She's tried to encourage my wife to drink excessively, Your Honor.'

'That's a rather unique statement,' he said. 'To be honest, I don't think I've ever heard anything quite like it. You're telling me the presence of a nun somehow has led your wife into problems with alcohol?'

'I think humor at the expense of others is beneath the court's dignity, Your Honor,' I said.

I saw the prosecutor's eyes light with anger.

'You're badly mistaken if you think I see humor in any of this, Detective. Step back, all of you,' the judge said. When he folded his hands, his knuckles looked like white dimes. 'I don't like my courtroom used as a theater. I don't like sloppy presentations, I don't like sloppy investigative work, I don't like police officers and prosecutors trying to obtain a special consideration or privilege from the court at the defendant's expense. I hope my meaning is clear. Bail is set at three hundred dollars.'

He flicked his gavel down on a small oak block.

On the way out of the courtroom the prosecutor caught my arm.

'Don't give it a second thought, Dave. I always enjoy calling a witness who makes me look like I've got my ass on upside down. Why didn't you flip Dautrieve's tie in his face while you were at it?' he said.

I followed the woman and her attorney out to the attorney's maroon Lincoln. The day was bright and clear, and leaves were bouncing across the freshly mowed lawn.

'Don't talk to him,' the attorney said, opening his door.

'It's all right. We're old pals, really. He and I share a lot of family secrets. About the wifey and that sort of thing,' she said. She put on a pair of black sunglasses and began tying a flowered bandanna around her hair.

'You share a big common denominator with most scam artists, Marie. You're cunning but you're not smart,' I said.

'Oh, hurt me deep inside, Dave,' she said, and pursed her lips at me.

'You didn't understand what I told you in there. Buchalter is going to be charged with murdering two of his own people. Bad P.R. when you're leading a cause. Even his lamebrain followers read newspapers.'

She hooked her purse on her wrist, then placed her hand on her hip.

'I've got a problem. My tractor don't get no traction. Can you give me a few minutes, baby-pie?' she said.

'Marie, don't spend any more time on this man,' her attorney said.

'How about it, Dave?' she said. 'It won't hurt your relationship with the sow. I think I remember somebody cranking a whole bunch of electricity into your batteries. Wouldn't you like a little sport fuck on the side?'

I opened her car door and fitted my hand tightly around her upper arm. Her skin whitened around the edges of my fingers. Pieces of torn color floated behind my eyes, like the tongues of orange flame you see inside the smoke of an oil fire, and I heard whirring sounds in my ears, like wind blowing hard inside a conch shell. I saw the top of the attorney's body across the car's rooftop, saw his Humpty-Dumpty head and wide tie and high collar, saw his mouth opening and a fearful light breaking in his eyes.

'There's no problem, Counselor. I just want to make sure y'all don't accuse us of a lack of courtesy in Iberia Parish,' I said, and sat the woman down hard in the passenger seat. Her sunglasses fell off her nose into her lap. 'Happy motoring, Marie. It's a grand day. Stay the fuck away from my house. Next time down, it's under a black flag.'

24

Late that afternoon Lieutenant Rankin of the Toronto Police Department called back and told me everything he had learned from others and the case record about the death of a robbery detective named James Mervain.

'This is what it comes down to,' he said. 'Mervain was one of those fellows whose life seemed to be going out of control – booze, a brutality charge, a wife in the sack with another cop, some suspicions that maybe he was gay – so when he got a little shrill, people dismissed what he had to say. You with me?'

'Yes.'

'He'd been working with a recruit named Kuhn or Koontz. Maybe he knew the guy off the job, too, through some kind of gay connection . . .'

'I don't understand, you're not sure of the name?'

'That's what's strange. A couple of cops around here still remember this recruit, and they're sure the name was Kuhn or Koontz, but the name's not in the computer. Maybe it got wiped out, I don't know. Anyway, Mervain started telling people that Kuhn, or whatever his name was, had some problems; in particular, he liked to hurt people. But if that was true, he never did it on the job. Which made everybody think Mervain had a secret life, out there in the gay bars somewhere, and he had some kind of personal or sexual grievance with this fellow.

'Then some rather serious weapons were stolen from a departmental arms locker – ten-gauge pumps, stun guns, three-fifty-sevens, nine-millimeter automatics, armor-piercing ammunition, stuff like that. Mervain maintained Kuhn was behind it. Actually, a custodian was arrested for it, but he died before he went to trial. This is about the time Kuhn disappeared, at least as far as anyone remembers.

'Then Mervain seemed to go crazy. He got arrested for drunk driving, he got beat up in a bar, he'd come to work so hungover nobody could talk to him till noon without getting their heads snapped off. He put his name on mailing lists of a half dozen hate groups, then he'd bring all this Nazi literature to the office and try to convince people Kuhn was part of an international conspiracy to bring back the Third Reich. The department sent him to a psychologist, but he just became more obsessed.

'Then one Monday he didn't come in to work. His ex-wife had no idea where he was, his apartment was empty, and some kids had stripped his car. Two weeks later the owner of a skid-row hotel called us. Maggots were crawling out from under the door crack in one of the rooms. Our people had to break open the door with a sledge. Mervain had nailed boards across the jamb. How much do you want in the way of detail?'

'Go ahead,' I said.

'The detective who did the investigation is still with the department. He says he never had a case like it before or since. Mervain hung himself, naked, upside down by the ankles with piano wire, then put a German Luger into his eye socket and let it off.'

'You're telling me y'all put this down as a suicide?'

'Forensics showed there's no question he fired the gun. The door was nailed shut. The window was locked from the inside. Both his personal and professional life were a disaster. How would you put it down?'

I tapped a paper clip on my desk blotter.

'Look, it bothered other people at the time, but there was no indication that anyone else could have been in that room,' he said.

'What do you mean *bothered*?'

'The room was full of Nazi and hate literature. The walls and floors were papered with it. But all his clothes, except what he'd been wearing, were gone. So were his billfold and the notebook that he always carried.'

'Does anyone remember what this man Kuhn looked like?'

'Two cops used the same words – "a big blond guy."'

'I'm going to fax y'all a composite. Would you send me everything you have on the Mervain case?'

'Sure. Look, there's one other thing. A couple of days after the death was ruled a suicide, the desk clerk called and said Mervain's coat was on the back of a chair in the lobby. He wanted to know what he should do with it.'

'Yes?'

'There was a napkin from a gay bar in one of the pockets. Mervain had written a note on it. Somebody stuck it in the case folder. I'll read it to you. "Schwert . . . Schwert . . . Schwert . . . His name is Schwert. I have become his fool and slave. I know he's out there now, flying in the howling storm. No one believes, I see no hope." Sounds kind of sad, doesn't it? You have any idea what it might mean?'

'What was Mervain's educational background?'

'Let's see . . . Bachelor's in liberal arts, a master's degree in administration of justice. Why?'

'I'm not sure.'

'Maybe we blew this one.'

'It's a big club. Thanks for your time, sir.'

Early the next morning I drove to New Orleans and, after going to the bail bonds office that fronted points for the Caluccis, I found Max at his mother's in an old residential neighborhood off Canal, not far from Mandina's restaurant. The house was late Victorian, with a wide gallery, a fresh coat of gray and white paint, and rose-bushes blooming all over the lawn.

The family was celebrating the birthday of a little boy and eating lunch on redwood picnic tables in the backyard. Balloons were tied to the trees and lawn furniture, and the tables were covered with platters of pasta and cream pastry, bowls of red sausage, beaded pitchers of lemonade and iced tea. Max Calucci sat in the midst of it all, in undershirt and slacks, the pads of hair on his brown shoulders as fine as a monkey's.

I had to hand it to him. His expression never changed when he saw me at the garden gate. He cut pieces of cake and handed them to the children, continued to tell a story in Italian to a fat woman in black and an elderly man on a thin walking cane, then excused himself, rubbed a little boy on the head, and walked toward me with a glass of lemonade in his hand.

'You got business with me?' he asked.

'If you've got business with Clete Purcel, I do.'

'He can't talk for himself?'

'You better hope he doesn't, Max.'

'Is this more hard guy stuff? You got your shovel with you?'

'Nope.'

His eyes were as black and liquid as wet paint.

'You got some kind of deal you want to cut? That why you're here?' he said.

'Maybe.'

He drank from his lemonade, his eyes never leaving mine. Then he pushed opened the short iron gate with his foot.

'It's a nice day, a special occasion. I got no bad feelings on a nice day like this. Eat a piece of cake,' he said.

'We can talk out here.'

'What, you too good to sit down at my nephew's birthday party?' he said.

I ate a custard-filled éclair in a sunny spot by the garden wall. The air was dry and warm, and the breeze blew through the banana trees along the wall and ruffled the water in an aboveground swimming pool. The guests around the tables were his relatives and family friends – working-class people who owned small grocery stores and cafés, carried hod, belonged to the plumbers' union, made the stations of the cross each Friday in Lent, ate and drank at every meal as though it were a pagan celebration, married once, and wore widow black with the commitment of nuns.

Max combed his hair back over his bald pate at the table, cleaned the comb with his fingers, then stuck the stub of a filter-tipped cigar in his mouth and motioned me toward a gazebo on the far side of the yard. The latticework was covered with purple trumpet vine; inside, the glass-topped table and white-painted iron chairs were deep in shadow, cold to the touch.

Max lit his cigar and let the smoke trail out of his mouth. His shoulders were brown and oily-looking against the white straps of his undershirt.

'Say it,' he said.

'I hear you and Bobo put out an open contract on Clete.'

'You get that from Lonighan?'

'Who cares where it came from?'

'Lonighan's a welsher and a bum.'

I leaned forward and rubbed my hands together.

'I'm worried about my friend, Max.'

'You should. He's got a radioactive brain or something.'

'I'm not here to defend what he does. I just want you guys to take the hit off him.'

'He's the victim? Have you seen my fucking car? It ain't a car no more. It's a block of concrete.'

'Come on, Max. You guys started it when you leaned on his girlfriend.'

'That's all past history. She paid the loan, she paid the back vig. All sins forgiven.'

'Here's the deal. You and Bobo tried to take out Nate Baxter. I think you probably did this without consent of the Commission. What if some reliable information ends up in their hands about a couple of guys in New Orleans trying to cowboy a police administrator?'

'That's what you got to work my crank with?' he said.

'Yeah, I guess so.'

'Then you got jack shit.'

'What's going to make you happy, Max?'

He smiled. I felt my pulse swelling in my throat; I rubbed the top of my knuckles with my palm. I kept my eyes flat and looked at the curtain of trumpet vine that puffed in the breeze.

'I want the two hundred large Tommy Lonighan owes me and Bobo,' he said. 'That fucking mick is gonna die and take the debt to the grave. You twist him right, we get our money, then I don't have no memory about troubles with Clete Purcel.'

'Big order, Max.'

'You know anything easy? Like they say, life's a bitch, then you get to be dead for a long time.'

The ash from his cigar blew on my slacks. I brushed it off, then put on my sunglasses and looked out into the sunlight.

'What, you sentimental about Lonighan or something?' he said.

'No.'

'That's good. Because he's been jobbing you. Him and Hippo Bimstine, both.'

'Oh?'

'That's a surprise? People like you rip me up, Robicheaux. You think Jews are martyrs, the Irish are fun guys singing "Rosie O'Grady" on the corner, and Italians are colostomy bags. Tell me I'm wrong.'

'You were going to say something about Tommy Blue Eyes?'

'Yeah, he got his fat mick mush full of booze and was laughing about how you trust Hippo Bimstine and think he's big shit because he's got all these liberal causes.'

'I see.'

'You see? I don't think you see shit. Lonighan says Hippo stole some stuff out of the public library about that Nazi sub so you wouldn't find out what's inside it.'

'No kidding?'

'*Yeah*, no fucking kidding.'

I leaned forward and picked at the calluses on my palm. The breeze was drowsy with the smell of chrysanthemums and dead birthday candles.

'You and I have something in common,' I said.

'I don't think so.'

'I went down on a murder beef once. Did you know that?'

'I'm supposed to be impressed?'

'Here's the trade, Max. Take the contract off Clete and I stay out of your life.'

'You ain't in my life.'

'Here's the rest of it.'

'I ain't interested,' he said. 'I tell you what. It's my nephew's birthday, you came out to my mother's house and showed respect, you didn't act like the drunk fuck everybody says you are. That means I'm letting all this stuff slide, and that includes what you done to me out at Lonighan's place. So you can tell dick-brain the score's even, he's getting a free pass he don't deserve, I got businesses to run and I don't have time for this shit. Are we clear on this now?'

'I hope you're a man of your word, Max.'

'Fuck you and get outta here.'

When I opened the gate and let myself out, I noticed a tangle of ornamental iron roses tack-welded in the center of the pikes. The cluster was uneven where one rose had been snapped loose from its base. I rubbed the ball of my thumb over the sharp edges of the broken stem and looked back at Max. His eyes had never left me. He rotated an unlit cigar in the center of his mouth.

The A.A. meeting is held on the second floor of a brick church that was used as a field hospital for Confederate wounded in 1863, then later as a horse stable by General Banks's Union cavalry. Outside, the streets are wet and cool and empty, the storefronts shuttered under the wood colonnades, the trees still dripping with rain against a sky that looks like a red-tinged ink wash.

It's a fifth step meeting, one in which people talk about stepping across a line and admitting to God, themselves, and another person the exact nature of their wrongs. For many, it's not an easy moment.

Some of them are still zoned out, their eyes glazed with residual fear; those sent by the court try to hide the resentment and boredom in their faces; others seem to have the exuberance and confidence of airplane wing walkers.

Bootsie sits next to me, her hands folded tightly in her lap. She showered after supper and put on makeup and a new yellow dress, but in her cheeks are pale discolorations, like slivers of ice, and there's a thin sheen of perspiration at her temples.

'You don't have to say anything. Just listen,' I whisper to her.

They start to unload. Some of it seems silly – overdue library books, cavalier attitudes toward bills – then it turns serious and you feel embarrassed and voyeuristic; you find your eyes dropping to the floor, and you try not to be affected by the level of pain in the speaker's voice.

The details sometimes make the soul wince; then you remember some of the things you did, or tried to do, or could have done, while drunk and you realize that what you hear in this room differs only in degree from the moral and psychological insanity that characterized your own life.

Only one speaker makes use of euphemism. That's because he's told his story before and he knows that not everyone in the room will be able to handle it. He was eighteen years old, ripped on reefer and pills, when he pushed a blindfolded VC suspect out the door of a Huey at five hundred feet; he so impressed the ARVN and American officer on board that they had him do it twice more the same afternoon.

Bootsie's eyes are filled with hidden thoughts. I slide my hand down her forearm and take her palm in mine. Her eyes move to the doorway and the darkened stairway at the front of the room. Her breath catches in her throat.

'What is it?' I ask.

Her eyes close, then open, like a doll's.

'A man at the door. Dave, I think—'

'What?'

'It was *him.*'

I get up from the folding chair and walk across the oak floor to the front of the room. I step through the open door, walk down the darkened stairway. The door to the street is open, and rain is blowing out of the trees onto the lawn. The violet air smells of wet stone and burning leaves.

I go back upstairs, and Bootsie looks at me anxiously. I shake my head.

Before the meeting ends, it's obvious she wants to speak. She raises her chin, her lips part. But the moment passes, and she lowers her eyes to her lap.

Later the room is empty. I turn out the lights and prepare to lock up. In the hallway downstairs she puts her arms around me and presses her face into my chest. I can feel her back shaking under my hands. A loose garbage can lid is bouncing down the street in the darkness.

'I feel so ashamed,' she says. Her face is wet against my shirt.

I went in to work early and looked at the notes I had taken during my conversation with the lieutenant at the Toronto Police Department.

It was time to try something different. On my yellow legal pad I made a list of aliases that Will Buchalter might have used. As a rule, the aliases used by a particular individual retain similarities in terms of initials or sound and phonetic value, or perhaps even cultural or ethnic identification, in all probability because most career criminals have a libidinal fascination with themselves.

I tried W. B. Kuhn, William Coon, Will Kuntz, Bill Koontz, then a dozen other combinations, making use of the same first and last names, in the same way that you would wheel pari-mutuel numbers in trying to hit a quiniela or a perfecta at the racetrack.

But more than a name it was a literary allusion written by the dead Canadian detective on the barroom napkin that gave me a brooding sense I almost did not want to confirm.

I began writing out the word *Schwert* with the combinations of first names and initials that I had already listed. The sheriff walked into my office with a cup of coffee in his hand and looked over my shoulder.

'That looks like alphabet soup,' he said. 'You going to run that through the NCIC?'

'Yeah, I want to go through the feds in New Orleans, too.'

'It can't hurt.' He gazed through the window at a black trusty in jailhouse issue sawing a yellowed palm frond from the tree trunk.

'You don't sound enthusiastic,' I said.

'I've got bad news. The tail we put on your girlfriend . . . She went through the front door of a supermarket in Lafayette, then out the back and *poof* . . . Gone.'

'Who was the tail?'

'Expidee Chatlin.'

I pressed my fingers into my temples.

'I didn't have anybody else available,' the sheriff said. 'I don't think it would have come out any different, anyway, Dave. Your gal's mighty slick.'

'I'd really appreciate your not calling her *my* gal or girlfriend.'

'Any way you cut it, she's one smart broad and she took us over the hurdles. That's just the way it plays out sometimes.'

'Too often.'

'Sir?'

I tried to concentrate on my legal pad.

'You and Bootsie have had a bad time. I don't think you should blame others for it, though,' he said.

'That wasn't my intention, Sheriff.' I could hear his leather gunbelt creak. I wrote the words *William B. Schwert* on the pad. He started to walk out of the room, then stopped.

'What've you got there, exactly?' he said.

'A Toronto cop wrote something on a napkin before he was found hanging by his ankles with a nine-millimeter round through his eye.' I glanced back at my notes. '"I know he's out there now, flying in the howling storm."'

'So?'

'It's from a poem by William Blake. It's about evil. As I remember it, it goes "O Rose, thou art sick.

The invisible worm
That flies in the night
In the howling storm

Has found out thy bed
Of crimson joy,
And his dark secret love
Does thy life destroy."'

'No, you misunderstood me, Dave. I was looking at the name you just wrote down there . . . Schwert. You never took any German at school?'

'No.'

'It means "sword," podna.'

He drank from his coffee cup and tapped me lightly on the shoulder with the flat of his fist.

But before I would get anything back from the FBI or the National Crime Information Center in Washington, D.C., Clete Purcel would write a new chapter in the history of the New Orleans mob and outdo even Clete Purcel.

25

Clete had been eating breakfast in Igor's on St Charles, his porkpie hat tipped down over one eye, when two of Max Calucci's bodyguards came in and sat at the table next to him. They were in a good mood, expansive, joking with the waitress, relaxed in Clete's presence. One of them accidentally knocked his chair into Clete's.

'Sorry, Purcel. Don't be getting the wrong signal. It ain't that kind of day,' he said.

Clete chewed his food and looked back at the men silently.

'I'm saying we got the word, okay?' the man said. He grinned.

Clete wiped his mouth with his napkin.

'There's some kind of comedy act here I don't know about?' he said.

'Cool your ovaries down. You want to join us? Your breakfast is on me.'

'I'll eat at that table after it gets scrubbed down with peroxide.'

'Suit yourself. It's a beautiful day. Why fuck a beautiful day?'

'Yeah, it was.'

The two men laughed and looked at their menus. Clete set his knife and fork down on his plate and put a matchstick in the corner of his mouth.

'Are we working on new rules here?' he said.

'Give it a break, Clete. You want some tickets to the LSU–Ole Miss game? Look, we're glad to hear it's over, that's all,' the second man said.

Clete removed the matchstick from his mouth and studied it.

'Who gave you permission to call me by my first name, and what's this stuff about something being over?' he said.

'Sorry we bothered you, Purcel,' the first man said. 'Robicheaux don't want to tell you he did a sit-down, that's between you and him. Hey, somebody got my fat ass out of the skillet, I'd count my blessings.'

The following is my best re-creation of the events, as described by Ben Motley and Lucinda Bergeron, that happened later out by Lake Pontchartrain.

Clete parked his convertible two blocks from Max Calucci's home, then took a cab to a construction site one mile away, on Robert E. Lee Boulevard, where the Caluccis supplied all the heavy equipment to the builder. He leaned against the trunk of a palm tree across the street, sucking on a think stick of peppermint candy, enjoying the morning, inhaling the breeze off the lake.

Then he casually strolled across the boulevard, the peppermint stick pointed upward like an erection, and hot-wired an enormous earthmover. It was outfitted with a steel blade that could strip baked hardpan down to bedrock, a great, saw-toothed bucket that could break and scoop up asphalt highway like peanut brittle, and huge balloon tires with studded welts for scouring trenches through piles of crushed stone and angle iron.

Before anyone realized what was happening, Clete had wheeled around the corner into the midday traffic and was hammering full throttle down the boulevard toward Max's house, diesel smoke flattening in a dirty plume from the stack.

The gateman at Max's was the first to see, or hear, the earthmover thundering down the quiet, oak-shaded residential street. Then, inside the steel-mesh protective cage, he recognized the powder blue porkpie hat, the round, pink face with the gray scar through one eyebrow like a strip of inner tube patch, and the massive shoulders that seemed about to split the seams on the Hawaiian shirt.

By this time the gateman was grabbing at the telephone box inset in the brick pillar by the edge of the driveway. But it was too late; Clete lowered the saw-toothed bucket, swung the earthmover into the drive, and blew the gates off their hinges.

No one at the house – the Vietnamese gardeners, three of Max's hired gumballs, a couple of coked-out dancers suntanning topless by the pool – could believe what was happening. Clete, bent low, like an ape, over the controls, headed across the lawn, grinding through flower beds, the patio furniture by the pool, crashing through a corner of the gazebo, splintering a birdbath into ceramic shards, raking off sprinkler heads, shredding garden hoses into chopped rubber bands.

He made a wide circle of lawn destruction and came to a halt twenty yards from the columned portico at the front of the house, the cap on the stack bubbling quietly. He lowered the bucket to clear his field of vision, sighted on the front entrance, raised the bucket into position again, shifted down, and gave it the gas.

The bucket exploded a hole the size of a garage door through the front wall. Then Clete backed off, gunning the engine, crunching over the crushed cinder blocks and plaster, got a good running start, and plunged into the house's interior.

He made U-turns, shifted from reverse to first, backed through walls and wet bars and bathrooms, ripped water pipes and drain lines out of the floors, and ground washing machines, television sets, and microwaves into sparking piles of electrical junk. He seemed to pause for a moment, perhaps to get his bearings, then he crashed through Max's mirror-walled bedroom, dropped the grader blade into position, and raked the eighteenth-century tester and oak floors through the French doors onto a domed sunporch, where he swung the bucket in a wide arc and sent cascades of glass onto the lawn.

By this time the gumballs and the topless suntanners were racing for the street. Clete bounced out onto the backyard, strips of fabric flying from the stack and the driver's cage like medieval streamers. He lit a cigarette with his Zippo, fitted his porkpie hat down on his brow, then demolished the garages and the garden shed, dropped the bucket squarely on top of a new Chrysler, ripped a long slice out of the greenhouse, and plowed trenches bristling with severed pink roots where hedges had been.

The Romans at Carthage couldn't have done a more thorough job.

Then he got down from the machine and strolled across the flattened fence at the back of the property toward his automobile, his hands in his pockets, gazing at the white chop out on the lake. Geysers of water from broken pipes in the yard were fountaining in the sunlight, glistening on the grass, blowing in the cool air like an unloosed rainbow.

After I heard from both Ben Motley and Lucinda Bergeron, I got an unexpected call.

'What do you want, Nate?' I said.

'Guess.'

'You got me.'

'You'd better tell that crazy sonofabitch to come in.'

'Tell him yourself.'

'Great suggestion. Except when we showed up at his apartment with a warrant last night, he climbed out the window and went across the rooftops. You're mixed up in this, Robicheaux. Don't pretend you're not.'

'I'm not.'

'You know how I can always tell when a drunk is lying? His lips are moving.'

'What else can I do for you this morning?'

'Tell that fat fuck you call a friend that he comes in or he gets no guarantees out on the street. You got my drift?'

'This must bother you, Nate.'

'What?' he said.

'Turning on your own people, taking it on your knees from the mob, doing grunt work for Max Calucci after he tried to have you whacked out.'

I could hear him breathing in the receiver, could almost smell the heat and nicotine coming through the perforations.

'Listen to me very carefully,' he said. 'The insurance adjuster estimates that Fuckhead did around a half million dollars' damage to that house. State Farm is not the Mafia, Robicheaux. They're corporate citizens, and they get seriously pissed and make lots of trouble when they have to pay out five hundred thousand large because a lunatic thinks he can wipe his shit on the furniture.'

'I'll pass on your remarks. Thanks for calling.'

'You never listen, do you? If I learn you have contact with Purcel and you don't report it, I'm charging you with aiding and abetting and being an accomplice after the fact.'

'Your problem isn't with me or Clete, Nate. When you took juice from the wise guys, you mortgaged your butt all the way to the grave,' I said, and hung up.

I went to the rest room and rinsed my face. I let the water run a long time. I even rinsed my ear where I had held the telephone receiver. Then I cupped a handful of water on the back of my neck and dried my skin with a handful of paper towels.

'You run the four-minute mile or something?' another detective said.

'That's right,' I said, and looked at him in the mirror.

'Who kicked on *your* burner?' he said.

Ten minutes later, my phone rang again.

'The wrong kind of people are looking for you,' I said. Through the receiver I could hear seagulls squeaking in the background.

'You heard about it?' Clete said.

'What do you think?'

'It'll cool down. It always does.'

'Baxter's got no bottom. He'll take you out, Clete.'

'You shouldn't try to cut deals with the greasebags on behalf of your old podjo.'

'Do you have a death wish? Is that the problem?'

'You want to go fishing? If the wind drops, I'm going after some specs in a couple of hours.'

'Fishing?'

'Yeah.'

I propped my forehead on my fingers and stared into space.

'You need any money?' I said.

'Not right now.'

'Why'd you do it, Clete? Baxter says the insurance company wants to hang you out to dry.'

'Who cares? They shouldn't do business with a bucket of shit like Max Calucci. You've had your shield too long, Streak. You're starting to think like an administrator.'

'What's that mean?'

'You think you or Motley or Lucinda Bergeron were ever going to get a search warrant on Max and Bobo? With Nate Baxter on their pad?'

'You were tossing the place with an earthmover?'

'So it was a little heavy-handed. But dig this. Just before I gutted Max's den, I emptied everything out of his desk into a garbage bag. I also took his Rolodex and all the videocassettes off the shelves. One of these videos is a documentary about this primitive Indian tribe down in South America. Before the missionaries got to them, these guys were known as the worst human beings on earth. They shrank heads and sawed people into parts; sometimes they'd boil them alive. They'd even kill their own children.'

'Go on.'

'They'd also cut the hearts out of their victims. What's Max doing with a tape like that? The mob's into anthropology?'

'You've queered it as evidence.'

'Nobody else cares, Dave. Except for you and Motley and Lucinda, everybody in New Orleans is happy these black pukes could find new roles as organ donors. History lesson, big mon. When they talk law and order, they mean Wyatt Earp leaving hair on the walls.'

Across the street, a black kid was flying a blood red kite high against a shimmering blue sky.

26

The information requests that I had made about a possible suspect named Schwert were answered, at first, in a trickle, in increments, unspecifically, as though we were pursuing a shadow that had cast itself over other cases and files without ever becoming a solid presence.

Then the computer printouts, the faxes, and the phone calls began to increase in volume, from the FBI, the NCIC, the Bureau of Alcohol, Tobacco and Firearms, the Immigration and Naturalization Service, and finally Interpol.

The sheriff looked down at the clutter of paper on my desk.

'Where'd you get your filing system? It looks like Fibber McGee's closet,' he said. He glanced up at my face. 'Sorry, that's one of those generational jokes, I guess.'

'The first time the name William Schwert shows up is in some phone taps the FBI and ATF had on some neo-Nazis in Idaho during the mideighties,' I said. 'Then ATF found it in the pocket of a guy who blew his face off while he was building a bomb in his basement in Portland.'

'Yeah, I think I remember that. He and some other guys were going to dynamite a synagogue?'

'That's right.'

'Schwert was involved?'

'No one's sure.'

The sheriff tilted his head quizzically.

'In a half dozen cases it's like he's standing just on the edge of the picture but he doesn't leave footprints,' I said.

The sheriff sniffed and blew his nose in a Kleenex.

'It doesn't sound like this is helping us a lot,' he said.

'It gets more interesting. The guy named Schwert seems to spend a lot of time overseas. Interpol has been tracking him for fifteen years. Berlin, London, Madrid, any place there're skinheads, Nazis, or Falangists.'

The light in the sheriff's eyes sharpened. He began poking in the papers on my desk.

'Where is it?' he said.

'What?'

'The Interpol jacket. The mug shots.'

'There aren't any. Nobody's nailed him.'

'This isn't taking us anywhere, Dave. It looks like what you've got here is more smoke. We don't even know if Schwert is Buchalter.'

'Interpol says a guy named Willie Schwert broke out of an asylum for the criminally insane in Melbourne, Australia, seventeen years ago. He tore the window bars out of a maximum security unit with his bare hands.'

'Then where's the sheet?'

'The records on the guy are gone. A fire in their computer system or something.'

'What is it, a computer virus wiping out all the information on this character?'

'You're not impressed?' I said.

'I wish I could say I was.'

'It's the same guy.'

'You're probably right. And it does diddle-squat for us. He's still out there, fucking up people in any way he can. I wish Purcel had dropped the hammer on this guy when he had him at close range . . . Pardon my sentiment. I'm becoming convinced I'm not emotionally suited for this job.'

'The people who are shouldn't be cops, Sheriff,' I said.

That evening, as Bootsie and I washed the dishes at the sink, the breeze through the screen was dry and warm and the clouds above my neighbor's tree line looked like torn plums in the sun's afterglow. Her hands were chaffed, her knuckles white in the dishwater. For a second time, she began to wash a saucer I had already dried. I took it from her hand and placed it back on the drain rack.

'You want to go to a meeting?' I asked.

'Not tonight.'

'You tired?'

'A little.'

'Do you want to lie down?' I said. I rested my hand on the top of her rump.

'Not really. Maybe I'll just read.' Her eyes focused on a solitary mockingbird that stood in the middle of the picnic table.

I nodded.

'I don't seem to have any energy,' she said. 'I don't know what it is.'

'Long day,' I said, and dried my hands and turned away from her.

'Yes,' she said. 'I guess that's it.'

Later, after she and Alafair had gone to bed, I sat in the living room by myself and stared at the television screen. A gelatinous fat man, with the toothy smile of a chipmunk, was denigrating liberals and making fun of feminists and the homeless. His round face was bright with an electric jeer when he broached the subject of environmentalists and animal rights activists. His live audience squealed with delight.

Eighteen million people listened to him daily.

I turned off the set and went into the kitchen. The moon was down, and I could hear the tree limbs outside the window knocking together in the wind.

When the phone rang on the counter, I knew who it would be. I almost looked forward to the encounter, like a man who has formed a comfortable intimacy with his bête noire.

His voice was indolent and ropy with saliva when he spoke. In the background I could hear the flat, tinny sound of Bix Beiderbecke's 'In a Mist.'

'I never saw tracks on your arm, Will. Do you shoot up in the thighs?'

'You never know.'

'How'd you get my number?' I said.

'People like to please. Not too much gets denied me, Dave.'

'It sounds like you might have done a good load of China pearl. Not a good sign for a guy who likes control.'

'Why did you do it?'

'What?'

'You spit in my face. When I tried to create a tender moment inside our pain.'

'I guess you're just that kind of guy. Besides that, you're probably insane.'

The phonograph stopped and started over again. Beiderbecke's trumpet rose off the record like sound ringing through crystal. Buchalter swallowed wetly, his mouth close to the receiver.

'It's not too late for us,' he said.

'It is for you, partner. Your threads are unraveling. We've got a make on you from Toronto and Interpol; we know about the asylum you broke out of in Australia. You're about to slide down the big ceramic bowl, Will.'

'You don't understand power. I can caress you in ways that'll make you beg for death. The auto garage was nothing.'

'Get off it, Buchalter. You're a hype. You're one day away any time your connection wants you.'

I heard his throat working again, words forming, then sticking unintelligibly in his mouth. Someone pulled the receiver from his hand.

'The wifey plowed again, Dave?' she said. Her voice was sweaty and hoarse, like a person high on her own glandular energies. 'You should have taken me up on my invitation. It'd give you something to fantasize about.'

'Your boyfriend's tracked shit over two continents, Marie,' I said. 'It looks like you're going to take the bounce with him.'

'Can she have orgasms while she's on the grog?'

'Save the comic book dialogue for after your trial. There's an amateur theatrical group at the women's prison in St Gabriel. You'll fit right in.'

'I keep having this dream. There's a pump handle in it. It feels hard in my hand, and it has moisture dripping off it. I wake up all hot, thinking of a big dark policeman. I get hot even talking about it. What's my dream mean, Dave?'

'I'll say adios now, Marie. Then I'll unplug the phones. Enjoy the time you have left with Buchalter. I bet he really knows how to capture a lady's heart.'

There was a pause, then I heard a match strike against an abrasive surface, the match head hissing, and her breath exhaling.

'Run the coordinates in the personals of *The Times-Picayune*,' she said. 'If you don't, we reach out and touch someone. No, not the sow or the little girl. Maybe the boogie and her son; maybe your uncontrollable friend, Purcel. Will would love to spend a few hours alone with Mr Purcel.'

'Be careful what you pray for.'

'You're so clever. And the wifey so sweet. I'm glad you're in the tropics where the sheep don't freeze up.'

I eased the receiver down in the cradle, then unplugged the phone jacks in both the kitchen and living room.

I undressed down to my skivvies and sat on the bed next to Bootsie in the dark. She was sleeping on her stomach, and I ran my hand down the smooth taper of her back and over her rump and bare thighs. Her skin felt hot, almost feverish, but she did not respond to my touch. Outside the window, the trees thrashed and swelled in the dry wind. I lay on top of the sheets and stared upward into the darkness, the backs of my fingers resting against Bootsie's leg, the words of the woman named Marie Guilbeaux like an obscene tongue in my ear.

The next morning I got up early and drove back to New Orleans. I stopped first at the library, or morgue, of *The Times-Picayune*, then drove down St Charles and found Hippo Bimstine working behind the candy counter at one of his drugstores in the Garden District. He wore a starched gray apron over his white shirt and tie and rotund stomach, and his hair was oiled and combed as tight as wire, his thick neck talcumed, his face cheerful and bright.

Hippo had the confident and jolly appearance of a man who could charm a snake into a lawn mower.

'Another nice day,' he said.

'It sure is,' I said.

'So why the dark look? You dump some money at the track?' His smile was inquisitive and full of play.

'I guess I get down when I find out a friend has tried to blindside me.'

'What are you talking here?' He tried to look me steadily in the eyes.

'Max Calucci's been saying peculiar things about you, Hippo.'

'Consider the source.'

'I am. He's got no reason to lie. He says Tommy Lonighan told him you removed some stuff about the Nazi U-boat from the public library.'

'I'm under arrest for library theft?'

'Buchalter and his buttwipes used up my sense of humor, partner.'

'We're talking in hieroglyphics here. You're mystifying me, Dave.'

'I found a nineteen fifty-six *States-Item* story on Jon Matthew Buchalter's death in the files at *The Times-Picayune*. When *The States-Item* folded, all its records were kept by *The Picayune*. But I was careless and missed the story the first time around. I have a feeling it's the one you took from the public library.'

'So you tripped over some big revelation from a rag of thirty-five years ago?'

'Not really. Jon Buchalter was raving on his deathbed about a large gold swastika on board a downed U-boat. Is that the secret you've been keeping from me?'

He considered for a moment and scratched at his neck with one finger. 'Yeah, that's about it. You satisfied?'

'No.'

'It's supposed to weigh forty-two pounds. It's got a gold wreath around it, and the wreath is set with jewels. Big fucking deal, huh?'

'You were willing to let me get involved with Nazis so you could salvage the gold in a World War II wreck?'

'You got some kind of malfunction with your thought processes, Dave. You keep forgetting it was you tried to squeeze every spendolie you could from a finder's fee.'

'I don't let my friends hang their butts in the breeze for money, either, Hippo.' I picked up a roll of mints from the counter and set a half-dollar down on the glass. 'Thanks for your time. See you around.'

I turned to go. Outside, the streetcar rattled down the neutral ground in the sunshine.

'You righteous cocksucker,' he said behind me. A woman with a magazine cupped in her hand replaced it on the rack and walked away.

'Excuse me?' I said.

'When you guys got nothing to support your own argument against a Jew, you always take your shot about money. It takes a while, but you always get to it.'

'You set me up, Hippo.'

'Fuck you I did.' He came around the edge of the counter. He touched his finger against my breastbone. 'You want the rest of the story? The gold in that swastika was pried out of the mouths of Polish Jews. It was a gift from Heinrich Himmler himself. You know what else's supposed to be in that sub? Hitler's plan for the United States. I don't let any man talk down to me because I'm a Jew, Dave. I don't want you in my store.'

'I'll try my best to stay out of your life.'

He went back behind the counter and began knocking open rolls of change and shaking them into the cash drawer. Then he stopped and slammed the drawer shut with the flat of his pudgy hand. I walked outside, my face burning, the eyes of a half dozen people fastened upon me.

Lucinda Bergeron was sanding the wood steps on the back of her house. The air was sunny and warm, and her hair looked damp and full with the heat from her body and her work. She wore flip-flops and a denim shirt that hung over her pink shorts, and blades of grass stuck to the tops of her feet. She kept glancing up at me while she sanded. The tiny gold chain and cross around her neck were haloed with perspiration against her black skin.

'You go back on duty tomorrow?' I said.

'That's right. All sins forgiven.'

'How do you feel?'

'You know, one foot in front of the other, a day at a time, all that jazz.'

I brushed off a step where she had already sanded and sat down. She wiped her eyes on her sleeve and wrapped a fresh piece of sandpaper around a block of wood. She made a circle with her thumb and forefinger and smoothed the paper against the grain.

'I want you to be careful, Lucinda.'

'Worry about yourself, hotshot.'

'It's a mistake to be cavalier about Buchalter, or Schwert, or whatever his name is. There's nothing predictable about this guy or the woman working with him.'

She raised her eyes to mine while her arm and hand kept a steady motion against the step. 'I can't tell you how much I'd love the opportunity,' she said.

'When you're forced to ... to pop a cap in the line of duty, something happens to you, at least if you're not a sociopath yourself. The next time it goes down, you get sweaty, you hesitate, you doubt your motivations. It's a dangerous moment.'

'You think I'll freeze up?'

'You tell me.'

'I don't have doubts about the man who hurt my child, believe me.'

'When are you going to quit calling Zoot a child?'

'When I feel like it, Mr Smart-ass.' She smiled, then worked the nozzle loose from the hose, turned on the faucet, and drank, with her body bent over, the backs of her thighs tight against her shorts, the water arching bright across her mouth. She wet a paper towel and wiped her face and neck and dropped it into a paper sack filled with garden cuttings.

'I have some tea made. Come inside,' she said.

The porcelain and yellow plastic surfaces of her kitchen gleamed in the sunlight through the windows, and the sills rang with red and blue dime-store vases. I sat at the breakfast table and watched her twist a handful of ice cubes in a towel and batter them on a chopping board with a rolling pin, then fill two tall glasses with the crushed ice and mint leaves and tea. The straps of her bra made a hard line across the wash-faded thinness of her denim shirt.

She turned toward me with the drink glasses in each hand. Her eyes looked at mine, and her expression sombered. She sat down across from me and folded her hands.

'I think you're a good person, Dave. That means some things aren't your style,' she said.

'I look like I have a clandestine agenda?'

'I've lived single for a long time. You recognize certain things in people. Even without being told.'

'I don't know if that's too complimentary.'

'Purcel was here yesterday.'

'There's a warrant on him.'

'I'm still suspended. I should worry about a warrant on Clete Purcel?'

'Why was he here?'

'He says one of the Caluccis' greasers will testify Nate Baxter's on a pad. He told me about your trouble at home.'

'Maybe some people should stay out of my private life.'

'Oh, that's perfect. Your closest friends shouldn't worry about you or try to help you?'

I felt my lips crimp together. I looked away from her unrelenting stare.

I stood up and took my seersucker coat off the back of the chair.

'Give me a call if Buchalter shows up,' I said, and walked toward the front door.

She followed me. The sun made slats of light on her face, causing her to squint as she looked up at me.

'Don't leave like this,' she said.

I took a breath. Her hair was scintillated with silver threads and curved thickly on her cheeks.

'What am I supposed to say, Lucinda?'

'Nothing. You're a good man. Good men don't need to say anything.'

The door was wide open so that nothing she did was hidden from view. She put her arms around my neck and bent my face to hers, raising herself on the balls of her feet, her knees pinching together, her thighs flexing and pressing against me unavoidably; then she kissed me on the cheeks, the bridge of the nose, the eyes, and finally once, a light adieu, on the mouth, as her hands came loose from my neck and my face felt as though it were covered with hot red dimes.

27

The chorus that condemns violence is multitudinous and unrelenting. Who can disagree with the sentiment? I think we're after the wrong enemy, though. It's cruelty, particularly when it's mindless and visited upon the defenseless, that has always bothered me most about human failure. But my viewpoint isn't exceptional. Anyone in law enforcement, social work, or psychiatric rehab of any kind carries with him or her a mental notebook whose pages never dim with the years.

Sometimes in the middle of the night I remember cases, or simply incidents, of twenty years ago that come aborning again like sins which elude remission, except either the guilt is collective in nature or the deed such a pitiful and naked admission of our tribal ignorance and inhumanity that the mere recognition of it leads to self-loathing.

Stephen Crane once suggested that few people are nouns; instead, most of us are adverbs, modifying a long and weary sequence of events in which the clearly defined culprit, with black heart and demonic intent, seldom makes himself available for the headsman.

I remember: a cop in the Lafayette police station laughing about how a friend rubbed his penis all over a black woman's body; a black street gang who videotaped their beating of a retarded Pakistani so they could show their friends their handiwork; an infant burned all over his body, even between his toes, with lighted cigarettes; a prosperous middle-class couple who forced the husband's parents to eat dog food; high school kids who held a drunk against a barroom picture window, then punched him through the glass; women and children sodomized, a coed shot through the face in Audubon Park (after she had surrendered her money), animals set on fire, a wounded cop flipped over on his back by his assailant, who then put a pillow under his head and slit his throat with a string knife.

I sincerely believe that we're attracted to films about the Mafia because the violence and evil portrayed in them seems to have an explanation and a beginning and an end. It's confined to one group of people, who in their fictional portrayal even have tragic proportions, and we're made to believe the problem is not endemic to the species.

But I think the reality is otherwise.

A random act of cruelty opened a door in the case I probably would not have gone through by myself.

It had started to sprinkle when I stopped at Igor's on St Charles for a po'-boy sandwich and to call Bootsie and tell her I was headed home.

'Call Ben Motley, Dave. He's left two messages,' she said.

'What's he want?'

'Something about Tommy Lonighan.'

'How you doing?'

'Fine.'

'You want to go out to eat tonight?'

'Sure. What's the occasion?' she said.

'Nothing special.'

'Is anything wrong?'

'No, why do you think that?'

'Because you always suggest going out to dinner when you feel guilty about something.'

'Not me.' I looked out at the rain striking against the half-opened windows of the streetcar.

'I'm sorry about last night,' she said.

'See you later, kiddo.'

'Hang on to your butt in the Big Sleazy.'

That's more like it, Boots, I thought.

I called Motley at headquarters in the Garden District.

'I got a strange story for you, Robicheaux,' he said. 'We've had some fag bashers running around the city. A couple of them are UNO pukes; the others are just ugly and stupid or probably latent queerbait themselves. Anyway, they're always on the prowl for fresh meat down in the Quarter. This time they picked up a transvestite on Dauphine and took him to a camp out in St Charles Parish. I think he blew a couple of them, then they got him stinking drunk, pulled his clothes off, and poured pig shit and chicken feathers all over him. Nice boys, huh?

'Anyway, the transvestite is no ordinary fruit. He looks like Frankenstein in a dress and panty hose. He starts sobering up and realizes this isn't a Crisco party. That's when he starts ripping puke ass, I mean busting slats out of the walls with these guys. The pukes made an instant conversion to law and order and called the sheriff's office.

'Right now Frankenstein's in a holding cell, scared shitless. Guess who he called to bail him out?'

'Lonighan?'

'Right. Then twenty minutes go by, and guess who calls back on the fruit's behalf?'

'I don't know, Ben.'

'A lawyer who works for the Calucci brothers. That's when the St Charles sheriff called us. Why do the Caluccis want to help a cross-dresser with feathers and pig flop in his hair?'

'Is the guy's name Manuel?'

'Yeah, Manuel Ruiz. The sheriff thinks he's a lobotomy case. He's probably illegal, too.'

'How long has he been in custody?'

'Two hours.'

'I'll get back to you. Thanks, Ben.'

An hour later Manuel Ruiz was still in the holding cell, a narrow, concrete, barred room with a wood bench against one wall and a drain hole and grate in the floor. There were dried yellow stains on the grate and on the cement around the hole. He was barefoot and wore a black skirt with orange flowers on it and a torn peasant blouse with lace around the neck; his hair was matted and stuck together in spikes. His exposed chest looked as hard and flawless in complexion as sanded oak.

'You remember me, Manuel?' I asked.

The eyes were obsidian, elongated, unblinking, lidless, his wide, expressionless mouth lipsticked like a fresh surgical incision.

'I just talked with the prosecutor's office,' I said. 'The boys aren't pressing charges. You can go home with me if you want.'

The skin at the corner of one eye puckered, like tan putty wrinkling.

'Or you can wait for the Caluccis' lawyer to get here. But he left word he's running late.'

'Caluccis no good. No want.' His voice sounded as though it came out of a cave.

'Not a bad idea. The other problem we might have is the INS, Manuel.'

He continued to stare at me, as though I were an anomaly caged by bars and not he, floating just on the edge of memory and recognition.

'Immigration and Naturalization,' I said, and saw the words tick in his eyes. 'Time to get out of town. Hump it on down the road. ¿*Vamos a casa?* Tommy's house?'

He hit at a fly with his hand, then looked at me again and nodded.

'I'll be back in a minute,' I said.

I walked back to the jailer's office. The jailer, a crew-cut man with scrolled green tattoos and black hair on his arms, sat behind his desk, reading a hunting magazine. By his elbow, a cigar burned in an ashtray inset in a lacquered armadillo shell.

'He's agreed to leave with me,' I said. 'How about a towel and a bar of soap and some other clothes?'

'He hosed down when he come in.' He looked back at his magazine, then rattled the pages. 'All right. We want everybody tidy when they leave. Hey, Clois! The Mexican's going out! Walk him down to the shower!' He looked back down at his magazine.

'What about the clothes?'

'Will you mail them back?'

'You got it.'

'Clois! Find something for him to wear that don't go with tampons!' He smiled at me.

It was cool and raining harder now as we drove toward New Orleans on old Highway 90. Manuel sat hunched forward, his arm hooked outside the passenger's door, his jailhouse denim shirt wet all the way to the shoulder. We crossed a bridge over a bayou, and the wind swirled the rain inside the cab.

'How about rolling up the window?' I said.

'Don't want smell bad in truck,' he said.

'You're fine. There's no problem there. Roll up the window please.'

He cranked the glass shut and stared through the front window at the trees that sped by us on the road's edge and the approaching gray silhouette of the Huey Long Bridge.

'Do you do some work for the Calucci brothers, Manuel?' I said.

'*Trabajo por* Tommy.'

'Yeah, I know you work for Tommy. But why do Max and Bobo want to get you out of jail, partner?'

His jug head remained motionless, but I saw his eyes flick sideways at me.

'Max and Bobo don't help people unless they get something out of it,' I said.

He picked up the paper sack that held his soiled clothes and clutched it in his lap.

'Where you from, Manuel?'

His face was dour with fatigue and caution.

'I'm not trying to trap you,' I said. 'But you're living with bad people. I think you need help with some other problems, too. Those boys who took you out in the marsh are sadists. Do you understand what I'm saying to you?'

But if he did, he gave no indication.

I shifted the truck into second and began the ascent onto the massive steel bridge that spanned the Mississippi. Down below, the water's surface was dimpled with thousands of rain rings, and the willow and gum trees on the bank were deep green and flattening in the wind off the gulf.

'Look, Manuel, Tommy Lonighan's got some serious stuff on his conscience. I think it's got to do with dope dealers and the vigilante killings in the projects. Am I wrong?'

Manuel's hands closed on the sack in his lap as though he were squeezing the breath out of a live animal.

'You want to tell me about it?' I said.

'*¿Quién es usted?*'

'My name's Dave Robicheaux. The man you saw at Tommy's house.'

'No. Where work? Who are?'

'I live in New Iberia. I'd like to help you. That's on the square. Do you understand me?'

'I go to jail because of boys?'

'Forget those guys. They're pukes. Nobody cares about them.'

'No jail?'

'That's right. What do you know about the vigilante, Manuel?'

He twisted his face away from me and stared out the passenger window, his lips as tight as the stitched mouth on a shrunken head. His leathery, work-worn hands looked like starfish clutched around the sack in his lap.

It was still raining a half hour later when I drove down Tommy Lonighan's drive, past the main house to the cottage where Manuel lived. Steam drifted off the coral-lined goldfish ponds; the door to the greenhouse banged like rifle shots in the wind. I cut the engine. Manuel sat motionless, with his hand resting on the door handle.

'Good luck to you,' I said.

'Why do?'

'Why do what?'

'Why help?'

'I think you're being used.' I took my business card out of my wallet and handed it to him. 'Call that telephone number if you want to talk.'

But it was obvious that he had little comprehension of what the words on the card meant. I slipped my badge holder out of my back pocket and opened it in front of him.

'I'm a police officer,' I said.

His hairline actually receded on his skull, like a rubber mask being stretched against bone; his nostrils whitened and constricted, as though he were inhaling air off a block of ice.

'All cops aren't bad, Manuel. Even those guys at the jail wanted to help you. They could have called Immigration if they had wanted.'

Bad word to use. The top of his left thigh was flexed like iron and trembling against his pants leg. I reached across him and popped the door open.

'Adios,' I said. 'Stay away from the pukes. Stay off Dauphine Street. Okay? Good-bye. *Hasta* whatever.'

I left him standing in the rain, his black hair splayed on his head like running paint, and drove back down the driveway. The gateman, a rain hat pulled down on his eyes, opened up for me. I rolled my window down as I drew abreast of him.

'Where's Tommy?' I said.

'He went out to the St Charles Parish jail to pick up the Indian. He's gonna be a little pissed when he gets back.'

'It's not Manuel's fault.'

'Tell me about it. I'm working his shift. The guy's a fucking savage, Robicheaux. He eats mushrooms off the lawn, he's got a fucking blowgun in his room.'

Way to go, Robicheaux, I thought. You frighten and confuse a retarded man, then leave him to the care of a headcase like Tommy Lonighan.

'Leave the gate open,' I said.

I made a U-turn in the street and headed back up the drive. I got out of the truck, a newspaper over my head, and walked toward Manuel's cottage. Then I stopped. At the rear of the greenhouse, kneeling in the rain, Manuel was chopping a hole through the roots of a hibiscus bush with a gardener's trowel. When the hole was as deep as his elbow, he dropped the trowel inside and began shoving the mound of wet dirt and torn roots in on top of it. The hibiscus flowers were red and stippled with raindrops, puffing and swelling in the wind like hearts on a green vine.

Ten minutes later I called Ben Motley from a pay phone outside a drugstore. A block away I could see the water whitecapping out on Lake Pontchartrain and, in the distance, the lights glowing like tiny diamonds on the causeway.

'Get a warrant on Tommy Lonighan's place,' I said.

'What for?'

I told him what I had seen and where they should dig.

'The vigilante is some kind of headhunter or cannibal?' he said.

'I don't know, Ben. But if you bust him, don't let the Caluccis or their lawyer bond him out.'

'The poor ignorant fuck.'

Welcome to Shit's Creek, Manuel.

28

The word *death* is never abstract. I think of my father high up on the night tower, out on the salt, when the wellhead blew and all the casing came out of the hole, the water and oil and sand geysering upward through the lights just before a spark flew from a metal surface and ignited a flame that melted the steel spars into licorice; I think of his silent form, still in hobnailed boots and hard hat, undulating in the groundswell deep under the gulf, his hand and sightless face beckoning.

Death is the smell that rises green and putrescent from a body bag popped open in a tropical mortuary; the luminescent pustules that cover the skin of VC disinterred from a nighttime bog of mud and excrement when the 105's come in short; the purple mushrooms that grow as thick and knotted as tumors among gum trees, where the boys in butternut brown ran futilely with aching breasts under a rain of airbursts that painted their clothes with torn rose petals.

But there are other kinds of endings that serve equally well for relocating your life into a dead zone where there seems to be neither wind nor sound, certainly not joy, or even, after a while, the capacity to feel.

You learn that the opposite of love is not hate but an attempt at surrogate love, which becomes a feast of poisonous flowers. You learn to make love out of need, in the dark, with the eyes closed, and to justify it to yourself, with a kiss only at the end. You learn that that old human enemy, ennui, can become as tangible and ubiquitous a presence in your life as a series of gray dawns from which the sun never breaks free.

I wasn't going to let it happen.

Bootsie and I met at a dance on Spanish Lake in the summer of '57. It was the summer that Hurricane Audrey killed over five hundred people in Louisiana, but I'll always remember the season for the twilight softness of its evenings, the fish fries on Bayou Teche and crab boils out on Cypremort Point, the purple and pink magic of each sunrise, the four-o'clocks that Bootsie would string in her hair like drops of blood, and the rainy afternoon we lost our virginity together on the cushions in my father's boathouse while the sun's refraction off the water spangled our bodies with brown light.

It was the summer that Jimmy Clanton's 'Just a Dream' played on every jukebox in southern Louisiana. I believed that death happened only to other

226

people, and that the season would never end. But it did, and by my own hand. Even at age nineteen I had learned how to turn whiskey into a weapon that could undo everything good in my life.

'What're you thinking about, bubba?' Bootsie said behind me.

'Oh, just one thing and another.' I stopped cleaning the spinning reel that I had taken apart on top of the picnic table. The air was wet and close, the willows dripping with water along the coulee.

'I called you twice through the window and you didn't hear me.'

'Sorry. What's up?'

'Nothing much. What's up with you?'

I turned around and looked at her. She wore a pair of white shorts and a T-shirt that was too small for her, which exposed her navel and her tapered, brown stomach.

'Isn't anything up with you?' she asked, and rested one knee on the bench, her arms on my shoulders, and leaned her weight into my back.

'What are you doing?' I said.

'Ummm,' she answered, and her hand moved down my chest.

I reached behind me and held the backs of her thighs and arched my neck and head between her breasts. She widened her legs and drew me tightly against her.

'Let's go inside,' she said, her voice husky and close to my ear.

'Alafair'll be home in a half hour.'

'A half hour will do just fine,' she said.

She drew the curtains in the bedroom, undressed completely, and pulled back the bedspread. Her skin was flushed and hot when I touched her.

'Are you okay, Boots?'

She pressed me down on the pillows and got on top of me, then cupped my sex with both hands and put it inside her. Her mouth opened silently, then her eyes became veiled and unfocused and she propped herself on her arms above me and adjusted her weight so that I was deep inside her, lost now in a place where breath and the heart's blood and the thin sheen of sweat on our bodies all became one. The only sound I could hear was a moist *click* in her throat when she swallowed, and the wind arching a thick, rain-slick oak limb against the window.

She came before I did, her breasts and nipples hard between her stiffened arms, her mouth wide, her hair curled damply on her cheeks. Then I felt it build and crest inside me, my loins dissolving like a hot ember burning through parchment. A sound unlike my own voice rose from my throat, and I pulled her close against me, my face buried in her hair, my mouth pressed like a hungry child's against her ear, while outside mockingbirds lifted clattering into the lavender sky.

I had believed that my will alone could solve the problem in our lives. As I lay beside her on top of the sheets, I realized that, as usual, I was wrong. But at a moment like that, who cares where gifts come from?

At five the next morning Clete Purcel knocked on my back screen. He wore canvas boat shoes without socks, a pair of baggy safari shorts covered with

227

snap-button pockets, his porkpie hat, and a sleeveless purple and gold Mike the Tiger jersey wash-faded to the thinness of cheesecloth. His face was unshaved and bright with fresh sunburn.

'You're not going to dime me, are you, Streak?'

'What do I know about warrants in Orleans Parish?' I stepped outside into the blue coolness of the morning and eased the screen shut behind me. 'Bootsie and Alf are still asleep. Let's walk down to the dock.'

We went down the slope through the deep shadow of the trees, stepping over the trip wire I had strung for Buchalter. Clete kept cracking his knuckles, as though they were big walnut shells. His eyes were red and irritated along the rims, as though he were hungover, but I could smell no alcohol on him.

'You look like you're getting a lot of sun,' I said.

'Why not? Life in the Quarter was turning me into a fat slug, anyway.'

Inside the shop I poured coffee and hot milk for both of us, and we took it out on to one of the spool tables by the water. He unsnapped a pocket on his shorts and unfolded a nautical chart on the table.

'Can you show me where that sub is?' His eyes looked at the chart and not at me.

'What are you up to?'

'What do you care?'

'You look wired, Clete. What's wrong?'

'I've got a warrant on me, my business is in the toilet, Nate Baxter's trained shitheads'll probably try to smoke me on sight, and you ask what's wrong?'

I smoothed the chart flat with my palm. The marsh was emerald green after last night's rain, and the cypress knees along the bayous were grained and dark and shining with water from a passing boat's wake.

'Don't get in any deeper,' I said.

'In for a penny, in for a pound. You going to show me where it is or not?' He lit an unfiltered cigarette and flicked the match hard into the air.

I took a mechanical pencil from my shirt pocket and made three marks on the chart.

'These are the places where either I saw it or Hippo's friend pinged it. You can see the pattern. There's probably a trench that bleeds back off the continental shelf. A guy with a depth finder could set up a zigzag pattern and probably locate it. Unless it drops off the shelf and only gets blown back in by a storm.'

He stared down at the chart, his hat cocked over one eye.

'What are you going to do?' I asked.

'Maybe I should remodel it with some C-4.'

'Is the preacher mixed up in this?'

'Not yet. But he was sure beautiful on the radio last night, you know, that call-in show where the geek in the street gets to express his opinion. Brother Oswald is telling people the Beast is about to rise from the sea.' He looked at me and tried to smile. 'Maybe he's talking about my ex.'

'What are you hiding from me, partner?'

He arched his cigarette out on the bayou and watched it hiss in the water and float downstream.

'I've got to quit this. My lungs feel like they've got battery acid in them,' he said.

'What's the gig, Clete?'

'I got to boogie, noble mon,' he said.

'Eat some breakfast.'

'Got to make it happen, Streak. Like you used to say, miles before I sleep and all that stuff. Hang loose.'

'How's Martina?'

He walked toward his convertible without answering, then turned, winked, and gave me the thumbs-up sign.

Just before noon, Ben Motley called me at the office.

'We got the trowel,' he said.

'Go on . . .'

'The blade was clean, but there was dried blood in a crack between the handle and the shaft. The lab says it's human.'

'What else?'

'Two types. One match. With a guy who had his heart taken out against the wall of the St Louis Cemetery.'

'Why not two matches?'

'You're assuming we've found all the victims.'

'Where's Manuel?'

'In custody . . . This one doesn't make me feel too good, Robicheaux. The guy's got strained carrots for brains. The interpreter says he speaks some Indian dialect from down in the fucking Amazon.'

'You think it's too easy?'

'I think maybe we're talking patsy here. Hey, Lonighan's a prick but he was genuinely upset, like in a personal way, when he found out we were charging the kid with murder. Does that sound like Tommy Bobalouba to you?'

Not bad, Mots, I thought.

'Have you had any contact with Clete Purcel?' I said.

'Who?'

'He found a videotape on South American Indians, a documentary of some kind, in Max Calucci's house.'

'There's static on the line. I couldn't hear what you said. You got me? I didn't fucking hear that, Robicheaux.'

'Lonighan borrowed two hundred thou for his casino from the Calucci brothers. I have a feeling he was paying the debt by helping them set up the brown scag trade in the projects.'

'You tell Purcel he tries to put turds in the punch bowl on this one, he won't have to worry about Nate Baxter. I'll send his butt to Angola myself.'

'Rough words, Mots.'

'What you don't understand is Purcel doesn't take a guy down because the guy broke the law. He takes him down because he doesn't like the guy. That's why he'll never carry a shield again.'

'How do you think the case against the Indian is going to stand up?'

'Circumstantial evidence, a retard on the stand, a defense attorney who lets the jury know the retard is a grunt for a rich gangster who actually drowned somebody with a fire hose and got away with it. Take a guess how the jury might vote.'

'Thanks for all the good news.'

'It's not all bad. The word on the street is Lonighan's dying.'

'For some reason that doesn't fill me with joy, partner.'

'Lonighan's mixed up with the Caluccis and the dope trade in the projects. Those black kids we bust all the time, they weren't addicts when they came out of their mamas' womb. Believe it or not, even those dead dealers had families, Robicheaux.'

Why argue with charity? I eased the receiver down in the cradle and stared out the window at the palm trees rattling in the wind. The bottom of the sky looked green over the gulf.

What was Clete Purcel doing?

I went home for lunch. When I came back the sheriff stopped me at the watercooler.

'The FBI just relayed some stuff to us from Interpol. They've got a fix on the woman,' he said.

'What?'

'Read it. It's on your desk. I thought stuff like that only went on in the Barker family.' He walked away and left me staring after him.

The statement from Interpol consisted of four paragraphs. There was nothing statistical or demonstrable about the information in them. As with all the other documents in the case, it was as though the writer were trying to describe an elusive presence that had been mirrored only briefly in the eyes of others.

But the images he used weren't those of the ordinary technical writer; they remained in the memory like splinters under the skin.

Two undercover antiterrorist agents in Berlin believed that the man known as William Buchalter and Willie Schwert and other variations operated inside a half dozen neo-Nazi groups with a half sister named Marie. A skinhead in a beer garden told a story of an initiation into a select inner group known in England and the United States as the Sword. A kidnapped Turkish laborer had knelt trembling on the dirt floor of a potato cellar, his wrists wired behind him, a burlap sack pulled over his face, while the initiates pledged their lives to the new movement. Then the woman named Marie had set the kidnapped man on fire.

I opened and closed my mouth, as though my ears were popping from cabin pressure in an airplane, and continued to read. The details in the last paragraph gave another dimension to the sweaty, hoarse voices that I had heard over the telephone.

The sheriff stood in my doorway with a coffee cup in his hand.

'You think that's our phony nun?' he said.

'Yeah, I do.'

'You believe that stuff at the end of the page?'

'They're perverse people. Why should anything they do be a surprise?'

'Did you know Ma Barker and one of her sons were incestuous? They committed suicide by machine-gunning each other. They were even buried together in the same casket, to keep the tradition intact. That's a fact.'

'Interesting stuff,' I said.

'You've got to have some fun with it or you go crazy. I got to tell you that?'

'No, you're right.'

He walked over and squeezed me on the shoulder. I could smell his leather gunbelt and pipe tobacco in his clothes.

'You sleeping all right at night?' he said.

'You bet.'

He grunted under his breath.

'That's funny, I don't. Well, maybe we'll drop that pair in their own box. Who knows?' he said.

He walked his fingernails across my desk and went back out the door.

The best lead on Buchalter, the only one, really, was still music.

Brother Oswald Flat, I thought.

I got his telephone number from long-distance information.

'Didn't you say you played with Jimmy Martin and the Sunny Mountain Boys?' I asked.

'What about hit?'

'Did you ever have any connection with jazz or blues musicians?'

'Son, I like you. I really do. But a conversation with you is like trying to teach someone the recipe for ice water.'

'I'm afraid I'm not following you.'

'That's the point. You never do.'

'I'll try to listen carefully, sir, if you can be patient with me.'

'Music's one club. Hit's like belonging to the church. Hit don't matter which room you're in, long as you're in the building. You with me?'

'You know some jazz musicians?'

'I'll have a go at hit from a different angle,' he said. 'I used to record gospel at Sam Phillip's studio in Memphis. You know who else recorded in that same studio? Elvis Presley, Carl Perkins, Johnny Cash, Jerry Lee Lewis, Jimmy Lee Swaggert. You want me to go on?'

'I think Will Buchalter has some kind of involvement with historical jazz or blues. But I don't know what it is.'

The phone was silent.

'Reverend?'

'Why didn't you spit hit out?'

This time I didn't answer. His voice had changed when he spoke again.

'I won't interrupt you or insult you again,' he said.

I recounted the most recent late-night phone call, with Beiderbecke's 'In a Mist' playing in the background; Buchalter's knowledge of early Benny Goodman and the proper way to handle old seventy-eights; the Bunk Johnson record that someone had left playing on my phonograph.

'You impress me, son. You *know*,' Oswald Flat said.

Again, I was silent.

'An evil man cain't love music,' he said. 'He's interested in hit for some other reason.'

'I think you're right.'

'There's a band plays on Royal Street. I mean, out in the street, when the cops put the barricades up and close off the traffic. They got a piano on a truck, a Chinese kid playing harmonica, some horns, a colored, I mean a black, man on slide guitar. The black man comes to my church sometimes. But he don't live in New Orleans. He's in Morgan City.'

'Yes?'

'If I call and see if he's home, can you meet me there in a couple of hours?'

'I think you'd better clarify yourself.'

'That's all you get. Holler till your face looks like an eggplant.'

'This is part of a police investigation, Reverend. You don't write the rules.'

'He's been in the penitentiary. He won't talk to you unless I'm there. You want my he'p or not?'

The black man's name was Jesse Viator, and he lived in a dented green trailer set up on concrete blocks thirty feet from the bayou's edge. He had only three teeth in his mouth, and they protruded from his gums like the hooked teeth in the mouth of a barracuda. We sat on old movie theater seats that he had propped up on railroad ties in his small, tidy backyard. A shrimp boat passed with its lights on, and near the far bank swallows were swooping above an oil barge that had rusted into a flooded shell.

Jesse Viator was not comfortable in the presence of a police officer.

'You remember that man you told me about, the one wanted you to record, the fellow you said bothered you the way he looked at you?' Brother Oswald said.

'Yeah, dude was up to no good,' he said.

'Why did you think that?' I asked. I smiled.

'Some people got their sign hanging out,' he answered. He pulled at the soft flesh under his chin and looked out at the bayou.

'Why was he up to no good, Jesse?' I said.

'Dude didn't say nothing mean. He was polite. But it was like there was heat in his face,' Viator said. 'Like a dry pan been setting on the gas burner.'

I showed him the composite drawing of Buchalter. He held it in the light from his trailer and studied it. His grizzled pate shone like tan wax.

'You do them composites with a machine, right? So a lot of them look alike,' he said.

'Who's the worst guy you ever met inside?' I said.

'They only get so bad. Then they all about the same. They end up in Camp J.'

'The guy I'm looking for is worse than anybody in Camp J. Do you believe me when I say that?'

He took the drawing back from my hand and tilted it to catch the light from the trailer. He tapped on the edges of the face. 'What's that?' he said.

'You tell me,' I said.

'Dude had dirt in his skin, what d' you call 'em, blackheads or something, made him look like he was wearing a mask around his eyes. Look, it was t'ree, four mont's back. I stopped thinking about it.'

'Tell him the rest of hit, Jesse,' Oswald Flat said.

'There ain't no *rest*,' he said. 'Dude say he give me a hundred dollars to record. I tole him I ain't interested. That's it. I don't want to talk about it no more.'

'Are you scared of this man?' I said, and kept my eyes on his.

He took a breath that was between anger and exasperation.

'You know the feeling that dude give me? It was like when a guy get made a slave up at Angola. When somebody turn out a kid, rape him, then tell him, "Haul your lil ass down the Walk. In a half hour come back with ten dollars. In another half hour, I want ten dollars more, then I want ten dollars more after that, or the next thing go in your mouth got a sharp point on it and it don't come out." That's what that dude's eyes made me think of.'

He became morose and sullen and would say little more. The moon was up, and road dust and a sheen of diesel oil floated on the dead current close under the willows. The air was cool and humid and smelled of bait shrimp someone had left in a bucket. I asked the reverend to wait for me out front.

'What'd you fall for, Jesse?' I said.

'Guy tried to joog me at a dance. I didn't want to, but I put him down. Lawyer tole me to plea to manslaughter.'

'You have a family?'

'My wife's at the Charity. She got heart trouble. Our two daughters is growed up and married, in California.'

'The man I want molested my wife. I'll show you what he does when he gets his hands on people.' I stood up from my chair.

'What you doing, man? Hey, you taking off your—'

'Buchalter used an electrical generator on me, Jesse. That's where he attached the terminals. It's quite an experience.'

He propped his hands on his thighs, twisted in his chair, and focused his eyes on a cane pole that was stuck deep in the roots of a cypress tree.

'Man, I'm serious, I don't want no more to do with this,' he said.

'You had this guy made from the jump. You've got to help me, Jesse.'

He wiped at his face as though insects were in his eyes.

'Dude comes up to me on Royal, right after the gig, offers me a hundred bucks to play a half hour of my slide at his studio. I say, A hundred bucks don't cut making a tape. He says it's a demo, he's gonna offer it around, he's doing me a favor, usually a guy's got to pay for his own demo.

'I'm looking into that cat's face, I'm thinking he ain't ever gonna use the word *nigger*, he ain't gonna call me boon or tree climber or spear chucker, that ain't his way. He got that lil smile playing around the corner of his mouth, just like them guys in the AB look at you up at the farm. They'll hoe next to you in the soybean row, won't say nothing to you, chopping all the time like their mind is full of cool thoughts. That night you go in the shower and that same dude waiting for you with a shank in his hand.'

'You've got to give me something, Jesse.'

'He say his studio was one hour away. One hour there, one hour back. He winked at me when he said it.'

'I think you're holding back on me.' I kept my eyes locked on his.

'I ain't. He called once, man, right here at the trailer. I tole him I still ain't interested. It sound like he was outdoors, pay phone maybe. I could hear waves flopping, like on a beach.'

'He never mentioned a place? How about Grand Isle?'

'Not unless they moved Grand Isle over to Miss'sippi.'

'I'm not with you.'

'That day on Royal. I didn't pay the car no mind, but the plates was from Miss'sippi. That good enough? 'Cause that's all there is.'

I gave him my business card and picked up my coat from the chair. He looked out into space while his hand closed and opened on the card. Then he pressed it back into my palm.

'My wife deserve a trip after all the sickness she been having. I think we going out to visit our children in California. Be gone quite a while. You understand what I'm saying?'

The next afternoon, which was Friday afternoon, Ben Motley called me from New Orleans.

'Max Calucci dropped the charges against Purcel for destroying his house,' he said.

'Quite a change of heart.'

'What's your take on it?'

'He probably started sweating marbles when he heard Lonighan's Indian was in custody. That is, if he's mixed up in the vigilante killings. The last thing he needs now is legal involvement with the prosecutor's office. What's the insurance carrier, State Farm, going to do?'

'They're out of luck if they want to put it on Purcel. The witnesses now say they don't remember what the guy on the grader looked like. But they're sure it wasn't Purcel. I left a message on his recorder, but he didn't call back.'

'He's holed up in a fish camp someplace.'

'I went by his office. A secretary, a temp, was in there. She said he retrieved the message off the machine. Why doesn't he answer his calls?'

'I don't know, he's a little irresponsible sometimes. What's the status on Manuel Ruiz?'

'No bond. We're holding him for the INS. By the way, tell Purcel it's all right he doesn't call me back. Since he's already got such good friends in the department. Like Nate Baxter.'

I left a message for Clete at both his office and his apartment.

That evening I put on my gym shorts and running shoes and did three sets of dead lifts, bench presses, and curls in the backyard. My neighbor was burning a pile of dried honeysuckle, and the air was hazy and sweet with the smoke.

Tie it down, *think*, I told myself. What were the ongoing connections in the Buchalter case?

Music, and now geography.

Two of Buchalter's hired meltdowns, Jack Pelley and Charles Sitwell, had been in the rock 'n' roll band in the Block at Angola. Buchalter evidently prowled stores that handled old records, like Jimmie Ryan's, and had tried to make a studio recording of the slide guitarist Jesse Viator.

He had been driving a car with Mississippi plates, had access to a studio an hour from New Orleans, and had made a telephone call within earshot of a beach.

The German skinhead who had been run down by his friends out on the salt had been diving from a cabin cruiser he and his friends had stolen from a berth in Biloxi.

Hippo Bimstine's friends had broken up a meeting of a hate group with baseball bats and expropriated their Nazi film footage in a cinder-block house north of Pascagoula.

I lowered the bar to my thighs, then curled it into my chest, released it slowly again, pausing in midair as the muscles in my arms burned and filled with blood. The air felt as cool as a knife blade in my lungs.

Maybe the circle was starting to tighten on Will Buchalter.

Before we went to bed, Bootsie and I ate a piece of pie at the kitchen table.

'Is something bothering you?' she said.

'I thought Clete might call.'

'Clete has his own way of doing things.'

'You're right about that.'

That night the wind blew hard out of the south, and I could hear our rental boats knocking against the pilings in the dock. Then it began to rain, and in my sleep I heard another sound, a distant one, metal striking methodically against metal, one pinging blow after another, muffled by the envelope of water it had to travel through.

In my dream I saw a group of Nazi sailors huddled in a half-flooded compartment, salt water pinwheeling through the leaks above their heads, their faces white with terror in the dimming light while they breathed their own stink and the coldness crept above their loins and one man kept whanging a wrench against the bulkhead.

I woke from the dream, my chest laboring for air. Through the clicking of the rain in the trees, I could still hear the rhythmic *twang* of metal hitting against metal. I slipped on my loafers and khakis, pulled a raincoat over my head, and, with a flashlight in my hand, ran from the back door to the collapsed barn by my duck pond. A sheet of corrugated tin roofing, purple with rust, was swinging from a broken beam against the remains of my father's old hay baler.

I pulled the broken beam and sheet of tin loose from the pile and threw them out into the field.

But I couldn't shake the dream. Why? What did I care about the fate of Nazis drowned fifty years ago?

The dream was not about submariners. Someone close to me was in trouble, maybe because of information I had given him, and I was trying to deny that simple fact.

Where was Clete Purcel?

29

Tommy Lonighan had turned up the heat inside his glassed-in sunporch, even though it was seventy-five degrees outside and he was wearing sweatpants and a long-sleeved flannel shirt. My face was moist with heat, but his skin looked dry and gray, almost flaccid, as though his glands had stopped secreting; he sat forward on his reclining chair, his eyes still trying to follow the action in a movie playing on his VCR, a furious conclusion working in his face.

'This is a piece of crap,' he said, pulled the cassette from the VCR, and flung it clattering into a pile of other cassettes. 'You saw that movie *Reservoir Dogs*? It's sickening. A bunch of made guys are beating up and torturing a cop. No mobbed-up guys would do something like that. The guy who wrote this don't know dick about crime. You know what I think, it's the guy wrote this is sick, not the fucking criminals.'

'Can you help me find Clete or not?'

'Where do you find an elephant? You go to the circus. How should I know where he is? Ask his punch, the one getting in my face about Jews.'

'I went by Martina's apartment this morning. No one's seen her in two or three days.'

''Cause she's with Purcel. 'Cause he's got a warrant on him, he don't wake up with a boner?'

'You're unbelievable, Tommy.'

'If Max or Bobo did something to him, I'd a heard about it, and I ain't.' He freed something from a nostril and sniffed dryly. 'Can I tell you something? I don't give a shit, either. I wish the Caluccis would try to hit somebody now. Maybe they'd get taken down like they deserve.'

'You're talking about my friend.'

'I should worry about Purcel? I got maybe three, four months, then the doctor says he'll start me on morphine. Maybe it ain't gonna do the job, either. You know why I got all this grief in my life? It's punishment 'cause I got mixed up with those fucking greasebags. They're immoral, they got no honor, they—'

'Then why not dime 'em and be done with it, Tommy?'

'I thought you knew.' His eyes were close-set, like BB's. Blotches of color broke in his face. 'You guys don't use telephones, you don't talk to each other?'

'What is it?' I said.

'Late yesterday, I spilled my guts, everything,' he said. 'I haven't been charged yet, but they'll do that Monday.'

I waited. The room was ablaze with sunlight and color – the deep blue tile floor, the cane deck furniture and canary yellow cushions – but in its midst Tommy looked stricken, like a man who had mistakenly thought the source of his abiding shame had at least become known and accepted if not forgiven.

'Max and Bobo wanted to scare the coloreds out of the trade in the projects,' he said. 'They used Manny to do three guys. They told him these coloreds were evil spirits and had to be killed 'cause they were selling dope and corrupting little kids. He comes from a bunch of headhunters or cannibals that's got a flower and death cult or something. Or maybe Max made him think he did after he got ahold of this documentary on these prehistoric people that's running around in South America. I don't know about that stuff.'

He scowled into space. White clouds were tumbling in the sky, leaves blowing across the freshly clipped lawn.

'You think I'm toe jam, don't you?' he said.

I kept my face empty and brushed at the crystal on my watch with my thumb.

'A couple of button guys did the other hits, I heard Jamaicans out of Miami,' he said. 'It's been putting boards in my head. I feel miserable. It's like nothing's any good anymore. There's some kind of smell won't wash out of my clothes. Here, you smell it?'

He extended his shirt cuff under my nose.

'Where you going?' he said.

'I've got to find Clete.'

'Stay. I'll fix some chicken sandwiches.'

'Sorry.'

He blew his nose in a Kleenex and dropped the Kleenex in a paper bag full of crumpled tissue, many of them flecked with blood.

'You seen Hippo?' he said.

'We're not on good terms, I'm afraid.'

'He ain't such a bad guy.' He stared disjointedly at the leaves blowing against the windows. 'You see him again, tell him I said that.'

'Sure.'

'You want to take some movie cassettes? I get them for two bucks from a guy sells dubs in Algiers.'

'Dubs?'

'What world you hang out in, Dave? Anything that's electronically recorded today gets dubbed and resold. Those music tapes you see in truck stops, you think Kenny Rogers sells his tapes for three-ninety-five? What, I'm saying the wrong thing again?'

'No, I just haven't been thinking clearly about something, Tommy. See you around.'

I went by Clete's office on St Ann in the Quarter. It was locked, the blinds drawn, the mailbox inside the brick archway stuffed with letters. I used a pay phone in Jackson Square to call Ben Motley at his home.

'Why didn't you tell me Lonighan made a statement yesterday?' I said.

'It happened late. I don't know how it's going to go down, anyway . . . Look, the bottom line is Lonighan implicated himself and the Indian. Lonighan's already a dead man, and the Indian's a retard. The interpreter says he'll testify he works for Spiderman if you want him to. The prosecutor's office isn't calling news conferences.'

'What's the status on the Caluccis?'

'That's what I'm trying to tell you, Robicheaux. There isn't any. We'll see what happens Monday. But we got an old problem, too. The Caluccis go down, Nate Baxter goes down. He's going to screw up the investigation any way he can.'

I felt my hand squeeze tightly around the receiver. The sunlight through the restaurant window was like a splinter of glass in the eye.

'Cheer up,' he said. 'We're getting there.'

'Purcel's completely off the screen.'

'Cover your own ass for a change. You know how Purcel'll buy it? He'll catch some kind of incurable clap when he's a hundred and fifty. Call me Monday.'

I drove up St Charles to Hippo's drugstore. He was sitting in the shade on a collapsible metal chair by the entrance, eating a spearmint snowball. Two streetcars were stopped at a sunny spot on the neutral ground, loading and unloading passengers. At first he ignored me and continued to eat the ice out of the paper cone; then he smiled and aimed his index finger and thumb at me like a cocked pistol.

'A weird place to sit, Hippo,' I said.

'Not for me. I love New Orleans. Look up and down this street – the trees, the old homes, the moss in the wind. There's not another street like it in the world.' He reached next to him and popped open a second metal chair. 'Sit down. What can I do for you?'

'You're okay, Hippo.'

'Why not?' His eyes squinted into slits with his smile.

'You know about almost every enterprise on the Gulf Coast, don't you?'

'Business is like spaghetti . . . pull on one piece, you move the whole plate.'

'Let me try a riddle on you. Mobbed-up guys don't torture cops, do they?'

'Not unless they're planning careers as crab bait.'

'Buchalter's not mobbed-up.'

'That's a breakthrough for you?'

'But what if Buchalter was selling duplicated recordings of historical jazz, or making blues tapes and screwing the musician on the copyright?'

'Dubs are in. Some lowlifes tried to get me to retail them in my drugstores. I don't think there's any big market for historical jazz, though.'

'Stay with me, Hippo. A guy selling dubs would have to piece off the action or be connected, right?'

'If he wants to stay in business.'

'So Buchalter's not part of the local action. Where's the biggest market for old blues and jazz?'

His eyes became thoughtful. 'He's selling it in Europe?'

'I think I've got a shot at him.'

He took another bite out of his cone and sucked his cheeks in.

'You want some backup? From guys with no last names?' he asked.

'Buchalter probably has a recording studio of some kind over on the Mississippi coast. I can go over there and spend several days looking through phone books and knocking on doors.'

He nodded without replying.

'Or I can get some help from a friend who has a lot of connections on the coast.'

'I provide information, then me and my friends get lost, that's what you're saying?'

'So far we don't have open season on people we don't like, Hippo.'

He crumpled up the paper cone in his hand, walked to a trash receptacle, and dropped it in.

'We'll use the phone at my place,' he said.

It didn't take long. He made four phone calls, then a half hour later a fax came through his machine with a list of addresses on it. He handed it to me, his sleek, football-shaped head framed by the corkboard filled with death camp photos behind him.

'There're seven of them, strung out between Bay St Louis and Pascagoula,' he said. 'It looks like you get to knock on lots of doors, anyway.'

I folded the fax and put it in my coat pocket.

'Did you hear about Tommy Bobalouba?' I said.

'He knew he had cancer two years ago. He shouldn't have fooled around with it.'

'That's kind of rough, Hippo.'

'I'm supposed to weep over mortality? Do you know what's going on in that mick's head? I win, he loses. But he wants me to know I win only because he got reamed by the Big C.'

'I saw him just a little while ago. He said you're not a bad guy. He wanted you to know he said that.'

He snipped off the tip of a cigar with a small, sharp tool, and didn't raise his eyes. He kept sucking his lips as though he had just eaten a slice of raw lemon rind.

It was three o'clock when I stopped at Bay St Louis. The bay was flat and calm, the long pier off old ninety dotted with fishermen casting two-handed rods and weighted throw nets into the glaze of sunlight on the surface; but in the south the sky was stained a chemical green along the horizon, the clouds low and humped, like torn black cotton.

The first address was a half block from the beach. The owners were elderly people who had moved recently from Omaha and had opened a specialty store that featured Christian books and records. They had bought the building two years ago from a man who had operated a recording studio at that address, but he had gone into bankruptcy and had since died.

I had a telephone number for the next address, which was in Pass Christian. I called before getting back on the highway; a recorded voice told me the number was no longer in service.

Thanks, Hippo.

I called his house to ask about the source of his information. His wife said he had left and she didn't know when he would be back. Did she know where he was?

'Why do you want to know?' she asked.

'It's a police matter, Mrs Bimstine.'

'Do you get paid for solving your own problems? Or do you hire consultants?'

'Did I do something to offend you?'

She paused before she spoke again. 'Somebody called from the hospital. Tommy Lonighan's in the emergency room. He wanted to see Hippo.'

'The emergency room? I saw Lonighan just a few hours ago.'

'Before or after he was shot?'

She hung up.

It was starting to rain when I drove into Gulfport to check the next address. The sky was gray now, and the beach was almost empty. The tide was out, and the water was green and calm and dented with the rain, but in the distance you could see a rim of cobalt along the horizon and, in the swells, the triangular, leathery backs of stingrays that had been kicked in by a storm.

I was running out of time. It was almost five o'clock, and many of the stores were closing for the weekend. At an outdoor pay phone on the beach, I called the 800 number for Federal Express and asked for the location of the largest FedEx station in the area.

There was only one, and it was in Gulfport. The clerk at the station was young and nervous and kept telling me that I should talk to his supervisor, who would be back soon.

'It's an easy question. Which of your customers sends the greatest volume of express packages overseas?' I said.

'I don't feel comfortable with this, Officer. I'm sorry,' he said, a pained light in his eyes.

'I respect your integrity. But would you feel comfortable if somebody dies because we have to wait on your supervisor?'

He went into the back and returned with a flat, cardboard envelope in his hand. He set it on the counter.

'The guy owns a music business in Biloxi,' he said. 'He sends a lot of stuff to Germany and France.'

'You know this guy?'

'No, sir.' His jawbone flexed against his skin.

'But you know something about him?'

He cleared his throat slightly. 'One of the black drivers said he'd quit before he'd go back to the guy's store.'

The sender's name on the envelope was William K. Guilbeaux.

Before driving into Biloxi, I called Hippo's house again. This time *he* answered. There was static on the line, and the rain was blowing in sheets against the windows of the phone booth.

'I can't understand you,' I said.

'I'm saying he had a priest with him. You're a Catholic, I thought you'd appreciate that.'

'Tommy's—'

'He had a priest there, maybe he'll get in a side door up in heaven. The spaghetti head didn't have that kind of luck, though.'

'What?'

30

On Saturdays Max and Bobo Calucci usually had supper, with their girlfriends and gumballs, at a blue-collar Italian restaurant off Canal near the New Orleans Country Club. It was a place with checker-cloth-covered tables, wood-bladed ceiling fans, Chianti served in wicker-basket bottles, a brass-railed mahogany bar, a TV sports screen high overhead, and a good-natured bartender who had once played for the Saints.

An off-duty uniformed police officer stood guard at the front door. The patrons were family people, and white; they celebrated birthdays and anniversaries at the restaurant; the mood was always loud and happy, almost raucous. It was like going through a door into a festive and carefree New Orleans of forty years ago.

Tommy Lonighan was by himself when he arrived in a rental stretch limo. Tommy Bobalouba, the stomp-ass kid from Magazine who could knock his opponent's mouthpiece into the fourth row, stepped out on the curb with the perfumed and powdered grace of castle Irish. He looked like an elegant resurrection of the 1940s, in a tailored white suit with purple pinstripes, a wide scarlet polka-dot tie, oxblood loafers, his face ruddy with a whiskey flush, his blue eyes as merry as an elf's. His lavender shirt seemed molded to his powerful physique.

Outside his shirt and under his tie, he wore a gold chain with what looked like two mismatched metal objects attached to it.

The cop at the door, who was nearing retirement, grinned and feigned a prizefighter's stance with him. When he walked through the tables, people shook his hand, pointed him out to each other as a celebrity; the bartender shouted out, 'Hey, Tommy, Riddick Bowe was just in here looking for you! He needs some pointers!'

Tommy sipped a whiskey sour at the bar, with one polished loafer on the rail, his smile always in place, his face turned toward the crowd, as though the collective din that rose from it was an extension of the adulation that had rolled over him in a validating crescendo many years ago, when thousands in a sweaty auditorium chanted, 'Hook 'im, Bobalouba! Hook 'im, Bobalouba! Hook 'im, Bobalouba!'

He gazed at the Caluccis' table with goodwill, bought a round for the bar, dotted a shrimp cocktail with Tabasco sauce, and ate it with a spoon like ice cream.

Then one of Max's people, a pale, lithe Neapolitan hood named Sal Palacio, walked up to him, his palms open, a question mark in the center of his face.

'We got a problem, Tommy?' he said.

'Not with me you don't,' Tommy answered, his dentures showing stiffly with his smile.

'Because Max and Bobo are wondering what you're doing here, since it ain't your regular place, you hear what I'm saying?'

Tommy looked at a spot on the wall, his eyelids fluttering. 'I need a passport in New Orleans these days?' he said.

'They said to tell you they got no hard feelings. They're sorry things ain't worked out, they're sorry you're sick, they don't want people holding no grudges.'

Tommy cocked his fists playfully; Sal's face popped like a rubber band.

'Man, don't do that,' he said.

'Take it easy, kid,' Tommy said, brushing Sal's stomach with his knuckles. 'You want a drink?'

'I got to ask you to walk into the washroom with me.'

'Hey, get this kid,' Tommy said to the people standing around him. 'Sal, you don't got a girlfriend?'

'It ain't funny, Tommy.'

Tommy pulled back his coat lapels, lifted his coattails, slapped his pockets, turned in a circle.

'Sal, you want to put your hand in my crotch?' he asked.

'You're a fucking lunatic,' he answered, and walked away.

But the Caluccis were becoming more and more nervous, self-conscious, convinced that each time Lonighan spoke into a cluster of people at the bar and they laughed uproariously, the Caluccis were the butt of the joke.

Max stood up from his chair, a bread stick in one hand, a pitcher of sangria in the other, working his neck against the starch in his collar.

'Hey, Tommy,' he said, over the heads of people at the other tables. 'You don't want to have a drink with your friends, you crazy guy?'

Tommy walked toward the Calucci table, still smiling, a dream-like luster in his eyes, his cheeks glowing from a fresh shave. He patted Max on the shoulders, pressed him into his chair, bent down and whispered in his ear, as though he were confiding in an old friend.

Few people noticed Tommy's left hand biting into the back of Max's neck or the charged and fearful light in Max's eyes, or Tommy raising his right knee and slipping a .38 one inch from the cloth holster strapped to his calf.

Then the conversation at the other tables died; people stopped eating and became immobile in their chairs, as though they were part of a film winding down on a reel; waiters set down their trays and remained motionless in the aisles. Tommy pushed Max's face into his plate as though he were bending the tension out of a spring.

243

The cop at the door had stepped inside out of the rain. He stared dumbfounded at Lonighan.

'Walk back outside, Pat. Or I pop him right now. I swear to God I will,' Tommy said.

'You're having some kind of breakdown, Tommy. This ain't your way,' Sal Palacio said.

'Put your piece in the pitcher, Sal. You other two fucks do the same,' Tommy said.

Sal and the other two bodyguards dropped their pistols into the sangria. Tommy twisted the barrel of the .38 into the soft place behind Max's ear and clicked back the hammer.

'This guy here, the one with the linguine in his face, him and his brother been killing the colored dealers in the projects,' he said. 'You think the city's shit now, wait till you see what it's like when the Caluccis got the whole dope trade to themselves.'

'Tommy, you're taking us all over the edge here,' the cop at the door said, his mouth parting dryly after his words had stopped.

'Hey, Pat, tell Nate Baxter I just fucked his meal ticket,' Tommy said, and pulled the trigger.

Max's mouth opened sideways on his plate, like that of a fish that had been thrown hard upon the bank. Tommy pulled the trigger again, with people screaming now, this time the barrel a half inch from the crown of Max's skull. A tuft of Max's hair jumped as though it had been touched by a puff of wind.

Then, with Bobo under the table and the cop drawing his weapon, Tommy went through the curtained hallway behind him, stepped inside the men's room, and bolted the door.

For some reason he did it in a toilet stall, seated on top of the stool, with his trousers still on, the revolver pointed awkwardly toward his throat. The impact of the round wedged his head into the corner of the stall; the recoil sent the .38 skittering in a red trail across the tiles; the hemorrhage from the wound covered his chest like a scarlet bib. Later the coroner lifted the gold chain from his neck with a fountain pen. Attached to it were a lead-colored army dog tag and a small gold boxing glove from the Golden Gloves of 1951.

I wondered if Tommy heard the roar of the crowd just as his thumb tightened inside the trigger housing, or the echo of Chinese bugles and small arms through a frozen arroyo, or perhaps the squeal of an ice truck's brakes on a street full of children in the Channel; or if he stared into the shadows, seeking the epiphany that had always eluded him, and saw only more shadows and motes of spinning dust and the graffiti scratched into the paint on the door, until he realized, just as the hammer snapped down on the brass cartridge, that the eruption of pain and fear and blood in his chest was simply the terminus of an ongoing war that he had waged for a lifetime against his own heart.

Later I mentioned my thoughts to Hippo.

'Don't complicate that dumb mick, Dave. He even screwed up his own suicide,' he answered. Then, with his face turned so I couldn't see his eyes,

'He apologized before he checked out. Just him and me in the room. Just like when we were boys.'

And he walked away.

31

The music store was located between an auto garage and a boarded-up café on a nondescript street north of Biloxi. It was still raining; only two cars were parked on the street, and the sidewalks were empty. A block farther north, there was a string of gray clapboard and Montgomery Ward brick houses, their lawns choked with weeds. A neon beer sign burned in the gloom above a pool hall that had virtually no patrons. The street reminded me of a painting I had once seen by Adolf Hitler; it contained buildings but no people. It was the kind of neighborhood where one's inadequacies would never find harsh comparisons.

Was this music store, with cracked and taped windows, moldy cardboard cartons piled by the front door, the headquarters of Will Buchalter, a man who moved like a political disease through a dozen countries?

I remembered a story about the Israeli agents who captured Adolf Eichmann as he was returning from his job in an automobile plant somewhere in South America. One of the agents was young and could not quite accept the fact that he was now face-to-face with the man who had murdered his parents.

'What job do you perform at the auto plant?' he asked.

'I'm one of the chrome polishers. We polish all the chrome surfaces on the new automobiles,' Eichmann answered.

According to the story, the agent began to weep.

The door to the store was locked, but I could see a man moving around behind a counter. The wind was blowing a wet, acrid stench through the space between the buildings. I tapped on the glass.

The man inside waved his hand negatively. I tapped again. He walked toward me, saying the word *Closed* so I could read his lips. He wore a sleeveless flannel shirt and black jeans that sculpted his sex. His blond hair was coated and waved with gel, his white arms wrapped with tattoos of green and red dragons.

I shook the doorknob when he tried to walk away.

'I'm a friend of Will's,' I said.

'He's gone,' the man said through the glass.

'Open up. I've got to leave him a message.'

'Sorry, we're closed. I don't know how else to say it.'

'Where's Marie?'

'Come back Monday,' he said, and dropped the venetian blinds down the glass.

I got back in my truck and drove three blocks up the street. Then I circled back, parked at the end of the alley, and walked toward the rear of the store under the eaves of the buildings. A rusted-out trash barrel was smoldering in the rain, and again I smelled a moist, acrid odor that was like the smell of a dead bat in an incinerator.

Just as I reached inside my raincoat for my .45, he stepped out the back door with a sack of trash in his hands. I slipped my hand back out of my coat and fixed a button with it.

'What's with you?' he said.

'I got to be back at the halfway house by dark, you hear what I'm saying?'

'No.'

'Maybe you think you're doing your job, but you're starting to piss me off,' I said.

'*Excuse* me.'

'Look, I was supposed to connect with him when I got out. I just had six fucking years of putting up with smart-ass watermelon pickers. I'm begging you, buddy, don't fuck up my day any worse than it already has been.'

'All right, I'm sorry, but it don't change anything. I got to lock up. Will ain't here. Okay? See the man Monday.'

He dropped the paper bag into the trash barrel and turned to go back inside. I shoved him hard between the shoulder blades, followed him inside, and laid the muzzle of the .45 against the back of his neck.

'Get down on your knees,' I said.

'I don't know who you are but—'

'You've got a serious hearing problem,' I said, kicked him behind the knee, and pushed him into the counter. His eyes widened with pain when his knees hit the floor.

'Where is he?' I said.

'He don't tell me that kind of stuff. I work for *him*, he don't work for me. Who are you, man?'

'What do you care, as long as you get to live?'

'I just finished a bit myself. Why you twisting me? Take your shit to Will.'

'But you're the only guy around,' I said. 'Which means you're all out of luck.'

I pulled my cuffs off my belt and hooked up his wrists. He was face down now, his eyelids fluttering against the dust and oil on the floor. The rain and the smoke from the trash barrel blew through the back door.

'What's that smell?' I said.

He bit down on his bottom lip.

I glanced around the store. The interior was cluttered with boxes of old seventy-eight records. In one corner was a glassed-in sound booth with an instrument panel and an elevated microphone inside. A mop inside a pail of dirty water was propped against a closed side door. I pulled back the slide on the .45 and eased a round into the chamber.

247

'I bought this in Bring Cash Alley in Saigon for twenty-five dollars,' I said. 'No registration, completely cold, you get my drift?'

His eyes squeezed shut, then opened again. 'Don't do this to me, man. Please,' he said.

My hand was tight and sweating on the knurled grips of the .45. I looked through the front window at the rain falling in the street. In the distance a stuck car horn was blaring, a stabbing, unrelieved sound in the inner ear like fingernails on a blackboard.

I eased the hammer back into place, clicked on the safety, and slipped the .45 back into my belt holster.

'I'm a police officer,' I said. 'Do you believe me when I say that?'

'Bust me. I ain't arguing.'

'But I'm beyond my parameters here. Do you know what that means?'

His eyes were filled with confusion.

'Will Buchalter and his sister have hurt my family,' I said. 'So we're not working on conventional rules anymore. Do you believe me when I say that?'

'Yes, sir. You got no trouble from me.'

'So what's that smell?'

'I was just trying to clean up ... The guy gets crazy sometimes ... He started hitting her with his fists for no reason, then he went in there with some scissors. I didn't have anything to do with it, man.'

'Hit who?'

'The broad ... I thought that's why you were here. The broad he's been holding.' He stared at the look on my face. 'Oh shit, man, this ain't my doing. You got to believe that.'

I scraped the pail and mop out of the way with my foot and opened the side door.

She was tied to a chair with clothesline, her mouth and eyes wrapped with silver tape, her reddish hair shorn and hacked to the scalp. One nostril was caked with dried blood, her neck and shoulders marbled with bruises the color of pomegranates. She turned her head toward my sound, like a blind person, her nostrils dilating with fear.

'Martina?' I said, my heart dropping.

She tried to talk through the tape.

I removed it first from her eyes, then her mouth. Her right eye was swollen shut, the inside of her lips gashed, her teeth pink, as though they had been painted with Mercurochrome. I opened my Puma knife and sliced the rope from the arms and back of the chair. She held me around the waist while I stroked her shorn head.

'It's all right,' I said. 'We'll get you to a hospital. I'll have somebody stay with you. You hear me? Buchalter's gone. Everything's going to be okay.'

She turned her face up to me. Her left eyeball jittered, as though a nerve in it were impaired. 'Where's Clete?' she said.

'I don't know. But we'll find him.'

'The man who beat me, he told me about the things he was going to do to Clete. He has pictures of what he's done to people.'

She leaned forward with her face in her hands, sobbing. There were white places the size of nickels with raw cuts inside them all over her scalp.

'I'll be right back,' I said.

The man in cuffs on the floor was trembling.

'I took her to the bathroom, I give her food when I wasn't supposed to,' he said.

'Where's your phone?'

'On the desk,' he said, exhaling the words like a man who knows the fury and intensity of the world is about to move past him.

I called 911 and asked for an ambulance and a sheriff's car.

'Here's how it shakes out, partner,' I said to the man on the floor. 'You're probably going down as an accessory to assault and battery, kidnapping, and anything else the locals can dream up. But no matter how you cut it, it's a serious bounce. You want to tell me where he is, I'll see what I can do for you later.'

'He knows how to get to people. Anywhere. Lockdown, isolation, Witness Protection Program. There's white guys even paid the Black Guerrillas to protect them. It didn't work.'

'Last chance.'

'Him and Marie, this morning, they got excited about something in a newspaper. Then they took off.'

'Where's the newspaper?'

'I burned it in the trash barrel. With her hair I swept up. I was trying to keep the place clean, and I go down on a kidnapping beef. You tell me that's fair, man.'

I heard sirens in the distance, outside the window, a black man was looking up the street.

'I don't want to be rough on you, but I'd reconsider my attitude about cooperating,' I said to the man in handcuffs. 'When we nail Buchalter, he's going to find out we talked to you first. Who do you think he's going to blame his problems on?'

His face turned ashen.

I rode in the ambulance with Martina to the hospital, then used the phone at the Harrison County Sheriff's Department to call home and Clete's office. I recorded a long message on his machine, assured him Martina was going to be all right, and left him the number of the hospital.

But I would soon discover that I wasn't thinking clearly. I called Ben Motley.

'It's Saturday afternoon. Believe it or not, Robicheaux, I'd like forty-eight hours without thinking about pus bags.'

'Buchalter doesn't take weekends off,' I said.

'You got the woman back. You traced Buchalter to his nest. Count your blessings. Ease up.'

'Now's the time to staple him to the wall, Ben. Call Fart, Barf, and Itch in New Orleans for me.'

'What else?'

'Nothing.' Then I happened to glance at a deputy across the room who was eating a sandwich with his feet on the desk and reading the sports page in the newspaper. 'Wait a minute. Do you have this morning's *Times-Picayune*?'

'What do you want?'

'Look in the personals for me.'

'That's what they do when they're bored over in Vice.'

'Come on, Ben.'

He put down the phone, then I heard newspaper pages rattling.

'Do you see anything in there that looks peculiar?' I said.

'That's like asking if there's any washroom graffiti that shouldn't be on a Hallmark card,' he said. 'Hold on ... Here's one that's all numbers. No message, just numbers.'

'Read them.' I could hear my own breath in the phone. I wrote the numbers down as he read them off. 'Those are the coordinates for that Nazi sub, Ben. You check with *The Times-Picayune*, you'll find Clete ran that ad.'

'I don't get it.'

'Buchalter kidnapped Martina and forced Clete to find out where I'd seen the sub. I gave him the coordinates. But it took a couple of days for the ad to come out. Look, we need to get a boat or a chopper out there.'

'Call your own department.'

'We don't have anything available.'

'You think I can snap my fingers on Saturday afternoon and come up with a boat or a helicopter? We don't have jurisdiction out on the salt, anyway.'

'You don't understand. I left a message on Clete's machine. I told him Martina's all right. As soon as he retrieves the message, you know where he's headed.'

'So let him light up the fun house. It's what Purcel does best.'

'He might lose, too. I need a boat.'

'You won't get it from me this weekend.'

'Motley—'

'It's *Motley* now? Why don't you call Nate Baxter? See what kind of help you get.'

I started back home. It was getting dark now, and the palm trees along the highway were beating in the wind, the rain spinning in my headlights. It would take me at least four and a half hours to reach New Iberia, then another seven, maybe more, with the bad weather, to get my boat down Bayou Teche and into the gulf south of Grand Isle.

I pulled into a filling station by the Pearl River and called Lucinda Bergeron's house. The gum trees around the phone booth were green and brightly lit by the filling station's signs, and the leaves were ripping like paper in the wind.

'Zoot?'

'Hey, Mr Dave, what's happenin'?'

'Where's your mom?'

'She ain't here. Something wrong?'

'I've got to get ahold of her. I need a boat.'

'She went to the grocery. What kind of boat you looking for?'

'A fast one,' I said.

'You ax the right man.'

'Oh?'

'I tole you at your house. But you wasn't listening real good, remember? I worked on all kinds of boats.'

'Who owns this boat, Zoot?'

'A man who don't mind lending it, I promise. When you coming?'

An hour and a half later I parked the truck at a boatyard way out in Jefferson Parish. It had quit raining; and the sky was dark, and water was dripping off the tin shed where Zoot waited in a cabin cruiser with the interior lights on. I took my Japanese field glasses from the glove compartment, then unlocked the iron box welded to the bed of my pickup and removed my old army field jacket and the AR-15 and my Remington twelve-gauge with the barrel sawed off right in front of the pump that I had wrapped in a canvas duffel bag. I dropped a box of .223 rounds and a box of double-ought buckshot into the bag and pulled the drawstring. When I walked out onto the dock under the shed I saw that Zoot wasn't alone.

'Hello, Lucinda,' I said, stepping down into the boat.

She was dressed in jeans, a purple sweater, and a nylon NOPD windbreaker. Zoot fixed his attention on the clearing sky, tapping his palms on the wheel, whistling quietly.

'What would you like to hear from me first?' she said.

'I beg your pardon?'

'You call my house and ask a seventeen-year-old to provide a boat for you?' she said.

'Believe what you want, Lucinda. I'm not up to an argument tonight.'

'You were willing to bring a minor and civilian into a potentially dangerous situation? With no consultation with anyone else?'

'I couldn't get a boat from Motley. I don't have time to go back to New Iberia. You think it's right Purcel may be out there by himself?'

'I can't quite tell you how angry I am,' she said.

'Then why'd you let him come?'

She didn't answer. I lowered my voice. 'Maybe nobody's out there. Maybe I should have waited for you to come home. Maybe I should have gone back to New Iberia,' I said. 'I did what I thought was best.'

I waited. Her arms were folded across her chest, her hands cupped on her elbows. I looked at Zoot, and he turned over the engines and backed us out of the slip. The wind was cool and damp and smelled of salt and dead gars that had been hit by boat propellers. Lights flickered across the clouds in the south.

We headed down Bayou St Denis. It was a beautiful boat, custom-built with teakwood and mahogany panels in the cabin, brightwork that had the soft glow of butter, wide beds down below, sonar, a pump toilet, a small galley, and twin two-hundred-horsepower Evinrude outboard engines that could hit fifty knots. When we entered Barataria Bay, Zoot tried to open her up.

'The chop's too heavy. You're going to beat us to death, partner,' I said.

The glass was beaded with the spray off the bow. The moon had broken from behind the clouds, and our wake glistened behind us like a long brown and silver trough. Zoot wore a black knitted cap rolled up on top of his head and chewed on a matchstick. When he eased back on the throttle, I saw the two ignition wires wrapped together and swinging loose at the bottom of the instrument panel.

'What kind of engineering do we have here, Zoot?' I said, raising my finger toward the wires.

'The man out of town right now. He forgot to leave the key where it's always at,' he said.

'I see.'

'That's a fact. He lets me take it all the time. I'll introduce y'all sometime.'

'That's very kind of you.'

I looked down below at Lucinda, who was sitting on a cushioned storage locker with her legs crossed, staring straight ahead. Her nickel-plated .357 revolver glinted in her belt holster. I realized that I had read her wrong.

I walked down the steps and sat on a bunk across from her. I could feel the steady vibration of the bow coursing through the chop.

'You're over the black dude in the motel?' I said.

Her mouth parted slightly.

'It's like anything else. It passes,' I said.

The skin wrinked at the corner of her left eye.

'The first time a guy dealt the play on me, I thought I'd wake up with his face in front of me every day of my life,' I said. 'Then one day it was gone. Poof. Three years later I put another guy down.'

'Why are you doing this?' she said.

'Because this boat's a little warm.'

'It's a little ...'

'Right. Warm. Not hot exactly. Terms like *borrowed* and *lend-lease* come to mind,' I said, and leaned forward on my hands. 'You've got your own agenda tonight, Lucinda.'

'He tortured my son.'

'You know when a good cop does it by the numbers? The day he thinks he *shouldn't* do it by the numbers.'

'I get this from the friend and advocate of Clete Purcel? Wonderful.'

'Don't let Buchalter remake you in his image.'

She looked into my face for a long time.

'Your advice is always good, Dave,' she said. 'But it's meant for others. It has no application for yourself, does it?'

We stared silently at each other as the hull of the boat veered toward the cut at Grand Terre.

It was a strange, cold dawn. With first light the sky looked streaked with india ink, then the wind dropped suddenly and the sun came up red and molten on the gulf's watery rim. The tide was coming in, rose-dimmed, heavy with the fecund smell of schooled-up trout, flecked with foam toward the shore, the air loud with the cry of gulls that glided and dipped over our wake. I watched the gray-green landmass of Louisiana fall away behind us.

Zoot stood erect in front of the wheel, his hooded workout jersey zipped up to his chin, his long hands resting lightly on the spokes. He had cranked open the glass, and the skin of his face looked taut and bright with cold.

'How you doing, Skipper?' I said.

'Not bad. She asleep?'

'Yes.'

'You know what she said about you the other day?'

'I wouldn't want to guess.'

'She say, "He's probably crazy but I wouldn't mind if I'd met him before he was married."'

'You'd better not be giving out your mama's secrets,' I said.

'Why you think she tell it to me?' he said.

Through my field glasses I could see the black, angular silhouettes of two abandoned drilling platforms against the sun and a freighter with rusty scuppers and a Panamanian flag to the far west. Zoot cut back on the throttle, and we rocked forward on our own wake.

'Look at the sonar, Mr Dave,' he said. 'We're in about forty feet now. But see where the line drops? That's a trench. I been over it before. It runs maybe two miles, unless it drifts over with sand sometimes.'

'You're pretty good at this.'

'I ain't even gonna say nothing. You and her just alike. Got one idea about everything, so every day you always surprised about something.'

'I think you're probably right.'

'*Probably?*' He shook his head.

But I wasn't listening now. Just off the port bow, beyond one of the drilling platforms, I saw the low, flat outline of a salvage vessel, one that was outfitted with side booms, dredges, and a silt vacuum that curved over the gunwale like the body of an enormous snake. I sharpened the image through the field glasses and saw that the ship was anchored bow and stern and was tilted slightly to starboard, as though it were straining against a great weight.

Then I saw something move on the drilling platform closest to us. I stepped outside the cabin and refocused the field glasses. The tide was washing through the pilings at the base of the platform, and upside-down in the swell, knocking against the steel girders, was the red and white hull of a capsized boat. I moved the glasses up a ladder to the rig itself and held them on a powerful, sunburned, bare-chested man whose Marine Corps utilities hung just below his navel.

'What is it?' Lucinda said behind me. The side of her face was printed with lines from her sleep.

I handed the glasses to her.

'Take a look at that first rig,' I said.

She balanced herself against the sway of the deck and peered through the glasses.

'It's Clete Purcel,' she said. 'He looks half frozen.'

'With a sunk boat,' I said. 'Clete's no sailor, either. Which means he probably went out with somebody who didn't make it to that ladder.'

'Who?'

'I don't like to think about it.'

'Who?'

'The elderly preacher comes to mind.' I went back inside the cabin. 'Zoot, take us on into the rig. But try to keep it between us and that salvage ship so whoever's onboard doesn't get a good look at us.'

'It's Buchalter and them Nazis?' he said. I saw his long, ebony hands tighten involuntarily on the wheel.

'Maybe it's just an ordinary salvage group trying to raise some drilling equipment.'

'There's some oil field junk down out here, but not yonder, Mr Dave.'

'Okay, podna.'

'I know what you got in that canvas bag. If the time come, is one of them for me?'

'You have any experience with firearms?'

'A lot.'

'With what kind?'

'The kind you shoot things wit' . . . Me and my cousin, we gone under the Huey Long Bridge and shot bottles all over the place.'

'Look, Zoot, we want the people on that salvage boat to think we're a fishing party. Can you set the outriggers and put some trolling rods in the sockets while I take the wheel?'

'Sure,' he said, but his eyes were still on the canvas bag.

'Just keep your hood tied on your head, too, in case they put binoculars on us.'

'You ain't gonna let me have one of them guns?'

'If that's Buchalter out there, we'll call the Coast Guard.'

'Then why you bring all them guns?'

I'd never guess you were Lucinda's son, I thought to myself.

I kept the bow pointed in a straight line at the rig and the salvage ship. The sun had broken through a bank of lavender and black clouds, and you could see flying fish and the stringlike tentacles and swollen pink air sacs of Portuguese man-o'-wars in the swell. The day should have warmed, but the wind had risen again and the tidal current looked green and cold flowing under the oil platform, rolling the capsized boat against the pilings and the steel ladder.

To the south there was a frothy white line along the horizon where the waves were starting to cap.

Zoot worked his way forward onto the bow, and I cut the gas and let the cabin cruiser drift into the ladder that extended out of the water, upward to the platform where Clete Purcel was leaning over the rail, staring down at us, the sandy curls of hair on his shoulders and chest blowing dryly in the wind.

He came down the ladder fast, his face pointed downward, his love handles flexing, his huge buttocks working as he clanged onto each rung.

When he dropped onto the bow, he kept his face pointed in the opposite direction from the salvage ship and made his way aft along the side of the cabin.

His teeth were chattering when he came through the hatchway.

'Streak, I love you,' he said. 'I knew my old podjo wouldn't let me down. I ain't kidding you, I was turning to an ice cube up there. I tried to wrap myself up in a piece of canvas, but it blew away.'

'What happened?'

'It's Buchalter. We found him about three this morning,' he said, pulling a blanket around his shoulders. 'We came up on him from the south. I thought we had him. There's a metal stairs on his port side. We were going to drift up to it, then take them from behind while all that machinery was roaring. Except we hit a log and punched a hole in the hull.'

He sat on top of a locker filled with life vests and scuba gear and worked the stopper from a bottle of Cutty Sark he had taken from the liquor cabinet. The scar through his eyebrow and across the bridge of his nose looked like a stitched strip of pink rubber.

'Who's we, Clete?'

'Brother Oswald.' His voice changed when he said the words. His eyes looked away from me, then at Lucinda and Zoot. Then he looked at the deck. He lifted the bottle to his mouth.

'Why didn't you wait?' I said.

'For what? The guy to blow the country?'

'You could have waited,' I said.

'Get real, Streak. You nail this guy under a black flag or he'll live to piss on your grave.'

'What's a black flag?' Zoot said.

Clete started to raise the Scotch again, then the color drained out of his face and he went through the hatchway and threw up over the stern. He came back inside, wiping his mouth with a towel.

'Excuse me, I swallowed some oil out there,' he said. 'When the boat turned over, I hung on to it. Brother Oswald had on a life preserver. He was drifting right past that stairs I was talking about. He didn't come out north of the ship, either.'

'You mean he's onboard with Buchalter?' Lucinda said.

'The tide was coming in real strong. He couldn't be anywhere else,' Clete said. 'I would have seen him. I know I would have.'

'I'll give our position to the Coast Guard,' I said.

'The old guy kept talking about Gog and Magog. What's Gog and Magog?' Clete said.

'It's a biblical prophesy about the war between good and evil,' I said.

'I don't know about no black flags and Magogs, but there's something I ain't mention yet,' Zoot said.

We all stared at him. In the silence a wave broke across the bow and streaked the glass.

'The radio don't work,' he said.

32

I was crouched behind Clete on the steps of the small passageway that gave onto the bow. He had put on my raincoat and a red wool shirt he found in a closet. His big hands were clenched on the stock and pump of the twelve-gauge shotgun. I could hear him breathing with expectation.

He glanced backwards at me and started to smile. Then stopped.

'Why the scowl, mon?'

'This is your fault.'

'I don't read it that way.'

'Why didn't you go take care of Martina? Why'd you have to go out on the salt with a fanatical old man?'

'I don't like what you're saying to me, Streak.'

'Too bad.'

'Remember the dude in New Iberia General? He got a hypodermic load of roach paste. Buchalter *ends* here.'

I punched him on the shoulder with my finger.

'We need to understand something, Clete. You're not going to re-create the O.K. Corral out here.'

He twisted around on his haunches.

'What do you want to do?' he said. 'Go all the way back to land to notify the Coast Guard, then hope they're not a hundred miles away? The old man's on his own up there. We go in there and blow up their shit.'

I punched him with one finger, hard, on the shoulder again. He turned and slapped my hand away, his green eyes suddenly disturbed and dark, as though he were looking at someone he didn't know.

'This whole gig started with you tearing up the Calucci brothers,' I said. 'It's not going to end that way. We're putting Buchalter in a cage.'

'Tell it to the Rotary Club,' he said, and looked upward toward the closed hatch.

We could hear Zoot cutting back the gas now, the exhaust pipes throbbing at the waterline, echoing off the steel hull of the salvage ship. Then we heard Lucinda making her way forward, picking up the bowline off the deck, as though it were natural to tie onto the metal steps that zigzagged down the side of the ship.

Clete eased the hatch upward a half inch.

'We found an injured man on an oil platform! We need your radio!' Lucinda shouted.

There was no answer. We could hear the sounds of an air compressor, a winch grinding, chains rattling through pulleys, a diesel engine working hard.

'It's a boat hand who doesn't know what to do,' Clete said. 'He probably went for somebody else.' He looked back at me again. 'Lighten up. I figure no more than five of them, including the diver in the water. Easy odds, mon.'

But the creases in the back of his neck were bright with sweat, his knuckles white and ridged on the shotgun's stock.

'We're calling it in for you!' someone yelled down at Lucinda.

'I'm a nurse! I need to describe his condition! I think he's had a coronary!'

'We're radioing your message! You can't come onboard!'

The hull bumped against the rubber tires that were roped to the bottom of the steps.

'Repeat . . . You can't come onboard! No one but company personnel are allowed! Your message is being transmitted!'

'This man may die!'

Clete's eyes were level with the crack between the deck and the hatch.

'She's tying on. That broad's got ice water in her veins,' he whispered. 'That's it, Lucinda, get on the steps, do it, do it, do it, do it . . . .'

'Mr Dave, leave me something 'case I got to come after y'all.'

I turned around. It was Zoot, bent down below the level of the passageway in the cabin.

'If it goes sour, partner, you get help,' I said.

It was very fast after that.

'Party time,' Clete said, and charged out onto the bow with the shotgun at port arms.

Lucinda had already reached the top of the stairs and was on the deck of the salvage ship, her .357 pointed straight out in front of her with both hands, her hair whipping in the wind, while she shouted at two paralyzed deckhands, 'Police officer, motherfucker! Down on your face, hands laced behind your neck! Are you deaf? Down on your face! Now! Or I blow your fucking head off!'

I hit the stairs running, right behind Clete, my .45 flopping in the pocket of my field jacket. I had already chambered a round in the AR-15, and my hand was squeezed tight on the grip and inside the trigger guard, my thumb poised on the safety. I could hear waves bursting against the stern and hissing along the hull.

The salvage ship was old, covered with tack welds, the scuppers orange with corrosion, the paint blistered and soft and flaking under the hand, the glass in the pilothouse oxidized and dirty with oil. The hatch to the engine room was open, and from below decks I could smell electrical odors, diesel fuel, stagnant water in a sump, a salty, rotten stench like a rat that's been caught in machinery.

Lucinda was standing above the two deckhands, her weapon moving back and forth between them while she worked her cuffs off her belt. I took them from her hand, hooked up one man, pulled his arm through a rail on the gate to the steps, then snipped the loose cuff on the second man's wrist.

'Where's the old-timer?' I said.

One man was bald and wore a chin beard; the other had an empty eye socket that was puckered and sealed shut as though it had been touched with a hot instrument. The bald man twisted his head and looked indifferently toward the south, where lightning was pulsating amid muted thunder on the horizon.

'Look at me when I talk to you,' I said. 'Where's the old man?'

He slowly turned his head and let his eyes drift over both me and Lucinda.

'Fuck you, nigger lover,' he said.

Then I heard Clete's weight shift above me and looked up just as he threw the shotgun against his shoulder and aimed at a man in a canvas coat and rain hood who stood in silhouette by the stern with a blue-black automatic in his hand.

Clete fired twice. Part of the double-ought buckshot razored lines of paint off the bulkhead like dry confetti, then the man in the canvas coat was knocked backwards as though he had been jerked by an invisible cable wrapped around his chest.

Clete ejected the spent easing onto the deck, pumped a fresh round into the chamber, then pressed two more shells into the magazine with his thumb.

'Three down,' he said. 'Streak, you and Lucinda go around the bow. I'll come up the other side. Watch the bridge. Don't let 'em get behind you.'

He didn't wait for an answer. He moved toward the stern, bearlike, his shotgun back at port arms, his scalp showing white in the wind, his utilities stiff with salt.

Lucinda glanced down at the cabin cruiser, which was rolling in the swells while Zoot kept gunning the engines to keep the stern from swinging into the salvage ship's hull.

'He's all right,' I said. 'My dad used to always say, "Don't ever treat brave people as less than what they are." '

'Cover your own ass,' she said.

We moved toward the bow. I could feel the deck vibrating under me from the machinery roaring on the other side of the ship. I paused at the steps that led onto the pilothouse, worked my way up them until I could see inside, then moved quickly through the open hatch.

I looked at the shape in the corner and lowered my rifle. I heard Lucinda behind me.

'Oh God,' she said.

'Check the starboard side,' I said, and knelt next to Brother Oswald. He lay on top of an oil-grimed tarp, his poached, round face filled with the empty, stunned, disbelieving expression that I had seen once in the faces of villagers who had been killed by airbursts in a rice field.

A switchblade knife, a made-in-Korea gut-ripper that you can buy for five dollars in Laredo, had been driven to the hilt just above his right lung. He had pressed a rag around the wound, and the rag had become sodden and congealed as though it had been dipped in red paint. I put my ear to his mouth and felt his breath touch my skin.

'We're going to medevac you out of here, partner,' I said. 'You hear me? We're going to secure the ship, then have you on a chopper in no time.'

His tongue stuck to his mouth when he tried to speak. I leaned down close to his face again. His breath smelled like dried flowers.

'. . . after the wrong one,' he whispered.

'I don't understand,' I said.

'Hit's the woman . . . She can speak in tongues . . . I heard her talk on the radio . . .'

'Who did this to you, Reverend?'

His lips moved, but no sound came out. His pale eyes looked like they were drowning.

'I can't see anybody on the starboard side,' Lucinda said.

I raised Brother Oswald's head with my palm, bunched up the tarp like a pillow, then turned his head sideways so his mouth could drain. I picked up the AR-15. The plastic stock felt cold and light and smooth in my hands.

'You know how to get the Coast Guard on the radio?' I said to Lucinda.

'Yes.'

'Tell them we're thirty miles south of Grand Isle. Describe the two oil platforms, and they'll know where to go.'

She nodded toward Brother Oswald, the question in her face.

I *don't know*, I said with my lips.

A moment later I crossed the deck in front of the pilothouse. I stepped out into the open, the iron sights of the AR-15 aimed at whoever might be standing between me and the stern.

But there was no one, except Clete Purcel, who was on one knee, his back toward me, amid a tangle of hoses, ropes, scuba and acetylene tanks, and salvage nets in pools of water. Two giant side booms towered above him, their cables almost bursting with the great weight anchored to them. Then beneath the sliding waves, the foam curling off the stern, the clouds of seaweed in the swells, glowing dimly under a bank of underwater lamps, I saw the long, tapered outline of the U-boat. It looked like the top of an enormous sand shark that had been torn out of the silt. I could see the forward deck gun shaggy with moss and crustaceans, air bubbles stringing from the torpedo tubes in the bow, the crushed steel flanges at the top of the conning tower, and the indistinct and dull glimmer of a swastika painted on the plates.

Clete's right arm was working furiously at a task that his body concealed from view. Then I saw the gasoline-powered generator and the air compressor just beyond where he was crouched on the deck, and I realized what he was doing.

I ran toward him, the rifle hanging loosely from my hand. With his single-bladed Case knife he had already sawed halfway through the air hose and the safety rope attached to it. The escaping pressure had blown a bare spot on the deck like a clean burn.

'Don't do it, Clete!'

'Too late, mon. Buchalter is about to do the big gargle.' He stood erect, ripped his knife through the remainder of the hose, and flung it like a severed snake into the water.

I stared over the side. Framed in silhouette against the bank of underwater lights, just aft of the conning tower, was a steel-mesh diver's platform, held aloft by a cable. In the middle of the platform, a diver in canvas suit, weighted boots, and hard hat was looking upward frantically, while a forgotten acetylene torch bounced like a sparkler across the sub's deck and the severed air hose spun limply downward into the darkness.

I dropped the rifle to the deck and tried to work the levers on the winch and spool that controlled the cable to the platform. I pushed the levers the wrong way, then corrected them and felt the engine buck into gear and start to retrieve the diver from below.

'Sorry, Dave, but this is one time you're wrong,' Clete said, pulling a fire ax from the wall above me. He tore all the connecting wires out of the winch's engine. Suddenly the spool locked in place, and the cable squeaked and oscillated slightly from side to side at the tip of the boom and trembled rigidly at the waterline. Then he swung the ax overhand into the spool and sheared the cable as neatly as you would coat hanger wire. It whipped free from the pulley on the boom and disappeared beneath the waves.

'It's homicide, Clete.'

'The hell it is. There's still at least one guy loose. All I did was keep a player off the board.'

But the story under the waves wasn't over. The platform had tipped sideways before it plummeted to the bottom, and the diver had managed to land on the deck, just behind the conning tower. I could see the brass helmet, the face glass, and the white hands waving in the tidal current, like a cartoon figure struggling at the bottom of a well.

I stripped off my field jacket, picked up a scuba tank and diving mask off the deck, checked the air gauge, and slipped my arms through the straps. I tied one end of a rope to the winch and the other around my waist.

'When I jerk, you pull us up,' I said.

'Big mistake,' Clete answered.

'I'll live with it. Don't let me down, Cletus.' He shrugged his shoulders and shook his head. I fitted the air hose into my mouth and went over the side.

The coldness was like a fist in the stomach, then I felt currents tear at me from several directions and I heard metal ringing, cable clanging on steel, plates grinding, perhaps a long-silenced propeller gouging a trench in packed sand, and I realized that the storm in the south was already destabilizing the sub's environment and was twisting the keel against the cables that Buchalter's crew had secured to the bow and stern.

I had no weight belt or flippers and had to struggle to gain depth. I blew the mask clear and swam deeper into the vortex of gold and brown light and spinning silt until I was only five feet away from the drowning figure in the diving suit. My head was aching with the cold, my teeth locked on the rubber mouthpiece to keep them from chattering, my ears pinging from the water pressure.

Then I saw what we had interrupted. The plates in the hull, just aft of the tower, probably already weak with strain and corrosion, had been cut with acetylene torches and prized out of the spars with jacks, exposing a compartment whose escape hatch into the tower was locked shut.

A battery-powered underwater light burned amid the drifting silt and softly molded skeletons of a dozen Nazi submariners.

Their uniforms were green rags now, their faces a yellow patina of pickled skin, their atrophied mouths puckered with rats' teeth.

I swam behind the diver, untied the rope from my waist, and slipped it under the canvas arms of the diver's suit, then knotted it hard in the spine. I felt the sub shift on its keel in a sudden surge of coldness from the gulf's bottom. As the deck listed to port, the diver turned in a slow pirouette and looked through the glass into my face.

The water had risen inside the suit to her neck, and her red hair floated like strands of dried blood against the glass. Her chin was twisted upward into the air, her cheeks pale, her mouth working like a guppy's.

It was too late to spin the wing nuts off the helmet and place my air hose in her mouth. I jerked hard on the rope and felt it come taut as Clete started to retrieve it topside. Then I tried to push both me and the woman who called herself Marie Guilbeaux to the surface.

Then, inches from my face, I saw the salt water climb to the top of the glass and immerse her head as though it were a severed and preserved specimen in a laboratory, her hair floating about her in a dark web. She fought and twisted, tried to hold her breath, her eyes bulging in their sockets; then a broken green balloon slipped suddenly from her mouth into the top of the helmet. Her arms locked about my neck in an almost erotic embrace, her body gathering against mine, her lips meshed against the glass like torn fruit, the teeth bare now, the loins shuddering, a wine-dark kiss from the grave.

A moment later I felt Clete stop pulling on the rope, then it was slipping free over the side of the salvage ship, curling down out of the waves toward me. I released the body of the woman called Marie Guilbeaux and watched it spin downward, the puffed arms extended sideways like a scarecrow's, the weighted boots pulling it past the bank of lights into the darkness, until the rope snapped taut again, and Marie's drowned figure swung back and forth against the bottom of the sub's hull.

I blew my glass clear again and swam upward to the surface. I popped through a wave into the wind, the groan of cables straining from the side booms, my mask streaked with water, my eyes searching the deck for Clete and Lucinda.

They were nowhere in sight. I climbed back aboard, breathless with cold, and slipped the straps to the air tank off my back. My AR-15 was gone.

I put on my field jacket, buttoned it against the wind, and took the .45 from the side pocket. A hollow-point round was already in the chamber. I cocked back the hammer and moved toward the stern, past the air compressor, the gasoline-powered generator, the winches, the piles of salvage nets and coils of acetylene hose, my shoulder brushing lightly against the base of the pilothouse, past an entrance to a room throbbing with the diesel motors that powered the side booms, past the galley, past a machine shop, finally to an open hatch that gave onto a small confined area that served as crew quarters.

No one.

I went inside the crew's quarters. It smelled of unwashed bedding and expectorated snuff. A color photograph of a nude black woman torn from a magazine was glued against one bulkhead. I went through another open hatch into a passageway that traversed the interior of the ship and led back toward the pilothouse and the bridge. The bulkheads were gray and cold with moisture, the deck patterned with the wet imprints of tennis shoes.

I opened or went through each hatch along the passageway.

Nothing.

The end of the passageway was unlighted, shrouded in gloom, as indistinct as fog. I didn't notice the broken lightbulb glass until the sole of my shoe came down on a piece of filament and cracked it against the deck. By then it was too late.

Buchalter stepped out from behind an open storage locker door, the stock of the AR-15 tight against his shoulder and cheek, one green eye as hard and bulbous as an egg behind the iron sights.

'You lose again, Dave. Throw it away,' he said, and kicked the door shut behind him, allowing me to see Lucinda and Clete on their knees by the ladder that led into the pilothouse, their fingers hooked behind their necks. There was a raw, skinned area above Clete's left eye.

'You want to take a chance and plant one in them?' Buchalter said.

'Don't give up your piece, Streak!' Clete shouted.

I held the .45 out to my side, bent slightly with my knees, and placed it carefully on the deck. Buchalter wore combat boots and khakis, a heavy gray wool shirt, and long underwear buttoned to the throat. His cheeks and chin were gold with the beginnings of a beard, the spray of blackheads fanning from his eyes like powder burns.

I smelled a bright, clean odor in the air, one that travels to the brain as quickly as a slap. Like the smell of white gas.

'Your friend killed my sister, Dave. What do you think of that?' he said. He looked at me with his lopsided grin.

'We tried to save her,' I said.

'Come join us,' he said.

'Maybe I shouldn't.'

'Oh, yes. It won't be complete without you. You and I have a date. All three of you do.' His thick tongue worked itself wetly along his lips.

'He soaked us with gasoline, Dave. Run!' Lucinda said.

'You know you're not going anywhere, Dave. Come closer. That's it, come on. The little boy is always inside the man. Don't be ashamed. You'd be surprised what people are willing to do under the right circumstances.' He held the rifle against his side by the pistol grip and worked a Zippo lighter out of his left pocket with his thumb.

'One's a Negro, the other a gentile who has intercourse with a Jew,' he said. 'They're going to die, anyway. Would you like to watch their performance with me, or be part of it? Nobody'll know, either, Dave.'

He pursed his lips and sucked in his cheeks, as though a mint lay on his tongue.

'The Coast Guard's on the way, Will.'

'I guess we should finish quickly then. Even when they catch my kind, you know what they do with us. Government hospitals. Clean drugs, maybe a horny nurse who needs a few extra dollars. Come on, kneel down with your friends, now.'

The heel of one boot clanked against a gasoline can. But then I heard another sound, too – behind me, at the far end of the passageway, a clumsy thud like an awkward person tripping across the bottom of a hatchway.

Buchalter heard it too, and his eyes shot past me, trying to focus on an image that they couldn't quite accept.

'Duck, Mr Dave!'

I dropped to the deck, curling in an embryonic ball, waiting for the quick, sharp report of the AR-15. Instead, I heard a sound like a strand of broken piano wire whizzing through the air.

I stared down the passageway at the frozen silhouette of Zoot Bergeron, the discharged speargun held in front of him.

I grabbed the .45 from the deck just as Will Buchalter stumbled along the bulkhead, through the gloom, toward the ladder, partly obscured by the open door on a locker. Then I saw both his hands clenched on the aluminum shaft that protruded from his mouth. He careened up the ladder, the tendons in his shoulders and neck knotted like the roots in a tree stump, his hands gathered in front of his mouth, his combat boots ringing like hammers on the iron steps.

I fired twice through the hatchway into the pilothouse and heard the hollow points shatter panes of glass out on the deck.

'Sorry, Streak. He came up behind me while I was pulling on that rope,' Clete said.

'Get the rifle,' I said, and went up the ladder after Buchalter.

But the chase was not to be a long one.

I found him out on the deck, his back slumped against the rail, like a lazy man taking a nap, the spearpoint protruding from the back of his neck in a bloody clot, the shaft trembling slightly with the vibrations from the engine room. His eyes were open and empty, staring at nothing, the gold down on his chin slick with the drainage from his wound.

It started to rain, and the spray off the stern was blowing hard in the wind. A cable snapped loose from a side boom and was gone below the water's surface in the wink of an eye.

I heard Clete behind me.

'Did you hit him?' he said.

'Nope.'

'A bad way for the black kid to get started,' he said, and looked at me.

I glanced up at the broken windows in the pilothouse. Lucinda and Zoot were still below.

'Let's do it,' I said.

We pulled Buchalter away from the rail and laid him flat on the deck, then rolled him over the side. His shirt was puffed with air, and a wave scudded the upper portion of his body along the hull of the ship; his mouth was locked open around the spear shaft as though he were yawning or perhaps considering one final thought before the waves pressed him under in a cascade of dirty foam.

'That storm looks mean. Time to cut loose from the Katzenjammer Kids,' Clete said. He paused. 'Is there some paperwork later that's going to cause a problem for me?'

'What do I know?' I said. I shielded my eyes against the rain and watched as he sliced the line that held the suspended body of the woman who called herself Marie Guilbeaux, shut down motors, released winches, chopped cables and ropes in half, his sandy hair blowing in the wind, his Marine Corps utilities flapping and flattening against his legs.

I felt the deck pitch under me when all the cables had snapped free from the submarine's weight. For just a moment I watched the mud and blackened seaweed and oil trapped in sand churn in clouds out of the gulf's bottom, and I knew that down below the U-boat's crew and Buchalter and his sister were setting sail again. But it wasn't a time to muse upon old historical warnings about protean creatures who rise from biblical seas or slouch toward Bethlehem to be born again.

Instead I mounted the steps into the pilothouse, where Lucinda and her son had fixed a blanket under Oswald Flat's head and pulled a second one up to his chin. They stood at one of the shattered windows, Zoot with his arm on his mother's shoulders, looking at a Coast Guard helicopter that was flying toward us from the east, just ahead of the impending storm.

Zoot's eyes searched my face.

'You saved our butts, partner, but you missed Buchalter completely,' I said.

'Then why ain't I seen the spear?'

'Who cares, podna? It's yesterday's box score now,' I said.

Down below, Clete stretched his big arms and shoulders, clenched the deck rail, and spit over the side.

'Good guys *über alles*,' he called up to us.

'What's that mean?' Zoot said.

'I think that's German for *Semper fi*, Mac,' I said, and hit him on the arm, trying not to intrude upon the affectionate smile in his mother's eyes.

Epilogue

The winter was mild that year; the days were balmy, the grass in the fields a soft green, the nights touched with a faint chill, a hint of smoke from a stump fire in my neighbor's pasture. Even during duck season, when the marsh should have been gray and thick with mist, the skies remained a porcelain blue and the cypress and gum and willow trees seemed to stay in leaf through Christmas, almost right up to the spring rains that begin in late February.

There was only one day when I truly felt winter's presence, and that presence was in the heart rather than the external world. For our anniversary Bootsie and Alafair and I treated ourselves to a weekend at the Pontchartrain Hotel on St Charles Avenue. We were having supper at an outdoor café down the street, and the day had been warm and bright, the camellia bushes thick with newly opened pink and blue flowers, the wonderful old green-painted iron streetcars clattering down the neutral ground under the overhang of the oak trees. Then the sun dropped behind the rooftops, the air became cold and heavy, and suddenly there was no traffic or sound in the streets, only dust and scraps of newspaper whirling in the wind through the tunnel of trees.

This is what it could become, I thought. All we had to do was stop believing in ourselves and let the charlatans and the manipulators convince us they have the answers that we don't. They aren't fashioned from anvil and chain in a devil's forge, either. Judas Iscariot was us; there was no metaphysical mystery to Will Buchalter and his sister and the Calucci brothers. Their souls had the wingspan of moths; they functioned because we allowed them to and gave them sanction; they stopped functioning when that sanction was denied.

'What's wrong, Dave?' Alafair said from across the table.

'Nothing, little guy. Everything seemed too quiet for a minute.'

'Then let's go hear the band at Preservation Hall,' she said.

'I think that's a fine idea,' I said, and rubbed the silky smooth top of her head.

One beautiful evening that spring we went to the New Orleans Jazz and Heritage Festival at the Fairgrounds. The Fat Man was up on the stage with his band, his sequined sports coat painted with a lavender glow, sweat streaking his walrus face like lines of clear plastic, his pudgy hands and ringed sausage fingers pounding on the piano keys. People began dancing in the infield, jitterbugging like kids out of the 1940s, doing the bop, the dirty boogie, the twist, the shag, arms and legs akimbo, full of fun and erotic innocence.

Everyone was there for it – Clete and Martina, Batist, Lucinda and Zoot (who wore his Marine Corps Reserve uniform), Pearly Blue and her ex-con pals from the Work the Steps or Die, Motherfucker group, Ben Motley, Hippo Bimstine and his family, black and white people, visitors from Europe, Japanese businessmen, zydeco and Dixieland musicians, granola hippies, Bourbon Street strippers, cross-dressers, French Quarter hookers, coon-ass bikers, Jimmie Ryan and Count Carbonna, the meltdowns, religious crazoids with placards warning of apocalyptic destruction, even Brother Oswald Flat and his wife, who strolled about the grounds, sharing a bag of pork rinds. The music rose into the sky until it seemed to fuse with the gentle and pervasive light spreading far beyond the racetrack, over oak-lined streets, paintless wood houses with galleries and green window shutters, elevated highways, the Superdome, the streetcars and palm-dotted neutral ground of Canal, the scrolled iron balconies, colonnades, and brick chimneys in the Quarter, Jackson Square and the spires of St Louis Cathedral, the Café du Monde, the wide mud-churned sweep of the Mississippi, the shining vastness of the wetlands to the south, and eventually the Gulf of Mexico, where later the moon would rise like an enormous pearl that had been dipped in a glass of burgundy.

It's funny what can happen when you lay bare the heart and join the Earth's old dance through the heavens.

Burning Angel

for Rollie and Loretta McIntosh

Commending myself to the God of the oppressed,
I bowed my head upon my fettered hands,
and wept bitterly.

— From *Twelve Years a Slave*, an autobiographical
account by Solomon Northup

1

The Giacano family had locked up the action in Orleans and Jefferson parishes back in Prohibition. Their sanction and charter came from the Chicago Commission, of course, and no other crime family ever tried to intrude upon their territory. Hence, all prostitution, fence operations, money laundering, gambling, shylocking, labor takeovers, drug trafficking, and even game poaching in south Louisiana became forever their special province. No street hustler, grifter, second-story creep, Murphy artist, dip, stall, or low-rent pimp doubted that fact, either, not unless he wanted to hear a cassette of what Tommy Figorelli (also known as Tommy Fig, Tommy Fingers, Tommy Five) had to say above the whine of an electric saw just before he was freeze-dried and hung in parts from the wood fan in his own butcher shop.

That's why Sonny Boy Marsallus, who grew up in the Iberville welfare project when it was all white, was a kind of miracle on Canal back in the seventies and early eighties. He didn't piece off his action, pimp, or deal in drugs or guns, and he told the old fat boy himself, Didoni Giacano, to join Weight Watchers or the Save the Whales movement. I still remember him out there on the sidewalk, down from the old Jung Hotel, on an electric-blue spring evening, with the palm fronds rattling and streetcars clanging out on the neutral ground, his skin as unblemished as milk, his bronze-red hair lightly oiled and combed back on the sides, always running some kind of game – craps, high-stakes bouree, washing Jersey money out at the track, bailing out mainline recidivists licensed bondsmen wouldn't pick up by the ears with Q-Tips, lending money with no vig to girls who wanted to leave the life.

Actually Sonny practiced the ethics that the mob falsely claimed for themselves.

But too many girls took a Greyhound out of New Orleans on Sonny's money for the Giacanos to abide Sonny's presence much longer. That's when he went south of the border, where he saw firsthand the opening of the Reagan theme park in El Salvador and Guatemala. Clete Purcel, my old partner from Homicide in the First District, hooked up with him down there, when Clete himself was on the run from a murder beef, but would never talk about what they did together, or what caused Sonny to become a subject of strange rumors: that he'd gone crazy on *muta* and *pulche* and psychedelic mushrooms, that he'd joined up with leftist terrorists, had served time in a shithole Nicaraguan jail, was working with Guatemalan refugees in southern Mexico, or was in a monastery in Jalisco. Take your choice, it all sounded unlike a Canal Street fixer with scars in his eyebrows and a coin-jingling rebop in his walk.

That's why I was surprised to hear he was back in town, fading the action again and putting deals together at the Pearl, where the old green-painted iron streetcar made its turn off St Charles onto the lovely hard-candy glitter and wind-blown palm-dotted sweep of Canal Street. When I saw him hanging in front of a game room two blocks up, his tropical suit and lavender shirt rippled with neon, he looked like he had never been under a hard sun or humped an M-60 or rucksack in a jungle where at night you burned leeches off your skin with cigarettes and tried not to think about the smell of trench foot that rose from your rotting socks.

Pool-room blacks leaned against parking meters and storefront walls, music blaring from boom boxes.

He snapped and popped his fingers and palms together and winked at me. 'What's happenin', Streak?' he said.

'No haps, Sonny. You didn't get enough of free-fire zones?'

'The city? It's not that bad.'

'Yeah, it is.'

'Drink a beer, eat some oysters with me.'

His accent was adenoidal, like most blue-collar New Orleans people whose English was influenced by the Irish and Italian immigrations of the late nineteenth century. He smiled at me, then puffed air out his mouth and cut his eyes up and down the street. He fastened his eyes on me again, still smiling, a man gliding on his own rhythms.

'Ouch,' he said, and stuck a stiffened finger in the middle of his forehead. 'I forgot, I heard you go to meetings now, hey, I love iced tea. Come on, Streak.'

'Why not?' I said.

We stood at the bar in the Pearl and ate raw oysters that were briny and cold, with flecks of ice clinging to the shells. He paid from a cash roll of fifties in his pocket that was wrapped with a thick rubber band. His jaws and the back of his neck gleamed with a fresh haircut and shave.

'You didn't want to try Houston or Miami?' I said.

'When good people die, they move to New Orleans.'

But his affected flamboyance and good humor weren't convincing. Sonny looked worn around the edges, a bit manic, maybe fried a little by his own velocity, the light in his eyes wary, his attention to the room and front door too pronounced.

'You expecting somebody?' I asked.

'You know how it is.'

'No.'

'Sweet Pea Chaisson,' he said.

'I see.'

He looked at my expression.

'What, that's a surprise?' he asked.

'He's a bucket of shit, Sonny.'

'Yeah, I guess you could say that.'

I was regretting my brief excursion into the illusionary pop and snap of Sonny Boy's world.

'Hey, don't go,' he said.

'I have to get back to New Iberia.'

'Sweet Pea just needs assurances. The guy's reputation is exaggerated.'

'Tell his girls that.'

'You're a cop, Dave. You learn about stuff after it's history.'

'See you around, Sonny.'

His eyes looked through the front window onto the street. He fitted his hand over my forearm and watched the barman drawing a pitcher of beer.

'Don't walk out now,' he said.

I looked through the front glass. Two women walked by, talking simultaneously. A man in a hat and raincoat stood on the curb, as though waiting for a taxi. A short heavyset man in a sports coat joined him. They both looked out at the street.

Sonny bit a hangnail and spit it off the tip of his tongue.

'Sweet Pea's emissaries?' I said.

'A little more serious than that. Come into the can with me,' he said.

'I'm a police officer, Sonny. No intrigue. You got a beef, we call the locals.'

'Save the rhetoric for Dick Tracy. You got your piece?'

'What do you think?'

'The locals are no help on this one, Streak. You want to give me two minutes or not?'

He walked toward the rear of the restaurant. I waited a moment, placed my sunglasses on top of the bar to indicate to anyone watching that I would be back, then followed him. He bolted the rest room door behind us, hung his coat from the stall door, and peeled off his shirt. His skin looked like alabaster, hard and red along the bones. A blue Madonna image, with orange needles of light emanating from it, was tattooed high up on his right shoulder.

'You looking at my tattoo?' he said, and grinned.

'Not really.'

'Oh, these scars?'

I shrugged.

'A couple of ex-Somoza technicians invited me to a sensitivity session,' he said.

The scars were purple and as thick as soda straws, crisscrossed on his rib cage and chest.

He worked a taped black notebook loose from the small of his back. It popped free with a sucking sound. He held it in his hand, with the tape hanging from the cover, like an excised tumor.

'Keep this for me.'

'Keep it yourself,' I said.

'A lady's holding a Xerox copy for me. You like poetry, confessional literature, all that kind of jazz. Nothing happens to me, drop it in the mail.'

'What are you doing, Sonny?'

'The world's a small place today. People watch CNN in grass huts. A guy might as well play it out where the food is right.'

'You're an intelligent man. You don't have to be a punching bag for the Giacanos.'

'Check the year on the calendar when you get home. The spaghetti heads were starting to crash and burn back in the seventies.'

'Is your address inside?'

'Sure. You gonna read it?'

'Probably not. But I'll hold it for you a week.'

'No curiosity?' he said, pulling his shirt back on. His mouth was red, like a woman's, against his pale skin, and his eyes bright green when he smiled.

'Nope.'

'You should,' he said. He slipped on his coat. 'You know what a barracoon is, or was?'

'A place where slaves were kept.'

'Jean Lafitte had one right outside New Iberia. Near Spanish Lake. I bet you didn't know that.' He stuck me in the stomach with his finger.

'I'm glad I found that out.'

'I'm going out through the kitchen. The guys out front won't bother you.'

'I think your frame of reference is screwed up, Sonny. You don't give a pass to a police officer.'

'Those guys out there ask questions in four languages, Dave. The one with the fire hydrant neck, he used to do chores in the basement for Idi Amin. He'd really like to have a chat with me.'

'Why?'

'I capped his brother. Enjoy the spring evening, Streak. It's great to be home.'

He unlocked the door and disappeared through the back of the restaurant.

As I walked back to the bar, I saw both the hatted man and his short companion staring through the front glass. Their eyes reminded me of buckshot.

Fuck it, I thought, and headed for the door. But a crowd of Japanese tourists had just entered the restaurant, and by the time I got past them the sidewalk was empty except for an elderly black man selling cut flowers out of a cart.

The evening sky was light blue and ribbed with strips of pink cloud, and the breeze off the lake balmy and bitten with salt, redolent with the smells of coffee and roses and the dry electric flash and scorch of the streetcar.

As I headed back toward my pickup truck, I could see heat lightning, out over Lake Pontchartrain, trembling like shook foil inside a storm bank that had just pushed in from the Gulf.

An hour later the rain was blowing in blinding sheets all the way across the Atchafalaya swamp. Sonny Boy's notebook vibrated on the dashboard with the roar of my engine.

2

The next morning I dropped it in my file cabinet at the Iberia Parish Sheriff's Department unread and opened my mail while I drank a cup of coffee. There was a telephone message from Sonny Boy Marsallus, but the number was in St Martinville, not New Orleans. I dialed it and got no answer.

I gazed out the window at the fine morning and the fronds on the palm trees lifting against the windswept sky. He was out of my jurisdiction, I told myself, don't get mixed up in his grief. Sonny had probably been out of sync with the earth since conception, and it was only a matter of time before someone tore up his ticket.

But finally I did pull the jacket on Sweet Pea Chaisson, which stayed updated, one way or another, because he was one of our own and seemed to make a point of coming back to the Breaux Bridge–St Martinville–New Iberia area to get in trouble.

I've never quite understood why behaviorists spend so much time and federal funding on the study of sociopaths and recidivists, since none of the research ever teaches us anything about them or makes them any better. I've often thought it would be more helpful simply to pull a half dozen like Sweet Pea out of our files, give them supervisory jobs in mainstream society, see how everybody likes it, then perhaps consider a more draconian means of redress, such as prison colonies in the Aleutians.

He had been born and abandoned in a Southern Pacific boxcar, and raised by a mulatto woman who operated a zydeco bar and brothel on the Breaux Bridge highway called the House of Joy. His face was shaped like an inverted teardrop, with white eyebrows, eyes that resembled slits in bread dough, strands of hair like vermicelli, a button nose, a small mouth that was always wet.

His race was a mystery, his biscuit-colored body almost hairless, his stomach a water-filled balloon, his pudgy arms and hands those of a boy who never grew out of adolescence. But his comic proportions had always been a deception. When he was seventeen a neighbor's hog rooted up his mother's vegetable garden. Sweet Pea picked up the hog, carried it squealing to the highway, and threw it headlong into the grille of a semi truck.

Nineteen arrests for procuring; two convictions; total time served, eighteen months in parish prisons. Somebody had been looking out for Sweet Pea Chaisson, and I doubted that it was a higher power.

In my mail was a pink memo slip I had missed. Written in Wally the dispatcher's childish scrawl were the words *Guess who's back in the waiting room?* The time on the slip was 7:55 a.m.

Oh Lord.

Bertha Fontenot's skin was indeed black, so deep in hue that the scars on her hands from opening oyster shells in New Iberia and Lafayette restaurants looked like pink worms that had eaten and disfigured the tissue. Her arms jiggled with fat, her buttocks swelled like pillows over the sides of the metal chair she sat on. Her pillbox hat and purple suit were too small for her, and her skirt rode up above her white hose and exposed the knots of varicose veins in her thighs.

On her lap was a white paper towel from which she ate cracklings with her fingers.

'You decide to pry yourself out your chair for a few minutes?' she said, still chewing.

'I apologize. I didn't know you were out here.'

'You gonna help me with Moleen Bertrand?'

'It's a civil matter, Bertie.'

'That's what you say before.'

'Then nothing's changed.'

'I can get a white-trash lawyer to tell me that.'

'Thank you.'

Two uniformed deputies at the water fountain were grinning in my direction.

'Why don't you come in my office and have some coffee?' I said.

She wheezed as I helped her up, then wiped at the crumbs on her dress and followed me inside my office, her big lacquered straw bag, with plastic flowers on the side, clutched under her arm. I closed the door behind us and waited for her to sit down.

'This is what you have to understand, Bertie. I investigate criminal cases. If you have a title problem with your land, you need a lawyer to represent you in what's called a civil proceeding.'

'Moleen Bertrand already a lawyer. Some other lawyer gonna give him trouble back 'cause of a bunch of black peoples?'

'I have a friend who owns a title company. I'll ask him to search the courthouse records for you.'

'It won't do no good. We're six black families on one strip that's in arpents. It don't show in the survey in the co'rthouse. Everything in the co'rthouse is in acres now.'

'It doesn't make any difference. If that's your land, it's your land.'

'What you mean *if*? Moleen Bertrand's grandfather give that land to us ninety-five years ago. Everybody knowed it.'

'Somebody didn't.'

'So what you gonna do about it?'

'I'll talk to Moleen.'

'Why don't you talk to your wastebasket while you're at it?'

'Give me your phone number.'

'You got to call up at the sto'. You know why Moleen Bertrand want that land, don't you?'

'No.'

'They's a bunch of gold buried on it.'

'That's nonsense, Bertie.'

'Then why he want to bulldoze out our li'l houses?'

'I'll ask him that.'

'When?'

'Today. Is that soon enough?'

'We'll see what we gonna see.'

My phone rang and I used the call, which I put on hold, as an excuse to walk her to the door and say good-bye. But as I watched her walk with labored dignity toward her car in the parking lot, I wondered if I, too, had yielded to that old white pretense of impatient charity with people of color, as though somehow they were incapable of understanding our efforts on their behalf.

It was two days later, at five in the morning, when a cruiser pulled a man over for speeding on the St Martinville highway.

On the backseat and floor were a television set, a portable stereo, a box of women's shoes, bottles of liquor, canned goods, a suitcase full of women's clothes and purses.

'There's a drag ball I haven't been invited to?' the deputy said.

'I'm helping my girlfriend move,' the driver said.

'You haven't been drinking, have you?'

'No, sir.'

'You seem a little nervous.'

'You've got a gun in your hand.'

'I don't think that's the problem. What's that fragrance in the air? Is it dark roast coffee? Would you step out of the car, please?'

The deputy had already run the plates. The car belonged to a woman named Della Landry, whose address was on the St Martin–Iberia Parish line. The driver's name was Roland Broussard. At noon the same day he was brought into our interrogation room by Detective Helen Soileau, a dressing taped high up on his forehead.

He wore dark jeans, running shoes, a green pullover smock from the hospital. His black hair was thick and curly, his jaws unshaved, his nails bitten to the quick; a sour smell rose from his armpits. We stared at him without speaking.

The room was windowless and bare except for a wood table and three chairs. He opened and closed his hands on top of the table and kept scuffing his shoes under the chair. I took his left wrist and turned up his forearm.

'How often do you fix, Roland?' I asked.

'I've been selling at the blood bank.'

'I see.'

'You got an aspirin?' He glanced at Helen Soileau. She had a broad face whose expression you never wanted to misread. Her blonde hair looked like a lacquered wig, her figure a sack of potatoes. She wore a pair of blue slacks and a starched short-sleeve white shirt, her badge above her left breast; her handcuffs were stuck through the back of her gunbelt.

'Where's your shirt?' I said.

'It had blood all over it. Mine.'

'The report says you tried to run,' Helen said.

'Look, I asked for a lawyer. I don't have to say anything else, right?'

'That's right,' I said. 'But you already told us you boosted the car. So we can ask you about that, can't we?'

'Yeah, I boosted it. So what else you want? Big fucking deal.'

'Would you watch your language, please?' I said.

'What is this, a crazy house? You got a clown making fun of me out on the road, then beating the shit out of me, and I'm supposed to worry about my fucking language.'

'Did the owner of the car load all her possessions in it and give you the keys so you wouldn't have to wire it? That's a strange story, Roland,' I said.

'It was parked like that in the driveway. I know what you're trying to do ... Why's she keep staring at me?'

'I don't know.'

'I took the car. I was smoking dope in it, too. I ain't saying anything else ... Hey, look, she's got some kind of problem?' He held his finger close to his chest when he pointed at Helen, as though she couldn't see it.

'You want some slack, Roland? Now's the time,' I said.

Before he could answer, Helen Soileau picked up the wastebasket by the rim and swung it with both hands across the side of his face. He crashed sideways to the floor, his mouth open, his eyes out of focus. Then she hit him again, hard, across the back of the head, before I could grab her arms. Her muscles were like rocks.

She shook my hands off and hurled the can and its contents of cigarette butts, ashes, and candy wrappers caroming off his shoulders.

'You little pissant,' she said. 'You think two homicide detectives are wasting their time with a fart like you over a car theft. Look at me when I talk to you!'

'Helen—' I said softly.

'Go outside and leave us alone,' she said.

'Nope,' I said, and helped Roland Broussard back into his chair. 'Tell Detective Soileau you're sorry, Roland.'

'For what?'

'For being a wiseass. For treating us like we're stupid.'

'I apologize.'

'Helen—' I looked at her.

'I'm going to the john. I'll be back in five minutes,' she said.

'You're the good guy now?' he said, after she closed the door behind her.

'It's no act, podna. I don't get along with Helen. Few people do. She smoked two perps in three years.'

His eyes looked up into mine.

'Here's the lay of the land,' I said. 'I believe you creeped that woman's duplex and stole her car, but you didn't have anything to do with the rest of it. That's what *I* believe. That doesn't mean you won't take the fall for what happened in there. You get my drift?'

He pinched his temples with his fingers, as though a piece of rusty wire were twisting inside his head.

'So?' I opened my palms inquisitively.

'Nobody was home when I went through the window. I cleaned out the place and had it all loaded in her car. That's when some other broad dropped her off in front, so I hid in the hedge. I'm thinking, What am I gonna do? I start the car, she'll know I'm stealing it. I wait around, she turns on the light, she knows the place's been ripped off. Then two guys roar up out of nowhere, come up the sidewalk real fast, and push her inside.

'What they done, I don't like remembering it, I closed my eyes, that's the truth, she was whimpering, I'm not kidding you, man, I wanted to stop it. What was I gonna do?'

'Call for help.'

'I was strung out, I got a serious meth problem, it's easy to say what you ought to do when you're not there. Look, what's-your-name, I've been down twice but I never hurt anybody. Those guys, they were tearing her apart, I was scared, I never saw anything like that before.'

'What did they look like, Roland?'

'Gimmie a cigarette.'

'I don't smoke.'

'I didn't see their faces. I didn't want to. Why didn't her neighbors help?'

'They weren't home.'

'I felt sorry for her. I wish I'd done something.'

'Detective Soileau is going to take your statement, Roland. I'll probably be talking to you again.'

'How'd you know I didn't do it?'

'The ME says her neck was broken in the bathroom. That's the only room you didn't track mud all over.'

I passed Helen Soileau on my way out. Her eyes were hot and focused like BB's on the apprehensive face of Roland Broussard.

'He's been cooperative,' I said.

The door clicked shut behind me. I might as well have addressed myself to the drain in the water fountain.

Moleen Bertrand lived in an enormous white-columned home on Bayou Teche, just east of City Park, and from his glassed-in back porch you could look down the slope of his lawn, through the widely spaced live oak trees, and see the brown current of the bayou drifting by, the flooded cane brakes on the far side, the gazebos of his neighbors clustered with trumpet and passion vine, and finally the stiff, blocklike outline of the old drawbridge and tender house off Burke Street.

It was March and already warm, but Moleen Bertrand wore a long-sleeve candy-striped shirt with ruby cuff links and a rolled white collar. He was over six feet and could not be called a soft man, but at the same time there was no muscular tone or definition to his body, as though in growing up he had simply bypassed physical labor and conventional sports as a matter of calling.

He had been born to an exclusionary world of wealth and private schools, membership in the town's one country club, and Christmas vacations in places the rest of us knew of only from books, but no one could accuse him of not having improved upon what he had been given. He was Phi Beta Kappa at Springhill and a major in the air force toward the end of the Vietnam War. He made the *Law Review* at Tulane and became a senior partner at his firm in less than five years. He was also a champion skeet shooter. Any number of demagogic politicians who were famous for their largess sought his endorsement and that of his family name. They didn't receive it. But he never gave offense or was known to be unkind.

We walked under the trees in his backyard. His face was cool and pleasant as he sipped his iced tea and looked at a motorboat and a water-skier hammering down the bayou on pillows of yellow foam.

'Bertie can come to my office if she wants. I don't know what else to tell you, Dave,' he said. His short salt-and-pepper hair was wet and freshly combed, the part a razor-straight pink line in his scalp.

'She says your grandfather gave her family the land.'

'The truth is we haven't charged her any rent. She's interpreted that to mean she owns the land.'

'Are you selling it?'

'It's a matter of time until it gets developed by someone.'

'Those black people have lived there a long time, Moleen.'

'Tell me about it.' Then the brief moment of impatience went out of his face. 'Look, here's the reality, and I don't mean it as a complaint. There're six or seven nigra families in there we've taken care of for fifty years. I'm talking about doctor and dentist bills, schooling, extra money for June 'Teenth, getting people out of jail. Bertie tends to forget some things.'

'She mentioned something about gold being buried on the property.'

'Good heavens. I don't want to offend you, but don't y'all have something better to do?'

'She took care of me when I was little. It's hard to chase her out of my office.'

He smiled and put his hand on my shoulder. His nails were immaculate, his touch as soft as a woman's. 'Send her back to me,' he said.

'What's this stuff about gold?'

'Who knows? I always heard Jean Lafitte buried his treasure right across the bayou there, right over by those two big cypress trees.' Then his smile became a question mark. 'Why are you frowning?'

'You're the second person to mention Lafitte to me in the last couple of days.'

'Hmmm,' he said, blowing air out his nostrils.

'Thanks for your time, Moleen.'

'My pleasure.'

I walked toward my truck, which was parked on the gravel cul-de-sac by his boathouse. I rubbed the back of my neck, as though a half-forgotten thought were trying to burrow its way out of my skin.

'Excuse me, didn't you represent Bertie's nephew once?' I asked.

'That's right.'

'His name's Luke, you got him out of the death house?'

'That's the man.'

I nodded and waved good-bye again.

He had mentioned getting people out of jail but nothing as dramatic as saving somebody from the electric chair hours before an electrocution.

Why not?

Maybe he was just humble, I said in response to my own question.

When I backed out of the drive, he was idly pouring his iced tea into the inverted cone at the top of an anthill.

I drove out on the St Martinville highway to the lime green duplex set back among pine trees where Della Landry had suddenly been thrust through a door into an envelope of pain that most of us can imagine only in nightmares. The killers had virtually destroyed the interior. The mattresses, pillows, and stuffed chairs were slashed open, dishes and books raked off the shelves, dresser drawers dumped on the floors, plaster and lathes stripped out of the walls with either a crowbar or claw hammer; even the top of the toilet tank was broken in half across the bowl.

Her most personal items from the bathroom's cabinets were strewn across the floor, cracked and ground into the imitation tile by heavy shoes. The sliding shower glass that extended across the tub had been shattered out of the frame. On the opposite side of the tub was a dried red streak that could have been painted there by a heavily soaked paintbrush.

When a homicide victim's life can be traced backward to a nether world of pickup bars, pimps, and nickel-and-dime hustlers and street dealers, the search for a likely perpetrator isn't a long one. But Della Landry was a social worker who had graduated in political science from LSU only three years ago; she attended a Catholic church in St Martinville, came from a middle-class family in Slidell, taught a catechism class to the children of migrant farm workers.

She had a boyfriend in New Orleans who sometimes stayed with her on the weekends, but no one knew his name, and there seemed to be nothing remarkable about the relationship.

What could she have done, owned, or possessed that would invite such a violent intrusion into her young life?

The killers could have made a mistake, I thought, targeted the wrong person, come to the wrong address. Why not? Cops did it.

But the previous tenants in the duplex had been a husband and wife who operated a convenience store. The next-door neighbors were Social Security recipients. The rest of the semirural neighborhood was made up of ordinary lower-middle-income people who would never have enough money to buy a home of their own.

A small wire book stand by the television set had been knocked over on the carpet. The titles of the books were unexceptional and indicated nothing other than a general reading interest. But among the splay of pages was a small newspaper, titled *The Catholic Worker*, with a shoe print crushed across it.

Then for some reason my eyes settled not on the telephone, which had been pulled loose from the wall jack, but on the number pasted across the telephone's base.

I inserted the terminal back in the jack and dialed the department.

'Wally, would you go down to my office for me and look at a pink message slip stuck in the corner of my blotter?'

'Sure. Hey, I'm glad you called. The sheriff was looking for you.'

'First things first, okay?'

'Hang on.'

He put me on hold, then picked up the receiver on my desk.

'All right, Dave.'

I asked him to read me the telephone number on the message slip. After he had finished, he said, 'That's the number Sonny Marsallus left.'

'It's also the number of the phone I'm using right now, Della Landry's.'

'What's going on? Sonny decide to track his shit into Iberia Parish?'

'I think you've got your hand on it.'

'Look, the sheriff wants you to head out by Spanish Lake. Sweet Pea Chaisson and a carload of his broads are causing a little hysteria in front of the convenience store.'

'Then send a cruiser out there.'

'It isn't a traffic situation.' He began to laugh in a cigar-choked wheeze. 'Sweet Pea's got his mother's body sticking out of the car trunk. See what you can do, Dave.'

3

Five miles up the old LaFayette highway that led past Spanish Lake, I saw the lights on emergency vehicles flashing in front of a convenience store and traffic backing up in both directions as people slowed to stare at the uniformed cops and paramedics who themselves seemed incredulous at the situation. I drove on the road's shoulder and pulled into the parking lot, where Sweet Pea and five of his hookers – three white, one black, one Asian – sat amidst a clutter of dirty shovels in a pink Cadillac convertible, their faces bright with sweat as the heat rose from the leather interior. A group of kids were trying to see through the legs of the adults who were gathered around the trunk of the car.

The coffin was oversize, an ax handle across, and had been made of wood and cloth and festooned with what had once been silk roses and angels with a one-foot-square glass viewing window in the lid. The sides were rotted out, the slats held in place by vinyl garbage bags and duct tape. Sweet Pea had wedged a piece of plywood under the bottom to keep it from collapsing and spilling out on the highway, but the head of the coffin protruded out over the bumper. The viewing glass had split cleanly across the middle, exposing the waxen and pinched faces of two corpses and nests of matted hair that had fountained against the coffin's sides.

A uniformed deputy grinned at me from behind his sunglasses.

'Sweet Pea said he's giving bargain rates on the broad in the box,' he said.

'What's going on?' I said.

'Wally didn't tell you?'

'No, he was in a comic mood, too.'

The smile went out of the deputy's face. 'He says he's moving his relatives to another cemetery.'

I walked to the driver's door. Sweet Pea squinted up at me against the late sun. His eyes were the strangest I had ever seen in a human being. They were webbed with skin in the corners, so that the eyeballs seemed to peep out from slits like a baby bird's.

'I don't believe it,' I said.

'Believe it,' the woman next to him said, disgusted. Her pink shorts were grimed with dirt. She pulled out the top of her shirt and smelled herself.

'You think it's Mardi Gras?' I said.

'I don't got a right to move my stepmother?' Sweet Pea said. His few strands of hair were glued across his scalp.

'Who's in the coffin with her?'

His mouth made a wet silent O, as though he were thinking. Then he said, 'Her first husband. They were a tight couple.'

'Can we get out of the car and get something to eat?' the woman next to him said.

'It's better you stay where you are for a minute,' I said.

'Robicheaux, cain't we talk reasonable here? It's hot. My ladies are uncomfortable.'

'Don't call me by my last name.'

'Excuse me, but you're not understanding the situation. My stepmother was buried on the Bertrand plantation 'cause that's where she growed up. I hear it's gonna be sold and I don't want some cocksucker pouring cement on top of my mother's grave. So I'm taking them back to Breaux Bridge. I don't need no permit for that.'

He looked into my eyes and saw something there.

'I don't get it. I been rude, I did something to insult you?' he said.

'You're a pimp. You don't have a lot of fans around here.'

He bounced the heels of his hands lightly on the steering wheel. He smiled at nothing, his white eyebrows heavy with sweat. He cleaned one ear with his little finger.

'We got to wait for the medical examiner?' he said.

'That's right.'

'I don't want nobody having an accident on my seats. They drunk two cases of beer back at the grave,' he said.

'Step over to my office with me,' I said.

'Beg your pardon?' he said.

'Get out of the car.'

He followed me into the shade on the lee side of the store. He wore white slacks and brown shoes and belt and a maroon silk shirt unbuttoned on his chest. His teeth looked small and sharp inside his tiny mouth.

'Why the hard-on?' he said.

'I don't like you.'

'That's your problem.'

'You got a beef with Sonny Boy Marsallus?'

'No. Why should I?'

'Because you think he's piecing into your action.'

'You're on a pad for Marsallus?'

'A woman was beaten to death last night, Sweet Pea. How you'd like to spend tonight in the bag, then answer some questions for us in the morning?'

'The broad was Sonny's punch or something? Why 'front me about it?'

'Nine years ago I helped pull a girl out of the Industrial Canal. She'd been set on fire with gasoline. I heard that's how you made your bones with the Giacanos.'

He removed a toothpick from his shirt pocket and put it in his mouth. He shook his head profoundly.

'Nothing around here ever changes. Say, you want a sno'ball?' he said.

'You're a clever man, Sweet Pea.' I pulled my cuffs from my belt and turned him toward the cinder-block wall.

He waited calmly while I snipped them on each wrist, his chin tilted upward, his slitted eyes smiling at nothing.

'What's the charge?' he asked.

'Hauling trash without a permit. No offense meant.'

'Wait a minute,' he said. He flexed his knees, grunted, and passed gas softly. 'Boy, that's better. T'anks a lot, podna.'

That evening my wife, Bootsie, and I boiled crawfish in a big black pot on the kitchen stove and shelled and ate them on the picnic table in the backyard with our adopted daughter, Alafair. Our house had been built of cypress and oak by my father, a trapper and derrick man, during the Depression, each beam and log notched and drilled and pegged, and the wood had hardened and grown dark with rainwater and smoke from stubble burning in the cane fields, and today a ball peen hammer would bounce off its exterior and ring in your palm. Down the tree-dotted slope in front of the house were the bayou and dock and bait shop that I operated with an elderly black man named Batist, and on the far side of the bayou was the swamp, filled with gum and willow trees and dead cypress that turned bloodred in the setting sun.

Alafair was almost fourteen now, far removed from the little Salvadorian girl whose bones had seemed as brittle and hollow as a bird's when I pulled her from a submerged plane out on the salt; nor was she any longer the round, hard-bodied Americanized child who read Curious George and Baby Squanto Indian books and wore a Donald Duck cap with a quacking bill and a Baby Orca T-shirt and red and white tennis shoes embossed with LEFT and RIGHT on each rubber toe. It seemed that one day she had simply stepped across a line, and the baby fat was gone, and her hips and young breasts had taken on the shape of a woman's. I still remember the morning, with a pang of the heart, when she asked that her father please not call her 'little guy' and 'Baby Squanto' anymore.

She wore her hair in bangs, but it grew to her shoulders now and was black and thick with a light chestnut shine in it. She snapped the tail off a crawfish, sucked the fat out of the head, and peeled the shell off the meat with her thumbnail.

'What's that book you were reading on the gallery, Dave?' she asked.

'A diary of sorts.'

'Whose is it?'

'A guy named Sonny Boy.'

'That's a grown man's name?' she asked.

'Marsallus?' Bootsie said. She stopped eating. Her hair was the color of honey, and she had brushed it up in swirls and pinned it on her head. 'What are you doing with something of his?'

'I ran into him on Canal.'

'He's back in New Orleans? Does he have a death wish?'

285

'If he does, someone else may have paid the price for it.'

I saw the question in her eyes.

'The woman who was killed up on the St Martin line,' I said. 'I think she was Sonny's girlfriend.'

She bit down softly on the corner of her lip. 'He's trying to involve you in something, isn't he?'

'Maybe.'

'Not maybe. I knew him before you did, Dave. He's a manipulator.'

'I never figured him out, I guess. Let's go into town and get some ice cream,' I said.

'Don't let Sonny job you, Streak,' she said.

I didn't want to argue with Bootsie's knowledge of the New Orleans mob. After she married her previous husband, she had found out he kept the books for the Giacano family and owned half of a vending machine company with them. She also discovered, when he and his mistress were shotgunned to death in the parking lot of Hialeah race track, that he had mortgaged her home on Camp Street, which she had brought free and clear to the marriage.

I didn't want to talk to Bootsie in front of Alafair about the contents of Sonny's notebook, either. Much of it made little sense to me – names that I didn't recognize, mention of a telephone tree, allusions to weapons drops and mules flying dope under U.S. coastal radar. In fact, the concern, the place names, seemed a decade out-of-date, the stuff of congressional inquiry during the mid-Reagan era.

But many of the entries were physical descriptions of events that were not characterized by ideology or after-the-fact considerations about legality or illegality:

The inside of the jail is cool and dark and smells of stone and stagnant water. The man in the corner says he's from Texas but speaks no English. He pried the heels off his boots with a fork and gave the guards seventy American dollars. Through the bars I can see the helicopters going in low across the canopy toward the village on the hillside, firing rockets all the way. I think the guards are going to shoot the man in the corner tomorrow morning. He keeps telling anyone who will listen he's only a marijuanista ...

We found six cane cutters with their thumbs wired behind them in a slough two klicks from the place where we picked up our ammunition. They'd had no connection with us. They had been executed with machetes while kneeling. We pulled out as the families were coming from the village ...

Dysentery ... water goes through me like a wet razor ... burning with fever last night while the trees shook with rain ... I wake in the morning to small-arms fire from the other side of an Indian pyramid that's gray and green and smoking with mist, my blanket crawling with spiders ...

'What are you thinking about?' Bootsie said on our way back from the ice cream parlor.

'You're right about Sonny. He was born to the hustle.'

'Yes?'

'I just never knew a grifter who deliberately turned his life into a living wound.'

She looked at me curiously in the fading light.

I didn't go directly to the department in the morning. Instead, I drove out past Spanish Lake to the little community of Cade, which was made up primarily of dirt roads, the old S.P. rail tracks, the dilapidated, paintless shacks of black people, and the seemingly boundless acreage of the Bertrand family sugar plantation.

It had rained earlier that morning, and the new cane was pale green in the fields and egrets were picking insects out of the rows. I drove down a dirt lane past Bertha Fontenot's weathered cypress home, which had an orange tin roof and a tiny privy in back. A clump of banana trees grew thickly against her south wall, and petunias and impatiens bloomed out of coffee cans and rusted-out buckets all over her gallery. I drove past one more house, one that was painted, and parked by a grove of gum trees, the unofficial cemetery of the Negro families who had worked on the plantation since before the War Between the States.

The graves were no more than faint depressions among the drifting leaves, the occasional wooden cross or board marker inscribed with crude lettering and numbers knocked down and cracked apart by tractors and cane wagons, except for one yawning pit whose broken stone tablet lay half buried with fallen dirt at the bottom.

But even in the deep shade I could make out the name *Chaisson* cut into the surface.

'I can hep you with something?' a black man said behind me. He was tall, with a bladed face, eyes like bluefish scale, hair shaved close to the scalp, his skin the dull gold cast of worn saddle leather. He wore a grass-stained pink golf shirt, faded jeans, and running shoes without socks.

'Not really,' I said.

'You ax Mr Moleen you can come on the property?' he said.

'I'm Detective Dave Robicheaux with the sheriff's department,' I said, and opened my badge holder in my palm. He nodded without replying, his face deliberately simple and empty of any emotion he thought I might read there. 'Aren't you Bertie's nephew?'

'Yes, suh, that's right.'

'Your name's Luke, you run the juke joint south of the highway?'

'Sometimes. I don't own it, though. You know lots of things.' When he smiled his eyes became veiled. Behind him, I saw a young black woman watching us from the gallery. She wore white shorts and a flowered blouse, and her skin had the same gold cast as his. She walked with a cane, although I could see no infirmity in her legs.

'How many people do you think are buried in this grove?' I asked.

'They ain't been burying round here for a long time. I ain't sure it was even in here.'

'Is that an armadillo hole we're looking at?'

'Miz Chaisson and her husband buried there. But that's the only marker I ever seen here.'

'Maybe those depressions are all Indian graves. What do you think?'

'I grew up in town, suh. I wouldn't know nothing about it.'

'You don't have to call me sir.'

He nodded again, his eyes looking at nothing.

'You own your house, podna?' I said.

'Aint Bertie say she own it since her mother died. She let me and my sister stay there.'

'She says she owns it, huh?'

'Mr Moleen say different.'

'Who do you believe?' I said, and smiled.

'It's what the people at the co'rthouse say. You want anything else, suh? I got to be about my work.'

'Thanks for your time.'

He walked off through the dappled light, his face turned innocuously into the breeze blowing across the cane field. Had I been a cop too long? I asked myself. Had I come to dislike someone simply because he'd been up the road?

No, it was the disingenuousness, the hostility that had no handles on it, the use of one's race like the edge of an ax.

But why expect otherwise, I thought. We'd been good teachers.

Five minutes after I walked into my office, Helen Soileau came through the door with a file folder in her hand and sat with one haunch on the corner of my desk, her wide-set, unblinking pale eyes staring at my face.

'What is it?' I said.

'Guess who bailed out Sweet Pea Chaisson?'

I raised my eyebrows.

'Jason Darbonne, over in Lafayette. When did he start representing pimps?'

'Darbonne would hitch his mother to a dogsled if the price was right.'

'Get this. The health officer wouldn't let Sweet Pea transport the coffin back to Breaux Bridge, so he got a guy to haul it for ten bucks in a garbage truck.'

'What's the file folder?'

'You wanted to question Pissant again? Too bad. The Feds picked him up this morning ... Hey, I thought that'd give your peaches a tug.'

'Helen, could you give a little thought as to how you speak to people sometimes?'

'I'm not the problem. The problem is that black four-eyed fuck at the jail who turned our man over to the FBI.'

'What does the FBI want with a house creep?'

'Here's the paperwork,' she said, and threw the folder on my desk. 'If you go over to the lockup, tell that stack of whale shit to get his mind off copping somebody's pud, at least long enough to give us a phone call before he screws up an investigation.'

'I'm serious, Helen ... Why not cut people a little ... Never mind ... I'll take care of it.'

After she left my office I went over to see the parish jailer. He was a three-hundred-pound bisexual with glasses as thick as Coke bottles and moles all over his neck.

'I didn't release him. The night man did,' he said.

'This paperwork is shit, Kelso.'

'Don't hurt my night man's feelings. He didn't get out of the eighth grade for nothing.'

'You have a peculiar sense of humor. Roland Broussard was witness to a murder.'

'So talk to the Feds. Maybe that's why they picked him up. Anyway, they just took him out on loan.'

'Where's it say that? This handwriting looks like a drunk chicken walked across the page.'

'You want anything else?' he asked, taking a wax paper-wrapped sandwich out of his desk drawer.

'Yeah, the prisoner back in our custody.'

He nodded, bit into his sandwich, and opened the newspaper on his desk blotter.

'I promise you, my man, you'll be the first to know,' he said, his eyes already deep in a sports story.

4

After you're a police officer for a while, you encounter certain temptations. They come to you as all seductions do, in increments, a teaspoon at a time, until you discover you made an irrevocable hard left turn down the road someplace and you wake up one morning in a moral wasteland with no idea who you are.

I'm not talking about going on a pad, ripping off dope from an evidence locker, or taking juice from dealers, either. Those temptations are not inherent in the job; they're in the person.

The big trade-off is in one's humanity. The discretionary power of a police officer is enormous, at least in the lower strata of society, where you spend most of your time. You start your career with the moral clarity of the youthful altruist, then gradually you begin to feel betrayed by those you supposedly protect and serve. You're not welcome in their part of town; you're lied to with regularity, excoriated, your cruiser Molotoved. The most venal bail bondsman can walk with immunity through neighborhoods where you'll be shot at by snipers.

You begin to believe there are those in our midst who are not part of the same gene pool. You think of them as subhuman, morally diseased, or, at best, as caricatures whom you treat in custody as you would humorous circus animals.

Then maybe you're the first to arrive on the scene after another cop has shot and killed a fleeing suspect. The summer night is hot and boiling with insects, the air already charged with a knowledge you don't want to accept. It was a simple B&E, a slashed screen in the back of a house; the dead man is a full-time bumbling loser known to every cop on the beat; the two wounds are three inches apart.

'He was running?' you say to the other cop, who's wired to the eyes.

'You goddamn right he was. He stopped and turned on me. Look, he had a piece.'

The gun is in the weeds; it's blue-black, the grips wrapped with electrician's tape. The moon is down, the night so dark you wonder how anyone could see the weapon in the hand of a black suspect.

'I'm counting on you, kid,' the other cop says. 'Just tell people what you saw. *There's* the fucking gun. Right? It ain't a mushroom.'

And you step across a line.

Don't sweat it, a sergeant and drinking buddy tells you later. It's just one more lowlife off the board. Most of these guys wouldn't make good bars of soap.

Then something happens that reminds you we all fell out of the same tree.

Imagine a man locked in a car trunk, his wrists bound behind him, his nose running from the dust and the thick oily smell of the spare tire. The car's brake lights go on, illuminating the interior of the trunk briefly, then the car turns on a rural road and gravel pings like rifle shot under the fenders. But something changes, a stroke of luck the bound man can't believe – the car bangs over a rut and the latch on the trunk springs loose from the lock, hooking just enough so that the trunk lid doesn't fly up in the driver's rearview mirror.

The air that blows through the opening smells of rain and wet trees and flowers; the man can hear hundreds of frogs croaking in unison. He readies himself, presses the sole of his tennis shoe against the latch, eases it free, then rolls over the trunk's lip, tumbles off the bumper, and bounces like a tire in the middle of the road. The breath goes out of his chest in a long wheeze, as though he had been dropped from a great height; rocks scour divots out of his face and grind red circles the size of silver dollars on his elbows.

Thirty yards up the car has skidded to a stop, the lid of the trunk flopping in the air. And the bound man splashes through the cattails into a slough by the side of the road, his legs tangling in dead hyacinth vines below the surface, the silt locking around his ankles like soft cement.

Ahead he can see the flooded stands of cypress and willow trees, the green layer of algae on the dead water, the shadows that envelop and protect him like a cloak. The hyacinth vines are like wire around his legs; he trips, falls on one knee. A brown cloud of mud mushrooms around him. He stumbles forward again, jerking at the clothesline that binds his wrists, his heart exploding in his chest.

His pursuers are directly behind him now; his back twitches as though the skin has been stripped off with pliers. Then he wonders if the scream he hears is his own or that of a nutria out on the lake.

They fire only one round. It passes through him like a shaft of ice, right above the kidney. When he opens his eyes, he's on his back, stretched across a cushion of crushed willows on top of a sand spit, his legs in the water. The sound of the pistol report is still ringing in his ears. The man who wades toward him in silhouette is smoking a cigarette.

Not twice. It's not fair, Roland Broussard wants to say. *I got a meth problem. That's the only reason I was there. I'm a nobody guy, man. You don't need to do this.*

The man in silhouette takes another puff off his cigarette, pitches it out into the trees, perhaps moves out of the moon's glow so Roland's face will be better illuminated. Then he sights along the barrel and puts another round from the .357 Magnum right through Roland's eyebrow.

He walks with a heavy step back up the embankment, where a companion has waited for him as though he were watching the rerun of an old film.

5

Clete listened, his powder blue porkpie hat slanted down on his forehead, his eyes roving out into the hall while I talked. He wore an immaculate pair of white tennis shorts and a print shirt covered with parakeets. The back of his neck and the tops of his immense arms were flaking with sunburn.

'Kidnapping a guy already in custody is pretty slick. Who do you figure these characters were?' he said, his eyes leaving two uniformed deputies on the other side of the glass.

'Guys who knew the drill, at least well enough to convince a night jailer they were FBI.'

'The greaseballs?'

'Maybe.'

'It's not their normal style. They don't like to stray into federal jurisdiction.' He glanced through the glass partition into the hall again. 'Why do I get the feeling I'm some kind of zoo exhibit?'

'It's your imagination,' I said, my face flat.

'I bet.' Then he winked and pointed at a deputy with one finger. The deputy looked down at some papers in his hand.

'Knock it off, Clete.'

'Why'd you ask me down here?'

'I thought you'd like to go fishing.'

He smiled. His face was round and pink, his green eyes lighted with a private sense of humor. A scar ran through part of his eyebrow and across the bridge of his nose, where he had been bashed with a pipe when he was a kid in the Irish Channel.

'Dave, I know what my old Homicide podjo is going to think before he thinks it.'

'I've got two open murder cases. One of the victims may have been Sonny Boy Marsallus's girlfriend.'

'Marsallus, huh?' he said, his face sobering.

'I tried to have him picked up by NOPD, but he went off the screen.'

He drummed his fingers on the arm of the chair.

'Leave him off the screen,' he said.

'What was he into down in the tropics?' I asked.

'A lot of grief.'

Helen Soileau came through the door, without knocking, and dropped the crime scene report on my desk.

'You want to look it over and sign it?' she said. Her eyes went up and down Clete's body.

'Do y'all know each other?' I said.

'Only by reputation. Didn't he work for Sally Dio?' she said.

Clete fed a stick of gum in his mouth and looked at me.

'I'll go over the report in a few minutes, Helen,' I said.

'We couldn't get a print off the cigarette butt, but the casts on the footprints and tire tracks look good,' she said. 'By the way, the .357 rounds were hollow-points.'

'Thanks,' I said.

Clete swiveled around in his chair and watched her go back out the door.

'Who's the muff-diver?' he said.

'Come on, Clete.'

'One look at that broad is enough to drive you to a monastery.'

It was a quarter to five.

'Do you want to pull your car around front and I'll meet you there?' I said.

He followed me in his old Cadillac convertible to the Henderson levee outside Breaux Bridge. We put my boat and outboard in the water and fished on the far side of a bay dotted with abandoned oil platforms and dead cypress trees. The rain was falling through shafts of sunlight in the west, and the rain looked like tunnels of spun glass and smoke rising into the sky.

Clete took a long-necked bottle of Dixie beer from the cooler and snapped off the top with his pocketknife. The foam slid down the inside of the neck when he removed the bottle from his mouth. Then he drank again, his throat working a long time. His face looked tired, vaguely morose.

'Were you bothered by that crack Helen made about Sally Dio?'

'So I ran security for a greaseball. I also had two of his goons slam my hand in a car door. Sometime when you have a chance, tell the bride of Frankenstein what happened when Sal and his hired gumballs were flying friendly skies.'

The plane had crashed and exploded in a fireball on a mountainside in western Montana. The National Transportation Safety Board said someone had poured sand in the gas tanks.

Clete finished his beer and blew out his breath. He pushed his hand down in the ice for another bottle.

'You okay, partner?' I said.

'I've never dealt real well with that bullshit I got involved with in Central America. Sometimes it comes back in the middle of the night, I mean worse than when I got back from Vietnam. It's like somebody striking a match on my stomach lining.'

There were white lines at the corners of his eyes. He watched his red-and-white bobber move across the water in the shade of an oil platform, dip below the surface and rise quivering again; but he didn't pick up his rod.

'Maybe it's time for the short version of the Serenity Prayer. Sometimes you just have to say fuck it,' I said.

'What's the worst day you had in 'Nam, I mean besides getting nailed by that Bouncing Betty?'

'A village chieftain called in the 105s on his own people.'

'Sonny Boy and I hooked up with the same bunch of gunrunners. It was like an outdoor mental asylum down there. Half the time I didn't know if we were selling to the rebels or the government. I was so strung out on rum and dope and my own troubles I didn't care, either. Then one night we got to see what the government did when they wanted to put the fear of God in the Indians.'

He pinched his mouth with his hand. His calluses made a dry sound like sandpaper against his whiskers. He took a breath and widened his eyes.

'They went into this one ville and killed everything in sight. Maybe four hundred people. There was an orphanage there, run by some Mennonites. They didn't spare anybody ... all those kids ... man.'

He watched my face.

'You saw this?' I asked.

'I heard it, from maybe a half mile away. I'll never forget the sound of those people screaming. Then this captain walked us through the ville. The sonofabitch didn't give it a second thought.'

He put a Lucky Strike in his mouth and tried to light it with a Zippo cupped in his hands. The flint scratched dryly and he took the cigarette back out of his mouth and closed his big hand on it.

'Let the past go, Cletus. Haven't you paid enough dues?' I said.

'You wanted to hear about Sonny Boy? Three weeks later we were with a different bunch of guys, I was so wiped out I still don't know who they were, Cubans maybe and some Belgians working both sides of the street. Anyway, we were on a trail and we walked right into an L-shaped ambush, M-60's, blookers, serious shit, they must have shredded twelve guys in the first ten seconds.

'Sonny was on point ... I saw this ... I wasn't hallucinating ... Two guys next to me saw it, too ...'

'What are you talking about?'

'He got nailed with an M-60. I saw dust jumping all over his clothes. I didn't imagine it. When he went down his shirt was soaked with blood. Three weeks later he shows up in a bar in Guatemala City. The rebels started calling him the red angel. They said he couldn't die.'

He took a long drink off the beer. The sunlight looked like a yellow flame inside the bottle.

'Okay, mon, maybe I fried my head down there,' he said. 'But I stay away from Sonny. I don't know how to describe it, it's like he's got death painted on his skin.'

'It sounds like another one of Sonny's cons.'

'There's nothing like somebody else telling you what you saw. You remember what an M-60 bouncing on a bungee cord could do to an entire ville? How about a guy who gets it from ten yards away? No, don't answer that, Dave. I don't think I can handle it.'

In the silence I could hear the *whir* of automobile tires on the elevated highway that spanned the swamp. The setting sun looked like lakes of fire in the clouds, then a shower began to march across the bays and willow islands and dance in a yellow mist on the water around us. I pulled up the sash weight I used for an anchor, cranked the engine, and headed back for the levee. Clete opened another bottle of Dixie, then reached deep down in the crushed ice, found a can of Dr Pepper, and tossed it to me. 'Sorry, Streak,' he said, and smiled with his eyes.

But the apology would be mine to make.

That night I put on my gym shorts, running shoes, and a T-shirt, and drove out toward Spanish Lake and the little community of Cade. I can't explain why I decided to jog there rather than along the bayou, by my house, south of town. Maybe it was because the only common denominator in the case, so far, was a geographical one. For no reason I understood, Sonny Boy had mentioned a barracoon, built near the lake by Jean Lafitte, then Sweet Pea Chaisson, who could never be accused of familial sentiment, other than a violent one, had decided to exhume his adoptive mother's remains from the Bertrand plantation and transport them in a garbage truck back to Breaux Bridge. Both men operated in a neon and concrete world where people bought and sold each other daily and lived by the rules that govern piranha fish. What was their interest or involvement in a rural community of poor black people?

I parked my truck and jogged along a dirt road between sugarcane acreage, over the railroad tracks, past a dilapidated clapboard store and a row of shacks. Behind me, a compact white automobile turned off the highway, slowed so as not to blow dust in my face, and drove toward the lighted houses on the lake. I could see the silhouettes of two people talking to each other.

The breeze was warm and smelled of horses and night-blooming flowers, freshly turned soil, and smoke blowing off a stump fire hard by a pecan orchard. The tree trunks seemed alive with shadows and protean shapes in the firelight, as though, if you let imagination have its way, the residents from an earlier time had not yet accepted the inevitability of their departure.

I've often subscribed to the notion that perhaps history is not sequential; that all people, from all of history, live out their lives simultaneously, in different dimensions perhaps, occupying the same pieces of geography, unseen by one another, as if we are all part of one spiritual conception.

Attakapas Indians, Spanish colonists, slaves who dredged mud from the lake to make bricks for the homes of their masters, Louisiana's boys in butternut brown who refused to surrender after Appomattox, federal soldiers who blackened the sky with smoke from horizon to horizon – maybe they were all still out there, living just a breath away, like indistinct figures hiding inside an iridescent glare on the edge of our vision.

But the lights I saw in a distant grove of gum trees were not part of a metaphysical speculation. I could see them bouncing off tree trunks and hear the roar and grind of a large machine at the end of the dirt lane that ran past Bertie Fontenot's house.

I slowed to a walk, breathing deep in my chest, and wiped the sweat out of my eyes at the cattle guard and wisteria-grown arched gate that marked the entrance to the Bertrand property. The dirt lane was faintly haloed with humidity in the moonlight, the rain ditches boiling with insects. I began jogging toward the lights in the trees, the steady thud of my shoes like an intrusion on a nocturnal plantation landscape that had eluded the influences of the twentieth century.

Then I had the peculiar realization that I felt naked. I had neither badge nor gun, and hence no identity other than that of jogger. It was a strange feeling to have, as well as to be forced into acknowledging simultaneously the ease with which my everyday official capacity allowed me to enter and exit any number of worlds where other people lived with an abiding trepidation.

The grinding sounds of the machine ceased and the headlights dimmed and then went off. I strained my eyes to see into the gum trees, then realized that the machine, a large oblong one with a cab and giant steel tracks, was parked beyond the trees in a field, its dozer blade glinting in the moonlight.

Bertie's house and the nephew's were dark. When I walked toward the grove I could see where the dozer blade had graded whole roadways through the trees, ripping up root systems, snapping off limbs, slashing pulpy divots out of the trunks, scooping out trenches and spreading the fill out into the cane field, churning and flattening and regrinding the soil and everything in it, until the entire ground area in and around the grove looked like it had been poured into an enormous bag and shaken out at a great height.

There was no one in sight.

I walked out onto the edge of the field by the earth mover. The moon was bright above the treetops and the new cane ruffled in the breeze. I picked up handfuls of dirt and sifted them through my fingers, touched the pieces of fractured bone, as tiny and brown as ancient teeth; strips of wood porous with rot and as weightless as balsa; the remains of a high button shoe, mashed flat by the machine's track.

The wind dropped and the air suddenly smelled of sour mud and humus and dead water beetles. The sky was a dirty black, the clouds like curds of smoke from an oil fire; sweat ran down my face and sides like angry insects. Who had done this, ripped a burial area apart, as though it had no more worth than a subterranean rat's nest?

I walked back down the dirt lane toward my truck. I saw the white compact car returning down the access road, slowing gradually. Suddenly, from a distance of perhaps forty yards, the person in the passenger's seat shined a handheld spotlight at me. The glare was blinding; I could see nothing except a circle of white red-rimmed heat aimed into my eyes.

No gun, no badge, I thought, a sweating late-middle-aged man trapped on a rural road like a deer caught in an automobile's headlights.

'I don't know who you are, but you take that light out of my eyes!' I shouted.

The car was completely stopped now, the engine idling. I could hear two people, men, talking to each other. Then I realized their concern had shifted from me to someone else. The spotlight went out, leaving my eyes filled with whorls of color, and the car shot forward toward my parked truck, where a man on foot was leaning through the driver's window.

He bolted down the far side of the railway, his body disappearing like a shadow into weeds and cattails. The white compact bounced over the train embankment, stopped momentarily, and the man in the passenger seat shined the spotlight out into the darkness. I used my T-shirt to wipe my eyes clear and tried to read the license plate, but someone had rubbed mud over the numbers.

Then the driver scorched a plume of oily dust out of the road and floored the compact back onto the highway.

I opened the driver's door to my truck. When the interior light flicked on, I saw curled on the seat, like a serpent whose back has been crushed with a car tire, a twisted length of rust-sheathed chain the color of dried blood. I picked it up, felt the delicate shell flake with its own weight against my palms. Attached to one end was a cylindrical iron cuff, hinged open like a mouth gaping in death.

I had seen one like it only in a museum. It was a leg iron, the kind used in the transportation and sale of African slaves.

6

The next morning was Saturday. The dawn was gray and there were strips of mist in the oak and pecan trees when I walked down the slope to help Batist open up the dock and bait shop. The sun was still below the treeline in the swamp, and the trunks on the far side of the bayou were wet and black in the gloom. You could smell the fecund odor of bluegill and sun perch spawning back in the bays.

Batist was outside the bait shop, poking a broom handle into the pockets of rainwater that had collected in the canvas awning that extended on guy wires over the dock. I had never known his age, but he was an adult when I was a child, as black and solid as a woodstove, and today his stomach and chest were still as flat as a boilerplate. He had farmed and trapped and fished commercially and worked on oyster boats all his life, and could carry an outboard motor down to the ramp in each hand as though they were stamped from plastic. He was illiterate and knew almost nothing of the world outside of Iberia Parish, but he was one of the bravest and most loyal men I ever knew.

He began wiping the dew off the spool tables, which we had inset with Cinzano umbrellas for the fishermen who came in at midday for the barbecue lunches that we sold for $5.95.

'You know why a nigger'd be setting in one of our boats this morning?' he asked.

'Batist, you need to forget that word.'

'This is a *nigger* carry a razor and a gun. He ain't here to rent boats.'

'Could you start over?'

'There's a high-yellow nigger wit' slacks on and shiny, pointy shoes,' he said, tapping his finger in the air with each word as though I were obtuse. 'He's setting out yonder in our boat, eating *boudin* out of a paper towel wit' his fingers. This is a nigger been in jail, carry a razor on a string round his neck. I ax what he t'inks he's doing. He look up at me and say, "You clean up round here?"

'I say, "Yeah, I clean trash out of the boat, and that mean you better get yo' worthless black ass down that road."

'He say, "I ain't come here to argue wit' you. Where Robicheaux at?"

298

'I say, "He ain't here and that's all you got to know." I say, "*Vas t'en, neg.*" That's it. We don't need them kind, Dave.'

He used a half-mooned Clorox bottle to scoop the ashes out of the split oil barrel that we used for a barbecue pit. I waited for him to continue.

'What was his name?' I said. 'What kind of car did he drive?'

'He didn't have no car, and I ain't ax him his name.'

'Where'd he go?'

'Wherever people go when you run them down the road with a two-by-fo'.'

'Batist, I don't think it's a good idea to treat people like that.'

'One like that always work for the white man, Dave.'

'I beg your pardon?'

'Everyt'ing he do make white people believe the rest of us ain't got the right to ax for mo' than we got.'

It was one of those moments when I knew better than to contend with Batist's reasoning or experience.

'Somet'ing else I want to talk wit' you about,' he said. 'Look in yonder my shelves, my pig feet, my *graton*, tell me what you t'ink of that.'

I opened the screen door to the shop but hated to look. The jar of pickled hogs' feet was smashed on the floor; half-eaten candy bars, hard-boiled eggs, and cracklings, called *graton* in Cajun French, were scattered on the counter. In the midst of it all, locked in a wire crab trap, Tripod, Alafair's three-legged coon, stared back at me.

I picked him up in my arms and carried him outside. He was a beautiful coon, with silver-tipped fur and black rings on his tail, a fat stomach and big paws that could turn doorknobs and twist tops off of jars.

'I'll send Alf down to clean it up,' I said.

'It ain't right that coon keep messing up the shop, Dave.'

'It looks to me like somebody left a window open.'

'That's right. *Somebody.* 'Cause I closed every one of them.'

I stopped.

'I didn't come down here last night, partner, if that's what you're saying.'

He straightened up from a table, with the wiping rag in his hand. His face seemed to gather with a private concern. Two fishermen with a minnow bucket and a beer cooler stood by the door of the shop and looked at us impatiently.

'You wasn't down here last night, Dave?' he asked.

'No. What is it?'

He inserted his thumb and forefinger in the watch pocket of the bell-bottom dungarees he wore.

'This was on the windowsill this morning. I t'ought it was somet'ing you found on the flo',' he said, and placed the oblong piece of stamped metal in my hand. 'What you call them t'ings?'

'A dog tag.' I read the name on it, then read it again.

'What's wrong?' he said.

I felt my hand close on the tag, felt the edges bite into my palm.

'You know I cain't read, me. I didn't want to give you somet'ing bad, no.'

'It's all right. Help those gentlemen there, will you? I'll be back down in a minute,' I said.

'It ain't good you not tell me.'

'It's the name of a man I was in the army with. It's some kind of coincidence. Don't worry about it.'

But in his eyes I could see the self-imposed conviction that somehow his own ineptitude or lack of education had caused me injury.

'I ain't mad about that coon, Dave,' he said. 'Coon gonna be a coon. Tell Alafair it ain't nobody's fault.'

I sat at the redwood table with a cup of coffee under the mimosa tree in the backyard, which was still cool and blue with shadow. The breeze ruffled the periwinkles and willows along the edge of the coulee, and two greenhead mallards, who stayed with us year-round, were skittering across the surface of the pond at the back of our property.

The stainless steel dog tag contained the name of Roy J. Bumgartner, his serial number, blood type, religion, and branch of service, the simple and pragmatic encapsulation of a human life that can be vertically inserted as neatly as a safety razor between the teeth and locked in place with one sharp blow to the chin.

I remembered him well, a nineteen-year-old warrant officer from Galveston, Texas, who had brought the slick in low out of the molten sun, the canopy and elephant grass flattening under the down draft while AK-47 rounds whanged off the ship's air-frame like tack hammers. Ten minutes later, the floor piled with wounded grunts, their foreheads painted with Mercurochromed *Ms* to indicate the morphine that laced their hearts, we lifted off from the LZ and flew back through the same curtain of automatic weapons fire, the helicopter blades thropping, the windows pocking with holes like skin blisters snapping.

My body was as dry and dehydrated as a lizard's skin, all the moisture used up by the blood-expander the medic had given me during the night, the way spilled water evaporates off a hot stove. The same medic, a sweaty Italian kid from Staten Island, naked to the waist, held me in his arms now, and kept saying, as much to convince himself as me, *You're gonna make it, Loot . . . Say good-bye to Shitsville . . . You're going home alive in sixty-five . . . Bum's chauffeuring this baby right into Battalion Aid . . . They got refrigeration, Loot . . . Plasma . . . Don't put your hands down there . . . I mean it . . . Hey, somebody hold his goddamn hands.*

With the ship yawing and grooves shearing out of the rotary and black smoke from an electrical fire spiraling back through the interior, the rice paddies and earthen dikes and burned-out hooches streaking by below us, I stared at the back of the pilot's head as though my thoughts, which were like a scream inside my skull, could penetrate his: *You can do it, pappy, you can do it, pappy, you can do it, pappy.*

Then he turned and looked behind him, and I saw his thin blond face inside his helmet, the dry lump of chewing tobacco in his cheek, the red field dressing across one eye, the bloodshot and desperate energies in the other, and I knew, even before I saw the waves sliding onto the beach from the South China Sea, that we were going to make it, that no one this brave could perish.

But that conclusion was born out of political innocence and a soldier's naive belief that he would never be abandoned by his own government.

Bootsie brought me another cup of coffee and a bowl of Grape-Nuts with milk and blackberries in it. She wore a pair of faded jeans and a beige sleeveless shirt, and her face looked cool and fresh in the soft light.

'What's that?' she said.

'A dog tag that's thirty years old.'

She touched the tag with the balls of her fingers, then turned it over.

'It belonged to a guy who disappeared into Laos,' I said. 'He never came back home. I think he's one of those who got written off by Nixon and Kissinger.'

'I don't understand,' she said.

'Batist found it on the windowsill in the bait shop this morning. It's thespian bullshit of some kind. Last night somebody put a rusted leg iron on the seat of my truck.'

'Did you tell the sheriff?'

'I'll talk to him Monday.'

I chewed a mouthful of Grape-Nuts and kept my face empty.

'Alafair's still asleep. You want to go back inside for a little while?'

'You bet.'

A few minutes later we lay on top of the sheets in our bedroom. The curtains were gauzy and white with small roses printed on them, and they puffed in the breeze that blew through the azaleas and pecan trees in the side yard. Bootsie kissed like no woman I ever knew. Her face would come close to mine, her mouth parting, then she would angle her head slightly and touch her lips dryly against mine, remove them, her eyes never leaving mine; then she'd brush my lips with hers one more time, her fingernails making a slow circle in the back of my hair, her right hand moving down my stomach while her tongue slid across my teeth.

She made love without inhibition or self-consciousness, and never with stint or a harbored resentment. She sat on top of me, took me in her hand, and placed me deep inside her, her thighs widening, a wet murmur breaking from her throat. Then she propped herself on both arms so that her breasts hung close to my face, her breath coming faster now, her skin bright with a thin sheen of sweat. I felt her heat spreading into my loins, as though it were she who was controlling the moment for both of us. She leaned closer, gathering herself around me, her feet under my thighs, her face flushed and growing smaller and turning inward now, her hair damp against her skin like swirls of honey. In my mind's eye I saw a great hard-bodied tarpon, thick and stiff with life, glide through tunnels of pink coral and waving sea fans, then burst through a wave in strings of foam and light.

Afterward, she lay inside my arm and touched what seemed to me all the marks of my mortality and growing age – the white patch of hair on the side of my head, my mustache, now flecked with silver, the puckered indentation from a .38 round below my left collarbone, the gray scar, like a flattened earthworm, from a pungi stick, on my stomach, and the spray of arrow-shaped welts on my thigh where steel shards from a Bouncing Betty still lay embedded. Then she rolled against me and kissed me on the cheek.

'What's that for?' I said.

'Because you're the best, *cher.*'

'You, too, Boots.'

'But you're not telling me something.'

'I have a bad feeling about this one.'

She raised up on one elbow and looked into my face. Her bare hip looked sculpted, like pink marble, against the light outside.

'These two murders,' I said. 'We're not dealing with local dimwits.'

'So?'

'It's an old problem, Boots. They come from places they've already ruined, and then it's our turn. By the time we figure out we're dealing with major leaguers, they've been through the clock shop with baseball bats.'

'That's why we hire cops like you,' she said, and tried to smile. When I didn't answer, she said, 'We can't remove south Louisiana from the rest of the world, Dave.'

'Maybe we should give it a try.'

She lay against me and placed her hand on my heart. She smelled of shampoo and flowers and the milky heat in her skin. Outside, I could hear crows cawing angrily in a tree as the sun broke out of the clouds like a heliograph.

7

It's probably safe to say the majority of them are self-deluded, uneducated, fearful of women, and defective physically. Their political knowledge, usually gathered from paramilitary magazines, has the moral dimensions of comic books. Some of them have been kicked out of the service on bad conduct and dishonorable discharges; others have neither the physical nor mental capacity to successfully complete traditional basic training in the U.S. Army. After they pay large sums of money to slap mosquitoes at a merc training camp in the piney woods of north Florida, they have themselves tattooed with death heads and grandiloquently toast one another, usually in peckerwood accents, with the classic Legionnaire's paean to spiritual nihilism, *Vive la guerre, vive la mort.*'

Miami is full of them.

If you want to connect with them in the New Orleans area, you cross the river over to Algiers into a neighborhood of pawnshops and Vietnamese-owned grocery stores and low-rent bars, and visit Tommy Carrol's Gun & Surplus.

It was Sunday evening, and Helen Soileau and I were off the clock and out of our jurisdiction. Tommy Carrol, whom I had never met, was locking up his glass gun cases and about to close. He wore baggy camouflage trousers, polished combat boots, and a wide-necked bright yellow T-shirt, like bodybuilders wear. His shaved head reminded me of an alabaster bowling ball. He chewed and snapped his gum maniacally, his eyes flicking back and forth from his work to Helen and me as we walked in file between the stacks of survival gear, ammunition, inflatable rafts, knife display cases, and chained racks of bolt-action military rifles.

'So I'm stuck again with the goddamn kids, that's what you're saying?' Helen said over her shoulder to me. She wore tan slacks, lacquered straw sandals, and a flowered shirt hanging outside her belt. She sipped from a can of beer that was wrapped in a brown bag.

'Did I say that? Did I say that?' I said at her back.

'You need something?' Tommy Carrol said.

'Yeah, a couple of Excedrin,' I said.

'Is there a problem here?' Tommy Carrol asked.

'I'm looking for Sonny Boy Marsallus,' I said.

'Don't tell us the herpes outpatient clinic, either. We already been there,' Helen said.

'Shut up, Helen,' I said.

'Did I marry Mr Goodwrench or not?' she said.

'What's going on?' Tommy asked, his gum snapping in his jaw.

'Doesn't Sonny hang in here?' I said.

'Sometimes. I mean he used to. Not anymore.'

'Helen, why don't you go sit in the car?' I said.

'Because I don't feel like changing diapers on your goddamn kids.'

'I've been out of the loop,' I said to Tommy. 'I'd like to get back to work.'

'Doing what?'

'Peace Corps. Isn't this the sign-up place?' I said.

He arched his eyebrows and looked sideways. Then he made a tent on his chest with the fingers of one hand. His eyes were like blue marbles.

'It makes you feel better to jerk my Johnson, be my guest,' he said. 'But I'm closing up, I don't have any contact with Sonny, and I got nothing to do with other people's family troubles.' He widened his eyes for emphasis.

'This is the guy knows all the mercs?' Helen said, and brayed at her own irony. She upended her beer can until it was empty. 'I'm driving down to the store on the corner. If you're not there in five minutes, you can ride the goddamn bus home.'

She let the glass door slam behind her. Tommy stared after her.

'For real, that's your wife?' he said, chewing his gum.

'Yeah.'

'What's your experience? Maybe I can help.'

'One tour in 'Nam. Some diddle-shit stuff with the tomato pickers.'

He pushed a pencil and pad across the glass countertop.

'Write your name and number down there. I'll see what I can come up with.'

'You can't hook me up with Sonny?'

'Like I say, I don't see him around, you know what I mean?' His eyes were as bright as blue silk, locked on mine, a lump of cartilage working in his jaw.

'He's out of town and nobody's missing him?' I smiled at him.

'You summed it up.'

'How about two guys who look like Mutt and Jeff?'

He began shaking his head noncommittally.

'The short guy's got a fire hydrant for a neck. Maybe he did some work for Idi Amin. Maybe Sonny Boy popped a cap on his brother,' I said.

His eyes stayed fixed on mine, but I saw his hand tic on the countertop, heard his heavy ring click on the glass. He picked up the notepad from the countertop and tossed it on a littered desk behind him.

'You shouldn't job me, man,' he said. His eyes were unblinking, his gum rolling on his teeth.

'You think I'm a cop?'

'You got it, Jack.'

'You're right.' I opened my badge holder on the countertop. 'You know who the guy with the sawed-off neck is, don't you?'

He dropped his ring of keys in his pocket and called out to a man sweeping the wood floors in front, 'Lock it up, Mack. I'm gonna see what the old woman's got for supper. The fun guy here is a cop. But you don't have to talk to him, you don't want.' Then he spat his chewing gum neatly into a trash bag and clanged through a metal door into the back alley.

I went through the door after him. He began to walk rapidly toward his car, his keys ringing in the pocket of his camouflage trousers.

'Hold on, Tommy,' I said.

Helen had parked her car by the end of the alley, next to a Dumpster and a stand of banana trees that grew along a brick wall. She got out of her car with her baton in her hand.

'Right there, motherfucker!' she said, breaking into a run. 'Freeze! Did you hear me? I said freeze, goddamn it!'

But Tommy Carrol was not a good listener and tried to make his automobile. She whipped the baton behind his knee, and his leg folded under him as though she had severed a tendon. He crashed into the side of his car door, his knee held up before him with both hands, his mouth open as though he were trying to blow the fire out of a burn.

'Damn it, Helen,' I said between my teeth.

'He shouldn't have run,' she said. 'Right, Tommy? You got nothing to hide, you don't need to run. Tell me I'm right, Tommy.'

'Lay off him, Helen. I mean it.' I helped him up by one arm, opened his car door, and sat him down in the seat. An elderly black woman, pulling a child's wagon, with a blue rag tied around her head, came off the side street and began rooting in the Dumpster.

'I'm going to file charges on you people,' Tommy said.

'That's your right. Who's the short guy, Tommy?' I said.

'You know what? I'm gonna tell you. It's Emile Pogue. Send the mutt here after him. She'll make a great stuffed head.'

I heard Helen move behind me, gravel scrape under her shoes.

'No,' I said, and held up my hand in front of her.

Tommy kneaded the back of his leg with both hands. A thick blue vein pulsed in his shaved scalp.

'Here's something else to take with you, too,' he said. 'Emile didn't work for Idi Amin. Emile trained him at an Israeli jump school. You jack-offs don't have any idea of what you're fooling with, do you?'

Monday morning I went to the Iberia Parish Court House and began researching the records on the Bertrand plantation out by Cade. Bertie Fontenot maintained that Moleen Bertrand's grandfather had given a strip of land to several black tenants, her ancestors included, ninety-five years ago, but I could find no record of the transfer. Neither could the clerk of court. The early surveys of the Bertrand property were crude, in French arpents, and made use of coulees and dirt roads as boundaries; the last survey had been done ten years ago for an oil company, and the legal descriptions were clear and the unit designations now in acres. But no matter – there had been no apparent subdivision of the plantation granting Bertie and her neighbors title to the land on which they lived.

The secretary at Moleen's law office told me he had gone out to the country club to join his wife for lunch. I found them by the putting green, he on a wood bench, only enough bourbon in his glass to stain the water the color of oak, she in a short white pleated skirt and magenta blouse that crinkled with light, her bleached hair and deeply tanned and lined face a deceptive and electric illusion of middle-aged health down in the Sunbelt.

For Julia Bertrand was at the club every day, played a mean eighteen as well as game of bridge, was always charming, and was often the only woman remaining among the male crowd who stayed at the bar through supper time. Her capacity was awesome; she never slurred her words or used profane or coarse language; but her driver's license had been suspended twice, and years ago, before I was with the sheriff's department, a Negro child had been killed in a hit-and-run accident out in the parish. Julia Bertrand had been held briefly in custody. But later a witness changed his story, and the parents dropped charges and moved out of state.

She bent over the ball, the breeze ruffling her pleated skirt against her muscular thighs, and putted a ten-footer, *plunk*, neatly into the cup. From the wood bench she picked up her drink, which was filled with fruit and shaved ice and wrapped with a paper napkin and rubber band, and walked toward me with her hand extended. Her smile was dazzling, her tinted contacts a chemical blue-green.

'How are you, Dave? I hope we're not in trouble,' she said. Her voice was husky and playful, her breath heavy with nicotine.

'Not with me. How you doing, Julia?'

'I'm afraid Dave's doing pro bono for Bertie Fontenot,' Moleen said.

'Dave, not really?' she said.

'It's gone a little bit beyond that,' I said. 'Some peculiar things seem to be happening out at your plantation, Moleen.'

'Oh?' he said.

'I went jogging on your place Friday night. I hope you don't mind.'

'Anytime,' he said.

'Somebody dropped a rusted leg iron on my truck seat.'

'A leg iron? Well, that's interesting, isn't it?' Moleen said, and drank from his glass. His long legs were crossed, his eyes impossible to read behind his sunglasses.

'Somebody was running a dozer blade through that grove of gum trees at the end of Bertie Fontenot's lane. It looks to me like there might have been some old graves in there.'

'I'm not quite sure what you're telling me or why, but I can tell you, with some degree of certainty, what *was* in there. My great-grandfather leased convicts as laborers after the Civil War. Supposedly there was a prison stockade right where those gum trees are today.'

'No kidding?' I said.

'A bad chapter in the family history, I'm afraid.'

'Oh, it was not. You liberals love collective guilt,' Julia said.

'Why would somebody want to put a leg iron in my truck?'

'Search me.' He took off his sunglasses, folded them on his knee, yawned, and looked at a distant, moss-hung oak by the fairway.

'It was probably just my night for strange memorabilia. Somebody left a dog tag on the windowsill of my bait shop. It belonged to a guy who flew a slick into a hot LZ when I was wounded.'

'That's quite a story,' he said.

He gazed down the fairway, seemingly uninterested in my conversation, but for just a moment there had been a brightening of color in his hazel eyes, a hidden thought working behind the iris like a busy insect.

'This guy got left behind in Laos,' I said.

'You know what, Dave?' he said. 'I wish I'd behaved badly toward people of color. Been a member of the Klan or a white citizens council, something like that. Then somehow this conversation would seem more warranted.'

'Dave's not out here for any personal reason, Moleen,' his wife said, smiling. 'Are you, Dave?'

'Dave's a serious man. He doesn't expend his workday casually with the idle rich,' Moleen said. He put a cigar in his mouth and picked a match out of a thin box from the Pontchartrain Hotel.

'Police officers ask questions, Moleen,' I said.

'I'm sorry we have no answers for you.'

'Thanks for your time. Say, your man Luke is stand-up, isn't he?'

'I beg your pardon?'

'Bertie Fontenot's nephew. He's loyal. I'd swear he was willing to see his sister and aunt and himself evicted rather than have you lose title to a strip of disputed land.'

The skin of Moleen's forehead stretched against the bone. The humor and goodwill had gone out of his wife's face.

'What's he talking about, Moleen?' she said.

'I haven't any idea.'

'What does that black man have to do with this?' she asked.

'Who knows? I believe Dave has a talent for manufacturing his own frame of reference.'

'My, you certainly have managed to leave your mark on our morning,' she said to me.

'A police investigation isn't preempted by a "members only" sign at a country club,' I said.

'Ah, now we get to it,' Moleen said.

'You know a dude named Emile Pogue?' I said.

He took his cigar out of his mouth and laughed to himself.

'No, I don't,' he said. 'Good-bye, Dave. The matinee's over. Give our best to your wife. Let's bust some skeet before duck season.'

He put his arm around his wife's waist and walked her toward the club dining room. She waved good-bye over her shoulder with her fingers, smiling like a little girl who did not want to offend.

Later that afternoon I went into Helen Soileau's office and sat down while she finished typing a page that was in her typewriter. Outside, the sky was blue, the azaleas and myrtle bushes in full bloom.

Finally, she turned and stared at me, waiting for me to speak first. Her pale adversarial eyes, as always, seemed to be weighing the choice between a momentary suspension of her ongoing anger with the world and verbal attack.

'I didn't get a chance to tell you yesterday, you'd make a great actress,' I said.

She was silent, her expression flat and in abeyance, as though my meaning had not quite swum into her ken.

'You had me convinced we were married,' I said.

'What's on your mind?'

'I talked with a couple of guys I know at NOPD. Tommy Carrol isn't pressing charges. He's got a beef pending on an automatic weapons violation.'

'That's the flash?'

'That's it.'

She began leafing through some pages in a file folder as though I were not there.

'But I've got a personal problem about yesterday's events,' I said.

'What might that be?' she said, not looking up from the folder.

'We need to take it out of overdrive, Helen.'

She swiveled her chair toward me, her eyes as intense and certain as a drill instructor's.

'I've got two rules,' she said. 'Shitbags don't get treated like churchgoers, and somebody tries to take me, a civilian, or another cop down, he gets neutralized on the spot.'

'Sometimes people get caught in their own syllogism.'

'*What?*'

'Why let your own rules lock you in a corner?'

'You don't like working with me, Dave, take it to the old man.'

'You're a good cop. But you're unrelenting. It's a mistake.'

'You got anything else on your mind?'

'Nope.'

'I ran this guy Emile Pogue all kinds of ways,' she said, the door already closed on the previous subject. 'There's no record on him.'

'Hang on a minute.' I went down to my office and came back. 'Here's the diary and notebook Sonny Boy Marsallus gave me. If this is what Della Landry's killers were after, its importance is lost on me.'

'What do you want me to do with it?'

'Read it or give it back, Helen, I don't care.'

She dropped it in her desk drawer.

'You really got your nose out of joint because I took down that gun dealer?' she said.

'I was probably talking about myself.'

'How about getting the corn fritters out of your mouth?'

'I've put down five guys in my career. They all dealt the play. But I still see them in my dreams. I wish I didn't.'

'Try seeing their victims' faces for a change,' she said, and bent back over the file folder on her desk.

The juke joint run by Luke Fontenot was across the railway tracks and down a dirt road that traversed green fields of sugarcane and eventually ended in a shell cul-de-sac by a coulee and a scattered stand of hackberry and oak trees. The juke joint was a rambling wood shell of a building on top of cinder blocks, the walls layered with a combination of Montgomery Ward brick and clapboard; the cracked and oxidized windows held together with pipe tape, still strung with Christmas lights and red and green crepe paper bells. A rusted JAX sign, with stubs of broken neon tubing on it, hung above the front screen door.

In back were two small dented tin trailers with windows and doors that were both curtained.

Inside, the bar was made of wood planks that had been wrapped and thumbtacked with oilcloth. The air smelled of the cigarette smoke that drifted toward the huge window fan inset in the back wall, spilled beer, okra and shrimp boiling on a butane stove, rum and bourbon, and melted ice and collins mix congealing in the bottom of a drain bin.

All of the women in the bar were black or mulatto, but some of the men were white, unshaved, blue-collar, their expressions between a leer and a smile directed at one another, as though somehow their presence there was part of a collective and private joke, not to be taken seriously or held against them.

Luke Fontenot was loading long-necked bottles of beer in the cooler and didn't acknowledge me, although I was sure he saw me out of the corner of his eye. Instead, it was his sister, who had the same gold coloring as he, who walked on her cane across the duckboards and asked if she could help me. Her eyes were turquoise, her shiny black hair cut in a pageboy, except it was shaped and curled high up on the cheek, the way a 1920s Hollywood actress might have worn it.

'I think Luke wanted to see me,' I said.

'He's tied up right now,' she said.

'Tell him to untie himself.'

'Why you want to be bothering him, Mr Robicheaux? He cain't do anything about Aint Bertie's land problems.'

'I'm sorry, I didn't get your name.'

'Ruthie Jean.'

'Maybe you've got things turned around, Ruthie Jean. I think Luke was out at my house at sunrise Saturday morning. Why don't you ask him?'

She walked with her cane toward the rear of the bar, and spoke to him while he kept lowering the bottles into the cooler, his face turning from side to side in case a hot bottle exploded in his face, her back turned toward me.

He wiped his hands on a towel and picked up an opened soft drink. When he drank from it he kept the left side of his face turned out of the light.

'I'm sorry Batist gave you a bad time out at my dock,' I said.

'Everybody get cranky with age,' he said.

'What's up, podna?'

'I need me a part-time job. I thought you might could use somebody at your shop.'

'I should have known that. You walked fifteen miles from town, at dawn, to ask me about a job.'

'I got a ride partway.'

A white man in an oil field delivery uniform went out the back screen door with a black woman who wore cutoff Levi's and a T-shirt without a bra. She took his hand in hers before they went into one of the tin trailers. Luke's sister glanced at my face, then closed the wood door on the screen and began sweeping behind where the door had been.

'What happened to your face?' I asked Luke.

'It get rough in here sometime. I had to settle a couple of men down.'

'One of them must have had a brick in his hand.'

He leaned on his arms and took a breath through his nostrils. 'What you want?' he said.

'Who dozered the cemetery by your house Friday night?'

'I done tole you, I don't know about no graves on that plantation. I grew up in town.'

'Okay, partner. Here's my business card. I'll see you around.'

He slipped it in his shirt pocket and began rinsing glasses in a tin sink.

'I ain't meant to be unpolite,' he said. 'Tell that to that old man work for you, too. I just ain't no hep in solving nobody's problems.'

'I pulled your jacket, Luke. You're a hard man to read.'

He raised his hand, palm outward, toward me.

'No more, suh,' he said. 'You want to ax me questions, come back with a warrant and carry me down to the jail.'

When I got into my pickup the sky was steel gray, the air humid and close as a cotton glove. Raindrops were hitting in flat drops on the cane in the fields.

Ruthie Jean came through the side door and limped toward me. She rested one hand on my window jamb. She had full cheeks and a mole by her mouth; her teeth were white against her bright lipstick.

'You saw something out here you gonna use against him?' she said.

The curtains were blowing in the windows and doors of the tin trailers in back.

'I was never a vice cop,' I said.

'Then why you out here giving him a bunch of truck?'

'Your brother's got a ten-year sheet for everything from concealed weapons to first-degree murder.'

'You saw on there he stole something?'

'No.'

'He hurt somebody didn't bother him first, didn't try cheat him out of his pay, didn't take out a gun on him at a bouree table?'

'Not to my knowledge.'

310

'But y'all make it come out like you want.'

'I'd say your brother's ahead of the game. If Moleen Bertrand hadn't pulled him out of the death house, with about three hours to spare, Luke would have been yesterday's toast.'

I felt myself blink inside with the severity of my own words.

'Y'all always know, always got the smart word,' she said.

'You're angry at the wrong person.'

'When y'all cain't get at the people who really did something, y'all go down into the quarters, find the little people to get your hands on, put inside your reports and send up to Angola.'

I started my truck engine. Her hand didn't move from the window jamb.

'I'm not telling the troot, no?' she said.

Her gold skin was smooth and damp in the blowing mist, her hair thick and jet black and full of little lights.

Her eyes roved over my face. 'You're not very good at this, if you ax me,' she said, and limped back toward the front door of the juke.

That afternoon, just before five, I received a call from Clete Purcel. I could hear seagulls squeaking in the background.

'Where are you?' I said.

'By the shrimp docks in Morgan City. You know where a cop's best information is, Streak? The lowly bail bondsman. In this case, with a fat little guy named Butterbean Reaux.'

'Yeah, I know him.'

'Good. Drive on down, noble mon. We'll drink some mash and talk some trash. Or I'll drink the mash while you talk to your buddy Sonny Boy Marsallus.'

'You know where he is?'

'Right now, handcuffed to a D-ring in the backseat of my automobile. So much for all that brother-in-arms bullshit.'

8

Clete gave me directions in Morgan City, and an hour later I saw his battered Cadillac convertible parked under a solitary palm tree by an outdoor beer and hot dog stand not far from the docks. The sky was sealed with gray clouds, and the wind was blowing hard off the Gulf, capping the water all the way across the bay. Sonny sat in the backseat of the Cadillac, shirtless, a pair of blue suspenders notched into his white shoulders. His right wrist was extended downward, where it was cuffed to a D-shaped steel ring inset in the floor.

Clete was drinking a beer on a wood bench under the palm tree, his porkpie hat slanted over his forehead.

'You ought to try the hot dogs here,' Clete said.

'You want to be up on a kidnapping charge?' I said.

'Hey, Sonny! You gonna dime me?' Clete yelled at the car. Then he looked back at me. 'See, Sonny's stand-up. He's not complaining.'

He brushed at a fleck of dried blood in one nostril.

'What happened?' I said.

'He'd rat-holed himself in a room over a pool hall, actually more like a pool hall and hot pillow joint. He said he wasn't coming with me. I started to hook him up and he unloaded on me. So I had to throw him down the stairs.'

He rubbed the knuckles of his right hand unconsciously.

'Why do you have it in for him, Clete?'

'Because he was down in Bongo-Bongo Land for the same reasons as the rest of us. Except he pretends he's got some kind of blue fire radiating around his head or something.'

I walked over to the car. Sonny's left eye was swollen almost shut. He grinned up at me. His sharkskin slacks were torn at the knee.

'How's the man, Streak?' he said.

'I wish you had come in on your own.'

'Long story.'

'It always is.'

'You going to hold me?'

'Maybe.' I turned toward Clete. 'Give me your key,' I called.

'Ask Sonny if I need rabies shots,' he said, and pitched it at me.

'You're not going to get clever, are you?' I said to Sonny.

'With you guys? Are you kidding?'

'You're the consummate grifter, Sonny,' I said, opened the door, and unlocked his wrist. Then I leveled my finger at his face. 'Who were the guys who killed Della Landry?'

'I'm not sure.'

'Don't you lie to me, Sonny.'

'It could be any number of guys. It depends who they send in. You didn't lift any prints?'

'Don't worry about what we do or don't do. You just answer my questions. Who's *they*?'

'Dave, you're not going to understand this stuff.'

'You're starting to piss me off, Sonny.'

'I don't blame you.'

'Get out of the car.' I patted him down against the fender, then slipped my hand under his arm and turned him toward my truck.

'Where we going?' he said.

'You're a material witness. You're also an uncooperative material witness. That means we'll be keeping you for a while.'

'Mistake.'

'I'll live with it.'

'Don't count on it, Dave. I'm not being cute, either.'

'He's a sweetheart,' Clete said from the bench. Then he rubbed the knuckles on his right hand and looked at them.

'Sorry I popped you, Cletus,' Sonny said.

'In your ear, Sonny,' Clete said.

We drove past boatyards then some shrimp boats that were knocking against the pilings in their berths. The air was warm and smelled like brass and dead fish.

'Can I stop by my room and pick up some things?' Sonny asked.

'No.'

'Just a shirt.'

'Nope.'

'You're a hard man, Streak.'

'That girl took your fall, Sonny. You want to look at her morgue pictures?'

He was quiet a long time, his face looking straight ahead at the rain striking the windshield.

'Did she suffer?' he said.

'They tore her apart. What do you think?'

His mouth was red against his white skin.

'They were after me, or maybe the notebook I gave you,' he said.

'I've got it. You've written a potential best-seller and people are getting killed over it.'

'Dave, you lock me up, those guys are going to get to me.'

'That's the breaks, partner.'

He was quiet again, his eyes focused inward.

'Are we talking about some kind of CIA involvement?' I said.

313

'Not directly. But you start sending the wrong stuff through the computer, through your fax machines, these guys will step right into the middle of your life. I guarantee it, Dave.'

'How's the name Emile Pogue sit with you?' I said.

He let out his breath quietly. Under his suspenders his stomach was flat and corded with muscle.

'Another officer ran him all kinds of ways and came up empty,' I said.

He rubbed the ball of his thumb across his lips. Then he said, 'I didn't eat yet. What time they serve at the lockup?'

Try to read that.

Two hours later Clete called me at home. It was raining hard, the water sluicing off the gutters, and the back lawn was full of floating leaves.

'What'd you get out of him?' Clete said.

'Nothing.' I could hear country music and people's voices in the background. 'Where are you?'

'In a slop chute outside Morgan City. Dave, this guy bothers me. There's something not natural about him.'

'He's a hustler. He's outrageous by nature.'

'He doesn't get any older. He always looks the same.'

I tried to remember Sonny's approximate age. I couldn't.

'There's something else,' Clete said. 'Where I hit him. There's a strawberry mark across the backs of my fingers. It's throbbing like I've got blood poisoning or something.'

'Get out of the bar, Clete.'

'You always know how to say it.'

I couldn't sleep that night. The rain stopped and a heavy mist settled in the trees outside our bedroom window, and I could hear night-feeding bass flopping back in the swamp. I sat on the edge of the bed in my skivvies and looked at the curtains puffing in the breeze.

'What is it, Dave?' Bootsie said behind me in the dark.

'I had a bad dream, that's all.'

'About what?' She put her hand on my spine.

'A captain I knew in Vietnam. He was a stubborn and inflexible man. He sent a bunch of guys across a rice field under a full moon. They didn't come back.'

'It's been thirty years, Dave.'

'The dream was about myself. I'm going into town. I'll call you later,' I said.

I took two paper bags from the kitchen pantry, put a clean shirt in one of them, stopped by the bait shop, then drove up the dirt road through the tunnel of oak trees and over the drawbridge toward New Iberia.

It was still dark when I reached the parish jail. Kelso was drinking a cup of coffee and reading a comic book behind his desk. His face looked like a walrus's in the shadows from his desk lamp, the moles on his neck as big as raisins.

'I want to check Marsallus out,' I said.

'Check him out? Like a book from the library, you're saying?'

'It's the middle of the night. Why make an issue out of everything?'

He stretched and yawned. His thick glasses were full of light. 'The guy's a twenty-four kick-out, anyway, isn't he?'

'Maybe.'

'I think you ought to take him to a shrink.'

'What'd he do?'

'He's been having a conversation in his cell.'

'So?'

'There ain't anybody else in it, Robicheaux.'

'How about bringing him out, Kelso, then you can get back to your reading.'

'Hey, Robicheaux, you take him to the wig mechanic, make an appointment for yourself, too.'

A few minutes later Sonny and I got in my truck and drove down East Main. He was dressed in his sharkskin slacks and a jailhouse denim shirt. There were low pink clouds in the east now and the live oaks along the street were gray and hazy with mist.

'There's a shirt in that bag by the door.' I said.

'What's this in the other one? You carrying around a junkyard, Dave?' He lifted the rusted chain and ankle cuff out of the bag.

I didn't answer his question. 'I thought you might enjoy some takeout from Victor's rather than eat at the slam,' I said, parking in front of a small cafeteria on Main across from the bayou. 'You want to go get it?'

'You're not afraid I'll go out the back door?'

'There isn't one.' I put eight one-dollar bills in his hand. 'Make mine scrambled eggs, sausage, grits, and coffee.'

I watched him walk inside, tucking my borrowed tropical shirt inside his rumpled slacks. He was grinning when he came back out and got in the truck.

'There *is* a back door, Streak. You didn't know that?' he said.

'Huh,' I said, and drove us across the drawbridge, over the Teche, into City Park. The bayou was high and yellow with mud, and the wake from a tug with green and red running lights washed over the banks into the grass. We ate at a picnic table under a tree that was alive with mockingbirds.

'You ever see a leg iron like that before, Sonny?'

'Yeah, in the museum at Jackson Square.'

'Why would you make it your business to know that Jean Lafitte operated a barracoon outside New Iberia?'

'Della told me. She was into stuff like that.' Then he wiped his face with his hand. 'It's already getting hot.'

'I read your notebook. It doesn't seem to have any great illumination in it, Sonny.'

'Maybe I'm a lousy writer.'

'Why do these bozos want to kill people over your notebook?'

'They're called cleanup guys. They hose a guy and everything around him right off the planet.'

'I'll put it to you, partner, that girl died a miserable death. You want to help me nail them or not?'

A pinched light came into his face. His hand tightened on the edge of the table. He looked out toward the bayou.

'I don't know who they were,' he said. 'Look, what I can tell you won't help. But you're a cop and you'll end up putting it in a federal computer. You might as well swallow a piece of broken glass.'

I took Roy Bumgartner's dog tag out of my shirt pocket and laid it on the table beside Sonny's Styrofoam coffee cup.

'What's that mean to you?' I asked.

He stared at the name. 'Nothing,' he said.

'He flew a slick in Vietnam and disappeared in Laos. Somebody left this in my bait shop for me to find.'

'The guy was an MIA or POW?'

'Yeah, and a friend of mine.'

'There's a network, Dave, old-time intelligence guys, mercs, cowboys, shitheads, whatever you want to call them. They were mixed up with opium growers in the Golden Triangle. Some people believe that's why our guys were left behind over there. They knew too much about ties between narcotics and the American government.'

I looked at him for a long time.

'What?' he said.

'You remind me of myself when I was on the grog, Sonny. I didn't trust anyone. So I seriously fucked up my life as well as other people's.'

'Yeah, well, this breakfast has started to get expensive.'

'I've got a few things to do in town. Can you take yourself back to the jail?'

'Take myself back to—'

'Yeah, check yourself in. Kelso's got a sense of humor. Tell him you heard the Iberia Parish lockup is run like the public library.' I stuck my business card in his shirt pocket. 'When you get tired of grandiose dog shit, give me a call.'

I picked up my coffee cup and walked back toward my truck.

'Hey, Dave, this isn't right,' he said behind me.

'You want to hang from a cross. Do it without me, partner,' I said.

At one that afternoon I called Kelso at the lockup.

'Did Marsallus make it back there?' I asked.

'Yeah, we're putting in a special cell with a turnstile for him. You're a laugh a minute,' he said.

'Kick him loose.'

'You know what kind of paperwork you make for me?'

'You were right, Kelso, the prosecutor says we can't hold him. He wasn't a witness to anything. Sorry to inconvenience you.'

'You know your problem, Robicheaux? You don't like doing the peon work like everybody else – filling out forms, punching clocks, going to coffee at ten a.m. instead of when you feel like it. So you're always figuring out ways to work a finger in somebody's crack.'

'Anything else?'

'Yeah, keep that punk out of here.'

'What's he done now?'

'Giving speeches to the wet-brains in the tank. I don't need that kind of shit in my jail. Wait a minute, I wrote the names down he was talking about to these guys. Who's Joe Hill and Woody Guthrie?'

'Guys from another era, Kelso.'

'Yeah, well, two or three like your redheaded friend could have this town in flames. The wet-brains and stew-bums are all trying to talk and walk like him now, like they're all hipsters who grew up on Canal Street. It's fucking pathetic.'

Two days later Helen Soileau called in sick. An hour later, the phone on my desk rang.

'Can you come out to my house?' she said.

'What is it?'

'Can you come out?'

'Yeah, if you want me to. Are you all right?'

'Hurry up, Dave.'

I could hear her breath against the receiver, heated, dry, suddenly jerking in the back of her throat.

9

She lived alone in a racially mixed neighborhood in a one-story frame house with a screened-in gallery that she had inherited from her mother. The house was Spartan and neat, with a new tin roof and a fresh coat of metallic gray paint, the cement steps and pilings whitewashed, the flower beds bursting with pink and blue hydrangeas in the shade of a chinaberry tree.

To my knowledge, she never entertained, joined a club, or attended a church. Once a year she left the area on a vacation; except for the sheriff, she never told anyone where she was going, and no one ever asked. Her only interest, other than law enforcement, seemed to lie in the care of animals.

She wore no makeup when she opened the door. Her eyes went past me, out to the street. Her face looked as hard and shiny as ceramic.

'Come inside,' she said.

Her nine-millimeter automatic was in a checkered leather holster on the couch next to an eight-by-eleven manila envelope. The interior of the house was immaculate, slatted with sunlight, and smelled of burnt toast and coffee that had boiled over on the stove.

'You had me worried a little bit, Helen,' I said.

'I had visitors during the night,' she said.

'You mean a break-in?'

'They didn't come inside.' Then her mouth twitched. She turned her face away and curled one finger at me.

I followed her through the kitchen and into the backyard, which was shaded by a neighbor's oak whose limbs grew across her fence. At the back of the lawn was a row of elevated screened pens where Helen kept rabbits, possums, armadillos, fighting cocks, or any kind of wounded or sick animal or bird that the humane society or neighborhood children brought her.

The tarps were pulled back on top of all the pens.

'It was warm with no rain in the forecast last night, so I left them uncovered,' she said. 'When I went out this morning, the tarps were down. That's when I saw that bucket on the ground.'

I picked it up and smelled it. The inside was coated with a white powder. My head jerked back involuntarily from the odor, my nasal passages burning, as though a rubber band had snapped behind my eyes.

'They sprinkled it through the wire, then pulled the canvas down,' she said.

The birds lay in lumps in the bottom of the pens, the way birds look after they've been shot in flight, their feathers puffing in the breeze. But the type of death the birds and animals died alike was more obvious in the stiffened bodies of the possums and coons. Their mouths were wide, their necks and spines twisted from convulsions, their claws extended as though they were defending themselves against invisible enemies.

'I'm sorry, Helen. It took a real sonofabitch to do something like this,' I said.

'Two of them. Look at the footprints. One of them must wear lead shoes.'

'Why didn't you call this in?'

Then once again I saw in her face the adversarial light and lack of faith in people that always characterized her dealings with others.

'I need some serious advice,' she said. I could hear her breathing. Her right hand opened and closed at her side. There were drops of perspiration on her upper lip.

'Go ahead, Helen.'

'I'll show you something that was under my door this morning,' she said, and led the way back into her living room. She sat on her rattan couch and picked up the manila folder. The sunlight through the blinds made bright yellow stripes across her face. 'Would you work with a queer?' she asked.

'What kind of question is that?'

'Answer it.'

'What other people do in their private lives is none of my business.'

'How about a bull or a switch-hitter?'

'I don't know where you're going with this, but it's not necessary.'

Her hand was inserted in the envelope, her teeth biting on the corner of her lip. She pulled a large glossy black-and-white photograph out and handed it to me.

'It was taken two nights ago. The grain's bad because he didn't use a flash. From the angle, I'd say it was shot through that side window.'

I looked down at the photo and felt my throat color. She kept her eyes on the far wall.

'I don't think that's any big deal,' I said. 'Women kiss each other. It's how people show affection.'

'You want to see the others?'

'Don't do this to yourself.'

'Somebody already has.'

'I'm not going to be party to an invasion of your private life, Helen. I respect you for what you are. These photographs don't change anything.'

'You recognize the other woman?'

'No.'

'She used to be a chicken for Sweet Pea Chaisson. I tried to help her get out of the life. Except we went a little bit beyond that.'

'Who cares?'

'I've got to turn this stuff in, Dave.'

'The hell you do.'

She was silent, waiting.

'Do you have to prove you're an honest person?' I said. 'And by doing so, cooperate with evil people in injuring yourself. That's not integrity, Helen, it's pride.'

She returned the photo to the envelope, then studied the backs of her hands. Her fingers were thick and ringless, square on the ends.

'The only guy who comes to mind is that paramilitary fuck, what's his name, Tommy Carrol,' she said.

'Maybe,' I said. But I was already remembering Sonny Boy's warning.

'But why would he put this note on the envelope?' She turned it over so I could read the line someone had written with a felt pen – *Keep your mind on parking tickets, Muffy.* 'Why the look?'

'Sonny Marsallus. He told me not to send anything on this guy Emile Pogue through the federal computer. All those informational requests had your name on them, Helen.'

She nodded, then I saw her face cloud with an expression that I had seen too often, on too many people, over the years. Suddenly they realize they have been arbitrarily selected as the victim of an individual or a group about whom they have no knowledge and against whom they've committed no personal offense. It's a solitary moment, and it's never a good one.

I worked the envelope out from under her hands.

'We could do all kinds of doo-dah with these photos, and in all probability none of it would lead anywhere,' I said. I slipped the photos face down out of the envelope and walked with them into the kitchen. 'So I'm making use of a Clete Purcel procedure here, which is, when the rules start working for the lowlifes, get a new set of rules.'

I took a lucifer match from a box on the windowsill above the sink, scratched it on the striker, and held the flame to the corner of the photographs. The fire rippled and curled across the paper like water; I separated each sheet from the other to let the air and heat gather on the underside, the images, whatever they were, shrinking and disappearing into blackened cones while dirty strings of smoke drifted out the screen. Then I turned on the faucet and washed the ashes down the drain, wiped the sink clean with a paper towel and dropped it in the trash.

'You want to have some early lunch, then go to the office?' I said.

'Give me a minute to change.' Then she said, 'Thanks for what you did.'

'Forget it.'

'I'll say this only once,' she said. 'Men are kind to women for one of two reasons. Either they want inside the squeeze box or they have genuine balls and don't have to prove anything. When I said thank you, I meant it.'

There are compliments you don't forget.

Before I drove away I put the stiffened body of one of the dead coons in a vinyl garbage sack and placed it in the bed of my truck.

The investigation had gone nowhere since the night of Della Landry's murder. I had made a mistake and listened to Sonny Boy's deprecation of the mob and his involvement with them. Sweet Pea Chaisson's name had surfaced again, and Sweet Pea didn't change toilet paper rolls without first seeking permission of the Giacano family. If the spaghetti heads had started to crash and burn back in the seventies, it was a secret to everyone except Sonny.

The heir to the old fat boy, Didoni Giacano, also known as Didi Gee, whose logo had been the bloodstained baseball bat that rode in the backseat of his Caddy convertible when he was a loan collector and who sometimes held down the hand of an adversary in an aquarium filled with piranhas, was his nephew, a businessman first, a gangster second, but with a bizarre talent for clicking psychotic episodes on and off at will – John Polycarp Giacano, also known as Johnny Carp and Polly Gee.

Friday morning I found him in his office out by a trash dump in Jefferson Parish. His eyes, nose, and guppy mouth were set unnaturally in the center of his face, compressed into an area the size of your palm. His high forehead was ridged and knurled even though he wasn't frowning. His hair was liquid black, waved on the top and sides, like plastic that had been melted, molded, and then cooled again.

When I knew him in the First District, he had been a minor soldier in the organization, a fight fixer, and a Shylock with jockies out at Jefferson Downs and the Fairgrounds. Supposedly, as a kid, he had been the wheelman on a couple of hundred-dollar hits with the Calucci brothers; but for all his criminal history, he'd only been down once, a one-year bit for possession of stolen food stamps in the late sixties, and he did the time in a minimum security federal facility, where he had weekend furloughs and golf and tennis privileges.

Johnny Carp was smart; he went with the flow and gave people what they wanted, didn't contend with the world or argue with the way things were. Celebrities had their picture taken with him. He lent money to cops with no vig and was never known to be rude. Those who saw his other side, his apologists maintained, had broken rules and earned their fate.

'You look great,' he said, tilting back in his swivel chair. Through the window behind him, seagulls were wheeling and dipping over mountains of garbage that were being systematically spread and buried and packed down in the landfill by bulldozers.

'When did you get into the trash business, Johnny?'

'Oh, I'm just out here a couple of days a week to make sure the johns flush,' he said. He wore a beige suit with thin brown stripes in it, a purple shirt and brown knit tie, and a small rose in his lapel. He winked. 'Hey, I know you don't drink no more. Me, neither. I found a way around the problem. I ain't putting you on: Watch.'

He opened a small icebox by the wall and took out an unopened quart bottle of milk. There were two inches of cream in the neck. Then he lifted a heavy black bottle of Scotch, with a red wax seal on it, from his bottom desk drawer. He poured four fingers into a thick water glass and added milk to it, smiling all the while. The Scotch ballooned and turned inside the milk and cream like soft licorice.

'I don't get drunk, I don't get ulcers, I don't get hangovers, it's great, Dave. You want a hit?'

'No thanks. You know why anybody would want to take down Sonny Boy Marsallus?'

'Maybe it's mental health week. You know, help out your neighborhood, kill your local lunatic. The guy's head glows in the dark.'

'How about Sweet Pea Chaisson?'

'Clip Sonny? Sweet Pea's a marshmallow. Why you asking me this stuff, anyway?'

'You're the man, Johnny.'

'Uncle Didi was the man. That's the old days we're talking about.'

'You have a lot of people's respect, Johnny.'

'Yeah? The day I go broke I start being toe jam again. You want to know about Marsallus? He came out of the womb with a hard-on.'

'What's that mean?'

'He's read enough books to sound like he's somebody he ain't, but he's got sperm on the brain. He uses broads like Kleenex. Don't let that punk take you over the hurdles. He'd stand in line to fuck his mother ... I say something wrong?'

'No,' I said, my face blank.

He folded his hands, his elbows splayed, and leaned forward. 'Serious,' he said, 'somebody's trying to whack out Sonny?'

'Maybe.'

He looked sideways out the window, thinking, his coat bunched up on his neck. 'It ain't anybody in the city. Look, Sonny wasn't never a threat to anybody's action, you understand what I'm saying? His problem is he thinks his shit don't stink. He floats above the ground the rest of us got to walk on.'

'Well, it was good seeing you, Johnny.'

'Yeah, always a pleasure.'

I pulled on my earlobe as I got up to go.

'It's funny you'd tell me Sonny uses women badly. That was never his reputation,' I said.

'People in the projects don't work. What do you think they do all day, why you think they have all them kids? He's a nickel-and-dime street mutt. The head he thinks with ain't on his shoulders. I'm getting through here?'

'See you around, Johnny.'

He cocked one finger at me, drank from his glass of milk and Scotch, his compressed features almost disappearing behind his hand and wrist.

I don't remember the psychological term for it, but cops and prosecutors know the mechanism well. It involves unintended acknowledgment of guilt through the expression of denial. When Lee Harvey Oswald was in custody after the assassination of President Kennedy, he seemed to answer truthfully many of the questions asked him by cops and newsmen. But he consistently denied ownership of the 6.5 millimeter rifle found on the sixth floor of the Texas Book Depository, the one piece of physical evidence to which he was unquestionably and inextricably linked.

Della Landry had been murdered, in all probability, because of her association with Sonny. The first remark out of Johnny's mouth had been a slur about Sonny's misuse of women, as if to say, perhaps, that the fate of those who involved themselves with him was Sonny's responsibility and not anyone else's.

But maybe I was simply in another cul-de-sac, looking for meaning where there was none.

As I got into my truck three of Johnny Carp's hoods were standing by the back of his Lincoln. They wore slacks with knife creases, tasseled loafers, short-sleeve tropical shirts, gold chains on their necks, and lightly oiled boxed haircuts. But steroids had become fashionable with the mob, too, and their torsos and arms were thick with muscle like gnarled oak about to split the skin.

They were taking turns firing a .22 revolver at tin cans and the birds feeding along the dirt road that led between the trash heaps. They glanced at me briefly, then continued shooting.

'I'd like to drive out of here without getting shot,' I said.

There was no response. One man broke open the revolver, shucked out the hulls, and began reloading. He looked at me meaningfully.

'Thanks, I appreciate it,' I said.

I drove down the road, tapping my horn as cattle egrets on each side of me lifted into the air. In my rearview mirror I saw Johnny Carp walk out of his office and join his men, all of them looking at me now, I was sure, with the quiet and patient energies of creatures whose thoughts you never truly wish to know.

Friday night I went to the parish library and began to read about Jean Lafitte. Most of the material repeated in one form or another the traditional stories about the pirate who joined forces with Andrew Jackson to defeat the British at the Battle of New Orleans, the ships he robbed on the high seas, the gangs of cutthroats he lived with in Barataria and Galveston, his death somewhere in the Yucatán.

He had been considered a romantic and intriguing figure by New Orleans society, probably because none of them had been his victims. But also in the library was an article written by a local historian at the turn of the century that did not treat Lafitte as kindly. His crimes did not stop with piracy and murder. He had been a blackbirder and was transporting African slaves into the country after the prohibition of 1809. He sold his stolen goods as well as human cargo on the banks of the Teche.

Milton and Shakespeare both said lucidity and power lay in the world of dreams. For me, that has always meant that sleep and the unconscious can define what daylight and rationality cannot. That night, as a wind smelling of salt and wet sand and humus blew across the swamp, I dreamed of what Bayou Teche must have been like when the country was new, when the most severe tool or weapon was shaped from a stone, the forest floor covered with palmettos, the moss-hung canopy so thick and tall that in the suffused sunlight the trunks looked like towering gray columns in a Gothic cathedral.

In the dream the air was breathless, like steam caught under a glass bell, an autumnal yellow moon dissected with a single strip of black cloud overhead, and then I saw a long wood ship with furled masts being pulled up the bayou on ropes by Negroes who stumbled along the banks through the reeds and mud, their bodies rippling with sweat in the firelight. On the deck of the ship were their women and children, their cloth bundles gathered among them, their eyes peering ahead into the bayou's darkness, as though an explanation for their fear and misery were somehow at hand.

The auction was held under the oaks at the foot of the old Voorhies property. The Negroes did not speak English, French, or Spanish, so indigenous histories were created for them. The other property did not offer as great a problem. The gold and silver plate, the trunks filled with European fashions, the bejeweled necklaces and swords and scrolled flintlocks, all had belonged to people whose final histories were written in water somewhere in the Caribbean.

In a generation or two the banks of Spanish Lake and Bayou Teche would be lined with plantations, and people would eat off gold plate whose origins were only an interesting curiosity. The slaves who worked the sawmills, cane fields, and the salt domes out in the wetlands would speak the language and use the names of their owners, and the day when a large sailing ship appeared innocuously on a river in western Africa, amidst a green world of birds and hummocks, would become the stuff of oral legend, confused with biblical history and allegory, and finally forgotten.

I believed the dream. I remembered the oak trees at the foot of the Voorhies property, when lengths of mooring chain, driven with huge spikes into the trunks, grew in and out of the bark like calcified rust-sheathed serpents. Over the years, the chains had been drawn deeper into the heart of the tree, like orange-encrusted iron cysts in the midst of living tissue or perhaps unacknowledged and unforgiven sins.

At breakfast Saturday morning Bootsie said, 'Oh, I forgot, Dave, Julia Bertrand called last night. She invited us out to their camp at Pecan Island next Saturday.'

The kitchen window was open, and the sky was full of white clouds.

'What'd you tell her?' I said.

'I thought it was a nice idea. We don't see them often.'

'You told her we'd come?'

'No, I didn't. I said I'd check to see if you had anything planned.'

'How about we let this one slide?'

'They're nice people, Dave.'

'There's something off-center out at Moleen's plantation.'

'All right, I'll call her back.' She tried to keep the disappointment out of her face.

'Maybe it's just me, Bootsie. I never got along well in that world.'

'*That* world?'

'They think they're not accountable. Moleen always gives me the impression he lives in rarefied air.'

'What are you talking about?'

'Nothing. Call Julia up and tell her we'll be out there.'

'*Dave*,' she said, the exasperation climbing in her voice.

'Believe me, it's part of a game. So we'll check it out.'

'I think this is a good morning to work in the garden,' she said.

It rained hard that night, and when I fell asleep I thought I heard a motorboat pass by the dock. After the rain stopped, the air was damp and close and a layer of mist floated on the bayou as thick as cotton. Just after midnight the phone rang. I closed the bedroom door behind me and answered it in the living room. The house was dark and cool and water was dripping off the tin roof of the gallery.

'Mr Robicheaux?' a man's voice said.

'Yeah. Who is this?'

'Jack.'

'Jack?'

'You found a dog tag. We tried to get your friend out. You want to hear about it?' There was no accent, no emotional tone in the voice.

'What do you want, partner?'

'To explain some things you probably don't understand.'

'Come to the office Monday. Don't call my house again, either.'

'Look out your front window.'

I pulled aside the curtain and stared out into the darkness. I could see nothing except the mist floating on the bayou and a smudged red glow from a gas flare on an oil rig out in the swamp. Then, out on the dock, a tall, angular man in raincoat and hat flicked on a flashlight and shined it upward into his face. He held a cellular phone to his ear and the skin of his face was white and deeply lined, like papier-mâché that has started to crack. Then the light clicked off again. I picked the phone back up.

'You're trespassing on my property. I want you off of it,' I said.

'Walk down to the dock.'

Don't fall into it, I thought.

'Put the light back on your face and keep your hands away from your sides,' I said.

'That's acceptable.'

'I'm going to hang up now. Then I'll be down in about two minutes.'

'No. You don't break the connection.'

I let the receiver clatter on the table and went back into the bedroom. I slipped on my khakis and loafers, and removed my holstered .45 automatic from the dresser drawer. Bootsie was sleeping with the pillow partially over her head. I closed the door quietly behind me, pulled back the slide on the .45 and chambered a round, eased the hammer back down, set the safety, then stuck the barrel inside the back of my belt.

I picked up the receiver.

'You still there, partner?' I said.

'Yes.'

'Turn on your flashlight.'

'What an excellent idea.'

I went out the front door and down the slope through the trees. He had moved out on the dirt road now and I could see him more clearly. He was well over six feet, with arms that seemed too thin for the sleeves of his raincoat, wide shoulders, a face as grooved and webbed with lines as dried putty. His left coat pocket sagged with the weight of the cellular phone and his left hand now held the flashlight. His lips were purple in the beam of the flashlight, like the skin of a plum. His eyes watched me with the squinted focus of someone staring through smoke.

'Put your right hand behind your neck,' I said.

'That's not dignified.'

'Neither are jerk-off games involving the death of a brave soldier.'

'Your friend could still be alive.'

He raised his right hand, hooked it above his lapel, and let it rest there. I watched him and didn't answer.

'Sonny Marsallus is a traitor,' he said.

'I think it's time we look at your identification.'

'You don't listen well.'

'You made a mistake coming here tonight.'

'I don't think so. You have a distinguished war record. Marsallus doesn't. He's for sale.'

'I want you to turn around, walk back to the dock, and place your hands on the rail ... Just do it, partner. It's not up for debate.'

But he didn't move. I could feel sweat running down my sides like ants, but the face of the man named Jack, who wore a hat and coat, was as dry as parchment. His eyes remained riveted on mine, like brown agate with threads of gold in them.

Then I heard a sound out in the shadows.

'Hey, Jack, what's shakin'?' a voice said.

Jack twisted his head sideways and stared out into the darkness.

'It's Sonny,' the voice said. 'Hey, Dave, watch out for ole Jack there. He carries a sawed-down twelve-gauge on a bungee rope in his right armpit. Peel back your raincoat, Jack, and let Dave have a peek.'

But that was not in Jack's plan. He dropped the flashlight to the ground and bolted past me up the road. Then I saw Sonny move out from under the overhang of a live oak, a Smith & Wesson nine-millimeter gripped at an upward angle with both hands.

'Get out of the way, Dave!' he shouted.

'Are you crazy? Put that down!'

But Sonny swung wide of me and aimed with both arms stretched straight out in front of him. Then he began firing, *crack, crack, crack, crack*, fire leaping out of the barrel, the empty brass cartridges clinking on the road.

He picked up the flashlight the man named Jack had dropped and shined it down the road.

'Look at the ground, Dave, right by that hole in the bushes,' he said. 'I think Jack just sprung a leak.' Then he called out into the darkness, 'Hey, Jack, how's it feel?'

'Give me the gun, Sonny.'

'Sorry, Streak . . . I'm sorry to do this to you, too . . . No, no, don't move. I'm just going to take your piece. Now, let's walk over here to the dock and hook up.'

'You're going across the line, Sonny.'

'There's just one line that counts, Dave, the one between the good guys and the shitbags.' He worked a pair of open handcuffs from the back pocket of his blue jeans. 'Put your hands on each side of the rail. You worried about procedure? That guy I just punched a drain hole in, dig this, you heard the Falangist joke down in Taco Tico country about the Flying Nun? This isn't a shuck, either. Some of the *junta* fucks in Argentina wanted a couple of nuns, human rights types, turned into object lessons. The guy who threw them out of a Huey at a thousand feet was our man Jack.

'See you around, Streak. I'll make sure you get your piece back.'

Then he disappeared through the broken bushes where the wounded man had fled. I raked the chain on the cuffs against the dock railing while mosquitoes droned around my head and my eyes stung with sweat and humiliation at my own failure and ineptitude.

10

After I had gone down to the office Sunday morning and made my report, a mail clerk at the post office called the dispatcher and said that during the night someone had dropped an army-issue .45 automatic through a post office mail slot. The .45 had been wrapped in a paper bag with my name written on the outside.

It was hot and bright at noon, with a breeze blowing out of the south, and Clete Purcel walked with me along the dirt road to the spot where Sonny and the man named Jack had entered the brush and run down the bayou's bank toward the four corners. The blood on the leaves was coated with dust from the road.

'It looks like Sonny really cored a hole in the guy. He didn't show up at a hospital?'

'Not yet.'

We walked through the brush and down to the bank. The deep imprints in the mud left by Sonny and the man named Jack were now crisscrossed with the shoe prints of the deputies who had followed Jack's blood trail to a break in the cattails where the bow of a flat-bottomed boat had been dragged onto the sand.

Clete squatted down heavily, slipped a piece of cardboard under one knee, and looked back up the bank toward the dock. He wore a pair of baggy, elastic-waisted shorts with dancing zebras printed on them. He took off his porkpie hat and twirled it on his index finger.

'Did you ever see the sawed-down twelve?' he asked.

'No.'

'You think he was carrying one?'

'I don't know, Clete.'

'But you know a guy like that was carrying a piece of some kind? Right?'

We looked at each other.

'So the question is, why didn't he try to pop Sonny with it? He could have waited for him in the dark and parked one in his brisket,' he said.

'Because he dropped it,' I said. Then I said, 'And why didn't anyone find it last night?'

He was spinning his hat on his finger now. His eyes were green and full of light.

'Because it fell in the water,' he said, and lumbered to his feet.

It didn't take long. Seventy feet back down the bank, where the water eddied around a sunken and rotted pirogue that was green and fuzzy with moss, we saw the barrel of the twelve-gauge glinting wetly among the reeds and the wake from a passing boat. The barrel was sawed off at the pump and impacted with sand. The stock had been shaved and shaped with a wood rasp and honed into a pistol grip. A two-foot length of bungee cord, the kind you use to strap down luggage, was looped and screwed into the butt.

Clete shook the sand out of the barrel and jacked open the breech. Yellow water gushed out of the mechanism with the unfired shell. Then he jacked four more rounds out on the ground. I picked them up and they felt heavy and wet and filmed with grit in my palm.

'Our man doesn't use a sportsman's plug,' Clete said. He looked at the shells in my hand. 'Are those pumpkin balls?'

'Yeah, you don't see them anymore.'

'He probably loads his own rounds. This guy's got the smell of a mechanic, Streak.' He peeled a stick of gum with one hand and put it in his mouth, his eyes thoughtful. 'I hate to say this, but maybe dick-brain saved your life.'

Down by the dock a teenage kid was holding up a stringer of perch for a friend to see. He wore a bright-chrome-plated watchband on his wrist.

'You don't think this guy's a button man, he's mobbed-up?' Clete asked.

'I was thinking about Sonny . . . the handcuffs . . . the way he took me down.'

Clete blew into the open breech of the shotgun, closed it, and snapped the firing pin on the empty chamber. He studied my face.

'Listen, Sonny's a walking hand-job. Stop thinking what you're thinking,' he said.

'Then why are you thinking the same thing?'

'I'm not. A guy like Sonny isn't born, he's defecated into the world. I should have stuffed him down a toilet with a plumber's helper a long time ago.'

'I've seen federal agents with the same kind of cuffs.'

'This guy's no cop. You buy into his rebop and he'll piss in your shoe,' he said, and put the shotgun hard into my hands.

Clete ate lunch with us, then I went down to the bait shop and picked up a Styrofoam cooler that I had filled with ice Friday afternoon. The corner of a black garbage bag protruded from under the lid. I walked back up the incline through the shade and set the cooler in the bed of my truck. Clete was picking up pecans from under the trees and cracking them in his hands.

'You want to take a ride to Breaux Bridge?' I asked.

'I thought we were going fishing,' he said.

'I hear Sweet Pea Chaisson has rented a place out by the old seminary.'

He smiled broadly.

We took the four-lane into Lafayette, then drove down the road toward Breaux Bridge, past Holy Rosary, the old Negro Catholic school, a graveyard with tombs above the ground, the Carmelite convent, and the seminary.

Sweet Pea's rented house was a flat-roofed yellow brick building shielded by a hedge of dying azalea bushes. The lot next door was filled with old building materials and pieces of iron that were threaded with weeds and crisscrossed with morning glory vines.

No one was home. An elderly black man was cleaning up dog feces in the yard with a shovel.

'He taken the ladies to the restaurant down on Cameron in Lafayette, down by the fo' corners,' he said.

'Which restaurant?' I said.

'The one got smoke comin' out the back.'

'It's a barbecue place?' I said.

'The man own it always burning garbage out there. You'll smell it befo' you see it.'

We drove down Cameron through the black district in Lafayette. Up ahead was an area known as Four Corners, where no number of vice arrests ever seemed to get the hookers off of the sidewalks and out of the motels.

'There's his Caddy,' Clete said, and pointed out the window. 'Check this place, will you? His broads must have rubber stomach liners.'

I parked in a dirt lot next to a wood frame building with paint that had blistered and curled into shapes like blown chicken feathers and with a desiccated privy and smoking incinerator in back.

'We're not only off your turf, big mon, we're in the heart of black town. You feel comfortable with this?' Clete said when we were outside the truck.

'The locals don't mind,' I said.

'You checked in with them?'

'Not really.'

He looked at me.

'Sweet Pea's a pro. It's not a big deal,' I said.

I reached inside the Styrofoam cooler and pulled the vinyl garbage bag out. It swung heavily from my hand, dripping ice and water.

'What are you doing?' Clete said.

'I think Sweet Pea helped set up Helen Soileau.'

'The muff-diver? That's the one who had her animals killed?'

'Give her a break, Clete.'

'Excuse me. I mean the lady who thinks I'm spit on the sidewalk. What's in the bag?'

'Don't worry about it.'

'I guess I asked for this.' He spit his gum out with a thropping sound.

We went through the door. It was a cheerless place where you could stay on the downside of a drunk without making comparisons. The interior was dark, the floor covered with linoleum, the green walls lined with pale rectangles where pictures had once hung. People whose race would be hard to define were at the bar, in the booths, and at the pool table. They all looked expectantly at the glare of light from the opening front door, as though an interesting moment might be imminent in their lives.

'Man, that Sweet Pea can pick 'em, can't he? I wonder if they charge extra for the roaches in the mashed potatoes,' Clete said.

In the light from the kitchen we could see Sweet Pea and another man sitting at a large table with four women. The other man was explaining something, his forearms propped on the edge of the table, his fingers moving in the air. The women looked bored, hungover, wrapped in their own skin.

'Do you make the dude with him?' Clete said close to my ear.

'No.'

'That's Patsy Dapolito, they call him Patsy Dap, Patsy Bones, Patsy the Baker. He's a button guy for Johnny Carp.'

The man named Patsy Dapolito wore a tie and a starched collar buttoned tightly around his neck. His face was pinched-looking, the nose thin, sharp-edged, the mouth down-turned, the teeth showing as though he were breathing through them.

'Stay out of overdrive, Dave. Dapolito's a headache,' Clete said quietly.

'They all are.'

'He baked another hood's bones in a wedding cake and sent it to a Teamster birthday party.'

Sweet Pea sat at the head of the table, a bib tied around his neck. The table was covered with trays of boiled crawfish and beaded pitchers of draft beer. Sweet Pea snapped the tail off a crawfish, sucked the fat out of the head, then peeled the shell off the tail. He dipped the meat into a red sauce, put it in his mouth, and never looked up.

'Y'all get yourself some plates, Mr Robicheaux,' he said. He wore cream-colored slacks and a bolo tie and a gray silk shirt that rippled with a metallic sheen. His mouth glistened as though it were painted with lip gloss.

I took the dead coon out of the bag by its hind feet. The body was leathery and stiff, the fur wet from the ice in the cooler. I swung it across the table right into Sweet Pea's tray. Crawfish shells and juice, beer, and coleslaw exploded all over his shirt and slacks.

He stared down at his clothes, the twisted body of the coon in the middle of his tray, then at me. But Sweet Pea Chaisson didn't rattle easily. He wiped his cheek with the back of his wrist and started to speak.

'Shut up, Sweet Pea,' Clete said.

Sweet Pea smiled, his webbed eyes squeezing shut.

'What I done to deserve this?' he said. 'You ruin my dinner, you t'row dead animals at me, now I ain't even suppose to talk?'

I could hear the air-conditioning units humming in the windows, a solitary pool ball rolling across the linoleum floor.

'Your buddies tried to hurt a friend of mine, Sweet Pea,' I said.

He wrapped a napkin around the coon's tail, then held the coon out at arm's length and dropped it.

'You don't want nothing to eat?' he asked.

'Fuck it,' Clete said beside me, his voice low.

Then I saw the expression on the face of the man called Patsy Dap. It was a grin, as though he both appreciated and was bemused by the moment that was being created for all of us. I felt Clete's shoe nudge against mine, his fingers pull lightly on my arm.

But it was moving too fast now.

'What d' we got here, the crazy person hour, fucking clowns abusing people at Sunday dinner?' Dapolito said.

'Nobody's got a beef with you, Patsy,' Clete said.

'What d' you call this, creating a fucking scene, slopping food on people, who the fuck is this guy?'

'We got no problem with you, Patsy. Accept my word on that,' Clete said.

'Why's *he* looking at me like that?' Dapolito said. 'Hey, I don't like that. Why you pinning me, man? . . . Hey . . .'

My gaze drifted back to Sweet Pea.

'Tell those two guys, you know who I'm talking about, not to bother my friend again. That's all I wanted to say,' I said.

'Hey, I said why you fucking pinning me. You answer my question,' Dapolito said.

Then his hand shot up from under the table and bit like a vise into my scrotum.

I vaguely recall the screams of the women at the table and Clete locking his big arms around me and dragging me backward through a tangle of chairs. But I remember my palm curving around the handle of the pitcher, the heavy weight of it swinging in an arc, the glass exploding in strings of wet light; I remember it like red shards of memory that can rise from a drunken dream. Then Dapolito was on his knees, his face gathered in his hands, his scarlet fingers trembling as though he were weeping or hiding a shameful secret in the stunned silence of the room.

11

'Why'd you do it, mon?' Clete said outside. We were standing between my truck and Sweet Pea's Cadillac convertible.

'He dealt it.' I wiped the sweat off my face on my sleeve and tried to breathe evenly. My heart was beating against my rib cage. So far we had heard no sirens. Some of the restaurant's customers had come out the front door but none of them wanted to enter the parking lot.

'Okay . . . this is the way I see it,' Clete said. 'You had provocation, so you'll probably skate with the locals. Patsy Dap's another matter. We'll have to do a sit-down with Johnny Carp.'

'Forget it.'

'You just left monkey shit all over the ceiling. We're doing this one my way, Streak.'

'It's not going to happen, Clete.'

'Trust me, big mon,' he said, lighting a cigarette. 'What's keeping the locals?'

'It probably got called in as barroom bullshit in the black district,' I said.

There was a whirring sound in my ears like wind blowing in seashells. I couldn't stop sweating. Clete propped his arm against the cloth top of Sweet Pea's car and glanced down into the backseat.

'Dave, look at this,' he said.

'What?'

'On the floor. Under those newspapers. There's something on the carpet.'

The exposed areas of the carpet, where people's feet had crumpled and bunched the newspaper, looked brushed and vacuumed, but there were stains like melted chocolate in the gray fabric that someone had not been able to remove.

'We took it this far. You got a slim-jim in your tool box?' Clete said.

'No.'

'So he needs a new top anyway,' he said, and snapped open a switchblade knife, plunged it into the cloth, and sawed a slit down the edge of the back window. He worked his arm deep inside the hole and popped open the door.

'Feel it,' he said a moment later, stepping aside so I could place my hand on the back floor.

The stain had become sticky in the enclosed heat of the automobile.

Hovering like a fog just above the rug was a thick, sweet smell that reminded me in a vague way of an odor in a battalion aid station.

'Somebody did some major bleeding back there,' Clete said.

'Lock it up again.'

'Wait a minute.' He picked up a crumpled piece of paper that was stuck down in the crack of the leather seat and read the carbon writing on it. 'It looks like Sweet Pea's got lead in his foot as well as his twanger. Ninety in a forty-five.'

'Let's see it,' I said.

He handed it to me. Then he looked at my face again.

'It means something?' he said.

'He got the ticket yesterday on a dirt road out by Cade. Why's he hanging around Cade?' In the distance I could hear a siren on an emergency vehicle, as though it were trying to find a hole through traffic at an intersection.

'Wait here. Everything's going to be copacetic,' Clete said.

'Don't go back in there.'

He walked fast across the lot, entered the side door of the restaurant, then came back out with his hand in one pocket.

'Why is it these dumb bastards always use the john to score? The owner's even got sandpaper glued on top of the toilet tank to keep the rag-noses from chopping up lines on it,' he said.

He stood between my truck and the Cadillac and began working open a small rectangular cellophane-sealed container with two silhouette lovers on it.

'You're one in a million, Cletus,' I said.

He unrolled a condom, then removed a piece of broken talc from his pocket, crushed it into fragments and powder, poured it with his palm into the condom, and tied a knot in the latex at the top.

'There's nothing like keeping everybody's eye on the shitbags. By the way, they wrapped one of those roller towels from the towel machine around Patsy's head. Think of a dirty Q-Tip sitting in a chair,' he said. He dropped the condom on the floor of the Cadillac with two empty crack vials and locked the door, just before an Acadian ambulance, followed by a Lafayette city police car, turned into the parking lot.

'Party time,' he said. He crinkled his eyes at me and brushed his palms softly.

The sheriff had never been a police officer before his election to office, but he was a good administrator and his general decency and sense of fairness had gotten him through most of his early problems in handling both criminals and his own personnel. He had been a combat marine, an enlisted man, during the Korean War, which he would not discuss under any circumstances, and I always suspected his military experience was related to his sincere desire not to abuse the authority of his position.

When I sat down in his office the sun was yellow and bright outside the window, and an array of potted plants on his windowsill stood out in dark silhouette against the light. His cheeks were red and grained and woven with tiny blue veins, and he had the small round chin of the French with a cleft in it.

He reread my report with his elbows on the desk blotter and his knuckles propped against his brow.

'I don't need this on Monday morning,' he said.

'It got out of hand.'

'Out of hand? Let me make an observation, my friend. Clete Purcel has no business here. He causes trouble everywhere he goes.'

'He tried to stop it, Sheriff. Besides, he knows Sonny Marsallus better than anyone in New Orleans.'

'That's not an acceptable trade-off. What's this stuff about a dead coon?'

I cleared a tic out of my throat. 'That's not in my report,' I said.

'Last night I got a call at home from the Lafayette chief of police. Let's see, how did he put it? "Would you tell your traveling clown to keep his circus act in his own parish?" You want to hear the rest of it?'

'Not really.' Because I knew my straying into another jurisdiction, or even the beer pitcher smashed into Patsy Dapolito's face, was not what was on the sheriff's mind.

'What have you held back from me?' he said.

I looked at him blankly and didn't answer.

'You're not the only one who chooses what to file a report on and what not to, are you?' he asked.

'Excuse me?'

'Saturday I ran into a friend of mine with the humane society. He's a friend of Helen Soileau's. He mentioned a certain event he thought I already knew about.'

The sheriff waited.

'I don't believe in using the truth to injure good people,' I said.

'What gives you the right to make that kind of decision?'

My palms felt damp on the arms of the chair. I could feel a balloon of heat rising from my stomach into my throat.

'I never enjoyed the role of pin cushion,' I said.

'You're being treated unfairly?'

I wiped my palms on my thighs and folded them in my lap. I looked out the window at the fronds on a palm tree lifting in the breeze.

'Somebody killed all her animals. You knew about it but you didn't report it and you went after Sweet Pea Chaisson on your own,' he said.

'Yes, sir, that's correct.'

'Why?'

'Because some shitheads set her up for blackmail purposes.'

He brushed at the corner of his eye with his fingertip.

'I have a feeling they didn't catch her in the sack with a boyfriend,' he said.

'The subject's closed for me, Sheriff.'

'Closed? Interesting. No, amazing.' He swiveled his chair sideways, rocked back in it, pushing against his paunch with his stiffened fingers. 'Maybe you ought to have a little more faith in the people you work for.'

'She sent some inquiries through the federal computer. Somebody doesn't want her to pursue it,' I said.

His eyes rested on the flowered teapot he used to water his plants, then they seemed to refocus on another concern. 'I've got the FBI bugging me about Sonny Marsallus. What's their interest in a Canal Street gumball?'

'I don't know.'

'They know a lot about him and I don't think it's off a rap sheet. Maybe he got loose from the witness protection program.'

'Sonny's not a snitch,' I said.

'Great character reference, Dave. I bet he took his grandmother to Mass, too.'

I rose from the chair. 'Are you going to tell Helen about our conversation?'

'I don't know. Probably not. Just don't try to take me over the hurdles again. Were you ever mixed up in army intelligence?'

'No, why?'

'This whole thing stinks of the federal government. Can you tell me why they have to track their shit into a town that's so small it used to be between two Burma-Shave signs?'

I sat back down. 'I want to get a warrant to search Sweet Pea Chaisson's car.'

'What for?'

'There's dried blood on the back floor.'

'How do you know?'

'Clete and I were inside it . . . Clete salted the shaft but the Lafayette cops didn't find what they were supposed to.'

'I don't believe what you're telling me.'

'You said you wanted it straight.'

'This is the last time we're going to have this kind of conversation, sir.'

I picked up my mail and walked down to my office. Five minutes later the sheriff opened my door just far enough to lean his head in.

'You didn't skate after all,' he said. 'Sweet Pea's lawyer, what's his name, that greasebag from Lafayette, Jason Darbonne, just filed a harassment complaint against you and the department. Another thing, too, Dave, just so we're clear on everything, I want this shit cleaned up and it'd better be damn soon.'

I couldn't blame him for his anger. The case drawers in our building were filled with enough grief, mayhem, perversity, and institutional failure to match the quality of life in the worst Third World nations on earth. Like case histories at a welfare agency, a police file, once opened, never seemed to close. Instead, it grew generationally, the same family names appearing again and again, the charges and investigations marking the passage of one individual from birth to adolescence to adulthood to death, crime scene photo upon mug shot, yellowing page upon yellowing page, like layers of sedimentary accretion formed by sewage as it flows through a pipe.

Children aborted with coat hangers, born addicted to crack, scalded under hot faucets; teenage mothers with pipe cleaner legs living between detox, the welfare agency, and hooking on the street; high school kids who can let off a .44 Magnum point-blank into their classmates at a dance and seriously maintain they acted in self-defense because they heard firecrackers popping in the parking lot; armed robbers who upgrade their agenda to kicking ballpoint pens into the eardrums of their victims before they execute them in the back of a fast-food restaurant; and the strangest and most baffling phenomenon of all, the recidivist pedophiles who are repeatedly paroled until they not only sodomize but murder a small child.

At one time local A.A. meetings were made up largely of aging drunks like myself. Now kids who should be in middle school are brought to the meetings in vans from halfway houses. They're usually white, wear burr haircuts, floppy tennis shoes, and oversize baseball caps sideways on their heads and look like refugees from an Our Gang comedy, except, when it's their turn to talk, they speak in coonass blue-collar accents about jonesing for crack and getting UA-ed by probation officers. You have the feeling their odyssey is just beginning.

Our best efforts with any of it seem to do no good. In dark moments I sometimes believed we should simply export the whole criminal population to uninhabited areas of the earth and start over again.

But any honest cop will tell you that no form of vice exists without societal sanction of some kind. Also, the big players would still be with us – the mob and the gambling interests who feed on economic recession and greed in politicians and local businessmen, the oil industry, which fouls the oyster beds and trenches saltwater channels into a freshwater marsh, the chemical and waste management companies that treat Louisiana as an enormous outdoor toilet and transform lakes and even the aquifer into toxic soup.

They all came here by consent, using the word *jobs* as though it were part of a votive vocabulary. But the deception wasn't even necessary. There was always somebody for sale, waiting to take it on his knees, right down the throat and into the viscera, as long as the money was right. The speeding ticket Clete had found in Sweet Pea's car had been written on the dirt road that led from the highway back to the juke joint operated by Luke and Ruthie Jean Fontenot. Before I left the office, I pulled the ten-year package we had on Luke.

He had been extricated from the death house while a convict barber was in the act of lathering and shaving his head, the state's final preparation for the moment when Luke would sit in an oak chair while men he didn't know screwed a metal cap down on his sweating pate and strapped his arms and shinbones so tightly into the wood that his own rigid configuration would seem part of the chair itself. The call had come from the governor's office after Moleen Bertrand had hand-delivered depositions from two witnesses who swore the victim, a white sharecropper, had brought a pistol out from under the bouree table. According to the witnesses, a wet-brain in the crowd had stolen the gun before the sheriff's deputies arrived.

Luke received not only a stay but eventually a new trial, and finally a hung jury and a prosecutorial decision to cut him loose. His debt to Moleen was a large one.

*

The morning was warm and humid and the breeze blew a fine dust out of the shell parking lot and powdered the leaves of the oak and hackberry trees that were clustered next to the juke joint. I drove through the empty lot and parked in the shady lee of the building. A trash fire was smoldering in a rusted oil barrel by one of the trailers. On the ground next to it, like a flattened snake with a broken back, was a long strip of crusted gauze. A black woman in purple shorts and an olive green V-neck sweater looked out the back screen and disappeared again. I kicked over the trash barrel, rolled it across the shells, and used a stick to pry apart a smoldering stack of newspaper and food-streaked paper plates, scorched *boudin* casings and pork rinds, until, at the bottom of the pile, I saw the glowing and blackened remains of bandages that dissolved into thread when I touched them with the stick.

I went through the screen door and sat at the empty bar. Motes of dust spun in the glare of light through the windows.

The woman had big arms and breasts, a figure like a duck, a thick and glistening black neck hung with imitation gold chains. She walked toward me in a pair of flip-flops, holding a cigarette with two fingers, palm upward, by the side of her face, her hoop earrings swinging on her lobes.

'You gonna tell me you the tax man, I bet,' she said.

'Nope.'

'You ain't the beer man.'

'I'm not that either.'

'Sorry, sugar, if you come down to check the jellyroll. It's too early in the morning.'

'I came down to see you,' I said, and smiled.

'I knowed it soon as you come in.'

'Is Luke here?'

'You see him?'

'How about Ruthie Jean?'

'They come in at night. What you gonna have?' she said, and folded her arms on the bar so that her breasts swelled like cantaloupes out of her sweater. A gold tooth glinted in the corner of her mouth. 'If you big enough, you can have anything you want. You big, ain't you?'

'How about a Dr Pepper?' I watched her uncap a bottle and fill a glass with ice, her thought patterns, her true attitudes toward whites, the plan or absence of a plan that governed her day, her feelings for a lover or a child, the totality of her life, all of it a mystery, hidden behind a coy cynicism that was as implacable as ceramic.

'Y'all don't have a gun-shot white man in one of those trailers, do you?' I said, and drank out of my glass.

'Don't know nothing about guns.'

'I don't blame you. Who bled all over those bandages?'

Her mouth was painted with purple lipstick. She pursed her lips into a large, thick button and hummed to herself. 'Here's a red quarter. Can you put it in the jukebox for me?' she said. 'It got fingernail polish on it so the jukebox man don't keep it when he picks up the coins.'

I opened my badge holder on the bar.

'Do you mind if I look in your trailers?' I said.

'I thought I had me a new boyfriend. But you just being on the job, ain't you?'

'I think there might be an injured man back there. So that gives me the right to go in those trailers. You want to help me?'

She pressed her fingertip on a potato chip crumb on the bar, looked at it, and flicked it away.

'I give away my heart and a man wipe his feet on it every time,' she said.

I went back outside. The windows in both trailers were open, the curtains blowing in the breeze, but the doors were padlocked. When I reentered the bar the woman was talking on the pay phone in back. She finished her conversation, her back to me, and hung up.

'Had to find me a new man,' she said.

'Can I have the key?'

'Sure. Why you ain't ax? You know how to put it in? Cain't every man always get it in by hisself.'

I unlocked and went inside the first trailer. It stunk of insecticide and moist garbage; roaches as fat as my thumb raced across the cracked linoleum. In the center of the floor was a double cot with a rubber air mattress on it and a tangled sheet spotted with gray stains. The small tin sink was full of empty beer cans, the drain stoppered with cigarette butts.

The second trailer was a different matter. The floor was mopped, the tiny bathroom and shower stall clean, the two trash cans empty. In the icebox was a gallon bottle of orange juice, a box of jelly doughnuts, a package of ground chuck steak. The sheets and pillow-cases had been stripped from the mattress on the bed. I grabbed the mattress by one end and rolled it upside down on the springs. In the center of the rayon cover was a brown stain the size of a pie plate that looked like the source had pooled and soaked deep into the fabric.

I opened my Swiss Army knife and grooved a line of crusted flakes onto the blade and wiped them inside a Ziploc bag. I locked the trailer and started to get in my truck, then changed my mind and went back inside the bar. The woman was mopping out the women's rest room, her stomach swinging under her sweater.

'He was a tall white man with a face full of wrinkles,' I said. 'He probably doesn't like black people much, but he had at least one nine-millimeter round in him and wasn't going to argue when Sweet Pea drove him out here. How am I doing so far?'

'It ain't my bidness, baby.'

'What's your name?'

'Glo. You treat me right, I light up. I light up your whole life.'

'I don't think you mean harm to anyone, Glo. But that man, the one with the wrinkles in his face, like old wallpaper full of cracks, he's a special kind of guy, he thinks up things to do to people, anybody, you, me, maybe even some Catholic nuns, I was told he threw two of them from a helicopter at a high altitude. Was the man in the trailer that kind of guy?'

She propped the head of the mop in a bucket of dirty water and worked her Lucky Strikes out of her shorts. Her right eye looked bulbous and watery as she held the Zippo's flame to the cigarette. She exhaled, pressed the back of her wrist to her eye socket, then cleared her throat and spat something brown into the wastebasket.

She tilted her chin up at me, her face unmasked, suddenly real, for the first time. 'That's the troot, what you saying about this guy?'

'As far as I know.'

'I'm locking up now, sugar, gotta take my little boy to the doctor today. There's a lot of grip going around.'

'Here my business card, Glo.'

But she walked away from me, her arms stiff at her sides, her hands extended at right angles, as though she were floating on currents of air, her mouth gathered into a silent pucker like a purple rose.

I drove across the cattle guard under the arched and wisteria-covered iron trellis at the entrance to the Bertrand plantation, down the dirt road to Ruthie Jean Fontenot's small white frame house, where I parked in the yard. The sun had gone behind a cloud, blanketing the fields with shadow, and the breeze felt moist and warm blowing across the tops of the cane.

Ruthie Jean opened her door on a night chain.

'What you want?' she said.

'Question and answer time.'

'I'm not dressed.'

'I'm not going away.'

'Aren't you suppose to have a warrant or something?'

'No.'

She made a face, closed the door hard, then walked into the back of the house. I waited ten minutes among the gum trees where the dirt had been bladed and packed smooth by the earthmover. I picked up the twisted tongue of an old shoe. It felt as dry and light as a desiccated leaf. I heard Ruthie Jean slip the night chain on the door.

Her small living room was cramped with rattan furniture that had come in a set. The andirons in the fireplace were stacked with stone logs, a blaze of scarlet cellophane pasted behind them to give the effect of flames. Ruthie Jean stood on her cane in a white dress with a lacy neckline, black pumps, and a red glass necklace. Her skin looked yellow and cool in the soft light.

'You look nice,' I said, and instantly felt my cheeks burn at the license in my remark.

'What you want down here this time?'

Before I could answer, a phone rang in back. She walked back to the kitchen to answer it. On a shelf above the couch were a clutter of gilt-framed family photographs. In one of them Ruthie Jean was receiving a rolled certificate or diploma of some kind from a black man in a suit and tie. They were both smiling. She had no cane and was wearing a nurse's uniform. At the end of the shelf was a dust-free triangular empty space where another photograph must have been recently removed.

'Are you a nurse?' I asked when she came back in the room.

'I was a nurse's aide.' Her eyes went flat.

'How long ago was that?'

'What you care?'

'Can I sit down, please?'

'Suit yourself.'

'You have a phone,' I said.

She looked at me with an incredulous expression.

'Your Aunt Bertie told me she didn't have a phone and I'd have to leave messages for her at the convenience store. But you live just next door. Why wouldn't she tell me to call you instead?'

'She and Luke don't get along.' Her cheek twitched when she sat down on the couch. Behind her head was the shelf with the row of framed photographs on it.

'Because he's too close to Moleen Bertrand?' I said.

'Ax them.'

'I want the white man named Jack,' I said.

She looked at her nails, then at her watch.

'This guy's an assassin, Ruthie Jean. When he's not leaking blood in one of your trailers, he carries a cut-down twelve-gauge under his armpit.'

She rolled her eyes, a whimsical pout on her mouth, and looked out the window at a bird on a tree branch, her eyelids fluttering. I felt my face pinch with a strange kind of anger that I didn't quite recognize.

'I don't understand you,' I said. 'You're attractive and intelligent, you graduated from a vo-tech program, you probably worked in hospitals. What are you doing with a bunch of lowlifes and white trash in a hot pillow joint?'

Her face blanched.

'Don't look injured. Sweet Pea Chaisson is supplying the girls at your club,' I said. 'Why are you letting these people use you?'

'What I'm suppose to do now, ax you to hep us, same man who say he doesn't need a warrant just 'cause he's down in the quarters?'

'I'm not the enemy, Ruthie Jean. You've got bad people in your life and they're going to mess you up in a serious way. I guarantee it.'

'There's nothing y'all don't know,' she said. But her voice was thick now, tired, as though a stone bruise were throbbing deep inside a vulnerable place.

I started in again. 'You're too smart to let a man like Sweet Pea or Jack run a game on you.'

She looked back out the window, a hot light in her eyes.

'Jack's got a friend who's built like an icebox. Did you see a guy who looks like that?' I said.

'I been polite but I'm axing you to leave now.'

'How do you think all this is going to end?'

'What you mean?'

'You think you can deal with these guys by yourself? When they leave town, they wipe everything off the blackboard. Maybe both you and your brother. Maybe Glo and your aunt, too. They call it a slop-shot.'

341

'You pretend you're different from other policemen but you're not,' she said. 'You pretend so your words cut deeper and hurt people more.'

I felt my lips part but no sound came out.

'I promise you, we'll nail this guy to the wall and I'll keep you out of it,' I said finally, still off balance, my train of thought lost.

She leaned sideways on the couch, her hands tight on her cane, as though a sliver of pain were working its way up her spine into her eyes.

'I didn't mean to insult or hurt you,' I said. I tried to organize my words. My eyes focused on the mole by her mouth and the soft curve of her hair against her cheek. She troubled me in a way that I didn't quite want to look at. 'This man Jack is probably part of an international group of some kind. I'm not sure what it is, but I'm convinced they're here to do grave injury to us. By that I mean all of us, Ruthie Jean. White people, black people, it doesn't matter. To them another human being is just a bucket of guts sewn up in a sack of skin.'

But it was no use. I didn't know what the man named Jack had told her, or perhaps had done to her, and I suspected his tools were many, but as was often the case, I knew I was witnessing another instance when the fear that moral cretins could inculcate in their victims was far greater than any apprehension they might have about refusing to cooperate with a law enforcement agency.

I heard a car outside and got up and looked outside the window. Luke, in a 1970s gas guzzler, had driven just far enough up the lane to see my truck, then had dropped his car in reverse and floorboarded it back toward the entrance to the plantation, dirt rocketing off the tires like shards of flint.

'I'm beginning to feel like the personification of anthrax around here,' I said.

'You what?'

'Nothing. I don't want to see y'all go down on a bad beef. I'm talking about aiding and abetting, Ruthie Jean.'

She got up on her cane, her hand locking hard into the curved handle.

'I cain't sit long. I got to walk around, then do some exercises and lie down,' she said.

'What happened to you?'

'I don't have any more to say.'

'Okay, you do what you want. Here's my business card in case you or Luke feel like talking to me later,' I said, weary of trying to break through her fear or layers of racial distrust that were generations in the making. And in the next few moments I was about to do something that would only add to them. 'Could I have a glass of water?' I asked.

When she left the room I looked behind and under the couch. But in my heart I already knew where I was going to find it. When the perps are holding dope, stolen property, a gun that's been used in an armed robbery or murder, and they sniff the Man about to walk into their lives, they get as much geography as possible between them and it. But Ruthie Jean wasn't a perp, and when her kind want to conceal or protect something that is dear to them, they stand at the bridge or cover it with their person.

I lifted up the cushion she had rested her back against. The gilt-frame color photograph was propped against the bamboo supports and webbing of the couch.

I had never seen him with a suntan. He looked handsome, leaner, his blue air force cap set at an angle, his gold bars, pilot's sunglasses, unbuttoned collar, and boyish grin giving him the cavalier and romantic appearance of a World War II South Pacific aviator rather than a sixties intelligence officer who to my knowledge had never seen combat.

I heard her weight on a floor plank. She stood in the doorway, a glass of water in her hand, her face now empty of every defense, her secrets now the stuff cops talk about casually while they spit Red Man out car windows and watch black women cross the street at intersections.

'It must have fallen off the shelf,' I said, my skin flexing against my skull. I started to replace the photograph in the dust-free spot at the end of the shelf. But she dropped her cane to the floor, limped forward off balance, pulled the photo from my hand, and hurled the glass of water in my face.

At the front door I looked back at her, blotted the water out of my eyes on my sleeve, and started to say something, to leave a statement hovering in the air that would somehow redeem the moment; an apology for deceiving her, or perhaps even a verbal thorn because she'd both disturbed and bested me. But it was one of those times when you have to release others and yourself to our shared failure and inadequacy and not pretend that language can heal either.

I knew why the shame and anger burned in her eyes. I believe it had little to do with me. In a flowing calligraphy at the bottom of the photo he had written, 'This was taken in some God-forsaken place whose name, fortunately, I forget – Always, Moleen.' I wondered what a plantation black woman must feel when she realizes that her white lover, grandiose in his rhetoric, lacks the decency or integrity or courage or whatever quality it takes to write her name and personalize the photo he gives her.

12

Clete called me from his office the next day.

'I'll buy you dinner in Morgan City after work,' he said.

'What are you up to, Clete?'

'I'm taking a day off from the colostomy bags. It's not a plot. Come on down and eat some crabs.'

'Is Johnny Carp involved in this?'

'I know a couple of guys who used to mule dope out of Panama and Belize. They told me some interesting stuff about fuckhead.'

'Who?'

'Marsallus. I don't want to tell you over the phone. There're clicking sounds on my line sometimes.'

'You're tapped?'

'Remember when we had to smoke that greaser and his bodyguard in the back of their car? I know IAD had a tap on me then. Sounds just like it. You coming down?'

'Clete—'

'Lighten up.'

He told me the name of the restaurant.

It was on the far side of Morgan City, just off the highway by a boat basin lined with docks, boat slips, and tin-roofed sheds that extended out over the water. Clete was at a linen-covered table set with flowers by the window. On the horizon you could see rain falling out of the sunlight like a cloud of purple smoke. He had a small pitcher of draft beer and an ice-filmed schooner and plate of stuffed mushrooms in front of him. His face was glowing with alcohol and a fresh sunburn.

'Dig in, noble mon. I've got some fried soft-shells on the way,' he said.

'What's the gen on Sonny?' I left my coat on to cover my .45.

'Oh, yeah,' he said, as though he had forgotten the reason for our meeting. 'These two mules, I know them because they're bondsmen now and handle a lot of the pukes dealing crack in the St. Bernard where I run down about three skips a week. They were flying reefer and coke out of Belize, which was some kind of stop-off place for a whole bunch of runs going in and out of Colombia and Panama. These guys say there were a lot of weird connections down there, CIA, military people, maybe some guys hooked into the White

House. Anyway, they knew asswipe and say everybody had him made for DEA.'

'"Asswipe" is Sonny Boy?'

His eyes fluttered. 'No, I'm talking about a Maryknoll missionary. Come on, Dave, stop letting this guy job you. His parents should have been sterilized or given a lifetime supply of industrial-strength rubbers.'

'You buy what these bondsmen say?'

'Not really. Marsallus never finished high school. The DEA hires college graduates, Notre Dame jocks with brains, not street mutts with tattoos and rap sheets.'

'Then why'd you have me come down here?' I asked.

But even as his eyes were drifting toward the door of the restaurant, I already knew the answer. John Polycarp Giacano had just come through the carpeted foyer, a raincoat draped on his shoulders as a movie actor might wear it. He was talking to a man behind him whom I couldn't see.

'Wait in the car. It's all right,' he said, his palms raised in a placating way. 'Fix yourself a drink. Then we'll catch some more fish.'

He slipped his coat off his shoulders and handed it to a waitress to hang up, never speaking, as though his intention should automatically be understood. He wore white boating shoes, pleated slacks that were the color of French vanilla ice cream, and a navy blue tropical shirt that was ablaze with big red flowers. He walked toward us, smiling, his close-set eyes, thick brows, nose, and mouth all gathered together like a facial caricature in the center of a cake.

'You shouldn't have done this, Clete,' I said.

'It's got to be cleared up, Streak. Patsy Dap listens to only one man. Just let me do the talking and everything's going to be cool.'

'How you doin', fellas?' Johnny Carp said, and sat down.

'What's the haps, John?' I said.

He picked up a stuffed mushroom with his fingers and plopped it in his mouth, his eyes smiling at me while he chewed.

'He asks me what's the haps,' he said. 'Dave, I love you, you fucking wild man.'

'Glad you could make it, Johnny,' Clete said.

'I love to fish,' he said. 'It don't matter redfish, gafftop, specs, white trout, it's the fresh air, the waves flopping against the boat, Dave, you're a fucking zonk, we ain't living in the days of the O.K. Corral no more, know what I'm saying?'

'I don't know what to tell you, Johnny,' I said.

'Hey, Clete, get us some drinks over here, some snapper fingers, some oysters on the half shell, make sure they're fresh, I got to talk to this crazy guy,' Johnny said.

'I don't think you do, John,' I said.

'What's he saying, Clete?'

'Streak doesn't like to bother people with his trouble, that's all, Johnny.'

'His trouble's my trouble. So let's work it out. I got a guy out in the car gonna have to have plastic surgery over in Houston. This is a guy nobody needs to have pissed off at him. I'm talking about a face looks like a basketball with stitches all over it. This guy couldn't get laid down at the Braille school. This ain't something you just blow out your ass because you happen to be a cop, Dave.'

'You're a generous man with your time, Johnny,' I said. 'But I didn't ask for a sit-down.'

'What, I'm here to play with my dick under the table?'

A family sitting close to us got up and left.

'Your man went across the line,' I said.

'I think we got a problem with pride here, Dave. It ain't good.'

'There're cops in New Orleans who would have blown out his candle, Johnny,' I said.

'You ain't in New Orleans. You degraded the man. He works for me. I got to square it, I'm being up-front here.'

'I don't think you're hearing me. I was off my turf. So your man's not down on an assault charge. End of subject, Johnny,' I said.

'You're burning up a lot of goodwill, Dave. That's the oil makes all the wheels turn. You're educated, I ain't got to tell you that,' Johnny said. 'The guy I got out in the car never had your advantages, he don't operate on goodwill, he operates out of respect for me. I don't honor that respect, then I don't get it from nobody else, either.'

'What do you think you're going to get here today?' I asked.

'I got an envelope with ten large in it. You give it to the guy for his hospital bill, just say you got no hard feelings. You ain't even got to say you're sorry. The money don't matter 'cause I'm paying his hospital bill anyway and he'll have to give me the ten back. So everybody wins, everybody feels better, and we don't have no problems later.'

'Are you serious?' I said.

'I throw a net over a guy makes some people wake up with cold sweats, pump him full of Demerol so he don't kick out my fucking windows, just so I can get him off your back, you have the fucking nerve to ask me if I'm serious?'

He took a comb out of his shirt pocket and ran it through his hair, touching the waves with his fingers simultaneously, his knurled forehead furrowing as his eyes bored into my face. The teeth of his comb were bright with oil.

'Come on, Johnny, Dave's not trying to dis anybody. The situation just got out of control. It happens.'

'He's not trying to *what*?' Johnny said.

'Dis anybody. He doesn't mean any disrespect.'

'I know what it means, why you using nigger language to me?'

Clete eased out his breath and lifted his shirt off his collarbone with his thumb. 'I got fried out in my boat today, Johnny,' he said. 'Sometimes I don't say things very well. I apologize.'

'I accept your invitation to dinner, you talk to me like I'm a goddamn nigger?'

The waiter set down a Scotch and milk in front of Johnny, another pitcher of beer for Clete, an iced tea for me, and a round tray of freshly opened oysters flecked with ice. Johnny reached across the table and popped Clete on top of the hand.

'You deaf and dumb?' he said.

Clete's green eyes roved around the room, as though he were appraising the fishnets and ship's life preservers hung on the wall. He picked up a oyster, sucked it out of the shell, and winked at Johnny Carp.

'What the fuck's that supposed to mean?' Johnny said.

'You're a lot of fun, John,' Clete said.

Johnny took a deep drink out of his Scotch and milk, his eyes like black marbles that had rolled together above the glass. He rubbed a knuckle hard across his mouth, then pursed his lips like a tropical fish staring out of an aquarium. 'I'm asking you in a nice way, you're giving me some kind of queer-bait signals here, you're ridiculing me, you just being a wiseass 'cause we're in public, what?' he said.

'I'm saying this was a bad idea,' Clete said. 'Look, I was there. Patsy Dap violated my friend's person, you know what I'm saying? That's not acceptable anywhere, not with your people, not with ours. He got what he deserved. You don't see it that way, Johnny, it's because you're fifty-two cards short of a deck. And don't ever put your fucking hand on me again.'

Five minutes later, under the porch, we watched Johnny Carp drive his Lincoln through the light rain toward the parking lot exit. He had rolled down the tinted windows to let in the cool air, and we could see Patsy Dapolito in the passenger seat, his face and shaved head like a bleached-out muskmelon laced with barbed wire.

'Hey, Patsy, it's an improvement. I ain't putting you on,' Clete yelled.

'You're a terrific intermediary, Clete,' I said.

'The Giacanos are scum, anyway. Blow it off. Come on, let's go out under the shed and throw a line in. Wow, feel that breeze,' he said, inhaling deeply, his eyes filling with pleasure at the soft twilit perfection of the day.

Clete was probably the best investigative cop I ever knew, but he treated his relationships with the lowlifes like playful encounters with zoo creatures. As a result, his attitudes about them were often facile.

The Giacanos never did anything unless money and personal gain were involved. The family name had been linked repeatedly to both a presidential assassination and the murder of a famous civil rights leader, and although I believed them capable of committing either one or both of those crimes, I didn't see how the Giacanos could have benefited financially from them and for that reason alone doubted their involvement.

But Johnny didn't do a sit-down with a rural sheriff's detective to prevent a meltdown like Patsy Dapolito from getting off his leash. Dapolito was morally insane but not stupid. When his kind stopped taking orders and started carrying out personal vendettas, they were shredded into fish chum and sprinkled around Barataria Bay.

Johnny Carp'd had another agenda when he came down to Morgan City. I didn't know what it was, but I was sure of one thing – one way or another, Johnny had become a player in Iberia Parish.

Jason Darbonne was known as the best criminal lawyer in Lafayette. He had the hard, grizzled body of a weight lifter and daily handball player, with thick upper arms and tendons like ropes in his shoulders. But it was his peculiar bald head that you remembered; it had the shape and color of an egg that had been hard-boiled in brown tea, and because he had virtually no neck, the head seemed to perch on his high collar like Humpty-Dumpty's.

A cold front had gone through the area early Wednesday morning, and the air was brisk and sunny when I ran into him and Sweet Pea Chaisson on the courthouse steps.

'Hey, Dave,' Sweet Pea said. 'Wait a minute, I forget. Is it your first name or your last name I ain't suppose to use?'

'What's your problem this morning?' I said.

'Don't talk to him,' Darbonne said to Sweet Pea.

'I didn't even know y'all sliced up my top till I went through the car wash. The whole inside of my car got flooded. Then the female attendant picks up this rubber that floats out from under the seat. I felt like two cents.'

'What's your point?' I said.

'I forgot to pay my State Farm. I'm gonna be out four t'ousand dollars. It ain't my way to go around suing people.' He brushed off Darbonne's hand. 'Just give me the money for the top and we'll forget it.'

'You'll forget it? You're telling me I'm being sued?' I said.

'Yeah, I want my goddamn money. The inside of my car's ruined. It's like riding around inside a sponge.'

I started inside the courthouse.

'What's the matter, there's something wrong with the words I use you don't understand?' he said.

His webbed, birdlike eyes focused earnestly on my face.

'I had nothing to do with damaging your car. Stay away from me, Sweet Pea,' I said.

He pressed the few strands of hair on his head flat with the palm of his hand and squinted at me as though he were looking through a dense haze, his mouth flexing in disbelief. Darbonne put his hand on Sweet Pea's arm.

'Is that a threat, sir?' he asked.

'No, it's just a request.'

'If you didn't do it, that fat fuck did,' Sweet Pea said.

'I'll pass on your remarks to Purcel,' I said.

'You're a public menace hiding behind a badge,' Darbonne said. 'If you come near my client again, you're going to wish your name was Job.'

Two women and a man passing by turned and looked at us, then glanced away. Darbonne and Sweet Pea walked out to a white Chrysler parked by the curb. The sun reflected hotly off the tinted back window like a cluster of gold needles. Darbonne was poised by the driver's door, waiting for an opportunity to open it in the traffic, his nostrils dilating at something in the breeze.

I walked toward him, looked across the Chrysler's roof into his surprised face.

'When I was a patrolman in New Orleans, you were a prosecutor for the United States attorney's office,' I said.

His hand was poised in midair, his sunglasses hanging from his fingers.

'What happened to you, sir?' I said.

He turned his face away from me and slipped his sunglasses on his nose, but not before I saw a level of injury in his eyes that I had not anticipated.

Helen Soileau sat on the corner of my desk. She wore a pair of tan slacks and a pink short-sleeve shirt.

'I took Marsallus's diary home last night and read it till two this morning,' she said. 'He's pretty good with words.'

'Sonny's not easy to put in one shoe box,' I said.

'Have you got all the paperwork on him?'

'Pretty much. None of it's very helpful, though. I got his family's welfare file if you want to look at it.'

'What for?'

'No reason, really.'

She picked up the folder from my blotter and began glancing through it.

'His mother was a prostitute?' she said.

'Yeah, she died of tuberculosis when he was a kid. His father was a blind man who sharpened knives and scissors on a grinder he used to wheel up and down Villere Street.'

Helen put the folder down.

'In the diary he talks about some songwriters. He quotes a bunch of their lyrics,' she said. 'Joe Hill and Woody Guthrie. Is Woody Guthrie related to Arlo?'

'Woody was his dad. Woody and Joe Hill wrote songs about farm migrants, the early unions, that sort of thing.'

'I don't get it,' she said.

'What?'

'Marsallus, he's not a wiseguy. He doesn't think like one. The stuff in that diary, it bothers me.'

'You mean the massacres in those villages?'

'Was that really going on down there?' she said.

'Everyone who was there tells the same story.'

'Marsallus said something about the nature of memory that I couldn't stop thinking about. "My cell partner told me today my head's like a bad neighborhood that I shouldn't go into by myself." There was a time in my life when I was the same way. I just didn't know how to say it.'

'I see,' I said, focusing my eyes at a point middistance between us.

She bounced her fingertips on the file folder.

'You want to go to lunch?' I said.

'No, thanks. Say, where's the portable cluster fuck these days?'

'I beg your pardon?'

'Clete Purcel.'

'Oh, he's around . . . Did you want me to tell him something?'

'I was just curious.'

I nodded, my face empty. She stood up from the corner of the desk, straightened her shoulders and flattened her stomach, tucked her shirt under her gunbelt with her thumbs.

'You looking at something?' she said.

'Not me.'

'I was too hard on the guy, that's all. I mean when he was in your office that time,' she said.

'He's probably forgotten about it, Helen.'

'Y'all go fishing a lot?'

'Once in a while. Would you like to join us?'

'I'm not much on it. But you're a cutie,' she said, walked her fingers across my shoulders, and went out the door.

Moleen Bertrand's camp was located down in the wetlands on a chenier, a plateau of dry ground formed like a barrier island by the tides from water-pulverized seashells. Except for the site of his camp, a four-bedroom frame building with a tin roof and screened-in gallery, the chenier was pristine, the black topsoil bursting with mushrooms and buttercups and blue bonnets, no different than it had been when the first Spanish and French explorers came to Louisiana. The woods were parklike, the trees widely spaced, the branches and trunks hung and wrapped with vines that had the girth of boa constrictors, the moss-covered canopy of live oaks hundreds of feet above the ground, which was dotted with palmettos and layered with rotting pecan husks. At the edge of the chenier were bogs and alligator grass and blue herons lifting above the gum trees and acres of blooming hyacinths that were impassable with a boat, and, to the south, you could see the long, slate green, wind-capped roll of the Gulf and the lightning that danced over the water like electricity trapped in a steel box.

Moleen and his wife, Julia, were flawless hosts. Their guests were all congenial people, attorneys, the owner of a sugar mill, an executive from a hot sauce company, their wives and children. Moleen fixed drinks at a bar on the gallery, kept a huge ice chest filled with soda and imported beer, barbecued a pig on a spit under a tin shed and roasted trays of wild ducks from the freezer. We busted skeet with his shotguns; the children played volleyball and sailed Frisbees; the air smelled of wildflowers and salt spray and the hot brassy odor of a distant storm. It was a perfect spring day for friends to gather on an untouched strip of the Old South that somehow had eluded the twentieth century.

Except for the unnatural brightness and confidence in Julia's face, the wired click in her eyes when she did not assimilate words or meaning right away, and Moleen's ongoing anecdotal rhetoric that seemed intended to distract from his wife's affliction. Each time she returned to the bar she poured four fingers of Jack Daniel's into her glass, with no water or soda, added a half cup of ice, a teaspoon of sugar, and a sprig of mint. We were eating in the main room when she said, out of no apparent context, 'Can any of y'all explain to me why this black congresswoman got away with refusing the Daughters of the Confederacy the renewal of their logo?'

'She didn't do it by herself,' Moleen said quietly, and touched his lips with his napkin.

'They went along with her, but she was behind it. That's what I meant, Moleen. I think it's ridiculous,' Julia said.

The other people at the table smiled, unsure of what was being said, perhaps faintly remembering a news article.

'Julia's talking about the Daughters of the Confederacy trying to renew the patent on their emblem,' Moleen said. 'The application was denied because the emblem has the Confederate flag on it.'

'That woman's a demagogue. I don't know why people can't see that,' Julia said.

'I think it's our fault,' a woman down the table said, leaning out over her plate to speak. 'We've let the Confederate flag become identified with all kinds of vile groups. I can't blame people of color for their feelings.'

'I didn't say I blamed people of color,' Julia said. 'I was talking about this particular black woman.'

'Julia makes a point,' Moleen said. 'The DOC's hardly a Fifth Column.'

'Well, I think we should do something about it,' Julia said. She drank from her glass, and the light intensified behind her chemical-green contact lenses.

'Oh, it gives them something to do in Washington,' Moleen said.

'It's not a joke, Moleen,' Julia said.

'Let me tell you something *she* did once,' Moleen said, spreading his napkin and replacing it on his lap. 'When she was a cheerleader at LSU. She and these other kids, they hooked up Mike the Tiger's empty cage to a pickup truck, with the back door flopping open, and drove all over nigger town on Saturday afternoon.' He blew a laugh out of his mouth. 'They'd stop in front of a bar or barbecue stand and say, "Excuse me, we don't want to alarm anyone but have y'all seen a tiger around here?" There were darkies climbing trees all over Baton Rouge.'

I stared at him.

'Don't tell that story. I didn't have anything to do with that,' Julia said, obviously pleased at the account.

'It's a campus legend. People make too much about race today,' he said.

'Moleen, that doesn't change what that woman has done. That's what I'm trying to say, which y'all don't seem to understand,' she said.

'For God's sakes, Julia, let's change the subject,' he said.

The table was quiet. Someone coughed, a knife scraped against a plate. The whites of Julia's eyes were threaded with tiny red veins, the lashes stuck together with mascara. I thought of a face painted on a wind-blown pink balloon that was quivering against its string, about to burst.

Later, outside, Moleen asked me to walk with him to the edge of the marsh, where his shotguns and skeet trap rested on top of a weathered picnic table. He wore laced boots, khaki trousers with snap pockets up and down the legs, a shooter's vest with twelve-gauge shells inserted in the cloth loops. He cracked open his double-barrel and plopped two shells in the chambers.

'Were you ever stationed in Thailand, Moleen?' I said.

'For a little while. Why do you ask?'

'A lot of intelligence people were there. I was just curious.'

He scratched at the corner of his mouth with a fingernail. 'You want to bust a couple?' he said.

'No thanks.'

'You looked a little steely-eyed at the table.'

I watched a nutria drop off a log and swim into a cluster of hyacinths.

'That little anecdote about Julia's cheerleading days bother you?' he asked.

'Maybe.'

'Come on, Dave, I was talking about a college prank. It's innocent stuff.'

'Not from you it isn't.'

'You have an irritating habit. You're always suggesting an unstated conclusion for other people to guess at,' he said. He waited. 'Would you care to explain yourself, Dave?'

'The problem isn't mine to explain, sir.' In the distance, out by the access road, I could see a heavyset man jogging in shorts and a T-shirt, a towel looped around his glistening neck.

'I think the role of human enigma would become kind of tiresome,' he said. He raised his shotgun to his shoulder, tracked the flight of a seagull with it, then at the last second blew the head off a clump of pampas grass. He cracked open the breech, picked the empty casing out, and flung it smoking into the mud.

'I believe I'll go back inside,' I said.

'I think you've made an unpleasant implication, Dave. I insist we clear it up.'

'I went back out to your plantation this week. I'm not sure what's going on out there, but part of it has to do with Ruthie Jean Fontenot.'

He looked into my eyes. 'You want to spell that out?' he said.

'You know damn well what I'm talking about. If you want to hide a personal relationship, that's your business. But you're hiding something else, too, Moleen, about that plantation. I just don't know what it is.'

He fitted the shortgun's stock to his shoulder, fired at a nutria that was swimming behind a half-submerged log, and blew a pattern of bird shot all over the pond. The nutria ducked under the water and surfaced again but it was hurt and swimming erratically. Moleen snapped open the breech and flung the casing out into the water.

'I don't take kindly to people insulting me on my own property,' he said.

'The insult is to that woman on the plantation. You didn't even have the decency to inscribe her name on the photograph you gave her.'

'You're beyond your limits, my friend.'

'And you're cruel to animals as well as to people. Fuck you,' I said, and walked back toward the camp.

I found Bootsie on the gallery.

'We have to go,' I said.

'*Dave*, we just ate.'

'I already said our good-byes. I have some work to do at the dock.'

'No! It's rude.'

Three women drinking coffee nearby tried not to hear our conversation.

'Okay, I'm going to put on my gym shorts and tennis shoes and jog a couple of miles. Pick me up out on the road.' She looked at me with a strangled expression on her face. 'I'll explain it later.'

We had come in Bootsie's Toyota. I unlocked the trunk, took out my running shoes and gym shorts, and changed in the lee of the car. Then I jogged across a glade full of buttercups, past a stand of persimmon trees that fringed the woods, and out onto the hard-packed dirt road that led off the chenier.

The wind was warm and the afternoon sky marbled with yellow and maroon clouds. I turned my face into the breeze, kept a steady pace for a quarter mile, then poured it on, the sweat popping on my forehead, the blood singing in my chest until Moleen Bertrand's words, his supercilious arrogance, became more and more distant in my mind.

I passed a clump of pecan trees that were in deep shadow, the ground under them thick with palmettos. Then in the corner of my vision I saw another jogger step out into the spangled light and fall in beside me.

I smelled him before I saw him. His odor was like a fog, gray, visceral, secreted out of glands that could have been transplanted from animals. His head was a tan cannonball, the shoulders ax-handle wide, the hips tapering down to a small butt that a woman could probably cover with both her hands. His T-shirt was rotted into cheesecloth, the armpits dark and sopping, the flat chest a nest of wet black hair.

His teeth were like tombstones when he grinned.

'You do it in bursts, don't you?' he said. His voice was low, full of grit, like a man with throat cancer. 'Me, too.'

His shoulder was inches away, the steady *pat-pat-pat-pat* of his tennis shoes in rhythm with mine, even the steady intake and exhalation of his breath now part of mine. He wrapped his towel over his head and knotted it under his chin.

'How you doin'?' I said.

'Great. You ever run on the grinder at Quantico?' He turned his face to me. The eyes were cavernous, like chunks of lead shot.

'No, I wasn't in the Corps,' I said.

'I knew a guy looked like you. That's why I asked.'

I didn't answer. Out over the salt a single-engine plane was flying out of the sun, its wings tilting and bouncing hard in the wind.

'Were you at Benning?' the man said.

'Nope.'

'I know you from somewhere.'

'I don't think so.'

'Maybe it was Bragg. No, I remember you now. Saigon, sixty-five. Bring Cash Alley. You could get on the pipe and laid for twenty bucks. Fucking A, I never forget a face.'

I slowed to a walk, breathing hard, my chest running with sweat. He slowed with me.

'What's the game, partner?' I said.

'It's a small club. No game. A guy with two Hearts is a charter member in my view.' He pulled his towel off his head and mopped his face with it, then offered it to me. I saw Bootsie's Toyota headed down the road toward us.

I backed away from him, my eyes locked on his.

'You take it easy, now,' I said.

'You too, chief. Try a liquid protein malt. It's like wrapping copper wire around your nuts, really puts an edge on your run.'

I heard Bootsie brake behind me. I got in the passenger seat beside her. My bare back left a dark wet stain on the seat.

'Dave, put on your shirt,' she said.

'Let's go.'

'What's wrong?'

'Nothing.'

She glanced in the rearview mirror. The man with the tan cannonball head was mopping the inside of his thighs with the towel.

'Yuck,' she said. '*Who's* that?'

'I have a feeling I just met Mr Emile Pogue,' I answered.

13

'This doesn't happen,' the sheriff said, his hands on his hips, looking at the manila folders and papers on my floor, the prise marks where a screwdriver had sprung the locks on the drawers in my desk and file cabinet. 'We have to investigate the burglary of our own department.'

It was 8 a.m. Monday morning and raining hard outside. The sheriff had just come into the office. I'd been there since seven.

'What's missing?' he asked.

'Nothing that I can see. The files on Marsallus and Della Landry are all over the floor, but they didn't take anything.'

'What about Helen's files?'

'She can't find her spare house key. She's going to have her locks changed today,' I said.

He sat down in my swivel chair.

'Do you mind?' he said.

'Not at all.' I began picking up the scattered papers and photographs from the floor and arranging them in their case folders.

He took a breath. 'All right, Wally says the cleaning crew came in about eleven last night. They vacuumed, waxed the floors, dusted, did the rest rooms, and left around two a.m. He's sure it was the regular bunch.'

'It probably was.'

'Then who got in here?'

'My guess is somebody else wearing the same kind of uniform came in and picked the locks, probably right after the cleaning crew left. Nobody pays much attention to these guys, so the only people who might have recognized the impostors were gone.'

The sheriff picked up my phone and punched a number.

'Come down to Dave's office a minute,' he said into the receiver. After he hung up he leaned one elbow on the desk and pushed a thumb into the center of his forehead. 'This makes me madder than hell. What's this country coming to?'

Wally opened my office door. He was a tall, fat man, with hypertension and a florid face and a shirt pocket full of cellophane-wrapped cigars. He was at the end of his shift and his eyes had circles under them.

'You're sure everybody on the cleaning crew was gone by two a.m.?' the sheriff said.

'Pretty sure. I mean after they went out the front door the hall down here was dark and I didn't hear nothing.'

'Think about it, Wally. What time exactly did the last cleaning person leave?' the sheriff said.

'I told you, two a.m., or a minute or two one side or another of it.'

'They all left together?' the sheriff said.

'The last guy out said good night at two a.m.'

'Was it the last guy or the whole bunch?' I asked.

He fingered the cigars in his pocket and stared into space, his eyes trying to concentrate.

'I don't remember,' he said.

'Did you know the guy who said good night?' I asked.

'He walked by me with a lunch pail and a thermos. A shooting came in two minutes earlier. That's how I knew the time. I wasn't thinking about the guy.'

'Don't worry about it,' I said.

Wally looked at the sheriff.

'It's not your fault, Wally. Thanks for your help,' the sheriff said. A moment later he said to me, 'What are these guys after?'

'They don't know that Marsallus gave me his notebook. But I bet they think we found a copy of it that they missed in Della Landry's house.'

'What's in it, though? You said it reads like St Augustine's *Confessions* among the banana trees.'

'You got me. But it must be information they need rather than information they're trying to keep from us. You follow me?'

'No.'

'If we have it, they know we've read it, maybe made copies of it ourselves. So that means the notebook contains something indispensable to them that makes sense only to themselves.'

'This guy you met jogging yesterday, you think he's this mercenary, what's his name, Pogue?'

'He knew the year I was in Vietnam. He even knew how many times I'd been wounded.'

The sheriff looked at the blowing rain and a mimosa branch flattening against the window.

'I see only one way through this,' he said. 'We find Marsallus again and charge him with shooting the man in front of your house. Then he can talk to us or take up soybean farming at Angola.'

'We don't have a shooting victim.'

'Find him.'

'I need a warrant on Sweet Pea's Cadillac.'

'You're not going to get it. Why aren't you sweating that black woman out at the Bertrand plantation on this?'

'That's a hard word,' I said.

'She's involved, she's dirty. Sorry to offend your sensibilities.'

'It's the way we've always done it,' I said.

'Sir?'

The air-conditioning was turned up high, but the room was humid and close, like a wet cotton glove on the skin.

'Rounding up people who're vulnerable and turning dials on them. Should we kick a board up Moleen Bertrand's butt while we're at it? I think he's dirty, too. I just don't know how,' I said.

'Do whatever you have to,' the sheriff said. He stood up and straightened his back, his eyes empty.

But no urgency about Moleen, I thought.

He read it in my face.

'We have two open murder cases, one involving a victim kidnapped from our own jail,' he said. 'In part we have shit smeared on our faces because you and Purcel acted on your own and queered a solid investigative lead. Your remarks are genuinely testing my level of tolerance.'

'If you want to stick it to Moleen, there's a way to do it,' I said. The sheriff waited, his face narrow and cheerless. 'Create some serious man-hours and reactivate the vehicular homicide file on his wife.'

'You'd do that?' he asked.

'No, I wouldn't. But when you sweat people, that's the kind of furnace you kick open in their face, Sheriff. It's just easier when the name's not Bertrand.'

'I don't have anything else to say to you, sir,' he said, and walked out.

Sometimes you get lucky.

In this case it was a call from an elderly Creole man who had been fishing with a treble hook, using a steel bolt for weight and chicken guts for bait, in a slough down by Vermilion Bay.

Helen and I drove atop a levee through a long plain of flooded sawgrass and got there ahead of the divers and the medical examiner. It had stopped raining and the sun was high and white in the sky and water was dripping out of the cypress trees the elderly man had been fishing under.

'Where is it?' I asked him.

'All the way across, right past them cattails,' he said. His skin was the color of dusty brick, his turquoise eyes dim with cataracts. 'My line went bump, and I thought I hooked me a gar. I started to yank on it, then I knew it wasn't no gar. That's when I drove back up to the sto' and called y'all.'

His throw line, which was stained dark green with silt and algae, was tied to a cypress knee and stretched across the slough. It had disappeared beneath the surface by a cluster of lily pads and reeds.

Helen squatted down and hooked her index finger under it to feel the tension. The line was snagged on an object that was tugging in the current by the slough's mouth.

'Tell us again what you saw,' she said.

'I done tole the man answered the phone,' he said. 'It come up out of the water. It liked to made my heart stop.'

'You saw a hand?' I said.

'I didn't say that. It looked like a flipper. Or the foot on a big gator. But it wasn't no gator,' he said.

'You didn't walk over to the other side?' Helen said.

'I ain't lost nothing there,' he said.

'A flipper?' I said.

'It was like a stub, it didn't have no fingers, how else I'm gonna say it to y'all?' he said.

Helen and I walked around the end of the slough and back down the far side to the opening that gave onto a canal. The current in the canal was flowing southward into the bay as the tide went out. The sun's heat rose like steam from the water's surface and smelled of stagnant mud and dead vegetation.

Helen shoved a stick into the lily pads and moved something soft under it. A cloud of mud mushroomed to the surface. She poked the stick into the mud again, and this time she retrieved a taut web of monofilament fishing line that was looped through a corroded yellow chunk of pipe casing. She let it slide off the stick into the water again. Then an oval pie of wrinkled skin rolled against the surface and disappeared.

'Why do we always get the floaters?' she said.

'People here throw everything else in the water,' I said.

'You ever see a shrink?'

'Not in a while, anyway,' I said. In the distance I could see two emergency vehicles and a TV news van coming down the levee.

'I went to one in New Orleans. I was ready for him to ask me about my father playing with his weenie in front of the kids. Instead, he asked me why I wanted to be a homicide detective. I told him it's us against the bad guys, I want to make a difference, it bothers me when I pull a child's body out of a sewer pipe after a sex predator has gotten through with him. All the while he's smiling at me, with this face that looks like bread pudding with raisins all over it. I go, "Look, Doc, the bad guys torture and rape and kill innocent people. If we don't send them in for fifty or seventy-five or ship them off for the Big Sleep, they come back for encores."

'He keeps smiling at me. I go, "The truth is I got tired of being a meter maid." He thought that was pretty funny.'

I waited for her to go on.

'That's the end of the story. I never went back,' she said.

'Why not?'

'You know why.'

'It still beats selling shoes,' I said.

She combed her hair with a comb from the back pocket of her Levi's. Her breasts stood out against her shirt like softballs.

'Fix your tie, cutie. You're about to be geek of the week on the evening news,' she said.

'Helen, would you please stop that?'

'Lighten up, Streak.'

'That's exactly what Clete Purcel says.'

'Cluster fuck? No kidding?' she said, and grinned.

Twenty minutes later two divers, wearing wet suits and air tanks and surgical gloves over their hands, sawed loose the tangle of monofilament fish line that had been wrapped around and crisscrossed over the submerged body and threaded through a daisy chain of junkyard iron. They held the body by the arms and dragged it heavily onto the bank, the decomposed buttocks sliding through the reeds like a collapsed putty-colored balloon.

A young television newsman, his camera whirring, suddenly took his face away from his viewer and gagged.

'Excuse me,' he said, embarrassed, his hand pinched over his mouth. Then he turned aside and vomited.

The divers laid the body front-down on a black plastic sheet. The backs of the thighs were pulsating with leeches. One of the divers walked away, took a cigarette from a uniformed deputy's mouth, and smoked it, his back turned toward us.

The pathologist was a tall white-haired man who wore a bow tie, suspenders, and a wide-brimmed straw hat with a thin black ribbon around the crown.

'I wonder why they didn't eviscerate him while they were at it,' he said.

The body was nude. The fingers and thumbs of both hands had been snipped off cleanly at the joints, perhaps with bolt cutters. The head had been sawed off an inch above the collarbones.

Helen bit a hangnail off her thumb. 'What do you think?' she said.

'Look at the size. How many guys that big end up as floaters?' I said.

Even in death and the gray stages of decomposition that take place under water in the tropics, the network of muscles in the shoulders and back and hips was that of a powerful, sinewy man, someone whose frame was wired together by years of calisthenics, humping ninety-pound packs in the bush, jolting against a parachute harness while the steel pot razors down on the nose.

I stretched a pair of white surgical gloves over my hands and knelt by the body. I tried to hold my breath, but the odor seemed to cling to my skin like damp wool, an all-enveloping hybrid stench that's like a salty tangle of seaweed and fish eggs drying on hot sand and pork gone green with putrefaction.

'You don't have to do that, Dave,' the pathologist said. 'I'll have him apart by five o'clock.'

'I'm just checking for a bullet wound, Doc,' I said.

I fitted both hands under the torso and flipped the body on its back.

'Oh shit,' a newsman said.

'Maybe the guy was having a female implant put in,' a uniformed deputy said.

'Shut up, asshole,' Helen said.

There was a single wound above the groin area. It had been cored out by a fish eel, whose head was embedded deep in the flesh while the tail flipped in the air like a silver whip.

'You might look for a nine-millimeter, Doc,' I said.

'You know this guy?' he asked.

359

'My guess is his name was Jack,' I said.

Helen brushed at his thigh with a piece of folded cardboard. 'Here's a tattoo his friends missed,' she said.

It was a faded green, red, and gold Marine Corps globe and anchor imposed upon a cone-shaped open parachute.

'The poor dumb fuck didn't even know who he was on a skivvy run,' Helen said.

Helen's therapist had asked her one of those questions for which an honest answer is seemingly disingenuous or so self-revealing that you don't wish to inhabit your own skin for a while.

My dreams seemed continuous, beginning with the first moments of sleep and ending at dawn, but the props and central characters always remained the same.

I stand at a brass-railed mahogany bar on a pink evening in the Philippines, the palm fronds in the courtyard waving slightly in the breeze. I knock back a shot glass of Beam and chase it with San Miguel on the side, rest my forearms on the coolness of the wood and wait for the rush, which, like an old friend, never disappoints, which always lasers straight to the nerve endings at the base of the brain and fills the glands and loins and the sealed corridors of memory with light and finally gives ease to the constricted and fearful heart.

For a while.

The bartender's face is pale yellow, the skin tight against the skull, the skin stretched into cat's whiskers, the mouth a stitched slit. The evening air is filled with the rustle of bead curtains and the silky whisper of the Oriental women who move through them; redolent with the thick, sweet smell of opium, like honey and brown sugar burned in a spoon, and the smoky scent of whiskey aged in charcoal barrels, the black cherries and sliced oranges and limes that you squeeze between your back teeth with an almost sexual pleasure, as though somehow they connect you with tropical gardens rather than places under the earth.

The dream always ends in the same way, but I never know if the scene is emblematic or an accurate recall of events that took place during a blackout. I see myself lifted from a floor by men with no faces who pitch me through a door into a stone-paved alley that reverberates with a clatter of metal cans and crones who scavenge through garbage. A pimp and a whore rifle my pockets while I stare up at them, as helpless as if my spine were severed; my hands are cuffed behind me in a chair in a Third World police station while I shake with delirium tremens and sweat as big as flattened marbles slides down my face.

When I wake from the dream my breath shudders in my throat, the air in the room seems poisoned with exhaled and rebreathed alcohol, and I sit on the edge of my bed and begin to rework the first three steps of the AA recovery program. But there are other images in my mind now, more disturbing than the ones from my sleep. It's like a red bubble rising out of a heated place just beyond the limits of vision; then it bursts in the back of the brain and I can see tracers lacing the night like strips of barroom neon and taste the bitterness of cordite on my tongue. The rush is just like the whiskey that cauterizes memory and transforms electrified tigers into figures trapped harmlessly inside oil and canvas.

My shield and my 1911-model army-issue .45 automatic sit on top of my dresser in the moonlight. I think it's not an accident they found their way into my life.

An hour after I got home that evening the phone rang in the kitchen.

'We dug out two rounds,' the medical examiner said. 'One of them's in good shape. But I'd say both are either nine-millimeter or .38 caliber.'

'Two?' I said.

'There was a second entry wound below the right armpit. It did the most damage. It flattened against something and toppled before it entered the chest cavity. Anyway, it pierced both his lungs. You still think this was the guy out at your house?'

'Yeah, the guy was carrying a cut-down twelve-gauge under his right arm. One of the rounds probably deflected off it.'

'I suspect he was wrapped awful tight, then.'

'I don't understand,' I said.

'He jacked a lot of adrenaline into his heart before he got hit. Otherwise, I don't know how he made it out of there. Anyway, tomorrow we'll see if we can match his blood to the specimens you gave me from Cade and the bushes in front of your house.'

'Thanks for your help, Doc.'

'Keep me posted on this one, will you?'

'Sure.'

'I wasn't passing on an idle thought about the adrenaline in this man's heart. I've read medical papers about the deaths of royalty who were executed during the French Revolution. Sometimes they were told if the headsman's blow was off the mark and they were able to get up and run, their lives would be spared. Some of them actually rose headless from the block and ran several yards before they collapsed.'

'Pretty grim stuff.'

'You're missing my point. I believe the man I took apart today was absolutely terrified. What could put that level of fear in a soldier of fortune?'

Not bad, podna, I thought.

After supper I sat on the gallery and watched Alafair currying her Appaloosa, whose name was Tex, out in the railed lot by the shed we had built for him. Tripod was off his chain and sitting on top of the rabbit hutch, his tail hanging down the side of the wire like a ringed banner. My neighbor had moved out of his house and put it up for sale, but each evening he returned to turn on his soak hoses and water sprinklers, filling the air with an iridescent mist that drifted across his hydrangeas onto our lawn. The sun had descended into a flattened red orb on the western horizon, and in the scarlet wash of the afterglow the flooded tree trunks in the swamp seemed suffused with firelight, and you could see an empty rowboat tied up in the black stillness of the bayou's far bank, the wood as dry and white as bone.

Bertie Fontenot's dinged and virtually paintless pickup truck bounced through the ruts in the road and turned into our drive. She got out, slammed the truck door, and labored up the incline, her elephantine hips rolling inside her print-cotton dress, her big lacquered straw bag with the plastic flowers on it gripped under her arm like an ammunition box.

'What you done about my title?' she said.

'Nothing.'

'That's all you got to say?'

'You don't seem to accept my word, Bertie. So I've given up explaining myself.'

She looked away at the horse lot.

'I seen you at Ruthie Jean's house. I thought maybe you was working on my title,' she said.

'A murder investigation.'

'Ruthie Jean don't know nothing about a murder. What you talking about?'

'You want to sit down, Bertie?'

'You finally axed,' she said.

I helped her up the steps into the swing. She wrapped one hand around the support chain and pushed herself back and forth in a slowly oscillating arc.

'This is a nice place for your li'l girl to grow up in, ain't it?' she said.

'Yes, it is.'

'How long your family own this?'

'The land was part of my grandfather's farm. My father built the house in nineteen thirty.'

'How'd you like it if somebody just took it away from you, say you ain't got no proof it was part of your gran'daddy's farm? Run a dozer through the walls and scrape away the ground just like none of y'all was ever here?'

'You've got to give me some time, Bertie. I'm doing the best I can.'

She snapped open the big clasp on her bag and reached inside.

'You don't believe Moleen after some treasure on our land, so I brought you something,' she said. 'I dug these out of my li'l garden early this spring.'

One at a time she removed a series of thin eight- or nine-inch objects individually wrapped in tissue paper and bound with rubber bands. Then she rolled the rubber bands off one and peeled back the paper and flattened it against the swing.

'What you think of that?' she said.

The spoon was black as a scorched pot with tarnish, but she had obviously rubbed the metal smooth and free of dirt with rags so you could clearly see the coat of arms and the letter *S* embossed on the flanged head of the handle.

'That's pretty impressive,' I said. 'How deep was this in the soil?'

'From my elbow to the tip of my finger.'

'Have you shown this to anybody else?'

'No, and I ain't going to. Not till I get a piece of paper that say that's my land.'

'There's an antique gun and coin store in New Orleans, Cohen's, it's on Royal Street. Can I take one of these spoons there if I don't tell them where I got it?'

'You give me your word on that?'

'Yes, ma'am.'

'How long that gonna take?' she said, fanning herself with a flowered handkerchief.

14

I checked out of the office early Tuesday afternoon and drove across the Atchafalaya Basin through Baton Rouge into New Orleans. I went first to Cohen's on Royal, whose collection of antique guns and coins and Civil War ordnance could match a museum's, then I met Clete at his office on St Ann and we walked through Jackson Square to a small Italian restaurant down from Tujague's on Decatur.

We sat in back at a table with a checkered cloth and ordered, then Clete went to the bar and came back with a shot glass of bourbon and a schooner of draft. He lowered the shot into the schooner with his fingertips and watched it slide and clink down the side to the bottom, the whiskey corkscrewing upward in an amber cloud.

'Why don't you pour some liquid Drāno in there while you're at it?' I said.

He took a deep hit and wiped his mouth with his hand.

'I had to pull a bail jumper out of a motel on the Airline Highway this afternoon. He had both his kids with him. I got to lose this P.I. gig,' he said.

'You did it when you had your shield.'

'It doesn't work the same way, mon. Bondsmen dime one guy just to bring in another. The shitbags are just money on the hoof.' He took another drink from his boilermaker and the light began to change in his eyes. 'Your ME matched up the blood on the floater?' he asked.

'Yeah, it's the guy named Jack. We got the media to sit on the story, though.'

He reached across the table and pulled the tissue-paper-wrapped spoon given me by Bertie Fontenot from my shirt pocket. He worked the paper off the embossed tip of the handle.

'What'd they tell you at Cohen's?' he said.

'It's eighteenth-century silverware, probably cast in Spain or France.'

He rubbed the ball of his thumb on the coat of arms, then stuck the spoon back in my pocket.

'This came off the Bertrand plantation, you say?' he said.

'Yep.'

'I think you're pissing up a flagpole, Streak.'

'Thanks.'

'You don't see it.'

'See what?'

'I think you've got a hard-on for this guy Bertrand.'

'He keeps showing up in the case. What am I supposed to do?'

'That's not it. He's the guy whose shit don't flush.'

'He's dirty.'

'So is the planet. Your problem is Marsallus and the mercs and maybe Johnny Carp. You got to keep the lines simple, mon.'

'What do you hear about Patsy Dapolito?' I said, to change the subject.

'I thought I told you. He's in jail in Houston. He told the plastic surgeon he'd put his eye out if he messed up the job.'

'The ME said the guy named Jack was probably terrified when he caught the two nine-millimeters.'

'You mean terrified of Sonny Boy?' he said.

'That's the way I'd read it.'

'There's another side to that guy, Streak. I saw him make a couple of captured army dudes, I mean they were real greaseballs, guys with children's blood splattered on their boots, so they probably had it coming, but you don't get something like that out of your memory easy – he made them scoop out a grave in the middle of a trail with pie plates and kneel on the edge, then from six inches he blew their brains all over the bushes with a .44 Magnum.'

Clete shook the image out of his face, then held up his empty shot glass at the bartender.

He'd had six boilermakers by the time we finished dinner. He started to order another round. His throat was red and grained, as though it were wind chafed.

'Let's get some coffee and beignets at the Café du Monde,' I said.

'I don't feel like it.'

'Yeah, you do.'

'Ole Streak, swinging through town like a wrecking ball, pretending everything's under control. But I love you anyway, motherfucker,' he said.

We walked under the colonnade of the French Market, then had coffee and pastry at the outdoor tables. Across the street, in Jackson Square, the sidewalk artists were still set up along the walkway, and at the end of the piked fence that surrounds the park you could see a gut-bucket string band playing adjacent to the cathedral. I walked with Clete back to his office and sat with him on the edge of a stone well in the courtyard while he told me a long-winded story about riding with his father on the father's milk delivery route in the Garden District; then the lavender sky began to darken and swallows spun out of the shadows and when the lights in the upstairs apartments came on I could see the alcohol gradually go out of Clete's eyes, and I shook hands with him and drove back to New Iberia.

When I got home from the office the next afternoon, Alafair was sitting in the swing on the gallery, snapping beans in a pot. Her face was scratched, and there were grass and mud stains on her Levi's.

'You look like you rode Tex through a briar patch, Alf,' I said.

'I fell down the coulee.'

'How'd you do that?' I leaned against the rail and a post on the gallery.

'A dog got after Tripod. I ran over in Mr LeBlanc's yard and tripped on the bank. I fell in a bunch of stickers.'

'The coulee's pretty steep over there.'

'That's what that man said.'

'Which man?'

'The one who got me out. He climbed down the side and got all muddy. He might buy Mr LeBlanc's house.'

I looked over into the neighbor's yard. A realtor I knew from town had just walked from the far side of the house with a clipboard in his hand. He was pointing at some features in the upstairs area, talking over his shoulder, when my eyes locked on the man behind him.

'Did this man say anything to you?' I said.

'He said I should be careful. Then he got Tripod out of the willow tree.'

'Where's Bootsie?' I said.

'She had to go to the store. Is something wrong, Dave?'

'No. Excuse me a minute.'

I went inside and called the dispatcher for a cruiser. Then I went back out on the gallery.

'I'm going next door. But you stay on the gallery, understand?' I said.

'He didn't do anything wrong, Dave.'

I walked across the grass toward my neighbor's property and the man with miniature buttocks and ax-handle shoulders and chunks of lead for eyes.

He was dressed in a pale blue summer sports coat, an open-collar white shirt with ballpoint pens in the pocket, gray slacks, shined brown wingtips that were caked with mud around the soles; except for the stains on his clothes, he could have been a working man on his way to a fine evening at the track.

The realtor turned and looked at me.

'Oh hello, Dave,' he said. 'I was just showing Mr Pogue the property here.'

'I'd like to thank the gentleman for helping my daughter out of the coulee,' I said.

'It was my pleasure,' the man with the buckshot eyes said, his mouth grinning, his head nodding.

'Mr Andrepont, could I talk with him in private a minute?' I said.

'I beg your pardon?' he said.

'It'll take just a minute. Thank you,' I said.

'I see, well, let me know when you're finished, sir.' He walked toward his car, averting his eyes to hide the anger in them.

'You're Emile Pogue,' I said.

'Why not?' The voice sounded like it came from rusted pipe.

'You get around a lot. Exercising out at Pecan Island, showing up at the house next door. What's your interest, Mr Pogue?'

'I'm retired, I like the weather, I like the price on this house.'

'Why is it I think you're full of shit?'

366

'Be fucked if I know.' He grinned.

'I'd like to ask a favor of you, take a ride down to our jail with me, we had a little problem there.'

'I was planning on having an early dinner with a lady friend,' he said.

'Change it to candlelight. Put your hands behind your head, please.'

'You got to have a warrant, don't you, chief?'

'I'm not big on protocol. Turn around.'

When he laced his fingers behind his neck his muscles almost split his coat. I rotated his left hand counterclockwise to the center of his back and pushed it into a pressure position between his shoulder blades. His upper arm had the tension and resistance of a wagon spring.

'Move your right hand higher, no, no, up behind your ear, Mr Pogue. That's right,' I said.

I cuffed his right wrist and moved it clockwise to his spine and then hooked it up to his left. I could see the cruiser coming up the road under the oak trees. I walked him down the sloping lawn to meet it, past the realtor, who stared at us open-mouthed.

'Is it true Sonny Marsallus popped a cap on your brother?' I said.

'Sounds like you left your grits on the stove too long,' he answered.

I rode in the back of the cruiser with him to the department, then took him down to my office and hooked him to the D-ring inset in the floor. I called the sheriff and Kelso, the jailer, at their homes. When I hung up the phone, Pogue was staring at me, his eyes taking my measure, one shoulder pulled lopsided by the D-ring. He gave off a peculiar smell, like testosterone in his sweat.

'We're going to have to wait a little bit,' I said.

'For what?'

I took out my time sheet from my desk drawer and began filling it in. We'd had a power failure earlier and the air-conditioning had been off for two hours.

'Wait for what?' he said.

I heard him shift in his chair, the handcuff clink against the steel D-ring. Five minutes later, he said, 'What's this, Psy Ops down in Bumfuck?' His sports coat was rumpled, his face slick with heat.

I put away my time sheet and opened a yellow legal pad on my desk blotter. I uncapped my fountain pen and tapped it idly on the pad. Then I wrote on several lines.

'You were an instructor at an Israeli jump school?' I said.

'Maybe. Thirty years in, a lot of different gigs.'

'Looks like you managed to stay off the computer.'

He worked his wrist inside the cuff.

'I'm maxing out here on this situation, chief,' he said.

'Don't call me that again.'

'You ever fish with a Dupont special, blow fish up into the trees? You cut to the chase, that's how it gets done. Who you think runs this country?'

'Why don't you clear that up for me?'

'You're a smart guy. Don't make like you ain't.'

'I see. You and your friends do?'

He smiled painfully. 'You got you a good routine. I bet the locals dig it.'

Through my window I saw the sheriff, Kelso, and the night man from the jail out in the hall. They were watching Emile Pogue. Kelso's eyes were distorted to the size of oysters behind his thick glasses. He and the night man shook their heads.

'We selling tickets? What's going on?' Pogue said.

'You ever work CID or get attached to a federal law enforcement agency?' I said.

'No.'

'Somebody with insider experience kidnapped a man out of our jail. They murdered him out at Lake Martin.'

His laugh was like the cough of a furnace deep under a tenement building.

'Don't tell me, the black guy looking out of the fishbowl has got to be the jailer,' he said.

Kelso and the night man went down the hall. The sheriff opened my door and put his head inside.

'See me on your way out, Dave,' he said, and closed the door again.

'It doesn't look like you're our man,' I said.

'I got no beef, long as we get this thing finished ... What you writing there?'

'Not much. Just a speculation or two.' I propped the legal pad on the edge of the desk and looked down at it. 'How's this sound? You probably enlisted when you were a kid, volunteered for a lot of elite units, then got into some dirty stuff over in 'Nam, the Phoenix Program maybe, going into Charlie's ville at night, slitting his throat in his sleep, painting his face yellow for his wife to find in the morning, you know the drill.'

He laughed again, then pinched the front of his shirt with his fingers and shook it to cool himself. I could see the lead fillings in his molars, a web of saliva in his mouth.

'Then maybe you went into poppy farming with the Hmongs over in Laos. Is that a possibility, Emile?'

'You like cold beer? At the White Rose they had it so cold it'd make your throat ache. You could get ice-cold beer and a blow job at the same time, that's no jive. You had to be up for it, though, know what I'm saying?'

'You should have gone out to Washington State,' I said.

'I'm a little slow this evening, you got to clue me.'

'That's where your kind end up, right, either in a root cellar in the Cascades or fucking up other people's lives in Third World countries. You shouldn't have come here, Emile.' I tore off the page on my legal pad, which contained a list of items I needed for the bait shop and couldn't afford, and threw it in the wastebasket. Then I unlocked his cuffed wrist from the D-ring.

He rose from the chair and his nostrils flared.

'I feel like I'm wrapped in stink,' he said.

'If you need a ride, a deputy will take you wherever you want,' I said.

368

'Thanks, I'll get a cab. Can I use your john? I got to wash up.'

I pointed toward the men's room, then I said, 'Let me ask a favor of you, Emile.'

'You got it.'

'You're a pro. Don't come through the wrong man's perimeter.'

'The house next to yours? Who the fuck wants to live on a ditch full of mosquitoes?'

He went down the hall and pushed through the men's room door. The light from inside framed him like a simian creature caught in the pop of a flashbulb.

I worked open the window to rid the office of the peculiar odor that Pogue left behind, like the smell of a warm gym that's been closed for days. Then I called home and went inside the men's room. It was usually clean and squared away, but around one basin soap and water were splashed on the mirror and walls and crumpled paper towels were scattered all over the floor. I walked down the darkened hall to the sheriff's office.

'Where's Pogue?' he said.

'Gone.'

'Gone? I asked you to see me before—'

'That's not what you said.'

'I was going to put a tail on the guy. I just called the FBI in Lafayette.'

'It's a waste of time.'

'Would you care to explain that?' he said.

'His kind don't disappear on you. I wish they would.'

'What are you talking about, Dave?'

'He's evil incarnate, Sheriff.'

Bootsie and Alafair and I had a cold supper of chicken salad sandwiches, bean salad, and mint tea on the redwood table in the backyard. The new cane in my neighbor's field was pale green and waving in the sun's afterglow; he had opened the lock in his irrigation canal and you could smell the heavy, wet odor of the water inching through the rows.

'Oh, I forgot, Dave. A man named Sonny called while you were gone,' Alafair said. She had showered and put on makeup and baby powder on her neck and a dark pair of blue jeans and a lavender blouse with primroses sewn on the sleeves.

'What'd he have to say?'

'Nothing. He said he'd call back.'

'He didn't leave a number?'

'I asked him to. He said he was at a pay phone.'

Bootsie watched my face.

'Where you going tonight?' I said to Alafair.

'To study. At the library.'

'You're going fifteen miles to study?' I said.

'Danny's picking me up.'

'Danny who? How old is this kid?'

369

'Danny Bordelon, and he's sixteen years old, Dave,' she said.

'Great,' I said. I looked at Bootsie.

'What's the big deal?' Alafair said.

'It's a school night,' I said.

'That's why we're going to the library,' she said.

Bootsie put her hand on my knee. After Alafair finished eating she went inside, then said good-bye through the window screen and waited on the gallery with her book bag.

'Ease up, skipper,' Bootsie said.

'Why'd you call me that?' I said.

'I don't know. It just came to mind.'

'I see.'

'I won't do it,' she said.

'I'm sorry. It's fine,' I said. But I could still hear that name on the lips of my dead wife, Annie, calling to me from the bed on which she was murdered.

'What's troubling you, Dave?' Bootsie said.

'It's Marsallus. We sat on the story about the body we pulled out of the slough by Vermilion Bay. It was the guy Sonny parked a couple of rounds in.'

She waited.

'He doesn't know we've got a murder charge against him. I might have to set him up, the same guy who possibly saved my life.'

Later, Bootsie drove to Red Lerille's Health and Racquet Club in Lafayette and I tried to find things to do that would take me away from the house and Sonny's call. Instead, I turned on the light in the tree, spread a cloth over the redwood table, and cleaned and oiled an AR-15 rifle I had bought from the sheriff and a Beretta nine-millimeter that Clete had given me for my birthday. But the humidity haloed the light bulb and my eyes burned with fatigue from the day. I couldn't concentrate and lost screws and springs in the folds of the cloth and finally gave it up just as the phone rang in the kitchen.

'Was that your kid I talked to?' Sonny said.

'Yes.'

'She sounds like a nice kid.'

I could hear traffic and the clang of a streetcar in the background.

'What's up?' I said.

'I thought I ought to check in. Something wrong?'

'Not with me.'

'I heard about what you did to Patsy Dap,' he said.

'Are you in New Orleans?'

'Sure. Look, I heard Patsy got out of jail in Houston and he's back in town. The guy's got the thinking processes of a squirrel with rabies.'

'I need to talk with you, Sonny.'

'Go ahead.'

'No, in person. We've got to work some stuff out.'

'You put me in the bag once, Dave.'

'I kicked you loose, too.'

He was silent. I could hear the streetcar clanging on the neutral ground.

'I'll be in the Pearl at ten o'clock in the morning,' I said. 'Be there or stay away, Sonny. It's up to you.'

'You got something on Della's murder?'

'How can I, unless you help me?'

'I eat breakfast at Annette's on Dauphine,' he said.

I rose early in the morning and helped Batist open up the shop, fire the barbecue pit, and bail the boats that had filled with rainwater during the night. The sky was clear, a soft blue, the wind cool and sweet smelling out of the south, and I tried to keep my mind empty, the way you do before having surgery or entering into situations that you know you'll never successfully rationalize.

He looked good at the table in Annette's, with a fresh haircut, in a lavender shirt and brown suit with dark stripes in it, eating a full breakfast of scrambled eggs with bloodred catsup and sausage patties and grits off a thick white plate; he even smiled, his jaw full of food, when Helen and I came through the entrance with a murder warrant and a First District NOPD homicide cop behind us.

He kept chewing, his eyes smiling, while I shook him down against the wall and pulled the nine-millimeter Smith & Wesson from the back of his belt and hooked up each of his wrists.

Then he said, 'Excuse me, I almost choked on my food there. Don't worry about this, Streak. A Judas goat has got to do its job.'

15

Thursday morning Julia Bertrand walked into my office, her tan face glowing with purpose. She sat down without asking, as though we were both there by a prearranged understanding.

'Could I help you, Julia?'

'I have a complaint,' she said, smiling prettily, her back erect, her hands uncertain.

'What might that be?'

'It's prostitution, if you ask me. Out by Cade, I'm talking about.' One hand fluttered on her thigh, then remained motionless.

'By Cade?'

'I drove our maid home yesterday. She lives on the dirt road by this bar. You know the one I'm talking about.'

'I think I do, Julia.'

'There were white men walking with these black women back to these trailers.'

When I didn't respond, she said, 'Dave, I'm not a prude. But this *is* our community.'

'Two doors down, there're a couple of guys inside you can talk to.'

'I suspect one of them is the same gentleman I spoke to earlier. He could hardly contain his yawn.'

'Some people believe it's better to know where the players are rather than spread them all over the community,' I said.

'The maid told me a black woman named Ruthie Jean Fontenot brings the prostitutes to the nightclub, or whatever you want to call it.'

I looked at her, at the manic, pinched energy in her face and the bleached hair spiked on the ends, the eyes bright with either residual booze or black speed, and I didn't doubt that the Furies waited for Julia each morning inside her dresser mirror.

'I'll ask someone to look into it,' I said.

'How kind.'

'Have I done something to offend you?'

'Of course not. You're a sweetie, Dave. I just wish I'd had a chance with you before Bootsie came along.'

'It's always good to see you, Julia.'

A few minutes later I watched through the window as she got into her yellow convertible and roared out into the traffic, her morning temporarily in place, as though reporting a crippled black woman to a rural sheriff's office had purged the earth of a great evil.

I had a cup of coffee, opened my mail, and went to the lockup. Kelso was chewing on a soda straw and reading from a folder opened on his desk. At the top of a page I could see Sonny's name.

'Robicheaux, my man, work out something, get his bail reduced, go the bail yourself, let him box up worms out at your dock, he don't belong here,' Kelso said.

'That's the way it shakes out sometimes, Kelso.'

'I got him in isolation like you asked, I'm even taking his food from my house to his cell. So what's he tell me? He wants to go back in main pop.'

'Bad idea.'

'He says it don't matter where I put him, his ticket's run out, he don't like small places. He wants to go back into main pop or he ain't gonna eat his food.'

'You've dealt with problem inmates before.'

'Here's the rest of it. My night man, he didn't make this cat Pogue, right, but now he says maybe he saw him around the jail earlier, maybe with some other guys. I go, "Why the fuck didn't you tell me this?" So now he says he don't remember anything, and besides that, his wife calls him in sick. I never had a hit in my jail, Robicheaux. You get this cocksucker out of here.'

I checked my weapon with Kelso, and a uniformed guard pulled the levers on a sliding barred door that gave onto a corridor of individual cells. The guard walked me past three empty cells to the last one on the row and let me in.

Sonny sat on the edge of his bunk in his skivvies, one bare foot pulled up on the thin mattress. His body looked hard and white, the scars on his rib cage and chest like a network of dried purple lesions.

I lowered the bunk from the opposite wall on its chain and sat down.

'You want to square with me?' I said.

'If you're here for absolution, I don't have the right collar for it,' he said.

'Who says I need it?'

'You work for the Man, Dave. You know how things really are, but you still work for the Man.'

'I'm going to be hard on you, Sonny. I think that girl in St Martinville is dead because of you, so how about getting your nose out of the air for a while?'

He put both his feet on the concrete floor and picked up an apple from a paper plate that contained two uneaten sandwiches and a scoop of potato salad.

'You want it? Kelso brought it from his house,' he said.

'You're really going on a hunger strike?'

He shrugged, let his eyes rove over the graffiti on the walls, looked at a cross somebody had scorched on the ceiling with a cigarette lighter. 'You're not a bad guy, Streak,' he said.

'Help us. Maybe I can get you some slack.'

'Hey, how about some prune-o? The sweep-up slipped me some.' He looked at the expression on my face. 'I got nothing I can help you with. That's what you don't hear.'

'What's in the notebook?'

He looked at me for a beat, considering his words, perhaps already dismissing their value. 'How close are the next-door neighbors?' he said.

'The next three cells are empty.'

'I did a gig with the DEA, not because they liked me, they just thought my city library card meant I probably had two or three brain cells more than the pipeheads and rag-noses they usually hire for their scut work. Anyway, considering the environment, it's not the kind of press I need, know what I'm saying?'

'Come on, Sonny.'

'Down in the tropics, the cocaine trail always leads back to guns. I met guys who'd been in Laos, the Golden Triangle, guys who'd helped process opium into heroin in Hong Kong. Then I started hearing stories about POWs who'd gotten written off by the government.

'I was carrying this shitload of guilt, so I thought I could trade it off by involving myself with these MIA-POW families. I helped put together this telephone tree, with all kinds of people on it who I didn't even know. I didn't realize some of them were probably ex-intelligence guys who'd been mixed up with these opium growers in Laos. You with me?'

'Yeah, I think so,' I said.

'Their consciences bothered them and they started telling the families about what went on over there. I was making out a death list and didn't know it. At least that's the best I can figure it. I burned the Xerox copy. Do the same with the original, Dave, before more people get hurt.'

'Guilt about what?' I said.

'I used people – Indians, peasant girls, people who'd always gotten the dirty end of the stick, anyway.'

He brushed at the top of his bare thigh.

'We walked into an ambush. I had a flak vest on. Everybody around me got chewed up,' he said.

'Sometimes a guy feels guilt when the guy next to him catches the bus. That's just the way it is, Sonny.'

'I was hit twice. When I went down, a half dozen other guys got shredded into horse meat right on top of me. Later, the Indians thought I had religious powers or I was an archangel or something. I played it for all it was worth, Streak. Look, my whole life I peddled my ass and ran games on people. Guys like me don't see a burst of light and change their hustle.'

He reached under the top of the mattress and took out a jar and unscrewed the cap. The smell was like soft fruit that had been mixed with lighter fluid and left in a sealed container on a radiator. After he drank from the jar the skin of his face seemed to flex against his skull.

'You called me a Judas goat. I have a hard time accepting that, Sonny.'

'Yeah, I don't like this cell too much, either.'

'You think I led you down the slaughter chute?'

'No, not really,' he said.

I nodded, but I couldn't look at his face. We both knew that had he not phoned me at the house to warn me about Patsy Dap, he might be riding on a breezy streetcar down St Charles Avenue.

'I'll tell you something else, Dave,' he said. 'I've whacked out five guys since I left the tropics. Jack and Pogue's brother were just two knots on the string.'

'You have a peculiar way of expiating your sins.'

'I don't want to hurt your feelings, for a roach you're a stand-up guy, but go write some parking tickets, or shuffle some papers, or take some of the Rotary boys out to supper and let them work your dork under the table. I'm probably going down for the big bounce. Don't drag your bullshit into my cell, Streak. This is one place where it's truly an insult.'

I hit on the bars with the side of my fist and called for the turnkey to open up. When I looked back at him, the cartilage working in my jaw, he was picking at a callus on his foot. The tattoo of the blue Madonna on his right shoulder, with needles of orange light emanating from it, looked like a painting on polished moonstone. I started to speak again, but he turned his eyes away from me.

Rufus Arceneaux had been a tech sergeant in the Marine Corps at age twenty-three. In the ten years he had been with the department he had gone from uniform to plainclothes and back to uniform again. He was a tall, raw-boned man, with a long nose and blond crewcut hair, whose polished gunbelt and holster fitted against his trim body as though it had been welded there. Rufus wore dark-tinted pilot's sunglasses and seldom smiled, but you always had the sense that his hidden eyes were watching you, taking your inventory, a suppressed sneer tugging at his mouth as soon as your back was turned.

It was Friday morning when Luke Fontenot called and told me his sister, Ruthie Jean, was in jail and that Rufus had been the arresting officer.

I walked down to his office and went inside without knocking. He was talking on the phone, one leg propped across an opened desk drawer. He glanced sideways at me, then returned to his conversation. I waited for him to finish. But he didn't.

His mouth dropped open when I tore the receiver out of his hand and hung it up in the cradle.

'What the hell you think you're doing, Robicheaux?'

'You busted Ruthie Fontenot for procuring?'

'So what?'

'You're intruding in a homicide investigation.'

'Tough shit. That place is crawling with nigger whores. It should have been cleaned out a long time ago.'

'You think Julia Bertrand is going to get you promoted?'

'Get the fuck out of my office.'

I leveled my finger at him. 'She'd better be kicked loose by five o'clock this afternoon. Don't underestimate your situation, Rufus.'

'*Fuck* you,' he said as I went out the door.

I talked with the sheriff and the prosecutor's office. Rufus had done his job well; he used another deputy as a witness to the sting, paid a prostitute at the juke to go in back, waited until she in turn passed the money to Ruthie Jean at the bar, and busted and Mirandized both the hooker and Ruthie Jean on the spot.

At eleven o'clock I got a surprise phone call.

'What can you do?' Moleen said.

'I don't know. Maybe nothing,' I said.

'She's not a procurer. What kind of crazy ideals do y'all operate on down there?'

'She took the money, she put it in the cash register.'

'You know what goes on in those places. She can't sanitize every dollar that goes through her hands.'

'You're getting on the wrong person's case, Moleen.'

'Yeah?'

I didn't speak. I could almost hear his anger building on the other end of the line.

'Goddamn it, you stop jerking me around, Dave.'

'Your wife was in here yesterday. I explained to her I didn't take vice complaints. I think she found the right person, though.'

'Are you telling me . . .' He couldn't get the sentence out.

'The arresting officer was Rufus Arceneaux. Talk to him, Moleen. In the meantime, you want to do some good, go her bail.'

'You self-righteous sonofabitch.'

'Thanks for your call,' I said, and hung up.

At noon, as I was leaving the building for lunch, I saw Luke Fontenot's paintless, smoking, 1970s gas-guzzler, its ruptured muffler roaring against the pavement, swing out of the traffic toward the curb.

He leaned down so he could see me through the passenger's window.

'I ain't gone hide no more,' he said. 'I got to talk. When you gone be back?'

'Talk about what?'

'He ain't want the baby. That's where it all gone bad, even before I had to shoot that man 'cause he was bad-mouthing my sister and blackmailing Mr Moleen at the same time.'

I opened the car door and got in beside him.

'How about I buy us both a po'-boy?' I said.

16

This is how Luke told it to me, or as best as I can reconstruct it.

The Bertrand family had always been absentee landowners and had left the general care of the plantation to an overseer named Noah Wirtz, a sharecropper from the Red River parishes who could pass or not pass for a person of color, whichever the situation required. Other than a few teachers at the rural elementary school, Ruthie Jean, at age eleven, had little immediate contact with white adults, until that smoky winter morning when Moleen came to the plantation with his college friends from Springhill to shoot doves.

He had been kneeling by the coulee's edge, his double-barrel propped against the trunk of a leafless sycamore, pouring a cup of coffee from his thermos while his dog hunted for the birds Moleen had just downed in the cane stubble, when he turned around and saw her watching him.

Her pigtails were tied with rubber bands, her plump body lost in a man's mackinaw.

'Why, good heavens, you gave me a start,' he said, although she knew it wasn't true. He winked at her. 'My friends and I are all out of coffee. Can you go ask your mama to fill this up?'

She took the thermos and wet cup from his hands, her eyes fascinated with his handsome face and the lifeless birds that he had charmed out of the sky into his canvas game pouch.

'Wait a minute,' he said, and slipped his thumb in his watch pocket and put a silver dollar in her palm. The ends of his slender fingers brushed her skin. She had not known a coin could be that heavy and big. 'That's for Christmas. Now, run along and tell your mama the coffee's for Mr Moleen.'

She didn't see him again for six years, then on a cold New Year's afternoon she heard guns popping on the far side of the cane field, out by the treeline, and when she went out on the gallery she saw four men walking abreast through the frozen stubble, while a frenzy of birds leaped into the air in front of them and tried to find invisibility against a pitiless blue sky.

The hunters unloaded canvas chairs, a cooler, a collapsible grill from the bed of a pickup, and drank whiskey and cooked two-inch bloodred steaks on a wood fire that whipped in the wind like a torn handkerchief. When the one named Moleen saw her from across the field and asked her to bring water, she went quickly into the kitchen and filled a plastic pitcher, her heart beating in her breast for a reason she didn't understand.

The faces of the hunters were red with windburn and bourbon, their eyes playful, their conversation roaming between the depth of drilling wells and the remembered adrenaline surge in the glands when they led a throbbing covey with ventilated-rib sights and, one-two-three-four-five, turned each bird into a broken smudge against the winter sun. She filled their glasses, now aware that her sense of alarm was not only baseless but vain, that their eyes never really took note of her, other than a glance to ensure the water didn't spill over their outstretched wrists.

But as she walked away, she heard a pause, a silence so loud that her ears popped, then the register dropped in one man's voice, and the muscles in her back seemed to gather and constrict inside her dress, as though the coarseness, the undisguised connotation of the remark had the power to shrink her in physical as well as emotional stature.

'*It's all pink inside, Moleen.*'

She kept her eyes straight ahead, focused on the gallery where her aunt and brother were husking and shelling pecans in a bucket, where the Christmas lights were still strung under the eaves, where her two cats played in a water oak that stood as stark against the winter light as a cluster of broken fingers.

She expected to hear the hunters laugh. Instead, there was silence again, and in the wind blowing at her back she clearly heard the voice of the man named Moleen:

'You've had too much to drink, sir. Regardless, I won't abide that kind of discourtesy toward a woman on my property.'

She never forgot that moment.

He came back from the service long after the other soldiers had returned. He never explained why, or told anyone exactly where he had been. But he had the quiet detachment of someone who has lived close to death, or perhaps of one who has watched the erosion of the only identity he ever had. He often sat alone in his car by the grove of gum trees, the doors open to catch the evening breeze, while he smoked a cigar in the drone of cicadas and stared at the molten sun descending over the cane fields.

One time Ruthie Jean opened an old issue of *Life* magazine and saw a picture taken in Indochina of a valley filled with green elephant grass and a sun like a red wafer slipping into the watery horizon. She walked with it to Moleen's car, almost as though she had picklocked his thoughts, and placed it in his hand and looked him directly in the face, as if to say the debt for the silver dollar and the rebuke of the drunken hunter was not being repaid but openly acknowledged as the bond between them that race and social station had made improbable.

He knew it, too. Whatever sin he had carried back from the Orient, blood that could not be rinsed from his dreams, a shameful and unspoken memory he seemed to see re-created in the fire of Western skies, he knew she looked into him and saw it there and didn't condemn him for it and instead by her very proximity told him he was still the same young man who was kind to a child on a hunter's dawn and who had struck dumb a peer whose words had the power to flay the soul.

The first time it happened was back beyond the treeline, toward the lake, in a cypress shack that had once been part of the old slave quarters and was later used as a corn crib. The two of them pulled the backseat out of his car and carried it inside, their bodies still hot from their first caresses only moments earlier. They undressed without speaking, their private fears etched in their faces, and when he found himself nude before she was, he couldn't wait, either out of need or embarrassment, and began kissing her shoulders and neck and then the tops of her breasts while she was still attempting to unsnap her bra.

She had never been with a white man before, and he felt strangely gentle and tender between her thighs, and when they came at the same time, she kissed his wet hair and pressed her palms into the small of his back and kept her stomach and womb tight against him until the last violent shudder in his muscles seemed to exorcise the succubus that fed at his heart.

He bought her a gold watch with sapphires set in the obsidian face, sent her gift certificates for clothes at Maison Blanche in New Orleans, and then one day an envelope with a plane ticket to Veracruz, money, and directions to a hotel farther down the coast.

Their rooms adjoined. Moleen said the owners of the hotel were traditional people whom he respected and to whom he did not want to lie by saying they were married.

The rented boat he took her out on was as white and gleaming as porcelain, with outriggers, fighting chairs, and a flying bridge. He would tie leader with the care and concentration of a weaver, bait the feathered spoons, then fling them into the boat's wake, his grin full of confidence and expectation. The curls of hair on his chest and shoulders looked like bleached corn silk against his tan skin.

On the first morning he showed her how to steer the boat and read the instrument panel. The day was boiling, the Gulf emerald green with patches of blue in it like clouds of ink, and while she stood at the wheel, her palms on the spokes, the engines throbbing through the deck, she felt his hands on her shoulders, her sides and hips, her breasts and stomach, then his mouth was buried in the swirls of her hair and she could feel his hardness grow against her.

They made love on an air mattress, their bodies breaking out with sweat, the boat rolling under them, the sky above them spinning with light and the cry of gulls. She came before he did, and then moments later she came again, something she had never done with another man.

Later, he fixed vodka and collins mix and cracked ice in two glasses, wrapped them in napkins with rubber bands, and they sat in their bathing suits in the fighting chairs and trolled across a coral reef whose crest was covered with undulating purple and orange sea fans.

She went below to use the rest room. When she came back up into the cabin, she saw another fishing boat off their port bow. A man and woman on the stern were waving at Moleen. He put his binoculars on them, then rose from his chair and came inside the cabin.

'Who's that?' she said.

'I don't know. They probably think we're someone else,' he said.

He took the wheel and eased the throttle forward. She watched the other boat drop behind them, the two figures on the stern staring motionlessly after them. She picked up the binoculars from the top of the instrument panel and focused them on the lettering on the boat's hull.

Later, she would not remember the boat's name, but the words designating its home port, *Morgan City, Louisiana*, filled her with a bitter knowledge that trysts among palm trees, or even the naked hunger that he would bring again and again to the plantation, on his knees in the corn crib, his hands clenching the backs of her thighs, would never efface.

Noah Wirtz was a lean, short man, with skin that looked like it had been singed by a gunpowder flash. He wore a black, short-billed leather cap, even in summer, and always smiled, as though the situation around him was fraught with humor that only he saw. He lived in a frame house at the head of the road with his wife, a fundamentalist Sunday school teacher from Mississippi who walked on a wooden leg. The black people on the plantation said, 'Mr Noah know how to make the eagle scream.' He and his wife spent nothing on movies, vacations, automobiles, liquor, outboard boats, pickup trucks, shotguns, even food that would make their fare better than the cornbread, greens, bulk rice and red beans, buffalo fish, carp, and low-grade meat most of the blacks ate. Every spare nickel from his meager salary went into the small grocery store they bought in Cade, and the profits from the store went into farm machinery, which he began to lease to sugar growers in Iberia and St Martin parishes.

It was a sweltering August night, the trees threaded with the electric patterns of fireflies, when Moleen discovered the potential of his overseer. He and Ruthie Jean had met in the shack beyond the treeline, and just as he had risen from her, his body dripping and limp, her fingers sliding away from his hips, he heard dry leaves breaking, a stick cracking, a heavy, audibly breathing presence moving through the undergrowth outside.

He put on his khakis, pulled his polo shirt on over his head, and ran out into the heated air and the aching drone of cicadas. Through the tree trunks, on the edge of the field, he saw Noah Wirtz getting into his battered flatbed truck, the points of his cowboy boots curled up into snouts on his feet, the armpits of his long-sleeved denim shirt looped with sweat.

'You! Wirtz!' Moleen shouted. 'You hold up there!'

'Yes, sir?' Wirtz smiled from under his leather cap, his skin as dark as if it had been smoked in a fire.

'What are you doing out here?'

'Cleaning up the trash the niggers threw on the ground at lunchtime.'

'I don't see any trash.'

'That's 'cause I buried hit. You want me to haul hit back to my house?' His seamed face was as merry as an elf's.

They looked at each other in the fading light.

'Have a good evening, cap'n,' Wirtz said, and spit a stream of Red Man before he got into the cab of his truck.

Moleen walked back through the trees to the shack. Even in the soft yellow afterglow through the canopy he knew, without looking, what he would find below the unshuttered and gaping shack window. The heels of the boots had bitten through the dry leaves into the wet underlayer, with the sharp and razored precision of a cleft-footed satyr.

The blackmail began later, after Moleen's marriage to Julia, but it was not overt, and never a difficult yoke to bear; in fact, it was so seemingly benign that after a while Moleen convinced himself that better it be Wirtz, who did what he was told, who was obsequious and contemptible (who sometimes even played the role of pimp and ensured their trysts would not be disturbed), than someone who was either more cunning or less predictable.

Moleen gave him a useless tractor that would have rusted into the weeds otherwise; a smoked ham at Christmas and Thanksgiving; venison and ducks when he had too much for his own freezer; the use of five acres that had to be cleared and harrowed first.

Ironically, the denouement of their arrangement came not because of Wirtz's avarice but because of his growing confidence that he no longer needed Moleen. He began selling liquor in his grocery store and lending money to black field hands and housemaids, on which they made five-percent interest payments one Saturday night a month until the principal was liquidated.

His farm machinery filled a rented tin shed up Bayou Teche.

Moleen heard the story first as rumor, then from the mouth of the sixteen-year-old girl who said Wirtz came to her house for his laundry when the parents were gone, then, after paying her and hanging the broomstick hung with his ironed shirts across the back of his truck cab, had gone back in the kitchen, not speaking, his eyes locked on the girl's, his breath now covering her face like a fog, and had clenched one of her wrists in his hand and simultaneously unzipped his overalls.

Moleen drove straight from the girl's house to Wirtz's and didn't even bother to cut the engine or close the door of his Buick behind him before he strode through the unpainted picket gate and up the narrow path lined with petunias to the gallery, where Wirtz, his face cool and serene in the shade, was eating from a box of Oreo cookies, his leather cap suspended on a nail above his head.

'The girl's too scared and ashamed to bring charges against you, but I want you off my property. In fact, I want you out of the parish,' Moleen said.

'Out of the parish, huh?' Wirtz said, and smiled so broadly his eyes were slits.

'Why in God's name I hired some white trash like you I'll never know,' Moleen said.

'White trash, huh? You hear this, cap'n. Befo' I'd put mine in that nigger, I'd cut hit off and feed hit to the dog.'

'Clean your house out. I want you gone by nightfall.'

Moleen started toward his car.

'You're a piece of work, Bertrand. You fuck down and marry up and don't give hit a second thought,' Wirtz said. He bit down softly on a cookie.

The blood climbed into Moleen's neck. He leaned inside the open door of the Buick, pulled the keys, and unlocked the trunk.

Noah Wirtz stared at him impassively, brushing his hands with a sound like emery paper, as Moleen came toward him with the horse quirt. He barely turned his face when the leather rod whipped through the air and sliced across his cheek.

'You ever speak to me like that again, I'll take your life,' Moleen said.

Wirtz pressed his palm to the welt, then opened and closed his mouth. His eyes seemed to study a thought inches in front of his face, then reject it. He laced his fingers together and cracked his knuckles between his knees.

'I got me a contract,' he said. 'Till the cane's in, I got a job and I got this house. You're trespassing, cap'n. Get your automobile off my turnaround.'

'The shooting,' I said to Luke, as he sat across from me at a picnic table under the pavilion in the park.

'I don't want to talk about that,' he said. He tried to light a cigarette, but the match was damp with his own perspiration and wouldn't ignite against the striker. 'They was gonna electrocute me. I still wake up in the middle of the night, I got the sheets tangled all over me, I can feel that man drawing his razor across my scalp.'

'Tell me what happened in that saloon, Luke.'

'He said it in front of all them men, about a woman ain't done anything to him, ain't ever hurt anybody.'

'Who?'

'Noah Wirtz, he talk about her at the bouree table like ain't even niggers gonna take up for her.'

'Said what, Luke?'

'"That bitch got a pumpkin up her dress, and I know the name of the shithog put it there." That's what he say, Mr Dave, looking me right in the eyes, a li'l smile on his mouth.'

Then he described that winter night in the saloon, almost incoherently, as though a few seconds in his life had been absorbed through his senses in so violent a fashion that he now believed the death he had been spared was in reality the only means he would ever have to purge and kill forever the memory that came aborning every night in his sleep.

It's the first Saturday of the month, and the bar and tables are crowded with blacks, mulattos, redbones, and people who look white but never define themselves as such. The air smells of expectorated chewing tobacco and snuff, animal musk, oily wood, chemically treated sawdust, overcooked okra, smoke, and unwashed hair. The video poker machines line an unadorned fiberboard wall like a magical neon-lit instrument panel that can transport the player into an electronic galaxy of wealth and power. But the big money is at the round, felt-covered bouree table, where you can lose it all – the groceries, the rent on a pitiful shack, the installment on the gas-guzzler, the weekly payment for the burial insurance collector, even the food stamps you can discount and turn into instant capital.

The man at the table with the cash is Noah Wirtz, and he takes markers in the form of bad checks, which he holds in lieu of payment on his loans and which he can turn over to the sheriff's office if the borrower defaults. Sometimes he uses a shill in the game, a hired man who baits a loser or a drunk and goads him into losing more, since bouree is a game in which great loss almost always follows recklessness and impetuosity.

Wirtz consoles, buys a drink for those who have lost all their wages, says, 'Come see me at the store in the morning. We'll work something out.' He knows how far to press down on a nerve, when to give it release. Until tonight, the cane harvest in, the contract with Bertrand finished, when perhaps his own anger, the quiet residual rage of his kind (and that had always been the word used to describe his social class), passed down like an ugly heirloom from one generation to the next, begins to throb like the blow of a whip delivered contemptuously across the face, and the name Moleen Bertrand and the world he represents to Wirtz and which Wirtz despises and envies becomes more important than the money he has amassed through stint and self-denial and debasing himself to the servile level of the blacks with whom he competes.

'What you got to say about it, Luke?' Wirtz says.

Luke's eyes can't focus, nor can he make the right words come out of his throat. His face contains the empty and deceptive intensity of a scorched cake pan.

'A certain white man didn't have to pull you off hit to get to hit hisself, did he?' Wirtz says.

Luke's one-inch nickel-plated .38 revolver, with no trigger guard and electrician's tape holding the handles together, is one step above scrap metal. But its power and short-range accuracy are phenomenal. The single steel-jacketed round he squeezes off splinters through the tabletop and felt cover and enters Wirtz's chin as though a red hole were punched there with a cold chisel.

Wirtz stumbles through the washroom door, a crushed fedora squeezed against the wound, his mouth a scarlet flower that wishes to beg for help or mercy or perhaps even forgiveness but that can only make unintelligible sounds that seem to have no human correspondent. He curls into a ball behind the toilet tank, his knees drawn up in front of him, his eyes pleading, his hands trembling on the fedora.

Luke pulls the trigger and the hammer snaps dryly on a defective cartridge. This time he cocks the hammer, feels the spring and cylinder and cogs lock into place, but the rage has gone, like a bird with hooked talons that has suddenly freed itself from its own prey and flown away, and he drops the pistol in the toilet bowl and walks into the larger room and the collective stare of people who realize they never really knew Luke Fontenot.

But the man he leaves behind closes and opens his eyes one more time, then expels a red bubble of saliva from his mouth and stares sightlessly at an obscene word scrawled in pencil on the wall.

'What happened to Wirtz's gun?' I said. 'Moleen found witnesses who saw Wirtz pull a gun.'

'Mr Moleen got money. You got money, you find anybody, anything you need.'

'I see,' I said. It was starting to sprinkle on the bayou. A mother opened an umbrella over her child, and the two of them ran for the cover of the trees. 'You mentioned a baby,' I said.

'I done tole you, he ain't want it.' Then his face became indescribably sad, unmasked, devoid of any defense or agenda. 'What they call that, "trimester," yeah, that's it, third trimester, she went did it wit' some man in Beaumont, cut up the baby inside her, cut her up, leave her walking on a cane, leave her with that baby crying in her head.'

He cleaned off his place and walked in the rain toward his car.

17

After Luke dropped me off at the department, I found a phone message from Clete Purcel in my mailbox. I called him at his office in New Orleans.

'You still got Marsallus in the bag?' he said.

'Yeah, he's on a hunger strike now.'

'The word's out Johnny Carp doesn't want anybody writing his bond.'

'I was right, then. Johnny's been after him from the jump.'

'He's probably already got somebody inside, or he'll get a local guy to bail him out. Any way you cut it, I think Sonny's floated into deep shit.'

'How do you figure Johnny's stake?' I said.

'Something to do with money. I hear his toilet seats are inset with gold pesos. He owned a lot with a thirty-foot Indian mound on it and sold it for landfill. It's a great life, isn't it, mon?'

Later, I gazed through the window at a rainbow arching across the sky into a bank of steel-colored clouds that were hung with wisps of rain. Sonny Boy was trussed and tagged and on the conveyor belt, like a pig about to be gutted, and the man who had kicked the machinery into gear was a police officer.

I crumpled up a letter inviting me to speak to the Rotary Club and threw it against the wall.

Moleen's law office was in a refurbished white-columned Victorian home, shaded by oaks, down the street from the Shadows on East Main.

I had to wait a half hour to see him. When the door opened, rather, when it burst back on its hinges, Julia Bertrand came through it as though she were emerging from the dry heat of a bake oven.

'Why, Dave,' she said, her makeup stretching on her features as though it had been painted there by a blind man. 'It's so appropriate for you to be here. You fellows can kick the war around. Moleen has all this guilt but he never got to kill anybody. How unfair of the gods.'

She brushed past me before I could answer.

I picked up the paper bag by my feet and closed Moleen's office door behind me. He sat behind a huge, dark red oak desk, his knitted brown tie pulled loose at the throat. His face was flushed, as though he had a fever.

'How's life, Moleen?'

'What do you want?'

'She's still in jail.'

He bit his thumbnail.

'Moleen?'

'I can't do anything.'

'She lives on your plantation. Bail her out. Nobody'll question your motivation.'

'Where the hell do you get off talking to me like that?' he said.

I sat down without being asked. I set the paper bag containing the leg iron on his desk. The manacle yawned out of the bag like a rusty mouth.

'Luke owned up to putting this in my truck. He said he doesn't care if I tell you about it or not.'

'I think you should see a therapist. I don't mean that unkindly, either,' he said.

'Luke's pretty sharp for a guy who didn't finish high school. He read a story in a magazine about a construction site that was shut down because there was an Indian mound on it. He thought he'd given me the means to put you out of business, whatever it is.'

'It's been a long day, Dave.'

'Is it a gambling casino?'

'Good-bye.'

'That's why you got rid of the cemetery.'

'Is there anything else you want to say before you leave?'

'Yeah. It's quarter to five on Friday afternoon and she's still in jail.'

He looked at me distractedly, breathing with his mouth open, his chest sunken, his stomach protruding over his belt like a roll of bread dough. When I got up to go, three buttons were flashing hot pink on his telephone, as though disembodied and cacophonous voices were waiting to converge and shout at him simultaneously.

After supper that night I put on my gym shorts and running shoes and did three miles along the dirt road by the bayou, then I did three sets of military presses, dead lifts, and arm curls with my barbells in the backyard. The western sky was streaked with fire, the air warm and close and alive with insects. I tried to rethink the day, the week, the month, my involvement with Sonny Boy Marsallus and Ruthie Jean and Luke and Bertie Fontenot and Moleen Bertrand, until each of my thoughts was like a snapping dog.

'What's bothering you, Dave?' Alafair said behind me.

'I didn't see you there, Alf.'

She held Tripod on her shoulder. He tilted his head at me and yawned.

'Why you worrying?' she asked.

'A guy's in jail I don't think belongs there.'

'Why's he in there then?'

'It's that fellow Marsallus.'

'The one who shot the –'

'That's right. The guy who was looking out for me. Actually, looking out for all of us.'

'Oh,' she said, and sat down on the bench, her hand motionless on Tripod's back, an unspoken question in the middle of her face.

'The man he shot died, Alf,' I said. 'So Sonny's down on a homicide beef. Things don't always work out right.'

Her eyes avoided mine. I could smell my own odor, hear my breathing in the stillness.

'It's not something I had a choice about, little guy,' I said.

'You said you wouldn't call me that.'

'I'm sorry.'

'It's all right,' she said, then picked up Tripod in her arms and walked away.

'Alafair?'

She didn't answer.

I put on a T-shirt without showering and began hoeing weeds out of the vegetable garden by the coulee. The air was humid and mauve colored and filled with angry birds.

'Time for an iced tea break,' Bootsie said.

'I'll be inside in a minute.'

'Cool your jets, Streak.'

'What's with Alf?'

'You're her father. She associates you with perfection.'

I chipped at the weeds with the corner of the hoe. The shaft felt hard and dry and full of sharp edges in my hands.

'Moleen's the problem, Dave. Not Sonny,' Bootsie said.

'What?'

'You think he's a hypocrite because he left the black woman in jail. Now maybe you're wondering about yourself and Sonny Boy.'

I looked up at her, squinted through the sweat in my eyes. I wanted to keep thudding the hoe into the dirt, let her words go by me as though they were illogical and unworthy of recognition. But there was a sick feeling in my stomach.

I propped my hands on the hoe handle, blotted my eyes on my forearm.

'I'm a police officer,' I said. 'I can't revise what happened. Sonny killed a man, Boots. He says he's killed others.'

'Then put it out of your mind,' she said, and went back inside the house.

Across the fence in my neighbor's field, I saw an owl swoop low out of the sun's last red light and, in a flurry of wings, trap and then scissor a field mouse in its beak. I could hear the mouse's voice squeaking helplessly as the owl flew into the sun.

Saturday morning I worked until noon at the bait shop, counting change twice to get it right, feigning interest in conversations I hardly heard. Then I put a Dr Pepper and two bottles of beer in a paper bag, with two ham and onion sandwiches, called the sheriff, and asked him to meet me up the road by the four corners.

He walked down the bank in a pair of floppy khaki shorts with zipper pockets, a white straw cowboy hat, and a denim shirt with the sleeves cut off at the armpits. He carried a spinning rod that looked like it belonged to a child.

'Beautiful day for it,' he said, lifting his face in the breeze.

The boat dipped heavily when he got into the bow. The tops of his arms were red with sunburn and unusually big for a man who did administrative work.

I took us through a narrow channel into the swamp, cut the engine, and let the boat drift on its wake into a small black lagoon surrounded with flooded cypress. A deserted cabin, built on pilings, was set back in the trees. A rowboat that was grayish blue with rot was tied to the porch and half-submerged in the water.

The sheriff bit into a ham sandwich. 'I got to admit this beats hitting golf balls in sand traps,' he said.

But he was an intelligent and perceptive man whose weekend humor served poorly the concern in his eyes.

Then I said it all, the way as a child I took my confused and labored thoughts into the confessional and tried to explain what both my vocabulary and loneliness made unexplainable. Except now, in order to undo a wrong, I was—

He said the word for me.

'Lying, Dave. We've never had that problem between us. I have a hard time dealing with this, podna.'

'The guy's grandiose, he's a huckster, he's got electrodes in his temples. But he's down on the wrong beef.'

'I don't give a goddamn what he is. You're violating your oath as a police officer. You're walking on the edges of perjury as well.'

I looked into the diffused green and yellow light on the rim of the lagoon. 'The eye remembers after the fact sometimes,' I said.

'You saw the cut-down twelve-gauge under the guy's coat? You felt you were in danger?'

'I'll put my revised statement in your mailbox this afternoon.'

'You missed your calling over in Vietnam. You remember those monks who used to set themselves on fire? You were born for it, Dave.'

'Marsallus doesn't belong in prison. At least not for popping the guy in front of my house.'

The sheriff set his fishing rod across his thighs and pulled up the anchor without my asking him. He stared into the water and the black silt that swirled out of the bottom, then wiped his face with his hand as though he were temporarily erasing an inevitable conclusion from his thoughts.

Monday morning I was suspended from the department without pay.

Monday night I drove out to the Bertrand plantation and returned the spoon Bertie Fontenot had given me. She fanned herself with a ragged magazine in the swing, her breasts hanging like watermelons inside her cotton dress.

'It's the right time period, but I don't think pirates buried those spoons in your garden,' I said.

'They growed there with my radish seeds?'

'The S on those spoons makes me think they're from the Segura plantation on the lake. During the Civil War, a lot of people buried their silverware and coins to keep them from the Yankees, Bertie.'

'They should have buried themselves while they was at it.'

I looked at the lights inside the house next door. Two shadows moved across the shades.

'A lawyer come down from Lafayette and got her out of jail this morning,' she said.

'Which lawyer?'

'I ain't ax his name. I seen him out here with Moleen once. The one look like he got grease on his bald head.'

'Jason Darbonne.'

'I'm going inside now. The mosquitoes is eating me up.' She paused in the square of light the door made, the white ends of her hair shiny with oil. 'They gonna run us off, ain't they?'

I had a half dozen answers, but all of them would have been self-serving and ultimately demeaning. So I simply said good night and walked to my truck by the grove of gum trees.

The moon was down, and in the darkness the waving cane looked like a sea of grass on the ocean's floor. In my mind's eye I saw the stubble burning in the late fall, the smoke roiling out of the fire in sulphurous yellow plumes, and I wanted to believe that all those nameless people who may have lain buried in the field – African and West Indian slaves, convicts leased from the penitentiary, Negro laborers whose lives were used up for someone else's profit – would rise with the smoke and force us to acknowledge their humanity and its inextricable involvement and kinship with our own.

But they were dead, their teeth scattered by plowshares, their bones ground by harrow and dozer blade into detritus, and all the fury and mire that had constricted their hearts and tolled their days were now reduced to a chip of vertebrae tangled in the roots of a sugarcane stalk.

18

Sonny Boy was sprung and I was now the full-time operator of a bait shop and boat-rental business that, on a good year, cleared fifteen thousand dollars.

He found me at Red Lerille's Gym in Lafayette.

'Jail wasn't that bad on you, Sonny. You look sharp,' I said.

'Get out of my face with that patronizing attitude, Dave.' He chewed gum and wore a tailored gray suit with zoot slacks and a blue suede belt and a T-shirt.

'I'm off the case, off the job, out of your problems, Sonny.'

I'd forgotten my speed bag gloves at home, but I began working the bag anyway, creating a circular motion with each fist, throbbing the bag harder and harder against the circular board it was suspended from.

'Who appointed you my caretaker?' he asked.

I skinned my knuckles on the bag, hit it harder, faster. He grabbed it with both hands.

'Lose the attitude. I'm talking to you. Who the fuck says you got to quit your job because of me?' he said.

'I didn't quit, I'm suspended. The big problem here is somebody pulled you down from your cross and you can't stand it.'

'I got certain beliefs and I don't like that kind of talk, Dave.'

I opened and closed my palms at my sides. My knuckles stung, my wrists pounded with blood. The gym echoed with the smack of gloves on leather, the ring of basketballs against the hardwood floor. Sonny's face was inches from mine, his breath hot on my skin.

'Would you step back, please? I don't want to hit you with the bag,' I said.

'I don't let anybody take my bounce, Dave.'

'That's copacetic, Sonny. I can relate to it. Hey, I don't want to offend you, but you're not supposed to be in here with street shoes on. They mark up the floors.'

'You can be a wiseass all you want, Dave. Emile Pogue is a guy who once put a flamethrower down a spider hole full of civilians. You think you're on suspension? In whose world?'

He walked across the gym floor, through a group of sweating basketball players who looked like their muscles were pumped full of hardening concrete.

I hit the speed bag one more time and felt a strip of skin flay back off my knuckle.

It rained hard the next morning. Lightning struck in the field behind my house and my neighbor's cows had bunched in the coulee and were lowing inside the sound of the rain. I read the paper on the gallery, then went back inside to answer the phone.

'You got to hear me, Dave,' Sonny said. 'Once they take me out, it'll be your turn, then the woman cop, what's-her-name, Helen Soileau, then maybe Purcel, then maybe your wife. They don't leave loose ends.'

'All right, Sonny, you made your point.'

'Another thing, this is personal, I'm no guy on a cross. In medieval times, I would have been one of those guys selling pigs' bones for saints' relics. The reality is I got innocent people's blood on my hands.'

'I don't know what to tell you, partner.'

'I'm not going away, Dave. You'll see me around.'

'That's what I'm afraid of,' I said. He didn't answer. For some reason I imagined him on a long, empty beach where the waves were lashed by wind but made no sound. 'Good-bye, Sonny,' I said, and replaced the receiver in the cradle.

An hour later the thunder had stopped and the rain was falling steadily on the gallery's tin roof. Clete's chartreuse Cadillac convertible, with fins and grillwork like a torn mouth, bounced through the chuckholes in the road and turned into my drive. He ran through the puddles under the trees, his keys and change jingling in his slacks, one hand pressed on top of his porkpie hat.

'They gave you the deep six, huh, big mon?' he said. He sat in the swing and wiped his face on his sleeve.

'Who told you?'

'Helen.'

'You're on a first-name basis now?'

'She met me at my office last night. She doesn't like seeing her partner get reamed. I don't either.' He looked at his watch.

'Don't put your hand in it, Clete.'

'You afraid your ole podjo's going to leave gorilla shit on the furniture?' I made a pocket of air in my cheek.

'You want to go partners in my agency?' he said. 'Hey, I need the company. I'm a grunt for Wee Willie Bimstine and Nig Rosewater. My temp's an ex-nun. My best friends are mutts in the city prison. The desk sergeant at First District wouldn't spit in my mouth.'

'Thanks, anyway, Cletus. I don't want to move back to New Orleans.'

'We'll open a branch here in New Iberia. Leave it to me, I'll set it up.'

Several nightmarish visions floated before my eyes. Clete looked at his watch. 'You got anything to eat?' he said.

'Help yourself.'

He walked through the house to the kitchen and came back on the gallery with a bowl of Grape-Nuts and a tall glass of coffee and hot milk. His teeth made a grinding sound while he ate. His eyes glanced at his watch again.

'Who you expecting?' I said.

'I'm meeting Helen in town. She's photocopying Sonny's diary for me.'

'Bad idea.'

He stopped chewing and his face stretched as tight as pig hide. He raised his spoon at me.

'Nobody fucks my podjo, pardon the word in your house,' he said.

I felt like the soldier who enlists at the outset of a war, then discovers, after his energies and blood lust have waned, that there is no separate peace, that he's a participant until the last worthless shot is fired on the last worthless day. Sonny was right. There are no administrative suspensions, no more so than when pistol flares burst overhead and flood the world with a ghostly white light and you turn into the skeletal, barkless shape of a tree.

When the rain stopped and the sky began to clear and gradually turn blue again, I took Alafair's pirogue and rowed it into the swamp. The stands of cypress were bright green and dripping with rainwater, and under the overhang every dead log and gray sand spit was covered with nutrias.

I slid the pirogue into a cove and ate a ham and onion sandwich and drank from a cold jar of sun tea.

Oftentimes when you work a case and the players and events seem larger than life, you leapfrog across what at first seems the minuscule stuff of police procedural novels. Details at a crime scene seldom solve crimes. The army of miscreants whose detritus we constantly process through computers and forensic laboratories usually close their own files by shooting themselves and one another, OD-ing on contaminated drugs, getting dosed with AIDS or busted in the commission of another crime, or perhaps turning over a liquor store where the owner had tired of being cleaned out and introduces the robber to Messieurs Smith & Wesson.

Several years ago the wire services reported rumors that Jimmy Hoffa's body had been entombed in concrete under the goal posts of a football stadium. Each time someone kicked the extra point, Hoffa's old colleagues would shout, 'This one's for you, Jimmy!'

It makes a good story. I doubt that it's true. The mob isn't given to poetics.

A New Orleans hit man, who admitted to murdering people for as little as three hundred dollars, told me Hoffa was ground up into fish chum and thrown by the bucket-load off the stern of a cabin cruiser, then the deck and gunnels hosed and wiped down a pristine white, all within sight of Miami Beach.

I believed him.

The body of the man named Jack had probably been mutilated by a professional, or at least the directions to do so had been given by one. But sinking the body with a tangle of fish line and scrap iron on the edge of a navigable channel had all the marks of an amateur, and probably a lazy one at that, or we would have never found it.

I called Helen at the department.

'What's ruthless, lazy, and stupid all over?' I asked.

'The guy taking your calls?'

'What?' I said.

'The old man assigned your open cases to Rufus Arceneaux.'

'Forget Rufus. We missed something when we pulled the floater out. He was tied up with scrap iron and fish line.'

'I'm not following you.'

'Let me try again. What's perverse, is not above anything, looks like a ghoul anyway, and would screw up a wet dream?'

'Sweet Pea Chaisson,' she said.

'Clete and I went to his house on the Breaux Bridge road before we had that run-in with him and Patsy Dap in Lafayette. I remember a bunch of building materials in the lot next door – building materials or maybe junk from a pipe yard.'

'Pretty good, Streak.'

'It's enough for a warrant,' I said.

'Then we toss his Caddy and maybe match the blood on the rug to the scraping you took from the trailer behind the juke. Dave, square your beef with the old man. I can't partner with Rufus.'

'It's not my call.'

'You heard Patsy Dap's in town?'

'No.'

'Nobody told you?' she said.

'No.'

'He got stopped for speeding on East Main yesterday. The city cop made him and called us. I'm sorry, I thought somebody told you.'

'Where is he now?'

'Who knows? Wherever disfigured paranoids hang out.'

'Keep me informed on the warrant, will you?' I said.

'You're a good cop, Dave. You get your butt back here.'

'You're the best, Helen.'

I walked down to the dock. The air was hot and still and down the road someone was running a Weed Eater that had the nerve-searing pitch of a dentist's instrument. So Patsy Dapolito was in New Iberia and no one had bothered to tell me, I thought. But why not? We did it all the time. We cut loose rapists, pedophiles, and murderers on minimum bail, even on their own recognizance, and seldom notified the victims or the witnesses to their crimes.

Ask anyone who's been there. Or, better yet, ask the victims or survivors about the feelings they have when they encounter the source of their misery on the street, in the fresh air, in the flow of everyday traffic and normal life, and they realize the degree of seriousness with which society treats the nature of their injury. It's a moment no one forgets easily.

My thoughts were bitter and useless.

I knew the origins of my self-indulgence, too. I couldn't get the word *disfigured* out of my mind. I tried to imagine the images that flashed through Patsy Dap's brain when he saw his face reflected in the mirror.

I helped Batist fill the coolers with beer and soda and scoop the ashes out of the barbecue pit, then I sat in the warm shade at one of the spool tables with a glass of iced tea and thought about Clete's offer.

19

The next morning I drove out to the Bertrand plantation to talk to Ruthie Jean, but no one was at home. I walked next door to Bertie's and knocked on the screen. When she didn't answer, I went around the side and saw her get up heavily from where she had been sitting on the edge of the porch. Her stomach swelled out between her purple stretch pants and oversize white T-shirt. She unhooked a sickle from the dirt and began slicing away the dead leaves from the banana trees that grew in an impacted clump against the side wall of the house.

I had the impression, however, she had been doing something else before she saw me.

'I'm worried about Ruthie Jean, Bertie,' I said. 'I think she nursed a man named Jack who died in the trailer behind the juke. She probably heard and saw things other people don't want her to talk about.'

'You done already tole her that.'

'She's not a good listener.'

'There's two kinds of trouble. What *might* happen, and what done *already* happen. White folks worry about *might*. It ain't the same for everybody, no.'

'You lost me.'

'It ain't hard to do,' she said. She ripped a tangle of brown leaves onto the ground, then lopped a stalk cleanly across the middle. The cut oozed with green water.

On the planks of the porch I saw a square of red flannel cloth, with a torn root and a tablespoon of dirt in the middle. I saw Bertie watch me out of the corner of her eye as I walked closer to the piece of flannel. Among the grains of dirt were strands of hair, what looked like a shirt button, and a bright needle with blood on it.

'I'm going to take a guess – dirt from a grave, root of a poison oak, and a needle for a mess of grief,' I said.

She whacked and lopped the dead stalks and flung the debris behind her.

'Did you get Moleen's hair and shirt button out of the shack by the treeline?' I asked.

'I ain't in this world to criticize. But you come out here and you don't do no good. You pretend like you know, but you playing games. It ain't no fun for us.'

'You think putting a gris-gris on Moleen is going to solve your problems?'

'The reason I put it on *him* is 'cause she ain't left nothing out here so I can put it on *her*.'

'Who?'

'Julia Bertrand.' She almost spit out the words. 'She already been out here once this morning. With that man work down the hall from you. Ruthie Jean ain't got her house no more. How you like that?'

I blew out my breath.

'I didn't know,' I said.

She tossed the sickle in the flower bed.

'That's my point,' she said, and went in her house.

A few minutes later, almost as though Bertie had planned Julia appearance's as part of my ongoing education about the realities of life on a corporate plantation, I saw Julia's red Porsche turn off the highway and drive down the dirt road toward me. Rufus Arceneaux sat next to her in a navy blue suit that looked like pressed cardboard on his body.

When she stopped next to me, her window down, her face cheerful, I tried to be pleasant and seem unknowing, to mask the embarrassment I felt for her and the level of vindictiveness to which she had devoted herself.

'Bertie doesn't have you digging holes after pirate's treasure, does she, Dave?' she said.

'She told me something disturbing,' I said, my voice bland, as though she and I were both concerned about the ill fortune of a third party. 'It looks like Ruthie Jean and Luke are being evicted.'

'We need the house for a tenant family. Ruthie Jean and Luke don't work on the plantation, nor do they pay rent. I'm sorry, but they'll have to find a new situation.'

I nodded, my face blank. I felt my fingers tapping on the steering wheel. I cut my engine.

'You already dropped the dime on her and had her locked up. Isn't that enough?' I said.

'Whatever do you mean?' she said.

I opened my door partway to let the breeze into the truck's cab. I felt my pulse beating in my neck, words forming that I knew I shouldn't speak.

'With y'all's background and education, with all Moleen's money, can't you be a little forgiving, a little generous with people who have virtually nothing?' I said.

Rufus bent down in the passenger's seat so I could see his face through the window. He had taken off his pilot's sunglasses, and his eyes looked pale green and lidless, the pupils as black and small as a lizard's, the narrow bridge of his nose pinched with two pink indentations.

'You're operating without your shield, Dave. That's something IA doesn't need to hear about,' he said.

She placed her hand on his arm without looking at him.

'Dave, just so you understand something, my husband is a charming man and a wonderful litigator who also happens to be a financial idiot,' she said.

'He has no money. If he did, he'd invest it in ski resorts in Bangladesh. Is Ruthie Jean home now?'

Her eyes fixed pleasantly on mine with her question. Her lipsticked smile looked like crooked red lines drawn on parchment.

I dropped the truck into low and drove under the wisteria-hung iron trellis of the Bertrand plantation, wondering, almost in awe, at the potential of the human family.

That afternoon Batist called me from the phone in the bait shop.

'Dave, there's a man out on the dock don't belong here,' he said.

'What's wrong with him?'

'I ax him if he want a boat. He says, "Give me a beer and a sandwich." An hour later he's sitting at the table under the umbrella, smoking a cigarette, he ain't eat the sandwich, he ain't drunk the beer. I ax him if there's anyt'ing wrong with the food. He says, "It's fine. Bring me another beer." I say, "You ain't drunk that one." He says, "It's got a bug in it. You got the afternoon paper here?" I say, "No, I ain't got the paper." He says, "How about some magazines?"'

'I'll be down in a minute,' I said.

'I ought to brought him a paper bag.'

'What d' you mean?'

'To put over his head. He looks like somebody took a sharp spoon and stuck it real deep all over his face.'

'Stay in the bait shop, Batist. You understand me? Don't go near this man.'

I hung up, without waiting for him to reply, called the department for a cruiser, took my .45 out of the dresser drawer, stuck it through the back of my belt, and hung my shirt over it. As I walked down the slope through the broken light under the pecan and oak trees, I could see a strange drama being played out among the spool tables on the dock. Fishermen who had just come in were drinking beer and eating smoked sausage and *boudin* under the umbrellas, their faces focused among themselves and on their conversations about big-mouth bass and goggle-eye perch, but in their midst, by himself, smoking a cigarette with the concentrated intensity of an angry man hitting on a reefer, was Patsy Dapolito, his mouth hooked downward at the corners, his face like a clay sculpture someone had mutilated with a string knife.

I remembered a scene an old-time gunbull had once pointed out to me on the yard, inside the Block, at Angola Penitentiary. Inmates stripped to the waist, their apelike torsos wrapped with tattoos, were clanking iron, throwing the shotput, and ripping into heavy bags with blows that could eviscerate an elephant. In the center of the lawn was a tiny, balding, middle-aged man in steel-rimmed spectacles, squatting on his haunches, chewing gum furiously, his jaws freezing momentarily, the eyes lighting, then the jaws moving again with a renewed snapping energy. When a football bounced close to the squatting man, a huge black inmate asked permission before he approached to pick it up. The squatting man said nothing and the football remained where it was.

'Forget about them big 'uns,' the gunbull told me. 'That little fart yonder killed another convict while he had waist and leg chains on. I won't tell you how he done it, since you ain't eat lunch yet.'

I looked down at Patsy Dapolito's ruined face. His pale eyes, which were round like an outraged doll's, clicked upward into mine.

'You made a mistake coming here,' I said.

'Sit down. You want a beer?' he said. He picked up a bottle cap from the tabletop and threw it against the screen of the bait shop. 'Hey, you! Colored guy! Bring us a couple more beers out here!'

I stared at him with my mouth open. Batist's head appeared at the screen, then went away.

'You've pulled some wiring loose, partner,' I said.

'What, I don't got a right to drink a beer in a public place?'

'I want you out of here.'

'Let's take a ride in a boat. I ain't never seen a swamp. You got swamp tours?' he said.

'*Adios*, Patsy.'

'Hey, I don't like that. I'm talking here.'

I had already turned to walk away. His hand clenched on my forearm, bit into the tendons, pulled me off balance into the table.

'Show some courtesy, act decent for a change,' he said.

'You need some help, Dave?' a heavyset man with tobacco in his jaw said at the next table.

'It's all right,' I said. People were staring now. My .45 protruded from under my shirt. I sat down on a chair, my arms on top of the spool table. 'Listen to me, Patsy. A sheriff's cruiser is on its way. Right now, you got no beef with the locals. As far as I see it, you and I are slick, too. Walk away from this.'

His teeth were charcoal colored and thin on the ends, almost as though they had been filed. His short, light brown hair looked like a wig on a mannequin. His eyes held on mine. 'I got business to do,' he said.

'Not with me.'

'With you.'

The fishermen at the other tables began to drift off toward their cars and pickup trucks and boat trailers.

'I want part of the action,' he said.

'What action?'

'The deal at the plantation. I don't care what it is, I want in on it. You're on a pad for Johnny Carp. That means you're getting pieced off on this deal.'

'A pad for—'

'Or you'd be dead. I know Johnny. He don't let nobody skate unless it's for money.'

'You're a confused man, Patsy.'

He pinched his nose, blew air through the nostrils, looked about at the sky, the overhang of the trees, a cloud of dust drifting from a passing pickup through a cane brake. 'Look, there's guys ain't even from the city in on this deal, military guys think they're big shit because they cooled out a few gooks and tomato pickers. I did a grown man with a shank when I was eleven years old. You say I'm lying, check my jacket.'

'It's Johnny you want to bring down, isn't it?' I said.

He kept huffing puffs of air through his nostrils, then he pulled a wadded handkerchief from his pocket and blew his nose in it.

'Johnny don't show it, but he's a drunk,' Dapolito said. 'A drunk don't look after anybody but himself. Otherwise you'd be fish bait, motherfucker.'

I walked out to meet the cruiser sent by the dispatcher. The deputy was a big redbone named Cecil Aguillard whose face contained a muddy light people chose not to dwell upon.

'You t'ink he's carrying?' Cecil said.

'Not unless he has an ankle holster.'

'What he's done?'

'Nothing so far,' I said.

He walked down the dock ahead of me, his gunbelt, holster, and baton creaking on his hips like saddle leather. The umbrella over Patsy's head tilted and swelled in the wind. Cecil pushed it at an angle so he could look down into his face.

'Time to go,' Cecil said.

Patsy was hunkered down over the tabletop, scowling into a state fish and game magazine. He made me think of a recalcitrant child in a school desk who was not going to let a nun's authority overwhelm him.

'Dave don't want you here,' Cecil said.

'I ain't done nothing.' His shoulders were hunched, his hands clenched into fists on the edges of the magazine, his eyes flicking about the dock.

Cecil looked at me and nodded his head toward the bait shop. I followed him.

'Clear everybody out of here, Dave, I'll take care of it,' he said.

'It won't work on this guy.'

'It'll work.'

'No, he'll be back. Thanks for coming out, Cecil. I'll call you later if I have to.'

'It ain't smart, Dave. You turn your back on his kind, he'll have your liver flopping on the flo'.'

I watched Cecil drive down the road in the deepening shadows, then I helped Batist seine the dead shiners out of our bait tanks and hose down the boats we had rented that day. Patsy Dapolito still sat at his table, smoking cigarettes, popping the pages in his magazine, wiping bugs and mosquitoes from in front of his face.

The sun had dipped behind my house, and the tops of the cypress in the swamp had turned a grayish pink in the afterglow.

'We're closing up, Patsy,' I said.

'Then close it up,' he said.

'We've got a joke out here. This fellow woke up on his houseboat and heard two mosquitoes talking about him. One said, "Let's take him outside and eat him." The other one said, "We'd better not. The big ones will carry him off for themselves."'

'I don't get it,' he said.

'Have a good one,' I said, and walked up the slope to the house.

Two hours later it was dark. I used the switch inside the house to turn on the string of lights over the dock. Patsy Dapolito still sat at his table, the Cinzano umbrella furled above his head. His hard, white body seem to glow with electrified humidity.

Later, Bootsie and Alafair pulled into the drive, the car loaded with bags of groceries they had bought in Lafayette.

'Dave, there's a man sitting on the dock,' Bootsie said.

'It's Patsy Dap,' I said.

'The man you—' she began.

'That's the one.'

'I can't believe it. He's on our *dock*?'

'He's not going to do anything,' I said.

'He's not going to have a chance to. Not if I have anything to do with it,' she said.

'I think Johnny Giacano's cut him loose. That's why he's here, not because of me. He couldn't think his way out of a wet paper bag, much less rejection by the only form of authority he's ever respected.'

But she wasn't buying it.

'I'll get rid of him,' I said.

'How?'

'Sometimes you've got to make their souls wince.'

'Dave?'

I carried a sack of groceries inside, then wrapped both my .45 and nine-millimeter Beretta inside a towel, took a tube of first-aid cream from the medicine cabinet, and walked down to the dock. Patsy's elbows were splayed on the table, his face pale and luminous with heat and perspiration. The tide was out and the current was dead in the bayou. Patsy worked a thumbnail between his teeth and stared at me.

'Put some of this stuff on those mosquito bites,' I said.

He surprised me. He filled both palms with white cream and rubbed it into his forearms and on his face and neck, his round chin pointed up in the air.

I unfolded the towel on the table. His eyes dropped to the pistols, then looked up at me.

'What, you got cold pieces for sale?' he said.

I released the magazine from the butt of each automatic so he could see the top round, inserted it again, chambered the round, set the safety, and placed both weapons butt to butt in the center of the table. Then I sat down across from him, my eyes stinging with salt. Up the slope, I could see Bootsie under the light on the gallery.

'If you want to square what I did to you, now's the time,' I said. 'Otherwise, I'm going to mop up the dock with you.'

He smiled and screwed a fresh cigarette in his mouth, crumpled up the empty pack. 'I always heard you were a drunk. That ain't your problem. You're fucking stupid, man,' he said.

'Oh?'

'I want to make somebody dead, I don't even have to get out of bed. Don't try to shine me off, worm man. Tell Johnny and those military asswipes they piece me off or I leave hair on the walls.'

He walked on the balls of his feet toward his automobile, lifting his arm to smell himself again.

Sometimes they don't wince.

20

Even inside the dream I know I'm experiencing what a psychologist once told me is a world destruction fantasy. But my knowledge that it is only a dream does no good; I cannot extricate myself from it.

As a child I saw the sun turn black against a cobalt sky and sink forever beyond the earth's rim. Years later the images would change and I'd revisit my brief time as a new colonial, see Victor Charles, in black pajamas, sliding on his stomach through a rice paddy, a French bolt-action rifle strapped across his back; two GIs eating C-rations in the shade of banyan trees after machine-gunning a farmer's water buffalo just for meanness' sake; three of our wounded after they'd been skinned and hung in trees like sides of meat by NVA.

In my dream tonight I can see the Louisiana coastline from a great height, as alluvial and new as it must have been after Jehovah hung the archer's bow in the sky and drew the waters back over the earth's edges, the rivers and bayous and wetlands shimmering like foil under the moon. But it's a view that will not hold at the center, because now I realize the cold light of the moon is actually the fire from chemical plants and oil refineries along the Mississippi, the shook foil of a dead Jesuit poet nothing more than industrial mercury systematically injected into the earth's veins. The roadways and ditches are blown with litter, the canals a depository for rubber tires, beer cans, vinyl sacks of raw garbage thrown from pickup trucks. A fish's gills are orange with fungus.

I wake from the dream and sit alone in the kitchen. I can hear thunder out of the Gulf and Tripod pulling his chain along the clothesline. Through the window my neighbor's freshly cut lawn smells like corn silk and milk. I sit on the back steps until the trees turn gray with the false dawn, then I go back inside and fall asleep just as the first raindrops *ping* against the blades of the window fan.

At noon Bootsie and I were eating lunch in the kitchen when Ruthie Jean Fontenot called.

'Moleen's at Dot's in St Martinville. You know where that's at, I'm talking about in the black section?' she said.

'I'm not his keeper, Ruthie Jean.'

'You can get him out.'

'Get him out yourself.'

'Some secrets suppose to stay secret. You know the rules about certain things that go on between white and black people.'

'Wrong man to call,' I said.

'The man owns the place is a friend of Luke's. He said Moleen's got a li'l pistol stuck down inside his coat. The man doesn't want to call the police unless he has to.'

'Forget Moleen and take care of yourself, Ruthie Jean. He's not worth—'

She hung up. I sat down at the table and started eating again. Bootsie watched my face.

'Moleen's a grown man,' I said. 'He's also a hypocritical sonofabitch.'

'He got her out of jail,' Bootsie said.

'He paid somebody else to do it. Which is Moleen's style. Three cushion shots.'

'Too harsh, Streak,' she said.

I drank out of my iced tea, sucked on a sprig of mint, finally squeezed my temples between my fingers.

'See you before five,' I said.

'Watch your ass, kiddo,' she said.

I took the old road into St Martinville, along Bayou Teche and through cane fields and pastureland where egrets stood like spectators on the backs of grazing cows. Dot's was a ramshackle bar toward the end of the main artery that traversed the black district and eventually bled into the square where Evangeline was buried with her lover behind the old French church. Ironically, the bar's geographical location, set like a way station between two worlds, was similar to the peculiar mix of blood and genes in the clientele – octoroons and quadroons, redbones, and people who were coal black but whose children sometimes had straw-colored curly hair.

Moleen sat in the gloom, at the far end of the bar, on a patched, fingernail-polish-red vinyl stool, his seersucker coat tight across his hunched shoulders, one oxblood loafer twisted indifferently inside an aluminum rung on the stool. I could smell his unwashed odor three feet away.

'She's worried about you,' I said, and sat down next to him.

He drank from a glass of bourbon and melted ice, pushed two one-dollar bills out of his change toward the bartender.

'You want a drink?' he said.

I didn't answer. I peeled back the edge of his coat with one finger. He glared at me.

'A .25 caliber derringer. That's dumb, Moleen,' I said. 'One of those is like bird shit hitting a brick.'

He pointed at his empty glass for the bartender. A deformed mulatto man with a shoe-shine box came through the front door in a burst of hot sunlight, let the door slam hard behind him, vibrating the glass and venetian blinds. His face was moronic, his mouth a wet drool, his arms like gnarled oak roots that were half the length they should have been. I looked away from him.

'You want your shoes shined?' Moleen said, a smile playing at the corner of his mouth.

'I think a remark like that is unworthy of you,' I said.

403

'I wasn't being humorous. His great-grandfather and mine were the same gentleman. If you think he's an eyeful, you should meet his mother. Hang around. She comes in about seven.'

'I can't stop you from fucking up your life, Moleen, but as a law officer, I want you to hand over your piece.'

'Take it. I've never fired a shot in anger, anyway.'

I slipped it from inside his belt, cracked open the breech below the lip of the bar.

'It's empty,' I said.

'Oh, yeah,' he said absently, and took two steel-jacketed rounds from his coat pocket and dropped them in my palm. 'They're going to take your friend Marsallus out.'

'Who?'

He tilted the glass to his mouth. His eyes were red along the rims, his face unshaved and shiny with a damp sweat.

'What's the worst thing you saw in Vietnam, Dave?' he asked.

'It's yesterday's box score.'

'You ever leave your own people behind, sell them out, scratch their names off a list at a peace conference, lie to their families?'

'Quit sticking thumbtacks in your head. Go public with it.'

'It *is* public, for God's sakes. Nobody cares.'

'Why do these guys want to kill Sonny?'

'He's a one-man firing squad. He gets them in his sights and they tend to dissolve in a red mist.'

'A good woman cares for you, Moleen. A guy could have worse problems,' I said.

'Which woman?'

'See you around, partner. Don't let them get behind you.' I started to get up.

'You're always the wiseguy, Dave. Try this. Ruthie Jean got her Aunt Bertie to file suit against the plantation. They retained a little sawed-off ACLU lawyer from New Orleans who can tie us up in court for years.'

'Sounds like a smart move.'

'Glad you think so. I know some gentlemen who probably won't agree with you. After they take Marsallus off the board, you may get to meet a few of them.'

'I already have. They're just not that impressive a crowd,' I said, got up off the stool, and collided into the deformed man. His wood shoe-shine box tumbled out of his hands; brushes, cans of wax and saddle soap, bottles of liquid polish clattered and rolled across the floor. His eyes had the panicked, veined intensity of hard-boiled eggs. He slobbered and made a moaning sound in his throat as he tried to pick up a cracked bottle of liquid polish that was bleeding into a black pool in the wood. But his torso was top-heavy, his arms too short and uncoordinated, and he stared helplessly at the dripping polish on his fingers as the bottle rolled farther from his grasp and left a trail of black curlicues across the floor.

I got down on my knees and began putting his things back in the box.

'I'm sorry, partner. We'll go down to the store and replace whatever I broke here. It's going to be okay,' I said.

His expression was opaque, his tongue thick as a wet biscuit on his teeth. He tried to make words, but they had no more definition than a man clearing a phlegmy obstruction from his throat.

I saw Moleen grinning at me.

'Racial empathy can be a sticky business, can't it, laddie?' he said.

I wanted to wipe him off the stool.

The anger, the inability to accept, would not go out of Bootsie's words. There were pale discolorations like melted pieces of ice in her cheeks. I couldn't blame her.

'Dave, she's only thirteen years old. She could have killed someone,' she said.

'But she didn't. She didn't chamber the round, either,' I said.

'That seems poor consolation.'

'I'll lock up all the guns,' I said.

It was eleven Friday night and we were in the kitchen. I had turned on the floodlight in the mimosa tree in the backyard. Alafair was in her room with the door closed.

I took another run at it.

'I know it's my fault. I left the Beretta where she could find it,' I said. 'But what if this guy had tried to come through the door or window?'

She washed a cup in hot water with her hands. Her skin was red under the tap. Her back looked stiff and hard against her shirt.

'You want to install a burglar alarm system?' I said.

'Yes!'

'I'll call somebody in the morning,' I said, and went into the backyard, where I sat for a long time at the picnic table and stared listlessly at the shadows of the mimosa tree shifting back and forth on the grass. It was not a good night to be locked up with your own thoughts, but I knew of nowhere else to take them.

In the morning I drove to New Iberia with Alafair to pick up an outboard engine from the freight agent at the train depot.

'You shouldn't have messed with the gun, Alf,' I said.

'I'd already called 911. What was I supposed to do next? Wait for him to kick the door in?' She looked straight ahead, her eyes dancing.

'I couldn't find any footprints.'

'I don't care. I saw him. He was out there in the trees. Tripod got scared and started running on his chain.'

'It wasn't the guy who got Tripod out of the coulee?'

'He was thinner. A car went by and his skin looked real white.'

'Did he have red hair?'

'I don't know. It was only a second.'

'Maybe it's time we learn how to use a pistol properly,' I said.

'Why's everybody mad at me? It's not fair, Dave.'

'I'm not mad at you, little guy . . . Sorry . . . Bootsie isn't, either. It's just—'

'Yes, she is. Don't lie about it. It makes it worse.'

'That's pretty strong, Alf.'

'Why'd y'all leave me alone, then? What am I supposed to do if bad people come around the house?' Her voice grew in intensity, then it broke like a stick snapping and she began to cry.

We were on East Main in front of the Shadows. I pulled into the shade of the oaks, behind a charter bus full of elderly tourists. The bus's diesel engine throbbed off the cement.

'I screwed up. I won't do it again,' I said.

But she kept crying, with both of her hands over her face.

'Look, maybe I won't go back with the department. I'm tired of being a punching bag for other people. I'm tired of the family taking my fall, too.'

She took her hands from her face and looked out the side window for a long time. She kept sniffing and touching at her eyes with the backs of her wrists. When she turned straight in the seat again, her eyes were round and dry, as though someone had popped a flashbulb in front of them.

'It's not true,' she said.

'What isn't?'

'You'll always be a cop, Dave. Always.'

Her voice was older than her years, removed from both of us, prescient with a joyless knowledge about the nature of adult promises.

By Sunday morning I still hadn't put the matter to rest. I woke early and tapped on Alafair's door.

'Yes?'

'It's Dave. You got a second?'

'Wait.' I heard her bare feet on the floor. 'Okay.'

Her shelves were filled with stuffed animals, the walls covered with posters featuring cats of all kinds. Alafair had propped a pillow behind her head and pulled up her knees so that they made a tent under the sheet. The curtains puffed in the breeze and the screen hung loose from the latch.

I sat in the chair by her homework desk.

'I was upset for another reason yesterday, one that's hard to explain,' I said. 'You didn't do anything wrong, Alf. I did.'

'You already said that.'

'Listen. When you kill another human being, no matter how necessary it might seem at the time, something goes out of your life forever. I never want that to happen to you. I still have dreams about the war, I have them about men I ran up against as a police officer. Their faces don't go underground with them.'

Her eyes blinked and went away from mine.

I saw the sheet ruffle and hump at the foot of the bed. It should have been a humorous moment, but it wasn't.

'Let's get this guy out of here so we can talk,' I said, and lifted Tripod from under the sheet. He hung heavily from my hands and churned his paws in the air as I walked to the window.

'He'll run down to the dock again,' she said, as if she could open a door out of our conversation.

'Batist can handle it,' I said, and dropped Tripod into the yard.

I sat back down. It was sunny and blue outside. In a short while we would be driving to Mass at St Peter's in New Iberia, then we'd have lunch at Victor's on Main. I didn't want to address the question in her eyes.

Her hands were pinched together on top of her knees. She looked at a poster of two calico kittens on the far wall.

'How many people, Dave, how many did you—'

'You never let yourself see a number in your mind, Alf. The day you do, the day it comes out of your mouth, that's the day you start being someone else,' I said.

Sonny Boy called the bait shop at three o'clock that afternoon.

'You've got a serious hearing problem,' I said. 'I want you out of my life. Don't come around my house anymore, you understand? You want to be a guardian angel, go to New York, put on a red beret, and buy a lot of subway tokens.'

'What do you mean come around your house?' he said. I could hear waves breaking against rocks or a jetty, then the sound of a door on a telephone booth closing.

'Friday night,' I said.

'I was in New Orleans,' he said.

'Don't give me that, Sonny.'

'I'm telling you the truth.'

'My daughter saw a guy in the trees. It wasn't Emile Pogue, it wasn't Patsy Dap, Patsy wants to do business and screw Johnny Carp, that leaves you.' But my words sounded hollow even to myself.

'They got lots of guys working for them, Streak, a lot of them in Florida. They get gooned-up like over-the-hill jarheads on a skivvy run, blow into town, give a guy a fatal accident, and catch the red-eye back to Tampa the same night.'

I could hear myself breathing against the receiver. Outside the screen window, the sunlight's reflection on the bayou was like a sliver of glass in the eye.

'Why'd you call?' I said.

'A rag-nose used to work for Johnny Carp told me Johnny's in on a deal to get some land by a train track. He said he heard Johnny tell a guy on the phone the land's got to be by a train track. That's the key.'

'To what?' I said.

'I don't know. You ought to see the rag-nose. He's got nostrils that look like tunnels going straight into his brain. The real reason I called, if my string runs out, like I bounce back treys and boxcars, know what I'm saying, I wanted to tell you I'm sorry for the trouble I caused other people.'

'Come on, Sonny, you got your ticket punched a long time ago. You'll be standing on Canal with a glass of champagne when they drive Johnny's hearse by ... Sonny?'

I heard the phone booth door rachet back violently on its hinges, the receiver clattering back and forth on its cord, then, almost lost in the crash of waves against rocks or a jetty, a sound like a string of firecrackers popping.

21

Early Monday morning the sheriff called and asked me to come to the department. I thought it was about Sonny. It wasn't.

He was scraping out the bowl of his pipe over the wastebasket with a penknife when I walked into his office.

'Sit down,' he said. He wiped the blade of the penknife on a piece of paper and folded it against the heel of his hand. 'This is a bad day, my friend . . . I wish I could tell you it's just a matter of IAD finding against you.'

I waited.

'You know the route,' he said. 'It's the kind of deal usually gets a guy a letter of reprimand in his jacket or a suspension.' He wadded up the piece of paper and tried to wipe the pipe's ashes out of his palm. 'This one's different.'

'Too many times across the line?'

'The problem is you're a police officer who doesn't like rules. You kept yourself on the job while you were officially suspended, didn't you?'

In my mind's eye I saw Rufus Arceneaux's face leaning across the seat inside Julia's automobile, the green eyes lighted with ambition and long-held grievance.

'There's something you're not saying, Sheriff.'

'I couldn't cover for you anymore, Dave. I told them about you and Purcel salting Sweet Pea's Caddy and queering the warrant.'

'I'm fired?'

'You can submit your resignation. It needs to be on my desk by five.'

I bounced my palms on my thighs.

'About queering the warrant,' I said. 'I made the connection between the scrap iron on the floater's body and a junk pile next to Sweet Pea's house. How'd that play out?'

'I'm afraid it's not your concern any longer.'

It was a windy day outside, and I could see the flag snapping and popping on the steel pole without making any sound.

'I'll box up my stuff,' I said.

'I'm sorry about this,' he said.

I nodded and opened the door to leave.

'Are you going to have that letter on my desk?' he asked.

'I don't think so,' I said.

On the way down the hall I picked up my mail and messages, found an empty cardboard box in a custodian's closet, unlocked my office door, and went inside.

It was all that quick, as though a loud train had gone past me, slamming across switches, baking the track with its own heat, creating a tunnel of sound and energy so intense that the rails seem to reshape like bronze licorice under the wheels; then silence that's like hands clapped across the eardrums, a field of weeds that smell of dust and creosote, a lighted club car disappearing across the prairie.

Or simply a man walking through glass doors into a sun-drenched parking lot, a box on his shoulder, and no one taking particular notice.

An electrical storm struck New Iberia that afternoon, and I sent Batist home and shut down the dock and watched a twenty-four-hour news station on the television set that I kept on top of the soda and lunch meat cooler. A lorry carrying three white men had gone into the black homelands of South Africa and had been shot up by black militia of some kind. The footage was stunning. One white man was already dead, crumpled over the steering wheel, his face pushed into a lopsided expression by the horn button; the two other men lay wounded on the pavement. One had propped his back against the tire and had his hands up, but he never spoke. The other man was on his stomach and having trouble raising his head so he could speak to the soldiers whose legs surrounded him. He was a large man, with a wild red beard, a broad nose, and coarse-grained skin, and he could hardly contain the rage in his throat.

'Will you call a fucking ambulance?' he said in a British accent. 'My friend's hurt. Did you hear me? We need the *fucking* ambulance. How do I say it to you? Call the fucking hospital for an ambulance ... Oh you have, have you? Well, *thank* you very much. Thank you fucking bloody very much.'

The militia shot him and his friend. Later, the replay of the tape did not show the bearded man getting in the face of his executioners. Instead, the newscaster said the victims had begged for their lives. That last line was repeated over and over throughout the afternoon. I kept waiting for it to be corrected. It never was, not to my knowledge. A brave man's death was revised downward to a shameful and humiliating one, either for categorical or dramatic purposes. The truth had become an early casualty.

What's the point?

I didn't know myself.

The thunder finally stopped and the rain roared on the tin roof and drenched the dock and spool tables and blew through the screens in a fine mist. I waited for it to slack off, then I locked up the bait shop and ran up the slope with a raincoat over my head and told Bootsie of the change in our circumstances.

That evening, which was unseasonably cool and marked by strange lights in the sky, Helen Soileau came out to the house and sat with me on the front steps, her thick forearms propped on her thighs like a ballplayer in a dugout, and told me the story about Sonny's phone call within earshot of waves bursting against a coastline.

The two shooters were pros, probably ex-military men, not the much-inflated contract wiseguys who undid their victims through treachery and had to press the muzzle into the hairline to ensure they didn't miss. They had him triangulated from forty yards out, with either AR-15s or .223 carbines. Had the target been anyone else, he would have been hurled backward, matted with shards of glass, and made to dance on invisible wires inside the phone booth. But one of the shooters probably blew it, shifted his sling to box the side of Sonny's face more tightly in his sights, to lock cartilage and jawbone and the almost feminine mouth, which made soundless words the shooter hated without even hearing them, lock them all into a narrow iron rectangle that would splinter into torn watermelon with the slightest pull of the shooter's finger.

But the inverted boat hull he was aiming across dented and made a thunking sound when he shifted the sling, and suddenly Sonny was on rock 'n' roll, his heart bursting with adrenaline, springing from the booth, his shoulders hunched, zigzagging through the boatyard, his hips swiveling like a football quarterback evading tacklers, his skin twitching as though someone had touched a hot match to it.

A witness down by the collapsed pier said Sonny seemed painted with magic. He raced between cinder-block tool shops and dry-docked shrimp boats that were eaten with rot, while the shooters tried to lock down on him again and whanged rounds off a welding truck, blew glass out of a watchman's hut, dissected the yawning door of a junked Coca-Cola machine, and stitched a row of bleeding holes across a corrugated tin paint shed.

Sonny bolted down the sandy slope to the riverbank and poured it on. But for some unexplainable reason he ran for the beach, the wheeling of gulls and other winged creatures, rather than back up the river to higher ground, and the sand became wetter and wetter under his feet, until his shoes sank up to the ankles in porridge.

Then they nailed him.

One shooter, a thick-bodied, truncated man, with knots of muscle through his back and skin-tight cutoffs rolled into his genitals, came over the riverbank in a breath-wheezing run, his rifle at port arms, and fired and fired until the breech locked open and shell casings littered the sand like broken gold teeth.

Sonny's Hawaiian shirt jumped and puffed as though carrion birds were pecking at it. His gait broke, his torso twisted momentarily, and he became a man ingesting a chunk of angle iron. But a long time ago, perhaps back in the Iberville welfare project, Sonny had learned the fate of those who go down in front of their adversaries' booted feet. He seemed to right himself, his face concentrating with a fragile inner balance, forcing a composed and single thought in front of his eyes; then he stumbled toward the surf and the crumpled pier that rang with the cries of frightened birds.

He waded through the breakers, his destroyed shirt billowing out into the tide like wings. The shooters fired twice more, wide and high, the rounds toppling and skipping across the water. But Sonny had become his own denouement. He struggled forward into the undertow, staining the world of fish and crabs and eels and stingrays with his blood, then simply stepped off into the depths, his red hair floating briefly beneath a wave like a windblown flower.

'You handling this, Dave?' Helen said.

'Sure.'

'He always lived on the edge. It was his way.'

'Yeah, I know what you mean,' I said. My voice seemed outside of my skin, my words spoken by someone else. After a while I said, 'Who pulled the body out?'

'They didn't find it.' I could feel her eyes moving on the side of my face. 'Forget it, Dave. He didn't make it. The Fed I talked to said the blood spore looked like dogs had been chewing on him.'

I felt my teeth scrape against one another. 'What was he doing in Mississippi?'

'The beach is full of casinos and greaseballs. Maybe he was tying another knot on his string. The Fed I talked to got pretty vague when I asked him the same thing.'

I bounced my forehead on my thumbs, looked at the sky that was metallic and burned-looking and flickering with lights. Helen stood up with her car keys in her hand.

'He pissed you off, he dragged his shit into your life, but you took his fall, anyway. Don't you dare put this on your conscience,' she said. She aimed her index finger at me.

She walked toward her car, then stopped and turned.

'Did you hear me?' she said.

'Sure.'

Her eyes fixed on mine, then her breasts rose and she walked through the wet leaves and pools of water to the drive, her shoulders squared with a moral certitude that I could only envy.

I woke at four in the morning and sat on the edge of the bed. I couldn't remember the details of the dream I'd just had, but in the center of my mind was an ugly and inescapable thought, like an angry man walking toward you in a darkened, wood-floored hallway.

We'd had him in custody. Then Johnny Giacano had put out the word he didn't want Sonny bailed out.

Question: What was the best way to make sure I heard what Johnny wanted?

Answer: Feed the information to Clete Purcel.

Had Johnny sucked me in?

I didn't know.

I couldn't accept Sonny's death. People like Sonny didn't die. They stayed high on their own rebop, heard Charlie Parker's riffs in the friction of the spheres, thrived without sunlight in the neon glaze of Canal and St Charles, fashioned sonnets out of street language, and proved to the rest of us that you could live with the full-tilt boogie in your heart and glide above the murderous fastenings of triviality.

They didn't find a body, I told myself. The sea always gives back its dead, and they didn't find Sonny's body.

You're dead when they unzip the bag, pry your dog tag out of your teeth, and drain your fluids through a grate in the bottom of a stainless steel trough. *That's* dead.

I lay back on the pillow with my forearm across my eyes and fell asleep. I dreamed I saw Sonny rise like Triton from the sea, his body covered with fish scales, a wreathed horn in his hand, already transforming into a creature of air and spun light.

The next afternoon Batist answered the phone in the bait shop, then handed me the receiver. The weather was hot and muggy, and I pressed a sweating can of Dr Pepper against my cheek and sat on a counter stool with the phone against my ear.

'Robicheaux?' the voice said.

There was no mistaking the thick, whiskey-and-cigarette-seared rasp, the words that rose like ash inside a chimney.

'Yes,' I said, and swallowed something stale and bitter in my throat.

'You must have run your thumb up somebody's hole. You got eighty-sixed out of your own department?'

'What's on your mind, Pogue?'

'I think you're not a bad dude. We need local guys to make it work. You want to piece off Purcel, it's copacetic with us.'

'Make what work? Who's us?'

'The whole fucking planet. Get with the program, ace.'

'I don't know what the program is.'

He laughed, his voice wheezing as though there were pinholes in his lungs.

'I like you, motherfucker,' he said. 'I told them to cut you in. I'd rather see you front points for us than y'all's resident cunt, what's the name, Bertrand?'

'Moleen?'

'Got to get the locals humping for you. Ever light up a ville with Zippo tracks? Something about the stink of fried duck shit really gets their attention.'

The phone receiver was warm and moist against my ear. Someone slammed the screen door behind me like the crack of a rifle.

'You were one of the shooters,' I said.

'The Marsallus gig? He took out some good men. He had it coming.'

'You fucked it up.'

I heard him shift the phone in his hand, his breath fan the mouthpiece in a dry, heated exhalation.

'Fucked it up, huh?'

'The Feds didn't find a body. I think Sonny'll be back to piss on your grave,' I said.

'You listen—' A nail caught in his throat and he began again. 'We busted his wheels, ace. I saw the bone buckle. That punk's down in the slime where he belongs.'

'He shows up when you don't expect him. Your buddy Jack got capped before he knew what hit him. Think about it,' I said, and hung up the receiver.

I hoped I left him with razors turning in his viscera.

22

At noon Tuesday a city cop picked up Ruthie Jean outside a restaurant on Main Street and took her to the city jail, where she was booked for disturbing the peace and disorderly conduct. He even cuffed her, put his hand hard inside her arm before he sat her down in the back of the cruiser and threw her cane across her lap and slammed the door to indicate his sympathies to anyone watching. I heard the story from a half dozen people, all of whom told it with a sense of genteel dismay, but I suspected they were secretly pleased, as small-town people are, when the sins of another are exposed and they no longer have to be complicit in hiding them.

People at first thought she was simply drunk, then they saw the feverish shine in the eyes, like someone still staring into the flame held to a crack pipe. An elderly woman who lived by Spanish Lake recognized and tried to counsel her, shushing her, patting her shoulders, trying to turn her away from Julia Bertrand, who had just parked her red Porsche at the curb in front of the Shadows and was walking cheerfully toward the restaurant, her mental fortifications in place, her long tan riding skirt whipping against her legs.

'Oh, it's all right,' she said to the other white woman. 'Ruthie Jean's upset about a tenant problem Moleen had to settle on the plantation. Now, you go on about your business, Ruthie Jean, and don't be bothering people. You want me to call somebody to drive you home?'

'You put me off the plantation, Julia. When you cut the balloon loose, it goes where it wants.'

'I'd appreciate it if you didn't address me by my first name.'

'You cain't hide from your thoughts. Not when he touches you in the dark, under the sheets, his eyes shut, and you know where his hand's been on me, you know he's thinking of me and that's why he does it to you with his eyes shut, he hurries it so he doesn't have to think about who he's doing it with, about how he's making a lie for both y'all, just like he hepped make my baby and kept pretending I could have it without a husband and live on the plantation like colored folks are suppose to do, like his ancestors did to us, like there wasn't any sin on the child, 'cause the child got Bertrand blood in him.'

'How dare you!'

'You cain't run away when you see that li'l boy in your headlights, either, see the fright in his li'l face, hear his voice speaking to you through the dirt they packed in his mouth. Liquor and drugs cain't keep a spirit in the grave. That li'l boy, his name was John Wesley, he sits on the floor by your nightstand and whispers all the secrets he learned down in the ground, all the things he didn't get to do, the questions he got about his momma and daddy and why they aren't there to take care of him or bring him things on his birthday 'cause your father run them out of the parish.'

'If you come close to me again, I'm going to slap your face.'

Julia crossed the street against the light, her waxed calves flashing like scissors.

But Ruthie Jean followed her, into the restaurant, through the linen-covered tables, past the framed charcoal sketches and pastel paintings of rural Louisiana on the walls, into an interior dining cul-de-sac.

Julia sat erectly in her chair, her menu held tightly in her fingers, a bitter thought clenched in her face. When Ruthie Jean took a chair at the next table, Julia began to laugh. It was a braying, disconnected sound, ongoing, like furniture falling down stairs.

'Is anything wrong, Miss Julia?' the owner asked.

'I thought this was a private dining room. It is a private dining room, isn't it?'

'Sometimes. When people reserve it for banquets and club meetings,' he answered.

'I'd like another table. Over there. By the window.'

'You bet. Are you sure everything's all right, Miss Julia?'

'Are you blind, sir?'

The owner held the chair for her at a table whose linen glowed in the sunlight. Now Ruthie Jean approached both of them, her dark eyes as bright as glass.

'John Wesley was buried in the rain in a casket made of papier-mâché and kite sticks,' she said. 'It's rotted away, eaten up with worms now, and that's how come he can visit in your room at night, sit right by your pillow and draw a picture in the air of the thing that got bounced up under your car and lost inside that sound that doesn't ever go out of your head.'

'You're a vicious, cunning, ungrateful nigra, Ruthie Jean. You can end in an asylum. Mark my word,' Julia said.

Someone was punching numbers on a telephone in the background.

'You cain't do nothing to stop Moleen from coming 'round my house again,' Ruthie Jean said. 'But I don't want him anymore. In Mexico one time he put a flower on my stomach and put his mouth on my nipples and put himself inside me and said I was all the food he'd ever need. Except he stole my nipples from my baby. That's 'cause y'all's kind of white people don't know how to love anything outside of what y'all need.'

After Ruthie Jean had been taken away in the cruiser, her soft black hair like the wig on a mannequin in the rear window, Julia sat numbed and motionless at the table in the deserted dining room; her lips were bloodless, her makeup dry and flaking from her facial hair, as though parched by an inner heat. One thumb kept digging into her cuticles, cutting half-moons into her knuckles, massaging a nest of thoughts that crawled through her veins like spiders.

She smiled and rose from the chair to meet her husband, who had just hurried from his law office down the street.

'Moleen, you dear,' she said. 'How good of you to come. Is something bothering you? Oh, what shall we do, dear boy?'

She used one sharpened fingernail to draw vertical red lines in the skin under his eyes, as though she were imprinting tears on a clown.

At dusk that same evening Clete Purcel's rust-eaten Caddy, with its mildewed and tattered top folded back at a twisted angle, throbbed into the drive and died like a sick animal.

He wore his porkpie hat and a tropical shirt with tiny purple seahorses printed all over it. He was eating an oyster po'-boy sandwich with one hand, tuning the radio with the other.

'Take a ride with me,' he said.

'What's up?'

'I need to talk, that's all.'

'Turn the radio down,' I said.

'Hey, you listen to Dr Boogie and the *Bon Ton* Soul Train?'

'No.'

He started the engine again and kept feeding it the gas while the Caddy's gutted muffler vibrated and rattled against the frame.

'Okay!' I said, above the noise, and got in beside him. A few minutes later we were approaching the drawbridge. 'Do you realize you always end up driving the same kind of cars greaseballs do?' I said.

'That's because I buy them off greaseballs. I'm lucky I can afford greaseball hand-me-downs.'

I waited for him to get to it. We turned into New Iberia, then headed out toward Spanish Lake. He bit down softly on his thumbnail, his face reflective and cool in the wind.

'I heard about Sonny. The guy didn't deserve to die like that,' he said. We were on the old two-lane road now. The azaleas and purple wisteria along the roadside were still in bloom and you could see the lake through the trees. Clete's voice was hoarse, down in his throat. 'Something else bothers me, too.' He turned and looked at me. 'I told you, when I hit Sonny, I got a red bruise on my knuckles, it looked like strawberry juice under the skin, it wouldn't go away?'

He shook his head, without waiting for me to answer.

'I was always pissed off at Sonny, I can't even tell you why. When I heard he got clipped, I felt really bad the way I treated him. I was in the can at Tujague's last night, washing my hands, and that strawberry bruise was gone.'

He held up the back of his hand in the sun's red glow off the dashboard.

'This stuff's in your mind, Clete.'

'Give me some credit, mon. My hand throbbed all the time. Now it doesn't. I think Johnny Carp used both of us to set up the whack.'

He turned left off the two-lane, drove past a collapsed three-story house that had been a gambling club in the sixties, then followed a dirt road to a woods where people had dumped raw garbage and mattresses and stuffed chairs in the weeds. Clete backed the Caddy into the gloom of the trees. The sun was below the horizon now, the air thick with birds.

'What are you doing?' I said.

'Helen Soileau got the warrant on Sweet Pea's house. Guess what? He'd ripped the carpet out of his Caddy.'

The radio was off now, and when he cut the engine I heard movement in the trunk, a shift of weight, the scrape of shoe leather against metal.

'This is a mistake,' I said.

'Watch the show. He's a geek. Geeks get off on being the center of attention.'

Clete took a can of beer from the Styrofoam cooler in the backseat and popped the trunk. Sweet Pea Chaisson's long body was curled between the tire wells, his webbed eyes glistening in the enclosed heat, his tin-colored silk shirt swampy with sweat. He climbed out over the bumper, his small mouth compressed as though he were sucking a mint.

'Hey, Dave. What's the word, babe?' he said.

Clete shoved him backward across a log, onto the ground.

'Streak lost his shield, Sweet Pea. We're operating on different rules now. Bad time to be a wiseass, know what I'm saying?' Clete said.

Sweet Pea inserted his little finger into an empty space in his teeth, then looked at the blood on the tip of it and spit in the weeds. He grinned up at Clete.

'I got to go to the bat'room,' he said.

'Do it in your clothes,' Clete said. Then to me, 'I found our man behind a colored juke joint. He was beating the shit out of one of his chippies with a rolled newspaper.'

'That was my wife,' Sweet Pea said.

Clete pitched the can of beer into his lap.

'Rinse your mouth out. Your breath's bad,' he said.

'T'anks, Purcel,' Sweet Pea said, ripped the tab, and drank deeply from the can. His face was covered with pinpoints of sweat and dirt. 'Where we at?' He looked off into the purple haze above the cane fields. 'Oh yeah, my mother's grave was right across them railway tracks.'

'Who put the whack on Sonny?' Clete said.

'I live in Breaux Bridge now. A crawfish getting run over on the highway is big news there. How do I know?'

Sweet Pea tipped the beer can to his mouth. Clete kicked it into his face. Sweet Pea's lips were suddenly bright red, his eyebrows dripping with beer foam, his face quivering with the force of the blow. But not one sound came from his throat. I pushed Clete away from him.

'No more,' I said.

'Take a walk down the road. Enjoy the evening. Stroll back in ten minutes,' he said. His blue-black .38 one-inch hung from his right hand.

'We take him back to wherever you got him. That's the way it is, Cletus.'

'You're screwing it up, Streak.'

Behind me, I heard Sweet Pea stirring in the weeds, getting to his feet.

'Stay where you are, Sweet Pea,' I said.

He sat on a log with his head between his legs and let the blood and saliva drain out of his mouth. When he looked up at me again, his face was changed.

'You're a pair of white clowns playing big shit out in the wood,' he said. His sharp, tiny teeth looked like they were stained with Mercurochrome.

Clete stepped toward him. I put my hand on his chest.

'What the fuck y'all know?' Sweet Pea said. 'Y'all ever hear there's a glow hanging over the ground at night on the Bertrand place? Where all them convicts was killed and buried in their chains. You t'ink you shit vanilla ice cream?'

'You're not making much sense, Sweet Pea,' I said.

'The juke where I bring my broads, how's it stay open? It's Bertrand's.'

'That's not true, partner. I've seen the deeds on all the land around here.'

'It's part of a con . . . a consor . . . something . . . what do you call it?' he said.

'Consortium.'

'Yeah,' he said. 'Hey, Purcel, you look like you need an enema. Why don't you shove that gun up your ass?'

Clete took a Lucky Strike out of his pocket and lit it. Then he pulled a strand of tobacco off his lip and dropped it in the air. The lighted windows of the Amtrak streamed by on the train tracks across the cane field. Sweet Pea sat on the log and looked at the train and scratched his cheek as though we were no longer there.

'You got a lot of luck, Sweet Pea,' I said.

'Yeah? Tell your wife I got an opening. For an older broad like that, I'll make an exception, too. Just straight dates, no sixty-nines,' he said.

I dream that night of people who live in caves under the sea. Their arms and shoulders are sheathed in silver feathers; their abalone skins dance with fiery sparks.

I once knew a helicopter pilot from Morgan City whose Jolly Green took an RPG right through the door. He had been loaded with ammunition and wounded civilians, and when they crashed in the middle of a river, most of the civilians burned to death or drowned. He became psychotic after the war and used to weigh and sink plastic statues of Jesus all over the waterways of southern Louisiana. He maintained that the earth was wrapped with water, that a bayou in the Atchafalaya Basin was an artery that led to a flooded rice plain in the Mekong Delta, that somehow the presence of a plastic statue could console those whose drowned voices still spoke to him from the silt-encrusted wreckage of his helicopter.

When he hung himself, the wire service story made much of his psychiatric history. But in my own life I had come to believe in water people and voices that can speak through the rain. I wondered if Sonny would speak to me.

It was a blue-gold morning, the sky clear, the wind balmy out of the south, when the sheriff parked his cruiser by the boat ramp and walked down the dock. I was shirtless, sanding dried fish scales out of the guardrail, the sun warm on my back, the day almost perfect. I didn't want to hear about someone else's troubles, their guilt, or even an apology for wrongs real or imagined.

'We've got Patsy Dapolito in lockup,' he said.

'That seems like a good place for him.'

'He says somebody stole the tip he left in the motel restaurant. He made quite a scene. Scared the shit out of everybody in the place. This guy is probably as close to Freddy Kruger as New Iberia will ever get.'

I drew the sandpaper along the grain of the wood and brushed the dust out into the sunlight.

'It doesn't concern you anymore, huh?' the sheriff said.

'Not unless he comes around here.'

'I wish I could tell you it's that easy, Dave.'

I started sanding again, my eyes on his.

'The FBI called yesterday. They thought you were still with us.' He shrugged off the discomfort of his own remark. 'They've got a tap on some of Johnny Carp's people. Your name came up in a conversation.'

'I'm not a player anymore, Sheriff. Maybe it's time you and the Feds got the word out.'

'The greaseballs think you know something you shouldn't. Or you're trying to queer their action over here.'

'They're wrong.'

'One of them said, "Let the Rambo fucks take care of it." They laughed, and another guy said, "Yeah, let 'em send in Charlie." Does that mean something to you?'

'Yeah, it does. I was fired. Y'all clean up your own mess.'

'I don't think anger will help us, Dave.'

'When a drunk gets eighty-sixed out of a bar, he's not supposed to buy drinks for the people still inside. You want a cup of coffee, Sheriff?'

Clete came by at noon, drank a beer under the awning on the dock, then insisted I drive into New Iberia with him.

'I've got to work,' I said.

'That's my point,' he said, crushing his beer can, his porkpie hat cocked over his scarred eyebrow, his face full of fun.

We drove down East Main, past the old Burke home and the Steamboat House, into the shade of live oaks, past the city library and the stone grotto dedicated to Christ's mother, which was the only remnant of the old Catholic elementary school and which in antebellum days had been the home of George Washington Cable, past the law offices of Moleen Bertrand and the Shadows into the full sunlight and practicality of the business district.

Clete parked by the side of a small office on the corner. The backs of the buildings were old, redbrick, still marked with nineteenth-century lettering. Fifty yards away a tugboat moved down Bayou Teche toward the drawbridge.

Two men in tennis shoes who were too slight to be professional movers were carrying furniture from a U-Haul van into the office.

'Clete?' I said.

'Your licenses will be a breeze. Till we get the paperwork done, I'll put you down as my associate or some bullshit like that.'

'You should have asked before you did this.'

'I did. You weren't listening,' he said.

'Who're these guys?'

'Uh, a package deal from Nig Rosewater Bail Bonds. Nig owes me for a couple of skips I ran down, in fact, it was these two guys right here, and the guys owe Nig for their bonds, so Nig threw in some furniture and everybody wins.'

'Clete, I really appreciate this but—'

'It's a done deal, big mon. Tell the guys where you want your desk and file cabinets. Make sure they don't walk out of here with any keys, either.' He looked at his watch, then glanced up the street. 'Here she comes. Look, take my car back to your house when you get finished, okay? Helen's taking me to lunch.'

He saw the look in my eyes.

'So she bats from both sides of the plate. Who's perfect?' he said.

The two of them drove away, waving out the windows as I stood on the sidewalk between Clete's junker Caddy and an office window that had already been lettered with the words ROBICHEAUX, PURCEL, AND ASSOCIATES INVESTIGATIVE AGENCY.

At twilight I drove out to the Bertrand plantation and parked by the grove of gum trees. I didn't have permission to be there, and didn't care. I had wanted to believe my involvement with Sonny Boy, Julia and Moleen, Luke and Ruthie Jean and Bertie Fontenot was over. But I knew better. Even Sweet Pea Chaisson did.

This piece of land was our original sin, except we had found no baptismal rite to expunge it from our lives. That green-purple field of new cane was rooted in rib cage and eye socket. But what of the others whose lives had begun here and ended in other places? The ones who became prostitutes in cribs on Hopkins Street in New Iberia and Jane's Alley in New Orleans, sliced their hands open with oyster knives, laid bare their shin bones with the cane sickle, learned the twelve-string blues on the Red Hat gang and in the camps at Angola with Leadbelly and Hogman Matthew Maxey, were virtually cooked alive in the cast-iron sweatboxes of Camp A, and rode Jim Crow trains North, as in a biblical exodus, to southside Chicago and the magic of 1925 Harlem, where they filled the air with the music of the South and the smell of cornbread and greens and pork chops fixed in sweet potatoes, as though they were still willing to forgive if we would only acknowledge their capacity for forgiveness.

Tolstoy asked how much land did a man need.

Just enough to let him feel the pull of the earth on his ankles and the claim it lays on the quick as well as the dead.

23

Even though my name was on the window, I didn't go to the office and, in fact, didn't formally accept the partnership, even though Bootsie and I needed the income.

Not until three days later, when Clete called the bait shop.

'Check this. Johnny Carp says he wants another sit-down. Eleven o'clock, our office,' he said.

'Tell him to stay out of town.'

'Not smart, big mon.'

'Don't try to negotiate with these guys.'

'The guy's rattled about something.'

'Who cares?' I said.

'Wake up, Dave. You got no radar anymore. You read the street while you got the chance or it eats you.'

I waited until almost eleven, then drove into New Iberia. John Polycarp Giacano's white stretch limo with the charcoal-tinted windows was double-parked in front of the office. A back window was partially lowered and two women with bleached hair and Frankenstein makeup were smoking on the backseat, looking straight ahead, bored, oblivious to each other. Three of Johnny's crew, wearing shades and boxed haircuts, stood on the sidewalk, looking up and down the street as though they were Secret Service agents.

I parked around the corner and walked back to the front door. One of them looked at me from behind his glasses, his expression flat, his hands folded in front of him. He chewed on a paper match in the corner of his mouth, nodding, stepping back to let me pass.

'Is that you, Frankie?' I said.

'Yeah. How you doing, Mr Robicheaux?' he answered.

'I thought you were away for a while.'

'This broad's conscience started bothering her and she changed her testimony. What're you gonna do?' He shrugged his shoulders as though a great metaphysical mystery had been placed on them.

'It might be a good idea to move the limo, Frankie.'

'Yeah, I was just going to tell the chauffeur that. Thanks.'

'When did Charlie start working with you guys?' I asked.

He held the tips of his fingers in the air, touched his cheek, gestured with his fingers again.

'*Who?*' he said. His mouth pursed into a small O the size of a Life Saver.

Inside the office, Clete sat behind an army-surplus metal desk, his hands hooked behind his neck. Johnny Carp sat across from him, his arms and legs set at stiff angles, his eyes filled with a black light, his knurled brow like ridges on a washboard. He wore a yellow shirt with the purple letter *G* embroidered on the pocket and a gray suit with dark stripes in it, a yellow handkerchief in the pocket. His shoes were dug into the floor like a man about to leap from a building.

'Dave, help me convince Johnny of something here,' Clete said. He smiled good-naturedly.

'What's happening, Johnny?' I said, and sat down on the edge of another metal desk.

'You guys tried to cowboy Patsy Bones,' he said.

'Wrong,' I said.

'Somebody put a nine-millimeter round six inches from his head. He thinks it come from me,' Johnny said.

'I can see that would be a problem,' I said.

'Don't crack wise with me, Dave.'

'I always treated you with respect, Johnny. But I'm out of the game now. You've got the wrong guy.'

'Hear what I'm saying.' His close-set eyes and mouth and nose seemed to shrink into an even smaller area in the center of his face. 'Don't try to scam us. You want something, you got a hard-on, bring it to the table. But you lay off this voodoo bullshit or whatever it is. I'm talking about Sonny here.'

I looked at Clete. He shook his head and turned up his palms.

'You've lost me, Johnny,' I said.

'A hooker says she saw him going by on the streetcar. Last night Frankie and Marco out there swear either him or his twin brother was walking into Louis Armstrong Park. What white person goes into Louis Armstrong Park at night? Then my wife tells me a redheaded guy was standing in our side yard, looking through our window.' A smile tugged at the corner of his mouth. 'What, y'all hire an actor or something?' Then his eyes clicked away from mine.

'Nope,' I said.

He wiped the front of his teeth with his index finger, rubbed it dry on his knee. His gaze roved around the room.

'This place is a shithole,' he said.

'Sonny's dead,' Clete said. 'You put the whack out, you ought to know, John.'

'You're a Magazine Street mick, Purcel, it ain't your fault you always got your foot up your own ass, so I don't take offense,' Johnny said. 'But, Dave, you got a brain. I'm asking you, no, I'm begging you, if you guys are trying to cowboy Patsy, or fuck with me, or fuck with anybody in my crew, stop it now. I'm in legitimate business. We put a lot of the old ways behind us, but don't provoke me.'

423

His words were those of a man in control. But I could smell a peculiar odor on his breath, like sour baby formula laced with booze.

'It's not us,' I said.

'The guy was a disease. Nobody else cared about him,' he said.

'Sonny was stand-up, Johnny. He took his own bounce and he didn't need Scotch and milk and a couple of chippies to get him through the morning,' I said.

Clete lit a cigarette with his Zippo, his broad shoulders hunched, seemingly unconcerned about the drift of the conversation, but through the smoke his eyes were fastened on Johnny's neck.

'You've developed a bad mouth, Dave. I'm here for accommodation, you don't want to listen, fuck you. Just don't try to run no games on me,' Johnny said.

'The problem's inside you, John. It's not with me or Clete.'

'You got an office and some furniture Nig Rosewater couldn't give away in colored town and you're a shrink now?'

'You've got blood on your hands. It doesn't wash off easily,' I said.

He rose from his chair, slipped two twenty-dollar bills out of his wallet, and laid them on Clete's desk.

'Y'all go up the street, have a nice lunch,' he said, and walked out into the sunlight.

Clete tipped his cigarette ashes in the tray. Then he scratched his eyebrow with his thumbnail, as though he didn't know which thought in his head to express first. 'You nailed him on that stuff about his chippies. He pays them a hundred bucks to blow him so he won't get AIDS,' he said. He tilted back in his swivel chair and stared at the wall. 'I can't believe this, the first person in our office is a psychotic greaseball.' He mashed out his cigarette and went outside with the two twenties wadded in his fist.

He caught the limo just as it was leaving the curb and knocked with his ring on the charcoal-tinted glass. Johnny Carp was bent forward on the seat when he rolled down the window, a smear of milk on his mouth.

'Hey, John, give this to your broads for their oral hygiene,' Clete said, and bounced the bills like soiled green Kleenex off Johnny Carp's face.

I cut the engine on the outboard and Alafair and I drift on the wake into a sandbar, then walk toward a line of willow and cypress trees. The sun is white, straight overhead, in a blue, cloudless sky. Behind the lacy movement of the trees, in a trapped pool of water, is the rusted, purple outline of a wrecked tow barge. I set up a cardboard box at the end of the sandbar, walk back to the boat, and unzip the carrying case from the Beretta nine-millimeter.

Once again, I show her the safeties and how the trigger mechanism disengages from the hammer, let her work the slide; then I take it from her and slip an empty magazine into the butt.

'Okay, what's the rule, Alf?' I say.

'Never assume a gun is unloaded. But never assume it's loaded, either.'

'You've got it. Do you remember how to clear the action?'

She pushes the release button on the butt, drops the magazine, works the slide twice, then peers into the empty chamber.

'Terrific,' I say.

This time I give her a loaded magazine. I stand behind her while she chambers a round and takes aim with both hands. She fires once and throws sand in the air by the side of the cardboard box.

'Aim a little higher and to your right, Alf.'

She misses twice and the rounds *whang* into the barge back in the trees. But the next round leaves a hole the size of a pencil in the cardboard. She starts to lower the pistol.

'Keep shooting till you're empty, Alf.'

The Beretta spits the empty casings into the sunlight, *pow, pow, pow*, each report echoes across the water. The breech locks open; a tongue of cotton white smoke rises from the chamber. The box is tilted sideways now, its clean surfaces peppered with black holes.

When Alafair smiles at me, I wonder if I have given away a knowledge that should never belong to a child.

She wants to reload.

It rained in the predawn hours this morning and the trees in the swamp were gray and shaggy with mist. Then the sun rose out of the steam and broke against the seal of clouds like a flattened rose.

I drop into the office on Main, a sojourner, still not quite accepting the reality of being a fired cop. The door is open to let in the clean smell of the rain tumbling out of the sunlight.

Clete is hooking paper clips in a chain on his desk blotter. I can feel his eyes flicking back and forth between his preoccupation and the side of my face.

'When you chase skips, you've got latitude no cop does,' he says. 'You can cross state lines, bust in doors without a warrant, pick up one perp to squeeze another. The Supreme Court will get a hand on it eventually, but right now it's kind of like being on point in a free-fire zone.'

He knows I'm not listening, but he continues anyway.

'We'll have a secretary in here tomorrow. I'm transferring some of the business from the New Orleans office. It just takes a while to make things come together,' he says.

I nod absently, try to avoid looking at my watch.

'You bother me, big mon,' he says.

'Don't start it, Clete.'

'It's not Sonny's death. It's not getting canned from your department, either. Even though that's what you want me to think.'

'I'm not up to it.' I splay my fingers in the air.

'The big problem is one that won't go away, Dave. You can't accept change. That's why you always got a firestorm inside you, that's why you ripped up Patsy Dap. You got to ease up, noble mon. You don't have a shield anymore. You smoke the wrong dude, you go down on a murder beef. Take it from a cat who's been there.'

'I think I'll go back to the bait shop now,' I say.

'Yeah, I guess you better.'

'I apologize for my attitude. You've been a real friend about this partnership.'

'No big deal. My business in New Orleans is going down the drain, anyway.'

Outside, the rain is blowing in the sunlight. When I look back through the office window, Clete is drinking coffee, staring at nothing, alone in the silence, a new, virtually unused white telephone on his army surplus desk.

I feel a pain in my chest and go back inside the office. Together, we walk down Main to Victor's for lunch.

Johnny Carp had made a pilgrimage to New Iberia, his second attempt at reconciliation. He was a mercurial headcase, a functioning drunk, a physiological caricature, a libidinous nightmare whose sexual habits you tried never to think about, but, most important, Johnny, like all drunks, was driven by a self-centered fear that made his kind see blood in tap water and dead men walking out of the surf.

I called Helen Soileau at the sheriff's department.

'What's the deal on Patsy Dapolito?' I asked.

'He has a rental dump by a pipeyard on the Jeanerette Road. Somebody popped one right through his bedroom window.'

'It was a nine-millimeter?'

'Or a .38. It was pretty beat up. Why?'

'Johnny Carp thinks Sonny was the shooter.'

'Big reach from the salt.' She paused. 'Sorry,' she said.

'Sonny's nine-millimeter is still in Possessions, isn't it?' I said.

'I hate to admit this, but I asked that question myself. No.'

'What happened to it?'

'We didn't charge him with carrying a concealed weapon because we busted him in Orleans Parish. So when he skated on the murder beef, he was home free and got his nine back. A Smith & Wesson, right?'

'What's the status on Dapolito?'

'We painted his doorknobs with roach paste so he can't go outside. Come on, Dave, what status? Even New Orleans doesn't know how to deal with this guy. We get three or four calls a day on him. He took a leak in the washbasin at Mulate's.'

'Thanks for your help, Helen.'

'It's not right what the old man did. I told him what I thought, too.'

'You shouldn't take my weight.'

She was quiet, as if she was deciding something, perhaps a choice about trust, which was always Helen's most difficult moment.

'I've got an awful feeling, Streak. It's like somebody put out a cigarette on my stomach lining. I get up in the morning with it.'

'Feeling about what?'

'They tore Della Landry apart with their bare hands. They took down

426

Sonny Marsallus in broad daylight. You watch your butt, you understand me?'

'Don't worry about me.'

I heard her hand clench and squeak on the receiver.

'I'm not explaining myself well,' she said. 'When I dropped those two perps, I saw my face on theirs. That's how I feel now. Do you understand what I'm talking about?'

I told her it was her imagination, to get away from that kind of thinking. I told her Batist was waiting for me down at the dock.

My answer was not an honest one.

Later, I sat in the backyard and tried to convince myself that my evasiveness was based on concern for a friend. A physician turns his eyes into meaningless glass, shows no expression when he listens through a stethoscope, I told myself. But that wasn't it. Her fear, whether for me or herself, had made me angry.

When you buy into premonitions, you jinx yourself and everyone around you. Ask anyone who's smelled its vinegar reek in the man next to him.

I remembered a helicopter hovering against a fiery red ball that could have been heated in a devil's forge, its blades thropping monotonously, the red dust and plumes from smoke grenades swirling into the air. But for those of us who lay on poncho liners, our wounds sealed with crusted field dressings and our own dried fluids, the dust was forming itself into an enormous, animate shape – domed, slack-jawed, leering, the nose a jagged hole cut in bone, a death's head that ballooned larger and larger above the clearing and called our names through the churning of the blades, the din of voices on the ground, the popping of small-arms fire that was now part of somebody else's war, just like the watery sound of a human voice speaking into an electric fan.

And if you did not shut out the syllables of your name, or if you looked into the face of the man next to you and allowed the peculiar light in his eyes to steal into your own, your soul could take flight from your breast as quickly as a dog tag being snipped onto a wire ring.

The sheriff called me early the next morning.

'I can't just deal you out, Dave. You need to be told this,' he said.

'What?'

'Sweet Pea and a black woman. We're not sure who she is yet.'

'Could you start over?' I said.

During the night a farmer had seen a cone of fire burning in an oak grove out by Cade. The heat was so intense the trees were scaled and baked into black stone. After the firemen covered the Cadillac with foam and stared through the smoke still billowing off the exploded tires, they made out the carbonized remains of two figures sitting erectly on the springs of the front seat, their lipless mouths wide with secrets that had risen like ash into the scorched air.

'The pathologist says double-ought bucks,' the sheriff said.

But he knew that was not the information I was waiting for.

'Sweet Pea had on a locket with his mother's name engraved on it,' he said. Then he said, 'I don't have any idea who she is, Dave. Look, I've already tried to find Ruthie Jean. She's disappeared. What else can I tell you? I don't like making this damn phone call.'

I guess you don't, I thought.

24

I called Clete at the small house he had rented by City Park and asked him to meet me at the office on Main. When I got there the newly hired secretary was hanging a curtain on the front window. She was a short, thick-bodied blond woman, with orange rouge on her cheeks and a pleasant smile.

'Clete didn't get here yet?' I said.

'He went for some coffee. Are you Mr Robicheaux?'

'Yes. How do you do? I'm sorry, I didn't get your name.'

'Terry Serrett. It's nice to know you, Mr Robicheaux.'

'You're not from New Iberia, are you?'

'No, I grew up in Opelousas.'

'I see. Well, it's nice meeting you,' I said.

Through the window I saw Clete crossing the street with a box of doughnuts and three sealed paper cups of coffee. I met him at the door.

'Let's take it with us,' I said.

He drove with one hand and ate with the other on the way out to Cade. The top was down and his sandy hair was blowing on his forehead.

'How are you going to pay a secretary?' I said.

'She works for five bucks an hour.'

'That's five bucks more than we're making,' I said.

He shook his head and smiled to himself.

'What's the joke?' I asked.

'We're going out to see where Sweet Pea Chaisson got turned into a human candle.'

'Yeah?'

'Are we on somebody's clock? Am I a dumb shit who's missed something?'

'You want to go back?'

He set his coffee cup in a wire ring that was attached to his dashboard and tried to put on his porkpie hat without losing it in the wind.

'You think they're wiping the slate clean?' he said.

'Their object lessons tend to be in Technicolor.'

'Why the black woman?'

'Wrong place, wrong time, maybe. Unless the dead woman is Ruthie Jean Fontenot.'

'I don't get it. Black people keep showing up in the middle of all this bullshit. Let's face it, mon. Ripping off the food stamp brigade isn't exactly the big score for those guys.'

'It's land.'

'For what?'

I didn't have an answer.

We drove down a gravel road through sugar and cattle acreage, then turned into an empty field where a section of barbed wire fence had been knocked flat. The weeds in the field were crisscrossed with tire tracks, and in the distance I could see the oak grove and a bright yellow strand of crime scene tape jittering in the wind.

Clete parked by the trees and we got out and walked into the shade. The fire-gutted, lopsided shell of Sweet Pea's convertible was covered with magpies. I picked up a rock and sailed it into the frame; they rose in an angry clatter through the leafless branches overhead.

Clete fanned the air in front of his face.

'I don't think the ME got everything off the springs,' he said.

'Look at this,' I said. 'There's glass blown into the backseat and a partial pattern on top of the door.' I inserted my little finger into a ragged hole at the top of the passenger door, then looked at the ground for empty shell casings. There weren't any.

'What a way to get it,' Clete said.

'You can see the angle of fire,' I said. 'Look at the holes in the paneling just behind the driver's seat.' I aimed over the top of my extended arm and stepped backward several feet. 'Somebody stood just about where I'm standing now and fired right into their faces.'

'I don't see Sweet Pea letting himself get set up like this,' Clete said.

'Somebody he trusted got in the backseat. Another car followed. Then the dice were out of the cup.'

'I got to get out of this smell,' Clete said. He walked back into the sunlight, spit in the weeds, and wiped his eyes on his forearm.

'You all right?' I said.

'In 'Nam I saw a tank burn. The guys inside couldn't get out. I don't like remembering it, that's all.'

I nodded.

'So I probably signed Sweet Pea's death warrant when I put him in the trunk of my car,' he said. 'But that's the breaks, right? One more piece of shit scrubbed off the planet.' With his shoe he rubbed the place where he had spit.

'You blaming yourself for the woman?' I asked.

He didn't have time to answer. We heard a car on the gravel road. It slowed, then turned through the downed fence and rolled across the field, the weeds rattling and flattening under the bumper.

'I know that guy, what's his name, he thinks we should be buddies because we were both in the Crotch,' Clete said.

'Rufus Arceneaux,' I said.

'Oh, oh, he doesn't look like he wants to be friends anymore.'

Rufus cut the engine and got out of the car. He wore tight blue jeans and a faded yellow polo shirt and his pilot's sunglasses, with his badge and holster clipped on a western belt. A small black boy of about ten, in an Astros baseball cap and oversize T-shirt, sat in the backseat. The windows were rolled up to keep the air-conditioning inside the car. But the engine was off now and the doors were shut.

'What the hell do you think you're doing?' Rufus said.

'The sheriff called me this morning,' I said.

'He told you to come out here?'

'Not exactly.'

'Then you'd better get out of here.'

'Did y'all find out who the broad was?' Clete said.

'It's not your business, pal,' Rufus said.

'*Pal*. Terrific,' Clete said. 'Who's the kid? He looks like he's about to melt.'

'Did y'all find any shell casings?' I said, and opened the back door to Rufus's car and brought the little boy outside. There was a dark, inverted V in his blue jeans where he had wet his pants.

'I don't know what it is with you, Robicheaux,' Rufus said. 'But, to be honest, I'd like to beat the living shit out of you.'

'What are you doing with the boy?' I said.

'His mother didn't come home. I'm taking him to the shelter. Now, y'all get the fuck out of here.'

I squatted down on my haunches and looked into the little boy's face. His upper lip was beaded with sweat.

'Where do you live, podna?' I asked.

'In the trailer, up yonder on the road.'

'What's your mama's name?'

'Gloria Dumaine. They call her "Glo" where she work.'

'Does she work at the juke?' I said.

'Yes, suh. That's where she gone last night. She ain't been back.'

I stood erect and put my fingers lightly on Rufus's arm, turned him toward the trees. I saw the skin stretch tight at the corners of his eyes.

'Walk over here with me,' I said.

'What . . .'

'I know his mother,' I said. 'She knew something about the decapitated floater we pulled out of the slough in Vermilion Parish. I think she was in the car with Sweet Pea.'

He removed his sunglasses, his eyes looking from the burned Caddy to the little boy. His mouth was a tight seam, hooked downward at the corners, his expression wary, as though a trap were being set for him.

'Take the little boy to the shelter. I'll call the sheriff and tell him what I told you,' I said.

'I'll handle it from here,' he said.

I walked over to Clete's convertible and got inside.

'Let's hit it,' I said.

As we drove across the field toward the gravel road, I looked back toward the oak grove. Rufus was squatting on his haunches, smoking a cigarette, staring at the scorched hulk in the trees, a man whose keen vision could snap the twine off Gordian knots. The little boy stood unnoticed and unattended in the sunlight, like a black peg tamped into the weeds, one hand trying to hide the wetness in his jeans.

They had killed Sweet Pea and Gloria. Who was next? I didn't want to think about it.

I drove to the office on Main with Clete, then walked down to Moleen Bertrand's law offices across from the Shadows. His secretary told me he had gone home for lunch. I drove across the drawbridge, past the old graystone convent, which was now closed and awaiting the wrecking ball, and followed the winding drive through City Park to Moleen's deep, oak-shaded lawn and rambling white house on Bayou Teche.

Julia was spading weeds out of a rosebed by the driveway, a conical straw hat on her head. She looked up and smiled at me as I drove by. Her shoulders were tan and covered with freckles and the skin above her halter looked dry and coarse in the sunlight. Behind her, balanced in the St Augustine grass, was a tall highball glass wrapped with a napkin and rubber band.

Moleen was eating a tuna fish sandwich on a paper plate inside the Plexiglas-enclosed back porch. He looked rested, composed, his eyes clear, almost serene. Outside, blue hydrangeas bloomed as big as cantaloupes against the glass.

'I'm sorry to bother you at home,' I said.

'It's no bother. Sit down. What can I do for you? You want something to eat?'

'You're looking good.'

'I'm glad you approve.'

'I'm not here to give you a bad time, Moleen.'

'Thank you.'

'Did you hear about a guy named Sweet Pea Chaisson getting whacked out by Cade?'

'I'm afraid not.'

'A black woman died with him.'

He nodded, the sandwich in his mouth. His eyes were flat. Against the far wall was a mahogany-and-glass case full of shotguns and bolt-action rifles.

'Call it off,' I said.

'What?'

'I think you have influence with certain people.'

'I have influence over no one, my friend.'

'Where's Ruthie Jean?'

'You're abusing my hospitality, sir.'

'Give it up, Moleen. Change your life. Get away from these guys while there's time.'

His eyes dropped to his plate; the ball of one finger worked at the corner of his mouth. When he looked at me again, I could see a nakedness in his face, a thought translating into words, a swelling in the voice box, the lips parting as though he were about to step across a line and clasp someone's extended hand.

Then it disappeared.

'Thanks for dropping by,' he said.

'Yeah, you bet, Moleen. I don't think you picked up on my purpose, though.'

'I didn't?' he said, wiping his chin with a linen napkin, his white shirt as crinkly and fresh as if he had just put it on.

'I have a feeling me and Clete Purcel might be on somebody's list. Don't let me be right.'

He looked at something outside, a butterfly hovering in a warm air current against the glass.

'Read *Faust*, Moleen. Pride's a pile of shit,' I said.

'I was never theologically inclined.'

'See you,' I said, and walked out into the humidity and the acrid reek of the chemical fertilizer Julia was feverishly working into her rosebushes.

But my conversation with him was not over. Two hours later he called me at the bait shop.

'I don't want to see you or your friend harmed. That's God's honest truth,' he said.

'Then tell me what you're into.'

'Dave, take the scales off your eyes. We don't serve flags or nations anymore. It's all business today. The ethos of Robert E. Lee is as dead as the world we grew up in.'

'Speak for yourself.'

He slammed the receiver down.

It was hot and dry that night, and through the bedroom I could see veins of heat lightning crawl and flicker through the clouds high above the swamp. Bootsie woke and turned toward me. The window fan made revolving shadows on her face and shoulders.

'Can't you sleep?' she said.

'I'm sorry, I didn't mean to wake you.'

'Are you worried about our finances?'

'Not really. We're doing okay.'

She placed one arm across my side.

'The department did you wrong, Dave. Accept it and let it go. We don't need them. What do you call that in A.A.?'

'Working the Third Step. But that's not it, Boots. I think Johnny Giacano or these military guys are starting to take people off the board.'

'They'd better not try it around here,' she said.

I looked into her face. It was calm, without anger or any display of self-manufactured feeling. Then she said, 'If one of those sonsofbitches tries to harm anyone in this family, he's going to think the wrath of God walked into his life.'

I started to smile, then looked at the expression in her eyes and thought better of it.

'I believe you, kiddo,' I said.

'Kiddo, yourself.' she answered.

She tilted her head slightly on the pillow and moved her fingers on my hip. I kissed her mouth, then her eyes and hair and ran my hands down her back.

Bootsie never did anything in half measures. She closed the door that gave onto the hallway – in case Alafair got up from bed and went into the kitchen for a drink of water – then pulled off her nightgown and stepped out of her panties in front of the window. She had the smoothest complexion of any woman I'd ever known, and in the spinning shadows of the window's fan's blades the curves and surfaces of her body looked like those of a perfectly formed statue coming to life against a shattering of primordial light.

I moved on top of her and she hooked her legs inside mine and pressed her palms into the small of my back, buried her mouth in my neck, ran her fingers up my spine into my hair, rolled her rump in a slow circle as her breath grew louder in my ear and her words became a single, heart-twisting syllable: 'Dave . . . Dave . . . Dave . . . oh Dave . . .'

It started to rain outside, unexpectedly, the water sluicing hard off the roof, splaying in front of the window fan. The wind-stiffened branches of the oak tree seemed to drip with a wet light, and I felt Bootsie lock her arms around my rib cage and draw me deeper inside her, into coral caves beneath the sea where there was neither thought nor fear, only an encompassing undulating current that rose and fell as warmly as her breast.

I had wired my house with a burglar alarm system that I couldn't afford and had taught my thirteen-year-old daughter how to use a weapon that could turn an intruder into potted meat product.

I also had dragged my insomnia and worry into the nocturnal world of my wife.

Who was becoming the prisoner of fear? Or, better put, who was allowing himself to become a spectator while others wrote his script?

Early Saturday morning Clete took one of my outboards down the bayou, with his spinning rod and a carton of red wigglers, and came back with a stringer of bream and sun perch that he lifted out of his cooler like a heavy, gold-green ice-slick chain. He knelt on the planks in the lee of the bait shop and began cleaning them in a pan of bloody water, neatly half-mooning the heads off at the gills.

'You should have gone out with me,' he said.

'That's like inviting the postman for a long walk on his day off,' I said.

He put an unlit cigarette in his mouth and smiled. The fish blood on his fingers made tiny prints on the cigarette paper.

'You look sharp, big mon. How about I take y'all to Possum's for lunch?' he said.

'Not today . . . I'm going to New Orleans in a few minutes. I told Bootsie you might hang around a little bit.'

He got to his feet and washed his hands under a faucet by the rail.

'What are you up to, Streak?'

'I'm tired of living in a bull's-eye.'

'Who's going to cover your back, mon?' he said, drying his hands on a rag.

'Thanks for watching the house,' I said, and walked back up the dock to my truck. When I looked in the rearview mirror, he was leaning against the dock rail, his face shadowed by his hat, one hand propped on his hip. The wind was hot blowing across the swamp and smelled of beached gars and humus drying in the sunlight. Just as I started my truck, the shadows of large birds streaked across the surface of the bayou. I looked into the sky and saw a circle of buzzards descending out of their pattern into the cypress, their wings clattering for balance just before they lighted on their prey.

There are a lot of ways to see New Orleans. At the right time of day the Quarter is wonderful. A streetcar ride up St Charles Avenue through the Garden District, past Audubon Park and Tulane, is wonderful anytime. Or you can try it another way, which I don't recommend.

Those who feed at the bottom of the food chain – the hookers, pimps, credit card double-billers, Murphy artists, stalls and street dips – usually work out of bars and strip joints and do a relatively minor amount of damage. They're given to the classical hustle and con and purloined purse rather than to physical injury.

One rung up are the street dealers. Not all of them, but most, are black, young, dumb, and carry a Jones themselves. The rock they deal in the projects almost guarantees drug-induced psychosis; anything else they sell has been stepped on so many times you might as well try to get high huffing baby laxative or fixing with powdered milk.

In another category are people who simply deal in criminal finance. They're usually white, older, have few arrests and own legitimate businesses of some kind. They fence stolen property, operate chop shops, and wash stolen and counterfeit money, which sells for ten to twenty cents on the dollar, depending on its origins or quality.

Then there is the edge of the Quarter, where, if you're drunk or truly unlucky, you can wander out of a controlled and cosmetic libertine environment into a piece of moral moonscape – Louis Armstrong Park or the St Louis cemeteries will do just fine – where kids will shoot a woman through the face at point-blank range for amounts of money you could pry out of a parking meter with a screwdriver. The murders receive national attention when the victim is a foreign tourist. Otherwise, they go on with unremarkable regularity, to the point that Louisiana now has the highest murder rate per capita in the United States.

Those at the top of the chain – dealers who form the liaison between Colombia and the wetlands, casino operators who front points for a Mafia-owned amusement company in Chicago – seldom do time or even have their names publicly connected with the forces they serve. They own newspaper people and literally employ the governor's children. Floating casino owners with state legislators on a pad work their shuck on morning television shows like good-natured Rotarians; Mafiosi who some think conspired to kill John Kennedy tend their roses and dine unnoticed in downtown restaurants.

It's not exaggeration.

I took the tour, thinking I could find information in the streets of New Orleans that had eluded me at home, and came up empty. But what should I have expected? Back alley hypes, graduates of City Prison, and prostitutes with AIDS (one of whom, with a haunted look in her eyes, asked me if the stories were true about this place called Lourdes) were people whose idea of a successful scam was to drill holes in their electric meters and pour honey inside so ants would foul and retard the mechanism or, more indicatively of the fear that defined their lives, wondered daily if the Mexican tar and water they watched bubbling in a heated spoon was not indeed the keyhole to the abyss where all the hungry gargoyles and grinding sounds of their childhoods awaited them.

It rained at dusk and I sat under the pavilion at the Café du Monde and ate a plate of beignets with powdered sugar and drank coffee *au lait*. I was tired and wet and there was a hum, a pinging sound in my head, the way your eardrums feel when you've stayed under water too long at a depth beyond your tolerance. St Louis Cathedral and the park in Jackson Square were gray in the rain, and a cold mist was blowing under the eaves of the pavilion. A young college couple with a portable stereo crossed against the light and ran breathlessly out of the rain into the cafe and sat at a table next to me. They ordered, and the boy peeled the cellophane off a musical tape and stuck it in his machine.

Anybody who grew up in south Louisiana during the fifties would remember those songs: 'Big Blue Diamond,' 'Shirley Jean,' 'Lawdy Miss Clawdy,' 'I Need Somebody Bad Tonight,' 'Mathilda,' 'Betty and Dupree,' and 'I Got the Rockin' Pneumonia and the Boogie Woogie, Too.'

I hadn't realized I was staring.

'You like those songs?' the boy said.

'Sure, you bet,' I said. 'They're hard to beat.'

'We bought them over on the corner. It's great stuff,' he said.

'I saw those guys. Cookie and the Cupcakes, Lloyd Price, Warren Storm. They used to play around here.'

They smiled and nodded, as though they were familiar with all those names, too, then tried to return to their own conversation without seeming impolite. I felt suddenly old and foolish.

I wanted to drive back home, mark off the day, forget all the faces I had looked into, erase the seared voices that could have been those of William Blake's lost souls on Lower Thames Street.

But I knew what I had to do. I was no longer a cop. My family was at risk as long as Johnny Carp thought I was a threat to one of his enterprises. I had told Moleen pride was a pile of shit. I wondered how good I would be at accepting my own admonition.

I walked back toward Esplanade, got in my truck, and headed up the entrance ramp to I–10 and Jefferson Parish. I thought I saw a chartreuse Cadillac convertible in my rearview mirror; then it disappeared in a swirl of rain.

The Giacano family had successfully controlled New Orleans for many reasons, one of which was the fact that they loved the appearance of normalcy and lived in upper-middle-class homes that didn't draw attention to their wealth. Johnny's limo stayed in a garage downtown; when he drove home from work, it was in his Lincoln. Johnny knew if there was one emotion that could overcome fear – which he instilled in his enemies with regularity – it was envy.

When whites began to flee New Orleans for Jefferson Parish and Metairie, the political base of David Duke, Johnny went with them. He joined any club he could buy his way into, pushed a basket around in the supermarket on Saturday mornings, played softball in the neighborhood park, and on Saturday nights threw huge dinners, where the tables with checkered cloths groaned with platters of pasta, sausage, meatballs, and baked lasagna, at a working-class Italian restaurant by the lake.

It was a strange evening. The rain was blowing harder now, and the swells in the lake were dark green and dimpled with rain, the causeway haloed with mist and electric lights all the way across the water to Covington, but the late sun had broken free of the clouds on the horizon and filled the western sky with a red glow like flames inside oil smoke.

It was a happy, crowded place, with wide verandas and high windows, private banquet rooms, a long railed bar, potted palms and plush maroon sofas by the cash register. I took off my seersucker coat in the men's room, dried my hair and face with paper towels, straightened my tie, tried to brush the powdered sugar from the Café du Monde off my charcoal shirt, then combed my hair and looked in the mirror. I didn't want to go back outside; I didn't want to say the words I would have to say. I had to look away from my own reflection.

Johnny was entertaining in a back room, with lacquered pine paneling and windows that gave onto the lake and the lighted sailboats that rocked in the swells. He was at the bar, in fine form, dressed in tailored, pegged gray slacks, tasseled loafers, plum-colored socks, a bright yellow dress shirt with bloodred cuff links as big as cherries. His marcelled hair gleamed like liquid plastic, his teeth were pink with wine. The hood at the door was in a jovial mood, too, and when I said, 'I got no piece, I got no shield, Max,' he smiled and answered, 'I know that, Mr Robicheaux. Johnny seen you outside. He wants you come on in and have a good time.'

I ordered a Dr Pepper and drank it five feet from where Johnny was holding a conversation with a half dozen people. My presence never registered in his face while he grinned and beamed and told a joke, rocking on the balls of his feet, his lips pursed as he neared the conclusion of his story, a clutch of fifty-dollar bills folded in a fan between his ringed fingers.

Again, I could hear a peculiar creaking sound in my head, like the weight of a streetcar pinging through steel track. I looked out the rain-streaked side window and thought I saw Clete Purcel staring back at me. When I blinked and widened my eyes, he was gone.

I finished my Dr Pepper and ordered another. I kept looking directly into Johnny's face. Finally I said it, gave recognition to his power, acknowledged my dependence on his mood and the enormous control he had over the lives of others: 'Johnny, I need a minute of your time.'

'Sure, Dave,' he said, and moved toward me along the bar, pointed toward his Manhattan glass for the bartender. 'How you doin'? You didn't bring that Irish ape, did you? Hey, just kidding. Purcel don't bother me. You ever know his mother? She was a wet-brain, used to sell out of her pants when her old man run off. Ask anybody in the Channel.'

'Can we talk somewhere?' I said.

'This is good.' Two of his hoods stood behind him, eating out of paper plates, salami and salad hanging off their lips. Their steroid-pumped upper arms had the diameter and symmetry of telephone poles inside their sports coats. 'Don't be shy. What's the problem?'

'No problem. That's what I'm saying, Johnny. I'm no threat to you guys.'

'What am I listening to here? I ever said you were a problem?' He turned to his men, a mock incredulous look on his face.

'My daughter saw a guy hanging around our house, Johnny. You think I have information, which I don't. They pulled my shield, I'm out of the game, I don't care what you guys do. I'm asking you to stay away from me and my family.'

'You hear this crazy guy?' he said to his hoods. Then to me, 'Eat some dinner, drink some wine, you got my word, anybody bother you with anything, you bring it to me.'

'I appreciate your attitude, Johnny,' I said.

My palms felt damp, thick, hard to fold at my sides. I was sweating inside my shirt. I swallowed and looked away from the smile on his face.

'I accused you of something that was in the imagination. I'm sorry about that,' he said. His men were grinning now.

'Excuse me?' I said.

'A redheaded guy, looked like Sonny Boy Marsallus, out at my house, walking around downtown, I asked you and Purcel if you'd hired an actor, remember?' he said.

I nodded.

'There he is,' he said, and pointed to a man in a white jacket busing a table. 'He's Sonny's cousin, a retard or something, I got him a job here. He looks just like him, except his brains probably run out his nose.'

'He looks like a stuffed head,' one of Johnny's men said.

'He'd make a great doorstop,' the other man said.

'Why was he at your house?' I said. The skin of my face burned and my voice felt weak in my throat.

'He was looking for a job. He'd been out there with Sonny once. Now he's making six bucks an hour and tips cleaning slops. So I done a good one for Sonny.'

One of the men behind Johnny gargled with his drink.

'Salt water's good for the throat,' he said to me. 'Take a glass-bottom boat ride, Robicheaux, ask Sonny if that ain't true.'

Johnny stripped a folded fifty out of the fan in his hand and dropped it on my forearm.

'Get something nice for your daughter,' he said. 'You done the right thing here tonight.' He reached out with one hand and adjusted the knot in my tie.

I saw the balloon of red-black color well up behind my eyes, heard a sound like wet newspaper ripping in my head, saw the startled and fearful look in his face just before I hooked him above the mouth, hard, snapping my shoulder into it, his nose flattening, his upper lip splitting against his teeth. I caught him again on the way down, behind the ear, then brought my knee into his face and knocked his head into the bar.

I kept waiting for his men to reach inside their coats, to pinion my arms, but they didn't move. My breath was heaving in my chest, my hands were locked on the lip of the bar, like a man aboard ship during a gale, and I was doing something that seemed to have no connection with me. He fought to get up, and I saw my shoe bite into his chin, his ear, his raised forearm, his rib cage, I felt Johnny Carp cracking apart like eggshell under my feet.

'Mother of God, that's enough, Dave!' I heard Clete shout behind me. Then I felt his huge arm knock me backward, away from Johnny's body, which was curled in an embryonic position next to the brass bar rail, his yellow shirt streaked with saliva and blood, his fists clenched on his head.

Then Clete laced his fingers under my arm, a paper bag crushed against the contour of his palm, and drew me back toward the door with him, a pistol-grip, sawed-down double-barrel twelve-gauge pointed at Johnny's men. The only sound in the room was the service door to the kitchen flipping back and forth on its hinges. The faces of the diners were as expressionless as candle wax, as though any movement of their own would propel them into a terrible flame. I felt Clete push me out into the darkness and the cold odor of an impending electric storm that invaded the trees like a fog. He shoved the sawed-down twelve-gauge into the paper bag and threw it on the seat of his convertible.

'Oh Dave,' he said. 'Noble mon . . .' He shook his head and started his car without finishing his sentence, his eyes hollow and lustrous with a dark knowledge, as though he had just seen the future.

25

By Monday morning nothing had happened. No knock at the door from New Orleans plainclothes, no warrant cut. To my knowledge, not even an investigation in progress.

The sky was clear and blue, windless, the day warm, the sun as bright as a shattered mirror on the bayou's surface. After the early fishermen had left the dock and I had started the fire in the barbecue pit for the lunches Batist and I would sell later, I called Clete at the office on Main.

'You need me for anything?' I said.

'Not really. It's pretty quiet.'

'I'm going to work at the dock today.'

'He's coming, Dave.'

'I know.'

The priest sits next to me on the weathered planks of the bleachers by the baseball diamond at New Iberia High. The school building is abandoned, the windows broken by rocks, pocked with BB holes. The priest is a tall, gray, crewcut man who used to be a submarine pitcher for the Pelicans back in the days of the Evangeline League and later became an early member of Martin Luther King's Southern Christian Leadership Conference. Today he belongs to the same A.A. group I do.

'Did you go to the restaurant with that purpose in mind?' he asks.

'No.'

'Then it wasn't done with forethought. It was an impetuous act. That's the nature of anger.'

It's dusk and the owner of the pawn and gun shop on the corner rattles the glass in his door when he slams and locks it. Two black kids in ball caps gaze through the barred window at the pistols on display.

'Dave?'

'I tried to kill him.'

'That's a bit more serious,' he says.

The black kids cross the street against the red light and pass close to the bleachers, in the shadows, oblivious to our presence. One picks up a rock, sails it clattering through a tree next to the school building. I hear a faint tinkle of glass inside.

'Because of your friend, what was his name, Sonny Boy?' the priest says.

'I think he put the hit on Sonny. I can't prove it, though.'

His hands are long and slender, with liver spots on the backs. His skin makes a dry sound when he rubs one hand on top of the other.

'What bothers you more than anything else in the world, Dave?'

'I beg your pardon?'

'Vietnam? The death of your wife Annie? Revisiting the booze in your dreams?'

When I don't reply, he lifts one hand, gestures at the diamond, the ruined school building that's become softly molded inside the fading twilight. A torn kite, caught by its string on an iron fire escape, flaps impotently against a wall.

'It's all this, isn't it?' he says. 'We're still standing in the same space where we grew up but we don't recognize it anymore. It's like other people own it now.'

'How did you know?'

'You want absolution for what you did to this guy?'

'Yes.'

'Dave, when we say the Serenity Prayer about acceptance, we have to mean it. I can absolve sins but I can't set either one of us free from the nature of time.'

'It has nothing to do with time. It's what we've allowed them to do – all of them, the dope traffickers, the industrialists, the politicians. We gave it up without even a fight.'

'I'm all out of words,' he says, and lays his hand on my shoulder. It has the weightlessness of an old man's. He looks at the empty diamond with a private thought in his eyes, one that he knows his listener is not ready to hear.

'Come on down to the office and talk to somebody for me, will you?' Clete said when I answered the phone early the next morning. Then he told me who.

'I don't want to talk to him,' I said.

'You're going to enjoy this. I guarantee it.'

Twenty minutes later I parked my truck in front of the office. Through the window I could see Patsy Dapolito sitting in a wood chair next to my desk, his brow furrowed as he stared down at the BB game that he tilted back and forth in his hands. His face looked like stitched pink rubber molded against bone.

I walked inside and sat behind my desk. The new secretary looked up and smiled, then went back to typing a letter.

'Tell Dave what's on your mind, get his thoughts on it,' Clete said to the back of Patsy's head.

'You guys hire operatives. Maybe we can work something out,' Patsy said.

'Like work for us, you mean?' I asked.

'Nobody catches any flies on you. I can see that,' he answered, and tilted more BBs into the tiny holes of his game.

Clete widened his eyes and puffed air in his cheeks to suppress the humor in his face.

'We're not hiring right now, Patsy. Thanks, anyway,' I said.

'Who tried to peel your box?' he said.

Clete and I looked at each other.

'You didn't know your place got creeped?' He laughed, then pointed with his thumb to the safe. 'You can punch 'em, peel 'em, or burn 'em. The guy tried to do this one was a fish. He should have gone through the dial.'

Clete got up from his desk and rubbed his fingers along the prised edge of the safe, then went to the front and back doors.

'How'd the guy get in?' he said to me, his face blank.

'It's called a lock pick, Purcel,' Patsy said.

'There're no scratches,' Clete said to me.

'Maybe the safe was already damaged when you got it from Nig,' I said. But Clete was already shaking his head.

Patsy lit a cigarette, held it upward in the cone of his fingers, blew smoke around it as though he were creating an artwork in the air.

'There's a hit on me. I got a proposition,' he said.

'Tell me who Charlie is,' I said.

'Charlie? What the fuck you talking about?'

'Would you watch your language, please,' I said.

'Language? That's what's you guys got on your mind, I use bad language?' he said.

'You're a beaut, Patsy,' I said.

'Yeah? Well, fuck you. The hit's coming from Johnny Carp. You stomped the shit out of him, Robicheaux; Purcel bounced money off his face. That gives all of us a mutual interest, you get my drift?'

'Thanks for coming by,' I said.

He stood up, ground his cigarette out in an ashtray, stabbing it into the ceramic as though he were working an angry thought out of his mind.

'Marsallus ever wash up on the shore?' he said.

'No, why?' I said.

'No reason. I wish I'd been there for it. It was time somebody broke that mutt's legs.'

'Get out,' I said.

When he walked past the secretary, he drew his finger, like a line of ice water, across the back of her neck.

When I closed the bait shop that night and walked up the dock toward the house, I saw Luke Fontenot waiting for me in the shadows of the oaks that overhung the road. He wore a pair of pink slacks, a braided cloth belt, a black shirt with the collar turned up on the neck. He flipped a toothpick out onto the road.

'What's up, partner?' I said.

'Come out to the plantation wit' me.'

'Nope.'

'Ruthie Jean and me want to bring all this to an end.'

442

'What are you saying?'

'Moleen Bertrand gonna fix it so it come out right for everybody.'

'I'm afraid I'm not one of his fans, Luke.'

'Talk to my Aint Bertie. If it come from you, she gonna listen.' I could hear the strain, like twisted wire, in his throat.

'To what? No, don't tell me. Somebody's going to give y'all a lot of money. Sounds great. Except Bertie's one of those rare people who's not for sale and just wants her little house and garden and the strip Moleen's grandfather gave y'all's family.'

'You ain't got to the part that counts most.'

He rubbed a mosquito bite on his neck, looked hotly into my face.

'Moleen and Ruthie Jean?' I said.

'That's what it always been about, Mr Dave. But if it don't go right, if Aint Bertie gonna act old and stubborn . . . There's some bad white people gonna be out there. I'm between Ruthie Jean and that old woman. What I'm gonna do?'

I followed him in my truck out to the Bertrand plantation. The sky was freckled with birds, the air heavy with smoke from a trash fire, full of dust blowing out of the fields. The grove of gum trees at the end of the road thrashed in black-green silhouette against the dying sun. While he told me a story of reconciliation and promise I sat with Luke on the tiny gallery of the house from which he and Ruthie Jean had been evicted, and I wondered if our most redeeming quality, our willingness to forgive, was not also the instrument most often used to lay bare and destroy the heart.

Moleen had found Luke first, then Ruthie Jean, the latter in a motel in a peculiar area of north Lafayette where Creoles and blacks and white people seemed to traverse one another's worlds without ever identifying with any one of them. He spent the first night with her in the motel, a low-rent 1940s cluster of stucco boxes that had once been called the Truman Courts. While he made love to her, she lay with her head propped up on pillows, her hands lightly touching his shoulders, her gaze pointed at the wall, neither encouraging nor dissuading his passion, which seemed as insatiable as it was unrequited.

Then in the middle of the night he sat naked on the side of the bed, his skin so white it almost glowed, his forearms on his thighs, his confession of betrayal and hypocrisy so spontaneous and devoid of ulterior motive that she knew she would have to forgive whatever injury he had done her or otherwise his sin would become her own.

She rose to her knees, pressed him back on the pillow, then mounted him and kissed his face and throat, made love to him almost as though he were a child.

When the light broke against the window curtains in the morning and she heard the sound of diesel trucks outside, car doors slamming, people talking loudly because they didn't care if others slept or not, all the hot, busy noise of another day in the wrong part of town, she could feel the nocturnal intimacy of their time together slipping away from her, and she knew he would shower soon, drink coffee with her, be fond, even affectionate, while the attention in his eyes wandered, then begin to refocus on the world that awaited him with all the guarantees of his race and position as soon as he left the motel.

But instead he drove them to Glaveston, where they ate lunch at a hotel restaurant on the beach, rented a boat and fished for speckled trout in the deep drop-off beyond the third sandbar, walked barefoot along the edge of the surf by the old World War I fort at sunset, and on a whim flew to Monterrey to watch a bullfight the next afternoon.

By the time they returned to Lafayette, Ruthie Jean believed her life had turned a corner she had not thought possible.

'He's leaving his wife?' I said.

'He give his word. He cain't stay with Miss Julia no more,' Luke said.

I didn't say anything for a long time.

'You're a smart man, Luke. Where's he going to take his law practice?'

'He sell the property, they ain't gonna have to worry.'

'I see.'

I had an indescribably sad feeling inside that I could not translate into words. Then I saw Ruthie Jean come out of Bertie's house and walk on her cane toward us. She looked beautiful. Her hair was brushed in thick swirls that curved on her high cheekbones, and the low-cut white knit dress she wore showed every undulation in her body. When she recognized me in the gloom, she went through the back door of the house.

'Are y'all staying here now?' I asked Luke.

'Yes, suh.'

'But it was Julia Bertrand who evicted y'all, wasn't it?'

He studied the grove of gum trees at the end of the road.

'So it must be with her knowledge y'all are back here. Does that make sense to you?' I said.

'Talk to Aint Bertie, Mr Dave.'

'I have too much respect for her. No offense meant. I'll see you, Luke.'

'Moleen Bertrand gonna keep his word.'

When I started my truck he was standing alone in his yard, a jailwise hustler, pulled from the maw of our legal killing apparatus, who grieved over his elderly aunt and put his trust in white people, whom a behaviorist would expect him to fear and loathe.

I wondered why historians had to look to the Roman arena for the seeming inexhaustible reservoirs of faith that can exist in the human soul.

The next evening, after I had closed the bait shop and dock, I put on my running shoes and gym shorts and worked out with my weights in the backyard. I did three sets of curls, dead lifts, and military presses, then jogged through the tunnel of trees by the bayou's edge. The sky was the color of gunmetal, the sun a crack of fire on the western horizon. I came out of the trees, the wind in my face, and headed for the drawbridge.

For some reason I wasn't even surprised when he came out of the shadows and fell in next to me, his tennis shoes powdering the dust in sync with mine, the granite head hunched down on his oily shoulders as though the neck had been surgically removed, his evenly measured breath warm with the smell of beer and tobacco.

'I saw you working out on the speed bag at Red Lerille's Gym,' he said. 'The trick's to do it without gloves.' He held out his square, blunt hands, his words bouncing up and down in his throat. 'I used to wrap mine with gauze soaked in lye water. Puts a sheath of callus on the outside like dry fish scale. The problem today is, some faggot cuts his hand on the bag, then you skin your hand on the same bag and you got AIDS, that's what these cocksuckers are doing to the country.'

'What's your problem, Pogue?'

'You gonna dime me?'

'I'm not a cop anymore, remember?'

'So the bar's open,' he said, and pointed toward a brown Nissan parked by the side of the road.

'I'm tied up.'

'I got the cooler on the backseat. Take a break, chief. Nobody's after your cherry,' he said.

Up ahead I could see the drawbridge and the bridge tender inside his little lighted house. Emile Pogue tugged his cooler out onto the road, stuck his corded forearm down into the water and melting ice, and pulled out two bottles of Coors.

'No, thanks,' I said.

He twisted off the cap on one bottle and drank it half-empty. His torso looked as taut and knurled as the skin on a pumpkin, crisscrossed with stitched scars, webbed with sinew like huge cat's whiskers above the rib cage. He worked his arms through a sleeveless, olive green shirt.

'You don't like me?' he said.

'No.'

He pinched his nostrils, flexed his lips back on his gums, looked up and down the road.

'Here's the deal,' he said. 'You put a stop to what's happening, I'll rat-fuck any greaseball you want, then I'm gone.'

'Stop what?'

'That demented guy, the one looks like a dildo you scrambled, Patsy Dapolito, he thinks Johnny Carp's got a hit on him. It ain't coming from Johnny, though.' His breath was like a slap, his body aura-ed with a fog of dried sweat and testosterone. He tapped me on the chest with his finger. 'Look at me when I'm talking to you. Sonny killed my brother. So I had a personal and legitimate hard-on for the guy.'

'I hear you.'

'But that ain't why Sonny's back.'

I stared at him, open-mouthed. His eyes had the dead quality of ball bearings. He breathed loudly through his nose.

'Back?' I said.

'Get you some Q-Tips, open up the wax. Don't tell me what I seen. Look, chief, till you been down in the bush with the Indians, done a few

445

mushrooms with these fuckers, I'm talking about on a stone altar where their ancestors used to tear out people's hearts, don't knock what somebody else tells you he sees.'

'You lost me.'

'I saw him at a camp I use out in the Atchafalaya. I looked out in the trees, inside all this hanging moss, there was a swarm of moths or butterflies, except they were on fire, then they formed a big cluster in the shape of a guy, and the guy walked right through the trunk of a tree into the water. It was Sonny Marsallus, he was burning like hundreds of little tongues of flame under the water. I ain't the only one seen it, either.'

His hand was squeezed like a huge paw around his beer bottle, his mouth an expressionless slit.

'I think we're talking about an overload of acid or steroids, Emile,' I said.

'You get word to Sonny,' he said. 'That Mennonite's words . . . they were a curse. I'm saying maybe I'm damned. I need time to get out of it.'

His breath was rife with funk, his eyes jittering, riveted on mine.

'What Mennonite?' I said.

Sometimes you pull aside the veil and look into the Pit. What follows is my best reconstruction of his words.

26

I had thirty guys strung out on the trail in the dark. It sounded like a traveling junkyard. I stopped them at the river, told the translator, Look, we got a problem here, two more klicks we're in Pinkville South, know what I'm saying, we go in, make our statement, then boogie on back across the river, the beer is five hours colder and we let the dudes from Amnesty International count up the score. In and out, that's the rhythm, none of our people get hurt, even the volunteers we took out of the last ville don't need to walk through any toe-poppers.

I'm talking to guys here who think the manual of arms is a Nicaraguan baseball player.

Look, ace, you got to understand, I didn't target the ville, it targeted itself. They were giving food to the people who were killing us. We warned them, we warned the American priest running the orphanage. Nobody listened. I didn't have no grief with the Mennonite broad. I saw her in the city once, I tipped my hat to her. I admired her. She was a homely little Dutch wisp of a thing working in a shithole most people wouldn't take time to spit on. The trouble came from a couple of liaison guys, officers who spent some time at a special school for greasers at Benning, listen, chief, I was an adviser, got me, I didn't get paid for interfering, you see these guys walk a dude into a tin shed that's got a metal bed frame in it, they close the door behind them, you'll hear the sounds way out in the jungle and pretend it's just monkeys shrieking.

Ellos! they'd yell when we came into the ville, and then try to hide. That was our name. As far as these poor bastards knew, I could have been Pancho Villa or Stonewall Jackson. Look, it got out of control. We were supposed to set up a perimeter, search for weapons, take one guy out in particular, this labor organizer, one object lesson, that's all, they used to call it a Christmas tree, a few ornaments hanging off the branches in the morning, you with me, but the guy runs inside the church and the priest starts yelling at our people out on the steps, and *pop pop pop*, what was I supposed to do, man? Suddenly I got a feeding frenzy on my hands.

You got to look at the overview to see my problem. It's in a cup of mountains, with nobody to see what's going on. That can be a big temptation. In the center of the ville is this stucco church with three little bell towers on it. The priest looks like a pool of black paint poured down the steps. The streets run off in all directions, like spokes on a wheel, and the guys did the priest are scared and start popping anybody in sight. Before I know it, they're down all the spokes, deep in the ville, the circus tent's on fire and I'm *one* fucking guy.

Geese and chickens are exploding out of the yards, pigs squealing, women screaming, people getting pulled into the street by their hair. She comes around a corner, like she's walking against a wind and it takes everything in her to keep walking toward the sounds that make most people cover their ears and hide. I ain't ever going to forget the look in her face, she had these ice blue eyes and hair like white corn silk and blood on her blouse, like it was thrown from an ink pen, but she saw it all, man, just like that whole street and the dead people in it zoomed right through her eyes onto a piece of film. The problem got made right there.

I pushed her hard. She had bones like a bird, you could hold her up against a candle and count them with your finger, I bet, and her face was a little pale triangle and I knew why she was a religious woman and I shoved her again. 'This is an accident. It's ending now. You haul your butt out of here, Dutchie,' I said.

I squeezed her arm, twisted her in the other direction, scraped her against the wall and saw the pain jump in her face. But they're hard to handle when they're light; they don't have any weight you can use against them. She pulled out of my hands, slipped past me, even cut me with her nails so she could keep looking at the things she wasn't supposed to see, that were going to mess all of us up. Her lips moved but I couldn't understand the words, the air between the buildings was sliced with muzzle flashes, like red scratches against the dark, and you could see empty shell casings shuttering across the lamplight in the windows. Then I heard the blades on the Huey before I felt the downdraft wash over us, and I watched it set down in a field at the end of this stone street and the two officers from the special school at Benning waiting for me, their cigars glowing inside the door, and I didn't have any doubt how it was going to go.

They said it in Spanish, then in English. Then in Spanish and English together. 'It is sad, truly. But this one from Holland is *communista*. She is also very *serio*, with friends in the left-wing press. *Entiede, Señor Pogue?*'

It wasn't a new kind of gig. You throw a dozen bodies out at high altitudes. Sometimes they come right through a roof. Maybe it saves lives down the line. But she was alive when they brought her onboard. Look, chief, I wasn't controlling any of it. My choices were I finish the mission, clean up these guys' shit and not think about what's down below, because the sun was over the ridges now and you could see the tile roof of the church and the body of the labor organizer hanging against the wall and Indians running around like an ants' nest that's been stepped on, or stay behind and wait for some seriously pissed-off rebels to come back into the ville and see what we'd done.

Two guys tried to lift her up and throw her out, but she fought with them. So they started hitting her, both of them, then kicking her with their boots. I couldn't take it, man. It was like somebody opened a furnace door next to my head. This stuff had to end. She knew it, too, she saw it in my eyes even before I picked her up by her shoulders, almost like I was saving her, her hands resting on my cheeks, all the while staring into my eyes, even while I was carrying her to the door, even when she was framed against the sky, like she was inside a painting, her hair whipping in the wind, her face jerking back toward the valley floor and what was waiting for her, no stopping any of it now, chief, and I could see white lines in her scalp and taste the dryness and fear on her breath, but her lips were moving again while I squeezed her arms tighter and moved her farther out into a place where nobody had to make decisions anymore, her eyes like holes full of blue sky, and this time I didn't need to hear the words, I could read them on her mouth, they hung there in front of me even while the wind tore her out of my hands and she became just a speck racing toward the earth: *You must change your way.*

27

Clete and I had breakfast the next morning at Victor's on Main. It was cool inside, and the overhead fans made shadows on the stamped tin ceiling.

'What'd he do then?' Clete said.

'Got in his car and drove away.'

'He confesses to a murder, tells you he sees flames burning under the water, then just drives away?'

'No, he repeated the Mennonite woman's words, then said, "How's that for a mind-fuck, chief?"'

The restaurant was almost empty, and a black woman was putting fresh flowers on the tables. Clete folded and unfolded his palms, bit down on the corner of his lip.

'You think Sonny's back?' I asked.

'*Back* from what? You don't come *back*. You're either alive or you're dead.'

'What set you off?'

'Nothing.'

'Look, somebody took a shot at Patsy Dap. Maybe with a nine-millimeter. Pogue says it didn't come from Johnny Carp,' I said.

His green eyes lingered on mine.

'You didn't?' I said.

'You said it a long time ago. They're all headcases. The object is to point them at each other,' he said.

'You can't orchestrate the behavior of psychopaths. What's the matter with you?'

'I did it when I had a few beers. I told you, nobody fucks my podjo.' He rolled his fork back and forth on the tablecloth, clicking it hard into the wood.

'What's worrying you?' I said.

'Pogue's a pro, he's got ice water in his veins. When's the last time a guy like that told you a dead man's trying to cap him?'

I went to a noon A.A. meeting and tried to turn over my problems to my Higher Power. I wasn't doing a good job of it. I had stomped and degraded Johnny Giacano in front of his crew, his friends and family. Were I still a police officer, I would have a marginal chance of getting away with it. But because of my new status, there was no question about the choices Johnny had before him. He would either redeem himself in an unmistakable, dramatic way or be cannibalized by his underlings.

As assassins, the Mafia has no peer. Their experience and sophistication go back to the Napoleonic wars; the level of physical violence imposed on their victims is usually grotesque and far beyond any practical need; the conviction rate of their button men is a joke.

The hit itself almost always comes about in an insidious fashion. The assassin is trusted, always has access, extends an invitation for a quiet dinner with friends, an evening at the track, a fishing trip out on the salt. The victim never suspects the gravity of his situation until, in the blink of an eye, he's looking into a face that's branded with an ageless design, lighted with energies that are not easily satiated.

I went to two meetings a day every day that week. When I got home Friday evening, Luke Fontenot was waiting for me in the bait shop.

He sat at a table in the corner, in the gloom, a cup of coffee in front of him. Batist was mopping down the counter when I came in. He looked back at me and shrugged, then dropped his rag in a bucket and went outside and lit a cigar on the dock.

'Aint Bertie got rid of her lawyer and signed a quit . . . what d'you call it?' Luke said.

'A quitclaim?'

'Yeah, that's it.'

He looked smaller in the weak light through the screened windows. His hair grew in small ringlets on the back of his neck.

'They give her twenty-five t'ousand dollars,' he said.

'Does she feel okay with that?'

'She don't want nothing to happen to me or Ruthie Jean.'

His eyes didn't meet mine. His face was empty, his mouth audibly dry when he spoke, like that of a person who's just experienced a moment for which he has little preparation.

'That lawyer from Lafayette, the one use to work for Sweet Pea Chaisson, Jason Darbonne, and some men from New Orleans come out to the place last night,' he said. 'They was standing by the gum trees, where the graves use to be, pointing out toward the train track. I went outside and ax them what they want. They say we got to be gone in thirty days, that strip of houses ain't gonna be nothing but broken bo'rds and tore-up water pipe.

'I tole them I ain't heard Moleen Bertrand tell me that, and the last I heard Moleen Bertrand own this plantation.

'One of them men from New Orleans say, "We was gonna copy you on all the documents, boy, but we didn't have your address."

'I said, "Moleen Bertrand tole my aunt she can stay on long as she likes."

'They didn't even hear me. They went on talking like I wasn't there, talking about pouring a foundation, cutting roads down to the train track, doing something with electric transformers. Then one guy stops the others

451

and looks at me. "Here's twenty dollars. Go down to the sto' and get us some cold beer. Keep a six-pack for yourself."

'You know what I said? "I ain't got my car." That's all the words I could find, like I didn't have no other kind of words, except to make an excuse for not running their errands.

'So the guy say, "Then go on in the house. You got no bidness out here."

'I said, "Moleen Bertrand done already talked to Aint Bertie. Y'all wasn't there, so maybe y'all don't know about it."

'Then the same guy, he walked real close to me, right up in my face, he was a big, blond guy with hair tonic on and muscles about to bust out of his shirt, he say, like we was the only two people on the earth and he knew exactly who he was talking to, he say, "Listen, you dumb nigger, you open your mouth again and you're gonna crawl back up those steps on your hands and knees."'

Luke raised his coffee cup, then set it back down without drinking from it. He looked through the screen window at the line of cypress trees across the bayou, at the sky above it that was like a crimson-streaked ink wash. His face had the lifeless quality of tallow.

'But that's not it, is it?' I asked.

'What ain't?'

'You've known white men like that before. You were stand-up even in the death house, Luke.'

'I called Moleen Bertrand at his office this morning. His secretary say he's in conference. I waited till eleven o'clock and called again. This time she say let me get your number. At three o'clock he still ain't called back. The next time I tried, she say he done gone for the day. I axed if he gone home. She waited a long time, then she say, No, he playing racquetball over in Lafayette.

'I knew where he play at. I was going in the front door when him and three other men was coming out, carrying canvas bags on their shoulders, their hair wet and combed, all of them smiling and stepping aside to let a lady pass.

'Moleen Bertrand shook hands with me and gone right on by. Just like that. Just like I was some black guy maybe he seen around once in a while.'

I got up from the table and turned on the string of lights over the dock. I heard Batist folding up the Cinzano umbrellas over the spool tables. Luke opened and closed his hand on a fifty-cent piece in his palm. Its edges left a circular print almost like an incision in his gold skin. I sat back down across from him.

'I don't think Moleen is in control of his life,' I said.

'He saved me from the electric chair. Didn't have nothing to gain for it, either. How come he start lying now?'

'He's involved with evil men, Luke. Get away from him.'

'I ain't worried about me.'

'I know you're not,' I said. Then I said, 'Where is she?'

'Out at the house, packing her new clothes, talking about some place in the Islands they're going to, pretending everything all right with Aint Bertie, pretending he fixing to come by anytime now.'

'I wish I had an answer for you.'

'I ain't ax you for one. I just wanted you to know something befo'hand. It ain't gonna end like Moleen want it to.'

'You'd better explain that.'

'You don't know Ruthie Jean, suh. Nobody do. Specially not Moleen Bertrand.'

He went out the screen door and walked down the dock under the string of light bulbs. I picked up the fifty-cent piece he had left for the coffee. It felt warm and moist from the pressure of his hand.

Saturday morning I was reading the newspaper on the front steps when Helen Soileau's cruiser came up the dirt road and turned in my drive. She closed the car door behind her and walked through the shade like a soldier on a mission, her dark blue slacks and starched white shirt, badge and black gunbelt and spit-shined black shoes and nickel-plated revolver as unmistakable a martial warning as the flat stare and the thick upper arms that rolled like a man's.

'Who's the in-your-face bitch-woman at your office?' she said.

'Beg your pardon?'

'You heard me, the one with the mouth on her.'

'Clete hired her. She didn't strike me that way, though.'

'Well, tell her to pull the splinters out of her ass or learn how to talk on the telephone.'

'How's life?' I said, hoping the subject would change.

'I'm working a double homicide with Rufus Arceneaux. I never quite appreciated the expression "dirt sandwich" before.'

'It sounds like you really got a jump start on the day. You want breakfast?'

She hooked one thumb in her gunbelt and thought about it. Then she winked. 'You're a sweetie,' she said.

I fixed coffee and hot milk and bowls of Grape-Nuts and blueberries for us on the picnic table in the backyard.

'There's something weird going on with Fart, Barf, and Itch,' she said. 'The RAC in New Orleans called me yesterday and asked if I'd heard anything about Sonny Boy Marsallus. I said, "Yeah, he's dead." He says, "We think that, too, but his body's never washed up. The tide was coming in when he got it."

'I say, "Think?"

'This guy is a real comedian. He says, "You remember that army-surplus character you bent out of round with your baton? Guy with a haircut like a white bowling ball, always chewing gum, Tommy Carrol? Somebody found him working late in his store last night and fried his mush."

'"Sorry, I don't remember a baton," I say.

'He thought that was real funny. He says, "Tommy Carrol did more than sell khaki underwear. He was mixed up with Noriega and some dope operations in Panama. After the ME dug him out of the ashes and opened him up, he found a nine-millimeter slug in what was left of his brain.'

'I knew what was coming but I go, "So?"

'He says, "I want to see if we got a match with the rounds from Marsallus's Smith & Wesson. Y'all still have those in your evidence locker, don't you?"

'I say, Sure, no problem, glad to do it. But guess who the department just hired to catalog evidence? Kelso's little brother threw them out.

'I called the comedian back and told him he was out of luck, then asked why he thought Marsallus could be involved. It was strange, he was quite a long time, then he said, "I guess I'd like to believe Sonny's not dead. I met him years ago in Guatemala City. He was a good guy."'

'He's heard something,' I said. 'Those ex-military guys believe Sonny's still out there.' I told her about my encounter with Emile Pogue by the drawbridge.

'Why do they want the Bertrand plantation?' she said.

'One day the country is going to bottom out and get rid of the dope trade. The smart ones are putting their money somewhere else.'

'In what?'

'You got me,' I said.

'Come back with the department.'

'The sheriff's the man.'

She grinned and didn't reply.

'What's that mean?' I said.

'He needs you. With guys like Rufus and Kelso and his brother on the payroll, give me a break. Stop thinking with your penis, Dave.' She put a spoonful of cereal and milk in her mouth.

That evening I drove past Spanish Lake and bought a Dr Pepper at a convenience store by the four corners in Cade and drank it in the cab of my truck. It had rained hard that afternoon, and the air was bright and clear and the sugarcane on the Bertrand acreage rippled in the wind like prairie grass.

I was convinced this was where the story would end, one way or another, just as it had started here when Jean Lafitte and his blackbirders had sailed up Bayou Teche under a veiled moon with their cargo of human grief.

Moleen didn't see it. His kind seldom did. They hanged Nat Turner and tanned his skin for wallets, and used their educations to feign a pragmatic cynicism and float above the hot toil of the poor whose fate they saw as unrelated to their own lives. The consequence was they passed down their conceit and arrogance like genetic heirlooms.

I wondered what it would be like to step through a window in time, into another era, into an age of belief, and march alongside Granny Lee's boys, most of them barefoot and emaciated as scarecrows, so devoted to their concept of honor and their bonnie blue flag they deliberately chose not to foresee the moment when their lives would be scattered by grapeshot like wildflowers blown from their stems.

As I finished my cold drink, I looked again at the red-tinged light on the fields and wondered if history might not be waiting to have its way with all of us.

28

Most people think it's a romantic and intriguing business. The imagination calls to mind the wonderful radio shows of the forties, featuring private investigators who were as gallant as their female clients were beautiful and cunning.

The reality is otherwise.

When I went into the office Monday morning Clete was talking to two men in their twenties who were slumped forward in their metal chairs, tipping their cigarette ashes on the floor, looking at their watches, at the secretary, at the door. One of them had three slender blue teardrops tattooed by the corner of his eye; the second man was blade-faced, his skin the color and texture of the rind on a smoked ham.

'So you guys got your bus tickets, your money for lunch, all the paperwork in case anybody stops you,' Clete said, his voice neutral, his eyes empty. 'But y'all check in with Nig soon as you arrive in New Orleans. We're clear on that, right?'

'What if Nig ain't in?' the man with the teardrops said.

'He's in,' Clete said.

'What if he ain't?'

'Let me try it another way,' Clete said. He popped a crick out of his neck, laced his fingers on his desk blotter, stared through the front window rather than address his listener. 'You're probably going to skate, even though you raped a two-year-old girl. Primarily because the child is too young to testify and the mother, who is your girlfriend, was too wiped out on acid to remember what happened. But the big factor here is Nig wrote your bond because you're willing to dime your brother, who skipped his court appearance and hung Nig out to dry for a hundred large.

'What does that all mean to a mainline con and graduate of Camp J like yourself? It means we don't have bars on the windows anymore. It also means you report in to Nig, you stay at the flop he's got rented for you, or I hunt your skinny, worthless ass down with a baseball bat.' Clete opened his palm, held it out in the air. 'Are we connecting here?'

The man with the teardrops studied his shoes, worked an incisor tooth against his lip, his eyes slitted with private thoughts.

'How about you, Troyce? Are you squared away on this?' Clete said to the second man.

'Sure.' He drew in on his cigarette, and you could hear the fire gather heat and crawl up the dry paper.

'If the woman you branded stands up, Nig will continue your bond on the appeal. But you got to get UA-ed every day. Don't come back to the halfway house with dirty urine, you okay with that, Troyce?' Clete said.

'She's not gonna stand up.'

'You boys need to catch your bus, check out the countryside between here and New Orleans,' Clete said.

The blade-faced man rose from his chair, offered his hand to Clete. Clete took it, looked at nothing when he shook it. Later, he went into the lavatory and came back out, drying his hands hard with a paper towel, his breath loud in his nose. He wadded up the towel and flipped it sideways toward the wastebasket, the unshaved back of his neck stippled with roses, as swollen against his collar as a fireplug.

An hour later I was walking toward my truck when Helen Soileau angled her cruiser out of the traffic and pulled to the curb. She leaned over and popped open the passenger door.

'Get in,' she said.

'What's wrong?'

'The old man had a heart attack. He got up to fix a sandwich at four this morning, the next thing his wife heard him crash across the kitchen table.'

'How bad is it?'

'They had to use the electric paddles. They almost didn't get him back.'

I looked through the windshield at the quiet flow of traffic on the street, the people gazing in shop windows, and felt, almost with a sense of shame, my unacknowledged and harbored resentment lift like a film of ash from a dead coal. 'Where is he now?' I asked.

'Iberia General . . . Hold on, that's not where we're going. He wants us to interview a guy in a county lockup in east Texas.'

'Us?'

'You got it, sweet cakes.'

'I need to talk with him, Helen.'

'Later, after we get back. This time we're doing it his way. Come on, shake it, you're on the clock, Streak.'

The county prison was an old, white brick two-story building just across the Sabine River, north of Orange, Texas. From the second-story reception room Helen and I could look down onto the exercise yard, the outside brick wall spiraled with razor wire, and the surrounding fields that were a shimmering violent green from the spring rains. Two guards in khaki uniforms without guns crossed the yard and unlocked a cast-iron, slitted door that bled rust from the jamb, and snipped waist and leg chains on a barefoot leviathan of a man in jailhouse whites named Jerry Jeff Hooker who trudged between them as though a cannonball were hung from his scrotum.

When the two guards, both of them narrow-eyed and cheerless piney woods crackers, brought him into the reception room and sat him down in front of a scarred wood table in front of us and slipped another chain around his belly and locked it behind the chair, which was bolted to the floor, I said it would be all right if they waited outside.

'Tell that to the nigger trusty whose arm he busted backward on a toilet bowl,' one of them said, and took up his position five feet behind Hooker.

'You want to run it by us, Jerry Jeff?' I said.

His skin was as pale as dough, his massive arms scrolled with green dragons, his pale blond eyebrows ridged like a Neanderthal's.

'I was the wheelman on the Marsallus hit,' he said. 'I testify against Emile Pogue, I walk on the vehicular homicide.'

'Wheelman?' I said.

'I drove. Emile chopped him.'

'Witnesses say there were two shooters,' Helen said.

'There was only one,' he said.

'We have trouble buying your statement, Jerry Jeff,' I said.

'That's your problem,' he said.

'You're copping to a murder beef,' Helen said.

'Marsallus ain't dead.'

I felt my heart quicken. He looked at my face, as though seeing it for the first time.

'He was still flopping around in the waves when we left,' he said. 'A guy in New Orleans, Tommy Carrol, got clipped the other night with a nine-Mike. That's Marsallus's trademark.'

'You a military man?' I said.

'Four-F,' he answered. He tried to straighten himself in his chains. His breath wheezed in his chest. 'Listen, these people here say I got to do a minimum two-bit in the Walls.'

'That doesn't sound bad for a guy who went through a red light drunk and killed a seventy-year-old woman,' I said.

'That's at Huntsville, my man, with the Mexican Mafia and the Black Guerrilla Liberation Army. For white bread it's the Aryan Brotherhood or lockdown. Fuck that.'

Helen and I let our eyes meet.

'You're jailwise but you got no sheet. In fact, there's no jacket of any kind on you anywhere,' I said.

'Who gives a shit?' he said.

'Who put out the hit?' I asked.

'Give me a piece of paper and a pencil,' he answered.

I placed my notebook and felt pen in front of him and looked at one of the guards. He shook his head.

'We need this, sir,' I said.

He snuffed down in his nose and unlocked Hooker's right wrist from the waist chain, then stepped back with his palm centered on the butt of his baton. Hooker bent over the pad and in a surprisingly fluid calligraphy wrote a single sentence, *You give me the name of the donkey you want and I'll pin the tail on him.*

'Bad choice of words,' I said, tearing the page from the pad.

'Emile used a .223 carbine. He had Marsallus trapped in a phone booth but he blew it,' he said.

'You'll rat-out Pogue to beat a two-year bounce?' I said.

His free hand rolled into a big fist, the veins in his wrist cording with blood, as though he were pumping a small rubber ball.

'I'm in the first stage of AIDS. I don't want to do it inside,' he said. 'What's it gonna be?'

'We'll think about it,' Helen said.

His nose was starting to run. He wiped it on the back of his wrist and laughed to himself.

'What's funny?' I said.

'Think about it? That's a kick. I'd do more than *think*, Muffy,' he said, his blue eyes threaded with light as they roved over her face.

'You killed my animals and birds,' she said.

He twisted his neck until he could see the guard behind him. 'Hey, Abner, get me a snot rag or walk me back to my cell,' he said.

The sheriff was in the Intensive Care unit when Helen and I visited him at Iberia General in the morning. Tubes dripped into his veins, fed oxygen into his nose; a shaft of sunlight cut across his forearm and seemed to mock the grayness of his skin. He looked not only stricken but also somehow diminished in size, shrunken skeletally, the eyes hollow and focused on concerns that floated inches from his face, like weevil worms.

I sat close to his bed and could smell an odor similar to withered flowers on his breath.

'Tell me about Hooker,' he whispered.

'It's time to let other people worry about these guys, skipper,' I said.

'Tell me.'

I did, as briefly and simply as possible.

'Say the last part again,' he said.

'He used the term "nine-Mike" for a nine-millimeter,' I said. '"Mike" is part of the old military alphabet. This guy came out of the same cookie cutter as Emile Pogue and the guy named Jack.'

He closed and opened his eyes, wet his lips to speak again. He tilted his head until his eyes were looking directly into mine. He was unshaved, and there were red and blue veins, like tiny pieces of thread, in the hollows of his cheeks.

'Last night I saw star shells bursting over a snowfield filled with dead Chinese,' he said. 'A scavenger was pulling their pockets inside out.'

'It was just a dream,' I said.

'Not just a dream, Dave.'

I heard Helen rise from her chair, felt her hand touch my shoulder.

'We should go,' she said.

'I was wrong. But so were you,' he said.

'No, the fault was mine, Sheriff, not yours,' I said.

'I squared it with the prosecutor's office. Don't let anybody tell you different.'

He lifted his hand off the sheet. It felt small and lifeless inside mine.

But I didn't go back to the office the next day. Instead, Batist and I took my boat all the way down Bayou Teche, through the vast green splendor of the wetlands, where blue herons and cranes glided above the flooded gum trees and the rusted wrecks of oil barges, into West Cote Blanche Bay and the Gulf beyond, while a squall churned like glazed smoke across the early sun.

My father, Aldous, was an old-time oil field roughneck who worked the night tower on the monkey board high above the drill platform and the sliding black waves of the Gulf of Mexico. The company was operating without a blowout preventer on the well-head, and when the bit punched into a natural gas dome unexpectedly, the casing geysered out of the hole under thousands of pounds of pressure, a spark danced off a steel surface, and the sky blossomed with a flame that people could see from Morgan City to Cypremort Point.

My father clipped his safety belt onto the Geronimo wire and jumped into the darkness, but the derrick folded in upon itself, like coat hanger wire melting in a furnace, taking my father and nineteen other men with it.

I knew the spot by heart; I could even feel his presence, see him in my mind's eye, deep below the waves, his tin hat cocked at an angle, grinning, his denim work clothes undulating in the tidal current, one thumb hooked in the air, telling me never to be afraid. Twice a year, on All Saints' Day and the anniversary of his death, I came here and cut the engines, let the boat drift back across the wreckage of the rig and quarterboat, which was now shaggy with green moss, and listened to the water's slap against the hull, the cry of seagulls, as though somehow his voice was still trapped here, waiting to be heard, like a soft whisper blowing in the foam off the waves.

He loved children and flowers and women and charcoal-filtered bourbon and fighting in bars, and he carried the pain of my mother's infidelity like a stone bruise and never let anyone see it in his eyes. But once on a duck hunting trip, after he got drunk and tried to acknowledge his failure toward me and my mother, he said, 'Dave, don't never let yourself be alone,' and I saw another dimension in my father, one of isolation and loneliness, that neither of us would have sufficient years to address again.

The water was reddish brown, the swells dented with rain rings. I walked to the stern with a clutch of yellow roses and threw them into the sun and watched a capping wave break them apart and scatter their petals through the swell.

Never alone, Al, I said under my breath, then went back into the cabin with Batist and hit it hard for home.

That night I had an old visitor, the vestiges of malaria that lived like mosquito eggs in my blood. I woke at midnight to the rumble of distant thunder, felt the chill on my skin and heard the rain tinking on the blades of the window fan, and thought a storm was about to burst over the wetlands to the south. An hour later my teeth were knocking together and I could hear mosquitoes droning around my ears and face, although none were there. I wanted to hide under piles of blankets even though my sheet and pillow were already damp with sweat, my mouth as dry as an ashtray.

I knew it would pass; it always did. I just had to wait and, with luck, I would wake depleted in the morning, as cool and empty as if I had been eviscerated and washed out with a hose.

Sometimes during those nocturnal hours I saw an electrified tiger who paced back and forth like a kaleidoscopic orange light behind a row of trees, hung with snakes whose emerald bodies were as supple and thick as an elephant's trunk.

But I knew these images were born as much out of my past alcoholic life as they were from a systemic return to the Philippines, just another dry drunk, really, part of the *guignol* that a faceless puppeteer in the mind put on periodically.

But tonight was different.

At first I seemed to see him only inside my head. He walked out of the swamp, his upper torso naked, with seaweed clinging to his ankles like serpents, his skin as bloodless as marble, his hair the same brightness and metamorphic shape as fire.

The storm burst over the swamp and I could see the pecan and oak trees flickering whitely in the yard, the tin roof on the bait shop leaping out of the darkness, wrenching against the joists in the wind. The barometer and the temperature seemed to drop in seconds, as though all the air were being sucked out of our bedroom, drawn backward through the curtains, into the trees, until I knew, when I opened my eyes, I would be inside a place as cold as water that had never been penetrated by sunlight, as inaccessible as the drop-off beyond the continental shelf.

What's the haps, Streak? he said.

You know how it is, you get deep in Indian country and you always think somebody's got iron sights on your back, I replied.

How about that Emile Pogue? Isn't he a pistol?

Why'd you play their game, Sonny? Why didn't you work with me?

Your heart gets in the way of your head, Dave. You've got a way of wheeling the Trojan horse through the gates.

What's that mean?

They want my journal. After they get it, somebody close to you will snap one into your brain pan.

Rough way to put it.

He picked my hand up by the wrist, drew it toward his rib cage.

Put your thumb in the hole, Dave. That's the exit wound. Emile caught me four times through the back.

I apologize, Sonny. I let you down.

Lose the guilt. I knew the score when I smoked Emile's brother.

We should have kept you in lockdown. You'd be alive now.

Who says I'm not? Stay on that old-time R and B, Streak. Don't stray where angels fear to tread. Hey, that's just a joke.

Wait, I said.

When I reached out to touch him, my eyes opened as though I had been slapped. I was standing in front of the window fan, whose blades were spinning in the mist that blew into the room. My hand was extended, lifeless, as though it were suspended in water. The yard was empty, the trees swollen with wind.

The sheriff had dreamed of star shells popping above the frozen white hills of North Korea. I had lied and sought to dispel his fear, as we always do when we see death painted on someone's face.

Now I tried to dispel my own.

At my foot was a solitary strand of brown seaweed.

29

I slept until seven, then showered, dressed, and ate breakfast in the kitchen. I could feel the day slowly come into focus, the predictable world of blue skies and wind blowing through the screens and of voices on the dock gradually becoming more real than the experience of the night before.

I told myself the gargoyles don't do well in sunlight.

Vanity, vanity.

Involuntarily I kept touching my wrist, as though I could still feel Sonny's damp fingers clamped around it.

'Were you walking around last night?' Bootsie said.

'A little touch of the mosquito.'

'You have anxiety about going back, Dave?'

'No, it's going to be just fine.'

She leaned over the back of my chair, folded her arms under my neck, and kissed me behind the ear. Her shampoo smelled like strawberries.

'Try to come home early this afternoon,' she said.

'What's up?'

'You never can tell,' she said.

Then she pressed her cheek against mine and patted her hand on my chest.

A half hour later Clete Purcel sat across from me in my office at the department.

'A strand of seaweed?' he said.

'Yep.'

'Dave, you were out on the Gulf yesterday. You tracked it into the house.'

'Yeah, that's probably what happened,' I said, and averted my eyes.

'I don't like this voodoo stuff, mon. We keep the lines simple. You got your shield back. It's time to stick it to Pogue and the greaseballs . . . Are you listening?'

'The problem's not coming from outside. It was already here.'

'This guy Bertrand again?'

'He's the linchpin, Clete. If he hadn't provided the opportunity, none of these others guys would be here.'

'He's a marshmallow. I saw him in the grocery the other day. His old lady was talking to him like he was the bag boy.'

'That doesn't sound right.'

'Maybe he has a secret life as a human poodle. Anyway, I got to deedee. Just keep gliding on that old-time R&B, noble mon.'

'What did you say?'

'Oh, that's just something Sonny Boy was always saying down in Guatemala,' he said, his eyes crinkling at the corners. 'I never thought I'd say this, but I miss that guy ... What's wrong?'

I spent the next two hours doing paperwork and trying to update my case files, half of which I had to recover from Rufus Arceneaux's office.

'I got no hard feelings,' he said as I was about to go back out the door.

'Neither do I, Rufus,' I said.

'We gonna work that double homicide at Cade together?' he said.

'No,' I said, and closed his door behind me.

I cleared off my desk, then covered it with all the case material I had on Johnny Giacano, Patsy Dapolito, Sweet Pea Chaisson, Emile Pogue, Sonny Boy Marsallus, the man named Jack whose decapitated body we pulled out of the slough, even Luke Fontenot – faxes, mug shots, crime scene photographs, National Crime Information Center printouts (the one on Dapolito was my favorite; while in federal custody at Marion he had tried to bite the nose off the prison psychologist).

What was missing?

A file on Moleen Bertrand.

It existed somewhere, in the Pentagon or at Langley, Virginia, but I would never have access to it. Neither, in all probability, would the FBI.

But there was another clerical conduit into the Bertrand home, a case file I should have looked at a long time ago.

Julia Bertrand's.

Helen Soileau and I spent the next hour sorting through manila folders and string-tied brown envelopes in a storage room that was stacked from the floor to the ceiling with cardboard boxes. Many were water damaged and tore loose at the bottom when you picked them up.

But we found it.

Halloween of 1983, on a dirt road between two cane fields out in Cade. Three black children, dressed in costumes, carrying trick or treat bags and jack-o'-lanterns, are walking with their grandfather toward the next house on the road. A blue Buick turns off the highway, fishtails in the dirt, scours a cloud of dust into the air. The grandfather hears the engine roar, dry clods of dirt rattling like rocks under the fenders, the tires throbbing across the baked ruts. The headlights spear through him and the children, flare into the cattails in the ditches; the grandfather believes the driver will slow, surely, pull wide toward the other side of the road, somehow abort what cannot be happening.

Instead, the driver accelerates even faster. The Buick flies by in a suck of air, a mushrooming cloud of sound and dust and exhaust fumes. The grandfather tries to close his ears as his grandchild disappears under the

Buick's bumper, sees a still-lighted and grinning jack-o'-lantern tumble crazily into the darkness.

I worked through lunch, read and reread the file and all the spiral notebook pages penciled by the original investigator.

Helen came back from lunch at 1 p.m. She leaned on her knuckles on top of my desk and stared at the glossy black-and-white photos taken at the scene. 'Poor kid,' she said.

The original accident report was brown and stiff on the edges from water seepage, the ink almost illegible, but you could still make out the name of the deputy who had signed it.

'Check it out,' I said, and inverted the page so Helen could read it.

'Rufus?'

'It gets more interesting,' I said, turning through the pages. 'A plainclothes named Mitchell was assigned the investigation. The grandfather remembered three numbers off the license plate, and the plainclothes made a match with Julia's Buick. Julia admitted she was driving her car out by Cade on Halloween night, but there was no apparent physical damage to link the car to the accident scene. The real hitch is in the old man's statement, though.'

'What?'

'He said the driver was a man.'

She rubbed the corner of her mouth with one finger, her eyes narrowing.

'The investigator, this guy Mitchell, was confused, too,' I said. 'His last note says, "Something sucks about this."'

'Mitchell was a good cop. I remember, it was about eighty-three he went to work for the Feds,' she said.

'Guess who replaced him on the case?' I said.

She studied my face. 'You're kidding?' she said.

'Our man Rufus again. Tell me, why would a cop who investigated a woman for hit-and-run vehicular homicide end up as her friend and confidant inside the department?'

'Dave, this really stinks.'

'That's not all. Later the grandfather said he didn't have on his glasses and wasn't sure about the numbers on the license plate. End of investigation.'

'You want to haul that sonofabitch in here?'

'Which one?' I said.

'Rufus. Who'd you think I meant?'

'Moleen Bertrand.'

He wasn't at his office. I drove to his home on Bayou Teche. A crew of black yardmen were mowing the huge lawn in front, raking leaves under the oaks, pruning back the banana trees until they were virtual stubs. I parked by the side garage and knocked. No one seemed to be inside. The speedboat was in the boathouse, snugged down under a tarp, wobbling in the bladed gold light off the water's surface.

'If you looking for Mr Moleen, he's out at Cade,' one of the black men said.

'Where's Miss Julia?' I asked.

'Ain't seen her.'

'Y'all look like you're working hard.'

'Mr Moleen say do it right. He ain't gonna be around for a while.'

I took the old highway out to Spanish Lake, past the restored antebellum homes on the shore and the enormous moss-strung oak trees that rippled in the breeze off the water. Then I turned down the corrugated dirt lane, under the rusted iron trellis, into the Bertrand plantation. Whoever Moleen's business partners were, they had been busy.

Bulldozers had cut swaths through the sugarcane, flattened old corn cribs and stables, splintered wild persimmon trees into torn root systems that lay exposed like pink tubers in the graded soil. I saw Moleen on horseback by the treeline, watching a group of land surveyors drive wood stakes and flagged laths in what appeared to be a roadway that led toward the train tracks.

I drove across the field, through the flattened cane, and got out of my truck. The sun was white in the sky, the air layered with dust. Moleen wore riding pants and boots and military spurs, a blue polo shirt, a bandanna knotted wetly around his neck, a short-brimmed straw hat with a tropical band. His right hand was curled around a quirt, his face dilated in the heat that rose from the ground.

'A hot day for it,' I said.

'I hadn't noticed,' he said.

A man operating a bulldozer shifted into reverse, made a turn by the treeline, and snapped a hackberry off at ground level like a celery stalk.

'I hate looking up at a man on horseback, Moleen,' I said.

'How about just saying what's on your mind?'

'After all these years, I finally figured you out.'

'With you, it always has to be an unpleasant moment. Why is that, sir?' he said, dismounting. He led his horse into the shade of the trees, turned to face me, a line of clear sweat sliding down his temple. Behind him, in the shadows, was the corn crib, strung with the scales of dead morning glory vines, where he and Ruthie Jean had begun their love affair years ago.

'I think Julia took your weight, Moleen.' He looked back at me, uncomprehending. 'When the child was run down, on Halloween night in eighty-three. You were the driver, not she.'

'I think you've lost your sanity, my friend.'

'It was a slick scam,' I said. 'A successful lie always has an element of truth in it. In that way, the other side can never figure out what's true and what's deception. Julia admitted to having driven the car that night, but y'all knew the witness said the driver was a man. So what appeared to be her honesty threw his account into question.'

'I think you need counseling. I genuinely mean that, Dave.'

'Then you got to Rufus Arceneaux and he twisted some screws on the witness. That's why you've never dumped your wife. She could get you disbarred, even sent up the road.'

His eyebrows were heavy with sweat, his knuckles white as slivers of ice on the quirt.

'I don't believe I can find adequate words to express my feelings about a man like you,' he said.

'Clean the peanut brittle out of your mouth. That child's death is on your soul.'

'Your problem is your own, sir. You don't respect the class you were born into. You look into the mirror and always see what you came from. I feel sorry for you.'

He waited, the quirt poised at his side.

'You're not worth punching out, Moleen,' I said.

I turned and walked back out into the field toward my truck, into the hot sunlight and the smell of diesel and the drift of dust from the machines that were chewing up the Bertrand plantation. My ears were ringing, my throat constricted as though someone had spit in my mouth. I heard Moleen's saddle creak as he mounted his horse. He sawed the reins and used his spurs hard at the same time, wheeling his horse and cantering toward the survey crew.

I couldn't let it go.

I walked after him through the destroyed cane, laced my hand inside the horse's bridle, felt it try to rear against my weight. The survey crew, men whose skin was a dark as chewing tobacco, paused in their work with chaining pins and transit and metal tapes, grinning good-naturedly, unsure of what was taking place.

Moleen wasn't prepared for an audience.

'If you're planning on a trip, I hope it's with Ruthie Jean,' I said.

He tried to jerk the horse's head free. I tightened my fingers inside the leather.

'Cops don't prevent crimes, they solve them after the fact,' I said. 'In this case, I'm creating an exception. Don't take either her or Luke Fontenot for granted because they're black. The person who kills you is the one at your throat before you ever know it.'

He raised his quirt. I flung the bridle from my hand, slapped his horse, and spooked it sideways among the surveyors.

I glanced back at him before I got into my truck. He was reining and soothing his horse, turning in a circle, his skin filmed with sweat and the dust that rose around him like a vortex, his face dark with shame and embarrassment.

But it was no victory. I was convinced Moleen had sold us out, was bringing some new form of evil into our lives, and there was nothing I could do about it.

An hour later I was in the Iberia Parish building permit office. All the applications for construction permits on Moleen's property had been filed by Jason Darbonne. The blueprints had the clean, rectangular lines that you associate with a high school drafting class; but they were also general in nature, and the interior seemed to be nothing more than a huge concrete pad, an empty shell, a question mark without function or purpose.

'What's the name of the company?' I asked the engineer.

'Blue Sky Electric,' he said.

'What do they do?'

'They work on electrical transformers or something,' he answered.

In small letters, in one corner of the blueprint, was the word *incinerator*.

'These plans have all the specifics of a blimp hangar,' I said.

He shrugged his shoulders.

'What's the problem?' he said.

'I wish I knew.'

Late that evening Bootsie looked out the kitchen screen into the backyard.

'Clete Purcel's sitting at our picnic table,' she said.

I went out the back door. Clete sat with his back to the house, hunched over a six-pack of Budweiser, an opened can in one hand, a Lucky Strike in the other. He wore elastic-waisted white tennis shorts, flip-flops, and a starched short-sleeve print shirt. By his foot was a cardboard box with tape across the top. The sun had dropped below my neighbor's treeline, and the sugarcane field behind my house was covered with a purple haze.

'What are you doing out here?' I asked.

'Figuring out how I should tell you something.'

I sat across from him. His green eyes were filled with an indolent, alcoholic shine. My foot accidentally hit the cardboard box under the table.

'You look like you made an early pit stop today,' I said.

'You remember those two geeks I put on the bus, the brander and the child rapist? I called Nig to see if they got there all right. Guess what? The brander's back in custody. He got to the victim and beat the living shit out of her. Of course, he asks Nig to write another bond for him. Nig tells him the guy is past his envelope, the guy's a flight risk, he's going down for sure this time, and, besides, even Nig can't stomach this barf bag any longer.

'So the barf bag gets cute, tells Nig, "Write the bond, I'll give up the guy's gonna do Purcel's buddy, what's-his-face, Robicheaux."

'Nig asks the barf bag who put him inside a whack on a cop, and the barf bag says, get this for lowlife class distinction, Patsy Dap used to piece off five-hundred-buck hits to him in the projects because Patsy thinks it's beneath him to do colored dope dealers.'

Clete drank from his beer can, looked at me over the tops of his fingers.

'Patsy's working for Johnny Carp again?' I said.

'It makes sense, mon. Patsy's a stir bug. Johnny puts Patsy back in the jar and takes you out at the same time.'

'They don't hit cops.'

'Dave, you rubbed shit in John Giacano's face in front of everybody he respects. You broke his nose and four of his ribs. A paramedic had to pry his bridge out of his throat. I didn't tell you everything the barf bucket said, either . . .

'The word is Johnny wants it in pieces, like the Giacanos did it to Tommy Fig, remember, they processed him into pork roasts and strung them from the ceiling fan in his own butcher shop, then had a big eggnog party while Tommy went spinning around in the air, except Johnny wants it to go down even worse, longer, on videotape, with an audio . . .'

Clete collapsed the aluminium beer can slowly in his huge hand, his eyes glancing away from mine uncertainly.

'Look, I need to be off the record here,' he said.

'About what?'

'I'm serious, Streak. When you operate with your shield you think too much like these Rotary cocksuckers . . . Excuse my language.'

'Will you just say it, Clete?'

He lifted the cardboard box from under the table, tore the tape, reached down inside the flaps.

'This afternoon I creeped the dump Patsy rents out on the Jeanerette Road,' he said. 'Don't worry, he was in a motel with his chippy at Four Corners in Lafayette. Dig this, big mon, a Tec-9, ventilated barrel, twenty-five-round nine-millimeter magazine, courtesy of an arms dealer in Miami who can provide them on the spot so the Jamaicans and the Cuban crazies don't have to wait on the mailman.'

He worked the action, snapped the firing pin on the empty chamber. 'It's got a "hell trigger" these guys out in Colorado make. You can fire bursts with it almost as fast as a machine gun. Fits neatly under a raincoat. Great for schoolyards and late-night convenience-store visits . . . Here's a set of Smith & Wesson handcuffs, state of the art, solid steel, spring-loaded. Aren't you glad to know a guy like Patsy can buy these at any police supply store . . .'

He put his hand back in the box and I saw his face change, his mouth form a seamed, crooked line, the scar through his eyebrow tighten against the bone. His hand was fitted through the handle of a stubby, cylindrical metal object shaped like a coffeepot.

'The receipt was stuck to the bottom, Dave. He bought it yesterday. Patsy Bones with a blowtorch? Put yourself inside his head—'

Through the kitchen window I could see Bootsie and Alafair washing dishes, talking to each other, the breeze from the attic fan blowing the curtains by the sides of their lighted faces.

Clete scratched his cheek with four fingers, like a zoo creature in a cage, his eyes waiting.

30

It was midmorning, the sun hazy through the oak trees that shaded the cluster of trailers and cottages where Patsy Dapolito lived east of town. Helen and I were parked in my truck behind a tin shed that had already started to creak with heat, watching Patsy shoot baskets in a dirt clearing by the side of a garage. His sockless ankles and white legs were layered with scar tissue and filmed with dust, his gym shorts knotted around his genitals like a drenched swimsuit, his T-shirt contoured against his hard body like wet Kleenex.

He whanged one more shot off the hoop, then dribbled the ball – *bing, bing, bing* – toward the door to his cottage. I got out of the truck, moved in fast behind him, and pushed him hard through the door. When he turned around, his mouth hooked like a cornered predator's, my .45 was pointed in the middle of his face.

'Oh, you again,' he said.

I shoved him into a wood chair. My hand came away damp from his T-shirt.

The floor was littered with movie and wrestling and UFO magazines, hamburger containers, empty Kentucky Fried Chicken buckets, dozens of beer and soda cans.

Helen came through the door with Clete's cardboard box hanging from her hand. She looked around the room.

'I think it needs a trough inset in the floor,' she said.

'This my get-out-of-Shitsville roust?' he said.

Helen gathered up his basketball, bounced it on the linoleum floor twice – *bing, bing* – then two-handed it off his forehead and caught the rebound between her palms. His head jerked, as though a thin wire had snapped behind his eyes, then he stared at her, with that bemused, inverted grin, the mouth turned downward at the corners, the teeth barely showing in a wet line above the lip.

'Your place got creeped, Patsy. We're returning your goods,' I said. I replaced my .45 in my clip-on holster and one at a time removed the Tec-9, the handcuffs, and the blowtorch from the cardboard box and set them on his breakfast table. He fingered the half-moon scars and divots on his face, watched me as though I were a strange shadow moving about on a surreal landscape that only he saw.

'The contract you took from Johnny is already sour, Patsy,' I said. 'There's a guy willing to give you up.'

'It must have been lard-ass that got in my place. He helped himself to the beer and potato salad in my icebox,' Patsy said. There was a red spot, like a small apple, in the middle of his forehead.

'You going to do me?' I said.

He picked at the calluses on his palm, looked up at me, breathed over the top of his teeth, his eyes smiling.

Helen caromed the ball off his head again.

'Hey!' he said, swatting the air, his face knotting. 'Lay off that!'

I reached back down in the cardboard box and retrieved a manila folder that was almost three inches thick. I pulled out a chair and sat in it, spread the folder on one thigh.

'You did a nickel on Camp J, you've gone out max-time twice, we're not going to insult you by treating you like a fish. I'm talking about the consequences of harming a police officer,' I said.

He crinkled his nose, looked at a spot three inches in front of his eyes. The shape of his head reminded me of a darning sock.

'But there's some weird stuff in your jacket, Patsy,' I said. 'You got picked up in a porno theater in New York once. The owner was connected to a child prostitution ring. You remember that gig?'

His eyes lifted into mine.

'When you were thirty-eight you went down for statutory rape. She was fourteen, Patsy. Then way back here . . .' I turned to the front of the folder, looked down at a page. 'It says here you got busted for abducting a little girl from a playground. The father wouldn't stand up so you walked. You see a pattern here?'

His hands shifted into his lap, his fingers netting together. Helen and I stared at him silently. His eyes blinked, looked back and forth between us, his nostrils whitening, as though he were breathing air off a block of ice.

'What?' he said. '*What?*'

'You're a button man, all right, but you're a pedophile first,' I said.

He churned the edges of his tennis shoes on the floor, his ankles bent sideways, his shoulders pinched forward, his neck hunched. I could hear him breathing, smell an odor like soiled cat litter that rose from his armpits. He started to speak.

'Here's the rest of it, Patsy. Your mother set fire to you in your crib,' I said.

His pale eyes stared back at me as though they had no lids. His mouth looked like a deformed keyhole in his face.

'You try to do me, all this becomes public knowledge,' I said. 'Anytime you're around Four Corners, you'll be picked up as a sex predator. We'll put you with every open molestation case we have, we'll make sure NOPD Vice gets in on it, too.'

'They'll have your picture in the T&A joints on Bourbon, Patsy,' Helen said.

'They made that up about my mother. There was a fire in the project,' he said.

470

'Yeah, she set it. That's why she died in the insane asylum,' I said.

'The message is, you're a geek. You start some shit, we'll finish it. You still think this is just a roust in Bumfuck?' Helen said, stepping toward him, her arms pumped.

When we left him, he was still seated in the chair, his head canted to one side, his mouth indented like a collapsed football bladder, his ankles folded almost flat with the floor, his eyes staring into tunnels and secret rooms that only Patsy Dapolito knew about.

Smoke 'em or bust 'em, make their puds shrivel up and hide, Clete used to say. But how do you take pride in wrapping razor wire around the soul of a man who in all probability was detested before he left the womb?

It rained after sunset, and the mist floated like smoke out of the cypress in the swamp. The air was cool when I closed up the bait shop, and I could hear bass flopping back in the bays. Through the screen I saw Alafair walking Tripod on his chain down the dock, while his nose sniffed at the dried blood and fish scales baked into the planks.

She came through the door, eased it back on the spring so it wouldn't slam, sat on a counter stool, and lifted Tripod into her lap. She had put on a fresh pair of blue jeans, a flowered cowboy shirt, and had tied her hair back with a blue ribbon. But her face looked empty, her brown eyes remote with thoughts she couldn't resolve.

'What's the trouble, Alf?' I said.

'It's gonna make you mad.'

'Let's find out.'

'A bunch of us were up by the bar, you know, Goula's, the other side of the drawbridge.'

'A bunch of you?'

'We were in Danny Bordelon's pickup truck. They wanted to get some beer.' She watched my face. 'Danny had his brother's ID card. He went inside the bar and got it.'

'I see.'

'They were going to drink it down the road.'

'What happened?'

'Are you going to be mad at Danny?'

'He shouldn't be buying beer for you guys.'

'I got out of the truck and walked. I was scared. They were mixing it with something called "Ever Clear," it's like pure grain alcohol or something.'

'Danny didn't try to take you home?'

'No.' She dropped her eyes to the floor.

'So we leave Danny alone in the future. You did the right thing, Alafair.'

'That's not all that happened, Dave . . . It started to rain and the wind was blowing real hard out of the swamp. A car came up the road with its lights on. The man who got Tripod out of the coulee, the man you handcuffed, he rolled down his window and said he'd take me home . . .'

'Did you get in the—'

'No. The way he looked at me, it was sickening. His eyes went all over me, like they were full of dirty thoughts and he didn't care if I knew it or not.'

I sat on the stool next to her, put my hand on her back.

'Tell me what happened, Alf,' I said.

'I told him I didn't want a ride. I kept walking toward the house. The rain was stinging my face and he kept backing up with me, telling me to get in, he was a friend of yours, I was gonna catch cold if I didn't get in.'

'You didn't do anything wrong, Alf. Do you understand me?'

'He started to open his door, Dave. Then this other man came out of nowhere. He had red hair and a black rain hat on with rain pouring off it, and he walked like he was hurt. He said, "I don't want it to go down in front of a kid, Emile. Time for you to boogie."'

'The man in the car turned white, Dave. He stepped on the gas and threw mud and water all over us. You could see sparks gashing off his bumper when he crossed the drawbridge.'

I looked out the window into the darkness, tried to clear an obstruction, like a fish bone, in my throat.

'Have you ever seen the man in the raincoat before?' I said.

'It was hard to see his face in the rain. It was pale, like it didn't have any blood ... He said, "You shouldn't be out here by yourself." He walked with me till we could see the lights on the dock. Then I turned around and he was gone.'

I took Tripod out of her lap and set him on the counter, then bent over her and hugged her against my chest, pressed my cheek against the top of her head.

'You're not mad?' she said.

'Of course not.'

Her eyes crinkled at the corners when she looked up at me. I smiled emptily, lest she sense the fear that hovered like a vapor around my heart.

The next morning the sun rose yellow and hot into a bone white sky. There was no wind, and the trees and flowers in my yard were coated with humidity. At 9 a.m. I glanced through my office window and saw Luke Fontenot park his car on the street and walk toward the entrance of the sheriff's department, his rose-colored shirt peppered with sweat. Just before he went through the door, he rubbed his mouth unconsciously.

When he sat down in the metal chair in front of my desk, he kept glancing sideways through the glass at the uniformed deputies who passed in the corridor.

'It's all right, Luke,' I said.

'I been in custody here. For killing a white man, back when things was a li'l different. You believe in the gris-gris, Mr Dave?'

'No.'

'Aint Bertie do. She put the gris-gris on Moleen Bertrand, now she say she cain't get it off.'

'That stuff's superstition, partner.'

'Come out to the cafe where she work.'

'Bertie can take care of herself.'

'I ain't worried about that old woman. It's Ruthie Jean. Suh, ain't it time you listen a li'l bit to what black folks got to say?'

Bertie Fontenot worked off and on in a black-owned clapboard cafe up Bayou Teche in Loreauville. She sat under a tarp extended on poles behind the building, next to a worktable and two stainless steel cauldrons that bubbled on a portable butane burner. The surrounding fields were glazed with sunlight, the shade under the tarp as stifling as a wool blanket on your skin.

Through the back screen I could hear the jukebox playing, *I searched for you all night in vain, baby. But you was hid out wit' another man.*

'Tell him,' Luke said.

'What for? Some people always know what they know,' she said.

She lifted her mammoth weight out of the chair and poured a wood basket filled with artichokes, whole onions, corn on the cob, and peeled potatoes into the cauldrons. Then she began feeding links of sausage into the steam, her eyes watering in the evaporation of salt and cayenne pepper. Stacked on the table were three swollen gunnysacks that moved and creaked with live crawfish.

'Aint Bertie, he took off from his work to come up here,' Luke said.

She wiped the perspiration off her neck with a tiny handkerchief and walked to her pickup truck, which was parked by an abandoned and partially collapsed privy, and came back into the shade with an old leather handbag drawn together at the top by a leather boot lace. She put her hand inside and removed a clutch of pig bones. They looked like long pieces of animal teeth against her coppery palm.

'It don't matter when or where I t'row them, they come up the same,' she said. 'I ain't got no power over what's gonna happen. I gone along with Ruthie Jean, even though I knowed it was wrong. Now I cain't undo any of it.'

She cast the bones from her hand onto the plank table. They seemed to bounce off the wood as lightly as sewing needles.

'See, all the sharp points is at the center,' she said. 'Moleen Bertrand dragging a chain I cain't take off. For something he done right here, it's got to do wit' a child, out on a dirt road, in the dark, when Moleen was drunk. There's a bunch of other spirits following him around, too, soldiers in uniforms that ain't nothing but rags now. Every morning he wake up, they sitting all around his room.'

'You told me you were worried about Ruthie Jean,' I said to Luke.

'She's in a rooming house in New Orleans, off Magazine by the river. Waiting for Moleen to get his bidness things together, take her to the Islands,' he said.

'Some people give they heart one time, keep believing when they ain't suppose to believe no more,' Bertie said. She unfolded the curved blade of a banana knife from its case, pulled a gunnysack filled with crawfish across the table toward her. 'Moleen gonna die. Except there's two bones in the middle of the circle. Somebody going wit' him.'

'Maybe Moleen thinks New Orleans is a better place for her right now. Maybe he's going to keep his word,' I said.

'You wasn't listening, Mr Dave,' Luke said. 'We ain't tole you Moleen Bertrand sent her to New Orleans. It was a police officer, he come down here at night, carried her on down to the airport in Lafayette.'

'Excuse me?' I said.

'You got him right down the hall from you, Mr White Trash himself, Rufus Arceneaux, same man run errands for Julia Bertrand,' she said.

She ripped the sack along the seam with her banana knife, then shucked it empty into the cauldron, where the crawfish stiffened with shock, as though they had been struck with electricity, and then roiled up dead in the churning froth.

That night the air was breathless, moonlit, filled with birds, stale with dust and the heat of the day that lingered in the baked wood and tin roofing of the house. It was long after midnight when the phone rang in the kitchen.

'You got the wrong signal, ace,' the voice said.

'Pogue?'

'Your little girl misunderstood.'

'No, you did. I told you not to come through the wrong man's perimeter.'

'I was there to help. They got a mechanic on you.'

'Come anywhere near my house, I'm going to take you off at the neck.'

'Don't hang up . . .' I could hear his breath rise and fall against the receiver. 'The Dutchie don't let me alone. I think I got only one way out. I cool out the hitter, I don't let nobody hurt your family. The problem is, I got no idea who they sent in. I need time, man, that's what you fucking don't hear.'

'Do you know what 'roid-induced psychosis is?' I said.

'No.'

'Too many injections in the butt. Then you drink a few beers and the snakes put on a special floor show. Don't call here again.'

'You got cement around your head? I ain't a bad guy. We went into Laos twice to get your friend back. You know anybody else who gave a shit about him?'

'You frightened my daughter. One way or another, that's going to get squared, Emile.'

'*Me?* Marsallus was there. She didn't tell you?'

'Your wheelman, Jerry Jeff Hooker, is in custody. He gave you up. Come in and maybe we can get you into a federal hospital.'

'I could smell Marsallus's breath, it was like the stink when you pop a body bag. The Dutchie turned him loose on me. Laos, Guatemala, colored town out there on the highway, it's all part of the same geography. Hell don't have boundaries, man. Don't you understand that?'

The phone was silent a long time. In the moonlight I saw an owl sink its razored beak into a wood rabbit in my neighbor's field. Then Emile Pogue quietly hung up.

474

31

The sheriff had been moved out of Intensive Care into an ordinary room at Iberia General, one that was filled with flowers and slatted sunlight. But his new environment was a deception. His whiskers were white against his flaccid skin, and his eyes had a peculiar cast in them, what we used to call the thousand-yard stare, as though he could not quite detach himself from old events that were still aborning for him on frozen hilltops that rang with bugles.

'Can you hand me my orange juice, please?' he said.

I lifted the glass straw to his lips, watched him draw the juice and melting ice into his mouth.

'I dreamed about roses under the snow. But then I saw they weren't roses. They were drops of blood where we marched out of the Chosin. It's funny how your dreams mix up things,' he said.

'It's better to let old wars go, skipper.'

'New Iberia is a good place.'

'It sure is.'

'We need to get these bastards out of here, Dave,' he said.

'We will.'

'Your daughter ID-ed Marsallus from his mug shot?'

'I shouldn't have told you that story,' I said.

'They couldn't pull him across the Styx. That's a good story to hear . . . Dave?'

'Yes?'

'I never told this to anyone except a marine chaplain. I sent three North Korean POWs to the rear once with a BAR man who escorted them as far as one hill. In my heart I knew better, because the BAR man was one of those rare guys who enjoyed what he did . . .'

I tried to interrupt, but he raised two fingers off the sheet to silence me.

'That's why I always sit on you, always try to keep the net over all of us . . . so we don't take people off behind a hill.'

'That's a good way to be,' I said.

'You don't understand. It's the rules get us killed sometimes. You got too many bad people circling you.'

475

His voice became weaker, and I saw the light in his eyes change, his chest swell, as he breathed more deeply.

'I'd better go now. I'll see you tomorrow,' I said.

'Don't leave yet.' His hand moved across my wrist. 'I don't want to fall asleep. During the day I dream about trench rats. It was twenty below and they'd eat their way inside the dead. That's how they live, Dave . . . By eating their way inside us.'

I went home for lunch, then walked down to the dock to talk to Alafair, who had just gotten out of school for the summer. Sitting under an umbrella at one of the spool tables was Terry Serrett, Clete's secretary. She wore pale blue shorts and a halter and her skin looked as white as a fish's belly. She read a magazine behind a pair of dark glasses while she idly rubbed suntan lotion on her thighs. When she heard my footsteps, she looked up at me and smiled. Her cheeks were roughed with orange circles like makeup on a circus clown.

'You're not working today?' I said.

'There's not much to do, I'm afraid. It looks like Clete is going to move back to New Orleans in a couple of weeks.'

'Can I bring you something?'

'Well, no, but . . . Can you sit down a moment?'

'Sure.'

The wind was warm off the water, and I was sweating inside my shirt even in the umbrella's shade.

'Clete's told me a little bit about this man Sonny Marsallus,' she said. 'Is it true he knows something about POWs in Southeast Asia?'

'It's hard to say, Ms Serrett.'

'It's Terry . . . We think my brother got left behind in Cambodia. But the government denies he was even there.'

'Sonny was never in the service. Anything he . . . knew was conjecture, probably.'

'Oh . . . I got the impression he had evidence of some kind.'

Her sunglasses were tinted almost black, and the rest of her face was like an orange and white mask.

'I'm sorry about your brother,' I said.

'Well, I hope I haven't bothered you,' she said, and touched my elbow softly.

'No, not at all.'

'I guess I'd better go before I burn up in this sun.'

'It's a hot one,' I said.

I watched her walk up the dock on her flats toward her car, a drawstring beach bag hanging from her wrist. The line of soft fat that protruded from her waistband was already pink with sunburn.

I went inside the bait shop. Alafair was stocking lunch meat and cold drinks in the wall cooler.

'Hi, Dave,' she said. 'Who was that lady?'

'Clete's secretary.'

She made a face.

'What's wrong?' I said.

She looked out the window screen. 'Where's Batist?' she said.

'Out on the ramp.'

'She was sitting inside a half hour ago, smoking one cigarette after another, smelling the whole place up. Batist gave me his Pepsi because he had to go put some man's boat in. After he went out, she said, "Better bring that over here, honey."

'I didn't know what she meant. I walked over to her table and she took the can out of my hand and got a bunch of napkins out of the holder and started wiping the top. She said, "You shouldn't drink after other people." Then she put it back in my hand and said, "There . . . Maybe now you won't have to scrub your gums with disinfectant. But I'd still pour it down the drain if I were you."

'What's she doing here, Dave?'

Rufus Arceneaux lived in a wood frame house on Bayou Teche just outside St Martinville. He had a gas light in his front yard, a new aluminum boat shed under his oak trees, an electric bug killer that snapped and hissed on his gallery. He did not resent his black neighbors because he considered himself superior to them and simply did not recognize their existence. Nor did he envy the rich, as he believed them the recipients of luck passed out by a society that was meant to be inequitable and often blessed the bumbling and the effete. His wary eye, instead, was directed at his peers and those among them who succeeded, he was sure, through stealth and design, and always at his expense.

He brought back a Japanese wife from Okinawa, a small, shy woman with bad teeth who worked briefly in a bakery and who lowered her eyes and covered her mouth when she grinned. One night the neighbors made a 911 call on Rufus's house, but the wife told the responding sheriff's deputies her television set had been tuned too loud, there was certainly no problem in the home.

One morning she did not report to work at the bakery. Rufus called the owner later and said she had mumps. When people saw her in town, her face was heavily made up, marbled with discolorations.

She left town on a Greyhound bus the following year. A Catholic priest who worked with Vietnamese refugees drove her to the depot in Lafayette and refused to tell anyone her destination.

For a while Rufus lived with a topless dancer from Morgan City, then a woman who had been fired from her position as a juvenile probation officer in Lake Charles. There were others, too, who came and went, all out of that seemingly endless supply of impaired or abused women who find temporary solace in the approval of a man who will eventually degrade and reject them. As an ex-NCO, Rufus was not one to argue with long-established systems. The only constants in Rufus's life were his two hunting dogs and his squared-away, freshly painted frame house.

It was twilight when I drove up his dirt drive and parked my truck in the trees and walked behind his house. He was drinking bottled beer in his undershirt on the cement pad that served as a back porch, his knees crossed, a pork roast hissing on a rotisserie barbecue pit. Rufus's shoulders were as smooth as stone, olive with tan, a gold and red Marine Corps emblem tattooed on his right arm. At the foot of his sloping yard a half-flooded pirogue lay in the shadows, its sides soft with green mold.

As was his way, he was neither friendly nor unfriendly. My presence in his life, off the clock, had no more significance than the whir of cars out on the state highway. A brunette woman with unbrushed hair, in cutoff blue jeans, came outside, set a small table with wood salad bowls and plates, and never looked at me. Nor did he attempt to introduce her.

He slid a metal chair toward me with his foot.

'There's some cold drinks in the cooler,' he said.

'I understand you drove Ruthie Jean Fontenot to the airport.'

He put a cigarette in his mouth, worked his lighter out of the watch pocket of his Levi's. It had a bronze globe and anchor soldered on its side.

'What's the problem on that, Dave?' he said.

'Are you working for the Bertrands?' I tried to smile.

'Not really.'

'I got you.'

'Just doing somebody a favor,' he said.

'I see. You think Ruthie Jean's getting set up?'

'For what?'

'The Bertrands have their own way of doing business.'

He drank from his beer, a slow, steady sip that showed neither need nor particular pleasure. He blew a cloud of cigarette smoke into the violet air. 'We're going to eat in a minute,' he said.

'I'm going to try to reopen the vehicular homicide case on Julia and Moleen.'

'Be my guest. They weren't involved.'

I looked at his rugged profile, the blond crewcut, the lump of cartilage in the jaw, the green eyes that were often filled with the lights of envy, and felt the peculiar sensation I was looking at an innocent who had no awareness of the lines he had stepped across.

'Moleen's mixed up with people who don't take prisoners, Roof,' I said.

'Are you kidding? He's a needle dick. His wife slides up and down the banister all morning to keep his lunch warm.'

'See you around,' I said.

I woke early the next morning and drove out to the Bertrand plantation. Why?

I really didn't know. The cement trucks, graders, and bulldozers were all idle and unattended now, sitting quietly among the swaths of destruction they had cut from the highway back to the treeline. Why had a company called Blue Sky Electric chosen this spot for its location? Access to the railroad? That was part of it, obviously. But there were a lot of train tracks in the state of Louisiana.

Maybe the answer lay in who lived here.

They were by and large disenfranchised and uneducated, with no political or monetary power. You did not have to be a longtime resident of Louisiana to understand their historical relationship to corporate industries.

Those who worked in the canneries were laid off at the end of the season, then told at the state employment office that their unemployment claims were invalid because their trade was exclusively that of professional canners; and since the canneries were closed for the season, the workers were not available for work, and hence ineligible for the benefits that had been paid into their fund.

This was the Orwellian language used to people who had to sign their names with an *X*.

For years the rice and sugar mills fired anyone who used the word *union* and paid minimum wage only because of their participation in interstate commerce. During the civil rights era, oil men used to joke about having 'a jig on every rig.' But the racial invective was secondary to the real logos, which was to ensure the availability of a huge labor pool, both black and white, that would work for any wage that was offered them.

The stakes today, however, were geographical. The natural habitat's worst enemies, the chemical plants and oil refineries, had located themselves in a corridor along the Mississippi known as Toxic Alley, running from Baton Rouge down to St Gabriel.

Almost without exception the adjacent communities were made up of blacks and poor whites.

I drove down the dirt road and stopped in front of Luke Fontenot's house. I saw his face at the window, then he opened the screen and walked out on the gallery, shirtless, barefoot, a jelly glass full of hot coffee in his hand.

'Something happen?' he said.

'No, I was just killing time. How you doing, Luke?'

'Ain't doing bad ... You just driving around?'

'That's about it.'

He inserted a thumbnail in his teeth, then folded his fingers and looked at the tops of his nails. 'I need legal advice about something.'

'Go ahead.'

'Got to have your promise it ain't going nowhere.'

'I'm a police officer, Luke.'

'You a police officer when you *feel* like being one, Mr Dave.'

'I'd better get to the office.'

He craned out over the railing, looked down the dirt road, measured the sun's height in the sky.

'Come on out back,' he said.

I followed him around the side of the house. He paused by the back porch, slipped a pair of toeless canvas shoes over his feet, and pulled a cane sickle out of a tree stump where chickens had been butchered.

'See where the coulee go, out back of the old privy?' he said, walking ahead of me. 'Yesterday they was running the grader along the edge of the coulee. The bank started caving, and the guy turned the grader out in the field and didn't do no more work here. Last night the moon was up and I seen something bright in the dirt.'

The coulee ran like a ragged wound in the earth to the edge of a cane field, where it had been filled in years ago so the cultivated acreage would not be dissected by a water drainage. The sides were eaten and scrolled with crawfish holes, the bottom thick with cattails and reeds, webs of dead algae, cane husks, and through the cattails a chain of stagnant pools that trembled with insects.

Luke looked back over his shoulder at the dirt road, then slid down the side of the coulee and stepped across a pool to the opposite bank.

'See where the machine crushed down the dirt?' he said. 'It look like a bottom lip hanging down, don't it?' He smiled up at me. 'Mr Dave, you gonna tell this to somebody?'

I squatted down on my haunches and didn't answer. He smiled again, blew out his breath, as though he were making an irrevocable commitment for both of us, then began working the tip of the sickle into the bank, scaling it away, watching each dirt clod that rolled down to his feet.

'What I found last night I stuck back in them holes,' he said. He sliced at the bank, and a curtain of dirt cascaded across his canvas shoes. 'Lookie there,' he said, his fingers grabbing at three dull pieces of metal that toppled and bounced into the water.

He stooped, his knees splayed wide, shoved his wrists into the reeds and the water that was clouding with gray puffs of mud, worked his fingers deeper into the silt, then held up an oblong, coinlike piece of silver and dropped it into my palm.

'What you call that?' he said.

I rubbed my thumb across the slick surface, the embossed cross and archaic numbers and lettering on it.

'It's Spanish or Portuguese, Luke. I think these were minted in Latin America, then shipped back to Europe,' I said.

'Aint Bertie been right all along. Jean Lafitte buried his treasure here.'

'Somebody did. What was the advice you wanted?'

'The wall of this coulee's probably full of them coins. But we talked Aint Bertie into giving up her claim.'

'This whole area is going to be covered with cement and buildings,' I said. 'The guys doing it don't care about the dead people buried here. Why should they care about the coins?'

'That's what I been thinking. No point bothering them.'

'I couldn't argue with that. How about I buy you some breakfast up on the highway, Luke?'

'I'd like that real fine. Yes, suh, I was fixing to ax you the same thing.'

Clete came into the office right after lunch. He wore a pair of seersucker slacks low on his hips and a dark blue short-sleeve silk shirt. He kept glancing back toward the glass partition into the hallway.

'Do I need a passport to get into this place?' he said. He got up, opened the door, and looked into a uniformed deputy's face. 'Can I help you with something?'

He returned to his chair, looked hard at the glass again, his face flushed.

'Ease up, Clete,' I said.

'I don't like people staring at me.' The soles of his loafers tapped up and down on the floor.

'You want to tell me what it is?'

'Emile Pogue's trying to set you up.'

'Oh?'

'You're going to step right into it, too.' He paced in front of my desk and kept snapping his fingers and hitting his hands together. 'I shouldn't have come in here.'

'Just tell me what happened.'

'He called my office. He said he wants to give himself up.'

'Why didn't he call me?'

'He thinks you're tapped.'

'Where is he, Clete?'

'I knew it.'

32

It was late afternoon when we put my boat into the Atchafalaya River and headed east into the basin and the huge network of bayous, bays, sandbars, and flooded stands of trees that constitute the alluvial system of the river. The sun was hot and bloodred above the willow islands behind us and you could see gray sheets of rain curving out of the sky in the south and waves starting to cap in the bay. I opened up both engines full throttle and felt the water split across the bow, hiss along the hull like wet string, then flatten behind us in a long bronze trough dimpled with flying fish that glided on the wind like birds.

Clete sat on a cushioned locker behind me, his Marine Corps utility cap on the back of his head, pressing rounds from a box of .223 ammunition into a second magazine for my AR-15. Then he inverted the magazine and jungle-clipped it with electrician's tape to one that was already in the rifle. He saw me watching him.

'Lose the attitude, big mon. You blink on this dude and he'll take your eyes out,' he said above the engine's noise.

I cut back on the throttle on the east side of the bay and let the wake take us into a narrow bayou that snaked through a flooded woods. Cottonmouth moccasins lay coiled on top of dead logs and the lowest cypress branches along the banks, and ahead I saw a white crane lift from a tiny inlet matted with hyacinths and glide for a time above the bayou, then suddenly rise through a red-gold, sunlit break in the canopy and disappear.

Clete was standing beside me now. There was no wind inside the trees, and I could smell mosquito dope running in his sweat. He wiped his eyes with the heel of his hand and swatted mosquitoes away from his hair.

'It's like being up the Mekong. It's got to be a setup,' he said.

'I think he's scared.'

'My ass. This guy's been killing people all his life. We can go around a corner and he can chop us into horse meat.'

'That's not it. He's had too many other chances.'

Clete pointed a finger at me, his eyes hard and big in his face, then went out of the cabin and worked his way forward to the bow, where he knelt on one knee with the AR-15 propped on his thigh, the sling wrapped around his forearm.

The sun fell through the canopy and illuminated a sunken houseboat and the pale, bloated carcass of a wild hog that had wedged under the porch roof. The metallic green backs of alligator gars rolled against the surface, then their long jaws and files of needlelike teeth parted as they went deep into the pocket where the hog's stomach used to be.

Up ahead was a blind corner. I began to believe Clete had been right. Not only were the risks all ours, I had allowed myself to be convinced that an amoral, pathological man was more human, more capable of remorse, than he had ever shown himself to be previously. This bayou, shut off from light, filled with insects and gars and poisonous snakes, vaguely scented with the smells of decay and death, a place Joseph Conrad would have well understood, was Pogue's chosen environment, and so far we were operating on his terms.

I cut the engines, and in the sudden quiet I heard our wake sliding back across the sandbars into the woods, a crescendo of birds' wings flapping in the trees, a 'gator slapping its tail in water. But I didn't hear the St Mary Parish sheriff's boat, with Helen Soileau on it, that should have been closing the back door on Emile Pogue.

I started to use the radio, then I saw Clete raise his hand in the air.

Someone was running in the woods, crashing through brush, splashing across a slough. I felt the bow bite into a sandbar and the boat become motionless. I went forward with Clete and tried to see through the tree trunks, the tangle of air vines, the leaves that tumbled out of the canopy, the pools of mauve shadow that seemed to take the shape of animals.

Then we heard the roar of an airboat out on the next bay.

'How do you figure that?' Clete said.

'Maybe he wants another season to run.'

We dropped off the bow onto the sandbar and worked our way along the bank and through the shallows to the corner. The back of Clete's neck was oily with sweat, inflamed with insect bites. He put an unlit cigarette in his mouth, paused at the bend in the bayou, then stepped out in the open, his face blank, his eyes flicking from one object to the next.

He pointed.

An aluminum boat with an outboard engine was tied with a chain to a cypress knee on the bank, and beyond it a shack was set back in the willows on pilings. The screens were webbed with rust, dead insects, and dirt, and the tin roof had long ago taken on the colors of a woods in winter. The base of the pilings glistened with a sheen like petroleum waste from the pools of stagnant water they sat in. Clete pressed a wadded handkerchief to his face. The dry ground behind the shack was blown with bottle flies and reeked of unburied excrement.

I slipped my .45 from my holster, pulled back the slide on a hollow-point round, and moved through the trees toward the rear of the shack while Clete approached the front. The water had receded only recently, and the sand was wet and curled over my tennis shoes like soft cement. I heard sound inside the shack, then realized a radio was playing. It was Ravel's *Bolero*, compelling and incessant, building like a painful obsession you can't let go of.

I came out of the trees ten feet from the rear of the shack and saw Clete poised by the front entrance, his face waiting. I held up my hand, then brought it down and we both went in at the same time.

Except my foot punched through a plank on the back step that was as soft as rotted cork. I stumbled into the interior still limping, my .45 pointed straight out with both hands. Clete was silhouetted against the broken light beyond the front door, his rifle hanging from his right hand. He was looking at something on the floor.

Then I saw him, amidst the litter of soiled clothes and fishing gear and barbells. He lay on his back by a small table with a shortwave radio on it, dressed in jeans, a sleeveless green T-shirt, suspenders, his bare feet like pale white blocks of wood. A dark pool shaped like a deformed three-leaf clover swelled from the back of his neck. I knelt beside him.

He opened his mouth and coughed on an obstruction deep in his throat. His tongue was as red and bright as licorice. I started to turn him on his side.

'Don't do it, chief,' he whispered. 'He broke the shank off inside.'

'Who did this to you, Emile?'

'Never saw him. A pro. Maybe that cocksucker Marsallus.'

His eyes came together like BBs, then refocused on my face.

'We're going to put you on my boat, then get you out in the bay so a chopper can pick you up,' I said.

But he was already shaking his head before I finished my words. His eyes slid off my face onto my shirt.

'What is it?' I said.

'Lean close.'

I lowered my ear toward his mouth, then realized that was not what he wanted. His hand lifted up and clenched around my religious medal and chain, knotted it across his knuckles, held me hovering above the shrunken pinpoints of his eyes.

'I ain't got the right words. Too many bad gigs, chief. I apologize for the Dutchie,' he whispered.

When his hand fell from my chain, his breath mushroomed out of his mouth and struck against my face like a fist. A bottle fly crawled across his eyes.

Clete clicked off the dial on the shortwave set. The dead radio tubes crackled in the silence.

33

The next morning Helen Soileau walked with me into Clete's office on Main. The front and back doors were open, and the papers in Clete's wire baskets lifted and ruffled in the breeze. Helen looked around the office.

'Where's Avon's answer to the Beast of Buchenwald?' she said.

'What's the problem?' Clete said from behind his desk, trying to smile.

'They knew we were coming, that's the problem,' she said.

'Terry? Come on,' he said.

'Where is she?' Helen said.

'Getting some stuff photocopied.'

'Does she have any scratches on her?' I said.

'You want me to strip-search my secretary?'

'It's not funny, Clete,' I said.

'She wasn't in the office when Pogue called,' he said.

'You're sure?' I said.

'She was across the street at the doughnut place.'

'You didn't tell her about it?' I asked.

'No . . .' His eyes looked into space. 'No, I'm sure of it. I never mentioned Pogue's name, never mentioned a place.'

Helen looked at me and made a sucking sound with her teeth. 'Okay,' she said. 'Maybe the hit was already on him. There's Marsallus to think about, too.'

'Not with a knife. We're talking about one of Pogue's buddies from the Phoenix Program,' Clete said. He leaned over in his chair and clicked on a floor fan, clamped his hand on top of a yellow legal pad by his telephone. The pages blew and rattled in the gust of air.

'Why would anyone try to take a guy like Pogue with a knife? Unless the killer knew we were in the vicinity?' I said.

Clete scratched at the scar that ran through his eyebrow, rested his chin on his knuckles.

'I guess you're right, you got a leak. How about that buttwipe who was in the Crotch?' he said.

'Rufus Arceneaux?' Helen said.

Clete and I drove to New Orleans at dawn, turned off I-10 onto St Charles

485

Avenue, and went uptown toward the Garden District, past the lovely old Pontchartrain Hotel and rows of antebellum and early Victorian homes with their narrow pillared galleries and oak-canopied yards that stayed black with shadow even in summer. We turned left across the neutral ground and the streetcar tracks and crossed Prytania, the street where Lillian Hellman grew up, then headed up Magazine, the old line of disembarkation into the Irish Channel, toward the levee and a different New Orleans, one of late-nineteenth-century paintless frame houses with ventilated shutters and hardpan dirt yards and tiny galleries propped up on bricks, clapboard corner bars that never closed or took down their Christmas lights, matchbox barbecue joints that smelled of hickory and ribs by 9 a.m., and graffiti-scrolled liquor stores whose windows were barred like jails.

I parked in front of the address Luke Fontenot had given me. A thundershower had just passed through the neighborhood and the air was gray and wet and steam rose from the roofs like smoke in winter. Clete rolled down the window and squinted at the rows of almost identical, weathered, coffee-colored houses, a ramshackle tin-roofed juke joint overgrown with banana trees on the corner, an elderly black man in a frayed suit and sneakers and baseball cap riding a bicycle with fat tires aimlessly up and down the street. I could see shadows and lights in Clete's face, like reflections that cling inside frost on a window.

'They say if you're ever black on Saturday night, you'll never want to be white again,' he said.

'You usually hear white people say that after they shortchange the yardman,' I said.

'Our house was one block over.'

I waited for him to go on, but he didn't.

'You want to come in?' I said.

'No, it's your show. I'm going to get a cup of coffee.'

'Something on your mind?'

He laughed down in his chest, rubbed a knuckle against his nose. 'My old man knocked me into next week because I dropped his bucket of beer in front of that juke joint. He was quite a guy. I was never big on nostalgia, Streak.'

I watched him walk toward the levee, his porkpie hat slanted on the crown of his head, his face lifted into the breeze off the river, his feelings walled up inside a private place where I never transgressed.

Ruthie Jean's address was a two-story house with a fire escape for an upstairs entrance and wash strung across the veranda and a single paint-blistered trellis that was spoked with red roses.

A police cruiser with the NOPD crescent on the door and a white cop in a sky blue shirt behind the wheel slowed by my pickup as I was locking the door behind me.

'Can I help you?' he said.

I opened my badge holder in my palm.

'On the job,' I said, and smiled.

'Work on your tan if you're coming back after sunset,' he said.

'Thanks,' I said, and felt conspiratorial and slightly ashamed at my own response.

A moment later Ruthie Jean opened the door at the head of the fire escape. She wore a pair of new blue jeans with a silver-tipped western belt and white tennis shoes and a burnt orange blouse and gold hoop earrings. This time there was no anger or recrimination in her face; in fact, I had the sense she expected me.

'I need to talk to you about Moleen,' I said.

'You surely don't give it up.'

'You don't have to talk to me, Ruthie Jean.'

'I know that. Come in, if you like.'

The living room was airy and cool, the upholstered couch and chairs patterned with flowers and decorated with doilies. The curtains puffed and twisted in the breeze, and you could see the top of the levee and hear boats with horns out on the river.

'Can I give you some coffee?' she said.

'That'd be nice.'

I sat in a deep chair while she fixed a tray in the kitchen. A steamer trunk lay opened by the couch. In a removable top compartment, which she had set at an angle to the sides in order to pack the bottom, was a clear plastic bag with folded blue and pink baby clothes inside. A withered camellia was pressed between the fabric and the plastic.

She limped into the living room with the tray; her eyes followed mine to the trunk. She lowered the tray down on the coffee table, then reset the wood compartment inside the trunk and closed the lid.

'Why you dislike Moleen so much?' she said.

'He thinks it's natural for other people to pay for his mistakes.'

'If you're talking about the abortion, it was me went over to Texas. Moleen didn't have anything to do with it.'

'Moleen ran down and killed the little boy out by Cade, not his wife.'

'I don't believe that.'

I leaned forward with my forearms on my thighs and rubbed my palm idly on my knuckles.

'I don't know how to tell you this,' I said. 'But I believe Julia Bertrand may try to do you grave injury. Maybe with Moleen's consent.'

'You cain't forgive him for the world he comes from, Mr Robicheaux. It's not his fault who he was born.'

I was at a loss.

'Do you have a gun?' I asked.

'No.'

Her face made me think of a newly opened dark flower about to be burned by a severe light.

'You're an admirable lady, Ruthie Jean. I hope you're going to be all right. Call me if I can ever help you in any way.'

'That's why you sent that other man?'

'Excuse me?'

'The one with the red hair and the skin look like milk. He was standing outside in the rain. I axed him what he was doing in this neighborhood at night. He said he was your friend and you were worried about me. He's your friend, isn't he?'

'Yes, I think he probably is.'

'Think?'

I started to explain, but I didn't. Then I simply said, 'I'd better be going now.'

Her turquoise eyes, gold skin, the mole by her mouth, her thick black hair that curved on her cheek were framed as though in a lens by the curtains that puffed and danced behind her head. Her eyes moved up to meet mine.

'You're a very good man,' she said.

'Good-bye, Ruthie Jean,' I said, and took her hand in mine. It was small and dry and I wanted to hold it a long time. I knew in a way that words could not explain that this was much more than a casual farewell.

We pulled into the circle drive of the yacht club and parked not far from the practice green. The yacht club was sparkling white in the sunlight, with flagstone terraces and tinted, glassed-in dining areas and fairways that looked like corridors of velvet between the oak trees. When we got out of the truck, Clete pulled his shirt down over the front of his slacks, smoothed it with his fingers, adjusted his belt with his thumb, looked down at his shirt again.

'How does a prick like Johnny Carp get in a joint like this?' he said.

'They recognize a closet Republican when they see one.'

'How do I look?' he said.

'Lean and mean, not a bump on you.'

'You sure you want to do this?'

'You got to do something for kicks,' I said.

'I'm starting to worry about you, big mon.'

We walked in the shade of the building toward the entrance. Sailboats were rocking in their slips out on Lake Pontchartrain. The maître d' stopped us at the door to the dining room.

'Do you gentlemen have reservations?' he said. His face and accent were European, his closed-shaved cheeks ruddy with color.

I opened my badge holder. 'We're here to see Polly Gee,' I said. He looked at me blankly. 'That's Johnny Carp . . . *John Giacano*. His secretary said he's having lunch here.'

His facial skin tightened against the bone. His eyes involuntarily glanced at a glass-domed annex to the main dining room. He cleared his throat softly.

'Is there going to be a problem, gentlemen?' he asked.

'We'll let you know if there is. Bring me a double Jack, with a Dixie on the side, and put it on Johnny's tab. He told me to tell you that,' Clete said.

The domed annex was empty, except for Johnny Carp and his crew, who were eating from gumbo appetizer bowls at a long linen-covered table set with flowers and pitchers of sangria. Johnny lowered his spoon from his mouth, his face dead. A scar, like a piece of black string, was crimped into his lip where I had hit him. One of Johnny's crew, a one-thousand-dollar-a-hit mechanic named Mingo Bloomberg, started to rise from his chair. He was a handsome, copper-haired man with ice blue eyes that were totally devoid of moral light.

'The man with the badge has a pass. You don't, Purcel,' he said.

'Don't get up on my account,' Clete said.

'A guy's got to try. It's nothing personal.'

'Put your hand on me and you're going to wear a metal hook, Mingo.'

'So we see how it shakes out,' Mingo said, and began to stand up.

Clete fitted his hand on Mingo's face and shoved him back down in his chair. Then he hit him twice with the flat of his hand, like a man swinging a fielder's glove filled with cement.

'You want another one?' he said. 'Tell me now, Mingo. Go ahead, open your mouth again.'

I cupped my palm around Clete's bicep. It felt like a grapefruit.

'I'm fed up with this shit. Somebody get security in here,' Johnny said.

'You're looking good, John,' I said.

'You're a lucky man, Dave.' He pointed his fork at me. 'You ought to burn a few candles at your church.'

'That's not quite how I see it, John,' I said. 'You don't want to queer your people's action in Iberia Parish by killing a police officer, but then again you're not always predictable. That means I need to do something about you, like maybe squeeze Patsy Dapolito until he gives you up. You think Patsy will give you up, John?'

'What's to give? He don't work for me no more. He never really did.'

'Oh?' I said.

'That's right, he's a malignant geek, a short-eyes, a freak. You gonna nail me with the testimony of a child molester? You know what my lawyer would do with a guy like that on the stand? When he gets excited he drools. Hey, you guys, picture star witness Patsy Bones drooling on the stand.' Johnny stretched his face out of shape and let his tongue roll wetly in his mouth while all his crew laughed. 'You two twerps get out of here.'

'It's always a pleasure, John,' I said.

Clete picked up a bread stick, dipped it in a sangria pitcher, and snapped it off in his jaw, winking at me while he grinned outrageously.

Outside in the parking lot, he pulled up his shirt and removed the tape recorder from under his belt, popped out the cassette, and flipped it in his palm.

'Isn't life grand?' he said.

34

I was filling out my time sheet the next day when Helen Soileau knocked on my office door, then sat on the corner of the desk and looked me in the face, her eyes seeming to focus on words or sentences in her head that would never become the right ones to use.

'Say it,' I said.

'I just got off the phone with Fart, Barf, and Itch in New Orleans. Marsallus is dead. They've got his body.'

I returned her stare and didn't answer.

'Dave?'

'Yeah.'

'Did you hear me?'

'I hear you. I don't believe it.'

'The body never washed up because it was wedged in the pilings of that collapsed pier.'

I looked out the window. The sky was thick with lead-colored clouds, the trees filmed with dust, motionless in the trapped heat. The traffic on the street seemed to make no sound.

'How'd they ID the body?' I said.

'Dental records.'

'What dental records?' I said, the irritation rising in my voice. 'Sonny grew up in a welfare project. He probably went to a dentist as often as he went to a gynecologist.'

'The agent says they're a hundred percent sure it's Sonny.'

'He worked for the Feds. He was an embarrassment to them. They want his file closed.'

'Do you know what denial is?'

'Yeah. With me it has to do with booze, not dead people.'

'You want to go to lunch?'

'No. Where's the body?'

'On its way to a mortuary in New Orleans. Leave it alone, Dave.' She watched my face. 'Water and fish and crabs do bad things.'

I rose from my desk and looked silently out the window until she was gone. Outside, a trusty from the parish lopped a dead banana stalk in half with a machete, revealing a swarm of fire ants that fed off the rotten pulp inside.

'You sure you want to see it?' the mortician, a middle-aged black man, said. It was late and he was tired. He wore a T-shirt and rumpled slacks without a belt, and there was stubble on his chin. 'Okay, if that's what you want. You say he was a friend?'

'Yes.'

He raised his eyebrows and opened the door to a back room where the temperature was twenty degrees lower than the front of the funeral home. It smelled of chemicals, stainless steel, the cool odor of scrubbed concrete.

Over his shoulder I could see an elevated flat-bottomed metal trough in the center of the room.

'It's going to be in a closed coffin. His relatives will never see inside it,' he said.

He stepped aside, and I saw the bloodless, shrunken form stretched out inside the trough, glowing in a cone of electric light that shone from overhead.

'There's morticians won't work on these kinds,' he said. 'I got a government contract, though, so I do everything they send me . . . Is that him?'

'That's not a human form anymore.'

'Your friend had red hair?'

I didn't reply. He waited. I heard him put on his glasses, fiddle with a fountain pen.

'I'll show you the bullet wounds. There're four,' he said. He leaned over the trough, pointing with the pen. 'Two through the chest, one in the groin, one through the side. They look like dimples in oatmeal now.'

'There weren't any rounds,' I said.

'Believe me, Mr Robicheaux, those are exit wounds. I worked in the mortuary at Chu Lai, Republic of South Vietnam. I took guys out of body bags been in there a long time, get my drift? . . . Look, the government doesn't make the kind of mistake you're thinking about.'

'Then how'd we all end up in Vietnam?' I asked.

He walked to the door and put his hand on the wall switch. 'I'm turning off the lights now. You coming?' he said.

I dreamed all night, then got up just before dawn and fixed coffee in the kitchen and drank it on the back steps. The sun was still below the treeline in the swamp and the air was moist and cool and smelled of milkweed and the cattle in my neighbor's field. I kept seeing Sonny's bloodless face and sightless eyes and red hair, like the head of John the Baptist on a metal tray. I flung my coffee into the flower bed and drove to Clete's apartment off East Main.

'You're starting the day like a thunderstorm, Streak,' he said, yawning in his Jockey underwear, pulling a shirt over his wide shoulders.

'Alafair and Pogue both saw him. So did Ruthie Jean Fontenot.'

'People see Elvis Presley. How about James Dean or Adolf Hitler, for God's sakes?'

'This is different.'

'You want to go crazy? Keep living inside your head like that.'

He slid a carton of chocolate milk and a box of jelly doughnuts out of the icebox and started eating.

'You want some?' he asked.

'I want to jump-start Patsy Dap.'

'How you going to feel if he takes down Johnny Carp?'

'I won't feel anything,' I said.

'Yeah, I bet.'

'I won't ever believe Sonny's dead,' I said.

'Don't talk to me about this stuff anymore.'

'One way or another, Sonny's out there, Clete.'

'I don't want to hear it, I don't want to hear it, I don't want to hear it,' he said, walking into the bathroom, working one hand into his shorts.

We drove in my truck out to Patsy Dapolito's rented cottage on the edge of town, but no one answered the door. Clete shielded the sun's glare from his eyes and squinted through the blinds on the side window.

'Look at the litter in there. I bet this guy takes a shit inside his clothes,' he said.

'I'll check with the landlord.'

'Patsy's in a trick pad in Lafayette.'

'How do you know?'

'A guy I wrote a bond on said he's got a couple of chippies at Four Corners who aren't too selective.'

'That doesn't mean he's there.'

'When your name is Patsy Dap, you're either thinking about getting laid or blowing out somebody's light. I'm seldom wrong about these guys. That bothers me sometimes.'

I looked at him strangely.

'Be happy you got your badge, Streak. It means you get to walk on the curb instead of in the gutter,' he said.

A half hour later we walked into the office of a motel at Four Corners in Lafayette. Raindrops were tinkling on the air-conditioner inset in the window. I showed my badge and a picture of Patsy Dap to the motel operator.

'Do you know this man?' I asked.

He crinkled his nose under his glasses, looked vague, shook his head.

'Lot of people come through here,' he said.

'You want to get your whole place tossed?' I said.

'Room six,' he replied.

'Give us the key ... Thanks, we're putting you down for a good citizen award,' Clete said.

We walked down to Dapolito's room as the rain blew underneath the overhang. I tapped with one knuckle on the door.

'It's Dave Robicheaux. Open up, Patsy,' I said.

It was quiet a moment, then he spoke in a phlegmy, twisted voice: 'Leave me alone 'less you got a warrant.'

I turned the key in the lock, nudged the door open with my foot, my hand on my .45.

'Ooops,' Clete said, peering over my shoulder.

'You guys get out of here,' Patsy said from the bed.

Clete pushed the door back slowly with the flat of his hand, sniffed at the air as we both stepped inside.

'You paying for your broads to smoke China white? High-grade stuff, my man,' Clete said.

She was not over sixteen, blond and beautiful in a rough way, with thick arms and shoulders, a heart-shaped face that wore no makeup, hands that could have been a farm girl's. She gathered the top sheet around her body. I pulled the bedspread off the foot of the bed, wrapped it around her, then handed her her clothes.

'Dress in the bathroom while we talk to this man,' I said. 'We're not going to arrest you.'

Her eyes were disjointed, one pupil larger than the other, glazed with fear and Oriental smack.

'Listen, this man kills people for a living. But if he didn't get paid, he'd do it for free. Don't ever come here again,' I said.

'Why the roust this time?' Patsy said. He sat with his back against the headboard, his hard, compact body as white as the skin on a toadstool, one hand kneading the sheet that covered his loins. A bluebird was tattooed above each of his nipples.

'I think you might still want to pop me, Patsy. Earn some points with Polly Gee,' I said.

'You're wrong. I'm going on a trip, all over the world, places I ain't ever got to visit.'

'Really?' I said.

'Yeah, I got an itinerary, everything. A Japanese travel service put it together. They even give you a booklet tells you how to get along with everybody, what things to watch out for. Don't get on elevators with Iranians 'cause of the BO they got. Don't shake hands with Arabs 'cause they wipe their ass with their bare hand.'

'Sounds great, except I don't believe you,' I said. I saw the girl go past the corner of my vision, out the door. 'Click on the tape, Clete.'

Clete set the portable tape player on the desk and snapped the play button. Patsy's scarred face looked confused at first as he heard Mingo Bloomberg's voice, then Clete's and Johnny Carp's and mine.

'What is this?' he said.

'I'll start it again. We don't want you to miss any of this. Particularly when they start laughing at you,' Clete said.

As Patsy listened, the skin on one side of his face seemed to crinkle like the surface of paint in a bucket. He lit a cigarette, one eye watering with the heat of the flame.

'You going to do hits for a guy like that?' Clete said.

Patsy's teeth protruded above his bottom lip like a ridge of bone. He huffed smoke out of the corner of his mouth.

'I don't want you thinking about whacking out Johnny, either. If Johnny gets capped, this tape goes to NOPD,' I said.

'I can hurt Johnny in ways you ain't thought about. You're stupid, Robicheaux. That's why you're a cop,' he said.

Clete and I walked outside and closed the door behind us. The rain was swirling in the wind.

'What do you think he meant?' Clete said.

'Who knows?'

'Dave, you going to be okay? You don't look too good.'

'I'm fine,' I said.

But I wasn't. I had no sooner closed the door to the pickup's cab when I had to open it again and vomit on the concrete. My face was cold with sweat. I felt Clete's big hand on my neck.

'What is it, Streak?' he said.

'The tattoo.'

'On fuckhead in there?'

'On Sonny's shoulder. A Madonna figure. I saw it in the mortuary.'

35

Later, I drove north of town to the sheriff's house on Bayou Teche and walked around his dripping live oaks to the gallery, where he sat in a straw chair with his pipe and a glass of lemonade. His house was painted yellow and gray, and petals from his hydrangeas were scattered like pink confetti on the grass; in back, I could see the rain dimpling on the bayou.

He listened while I talked, never interrupting, snuffing down in his nose sometimes, clicking his pipe on his teeth.

'Do like Purcel and Helen tell you, Dave. Let Marsallus go,' he said.

'I feel to blame.'

'That's vain as hell, if you ask me.'

'Sir?'

'You're a gambler, Dave. Marsallus faded the backline and bet against himself a long time ago.'

I looked at the rain rings out on the bayou, at a black man in a pirogue under a cypress overhang who was tossing a handline and baited treble hook into the current.

'And as far as this supernatural stuff is concerned, I think Marsallus is alive only in your head,' he said.

'People have seen him.'

'Maybe they see what you want them to see.'

Wrong, skipper, I thought. But this time I kept my own counsel.

'Somebody knew we were coming for Pogue,' I said. 'Maybe we've got a leak in the department.'

'Who?'

'How about Rufus Arceneaux?'

He thought for a moment, adjusted his shirt collar with his thumb.

'Rufus would probably do almost anything, Dave, as long as he thought he was in control of it. He'd be out of his depth on this one.'

'How'd they know we were coming?'

'Maybe it was just coincidence. We don't solve every crime. This might be one of them.'

'They're wiping their feet on us, Sheriff.'

He ran a pipe cleaner through the stem of his pipe and watched it emerge brown and wet from the metal airhole.

'You're lucky you don't smoke,' he said.

After work I went home and put on my gym shorts and running shoes and worked out with my weight set in the backyard. It had stopped raining and the sky was rippled with purple and crimson clouds and loud with the droning of tree frogs. Then I went inside and showered and put on a fresh pair of khakis and began poking through the clothes hangers in the closet. Boots sat on the bed and watched me.

'Where's my old charcoal shirt?' I asked.

'I put it in your trunk. It's almost cheesecloth.'

'That's why I wear it. It's comfortable.'

The trunk was in the back of the closet. I unlocked it and saw the shirt folded next to my AR-15 and the holstered nine-millimeter Beretta I had taught Alafair how to shoot. I removed the shirt, locked the trunk, and dropped the key in a dresser drawer.

'You still thinking about Sonny?' she said.

'No, not really.'

'Dave?'

'It's not my job to explain what's unexplainable. St Paul said there might be angels living among us, so we should be careful how we treat one another. Maybe he knew something.'

'You haven't said this to anybody else, have you?'

'Who cares?'

I started to button my shirt, but she got off the bed and began buttoning it for me.

'You're too much, Streak,' she said, nudging my leg with her knee.

In the morning I called a half dozen licensing agencies in Baton Rouge for any background I could get on Blue Sky Electric Company. No one seemed to know much about them, other than the fact they had acquired every permit they needed to begin construction on their current site by Cade.

What was their history?

No one seemed to know that, either.

Where had they been in business previously?

Eastern Washington and briefly in Missoula, Montana.

I called a friend in the chemistry department at the University of Southwestern Louisiana in Lafayette, then met him for lunch in the student center, which looked out upon a cypress-filled lake on the side of old Burke Hall. He was an elderly, wizened man who didn't suffer fools and was notorious for his classroom histrionics, namely, kicking his shoes across the lecture room the first day of class and gracefully flipping the text over his shoulder into a wastebasket.

'What do these guys make?' he said.

'Nobody seems to know.'

'What do they un-make?'

'I beg your pardon?'

'It's not a profound concept, Dave. If they don't make things, they dispose of things. You said they had an incinerator. Who besides Satan needs an incinerator in a climate like this?'

'They do something with electrical transformers,' I said.

His eyes looked like slits, his skin webbed like dry clay.

'If they're incinerating the oil in the transformers, they're probably emitting PCBs into the environment. PCBs not only go into the air, they go into the food chain. Anticipate a change in local cancer statistics,' he said.

Back at my office I called the EPA in Washington, D.C., then newspapers and wire services in Seattle and Helena, Montana. Blue Sky Electric had changed its corporate name at least seven times and had been kicked out of or refused admission to thirteen states. Each time it departed an area, it left behind a Superfund cleanup that ran into millions of dollars. The great irony was that the cleanup was contracted by the same corporation that owned the nonunion railroad that transported the transformers to Blue Sky Electric.

The last place they had tried to set up business was in Missoula, where they had been driven out of town by a virtual lynch mob.

Now they had found a new home with the Bertrand family, I thought.

'What are you going to do?' Helen said.

'Spit in the punch bowl.'

I called the *Daily Iberian*, the Baton Rouge *Morning Advocate*, the New Orleans *Times-Picayune*, the Sierra Club, an ACLU lawyer who delighted in filing class action suits on behalf of minorities against polluters, and a RICO prosecutor with the U.S. attorney general's office.

After work, Rufus Arceneaux stopped me on the way to my truck in the parking lot. His armpits were dark with sweat rings, his breath as rank as an ashtray.

'I need to talk with you,' he said.

'Do it on the clock.'

'This is private. I got no deep involvement with the Bertrands. I did a little security for them, that's all.'

'What are you telling me, Roof?'

'Any kind of shit coming down on their head, problems with the greaseballs, it's got nothing to do with me. I'm out. Understand what I'm saying?'

'No.'

I could smell the fear in his sweat. He walked away from me, his GI haircut as slick as a peeled onion against the late sun.

That evening I helped Batist bail and chain-lock our rental boats and close up the bait shop. The air was dry and hot, the sky empty of clouds and filled with a dull white light like a reflection off tin. My hands, my chest, seemed to burn with an energy I couldn't free myself from.

'What's got your burner on, Streak?' Bootsie said in the living room.

'Rufus Arceneaux's trying to disassociate himself from the Bertrands. He knows something's about to hit the fan.'

'I don't un—' she began.

'Clete and I shook up Patsy Dapolito. He said he could hurt Johnny Carp in ways I hadn't thought about.'

'That psychopath is after Julia and Moleen?'

'I don't know,' I said. I went into the bedroom, picked up my .45 in its holster, and drove into New Iberia.

It was dusk when I turned into Moleen's drive and parked by his glassed-in back porch. Every light was on in the house, but I saw Moleen out on his sloping lawn, raking pine needles into a pile under a tree. Behind him a shrimp boat with green and red running lights on was headed down Bayou Teche toward the Gulf.

'Is there some reason I should have been expecting you?' he said.

'Patsy Dap.'

'Who?'

'I kicked a two-by-four up his butt yesterday. I think he might try to square a beef with Johnny by going through you.'

'You have problems with your conscience, sir?'

'Not over you.'

'A matter of principle, that sort of thing?'

'I've said what I had to say.'

'You loathed us long before any of this began.'

'Your friends murdered Sonny Boy Marsallus. Either you or Julia ran down and killed a child. One of these days the bill's going to come due, Moleen.'

I walked back toward my truck. Through the lighted windows I could see Julia, in a yellow dress, a drink in her hand, talking brightly on the phone.

I heard Moleen behind me, felt his hand bite into my arm with surprising strength.

'Do you think I wanted any of this to happen? Do you know what it's like to wake up every morning with your whole—' He waved his arm vaguely at the air, as a drunk man might. Then he blanched, as though he were watching himself from outside his own skin.

'I don't think you're well, Moleen. Get some help. Go into the witness protection program.'

'What do you suggest about Ruthie Jean?'

'If that's her choice, she can go with you.'

'You have no idea how naive you are, sir,' he said.

He wore a stained white shirt and a pair of baggy seersucker slacks with no belt. For just a moment, in the deepening shadows, with the splayed cane rake propped in his hand, a drop of sweat hanging on his chin, he no longer looked like the man whom I had resented most of my life.

'Is there anything I can do?' I said.

'No, but thank you, anyway, Dave. Good night.'

I held out my business card. He hesitated, then took it, smiling wanly, and inserted it in his watch pocket.

'Good night, Moleen,' I said.

I woke early Saturday morning and went to Red's Gym in Lafayette and worked out hard on the speed and heavy bag, did three miles on the outdoor track, then drove back home and helped Alafair and Batist fix lunch for the fishermen who returned to the dock during the midday heat. But I couldn't rid myself of a nameless, undefined red-black energy that made my palms ring, the pulse beat in my wrists. The only feeling I'd had like it was on benders of years ago when my whiskey supply was cut off, or in Vietnam, when we were moved into a free-fire zone only to learn that the enemy had gone.

I called Moleen's house.

'I'm afraid you've missed him,' Julia said.

'Would you have him call me when he comes back?'

'I've just hired an auctioneer to get rid of his things. Oh, I'm sorry, would you like to come out before the sale and pick up a bargain or two?'

'There's a New Orleans greaseball in town named Patsy Dapolito.'

'I'm supposed to be on the first tee by one o'clock. Otherwise, I'd love to chat. You're always so interesting, Dave.'

'We can put a cruiser by your house. There's still time for alternatives, Julia.'

'You're such a dear. Bye-bye now.'

Later, Alafair went to a picture show in town and Bootsie and I fixed deviled eggs and ham and onion sandwiches and ate them on the kitchen table in front of the floor fan.

'You want to go to Mass this afternoon instead of in the morning?' she said.

'Sure.'

She swallowed a small bite from her sandwich and fixed her eyes on my face. Her hair moved in the breeze from the fan. She started to speak.

'I've made my peace about Sonny,' I said. 'He was brave, he was stand-up, he never compromised his principles. That's not a bad recommendation to take into the next world.'

'You're special, Streak.'

'So are you, kiddo.'

After we did the dishes she walked down to the vegetable garden at the end of the coulee, with the portable phone in her hand in case I was down at the dock when Alafair called from the show.

A blue Plymouth turned into the drive, and a moment later I saw Terry Serrett walk across the grass toward the gallery. She was dressed in loose-fitting pink-striped shorts, a white blouse, and red sandals; her drawstring beach bag swung against her thigh. Before she mounted the steps, she paused, looked back at the road and down at the dock.

I came to the screen door before she knocked. Her sunglasses were black in the shade; her mouth, which was bright red with lipstick, opened in surprise.

'Oh, there you are!' she said.

'Can I help you?'

'Maybe, if I could come in a minute.'

499

I looked at my watch and tried to smile. 'What's up?' I said. But I didn't open the screen.

She looked awkward, uncomfortable, her shoulders stiffening, an embarrassed grin breaking on the corner of her mouth.

'I'm sorry to ask you this, but I *have* to use your rest room.'

I opened the door and she walked past me into the living room, her eyes seeming to adjust or focus behind her glasses, as though she were examining the furniture in the room or perhaps in the hallway or in the kitchen.

'It's down the hall,' I said.

A moment later I heard the toilet flush and the water in the lavatory running.

She walked back into the living room.

'That's better,' she said. She examined the room, listening. 'It's so quiet. Are you Saturday house-sitting?'

'Oh, I'll be going down to work at the dock in a little while.'

She was absolutely immobile, as though she were caught between two antithetical thoughts, her thickly made-up face as white and as impossible to penetrate as a Kabuki mask.

The phone rang on the table by the couch.

'Excuse me a minute,' I said, and sat down and picked up the receiver from the hook. Through the front screen I saw Batist walking from the dock, up the slope toward the house.

'Dave?' the voice said through the receiver.

'Hey, Clete, what's happening?' I said.

'You remember Helen gave me a Xerox of Sonny's diary? All this time I had it under my car seat. This morning I brought it in and told Terry to stick it in the safe. A little while later I check, guess what, it's gone and so is she. I'm sitting at the desk by the safe, feeling like a stupid fuck, and I look down at the notepad there, you know, the one I took directions to Pogue's place on, and I realize the top sheet's clean. I'm sure I haven't used that pad since Pogue called. Somebody tore off the page that had my pencil impressions on it . . .

'You there?'

36

She pointed the Ruger .22 caliber automatic at my stomach.

'So you're Charlie,' I said.

She didn't answer. Her body was framed against the light through the window, as though crystal splinters were breaking over her shoulders. She looked out the window at Batist walking through the shade trees toward the gallery.

'Tell him you're busy, you'll be down at the dock later,' she said. 'Use those exact words.'

'None of this serves your cause.'

She picked up a pillow from a stuffed chair.

'You need to get rid of the black man,' she said.

I rose to my feet. She backed against the front wall, the pillow folded across the top of the Ruger. Her mouth was parted slightly, as though she used air only in teaspoons. I stood in the door and called through the screen: 'I'll be down at the dock later, Batist.'

'The air pump gone out on the shiner tank,' he said.

I hesitated, opened and closed my hands at my sides, felt the trees, the yard, the fractured blue of the sky almost pulling me through the screen. The woman named Terry raised the Ruger level with the side of my head, whispered dryly: 'He won't make three steps after I do you.'

'Give me a few minutes,' I called.

'One of us got to go in town.'

'I know that, podna.'

'Long as you know,' he said, and walked back down the slope.

I could hear the wood in the floor creak under my feet, the wind scudding leaves across the gallery.

'Back away from the door,' the woman said.

'We've still got the original manuscript,' I said.

'Nobody else cares about it. Back away from the door and sit in the stuffed chair.'

'Fuck you, Terry, or whatever your name is.'

Her face was as opaque as plaster. She closed the ends of the pillow around the Ruger, brought the barrel's tip upward until it was aimed at my throat.

I felt my eyes water and go out of focus.

Outside, Tripod raced on his chain up and down the clothesline. Her face jerked at the sound, then she shifted her weight, glanced quickly at the side window, an incisor tooth biting down on her lip, inadvertently moved the barrel's aim two inches to the side of my throat.

Bootsie fired from the hallway, the Beretta pointed in front of her with both hands.

The first round hit the woman high up in the right arm. Her blouse jumped and colored as though a small rose had been painted in the cloth by an invisible brush. But she swallowed the sound that tried to rise from her throat, and turned toward the hallway with the Ruger still in her hand.

Bootsie fired again, and the second round snapped a brittle hole through the left lens of the black-tinted sunglasses worn by the woman named Terry. Her fingers splayed stiffly at odd angles from one another as though all of her nerve connections had been severed; then her face seemed to melt like wax held to a flame as she slipped down between the wall and the stuffed chair, a vertical red line streaking the wallpaper.

My hands were shaking when I set the safety on the Beretta and removed it from Bootsie's grasp, pulled the magazine and ejected the round from the chamber.

I squeezed her against me, rubbed my hands over her hair and back, kissed her eyes and the sweat on her neck.

She started toward the woman on the floor.

'No,' I said, and turned her toward the kitchen, the light pouring through the western windows, the trees outside swelling with wind.

'We have to go back,' she said.

'No.'

'Maybe she's still . . . Maybe she needs . . .'

'No.'

I made her sit down on the redwood picnic bench while I walked to the garden by the coulee and found the portable phone where she had dropped it in the grass, the transmission button still on. But before I could punch in 911 I heard sirens in the distance and saw Batist come out the back door with a dogleg twenty-gauge in his hand.

'It's okay,' I said. 'Send the deputies inside.'

His eyes went from me to Bootsie.

'We're fine here, Batist,' I said.

He nodded, cracked open the barrel of the shotgun, and walked down the drive, the open breech crooked over his forearm, peeling the cellophane off a cigar with his thumbnail.

I put my palm on Bootsie's neck, felt the wetness of her hair, her skin that was as hot as a lamp shade.

'It's going to pass,' I said.

'What?' She looked at me blankly.

'You didn't have a choice. If you hadn't picked up Clete's call, I'd be dead.'

'Clete? Clete didn't . . . The phone rang out in the garden and he said, "Dave's in trouble. I can't help him. It's too far to come now. You have to do it."'

'Who?'

'I can't handle this. You said you saw his tattoo on the remains in the morgue. You swore you did. But I know that voice, Dave. My God . . .' But she didn't finish. She pressed the heels of her hands into her eyes and began to weep.

37

I believe Moleen Bertrand was like many of my generation with whom I grew up along Bayou Teche. We found ourselves caught inside a historical envelope that we never understood, borne along on wind currents that marked our ending, not our beginning, first as provincial remnants of a dying Acadian culture, later as part of that excoriated neo-colonial army who would go off to a war whose origins were as arcane to us as the economics of French poppy growers.

When we finally made a plan for ourselves, it was to tear a hole in the middle of our lives.

I don't know why Moleen chose to do it in an apartment off Rampart, near the edge of the Quarter, not far from the one-time quadroon brothels of Storyville and the Iberville Project where Sonny Boy grew up. Perhaps it was because the ambiance of palm fronds, rusting grillwork, and garish pastels that tried to cover the cracked plaster and crumbling brick was ultimately the signature of Moleen's world – jaded, alluring in its decay, seemingly reborn daily amidst tropical flowers and Gulf rainstorms, inextricably linked to a corrupt past that we secretly admired.

At five in the morning I got the call from an alcoholic ex-Homicide partner at First District Headquarters.

'The coroner won't be able to bag it up till after eight, in case you want to come down and check it out,' he said.

'How'd you know to call me?' I said.

'Your business card was on his nightstand. That and his driver's license were about all he had on him. The place got creeped before we arrived.' He yawned into the phone. 'What was he, a pimp?'

The flight in the department's single-engine plane was only a half hour, but the day was already warm, the streets dense with humidity, when Helen Soileau and I walked through the brick-paved courtyard of the building, into the small apartment whose walls were painted an arterial red and hung with black velvet curtains that covered no windows.

Moleen and Ruthie Jean lay fully clothed on top of the double bed, their heads wrapped in clear plastic bags. A crime scene photographer was taking their picture from several angles; each time his flash went off their faces seemed to leap to life inside the folds of the plastic.

'He was a lawyer, huh? Who was the broad?' my ex-partner said. He wore a hat and was drinking coffee from a Styrofoam cup.

'Just a farm girl,' I said.

'Some farm girl. She did both of them.'

'She did what?' I said.

'His bag was tied from behind, hers in front. I hope she was a good piece of ass,' he said.

'Shut up,' Helen said. 'Did you hear me? Just shut the fuck up.'

Later, Helen and I turned down an offer of a ride to the airport and instead walked up to Canal to catch a cab. The street was loud with traffic and car horns, the air stifling, the muted sun as unrelenting and eye-watering as a hangover. The crowds of people on the sidewalks moved through the heat, their faces expressionless, the gaze in their eyes introspective and dead, preset on destinations that held neither joy nor pain, neither loss nor victory.

'What are you doing, Streak?' Helen said.

I took her by the hand and crossed to the neutral ground, drew her with me into the belly of the great iron streetcar from the year 1910 that creaked on curved tracks past the Pearl, with its scrolled black colonnade on the corner of Canal and St Charles, where Sonny Boy used to put together deals under a wood-bladed fan, on up the avenue, clattering past sidewalks cracked by oak roots as thick as swollen fire hoses, into a long tunnel of trees and heliographic light that was like tumbling through the bottom of a green well, to a place where, perhaps, the confines of reason and predictability had little application.

Epilogue

Late fall is a strange time of year in southern Louisiana. After first frost robins fill the trees along the bayou and camellias that seem fashioned from crepe paper bloom with the colors of spring, even though winter is at hand. The sky is absolutely blue and cloudless, without an imperfection in it, but at evening the sunlight hardens and grows cold, as it might in a metaphysical poem, the backroads are choked with cane wagons on their way to the mill, and the stubble fires on the fields drench the air with an acrid, sweet smell like syrup scorched on a woodstove.

Bootsie and I took Alafair to the LSU–Ole Miss game that year and later stopped for crawfish at Possum's on the St Martinville Road. It had been a wonderful day, the kind that memory will never need to improve upon, and when we got home we lighted Alafair's jack-o'-lanterns on the gallery and fixed hand-crank ice cream and frozen blackberries in the kitchen.

Maybe it was the nature of the season, or the fact that quail and dove freckled the red sun in my neighbor's field, but I knew there was something I had to do that evening or I would have no rest.

And like some pagan of old, weighing down spirits in the ground with tablets of stone, I cut a bucket full of chrysanthemums and drove out to the Bertrand plantation, down the dirt road past the tenant houses, to the grove of gum trees that had once been a cemetery for slaves. When I got out of the truck the air was damp and cold and smelled like dust and rain; curlicues of sparks fanned out of the ash in the fields and I could hear leaves swirling dryly across the concrete pad abandoned by the construction company.

I put in my raincoat and hat and walked across the field to the treeline and the collapsed corn crib where Ruthie Jean and Moleen had begun their affair, where they had been spied on by the overseer whom Luke Fontenot would later kill, where they had reenacted that old Southern black-white confession of need and dependence that, in its peculiar way, was a recognition of the simple biological fact of our brotherhood.

And for that reason only, I told myself, I stuck the flowers by their stems in what was left of the crib's doorway, then began walking back toward my truck just as the first raindrops clicked against the brim of my hat.

But I knew better. *All* our stories began here – mine, Moleen's, the Fontenot family's, even Sonny's. Born to the griff, pool halls, and small-time prize rings, he somehow stepped across an unseen line and became someone whom even he didn't recognize. The scars on his body became lesions on our consciences, his jailhouse rebop a paean for Woody Guthrie and Joe Hill.

If I learned anything from my association with Moleen and Ruthie Jean and Sonny Boy, it's the fact that we seldom know each other and can only guess at the lives that wait to be lived in every human being.

And if you should ever doubt the proximity of the past, I thought to myself, you only had to look over your shoulder at the rain slanting on the fields, like now, the smoke rising in wet plumes out of the stubble, the mist blowing off the lake, and you can see and hear with the clarity of a dream the columns marching four abreast out of the trees, barefoot, emaciated as scarecrows, their perforated, sun-faded colors popping above them in the wind, their officers cantering their horses in the field, everyone dressing it up now, the clatter of muskets shifting in unison to the right shoulder, yes, just a careless wink of the eye, just that quick, and you're among them, wending your way with liege lord and serf and angel, in step with the great armies of the dead.

Purple Cane Road

for old-time University of Missouri pals
Harold Frisbee and Jerry Hood

1

Years ago, in state documents, Vachel Carmouche was always referred to as the electrician, never as the executioner. That was back in the days when the electric chair was sometimes housed at Angola. At other times it traveled, along with its own generators, on a flatbed semitruck from parish prison to parish prison. Vachel Carmouche did the state's work. He was good at it.

In New Iberia we knew his real occupation but pretended we did not. He lived by himself, up Bayou Teche, in a tin-roofed, paintless cypress house that stayed in the deep shade of oak trees. He planted no flowers in his yard and seldom raked it, but he always drove a new car and washed and polished it religiously.

Early each morning we'd see him in a cafe on East Main, sitting by himself at the counter, in his pressed gray or khaki clothes and cloth cap, his eyes studying other customers in the mirror, his slight overbite paused above his coffee cup, as though he were waiting to speak, although he rarely engaged others in conversation.

When he caught you looking at him, he smiled quickly, his sun-browned face threading with hundreds of lines, but his smile did not go with the expression in his eyes.

Vachel Carmouche was a bachelor. If he had lady friends, we were not aware of them. He came infrequently to Provost's Bar and Pool Room and would sit at my table or next to me at the bar, indicating in a vague way that we were both law officers and hence shared a common experience.

That was when I was in uniform at NOPD and was still enamored with Jim Beam straight up and a long-neck Jax on the side.

One night he found me at a table by myself at Provost's and sat down without being asked, a white bowl of okra gumbo in his hands. A veterinarian and a grocery store owner I had been drinking with came out of the men's room and glanced at the table, then went to the bar and ordered beer there and drank with their backs to us.

'Being a cop is a trade-off, isn't it?' Vachel said.

'Sir?' I said.

'You don't have to call me "sir" . . . You spend a lot of time alone?'

'Not so much.'

'I think it goes with the job. I was a state trooper once.' His eyes, which were as gray as his starched shirt, drifted to the shot glass in front of me and the rings my beer mug had left on the tabletop. 'A drinking man goes home to a lot of echoes. The way a stone sounds in a dry well. No offense meant, Mr Robicheaux. Can I buy you a round?'

The acreage next to Vachel Carmouche was owned by the Labiche family, descendants of what had been known as free people of color before the Civil War. The patriarch of the family had been a French-educated mulatto named Jubal Labiche who owned a brick factory on the bayou south of New Iberia. He both owned and rented slaves and worked them unmercifully and supplied much of the brick for the homes of his fellow slave owners up and down the Teche.

The columned house he built south of the St Martin Parish line did not contain the Italian marble or Spanish ironwork of the sugar growers whose wealth was far greater than his own and whose way of life he sought to emulate. But he planted live oaks along the drives and hung his balconies and veranda with flowers; his slaves kept his pecan and peach orchards and produce fields broom-sweep clean. Although he was not invited into the homes of whites, they respected him as a businessman and taskmaster and treated him with courtesy on the street. That was almost enough for Jubal Labiche. Almost. He sent his children North to be educated, in hopes they would marry up, across the color line, that the high-yellow stain that limited his ambition would eventually bleach out of the Labiche family's skin.

Unfortunately for him, when the federals came up the Teche in April of 1863 they thought him every bit the equal of his white neighbors. In democratic fashion they freed his slaves, burned his fields and barns and corncribs, tore the ventilated shutters off his windows for litters to carry their wounded, and chopped up his imported furniture and piano for firewood.

Twenty-five years ago the last adult members of the Labiche family to bear the name, a husband and a wife, filled themselves with whiskey and sleeping pills, tied plastic bags over their heads, and died in a parked car behind a Houston pickup bar. Both were procurers. Both had been federal witnesses against a New York crime family.

They left behind identical twin daughters, aged five years, named Letty and Passion Labiche.

The girls' eyes were blue, their hair the color of smoke, streaked with dark gold, as though it had been painted there with a brush. An aunt, who was addicted to morphine and claimed to be a *traiture*, or juju woman, was assigned guardianship by the state. Often Vachel Carmouche volunteered to baby-sit the girls, or walk them out to the road to wait for the Head Start bus that took them to the preschool program in New Iberia.

We did not give his attentions to the girls much thought. Perhaps good came out of bad, we told ourselves, and there was an area in Carmouche's soul that had not been disfigured by the deeds he performed with the machines he oiled and cleaned by hand and transported from jail to jail. Perhaps his kindness toward children was his attempt at redemption.

Besides, their welfare was the business of the state, wasn't it?

In fourth grade one of the twins, Passion, told her teacher of a recurrent nightmare and the pain she awoke with in the morning.

The teacher took Passion to Charity Hospital in Lafayette, but the physician said the abrasions could have been caused by the child playing on the seesaw in City Park.

When the girls were about twelve I saw them with Vachel Carmouche on a summer night out at Veazey's ice cream store on West Main. They wore identical checkered sundresses and different-colored ribbons in their hair. They sat in Carmouche's truck, close to the door, a lackluster deadness in their eyes, their mouths turned down at the corners, while he talked out the window to a black man in bib overalls.

'I've been patient with you, boy. You got the money you had coming. You calling me a liar?' he said.

'No, suh, I ain't doing that.'

'Then good night to you,' he said. When one of the girls said something, he popped her lightly on the cheek and started his truck.

I walked across the shell parking area and stood by his window.

'Excuse me, but what gives you the right to hit someone else's child in the face?' I asked.

'I think you misperceived what happened,' he replied.

'Step out of your truck, please.'

'My cotton-pickin' foot. You're out of your jurisdiction, Mr Robicheaux. You got liquor on your breath, too.'

He backed his truck out from under the oak trees and drove away.

I went to Provost's and drank for three hours at the bar and watched the pool games and the old men playing bouree and dominoes under the wood-bladed fans. The warm air smelled of talcum and dried perspiration and the green sawdust on the floor.

'Have any locals pulled in Vachel Carmouche?' I asked the bartender.

'Go home, Dave,' he said.

I drove north along Bayou Teche to Carmouche's home. The house was dark, but next door the porch and living room lights were on at the Labiche house. I pulled into the Labiche driveway and walked across the yard toward the brick steps. The ground was sunken, moldy with pecan husks and dotted with palmettos, the white paint on the house stained with smoke from stubble fires in the cane fields. My face felt warm and dilated with alcohol, my ears humming with sound that had no origin.

Vachel Carmouche opened the front door and stepped out into the light. I could see the twins and the aunt peering out the door behind him.

'I think you're abusing those children,' I said.

'You're an object of pity and ridicule, Mr Robicheaux,' he replied.

'Step out here in the yard.'

His face was shadowed, his body haloed with humidity in the light behind him.

'I'm armed,' he said when I approached him.

I struck his face with my open hand, his whiskers scraping like grit against my skin, his mouth streaking my palm with his saliva.

He touched his upper lip, which had broken against his overbite, and looked at the blood on his fingers.

'You come here with vomit on your breath and stink in your clothes and judge me?' he said. 'You sit in the Red Hat House and watch while I put men to death, then condemn me because I try to care for orphan children? You're a hypocrite, Mr Robicheaux. Be gone, sir.'

He went inside and closed the door behind him and turned off the porch light. My face felt small and tight, like the skin on an apple, in the heated darkness.

I returned to New Orleans and my problems with pari-mutuel windows and a dark-haired, milk-skinned wife from Martinique who went home with men from the Garden District while I was passed out in a houseboat on Lake Pontchartrain, the downdraft of U.S. Army helicopters flattening a plain of elephant grass in my dreams.

I heard stories about the Labiche girls: their troubles with narcotics; the bikers and college boys and sexual adventurers who drifted in and out of their lives; their minor roles in a movie that was shot outside Lafayette; the R&B record Letty cut in prison that made the charts for two or three weeks.

When I bottomed out I often included the girls in my prayers and regretted deeply that I had been a drunk when perhaps I could have made a difference in their lives. Once I dreamed of them cowering in a bed, waiting for a man's footsteps outside their door and a hand that would quietly twist the knob in the jamb. But in daylight I convinced myself that my failure was only a small contributing factor in the tragedy of their lives, that my guilty feelings were simply another symptom of alcoholic grandiosity.

Vachel Carmouche's undoing came aborning from his long-suppressed desire for publicity and recognition. On a vacation in Australia he was interviewed by a television journalist about his vocation as a state executioner.

Carmouche sneered at his victims.

'They try to act macho when they come into the room. But I can see the sheen of fear in their eyes,' he said.

He lamented the fact that electrocution was an inadequate punishment for the type of men he had put to death.

'It's too quick. They should suffer. Just like the people they killed,' he said.

The journalist was too numb to ask a follow-up question.

The tape was picked up by the BBC, then aired in the United States. Vachel Carmouche lost his job. His sin lay not in his deeds but in his visibility.

He boarded up his house and disappeared for many years, where to, we never knew. Then he returned one spring evening eight years ago, pried the plywood off his windows, and hacked the weeds out of his yard with a sickle while the radio played on his gallery and a pork roast smoked on his barbecue pit. A black girl of about twelve sat on the edge of the gallery, her bare feet in the dust, idly turning the crank on an ice cream maker.

After sunset he went inside and ate dinner at his kitchen table, a bottle of refrigerated wine uncapped by his plate. A hand tapped on the back door, and he rose from his chair and pushed open the screen.

A moment later he was crawling across the linoleum while a mattock tore into his spine and rib cage, his neck and scalp, exposing vertebrae, piercing kidneys and lungs, blinding him in one eye.

Letty Labiche was arrested naked in her backyard, where she was burning a robe and work shoes in a trash barrel and washing Vachel Carmouche's blood off her body and out of her hair with a garden hose.

For the next eight years she would use every means possible to avoid the day she would be moved to the Death House at Angola Penitentiary and be strapped down on a table where a medical technician, perhaps even a physician, would inject her with drugs that sealed her eyes and congealed the muscles in her face and shut down her respiratory system, causing her to die inside her own skin with no sign of discomfort being transmitted to the spectators.

I had witnessed two electrocutions at Angola. They sickened and repelled me, even though I was involved in the arrest and prosecution of both men. But neither affected me the way Letty Labiche's fate would.

2

Clete Purcel still had his private investigator's office in the Quarter, down on St Ann, and ate breakfast every morning in the Café du Monde across from Jackson Square. That's where I found him, the third Saturday in April, at a shady outdoor table, a cup of coffee and hot milk and pile of powdered beignets on a plate in front of him.

He wore a blue silk shirt with huge red flowers on it, a porkpie hat, and Roman sandals and beige slacks. His coat was folded over an empty chair, the handkerchief pocket torn loose from the stitching. He had sandy hair that he combed straight back and a round Irish face and green eyes that always had a beam in them. His arms had the girth and hardness of fire plugs, the skin dry and scaling from the sunburn that never quite turned into a tan.

At one time he was probably the best homicide investigator NOPD ever had. Now he ran down bail skips in the projects for Nig Rosewater and Wee Willie Bimstine.

'So I'm hooking up Little Face Dautrieve when her pimp comes out of the closet with a shank and almost cuts my nipple off,' he said. 'I paid three hundred bucks for that suit two weeks ago.'

'Where's the pimp?' I asked.

'I'll let you know when I find him.'

'Tell me again about Little Face.'

'What's to tell? She's got clippings about Letty Labiche all over her living room. I ask her if she's morbid and she goes, "No, I'm from New Iberia." So I go, "Being on death row makes people celebrities in New Iberia?" She says, "Brush your teeth more often, Fat Man, and change your deodorant while you're at it." '

He put a beignet in his mouth and looked at me while he chewed.

'What's she down on?' I asked.

'Prostitution and possession. She says the vice cop who busted her got her to lay him first, then he planted some rock in her purse. He says he'll make the possession charge go away if she'll provide regular boom-boom for him and a department liaison guy.'

'I thought the department had been cleaned up.'

'Right,' Clete said. He wiped his mouth with a paper napkin and picked up his coat. 'Come on, I'll drop this at the tailor's and take you out to the project.'

'You said you hooked her up.'

'I called Nig and got her some slack . . . Don't get the wrong idea, mon. Her pimp is Zipper Clum. Little Face stays on the street, he'll be back around.'

We parked under a tree at the welfare project and walked across a dirt playground toward the two-story brick apartment building with green window trim and small green wood porches where Little Face Dautrieve lived. We passed a screen window and Clete fanned the air in front of his face. He stared through the screen, then banged on the frame with his fist.

'Lose the pipe and open the front door,' he said.

'Anything for you, Fat Man. But don't get on my bat'room scale again. You done broke all the springs,' a voice said from inside.

'My next job is going to be at the zoo. I can't take this anymore,' Clete said when we were on the front porch.

Little Face pushed open the door and held it while we walked inside. She wore cut-off blue jeans and a white T-shirt and had very dark skin and lustrous, thick hair that she wore on her shoulders. Her eyes were no bigger than dimes.

'This is Dave Robicheaux. He's a homicide detective in Iberia Parish,' Clete said. 'He's a friend of Letty Labiche.'

She tilted up her profile and pursed her lips and brushed back her hair with her fingers. She had on heels, and her rump and the backs of her thighs were taut against her shorts.

'How about flexing your brain instead of your stuff for a change?' Clete said.

'What he want wit' me?' she said.

'Why would you keep all those newspaper clippings about Letty?' I asked.

'They for Zipper,' she replied.

'You know how Zipper got his name? He carved all over a girl's face with a razor blade,' Clete said to her.

'We still love you, Fat Man. Everybody down here do,' she said.

'I hate this job,' Clete said.

I placed my hands lightly on the tops of Little Face's arms. For a moment the cocaine glaze went out of her eyes.

'Letty Labiche is probably going to be executed. A lot of people think that shouldn't happen. Do you know something that can help her?' I said.

Her mouth was small and red, and she puckered her lips uncertainly, her eyes starting to water now. She pulled out of my grasp and turned away.

'I got an allergy. It makes me sneeze all the time,' she said.

The mantel over the small fireplace was decorated with blue and red glass candle containers. I stooped down and picked up a burned newspaper photo of Letty from the hearth. Her image looked like it was trapped inside a charcoal-stained transparency. A puff of wind blew through the door, and the newspaper broke into ash that rose in the chimney like gray moths.

'You been working some juju, Little Face?' I asked.

' 'Cause I sell out of my pants don't mean I'm stupid and superstitious.'

Then she said to Clete, 'You better go, Fat Man. Take your friend wit' you, too. You ain't funny no more.'

Sunday morning I went to Mass with my wife, Bootsie, and my adopted daughter, Alafair, then I drove out to the Labiche home on the bayou.

Passion Labiche was raking pecan leaves in the backyard and burning them in a rusty barrel. She wore men's shoes and work pants and a rumpled cotton shirt tied under her breasts. She heard my footsteps behind her and grinned at me over her shoulder. Her olive skin was freckled, her back muscular from years of field work. In looking at the brightness of her face, you would not think she grieved daily on the plight of her sister. But grieve she did, and I believed few people knew to what degree.

She dropped a rake-load of wet leaves and pecan husks on the fire, and the smoke curled out of the barrel in thick curds like damp sulfur burning. She fanned her face with a magazine.

'I found a twenty-year-old hooker in New Orleans who seems to have a big emotional investment in your sister's case. Her name's Little Face Dautrieve. She's originally from New Iberia,' I said.

'I don't guess I know her,' she said.

'How about a pimp named Zipper Clum?'

'Oh, yes. You forget Zipper about as easy as face warts,' she said, and made a clicking sound and started raking again.

'Where do you know him from?' I said.

'My parents were in the life. Zipper Clum's been at it a long time.' Then her eyes seemed to go empty as though she were looking at a thought in the center of her mind. 'What'd you find out from this black girl?'

'Nothing.'

She nodded, her eyes still translucent, empty of anything I could read. Then she said, 'The lawyers say we still got a chance with the Supreme Court. I wake up in the morning and think maybe it's all gonna be okay. We'll get a new trial, a new jury, the kind you see on television, full of people who turn abused women loose. Then I fix coffee and the day's full of spiders.'

I stared at her back while she raked. She stopped and turned around.

'Something wrong?' she said.

'I didn't mention Little Face Dautrieve was black,' I said.

She removed a strand of hair from the corner of her mouth. Her skin looked dry and cool inside the smoke from the fire, her hands resting on the rake, her shoulders erect.

'What are the odds she work for Zipper and she white?' she said.

When I didn't reply her eyes wandered out into the yard.

'I'll stay in touch,' I said finally.

'You bet, good-looking man, you.'

I operated a boat-rental and bait business on the bayou down toward Avery Island, south of New Iberia. The house my father had built of cypress sat up on a slope above the dirt road, its wide gallery and rusted corrugated roof shaded by live-oak and pecan trees. The beds were planted with roses, impatiens, hydrangeas, and hibiscus, and we had a horse lot for Alafair's Appaloosa and a rabbit hutch and a duck pond at the foot of the backyard. From the gallery we could look down through the tree trunks in the yard to the dock and concrete boat ramp and the bait shop and the swamp on the far side. At sunset I pulled back the awning on the guy wires that ran above the dock and turned on the string of overhead lights and you could see the bream feeding on the insects around the pilings and the water hyacinths that grew in islands among the cypress knees. Every night the sky over the Gulf danced with heat lightning, white sheets of it that rippled silently through hundreds of miles of thunderheads in the wink of an eye.

I loved the place where I lived and the house my father had built and notched and grooved and pegged with his hands, and I loved the people I lived with in the house.

Sunday night Bootsie and I ate supper on the picnic table under the mimosa tree in the backyard. The wind was balmy and smelled of salt and fish spawning, and the moon was up and I could see the young sugarcane blowing in my neighbor's field.

Bootsie set out a tray of deviled eggs and sliced ham and onions and tomatoes on the table and poured two glasses full of crushed ice and sun tea and put sprigs of mint in them. Her hair was the color of honey and she had cut it so it was short and thick on the back of her neck. She had the most lovely complexion of any woman I had ever known. It had the pinkness of a rose petal when the rose first opens into light, and a faint flush came into her cheeks and throat when she made love or when she was angry.

'You saw Passion Labiche today?' she asked.

'Yeah. It bothered me a little bit, too,' I said.

'Why?'

'A hooker in New Orleans, a bail skip Clete ran down, had saved all these clippings about Letty. I asked Passion if she knew her. She said she didn't, but then she slipped and referred to the girl as being black. Why would she want to lie?'

'Maybe she was just making an assumption.'

'People of color usually make derogatory assumptions about their own race?' I said.

'All right, smart,' she said.

'Sorry.'

She hit the top of my hand with her spoon. Just then the phone rang in the kitchen.

I went inside and picked it up.

'I got the word on Zipper Clum. He's going to be in a fuck pad in Baton Rouge about two hours from now. Out towards where Highland Road runs into the highway . . . You there?' Clete said.

'Yeah. I'm just a little tired.'

'I thought you wanted the gen on those news clippings.'

'Can we nail this guy another time?'

'The Zip's a moving target,' he said.

*

I put my army-issue .45 that I had brought home from Vietnam on the seat of my truck and took the four-lane to Lafayette, then caught I-10 across the Atchafalaya Basin. The wind came up and it started to rain, dimpling the bays on each side of the causeway. The islands of willows and flooded cypress were in early leaf, whipping in the wind, and there was a hard chop in the bays that broke against the pilings of abandoned oil platforms. I crossed the Atchafalaya River, which had swollen over its banks into the woods, then the wetlands began to fall behind me and I was driving through pasture and farmland again and up ahead I could see the bridge across the Mississippi and the night glow of Baton Rouge against the sky.

I drove through the city, then east on Highland, out into the country again, and turned on a shell road that led back into a grove of trees. I saw Clete's maroon Cadillac parked by a white cinder-block apartment building whose windows were nailed over with plywood. A second car, a new Buick with tinted windows, was parked next to a cluster of untrimmed banana trees. A light burned behind the plywood on the second floor of the building, and another light was turned on inside a shed that had been built over the stairwell on the roof.

I clipped my holster on my belt and got out of the truck and walked toward the front entrance. It had stopped raining now, and the wind puffed the trees over my head. The dark blue paint of the Buick was luminous with the rainwater that had beaded into drops as big as quarters on the wax.

I heard feet scraping on the roof, then a man's voice yell out and a sound like a heavy weight crashing through tree limbs.

I slipped the .45 out of its holster and went to the side of the building and looked up toward the roof. I saw Clete Purcel lean over the half-wall that bordered the roof, stare at something down below, then disappear.

I went in the front door and climbed the stairs to a hallway that was littered with garbage and broken plaster. Only one room was lighted. The door was open and a video camera on a tripod was propped up by a bed with a red satin sheet on it.

I went up another stairwell to the roof. I stepped out on the gravel and tar surface and saw Clete grab a black man by his belt and the back of his collar and run him toward the wall, then fling him, arms churning, into a treetop down below.

'What are you doing?' I said incredulously.

'They were gang-banging a pair of sixteen-year-old girls down there and filming it. Zipper and his pals have gone into the movie business,' Clete said. He wore a blue-black .38 in a nylon and leather shoulder holster. A flat-sided sap stuck out of his back pocket. 'Right, Zip?'

He kicked the sole of a mulatto who was handcuffed by one wrist to a fire-escape rung. The mulatto's eyes were turquoise, the irises ringed with a frosted discoloration. A puckered, concentric gray scar was burned into one cheek. His hair was almost white, straight, like a Caucasian's, cut short, his body as taut and shiny as wrapped plastic, his arms scrolled with jailhouse art.

'Robicheaux?' he said, focusing on my face.

'Why's Little Face Dautrieve collecting news articles on Letty Labiche?' I asked.

'Her brains are in her ass. That's where they suppose to be. Say, your man here kind of out of control. How 'bout a little intervention?'

'I don't have much influence with him,' I said.

'It's your flight time, Zipper. I'm not sure I can hit that tree again, though,' Clete said. He pulled his revolver from his shoulder holster and threw it to me, then leaned down and unlocked the cuff on Zipper's wrist and jerked him to his feet.

'Look over the side, Zipper. It's going to break all your sticks, guaranteed. Last chance, my man,' Clete said.

Zipper took a breath and raised both hands in front of him, as though placating an unteachable adversary.

'I tole you, Little Face got her own groove. I don't know why she do what she do,' he said.

'Wrong answer, shithead,' Clete said, and hooked one hand under Zipper's belt and clenched the other tightly on the back of his neck.

Zipper's face twisted toward mine, the rictus of his mouth filled with gold and silver, his breath a fog of funk and decayed shrimp.

'Robicheaux, your mama's name was Mae . . . Wait, it was Guillory before she married. That was the name she went by . . . Mae Guillory. But she was your mama,' he said.

'What?' I said.

He wet his lips uncertainly.

'She dealt cards and still hooked a little bit. Behind a club in Lafourche Parish. This was maybe 1966 or '67,' he said.

Clete's eyes were fixed on my face. 'You're in a dangerous area, sperm breath,' he said to Zipper.

'They held her down in a mud puddle. They drowned her,' Zipper said.

'They drowned my . . . Say that again,' I said, my left hand reaching for his shirt, my right lifting Clete's .38 toward his face.

'These cops were on a pad. For the Giacanos. She saw them kill somebody. They held her down in the mud, then rolled her into the bayou,' Zipper said.

Then Clete was between me and Zipper Clum, shoving me in the chest, pushing away the gun in my hand as though it were attached to a spring. 'Look at me, Streak! Get out of it! Don't make me clock you, noble mon . . . Hey, that's it. We're copacetic here, yes indeedy. Nothing rattles the Bobbsey Twins from Homicide.'

3

My father was an enormous, black-haired, illiterate Cajun whose saloon brawls were not only a terrifying experience for his adversaries but beautiful to watch. He would back against a wall in Provost's or Slick's or Mulate's and take on all comers, his hamlike fists crashing against the heads of his opponents, while cops and bouncers tried to nail him with pool cues and chairs and batons before he destroyed the entire bar. Blood would well out of his scalp and glisten in his beard and wild, curly hair; the more his adversaries hit him, the more he would grin and beckon the brave and incautious into range of his fists.

That was the Aldous Robicheaux people saw publicly, fighting, his shirt and striped overalls ripped off his back, his wrists handcuffed behind him while a half dozen cops escorted him to a police car. They never saw what my father and mother did to each other at home before my father went to the saloon to find a surrogate for the enemy he couldn't deal with inside his own breast.

My mother was a plump, attractive woman who worked for thirty cents an hour in a laundry that employed mostly Negro women. She loved to dress up and wear her lavender pillbox hat, one with a stiff white net on it, and go to dance halls and crawfish boils and the *fais-dodo* in Breaux Bridge. While my father was in the parish prison, other men came to our house, and two of them offered my mother access to what she thought was a much better world than the one she shared with my father.

Hank was a soldier stationed at Fort Polk, a tall, sun-browned man with a red, welted scar from Omaha Beach on his shoulder who told my mother he belonged to the stagehands union in Hollywood. In the morning he would go into the bathroom when my mother was already in there, and I would hear them laughing through the door. Then he would stay in there a long time by himself, filling the room with steam. When I went in to bathe before school, no warm water was left in the tank, and he would tell me to heat a pan on the stove and wash with a rag at the kitchen sink.

'Mama wants me to take a whole bath,' I said one morning.

'Suit yourself, kid. Scrub out the tub when you get finished. I don't like sitting in somebody else's dirt,' he replied.

He smelled of testosterone and shaving cream and the cigarette he kept balanced on the lavatory while he combed Lucky Tiger into his hair in front of the mirror, a towel wrapped around his hips. He saw me watching him in the mirror and he turned and cocked his fists like a prizefighter's.

He and my mother boarded the Sunset Limited in 1946 and went out to Hollywood. On the platform she hugged me against her and kept patting me on the head and back as though her hands could convey meaning her words could not.

'I'm gonna send for you. I promise, Davy. You gonna see movie stars and swim in the ocean and go on roller-coaster rides out over the water, you. It ain't like here, no. It don't never rain and people got all the money they want,' she said.

When she returned to New Iberia on the bus, the ticket purchased with money my father had to wire a priest, she showed me postcards of Angel's Flight and Grauman's Chinese Theater and the beach at Malibu, as though these were magic places that had defined her experience in California rather than a garage apartment by a downtown freeway where Hank had left her one morning with the icebox empty and the rent unpaid.

But it was a thin, small-boned bouree dealer named Mack who took her away from us permanently. He owned a car and wore a fedora and two-tone shoes and had a moustache that looked like it had been drawn above his lip with grease pencil. I hated Mack more than any of the others. He feared my father and was cruel in the way all cowards are. He knew how to inflict injury deep into the bone, and he always had an explanation to mask the nature of his real agenda, like a man who tickles a child incessantly and says he means no harm.

My calico cat gave birth to her litter in the barn, but Mack found them before I did. He put them in a paper sack and weighted the sack with a rock and sank it in the coulee, pushing me away with his palm, then raising a cautionary finger at my face.

'Don't touch me again, no, 'cause I'm gonna hit you,' he said. 'Them kittens gonna grow up and kill the chicks, just like their mama been doin'. You gonna buy more chickens, you? You gonna put food on the table, you?'

He and my mother drove away one summer's day in a rooster tail of dust to Morgan City, where Mack got her a job at a beer garden. I didn't see her again until many years later, when I was in high school and I went to a roadhouse on the Breaux Bridge Highway with some other boys. It was a ramshackle gambling and pickup place, where the patrons fought over whores with bottles and knives in the parking lot. She was dancing with a drunk by the jukebox, her stomach pressed into his loins. Her face was tilted up into his, as though she were intrigued by his words. Then she saw me looking at her from the bar, saw my hand lift from my side to wave at her, and she smiled back at me briefly, her eyes shiny and indolent with alcohol, a vague recognition swimming into her face and disappearing as quickly as it came.

I never saw her again.

Monday morning the sheriff called me into his office. He wore a striped, black suit with a purple-and-white-striped snap-button shirt and a hand-tooled belt and half-topped boots. The windowsill behind his head was lined with potted plants that glowed in the thinly slatted light through the blinds. He had run a dry-cleaning business before he was elected sheriff and was probably more Rotarian than lawman; but he had been in the First Marine Division at the Chosin Reservoir and no one questioned his level of integrity or courage or the dues he had paid and never spoke about (except, to my knowledge, on one occasion, when he'd had a coronary and thought he was dying and he told me of pink airbursts high above the snow on the hills and Chinese bugles blowing in the darkness and winds that could swell fingers into purple balloons).

His stomach hung over his belt and his cheeks were often flushed from hypertension, but his erect posture, either sitting or standing, always gave him the appearance of a much greater level of health than he actually possessed.

'I just got off the phone with the East Baton Rouge sheriff's office,' he said, looking down at a yellow legal pad by his elbow. 'They say a couple of black lowlifes were thrown off a roof east of town last night.'

'Oh?'

'One of them has a broken arm, the other a concussion. The only reason they're alive is they crashed through the top of an oak tree.'

I nodded, as though unsure of his larger meaning.

'The two lowlifes say Clete Purcel is the guy who made them airborne. You know anything about this?' the sheriff said.

'Clete's methods are direct sometimes.'

'What's most interesting is one of them took down the license number of your truck.' The sheriff's eyes dropped to his legal pad. 'Let's see, I jotted down a quote from the East Baton Rouge sheriff. "Who told your homicide investigator he could come into my parish with an animal like Clete Purcel and do business with a baseball bat?" I didn't quite have an answer for him.'

'You remember my mother?' I asked.

'Sure,' he replied, his eyes shifting off mine, going empty now.

'A pimp named Zipper Clum was on that roof. He told me he saw my mother killed. Back in 1966 or '67. He wasn't sure of the year. It wasn't an important moment in his career.'

The sheriff leaned back in his chair and lowered his eyes and rubbed the cleft in his chin with two fingers.

'I'd like to believe you trusted me enough to tell me that up front,' he said.

'People like Zipper Clum lie a lot. He claims two cops drowned her in a mud puddle. They shot somebody and put a throw-down on the corpse. My mother saw it. At least that's what Clum says.'

He tore the top page off his legal pad and crumpled it up slowly and dropped it in the wastebasket.

'You want some help on this?' he asked.

'I'm not sure.'

'Ernest Hemingway said chasing the past is a bum way to live your life,' the sheriff said.

'He also said he never took his own advice.'

The sheriff rose from his swivel chair and began watering his plants with a hand-painted teakettle. I closed the door softly behind me.

I took a vacation day Friday and drove back to New Orleans and parked my truck on the edge of the Quarter and walked through Jackson Square and Pirates Alley, past the deep green, shaded garden behind St Louis Cathedral, and down St Ann to Clete Purcel's office.

The building was tan stucco and contained an arched foyer and flagstone courtyard planted with banana trees. An 'Out to Lunch' sign hung in the downstairs window. I went through the foyer and up the stairs to the second floor, where Clete lived in a one-bedroom apartment with a balcony that gave onto the street. The ironwork on the balcony was overgrown with bougainvillea, and in the evening Clete put on a pair of blue, baggy, knee-length boxing trunks and pumped barbells out there under a potted palm like a friendly elephant.

'You really want to 'front this vice cop over Little Face Dautrieve?' he asked. He had unwrapped two fried-oyster po'boy sandwiches, and he set them on the table with two cardboard containers of dirty rice.

'No, I want to find out why she has this personal involvement with Letty Labiche.'

He sat down at the table and hung a napkin like a bib from his shirt collar. He studied my face.

'Will you stop looking at me like that?' I said.

'I can hear your wheels turning, big mon. When you can't get it to go your way, you find the worst guy on the block and put your finger in his eye.'

'I'm the one who does that?'

'Yeah, I think that's fair to say.' He chewed a mouthful of oysters and bread and sliced tomatoes and lettuce, a suppressed smile at the corner of his mouth.

I started to speak, but Clete put down his sandwich and wiped his mouth and his eyes went flat. 'Dave, this vice cop is a real prick. Besides, a lot of guys at NOPD still think we're the shit that wouldn't flush.'

'So who cares if we rumple their threads?' I said.

He blew out his breath and slipped his seersucker coat over his shoulder holster and put on his porkpie hat and waited for me by the door.

We went down to First District Headquarters on North Rampart, not far from the Iberville Welfare Project, but the detective we were looking for, a man named Ritter, had gone to Mississippi to pick up a prisoner. Clete's face was dark, his neck red, when we came back outside.

'I thought you'd be relieved,' I said.

He bit a hangnail off his thumb.

'You see the way those guys were looking at me in there? I don't get used to that,' he replied.

'Blow 'em off.'

'They were down on you because you were honest. They were down on me because they thought I was dirty. What a bunch.'

We got in my truck. A drop of perspiration ran out of the lining of his hat into his eye. His skin looked hot and flushed, and I could smell his odor from inside his coat.

'You said Little Face was supposed to come across for both Ritter and a liaison guy. Who's the liaison guy?' I said.

'A political fuck named Jim Gable. He's an insider at City Hall. He was in uniform at NOPD before we came along.'

'A City Hall insider is extorting sexual favors from a street hooker?'

'This guy's had his Johnson out for thirty years. You want to brace him?'

'You up for it?' I asked.

Clete thought about it. 'He's on vacation, over at his home in Lafourche Parish.' Clete pressed his palms together and twisted them back and forth, the calluses scraping audibly. 'Yeah, I'm up for it,' he said.

We drove out of the city, south, to Bayou Lafourche, then followed the state highway almost to Timbalier Bay and the Gulf of Mexico. We turned down a dirt road through farmland and clusters of paintless cabins and clearings in the sugarcane that were filled with tin-roofed sheds and farm equipment. It was late afternoon now, and the wind had kicked up and the cane was blowing in the fields. Clouds moved across the sun and I could smell rain and salt in the air and the odor of dead animals in the ditches. Off in the distance, silhouetted against the dull shimmer of the bay, was a three-story coffee-colored, purple-tiled house surrounded by palm trees.

'How's a cop own a house like that?' I asked.

'It's easy if you marry an alcoholic with heart disease in her family,' Clete said. 'Stop up at that grocery. I'm going to have a beer and shot. This guy turns my stomach.'

'How about easing up, Clete?'

I pulled into the grocery store and he got out without answering and went inside. The store was weathered gray, the nail holes leaking rust, the wide gallery sagging on cinder blocks. Next to it was an abandoned dance hall, the Montgomery Ward brick peeled away in strips, the old red and white Jax sign perforated with bird shot.

Behind the nightclub was a row of cabins that looked like ancient slave quarters. The wind was blowing harder now, flecked with rain, and dust lifted in clouds out of the fields.

Clete came out of the store with a half pint of bourbon in a paper bag and an open can of beer. He took a hit out of the bottle, finished the beer, and put the bottle under the front seat.

'I called Gable. He says to come on down,' Clete said. 'Something wrong?'

'This place . . . It's like I was here before.'

'That's because it's a shithole where whitey got rich while a lot of peons did the grunt work. Like where you grew up.'

When I ignored his cynicism, his eyes crinkled at the corners and he sprayed his mouth with breath freshener. 'Wait till you meet Jim Gable. Then tell me he's not a special kind of guy,' he said.

*

The light had faded from the sky and rain slanted across the flood lamps that were anchored high in the palm trees when we pulled through the iron gates into Jim Gable's drive. He opened the side door onto the porte cochere, grinning with a gap-toothed smile, a man dressed in white slacks and a blue-striped sports coat. His head was too large for his narrow shoulders.

He shook my hand warmly.

'I've heard a great deal about you, Mr Robicheaux. You had quite a war record, I understand,' he said.

'Clete did. I was over there before it got hot,' I replied.

'I was in the National Guard. We didn't get called up. But I admire the people who served over there,' he said, holding the door open for us.

The inside of the house was softly lit, the windows hung with red velvet curtains; the rooms contained the most beautiful oak and cypress woodwork I had ever seen. We walked through a library and a hallway lined with bookshelves into a thickly carpeted living room with high French doors and a cathedral ceiling. Through a side door I saw a woman with a perfectly white, death-like face lying in a tester bed. Her hair was yellow and it fanned out on the pillow from her head like seaweed floating from a stone. Gable pulled the door shut.

'My wife's not well. Y'all care for a whiskey and soda?' he said from the bar, where he tonged cubes of ice into a highball glass. His hair was metallic gray, thick and shiny, and parted sharply on the side.

'Not for me,' I said. Clete shook his head.

'What can I help y'all with?' Gable asked.

'A pimp named Zipper Clum is throwing your name around,' I said.

'Really?'

'He says you and a vice cop in the First District have an interest in a prostitute named Little Face Dautrieve,' I said.

'An interest?'

'Zipper says she gets into the sack with you guys or she goes down on a possession charge,' I said.

Gable's eyes were full of irony. 'One of my men held Zipper's face down on an electric hot plate. That was fifteen or twenty years ago. I fired the man who did it. Zipper forgets that,' Gable said. He drank from his glass and lit a thin cigar with a gold lighter. 'You drove over from New Iberia to check on corruption in the New Orleans Police Department, Mr Robicheaux?'

'I think the prostitute has information that might be helpful in the case of Letty Labiche,' I said.

He nodded, his eyes unfocused with half-formed thoughts.

'I hear Labiche is born again,' he said.

'That's the word,' I said.

'It's funny how that happens on death row. As far as I'm concerned, Letty Labiche doesn't deserve to die by lethal injection. She killed a lawman. I think she should be put to death in the electric chair, and not all at once, either,' he said.

Clete looked at me, then at the door.

'A lot of people think different,' I said.

'Fortunately it's not my obligation to argue with them,' Gable replied. 'On another subject, would you care to look at my collection of ordnance?' He was grinning again now, his callousness or meanness of spirit or whatever moral vacuity that seemed to define him once more hidden in the smiling mask that he wore like ceramic.

'Another time,' I said.

But he wasn't listening. He pushed open two oak doors with big brass handles on them. The inside of the room was filled with glass gun cases, the walls hung with both historical and modern weapons. One mahogany rack alone contained eight AK-47 rifles. On a table under it was a huge glass jar, the kind used in old-time drugstores, filled with a yellow fluid. Gable tapped on the lid with his fingernail so the object inside vibrated slightly and moved against the glass.

I felt a spasm constrict the lining of my stomach.

'That's a VC head. My cousin brought it back. He was in the Phoenix Program,' Gable said.

'We've got all we need here,' Clete said to me.

'Have I offended you?' Gable asked.

'Not us. I wish you'd made it over there, Jim. It was your kind of place,' Clete said.

Clete and I both turned to go and almost collided with Gable's wife. She wore a white silk robe and silver slippers and supported herself on a cane with a rubber-stoppered tripod on it. Her rouged cheeks and lipstick made me think of cosmetics applied in a desperate fashion to a papier-mache doll. Her yellow hair was like wisps of corn silk. When she smoothed it back, lifting it coyly into place, her temples pulsed with tiny blue veins.

'Have you invited the gentlemen for a late supper?' she asked her husband.

'They're just here on business, Cora. They're leaving now,' Gable replied.

'I apologize for not coming out to welcome you. I didn't realize you were here,' she said.

'That's quite all right,' I said.

'You mustn't pay attention to Jim's war souvenirs. They were given to him or he purchased them. He's a gentle man by nature,' she said.

'Yes, ma'am,' I said.

She placed her hand in mine. It had no more weight or density than a bird's wing.

'We'd love to see you again, sir,' she said. Her fingers tightened on mine, her eyes more than earnest.

The sky was dark and streaked with rain when Clete and I went back outside. The air smelled of ozone and schooled-up fish out in the bay. Lightning leaped from the horizon to the top of the sky, and I looked out at the pale green color of the sugarcane blowing in the wind and at the crossroads in the distance where we had stopped at the general store next to the abandoned nightclub with the cabins in back, and I remembered when I had been there before.

'My mother ran off with a man named Mack when I was a little boy,' I said to Clete. 'She came back for me once and we stayed in one of those cabins behind the nightclub.'

'Let it go, Streak,' he said.

'My father was in jail. Mack dealt cards at that club. My mother was a waitress there.'

'That was a long time before she died, big mon. Don't hurt yourself like this.'

We had backed out almost to the front gate. I stopped the truck and walked to the front door in the rain and knocked loudly on the door.

Jim Gable opened it with a turkey drumstick wrapped in a paper napkin in his hand. He was grinning.

'You forgot something?' he said.

'You're from Lafourche Parish, Mr Gable?'

'I grew up right down this road.'

'My mother's name was Mae Guillory. I think she was murdered somewhere close by. Zipper says it was around '66 or '67. Did you know a woman named Mae Guillory?'

His face transformed itself into the smiling, disingenuous countenance that all dishonest people know how to affect, the light in his eyes deliberately unfocused, the lips parted solicitously.

'Why, no, I don't think I ever knew anyone by that name. Mae? No, I'm sure of it,' he replied.

I got back into the truck and backed into the road and headed toward the crossroads.

Clete reached under the seat and removed his half pint bottle of whiskey and unscrewed the cap with one thumb, his eyes on the sugarcane and the rain ditches that swept past both sides of the truck. He took a sip from the bottle and put a Lucky Strike in his mouth.

'How about eighty-sixing the booze while we're driving?' I said.

'Gable knows something about your mother's death?' he said.

'Put it in the bank,' I said.

4

On Monday I drove to the women's prison at St Gabriel, ten miles south of Baton Rouge, and waited for a female guard to walk Letty Labiche from a lockdown unit to an interview room. While I waited a television crew and a male and female journalist from a Christian cable channel were packing up their equipment.

'You interviewed Letty?' I asked the woman.

'Oh, yes. Her story's a tragic one. But it's a beautiful one, too,' she replied. She was middle-aged, blond and attractive, her hard, compact body dressed in a pink suit.

'Beautiful?' I said.

'For a Christian, yes, it's a story of forgiveness and hope.' Her face lifted into mine, her blue eyes charged with meaning.

I looked at the floor and said nothing until she and the other journalist and their crew were gone.

When Letty came into the room with the female guard she was wearing prison denims and handcuffs. The guard was as broad as an ax handle, pink-complected, with chestnut hair, and arms like an Irish washerwoman. She turned the key in the handcuff locks and rubbed Letty's wrists.

'I got them a little tight. You gonna be okay here, hon?' she said.

'I'm fine, Thelma,' Letty said.

I could not tell the difference between Letty and her twin sister, except for a rose with green leaves tattooed on her neck. They had the same skin, the same smoke-colored, wavy, gold-streaked hair, even the same powerful, physical presence. She sat down with me at a wood table, her back straight, her hands folded in front of her.

'You're going to be on cable television, huh?' I said.

'Yes, it's pretty exciting,' she said.

But she caught the look in my eyes.

'You don't approve?' she said.

'Whatever works for you is the right thing to do, Letty.'

'I think they're good people. They been kind to me, Dave. Their show goes out to millions of homes.'

Then I saw the consuming nature of her fear, her willingness to believe that exploitative charlatans could change her fate or really cared what happened to her, the dread and angst that congealed like a cold vapor around her heart when she awoke each morning, one day closer to the injection table at Angola. How much time was left? Six weeks? No, it was five weeks and four days now.

I remembered a film clip that showed Letty at a religious service in the prison chapel, rising from her knees in front of the cross, her clasped hands extended high above her head in a histrionic portrayal of prayer. It was almost embarrassing to watch. But I had learned long ago that unless you've had your own ticket punched in the Garden of Gethsemane, you shouldn't judge those whose fate it is to visit there.

'What can you tell me about a black woman named Little Face Dautrieve?' I asked.

'Tell you?'

'You know her, don't you?'

'The name's not real familiar,' she said.

'Why do you and Passion refuse to confide in me?' I said.

She looked at the tops of her big-boned hands. 'The information you're after won't help. Leave it alone,' she said.

One hand opened and closed nervously on the table-top. Her palm was gold, shiny with moisture, her nails trimmed close to the cuticle. I took her fingers in mine.

'You all right?' I asked.

'Sure.'

But she wasn't. I could see her pulse beating in her neck, the white discoloration on the rim of her nostrils. She swallowed dryly when she looked back into my face, her eyes working hard to retain the light that the reborn seemed to wear as their logo.

'No one has to be brave all the time. It's all right to be afraid,' I said.

'No, it's not. Not if you have faith.'

There was nothing for it. I said good-bye and walked outside into the world of wind and green lawns and sunlight on the skin and trees bending against the sky. It wasn't an experience I took for granted.

When I got home that evening Clete Purcel was leaning on the rail at the end of my dock, eating from a paper sack filled with hog cracklings, brushing the crumbs off his hands into the bayou. The sun was red behind the oaks and pecan trees in my yard, and the swamp was full of shadows and carrion birds drifting above the tops of the dead cypress.

I walked down the dock and leaned against the rail next to him.

'The moon's rising. You want to try some surface lures?' I said.

'I got a call from Zipper Clum today. He says a shitload of heat just came down on his head and we're responsible for it.' He pulled a crackling out of the sack and inserted it in his mouth with his thumb and forefinger.

'Gable sicced some cops on him?'

'They rousted him and put him in a holding cell with a bunch of Aryan Brotherhood types. Zipper left a couple of teeth on the cement.'

'Tell him to give us something and we'll help him.'

'The guy's a bottom-feeder, Dave. His enemy's his mouth. He shoots it off, but he doesn't have anything to give up.'

'Life's rough.'

'Yeah, that's what I told him.' Clete tore the tab on a beer can and leaned his elbows on the handrail. The wind rippled the bamboo and willow trees along the bayou's edge. 'Zipper thinks he might get popped. I say good riddance, but I don't like to be the guy who set him up. Look, the guy's conwise. If he's wetting his pants, it's for a reason. Are you listening to me?'

'Yeah,' I said abstractly.

'You stuck a broom up Jim Gable's ass. He plans to be head of the state police. You remember that black family that got wiped out with shotguns about ten years back? Out by the Desire Project? The husband was snitching off some narcs and they wasted him and his wife and kid. I heard Gable ordered the clip on the husband and it got out of control.'

'Let me tell Bootsie I'm home and we'll put a boat in the water,' I said.

Clete finished his cracklings and wadded up the sack and popped it with the flat of his hand into a trash barrel.

'I've always wondered what it was like to have a conversation with a wood post,' he said.

At that time the governor of the state was a six-foot-six populist by the name of Belmont Pugh. He had grown up in a family of sharecroppers in a small town on the Mississippi River north of Baton Rouge, feckless, illiterate people who sold pecans off the tailgates of pickup trucks and pulled corn and picked cotton for a living and were generally referred to as poor white trash. But even though the Pughs had occupied a stratum below that of Negroes in their community, they had never been drawn to the Ku Klux Klan, nor were they known to have ever been resentful and mean-spirited toward people of color.

I had known Belmont through his cousin Dixie Lee Pugh at SLI when we were all students there during the late 1950s. Dixie Lee went on to become the most famous white blues singer of his generation, second only to Elvis as a rock 'n' roll star. Belmont learned to play piano in the same Negro juke joint that Dixie Lee did, but he got hit with a bolt of religion and turned to preaching as a career rather than music. He exorcised demons and handled snakes and drank poisons in front of electrified rural congregations all over Louisiana. He baptized Negroes and poor whites by immersion in bayous so thick with mud they could clog a sewer main, while cottonmouth moccasins and alligators with hooded eyes watched from among the lily pads.

But the donations he received from church people were small ones and he made his living by selling detergent, brooms, and scrub brushes out of his automobile. Occasionally he would stop by New Iberia and ask me to have lunch with him at Provost's Bar. He had attended college only one year, but he was proud of what he called his 'self-betterment program.' He read a library book thirty minutes before breakfast each morning and thirty minutes before going to bed. He learned one new word from a thesaurus each day, and to improve what he called his 'intellectual thinking skills,' he did his business math in his head. He performed one good deed a day for somebody else, and, in his words, 'as a man on his way up, one good deed for my own self.'

To save money he slept in his car, ate fifty-cent lunches in poolrooms, and sometimes bathed and shaved with a garden hose behind a church house fifteen minutes before his sermon.

Then Belmont discovered the carnival world of Louisiana politics, in the way a mental patient might wander into a theme park for the insane and realize that life held more promise than he had ever dreamed.

Newspeople called Belmont the most mesmerizing southern orator since Huey Long.

During his run for his second term as governor, the opposition spread rumors that Belmont was not only a drunk but that his mulatto mistress, whom he had stashed over in Vicksburg, had borne him twins. *Time* magazine said he was finished. Fundamentalist preachers, once his colleagues, denounced him from every pulpit in the state. Belmont appeared on a nationally telecast religious show and tried to rinse his sins in public. His contrition was a flop.

He held a July Fourth political rally and barbecue in Baton Rouge. The beer, the corn on the cob, the chicken, and the links were free, paid for, some said, by casino interests in Chicago and Las Vegas. Belmont climbed up onto a flatbed truck while his string band belted out 'The Orange Blossom Special.' He played harmonica into the microphone, his face reddening, sweat leaking out of his Stetson hat. When the song ended, the applause was no more than a ripple, while the audience waited to hear what Belmont Pugh had to say about his misdeeds.

He wore shined oxblood cowboy boots, a white suit, a blue shirt, and a flowered necktie. He was too tall to speak comfortably into the microphone, and he removed it from the stand and held it in his huge hand.

His face was solemn, his voice unctuous.

'I know y'all heered a lot of stories about your governor,' he said. 'I won't try to fool you. They grieve me deeply. I'm talking heartfelt pain.'

He paused, taking a breath. Then his knees bent slightly, as though he were gathering a huge volume of air in his lower parts.

'But I'm here to tell y'all right now ... That *any*time, *any*where, *any*body ...' He shook his head from side to side for emphasis, his voice wadding in his throat as though he were about to strangle on his own emotions. 'I mean *anybody* sets a trap for Belmont Pugh with whiskey and women ...' His body was squatted now, his face breaking into a grin as wide as an ax blade. 'Then by God they'll catch him every time!' he shouted.

The audience went wild.

The price of domestic oil rose the same week and the economy bloomed. Belmont was re-elected by a landslide.

Late the next afternoon I looked through the screen window of the bait shop and saw Belmont's black Chrysler park by the boat ramp and Belmont walk down the dock toward the shop. His aides had started to follow him but he waved them off with his Stetson hat, then began slapping the hat against his thigh, as though pounding dust off his clothes. His brow was furrowed, his eyes deep in his face. He blew out his breath and punched and shaped the crown of his hat with his fist and fitted it back on his head just before entering the shop, his easy smile back in place.

Fifteen minutes later we were a mile down the bayou, the outboard pulled into a cove of cypress and willow trees. Belmont sat on the bow and flipped his lure toward the edge of the lily pads and retrieved it slowly through the dark water. He had a lean face and long teeth and pale eyes and graying hair that hung over his ears. His Stetson, which he wore virtually everywhere, was shapeless and stained with sweat and wrapped with a silver cord around the crown.

'You a student of Scripture, Dave?' he asked.

'Not really.'

'The Old Testament says Moses killed maybe two hundred people when he come down off Mount Sinai with the Ten Commandments still smoking in his hands. God had just talked to him from the burning bush, but Moses saw fit to put them people to death.'

'I'm not following you, Belmont.'

'I've signed death warrants on a half dozen men. Every one of them was a vicious killer and to my mind deserved no mercy. But I'm sorely troubled by the case of this Labiche woman.'

I lay my rod across the gunnels of the boat. 'Why?' I asked.

'*Why?* She's a woman, for God's sakes.'

'That's it?'

He fanned a mosquito out of his face.

'No, that's not it. The minister at my church knows her and says her conversion's the real thing. That maybe she's one of them who's been chosen to carry the light of God. I got enough on my conscience without going up to judgment with that woman's death on me.'

'I know a way out.'

'How?'

'Refuse to execute anyone. Cut yourself loose from the whole business.'

He threw his rod and reel against the trunk of a cypress and watched it sink through a floating curtain of algae.

'Send me a bill for that, will you?' he said.

'You can bet on it,' I replied.

'Dave, I'm the governor of the damn state. I cain't stand up in front of an auditorium full of police officers and tell them I won't sign a death warrant 'cause I'm afraid I'll go to hell.'

'Is there another reason?'

He turned his face into the shadows for a moment. He rubbed the curls on the back of his neck.

'Some people say I might have a shot at vice president. It ain't a time to be soft on criminals, particularly one who's chopped up an ex-state trooper.'

'I don't know what to tell you,' I said, trying to conceal the disappointment in my voice.

He beat at the air with both hands. 'I'm gonna call the Mosquito Control down here and bomb this whole place,' he said. 'Lord God Almighty, I thought liquor and women's thighs were an addiction. Son, they don't hold a candle to ambition.'

The next morning a young black woman walked through the front door of the Iberia Parish Sheriff's Department and down the hall to my office and tapped on the glass with one ringed finger. She wore a lavender shirt and white blouse and lavender pumps, and carried a baby in diapers on her shoulder.

'Little Face?' I said when I opened the door.

'I'm moving back here. Out at my auntie's place in the quarters at Loreauville. I got to tell you something,' she said, and walked past me and sat down before I could reply.

'What's up?' I said.

'Zipper Clum is what's up. He say he gonna do you and Fat Man both.'

'Clete Purcel is "Fat Man"?'

'Fat Man shamed him, slapped his face up on that roof, throwed his pimp friends crashing down through a tree. I ax Zipper why he want to hurt you. He say you tole some people Zipper was snitching them off.'

'Which people?'

She rolled her eyes. 'Zipper's gonna tell me that? He's scared. Somebody done tole him he better clean up his own mess or Zipper ain't gonna be working his street corners no more. Anybody who can scare Zipper Clum is people I wouldn't want on my case.'

She shifted her baby to her other shoulder.

'You're an intelligent lady, Little Face.'

'That's why I'm on welfare and living with my auntie in the quarters.'

'The day Vachel Carmouche was killed a black girl of about twelve was turning an ice cream crank on his gallery. That was eight years ago. You're twenty, aren't you?'

'You been thinking too much. You ought to go jogging with Fat Man, hep him lose weight, find something useful for you to do so you don't tire out your brain all the time.'

'What happened inside Vachel Carmouche's house that night? Why won't you tell me?'

'He wanted to live real bad, that's what happened. But he didn't find no mercy 'cause he didn't deserve none. You ax me, a man like that don't find no mercy in the next world, either.'

'You saw him killed, didn't you?'

'Mine to know.'

'Did he molest you? Is that why Letty came to Carmouche's back door that night?'

Her small face seemed to cloud with thought.

'I got to come up wit' a name for you. Maybe an Indian one, something like "Man Who's Always Axing Questions and Don't Listen." That's probably too long, though, huh? I'll work on it.'

'That's real wit,' I said.

'It ain't your grief, Sad Man. Stay out of it before you do real damage to somebody. About Zipper? Some snakes rattle before they bite. Zipper don't. He's left-handed. So he's gonna be doing something wit' his right hand, waving it around in the air, taking things in and out of his pockets. You gonna be watching that hand while he's grinning and talking. Then his left hand gonna come at you just like a snake's head. Pow, pow, pow. I ain't lyin', Sad Man.'

'If Vachel Carmouche molested you, we'd have corroborating evidence that he molested Letty and Passion,' I said.

'I got to feed my baby now. Tell Fat Man what I said. It won't be no fun if he ain't around no more,' she said.

She rose from her chair and hefted her baby higher on her shoulder and walked back out the door, her face oblivious to the cops in the hall whose eyes cut sideways at her figure.

Connie Deshotel was the attorney general of Louisiana. Newspaper accounts about her career always mentioned her blue-collar background and the fact she had attended night school at the University of New Orleans while working days as a patrolwoman. She graduated in the upper five per cent of her law class at LSU. She never married, and instead became one of those for whom civil service is an endless ladder into higher and higher levels of success.

I had met her only once, but when I called her office in Baton Rouge Wednesday afternoon she agreed to see me the next day. Like her boss, Belmont Pugh, Connie Deshotel was known as an egalitarian. Or at least that was the image she worked hard to convey.

Olive-skinned, with metallic-colored hair that had been burned blond on the ends by the sun, she was dressed in a gray suit with a silver angel pinned on her lapel. When I entered her office, her legs were crossed and her hand was poised with a pen above a document on her desk, like a figure in a painting who emanates a sense of control, repose, and activity at the same time.

But unlike Belmont Pugh, the sharecropper populist who was so untraveled and naive he believed the national party would put a bumbling peckerwood on its ticket, Connie Deshotel's eyes took your inventory, openly, with no apology for the invasion of your person and the fact you were being considered as a possible adversary.

'We met once, years ago, during Mardi Gras,' she said.

My gaze shifted off hers. 'Yeah, I was still with NOPD. You were in the city administration,' I said.

She touched a mole at the corner of her mouth with a fingertip.

'I was drunk. I was escorted out of a meeting you were chairing,' I said.

She smiled faintly, but her eyes hazed over, as though I were already disappearing as a serious event in her day.

'What can I do for you, Detective Robicheaux? That's your grade, *detective*, right?' she asked.

536

'Yeah. An informant told me two cops on a pad for the Giacanos killed a woman in Lafourche Parish in 1966 or '67. Her maiden name was Mae Guillory.'

'Which department were they with?'

'He didn't know.'

'Did you find a record of the crime?'

'None.'

'How about the body?'

'To my knowledge, none was ever found.'

'Missing person reports?'

'There's no paperwork on this at all, Ms Deshotel.'

She put down her pen and sat forward in her swivel chair. She looked into space.

'I'll call the authorities in Lafourche Parish. It sounds like a blind alley, though. Who's the informant?'

'A pimp in New Orleans.'

'Why's he coming forward now?'

'A friend of mine was going to throw him off a roof.'

'Ah, it's becoming a little more clear now. Is this friend Clete Purcel?'

'You know Clete?'

'Oh, yes. You might say there's a real groundswell for revocation of his P.I. license. In fact, I have his file right here.' She opened a desk drawer and removed a manila folder filled with police reports, a thickly folded printout from the National Crime Information Center, and what looked like letters of complaint from all over the state. 'Let's see, he shot and killed a government witness, stole a concrete mixer and filled a man's convertible with cement, and destroyed a half-million-dollar home on Lake Pontchartrain with an earth grader. He also slim-jimmed Bobby Earl's car at the Southern Yacht Club and urinated on the seats and dashboard. You say he's been throwing people off of roofs recently?'

'Maybe I misspoke on that,' I said.

She glanced at her watch.

'I'm sorry. I'm late for a luncheon. Give me your card and I'll call you with any information I can find,' she said.

'That's good of you,' I said.

'What was the victim's name again?'

'Mae Guillory was her maiden name. Her married name was Robicheaux.'

'Are you related?'

'She was my mother. So I'll be hanging around on this one, Ms Deshotel.'

The inquisitory beam came back in her eyes, as though the earlier judgment she had passed on me had suddenly been set in abeyance.

5

As a little boy Zipper Clum tap-danced for coins on the sidewalks in the French Quarter. The heavy, clip-on taps he wore on his shoes clicked and rattled on the cement and echoed off the old buildings as though he were in a sound chamber. He only knew two steps in the routine, but his clicking feet made him part of the scene, part of the music coming from the nightclubs and strip joints, not just a raggedy black street hustler whose mother turned tricks in Jane's Alley.

Later on, Zipper Clum came to fancy himself a jazz drummer. He took his first fall in Lake Charles, a one-bit in the Calcasieu Parish Prison, before the civil rights era, when the Negroes were kept in a separate section, away from the crackers, who were up on the top floor. That was all right with Zipper, though. It was cooler downstairs, particularly when it rained and the wind blew across the lake. He didn't like crackers, anyway, and at night he could hear the music from the juke joint on Ryan Street and groove on the crash of drums and the wail of horns and saxophones.

His fall partner was a junkie drummer who had sat in with the Platters and Smiley Lewis. Zipper was awed by the fact that a rag-nose loser with infected hype punctures on his arms could turn two drumsticks into a white blur on top of a set of traps.

In the jail the junkie created two makeshift drumsticks from the wood on a discarded window shade and showed Zipper everything he knew. There was only one problem: Zipper had desire but only marginal talent.

He feigned musical confidence with noise and aggressiveness. He sat in with bands on Airline Highway and crashed the cymbals and bass drum and slapped the traps with the wire brushes. But he was an imitator, a fraud, and the musicians around him knew it.

He envied and despised them for their gift. He was secretly pleased when crack hit New Orleans like a hurricane in 1981. Zipper was clean, living on his ladies, pumping iron and drinking liquid protein and running five miles a day while his pipehead musician friends were huffing rock and melting their brains.

But he still loved to pretend. On Saturday mornings he sat in the back of his cousin's lawn-mower shop off Magazine and plugged in a cassette of Krupa or Jo Jones or Louie Bellson on his boom box, simultaneously recording himself on a blank tape while he flailed at his set of drums.

Witnesses later said the white man who parked a pickup truck out front wore Levi's low on his hips, without a belt, a tight-fitting white T-shirt, cowboy boots, and combed his hair like a 1950s greaser. One witness said he was a teenager; two others described him as a man in his thirties. But when they talked to the police artist, they all agreed he had white skin, a mouth like a girl's, and that he looked harmless. He smiled and said hello to an elderly woman who was sitting under an awning, fanning herself.

The bell tinkled over the front door and Zipper turned down the boom box and shouted from the back, 'My cousin's next door.'

But some crackers just don't listen.

'Hey, don't come around that counter, man,' Zipper said. 'Say, you not hearing me or something? The man who own this store ain't here right now.'

'Sorry.'

'Yeah, just stay out there in front. Everything gonna be cool.'

'When's he gonna be back?'

'Maybe two or three minutes, like the sign on the door say.'

'You play drums?'

There was a pause. 'What you want in here, cracker?' Zipper asked.

'Your cousin's got a big tab with Jimmy Fig. He's got to pay the vig to the Fig.'

Zipper got up from the stool he was sitting on and walked to the service counter. The counter was lined with secondhand garden tools that had been wire-brushed on a machine, sharpened, oiled, and repainted.

'Jimmy Fig don't lend money. He sells cooze,' Zipper said.

'If you say so. I just go where they tell me.'

'Don't grin at me, man.'

'No problem.'

'Hey, take your hand out where I can see it,' Zipper said.

'I delivered the message. I'm going now. Have a good day.'

'No, I want to show you something. This is a twenty-dollar gold piece. Bet you fifty dollars I can roll it across the top of my fingers three times without dropping it. I lose, I put in the gold piece, too. Damn, I just dropped it. You on, my man?'

'Fifty dollars? Without touching it with the other hand?'

'You got it, bo.'

'You give me the gold piece, too?'

'My word's solid, bo. Ask anybody about Zipper Clum.'

'All right, there's my fifty bucks. This isn't a hustle, is it?'

Zipper smiled to himself and began working the gold piece across the tops of his fingers, the edges of the coin tucking into the crevices of skin and flipping over like magic. At the same time his left hand moved under the counter, where his cousin had nailed a leather holster containing a .38 revolver. Zipper felt his palm curve around the checkered wood handles and the smooth taper of the steel.

'Oops, I dropped it again. I done made you rich, cracker,' he said, and slipped the .38 from the leather.

It was a good plan. It had always worked before, hadn't it? What was wrong?

His mind could not assimilate what had just happened. The gold piece had dropped off the tops of his fingers and bounced on the counter and rolled dryly across the wood. But the cracker had not been watching the coin. He had just stood there with that stupid grin on his face, that same, arrogant, denigrating white grin Zipper had seen all his life, the one that told him he was a dancing monkey, the unwanted child of a Jane's Alley whore.

He wanted to snap off a big one, right in the cracker's mouth, and blow the back of his head out like an exploding muskmelon.

But something was wrong in a way he couldn't focus on, like a dream that should illuminate all the dark corners of your consciousness but in daylight eludes your memory. His left hand wouldn't function. The coldness of the steel, the checkering on the grips had separated themselves from his palm. One side of him was lighter than the other, and he was off balance, as though the floor had tilted under his feet. He closed his eyes and saw the scene take place again, watching it now through a red skein on the backs of his eyelids, the cracker lifting a machete off the counter, one his cousin had honed on an emery wheel, swinging it across Zipper's forearm, chopping through tendon and bone like a butcher's cleaver.

Zipper stared down at the .38 and his severed arm and the fingers that now seemed to be trying to gather up the gold twenty-dollar piece from the countertop. Zipper's boom box was playing Louie Prima's 'Sing, Sing, Sing,' and he remembered a little boy on Bourbon Street stooping in mid-dance to catch the coins that bounced out of the cigar box by his feet and rolled across the sidewalk.

'It was supposed to be a clean hit. That's the way I work. So it's on you,' the cracker said, and came quickly behind the counter and shoved Zipper to the floor.

The cracker pulled back the slide on a .25 automatic and bent over and pulled the trigger, straddling Zipper, his cowboy boots stenciling the floor with Zipper's blood. But the gun clicked and did not fire.

The cracker ejected the shell, then aimed the muzzle an inch from Zipper's forehead and shielded his face with one hand to avoid the splatter.

'You the trail back to Robicheaux's mama. You got a mouth like a girl. You got blue eyes. You got skin like milk. You never done no outside work. You six feet tall. Boy, you one badass motherfucker,' Zipper said.

'You got that last part right,' the cracker said.

It was funny how loud a .25 was. A couple of pops and you couldn't hear for an hour. The shooter recovered his empty brass and the ejected dud from the floor, pulled off his T-shirt, which was now splattered with blood, wiped off the machete's handle, and walked to his truck with his shirt wadded up in his hand.

Then something bothered him. What was it? He went back inside and kicked the boom box on the floor and smashed its guts out with his boot heel. Still, something wasn't right. Why had the pimp started taking his inventory? A mouth like a girl's? What was that stuff about somebody's mama? Maybe the pimp was a latent fudge packer. There was a lot of weirdness around these days. Well, that's the way the toilet flushed sometimes.

The old woman outside, who was deaf, waved to him as he twisted the steering wheel of his truck, a pocket comb in his teeth, and turned into the traffic.

6

Monday morning an old-time NOPD homicide investigator named Dana Magelli sat down in my office and played the recording tape that had been recovered from the destroyed boom box at the murder scene off Magazine Street. Magelli had dark, close-clipped hair and dark skin and wore a neat mustache and still played an aggressive handball game three days a week at the New Orleans Athletic Club. Photos from the crime scene and a composite sketch of the shooter were spread on top of my desk.

'Why would Zipper call the hitter the trail back to your mother?' he asked.

'Zipper says "Robicheaux" on the tape. He doesn't mention a first name. Why do you connect the tape to me?' I replied.

'You and Clete Purcel were at First District asking questions about him.'

'He told me he saw two cops kill my mother back in the sixties.'

'I see,' Magelli said, his eyes going flat. 'Which leads you to conclude what?'

'That maybe the guys who did it put the hitter on Zipper Clum.'

'Who might these guys be?'

'Search me,' I said, my eyes not quite meeting his.

He wore a beige sports jacket and tan slacks. He leaned forward in his chair and rested his elbows on my desk.

'You're a good cop, Dave. You always were. You got a rotten deal. A lot of guys would like to see you reinstated in the department,' he said.

'How about Purcel?'

'Purcel was a wrong cop.'

'The whole department was wrong,' I said.

'It's not that way now. Maybe a few guys are still dirty, but the new chief has either suspended or put most of the real slimebags in jail.'

'What's your point, Dana?'

'You'd better not be squaring a personal beef on your own in Orleans Parish.'

'I guess you never know how it's going to shake out,' I said.

'Bad answer from a guy with your mileage,' he said.

'Find my old jacket and put a letter in it,' I said.

But he wasn't listening now. 'We've run the shooter through the computer system every way we could,' he said. 'Nothing. He's got the look of a genuine sociopath, but if there's paperwork on him anywhere, we can't find it.'

'I think he's a new guy, just starting out, making his bones with somebody,' I said. 'He was personally upset he couldn't make a clean hit. But he was still doing everything right until he went back to smash the boom box. He knew he was leaving something behind, but his head was on the full-tilt boogie and he couldn't think his way through the problem. So he tore up the boom box but he left us the tape. He's an ambitious, new player on the block who doesn't quite have ice water in his veins yet.'

Magelli rubbed his chin with two fingers.

'I had a Tulane linguist listen to the tape,' Magelli said. 'He says the accent is Upper South, Tennessee or Kentucky, reasonably educated, at least for the kind of dirt bags we usually pull in. You think he's mobbed-up?'

'No,' I said.

'Why not?'

'Because he talks about paying "the vig to the Fig." Everybody in the life knows Jimmy Figorelli is a pimp, not a shylock.'

Magelli smiled.

'Come back to work for us,' he said.

'Take Purcel, too. You get two for one.'

'You wouldn't come if we did, would you?'

I took my eyes off his to change the subject. 'There's another possibility in this case,' I said. 'It was Zipper Clum's perception the hitter was sent by the people who killed my mother. That doesn't make it so. A lot of people would enjoy breaking champagne bottles on Zipper's headstone.'

'Zipper was a ruthless bucket of shit. But he was the smartest pimp I ever met. He knew who paid his killer. You know it, too,' Magelli said. He cocked his finger at me like a pistol as he went out the door.

Just as I was going into Victor's on Main Street for lunch, Clete Purcel's maroon Cadillac pulled to the curb, his salt-water fishing rods sticking out of the back windows. He'd bought the Cadillac, the only type of car he ever drove, for eight hundred dollars from a mortician who had bought it off the family of a mobbed-up suicide victim. The steel-jacketed .357 round had exited through the Cadillac's roof, and Clete had filed down the jagged metal and filled the hole with body solder and sanded it smooth and sprayed it with gray primer so the roof looked like it had been powdered from the explosion of a large firecracker.

'What are you doing here?' I asked.

'I had to get out of New Orleans for a while. This homicide guy Magelli was bugging me yesterday about Zipper Clum getting popped. Like I have knowledge about every crime committed in Orleans and Jefferson parishes,' Clete said.

'You usually do.'

'Thanks. Let's get something to go and eat in the park. I want to have a talk with you, big mon.'

'About what?'

'I'll tell you in the park.'

We ordered two Styrofoam containers of fried catfish and coleslaw and dirty rice and drove across the drawbridge that spanned Bayou Teche at Burke Street. The bayou was dented with rain rings. Clete parked the Cadillac by one of the picnic shelters under the oaks in City Park, and we sat under the tin roof in the rain and warm breeze and ate lunch. Inside all of Clete's outrageous behavior was the secular priest, always determined to bail his friend out of trouble, no matter how unwanted his help was. I waited for the sermon to begin.

'Will you either say it or stop looking at me like that?' I said finally.

'This homicide hotshot, Magelli? He's heard you've been moving the furniture around about your mother's death. He thinks you might just do a number on somebody.'

'Who cares what he thinks?'

'I think he's right on. You're going to coast along, not saying anything, stonewalling people, then when you think you've found out enough, you're going to blow up their shit.'

'Maybe you're right.'

'It's not your style, noble mon. That's why I'm going to be in town for a little while. I was out at Passion Labiche's place early this morning.'

'What for?'

'Because I'm not sure the hit on Zipper Clum is related to your mother's death. These political fucks in Baton Rouge want Letty Labiche executed, body in the ground, case closed, so they can get back full-time to the trough. You keep turning over rocks, starting with sticking a gun in Zipper Clum's mouth up on that roof.'

'Me?'

'So I helped a little bit. That Passion Labiche is one hot-ass-looking broad, isn't she? Is she involved with anybody?'

'Why don't you give some thought to the way you talk about women?'

'It was a compliment. Anyway, you're right, she's hiding something. Which makes no sense. What do she and her sister have to lose at this point?'

I shook my head.

'I think we should start with the hitter, the cracker on the tape,' I said.

'I got a question for you. Jack Abbott, this mainline con a writer got out of the Utah Pen some years back? Where'd he go after he knifed a waiter to death in New York?'

'Morgan City.'

'What can I say? Great minds think alike. I already put in a couple of calls,' Clete said, grinning while he wiped food off his mouth.

But I didn't have great faith in finding the killer of Zipper Clum in Morgan City, even though it was known as a place for a man on the run to disappear among the army of blue-collar laborers who worked out of there on fishing vessels and offshore drilling rigs. Clete had not heard the tape on which Zipper had said his killer had never done outside work and had skin like milk. I also believed Clete was more interested in monitoring me than the investigation into my mother's death. He came to the sheriff's department at quitting time, expecting to drive down together to Morgan City.

'I can't go today,' I said.

'Why not?' he asked.

'Commitments at home.'

'Yeah?' He was standing in the middle of my office, his porkpie hat slanted down on his head, his stomach hanging over his belt, an unlit Lucky Strike in his mouth. He tossed the cigarette end over end into the wastebasket. 'I refuse to light one of these things ever again. Why are you giving me this bullshit, Streak?'

'Come have dinner with us.'

'No, I'm meeting this retired jigger an hour from now. You coming or not?'

'A bank jigger?'

'More serious. He was the lookout man for a couple of hit teams working out of Miami and New Orleans.'

'Not interested.'

'Where do you think we're supposed to get information from, the library?'

When I didn't reply, he said, 'Dave, if you want me out of town, just say so.'

'Let's talk about it tomorrow.'

'*You* talk about it. I'm meeting the jigger. You don't want to hear what I find out, no problem.'

After he closed the door behind him, his heat and anger remained like a visible presence in the room's silence.

That evening Alafair, Bootsie, and I were eating supper in the kitchen when we heard a heavy car on the gravel in the driveway. Alafair got up from the table and peered out the window. She was in high school now and seemed to have no memory anymore of the civil war in El Salvador that had brought her here as an illegal refugee, nor of the day I pulled her from the submerged wreckage of an airplane out on the salt. Her Indian-black hair was tied up on her head with a blue bandanna, and from the back, when she raised up on the balls of her feet to see better through the blinds, her body looked like that of a woman ten years her senior.

'It's somebody in a limousine, with a chauffeur. She's rolling down the window. It's an old woman, Dave,' she said.

I went out the back door and walked around the side of the house to the limousine. It was white, with charcoal-tinted windows, and the chauffeur wore a black suit and cap and tie and white shirt. Oddly, his face was turned away, as though he did not want me to see it.

Through the limousine's open back window I saw Jim Gable's wife, in a white dress and gloves, drinking sparkling burgundy from a crystal glass with a long stem. The late sun's glow through the trees gave her skin a rosy tone it did not naturally possess, and her mouth was soft, full of wrinkles, when she smiled at me. What was her name? Corrine? Colinda?

'Micah, open the door so Mr Robicheaux can get in,' she said to the chauffeur.

He stepped out of the driver's seat and opened the back, his face still averted. When I was inside, on the rolled leather seat, he walked down toward the dock just as a flight of snow egrets flew across the water, their wings pink in the sunset.

'How you do, Miss Cora?' I said.

'I couldn't stand staying another day alone while Jim's in the city. So I got Micah to drive me on a little tour of your lovely area. Join me in a glass of burgundy, Mr Robicheaux,' she said.

I realized, listening to her voice, that her Deep South accent came and went arbitrarily, even though her eyes, which were violet, never seemed to vary in their level of warmth and sincerity.

'No, thanks. Would you like to come in and have a bite to eat?' I replied.

'I'm afraid I've intruded. I do that sometimes. Lack of an audience, that sort of thing.' She watched my face to see if I had inferred a second meaning. Obviously I had not.

'Audience?' I said, confused.

'It's a vanity of mine. I assume everyone on the planet spends time thinking about old movies.' She opened a scrapbook and turned several pages that were thick and stiff with glued news articles and black-and-white photographs. She turned another page, and I looked down at a stunning color photograph of a woman with long blond hair in a black nightgown, reclining seductively on a divan with one arm behind her head. Her eyes were violet, her lipsticked mouth waiting to be kissed.

'You're Cora Perez. You were a movie star. I saw you in a film with Paul Muni,' I said.

'That was at the end of Paul's career. He was such a wonderful man to work with. He knew how nervous and unsure I was, and he used to bring a flower to me each morning at the set,' she said.

'It's an honor to know you, Miss Cora,' I said, still unsure of the reason for her visit. My eyes drifted to the kitchen window, where Alafair's and Bootsie's silhouettes were visible at the table.

'I mustn't keep you,' she said, and touched me lightly on the back of the hand. 'Sometimes I just need someone to reassure me I'm not indeed of diminished capacity.'

'Pardon?'

'I'm being declared as such by the court. It's not flattering, of course. But perhaps they're right. How does one accused of being mentally impaired prove she is not mentally impaired? It's like trying to prove a negative.'

'I don't think you're impaired at all, Miss Cora. You strike me as a remarkable person.'

'Why, you're obviously a man of great wisdom, Mr Robicheaux.'

I thought she would say more and explain her presence or whatever need it was that hovered around the edges of her sentences, but she didn't. I shook hands with her and got back out of the car, which the chauffeur took as his signal to walk back up from the dock. He fixed his cap down on his forehead and pretended he was studying the details of the dirt road and trees and canebrakes on either side of him as he approached the limousine.

'Try not to stare at Micah. He has a deformity of the face. Jim calls him "Cyclops," even though I don't allow him to do it in my presence,' Miss Cora said.

Just as she finished speaking Micah tilted his chin into the light and I saw the nodulous skin growth that covered the right side of his face, like a strawberry-colored skein that had hardened and pinched the eye shut, tightening the cheek so that the teeth on the right side of the lip were exposed.

I pulled my eyes away and looked deliberately through the back window into Miss Cora's face.

'Good-bye, Miss Cora,' I said.

'Come see me. Please do. You impress me greatly, sir,' she replied.

I went back inside the house and sat down at the table with Alafair and Bootsie.

'Who was that?' Bootsie asked.

'Her stage name was Cora Perez. She was pretty big stuff in Hollywood back in the late forties and early fifties,' I said.

'I remember her. Where'd you meet her?' Bootsie said.

'Clete and I had to run down some character by the name of Jim Gable. Clete says Gable married her for her money when he knew she had cancer.'

Bootsie looked down at her plate and picked up her fork. Her hair was the color of honey and it moved in the breeze through the window.

'Did I say something wrong?' I asked.

'No, not at all,' she replied. She put a very small piece of food in her mouth with the tip of her fork and kept her eyes on her plate.

That night, in bed, Bootsie rested her arm across her forehead and looked up at the ceiling. The moon was rising in the east and the revolving blades of the window fan marbled her body with shadows. I put my hand on her shoulder and she rolled toward me and rested her head under my chin. I raised her slip on her thigh and felt the tapered smoothness of her skin. But her hands were folded together and she didn't respond as she normally did.

'What's the problem, Boots?' I asked.

'This Jim Gable you were talking about? Was he a policeman in New Orleans at one time?' she said.

'He still is. A liaison wheel with the mayor's office.'

'I used to know him,' she said.

'Oh?'

'After my second husband was killed.'

She didn't continue. She seldom spoke of her earlier marriages. Her first husband had been an oil field helicopter pilot who crashed offshore, but the second one had been Ralph Giacano, nephew of Didi Gee, a gangster who held his enemies' hands down in an aquarium filled with piranha and who some people believe was mixed up in the assassination of President Kennedy. The nephew, Ralph, was not only a degenerate gambler who bankrupted Bootsie, but he also tried to take the Colombians over the hurdles and was shotgunned to death, along with his mistress, in the parking lot of Hialeah racetrack.

'What about Jim Gable?' I asked.

'He came to the house a lot after Ralph was killed. He was part of a special unit that was assigned to watch the Mob. We started seeing each other . . . No, that's not an honest way to put it. We had an affair.'

Her knees were drawn up against me, her body motionless. I could feel her breath on my chest.

'I see,' I said.

'I don't like hiding things from you.'

'It was all a long time ago,' I replied. I tried to keep my voice neutral and ignore the tight feeling in my face and the needles in my throat.

'Does Jim Gable bother you because Clete says he's an opportunist?' she asked.

'He keeps the head of a Vietnamese soldier in a jar of chemicals. He said he'd like to see Letty Labiche electrocuted in stages. I think he lied about his knowledge of my mother's death,' I said.

Bootsie lay very quiet in the dark, then rolled away from me and stared up at the ceiling. She sat on the side of the bed with her back to me for a long time. I started to touch her with my hand, but she reached behind her and picked up her pillow and went into the living room.

7

The next afternoon, just before quitting time, Clete came into my office.

'The jigger's name is Steve Andropolis. He worked for the Giacanos and did freelance stuff in Miami when it was an open city. You remember him?' he said.

'Vaguely.'

'I had the wrong address last night. He agreed to show up again tonight. The guy's a shitbag, Streak, but he's a gold mine of information.'

'Why's he want to help us?'

'He's into Wee Willie Bimstine for four large. I got him a one-month extension with no vig.'

'It sounds good, Cletus,' I said.

He smiled and put a breath mint on his tongue.

We drove south to Morgan City as the evening cooled and the clouds over the Gulf turned a deeper red in the sunset. The man named Steve Andropolis was waiting for us in the back of a diner set on pilings by the water's edge. A half-empty green beer bottle and a white plate filled with fried shrimp tails sat in front of him. The hard, rounded surfaces of his face reminded me of an old baseball. He wore a new golf cap and a bright yellow golf shirt and gray slacks and tan loafers, as though affecting the appearance of a Florida retiree, but he had big-knuckled hands, a faded blue tattoo of a nude girl on his forearm, and close-set, pig's eyes that took the inventory of everyone in the diner.

When Clete introduced me, I didn't take his hand. He let his hand remain in the air a moment, then parted his lips slightly and wiped at something on the corner of his mouth.

'I know you?' he said.

'From a long time ago. You had a DWI and the court sent you to a twelve-step program in the Quarter. You stole two-hundred dollars from the group's treasury.'

Andropolis turned to Clete. 'What's the deal?' he asked.

'There's no problem here, Steve. We just want to know what you've heard about this guy who did Zipper Clum,' Clete said.

'His name's Johnny Remeta. He's out of Michigan. They say he's got a lot of talent,' Andropolis said.

549

'A lot of talent?' I said.

'Is there an echo in here?' Andropolis said.

'This doesn't fit, Steve. The guy we're looking for is a hillbilly,' Clete said.

'You wanted to know who was the new kid in town, I told you. He's done hits for the greaseballs out on the coast, maybe a couple of pops in Houston. He don't have a sheet, either,' Andropolis said.

'Where is he?' Clete asked.

'A guy who blows heads? He ain't like other people. He does the whack, gets his ashes hauled, and visits Disneyland.'

Andropolis' eyes kept returning to my face as he spoke.

'Why's he looking at me like that?' he asked Clete.

'Streak's just being attentive. Right, Dave?' Clete said, and gave me a deliberate look.

'Right,' I said.

'Y'all want to know anything else?' Andropolis asked.

'I think I remember some other things about you, Steve. Weren't you in the Witness Protection Program? What happened on that deal?' I said.

'What do you mean "what happened"?'

'You were one of the guys who gave up Didi Gee. But you're obviously not a federally protected witness anymore.'

'Because that tub of guts had his insides eaten out by the Big C. I heard the mortuary had to stuff his fat ass into a piano crate,' he replied.

'You go way back with the Giacano family?' I asked.

'Yeah, I knew Didi when he used to carry a blood-stained baseball bat in the backseat of his convertible.'

'Ever hear about a couple of cops on a pad snuffing a woman in Lafourche Parish back in the sixties?' I asked.

His eyes cut sideways out the window. He seemed to study the swirls of color in the sky. The sun was almost down now, and small waves from a passing tugboat rippled back over the mudflat under the diner's pilings.

'Yeah, I remember that. A whore?' he said.

'Yeah, Zipper said the same thing. They killed a whore,' I said, my face expressionless, the skin tight against the bone, my hands folded one on top of the other.

'She had something on them. That's all I remember,' he said.

'No names?' I said.

'No, I don't know anything else about it.'

'But you're sure she was a whore? That's what you called her, right?' I said.

'You got some trouble with that word?' he asked.

'No, not really,' I said, and took my eyes off his and scratched a place on my forehead.

He raised a finger to the counterman to order a beer for himself, then said, 'I got to take a drain.'

Clete leaned forward in the booth.

'Quit baiting the guy,' he said.

'He knows more,' I said.

'He's a gumball. You get what you see. Be thankful. We got the name of the shooter.'

'Excuse me,' I said, and followed Steve Andropolis into the men's room and shot the dead bolt behind me. The room was small, the air fetid and warm, with a wood enclosure around the toilet. I reached under my seersucker coat and slipped my .45 from its clip-on holster. I pulled back the slide and released it, chambering the top round on the magazine.

I stood back from the door on the toilet enclosure and kicked it open. Andropolis had been tucking his shirt into his trousers when the door hit him in the back and knocked him off balance against the wall. He tried to push the door back into my face, but I stomped it again, harder this time, ripping the top hinge and screws loose, pinning him in a half-crumpled position against the toilet bowl. I held on to the side of the stall with my left hand and drove my shoe through the door, again and again, splintering plywood into his face.

Then I flung the door off him and pointed the .45 at his mouth. A twelve-inch strip of desiccated wood was affixed to his cheek with three rusty nails.

'I wanted to apologize to you, Steve. I lied out there. I *was* bothered by the word "whore." When a subhuman sack of shit calls my dead mother a whore, that bothers me. Does that make sense to you, Steve?'

He closed his eyes painfully and pulled loose the splintered board that was nailed to his cheek.

'I've heard about you, you crazy sonofabitch. What do I know about your mother? I'm a spotter. I never capped anybody in my life.'

'You tell me who killed her, Steve, or your brainpan is going to be emptied into that toilet bowl in ten seconds.'

He began getting to his feet, blood draining in a long streak from his cheek.

'Fuck you, Zeke,' he said, and drove his fist into my scrotum.

My knees buckled, and a wave of pain rose like a gray, red-veined balloon out of my loins, took all the air from my lungs, and spread into my hands. I fell against the wall, the backs of my legs quivering, the .45 on the floor by my foot, the hammer on full cock.

Andropolis kicked the screen out of the window, placed one foot on the jamb, and leaped outside.

He stared back at me, the clouds etched with purple fire behind his head.

'When your mother died? I hope it didn't go like I think it probably did. I hope they hurt her,' he said.

He ran through the shallow water across the mudflat toward a distant clump of willow trees. The water splashing from under the impact of his feet had the same amber brilliance in the sunlight as whiskey splashed in a thick beer glass. I sighted the .45 on the middle of his back and felt my finger begin to tighten inside the trigger guard.

Clete Purcel exploded the dead bolt off the men's room door frame with one thrust of his massive shoulder.

'What are you doing, Dave?' he said incredulously.

I lay my forehead down on my arms and closed my eyes, my heart thundering in my ears, a vinegar-like odor rising from my armpits.

The next afternoon I drove out to the Labiche house on the bayou and was told by a black kid watering down the azaleas in front that Passion was at the cafe and nightclub she owned outside St Martinville. I drove to the club, a flat-roofed, green building with rusty screens and a fan-ventilated, hardwood dance floor. The sun's glare off the shale parking lot was blinding. I went in the side door and walked across the dance floor to the bar, where Passion was breaking rolls of quarters and dumping them into her cash drawer.

In the far corner stood the ancient piano that Letty used to play nightly. The keys were yellow, the walnut edges of the casement burned by cigarettes. Letty was one of the best rhythm-and-blues and boogie-woogie piano players I had ever seen perform. You could hear Albert Ammons, Moon Mulligan, and Jerry Lee Lewis in her music, and whenever she did 'Pine Top's Boogie,' the dance floor erupted into levels of erotic behavior that would have received applause at the baths of Caracalla.

Passion sometimes played in the house band as a bass guitarist, but she had never possessed her sister's talent. To my knowledge, no one had sat seriously at the piano since Letty had been arrested for the murder of Vachel Carmouche. At least not until today.

'You're walking with a list, chief,' Passion said.

'Really?' I said.

'You get hurt or something?'

'I'm doing fine. How about you, Passion?'

I sat at the bar and looked at an empty, oversized beer mug in front of me. The near side of the mug was coated with a thick, orange residue of some kind.

'The governor of Louisiana just drank out of that. I'm not sure if I should boil it for germs or not,' Passion said. She wore a white cotton dress printed with flowers. The light colors made her look even bigger than she was, and, in a peculiar way, more attractive and forceful.

'Belmont Pugh was here?' I said.

'He played Letty's piano. He's not bad.'

'What did he want from you?'

'What makes you think he wanted anything?' she asked.

'Because I know Belmont Pugh.'

Then she told me. It was vintage Belmont.

His black Chrysler had braked to a stop in the shell parking lot, drifting a dry, white cloud of dust across the building, and Belmont had come through the front door, stooping under the door frame, moisture leaking out of his hat, his silver shirt glued to his skin, a sweaty aura of libidinal crudeness and physical power emanating from his body.

'I'm in need of massive liquids, hon,' he said, and sat with his face in his hands while Letty drew a draft beer for him. 'Sweetheart, that little-bitty glass ain't gonna cut it. Give me that big 'un yonder, bust three raw eggs in it, and tell my family I died in your arms.'

She laughed, her arms folded across her chest.

'I always heard you were unusual,' she said.

'That's why my wife throwed me out, God bless her. Now what am I gonna do – heartbroken, hungover, too old to have a beautiful, young Creole thing like you in his life? It's a misery, girl. Fill this up again, will you? Y'all got anything good to eat?'

He played the piano while she fixed him a sandwich in the café. She put the sandwich on a plate and set the plate on the end of the bar. He sat down on the stool again and removed his hat and mopped his face with a handkerchief. The skin across the top of his forehead was as pale as a cue ball.

'That record your sister cut in jail? She's a major talent, if you ask me. The minister at my church says she's a fine woman, too,' he said.

Passion looked at him silently, her rump resting against the tin wash bin behind her.

'You wondering why I'm here? I don't want to see a good woman die. It's that simple. But y'all gotta hep me and give me something I can use,' he said.

'How?' Passion asked.

'That story y'all told the jury didn't do nothing but leave skid marks on the bowl. There wasn't no evidence Carmouche ever molested anybody else. It's hard to believe after all those years your sister would suddenly decide to take the man apart with a mattock. Like she was bored and it just come to mind as the thing to do.'

'Would you like me to describe what he did to me and Letty?'

'Lord, it's hot in here. Why don't you fix your air conditioner? No, I don't want you to describe it. I suspect the man was everything you say he was. That's why I want you to find somebody who can support your story. Round up a mess of black people, talk to 'em, you hear what I'm saying, sometimes folks shut out bad memories, you gotta remind them of what happened. They call it "recovered memory." People get rich suing over it.'

'You want me to get some black people to lie for us?'

'Girl, please don't use that word. And I don't care if they're white or black. I'll get state investigators down here to take their deposition. But y'all gotta understand my situation. I cain't give clemency to a woman 'cause I like the way she plays the piano. People in the last election was already calling me the Silver Zipper.'

'Letty won't go along with it.'

'You better hear what I'm saying, Miss Passion, or it's gonna be on y'all's own self. Them sonsofbitches in Baton Rouge is serious.'

'You want a refill, Governor?'

His face was tired and poached-looking in the warm gloom of the bar. He pulled his shirt out from his chest with his fingers and shook the cloth, his mouth down-turned at the corners. 'Damn if I can ever find the right words to use to people anymore,' he said, and pushed his Stetson on his head and walked back out of the club, the electric fan by the door flapping back his coat just before he stepped into the heated whiteness of the day outside.

Passion walked to the door.

'I'll tell her,' she said as his car scoured dust out of the parking lot.

But Belmont did not hear her.

'Maybe Belmont's a little corrupt, but he's got his hand on it,' I said.

'Meaning?' she said, her face in a pout.

'Nobody bought y'all's story. Vachel Carmouche had been gone from here for years. The very night he returned, your sister killed him. Over deeds done to her as a child?'

'You came out here to put this in my face?'

'No. Little Face Dautrieve inasmuch told me she was there that night. But that's all she'll say. What happened that night? Is Little Face protecting somebody?'

'Ax her.'

'You want it this way?' I said.

'Pardon?'

'That I be your adversary? The guy you don't trust, the guy who makes a nuisance of himself?'

'I didn't mean to make you mad,' she said.

'Give me a Dr Pepper, will you?'

'There isn't no way out for us, Dave. My sister's gonna die. Somebody got to pay for that nasty old piece of white trash.'

She walked on the duckboards to the end of the bar, her back turned toward me so I couldn't see her face. Her large body was framed against the white glare of the parking lot, her smoke-colored hair wispy with light. She picked a rose out of a green bottle on the liquor counter and stared at it dumbly. The petals were dead, the color of a bruise, and they fell off the stem of their own weight and drifted downward onto the duckboards.

8

I got home late from work that evening. Alafair had gone to the City Library and Bootsie had left a note on the kitchen blackboard that said she was shopping in town. I fixed a cup of coffee and stirred sugar in it and sat on the back steps in the twilight and watched the ducks wimpling the water on the pond at the foot of our property.

But sometimes I did not do well in solitude, particularly inside the home where my original family had come apart.

In the gathering shadows I could almost see the specters of my parents wounding each other daily, arguing bitterly in Cajun French, each accusing the other of their mutual sins.

The day my mother had gone off to Morgan City with Mack, the bouree dealer, my father had been hammering a chicken coop together in the side yard. Mack's Ford coupé was parked on the dirt road, the engine idling, and my mother had tried to talk to him before she left me in his care.

My father was heedless of her words and his eyes kept lifting from his work to Mack's car and the sunlight that reflected like a yellow flame off the front windows.

'That li'l gun he carry? See what good it gonna do him he step his foot on my property,' he said.

The day was boiling hot, the air acrid with a smell like fresh tar and dust blowing off a gravel road. My father's skin was glazed with sweat, his veins swollen with blood, his size seeming to swell inside his overalls with the enormous range his anger was capable of when his pride had been injured.

I sat on the front steps and wanted to cover my ears and not hear the things my parents said to each other. I wanted to not see Mack out there on the road, in his fedora and two-tone shoes and zoot slacks, not think about the pearl-handled, two-shot derringer I had seen once in his glove box.

But my father looked from his work to me, then out at Mack and back at me again, and the moment went out of his face and he lay his ball peen hammer on a bench and picked up the side of the chicken coop and examined its squareness and felt its balance. I pushed my hands under my thighs to stop them from shaking.

When my mother drove away with Mack, I thought there might still be hope for our family. My father, Big Aldous, the grinning, irresponsible derrick man and saloon brawler, was still my father. Even at that age I knew he had chosen me over an act of violence. And my mother, Mae, was still my mother. Her lust and her inability to deal with my father's alcoholism made her the victim of bad men, but she was not bad herself. She loved me and she loved my father, or she would not have fought with him.

But now there were people who called my mother a whore.

I had never heard that word used in association with her. During my mother's lifetime whores didn't work in laundries for thirty cents an hour or wait tables in beer gardens and clapboard bars and hoe out victory gardens for a sack of string beans.

Had it not been for Clete Purcel, I would have squeezed off my .45 on the back of the jigger named Steve Andropolis because he called my mother a whore. In my mind's eye I still saw myself doing it. I saw a worthless, running, pitiful facsimile of a human being look back at me, his mouth round with a silent scream, his arms spread against a bloodred sky. I looked down at my hand, and it was tightened into a ball, the forefinger kneading against the thumb.

I threw my coffee into the flower bed and tried to rub the fatigue out of my face.

Bootsie's car turned into the drive and stopped in front, then I heard the crinkle of paper bags as she unloaded the groceries and carried them across the gallery. Normally she would have driven to the back of the house to unload, but our conversations had been few since the night of her revelation about her affair with Jim Gable.

Why had I demeaned him as Bootsie and I lay there in the dark? It had been the same as telling her she had somehow willingly shared her life and person with a degenerate. Her second husband, Ralph Giacano, had lied his way into her life, telling her he had a degree in accounting from Tulane, that he owned half of a vending machine company, that, in effect, he was an unexciting, ordinary but decent middle-class New Orleans businessman.

He was an accountant, all right, but as a bean counter for the Mob; the other half of the vending machine operation was owned by Didi Gee.

She had to fly to Miami to identify the body after the Colombians blew Ralph's face off. She also found out his dead mistress had been the bank officer who had set up the second mortgage on her house in the Garden District and had helped Ralph drain her accounts and the equity portfolio the bank managed for her.

She had been betrayed, degraded, and bankrupted. Was it any wonder a man like Gable, a police officer of detective grade, supposedly a man of integrity, could insinuate his way into her life?

Bootsie opened the screen door behind me and stood on the top step. Out of the corner of my eye I could see her ankles and the tops of her feet inside the moccasins she wore.

'Did you eat yet?' she said.

'I had that potato salad in the icebox.'

'You might have to do an extra mile on your run,' she replied.

I leaned forward on my forearms and folded my hands between my knees.

The ducks were turning in circles on the pond, their wings fluttering, sprinkling the water's surface.

'I think you're a great lady, Boots. I don't think any man deserves you. I know I don't,' I said.

The light had washed out of the sky; the wind blowing across my neighbor's cane field was touched with rain and smelled of damp earth and the wildflowers that grew along the coulee. Bootsie sat down on the step behind me, then I felt her fingertips on the back of my neck and in my hair.

'You want to go inside?' she asked.

Later that night the weather turned unseasonably cool and it started to rain, hard, sheets of it marching across marshlands, cane fields, tin roofs, bayous, and oak-lined communities up the Teche. In the little town of Loreauville, a man parked his pickup truck outside a clapboard bar and walked through the rain to the entrance. He wore jeans low on his hips, exposing his midriff, and pointed boots and black-rimmed glasses and a straw cowboy hat.

When he sat at the bar, which was deserted because of the bad weather, he removed his hat and set it crown-down on the stool next to him. He wiped his glasses with a paper napkin, then forgot they were dry and picked them up and wiped them again, his expression seemingly troubled by a concern or problem he couldn't resolve. Later the bartender described the man as 'handsome, with kind of a ducktail haircut ... Likable, I guess, but I wouldn't make him for no dishware man.'

The man ordered a diet soda and opened a vinyl folder wrapped with rubber bands and filled with invoices of some kind.

'You know a family named Grayson back in the quarters?' he said.

'Cain't say I do,' the bartender replied.

The man looked down at his invoice folder, widening his eyes, as though bemused. 'They live next door to the Dautrieve family,' he said.

'Oh, yeah. Go back up the road till you see some shotgun cabins. The Dautrieves are on the second row,' the bartender said.

'They won a bunch of dishware.'

'Who?'

'The Graysons.' The man held up a brochure with pictures of dishes and cups on it to make his point.

The bartender nodded vaguely. The man with the invoice folder stared into space, as though he saw meaning in the air, in the lightning that trembled in the trees along the bayou. He paid for his diet drink and thanked the bartender and drove up the road, in the opposite direction from the quarters.

It was still raining the next night when Little Face Dautrieve's aunt left for her janitorial job at the hospital in New Iberia and Little Face changed her baby's diaper, put a pacifier in his mouth, and lay him down in his crib. The cabin had been built in the last century, but it stayed warm and dry and snug in bad weather. When it rained Little Face liked to open the bedroom window partway and let the breeze blow across the baby's crib and her bed.

In the middle of the night she thought she heard a truck engine outside and tires crunching on clamshells, then the sound disappeared in the thunder and she fell asleep again.

When she awoke he was standing over her, his form-fitting T-shirt molded wetly against his torso. His body had a fecund odor, like water in the bottom of a coulee; a nickel-plated revolver, the handles wrapped with electrician's tape, hung from his gloved right hand.

'I came in out of the rain,' he said.

'Yeah, you done that. There ain't no rain in the house,' she replied, raising herself up on her hands, a wishbone breaking in her throat.

'You mind if I stay here? I mean, stay out of the rain?' he asked.

'You here, ain't you?'

His palm opened and closed on the grips of the pistol, the edges of the tape sticking, popping on his skin. His face was pale, his mouth soft and red in the flashes of lightning outside. He wet his lips and cut his eyes at the window, where mist was drifting across the sill and dampening the baby's mattress.

The man pushed the window tight and gazed down at the baby, who slept with his rump in the air. A pillow was stuffed into an empty space where one of the wood runners was missing. For some reason, perhaps because of the noise the window made, the baby woke and started to cry. The man pried the pillow loose and kneaded it in his left hand and turned toward Little Face.

'Why'd you get mixed up with a bunch of geeks? Why'd you run your mouth?' the man said. His black hair was combed back neatly on both sides, his skin glistening with water, his navel rising and falling above his jeans.

'Write out a list of the people ain't geeks. I'll start hanging 'round wit' them,' she replied.

'Make that baby be quiet.'

'You done woke him up. Babies gonna cry when they get woke up.'

'Just shut him up. I can't think. Why don't you have a man to take care of you?'

'I can have all the men I want. Trouble is, I ain't met none I want, including present company.'

He looked at the baby again, then closed and opened his eyes. He took a breath of air through his mouth, holding it, as though he were about to speak. But no sound came out. He folded the pillow around the pistol and held both ends together with his left hand. The rims of his nostrils whitened, as though the temperature had dropped precipitously in the room.

'You make me mad. You're too dumb to understand what's happening. Get that look off your face,' he said.

'It's my house. I ain't axed you in it. Go back in the rain you don't like it,' she said quietly.

Then she saw into his eyes and her throat went dry and became constricted like a piece of crimped pipe and she remembered the word 'abyss' from a sermon at a church somewhere and she knew now what the word meant. She tried to hold her gaze evenly on his face and stop the sound that thundered in her ears, that made her own words distorted and unintelligible to her.

Her hands knotted the sheet on top of her stomach.

'My baby ain't part of this, is he?' she said.

The man drew an enormous breath of air through his nose, as though he were hyperventilating. 'No, what do you think I am?' He held up the pillow as though he had just discovered its presence. 'Don't put something like this in a crib. That's how babies suffocate,' he said, and flung the pillow across the room.

He shoved the revolver in his blue-jeans pocket, the butt protruding just above the edge of the cloth, his booted feet wide-spread, as though he were confronting an adversary that no one else saw.

'You gonna just stand there, Rain Man?' she asked, because she had to say something or the sound roaring in her ears would consume her and the shaking in her mouth would become such that her jawbones would rattle.

He waited a long time to answer her. 'I don't know what I'm gonna do. But you shouldn't be messing with my head, lady. You really shouldn't be doing that at all,' he said.

Then he went out the screen door into the storm and drove his truck in reverse down the clamshells to the two-lane state road, the rain blowing like shattered crystal in his backup lights.

I spent the next morning, along with my partner, Helen Soileau, interviewing Little Face and anyone else in Loreauville who might have seen the intruder into Little Face's home. Helen had started her career as a meter maid at NOPD, then had put in seven years as a patrolwoman in the Garden District and the neighborhood around the Desire Welfare Project, an area so dangerous and violent that black city councilmen tried to persuade President Bush to clean it out with federal troops. Finally she returned to New Iberia, where she had grown up, and was hired as a plainclothes investigator by the sheriff's department.

Helen wore slacks and khakis and jeans to work, was thick-bodied and muscular, and looked boldly into the world's face, her arms pumped, her waved, lacquered blond hair her only visible concession to femininity. As a rule, she had trouble with difficult people only once. She had shot and killed three perpetrators on the job.

We stood in the parking lot of the bar the intruder had visited the night before he had wedged a screwdriver blade into the lock on Little Face's cabin door. The sun was out, the air cool and rain-washed, the sky blue above the trees.

'You think he's the same guy who did Zipper Clum, huh?' Helen said.

'That's my read on it,' I said.

'He tells the bartender he's delivering dishware to a family named Grayson, who don't exist, then casually mentions the Graysons live next to the Dautrieves, and that's how he finds Little Face. We're dealing with a shitbag who has a brain?'

She didn't wait for me to answer her question. She looked back at the bar, tapping her palm on the top of the cruiser.

'How do you figure this guy? He must have known his contract was on a woman, but then he walks out on the job,' she said.

'She had the baby in the room with her. It sounds like he wasn't up to it.'

'All we need is another piece of shit from New Orleans floating up the bayou. What do you want to do now, boss man?'

'Good question.'

Just as we started to get in the cruiser, the bartender opened the screen door and leaned outside. He held up a brightly colored brochure of some kind in his hand.

'Is this any hep to y'all?' he asked.

'What you got there?' I said.

'The man you was axing about? He left it on the counter. I saved it in case he come back,' the bartender said.

Helen's usual martial expression stretched into a big smile. 'Sir, don't handle that any more than you need to. There you go. Just let me get a Ziploc bag and you can slip it right inside . . . That's it, plop it right in. Lovely day, isn't it? Drop by the department for free doughnuts any time. Thank you very much,' she said.

It's called the Automated Fingerprint Identification System, or AFIS. It's a miracle of technology. A latent fingerprint can be faxed to a computer at a regional pod and within two hours be matched with a print that is already on file.

If the fingerprint has a priority.

Priorities are usually given to homicide cases or instances when people are in custody and there is a dramatic need to know who they are.

The man who had prized open Little Face Dautrieve's cabin door was de facto guilty of little more than breaking and entering. The possibility that he was the same man who killed Zipper Clum was based only on my speculation. Also, the Clum homicide was not in our jurisdiction.

No priority for the latent print we took off the dishware brochure the bartender had saved. Get a number and wait. The line in Louisiana is a long one.

I called the office of Connie Deshotel, the attorney general, in Baton Rouge.

'She's out right now. Can she call you back?' the secretary said.

'Sure,' I replied, and gave her my office number.

I waited until quitting time. No call. The next day was Saturday.

I tried again Monday morning.

'She's out,' the secretary said.

'Did she get the message I left Friday?' I asked.

'I think she did.'

'When will she be back?'

'Anytime now.'

'Can you have her call me, please?'

'She's just been very busy, sir.'

'So are we. We're trying to catch a murderer.'

Then I felt stupid and vituperative for taking out my anger on a secretary who was not to blame for the problem.

Regardless, I received no return call. Tuesday morning I went into Helen's office. Her desk was covered with paperwork.

'You want to take a ride to Baton Rouge?' I asked.

Connie Deshotel's office was on the twenty-second floor of the state capitol building, high above the green parks of the downtown area and the wide sweep of the Mississippi River and the aluminum factories and petroleum refineries along its shores. But Connie Deshotel was not in her office. We were told by the secretary she was in the cafeteria downstairs.

'Is there a line to kiss her ring?' Helen asked.

'Excuse me?' the secretary said.

'Take it easy, Helen,' I said in the elevator.

'Connie Deshotel was born with a hairbrush up her ass. Somebody should have straightened her out a long time ago,' she replied.

'You mind if I do the talking?' I asked.

We stood at the entrance to the cafeteria, looking out over the tables, most of which were occupied. Connie Deshotel was at a table against the back wall. She wore a white suit and was sitting across from a man in a blue sports coat and tan slacks whose thinning hair looked almost braided with grease.

'You make the gel head?' Helen said.

'No.'

'Don Ritter, NOPD Vice. He's from some rat hole up in Jersey. I think he's still in the First District.'

'That's the guy who busted Little Face Dautrieve and planted rock on her. He tried to make her come across for him and Jim Gable.'

'Sounds right. He used to shake down fudge packers in the Quarter. What's he doing with the attorney general of Louisiana?'

'Go easy, Helen. Don't make him cut and run,' I said.

'It's your show,' she said, walking ahead of me between the tables before I could reply.

As we approached Connie Deshotel, her eyes moved from her conversation onto my face. But they showed no sense of surprise. Instead, she smiled good-naturedly.

'You want some help with access to AFIS?' she said.

'How'd you know?' I asked.

'I called your office this morning. But you'd already left. The sheriff told me about your problem. I had him fax the latents to the pod. The ID should be on your desk when you get back to New Iberia,' she said.

The confrontation I had been expecting was suddenly gone. I looked at her in dismay.

'You did it,' I said.

'I'm glad my office could help. I'm only sorry I couldn't get back to you

561

earlier. Would you like to join us? This is Don Ritter. He's at the First District in New Orleans,' she said.

Ritter put out his hand and I took it, in the way you do when you suppress your feelings and know that later you'll wish you hadn't.

'I already know Helen. You used to be a meter maid at NOPD,' he said.

'Yeah, you were tight with Jim Gable,' she said, smiling.

I turned and looked directly into Helen's face. But she didn't allow herself to see my expression.

'Jim's working liaison with the mayor's office,' Ritter said.

'How about that Zipper Clum getting wasted? Remember him? You and Jim used to leave him hooked up in the cage,' Helen said.

'A tragic event. Everybody laughed for five minutes at roll call the other day,' Ritter said.

'We have to go. Thanks for your help, Ms Deshotel,' I said.

'Anytime, Mr Robicheaux,' she replied. She looked lovely in her white suit, her olive skin dark with tan, the tips of her hair burned by the sun. The silver angel pinned on her lapel swam with light. 'Come see us again.'

I waited until we were in the parking lot before I turned my anger on Helen.

'That was inexcusable,' I said.

'You've got to make them wince sometimes,' she said.

'That's not your call, Helen.'

'I'm your partner, not your driver. We're working the same case, Dave.'

The air rising from the cement was hot and dense with humidity and hard to breathe. Helen squeezed my upper arm.

'In your mind you're working your mother's case and you think nobody's going to help you. It's not true, bwana. We're a team. You and I are going to make them religious on this one,' she said.

If indeed the man who had broken into Little Face's cabin was the same man who murdered Zipper Clum, the jigger named Steve Andropolis had been halfway right about his identity. The National Crime Information Center said the print we had sent through AFIS belonged to one Johnny O'Roarke, who had graduated from a Detroit high school but had grown up in Letcher County, Kentucky. His mother's maiden name was Remeta. At age twenty he had been sentenced to two years in the Florida State Penitentiary at Raiford for robbery and possession of burglar tools and stolen property.

While in prison he was the suspect in the murder of a six-and-one-half-foot, 280-pound recidivist named Jeremiah Boone, who systematically raped every fish, or new inmate, in his unit.

Helen sat with one haunch on the corner of my desk, reading from the sheets that had been faxed to us by the Florida Department of Corrections in Tallahassee.

'The rapist, this guy Boone? He was Molotoved in his cell. The prison psychologist says O'Roarke, or Remeta, was the regular punch for eight or nine guys till somebody turned Boone into a candle. Remeta must have made his bones by torching Boone,' she said, then waited. 'You listening?'

'Yeah, sure,' I replied. But I wasn't. 'Connie Deshotel seemed to be on the square. Why's she hanging around with a wrong cop, the gel head, what's his name, Ritter?'

'Maybe they just ran into each other. She started her career at NOPD.'

'She stonewalled us, then fell over backwards to look right,' I said.

'She got us the ID. Forget it. What do you want to do about Remeta, or O'Roarke, or whatever he calls himself?' Helen said.

'He probably got front money on the Little Face hit. Somebody besides us isn't happy with him right now. Maybe it's a good time to start jacking up the other side.'

'How?' she said.

I glanced out the window just as Clete Purcel's maroon Cadillac pulled to the curb, with Passion Labiche in the passenger's seat.

9

I walked down the hallway toward the building's entrance, but the sheriff cut me off.

'Purcel's out there,' he said.

'I know. I'm going to meet him,' I said.

'Keep him out of here,' he replied.

'You're too hard on him.'

'You want my job, run for office. I don't want him in the building.'

I looked at his back as he walked away, his words stinging in my face. I caught up with him.

'It's not Purcel. It's who he's with. I think she bothers a few people's conscience around here,' I said.

'You're out of line.'

'With respect, so are you, sir,' I replied, and went outside.

Clete was walking toward me from the curb. He wore a light suit and a tan silk shirt and a dark tie with tiny flowers on it, and his porkpie hat had been replaced by a Panama with a green-tinted visor built into the brim.

'What are you doing with Passion?' I asked.

'I took her to the clinic over in Lafayette.'

'What for?'

'She sees a dermatologist there or something. She didn't want to talk about it.'

'You didn't answer my question. What are you doing with her?'

'None of your damn business, Streak.'

We stood there like that, in the heat of the afternoon, the shadows of the huge white courthouse falling on the lawn behind us. Then Clete's face relented and his eyes went away from me and came back again.

'I took her for a drive because I like her. We're going to dinner and a movie. You want to tag along?' he said.

'I want to talk to you in private.'

'Yeah, anytime I can be useful. Thanks for the hospitality,' he said, and got back into the Cadillac and drove away. Passion smiled at me, brushing her hair out of one eye with the ends of her fingers.

Clete came into the bait shop when I was closing up that night. He opened a bottle of Dixie beer and drank it at the counter. I sat down next to him with a Dr Pepper.

'I'm sorry about today. I just worry about you sometimes, Cletus,' I said.

'You think I'm over-the-hill for Passion?'

'You carried me down a fire escape with two bullets in your back. I don't like to see you get hurt.'

'She makes me feel young. What's wrong in that?'

I cupped my hand on the back of his neck. The baked scales on his skin were as stiff as blistered paint.

'Nothing's wrong with it,' I said.

'So why did you want to talk in private?'

'We think the Zipper Clum shooter is a Kentucky product by way of Michigan. His real name is Johnny O'Roarke but he goes by Remeta. He did a two-bit in Raiford. He also got to be an expert in jailhouse romance.'

'Same guy who was going to do Little Face?'

'That's the way I see it.'

'The jigger said Remeta didn't have a sheet.'

'You ever know a gumball yet who had the whole story right?'

'So Remeta blew off the hit and now he's in the shithouse with whoever gave him the contract. Is that what you were going to tell me?'

'That's about it.'

He grinned and drank out of his beer. 'And you think we should make life as messed up as possible for all bad guys involved?'

'Who's the best source for cold pieces around New Orleans?' I asked.

'It used to be Tommy Carrol, till somebody flushed his grits for him. Right now?' He scratched his hairline and thought. 'You ever hear of the Eighteenth Street gang in Los Angeles? They're here, kind of like sewer growth metastasizing across the country. I never thought I'd miss the greaseballs.'

I drove down East Main at sunrise the next day, under the arched canopy of live oaks that lined the street, and picked Clete up at the apartment he had rented downtown. The moon was still up, the air heavy with the smell of night-blooming flowers and wet trees and bamboo and water that has seeped deep into the soil and settled permanently around stone and brickwork.

But three hours later Clete and I were in a rural area north of New Orleans that in terms of toxicity probably has no environmental equivalent in the country. The petrochemical plants on the edge of the wetlands bleed their wastes into the drainages and woods, systemically killing all life in them, layering the soil with a viscous, congealed substance that resembles putty veined with every color in the rainbow.

The man we were looking for, Garfield Jefferson, lived at the end of a row of tin-roofed shotgun shacks left over from the days of corporate plantations. The rain ditch in front was blown with Styrofoam litter, the yard heaped with upholstered furniture.

'This guy's a gun dealer?' I said.

'He creates free-fire zones for other people to live in and keeps a low profile in Shitsville. Don't be deceived by his smile, either. He's a mainline grad of Pelican Bay,' Clete said.

Garfield Jefferson's skin was so black it gave off a purple sheen, at least inside the colorless gloom of his tiny living room, where he sat on a stuffed couch, legs spread, and grinned at us. The grin never left his face, as though his mouth were hitched on the corners by fishhooks.

'I'm not following y'all. You say you a cop from New Iberia and some dude give you my name?' he said.

'Johnny Remeta says you sold him the piece he did Zipper Clum with. That puts you deep down in the bowl, Garfield,' I said.

'This is all new to me, man. How come the guy is telling you this, anyway? He just running around loose, popping people, calling in information from the phone booth?' Jefferson said.

'Because he fucked up a hit for the wrong people and he knows his ass is hanging over the fire. So he wants to cut a deal, and that means he gives up a few nickel-and-dime pus heads like yourself as an act of good faith,' Clete said.

Jefferson looked out the window, grinning at nothing, or perhaps at the outline of a chemical plant that loomed over a woods filled with leafless trees. His hair was shaved close to the scalp, his wide shoulders knobby with muscle under his T-shirt. He fitted a baseball cap backwards on his head and adjusted it, his eyes glowing with self-satisfaction.

'A turned-around cap in Louisiana mean a guy don't do drugs. You white folks ain't caught on to that. You see a nigger with his hat on backwards, you think "Mean-ass motherfucker, gonna 'jack my car, get in my daughter's bread." I ain't dealt no guns, man. Tell this cracker he be dropping my name, I be finding his crib. I got too much in my jacket to sit still for this shit,' he said. He grinned innocuously at us.

Clete stood up from his chair and remained standing on the corner of Jefferson's vision. He picked up a ceramic lamp, the only bright object in the room, and examined the motel logo on the bottom of it.

'You got a heavy jacket, huh?' I said.

'Eighteen Streeters always get Pelican Bay. Twenty-three hour lockdown. But I'm through with all that. I come back here to be with the home folks,' Jefferson said.

Clete smashed the lamp across the side of Jefferson's head. Pieces of ceramic showered on the couch and in Jefferson's lap. For a moment his face was dazed, his eyes out of focus, then the corners of his mouth stretched upward on wires again.

'See, when people got a weight problem, they go around pissed off all the time, big hard-on 'cause they fat and ugly and don't want no full-length mirrors in their bathrooms,' Jefferson said.

'You think you're funny?' Clete said, and hit him with the flat of his hand on the ear. 'Tell me you're funny. I want to hear it.'

'Clete,' I said softly.

'Butt out of this, Streak.' Then he said to Jefferson, 'You remember those three elementary kids got shot at the playground off Esplanade? The word is you sold the Uzi to the shooter. You got something to say about that, smart-ass?'

'Free enterprise, motherfucker,' Jefferson said, evenly, grinning, his tongue thick and red on his teeth.

Clete knotted Jefferson's T-shirt with his left hand and drove his right fist into Jefferson's face, then pulled him from the couch and threw him to the floor. When Jefferson started to raise himself on his arms, Clete crashed the sole of his shoe into his jaw.

'It looks like you just spit some teeth there, Garfield,' Clete said.

'Get away from him, Clete,' I said.

'No problem. Sorry I lost it with this outstanding Afro-American. Do you hear that, Garfield? I'll come back later sometime and apologize again when we're alone.'

'I mean it, Clete. Wait for me in the truck.'

Clete went out into the yard and let the screen slam behind him. He looked back at me, his face still dark, an unlit Lucky Strike in his mouth. I helped Jefferson back onto the couch and found a towel in the bathroom and put it in his hand.

'I'm sorry that happened,' I said.

'You the good guy in the act, huh?' he replied.

'It's no act, partner. Clete will tear you up.'

Jefferson pushed the towel tight against his mouth and coughed on his own blood, then looked up at me, this time without the grin, his eyes lackluster with the banal nature of the world in which he lived.

'I didn't sell the piece to the cracker. He wanted one, but he ain't got it from me. He got some wicked shit in his blood. I don't need his grief,' he said.

'What are you talking about?'

'He do it for hire. But if there wasn't no money in it, he'd do it anyway. You say he fucked up a hit? I don't believe it. He gets off on it, man. Somebody done reamed that dude good.'

Clete and I drove into the French Quarter, then across the river into Algiers. We talked to hookers, pimps, house creeps, stalls, dips, strong-arm robbers, fences, money washers, carjackers, petty boosters and addicts and crack dealers, all the population that clings to the underside of the city like nematodes eating their way through the subsoil of a manicured lawn. None of them seemed to know anything about Johnny Remeta.

But an ex-prizefighter who ran a saloon on Magazine said he'd heard a new button man in town had bought a half dozen clean guns off some black kids who'd burglarized a sporting goods store.

'Who's he working for, Goldie?' I asked.

'If he waxed Zipper Clum, the human race,' he answered.

At dusk, when the sun was only an orange smudge over the rooftops and the wind was peppered with grit and raindrops, we found one of the kids who had broken into the sporting goods store. Clete pulled him out of a fig tree down the street from the St Thomas Welfare Project.

He was fourteen years old and wore khaki short pants and tennis shoes without socks. Sweat dripped out of his hair and cut lines in the dust on his face.

'This is the mastermind of the group. The ones who got away are younger than he is,' Clete said. 'What's your name, mastermind?'

'Louis.'

'Where's the guy live you sold the guns to?' Clete asked.

'Probably downtown somewhere.'

'How do you know that?' I asked.

' 'Cause he drove toward downtown. The same direction the streetcar go to.'

'Pretty smart deduction, Louis. How much did he give you for the guns?' Clete said.

'A hunnerd dollars.'

'For six guns?' Clete said.

'He said he didn't have no more money. He showed us his wallet. It didn't have no more money in it.'

'One of those guns was used to kill somebody, Louis,' I said.

He looked into space, as though my words and the reality they suggested had nothing to do with his life. He must have weighed eighty pounds. He looked like an upended ant, with small ears, hooked teeth, and eyes that were too large for his face. His knees and elbows were scabbed, his T-shirt glued to his chest with dried food.

'What'd you do with the money, partner?' I asked.

'Didn't get no chance to do nothing. Big kids took it. We was going to the show. Y'all got any spare change?'

His eyes blinked in the silence while he waited for an answer.

What had we accomplished? There was no way to tell. We had put the word on the street that Johnny Remeta was willing to give up people in the New Orleans underworld. Maybe either he or the people who had given him the contract on Zipper Clum and Little Face Dautrieve would be forced into the sunlight. But that night I was too tired to care.

When I was nineteen I worked on an offshore seismograph rig, called a doodlebug outfit in the oil field. It was the summer of 1957, the year that Hurricane Audrey pushed a tidal wave out of the Gulf of Mexico on top of Cameron, Louisiana, crushing the town flat, killing hundreds of people.

For weeks afterward bodies were found in the forks of gum trees out in the swamp or inside islands of uprooted cypress that floated out of the wetlands into the Gulf. Sometimes the long, rubber-coated recording cables we strung from the bow and stern of a portable drill barge got hung on a sunken tree in the middle of a bay or river and a crew member on the jugboat would have to go down after them.

The water was warm with the sun's heat, dark brown with mud and dead hyacinths. The kid who went over the gunnel and pulled himself hand over hand down to the fouled place on the cable did so without light. The sun, even though it was absolutely white in the sky, could not penetrate the layers of silt in the water, and the diver found himself swimming blindly among the water-sculpted and pointed ends of tree branches that gouged at his face like fingers. If he was lucky, the cable came loose with one hard tug in the right direction.

On a late July afternoon I swam down fifteen feet until I touched the smooth, mud-encased trunk of an enormous cypress. I felt my way along the bark until I bumped into the root system, then unwrapped the cable and slid it toward me off the sides of a taproot.

A gray cloud of mud mushroomed around me, as though I had disturbed an envelope of cold air trapped inside the maw of the tree's root system. Suddenly the body of a woman rose out of the silt against mine, her hair sliding across my face, her dress floating above her underwear, the tips of her ringed fingers glancing off my mouth.

No one on the jugboat saw her and some of the crew did not believe the story I told them. But the woman who had been gripped and held fast by the cypress tree, set free only to be lost again, lived with me in my dreams for many years. Her memory had the power to close my windpipe and steal the air from my lungs.

Tonight she was back, although in a different form.

It was nighttime in the dream, the air thick and acrid and sweet at the same time with smoke from a distant stubble fire. I saw my mother, Mae Robicheaux, on a dirt road that led past a neon-lit dance hall. The road was bordered on each side by fields that were bursting with fat stalks of purple cane, their leaves rustling with wind. She was running down the dirt road in the pink uniform she wore to work at the beer garden, her hands outstretched, her mouth wide with a desperate plea. Two cops ran behind her, their hands holding their revolvers in their holsters to prevent them from falling out on the ground.

I was unable to move, watching impotently as a torrent of water surged out of the bay at the end of the dirt road and roared toward her between the walls of sugarcane. She tripped and fell and the root systems from the fields wrapped her body like white worms and held her fast while the water coursed around her thighs, her hips and breasts and neck.

I could see her eyes and mouth clearly now and read my name on her lips, then the current closed over her head and I sat up in bed, my face popping with sweat, my lungs burning as though acid had been poured in them.

I sat in the kitchen, in the dark, my heart twisting in my chest. I went into the bedroom and came back again, with my .45 in my hand, my palm damp on the grips. In my mind I saw the two cops who had chased my mother down the road, saw the sky blue of their uniforms, the glint of the moon on their shields and revolver butts and waxed gun belts, saw everything about them except their faces. I wanted to fire my weapon until the barrel was translucent with heat.

When Bootsie lay her hand on my back, I twitched as though touched with a hot iron, then placed the .45 on the table and buried my face in her stomach.

10

On Saturday I woke early, before sunrise, to help Batist, the elderly black man who worked for me, open the bait shop and fire the barbecue pit on which we prepared chickens and links for our midday customers. I unhooked Tripod, Alafair's pet three-legged coon, from his chain and set him on top of the rabbit hutch with a bowl of water and a bowl of fish scraps. But he hopped down on the ground and walked ahead of me through the pecan and oak trees and across the dirt road to the dock, his tail and rear end swaying.

He and Batist had been at war for years, Tripod flinging boudin all over the counter, destroying boxes of fried pies and candy bars, Batist chasing him down the dock with a broom, threatening to cook him in a pot. But finally they had declared a truce, either out of their growing age or their recognition of their mutual intractability. Now, whenever Alafair or I turned Tripod loose, he usually headed for the dock and worked the screen open and slept on top of the icebox behind the counter. Last week I saw Batist roaring down the bayou in an outboard, with Tripod sitting on the bow, his face pointed into the breeze like a hood ornament.

When I went inside the shop Batist was drinking a cup of coffee, looking out the screen window at the swamp.

'You ever seen a red moon like that this time of year?' he said.

'The wind's up. There's a lot of dust in the air,' I said.

He was a big man, the muscles in his upper arms like croquet balls; his bell-bottomed dungarees and white T-shirt looked sewn to his skin.

'Old people say back in slave days they poured hog blood in the ground under a moon like this,' he said.

'Why?' I asked.

'Make the corn and cane bigger. Same reason people kill a gator and plant it in the field,' he replied. 'I seen Clete Purcel with Passion Labiche.'

'Really?'

'Them girls are trouble, Dave. Their folks was pimps.'

'A good apple can come off a bad tree,' I said.

'Tell that to the man got his parts chopped up all over the flo'.'

'I think he had it coming,' I replied.

Tripod had crawled up on the counter and was sniffing a jar of pickles. Batist hefted him up in the crook of his arm. Tripod's tail was ringed with silver bands and it flipped back and forth between his upended legs.

'We was ten of us when I was growing up. My mama made a big pan of biscuits for breakfast every morning but we didn't have nothing to put on them. So she kept a jar of fig preserves on the table. We rubbed the biscuit on the side of the jar, then ate it. We all laughed when we done that. Everybody's road got glass on it, Dave. Don't mean you got the right to kill nobody,' he said.

'What does that have to do with Clete seeing Passion, Batist?'

'I knowed them girls since they was little. You seen one, you seen the other. They wasn't never more than a broom handle apart.'

'It's too early in the morning to argue with you, partner,' I said.

'I ain't arguing. The troot's the troot. I ain't got to prove nothing, me.'

He walked outside into the soft blue light and set Tripod on the handrail and began hosing down the spool tables on the dock, the moon dull red behind his head.

Later that morning I filled an envelope full of black-and-white photos taken at the Vachel Carmouche murder scene and drove out to Carmouche's boarded-up house on the bayou. The property itself seemed physically stricken by the deed that had been committed there. The yard was waist-high in weeds, the gallery stacked with old tires and hay bales that had gone gray with rot. Nests of yellow jackets and dirtdobbers buzzed under the eaves and a broken windmill clanged uselessly in a dry, hot wind.

I walked around back, re-creating in my mind's eye the path that Letty must have taken from the back porch to the rear of her house, where she stripped off her shoes and robe and washed the blood from her hair and body with a garden hose. The lock was already broken on the back door of Carmouche's house, and I pushed the door open, scraping it back on the buckled linoleum.

The air was stifling, like the inside of a privy in summer, rife with the smell of bat guano and pools of settled water under the floor, superheated by the tin roof and the closed windows. A green plant, as dark as spinach, had blossomed from the drain in the sink.

But the signs of Carmouche's agony from his crawl were still visible on the linoleum, like smeared reddish black paint that had dried and taken on the crisp, razored design of broken leaves. But there were other stains in the kitchen, too – a tentacle of connected dots on the wall by the stove and two similar streakings on the ceiling. I touched my fingers on the dots by the stove and felt what I was sure were the crusted, physical remains of Louisiana's most famous electrician.

I looked through the crime scene photos again. Blood had been slung all over the floor, the walls, the curtains on the cabinets, the icebox, and even the screen of the television set, which had been tuned to an old Laurel and Hardy comedy when the photo was taken. But how would blood from a mattock, a heavy, two-handed tool used to bust up stumps and root systems, create whipped patterns like those on the ceiling and the wall?

I walked across the yard to the back of the Labiche house. The faucet where Letty had washed herself dripped water into the dust; the oil drum she had tried to destroy her robe and shoes in now smoldered with burning leaves; the house she had grown up in was ringed with roses and gardenias, and red squirrels leaped from the branches of the live oaks and clattered across the roof.

The home was weathered, the woodwork termite-eaten and the white paint cracked by the sun and dulled by smoke from stubble fires, but it was still a fine place in which to live, a piece of history from antebellum times, if only Letty were here to enjoy it, if only she had not traded off her life in order to kill a worthless man like Vachel Carmouche.

'You prowling 'round my house for a reason?' someone said behind me.

'What's the haps, Passion?' I said.

She wore sandals and baggy jeans and stood with her big-boned hands on her hips.

'Clete says you think he's a cradle robber, that I'm too young a chick for a man his age.'

'He tells that to women all the time. It makes them feel sorry for him,' I replied.

'What were you doing over at Carmouche's place?' she asked.

'An elderly black friend of mine was mentioning how you and Letty were inseparable. How if somebody saw one of you, he automatically saw the other.'

'So?'

'What were you doing the night Carmouche got it?'

'Read the trial report. I'm not interested in covering that same old territory again. Tell me something. You got a problem with your friend seeing me 'cause I'm Creole?'

'You'll have to find another pin cushion, Passion. See you around,' I said, and walked across the yard under the shade trees toward my truck.

'Yeah, you, too, big stuff,' she said.

When I drove back up the road, she was carrying a loaded trash can in each hand to the roadside, her chest and heavy arms swollen with her physical power. I waved, but my truck seemed to slide past her gaze without her ever seeing it.

That afternoon Governor Belmont Pugh held a news conference, supposedly to talk about casinos, slot machines at the state's racetracks, and the percentage of the gambling revenue that should go into a pay raise for schoolteachers.

But Belmont did not look comfortable. His tie was askew, the point of one collar bent upward, his eyes scorched, his face the color and texture of a boiled ham. He kept gulping water, as though he were dehydrated or forcing down the regurgitated taste of last night's whiskey.

Then one reporter stood up and asked Belmont the question he feared: 'What are you going to do about Letty Labiche, Governor?'

Belmont rubbed his mouth with the flat of his hand, and the microphone picked up the sound of his calluses scraping across whiskers.

'Excuse me, I got a sore throat today and cain't talk right. I'm granting an indefinite stay of execution. Long as she's got her appeals up there in the courts. That's what the law requires,' he said.

'What do you mean "indefinite," Governor?'

'I got corn fritters in my mouth? It means what I said.'

'Are you saying even after her Supreme Court appeal, you're going to continue the stay, or do you plan to see her executed? It's not a complicated question, sir,' another reporter, a man in a bow tie, said, smiling to make the insult acceptable.

Then, for just a moment, Belmont rose to a level of candor and integrity I hadn't thought him capable of.

'Y'all need to understand something. That's a human life we're talking about. Not just a story in your papers or on your TV show. Y'all can take my remarks any damn way you want, but by God I'm gonna do what my conscience tells me. If that don't sit right with somebody, they can chase a possum up a gum stump.'

An aide stepped close to Belmont and spoke into his ear. Belmont's face had the flatness of a guilty man staring into a strobe light. It didn't take long for the viewer to realize that a rare moment had come and gone.

Belmont blinked and his mouth flexed uncertainly before he spoke again.

'I'm an elected official. I'm gonna do my duty to the people of Lou'sana. That means when the appeal is over, I got to uphold the law. I don't got personal choices . . . That's it. There's complimentary food and drink on a table in the back of the room.' He swallowed and looked into space, his face empty and bloodless, as though the words he had just spoken had been said by someone else.

The next morning I read the coroner's report on the death of Vachel Carmouche. It was signed by a retired pathologist named Ezra Cole, a wizened, part-time deacon in a fundamentalist congregation made up mostly of Texas oil people and North Louisiana transplants. He had worked for the parish only a short time eight or nine years ago. But I still remembered the pharmacy he had owned in the Lafayette Medical Center back in the 1960s. He would not allow people of color to even stand in line with whites, requiring them instead to wait in the concourse until no other customers were inside.

I found him at his neat gray and red bungalow out by Spanish Lake, sanding a boat that was inverted on sawhorses. His wife was working in the garden behind the picket fence, a sunbonnet on her head. Their lawn was emerald green from soak hoses and liquid nitrogen, their bamboo and banana trees bending in their backyard against the blueness of the lake. But in the midst of this bucolic tranquillity, Ezra Cole waged war against all fashion and what he saw as the erosion of moral tradition.

'You're asking me how blood got on the ceiling and the wall by the stove? The woman slung it all over the place,' he said.

He wore suspenders over a white dress shirt and rubber boots with the pants tucked inside. His face was narrow and choleric, his eyes busy with angry thoughts that seemed to have less to do with my questions than concerns he carried with him as a daily burden.

'The pattern was too thin. Also, I don't know how she could throw blood on the ceiling from a heavy tool like a mattock,' I said.

'Ask me how she knocked the eyeball out of his head. The answer is she probably has the strength of three men. Maybe she was full of dope.'

'The drug screen says she wasn't.'

'Then I don't know.'

'Was there a second weapon, Doctor?'

'It's all in the report. If you want to help that woman, pray for her soul, 'cause I don't buy death row conversions.'

'I think the blood on the ceiling was thrown there by a knife or barber's razor or weed sickle,' I said.

His face darkened; his eyes glanced sideways at his wife. His hand pinched hard into my arm.

'Step over here with me,' he said, pushing and walking with me toward my truck.

'Excuse me, but take your hand off my person, Dr Cole.'

'You hear my words, Mr Robicheaux. I know Vachel Carmouche's relatives. They don't need to suffer any more than they have. There's nothing that requires a pathologist to exacerbate the pain of the survivors. Are you understanding me, sir?'

'You mean you lied on an autopsy?'

'Watch your tongue.'

'There *was* a second weapon? Which means there might have been a second killer.'

'He was sexually mutilated. While he was still alive. What difference does it make what kind of weapon she used? The woman's depraved. You're trying to get her off? Where's your common sense, man?'

At sunset that same day Batist phoned up from the dock.

'Dave, there's a man down here don't want to come up to the house,' he said.

'Why not?'

'Hang on.' I heard Batist put the receiver down on the counter, walk away from it, then scrape it up in his hand again. 'He's outside where he cain't hear me. I t'ink he's a sad fellow 'cause of his face.'

'Is his name Mike or Micah or something like that?'

'I'll go ax.'

'Never mind. I'll be right down.'

I walked down the slope toward the dock. A purple haze hung in the trees, and birds lifted on the wind that blew across the dead cypress in the swamp. The man who was the chauffeur for Cora Gable was leaning on the rail at the end of the dock, looking out at the bayou, his face turned into the shadows. His shirtsleeves were rolled and his biceps were tattooed with coiled green and red snakes whose fangs were arched into their own tails.

'You're Micah?' I said.

'That's right.'

'Can I help you?' I asked.

'Maybe you can Ms Perez.'

'Jim Gable's wife?'

'I call her by her screen name. The man who marries her ought to take her name, not the other way around.'

His right eye glimmered, barely visible behind the nodulous growth that deformed the side of his face and exposed the teeth at the corner of his mouth. His hair was straw-colored and neatly barbered and combed, as though his personal grooming could negate the joke nature had played upon him.

'It's all about a racetrack. Outside of Luna Mescalero, New Mexico,' he said.

'Pardon?'

'Mr Gable got her to buy a spread out there. He's building a racetrack. He's been trying to do it for years. That's where I'm from. I was a drunkard, a carnival man, what they call the geek act, before that woman come into my life.'

'She seems like a special person,' I said.

He turned his face into the glow of the electric lights and looked me directly in the eyes.

'I did nine months on a county road gang, Mr Robicheaux. One day I sassed a hack and he pulled me behind the van and caned knots all over my head. When I tried to get up he spit on me and jabbed me in the ribs and whipped me till I cried. Ms Perez seen it from her front porch. She called the governor of New Mexico and threatened to walk in his office with a reporter and slap his face unless I was released from jail. She give me a job and an air-conditioned brick cottage to live in when other people would hide their children from me.'

'I don't know what I can do, Micah. Not unless Jim Gable has committed a crime of some kind.'

He chewed the skin on the ball of his thumb.

'A man who doesn't respect one woman, won't respect another,' he said.

'Excuse me?'

He looked out into the shadows again, his head twisting back and forth on his neck, as though searching for words that would not injure.

'He speaks disrespectfully of Ms Perez in front of other men. She's not the only one. Is your wife's first name Bootsie?'

'Yes,' I replied, the skin tightening around my temples.

'He said dirty things about her to a cop named Ritter. They laughed about her.'

'I think it's time for you to go.'

He splayed open his hand, like a fielder's glove, and stared at it and wiped dirt off the heel with the tips of his fingers.

'I've been told to get off better places. I come here on account of Ms Perez. If you won't stand up for your wife, it's your own damn business,' he said, and brushed past me, his arm grazing against mine.

'You hold on,' I said, and lifted my finger at him. 'If you've got a beef to square with Jim Gable, you do it on your own hook.'

He walked back toward me, the teeth at the corner of his mouth glinting in the purple dusk.

'People come to the geek act so they can look on the outside of a man like me and not look at the inside of themselves. You stick your finger in my face again and I'll break it, policeman be damned,' he said.

It stormed that night. The rain blew against the house and ran off the eaves and braided and whipped in the light that fell from the windows. Just as the ten o'clock news came on, the phone rang in the kitchen.

The accent was East Kentucky or Tennessee, the pronunciation soft, the 'r' sound almost gone from the words, the vowels round and deep-throated.

'There's no point in trying to trace this call. I'm not using a ground line,' he said.

'I'm going to take a guess. Johnny Remeta?' I said.

'I got a hit on me. Maybe you're responsible. I can't be sure.'

'Then get out of town.'

'I don't do that.'

'Why'd you call me?'

'Sir, you told folks I was a snitch. What gives you the right to lie like that? I don't even know you.'

'Come in. It's not too late to turn it around. Nobody's mourning Zipper Clum.'

'You've got to set straight what you've done, Mr Robicheaux.'

'You're in the wrong line of work to demand redress, partner.'

'Demand what?'

'Listen, you wouldn't go through with the job at Little Face Dautrieve's place. Maybe you have qualities you haven't thought about. Meet me someplace.'

'Are you kidding?'

I didn't reply. He waited in the silence, then cleared his throat as though he wanted to continue talking but didn't know what to say.

The line went dead.

A hit man who calls you 'sir'?

11

At eight o'clock Monday morning the sheriff stopped me just as I walked in the front door of the department. A small square of blood-crusted tissue paper was stuck to his jawbone where he had cut himself shaving.

'Come down the hall and talk with me a minute,' he said.

I followed him inside his office. He took off his coat and hung it on a chair and gazed out the window. He pressed his knuckles into his lower spine as though relieving himself of a sharp pain in his back.

'Close the door. Pull the blind, too,' he said.

'Is this about the other day?'

'I told you I didn't want Clete Purcel in here. I believe that to be a reasonable request. You interpreted that to mean I have problems of conscience over Letty Labiche.'

'Maybe you just don't like Purcel. I apologize for implying anything else,' I said.

'You were on leave when Carmouche was killed. You didn't have to put your hand in it.'

'No, I didn't.'

'The prosecutor asked for the death penalty. The decision wasn't ours.'

'Carmouche was a pedophile and a sadist. One of his victims is on death row. That one just won't go down, Sheriff.'

The color climbed out of his neck into his face. He cut his head to speak, but no words came out of his mouth. His profile was as scissored as an Indian's against the window.

'Don't lay this off on me, Dave. I won't abide it,' he said.

'I think we ought to reopen the case. I think a second killer is out there.'

He widened his eyes and said, 'You guys in A.A. have an expression, what is it, "dry drunks"? You've got a situation you can't work your way out of, so you create another problem and get emotionally drunk on it. I'm talking about your mother's death. That's the only reason I'm not putting you on suspension.'

'Is that it?' I said.

'No. A New Orleans homicide cop named Don Ritter is waiting in your office,' he replied.

'Ritter's Vice.'

'Good. Clear that up with him,' the sheriff said, and leaned against the windowsill on his palms, stretching out his frame to ease the pain in his lower back.

Don Ritter, the plainclothes detective Helen called the gel head, was sitting in a chair in front of my desk, cleaning his nails over the wastebasket with a gold penknife. His eyes lifted up at me. Then he went back to work on his nails.

'The sheriff says you're Homicide,' I said.

'Yeah, I just changed over. I caught the Zipper Clum case.'

'Really?'

'Who told you and Purcel to question people in New Orleans about Johnny Remeta?'

'He's a suspect in a house invasion.'

'A house invasion, huh? Lovely. What are we supposed to do if you scare him out of town?'

'He says that's not his way.'

'He says?'

'Yeah, he called me up last night.'

Ritter brushed the detritus from his nails into the basket and folded his penknife and put it in his pocket. He crossed his legs and rotated his ankle slightly, watching the light reflect on his shoe shine. His hair looked like gelled pieces of thick twine strung back on his scalp.

'The home invasion? That's the break-in at Little Face Dautrieve's place?' he said.

'Little Face says you planted rock on her. She's trying to turn her life around. Why don't you stay away from her?'

'I don't know what bothers me worse, the bullshit about talking to Remeta or the injured-black-whore routine. You want to nail this guy or not?'

'You see Jim Gable?'

'What about it?'

'Tell him I'm going to look him up on my next trip to New Orleans.'

He chewed with his front teeth on something, a tiny piece of food perhaps.

'So this is what happens when you start over again in a small town. Must make you feel like staying in bed some days. Thanks for your time, Robicheaux,' he said.

I signed out of the office at noon and went home for lunch. As I drove down the dirt road toward the house, I saw a blue Lexus approach me under the long line of oak trees that bordered the bayou. The Lexus slowed and the driver rolled down her window.

'How you doin', Dave?' she said.

'Hey, Ms Deshotel. You visiting in the neighborhood?'

'Your wife and I just had lunch. We're old school chums.'

She took off her sunglasses, and the shadows of leaves moved back and forth on her olive skin. It was hard to believe her career in law enforcement went back into the 1960s. Her heart-shaped face was radiant, her throat unlined, her dark hair a reminder of the health and latent energy and youthful good looks that her age didn't seem to diminish.

'I didn't realize y'all knew each other,' I said.

'She didn't remember me at first, but . . . Anyway, we'll be seeing you. Call me for anything you need.'

She drove away with a casual wave of the hand.

'You went to school with Connie Deshotel?' I asked Bootsie in the kitchen.

'A night class at LSU-NO. She just bought a weekend place at Fausse Pointe. You look puzzled.'

'She's strange.'

'She's a nice person. Stop being psychoanalytical,' Bootsie said.

'She was having lunch in Baton Rouge with an NOPD cop named Don Ritter. He's a genuine lowlife.'

She hung a dishrag over the faucet and turned toward me and let her eyes rove over my face.

'What did he do?' she asked.

'He twists dials on black hookers. Helen says he used to extort gays in the Quarter.'

'So he's a dirty cop. He's not the only one you've known.'

'He's buds with Jim Gable.'

'I see. That's the real subject of our conversation. Maybe you should warn me in advance.'

'Gable has personal knowledge about my mother's death. I'm absolutely convinced of that, Boots.'

She nodded, almost to herself, or to the room, rather than to me, then began slicing a roast on the counter for our sandwiches. She cut harder, faster, one hand slipping on the knob of bone she used for a grip, the blade of the butcher knife knocking against the chopping board. She slid the knife in a long cut through a flat piece of meat and halved and quartered a bloodred tomato next to it, her knuckles whitening. Then she turned around and faced me. 'What can I tell you? That I loathe myself for the fact I slept with him? What is it you want me to say, Dave?'

At the end of the week I received a call from Connie Deshotel at the office.

'Dave, maybe we've had some luck. Do you know of a recidivist named Steve Andropolis?' she said.

'He's a spotter, what used to be called a jigger.'

'He's in custody in Morgan City.'

'What for?'

'Possession of stolen weapons. He says he knows you. This is his fourth time down. He wants to cut a deal.'

'Andropolis is a pathological liar.'

'Maybe. He says he has information on the Zipper Clum murder. He also says he knows how your mother died.'

The sun was high and bright in the sky, the tinted windows of the cars in the parking lot hammered with white daggers. I felt my hand tighten on the telephone receiver.

'How did he come by his information?' I asked.

'I don't know. Two detectives from NOPD are going to interview him this afternoon. You want to meet them there?'

'Is one of them Ritter?'

'Probably. He caught the case.'

'What's Andropolis' bond?'

'None. He's a flight risk.'

'I'll make arrangements to go over there in the next two or three days. Thanks for passing this on, Ms Deshotel,' I said.

'You seem pretty casual.'

'His crime isn't in our jurisdiction. I don't have the legal power to do anything for him. That means he wants to use me against somebody else. Let him sweat awhile.'

'You should have been a prosecutor,' she said.

'What's he have to offer on Remeta?' I said as an afterthought.

'Ritter thinks he might have sold Remeta the weapon used in the Clum killing. Maybe he knows who ordered the hit.'

'The piece came from a sporting goods break-in. The thieves were black kids from the St Thomas Project. Andropolis is taking Ritter over the hurdles.'

'I thought I might be of help. Good luck with it, Dave. Give my best to your wife,' she said, and quietly hung up.

That evening the sky was filled with yellow and red clouds when Clete Purcel and I put a boat in the water at Lake Fausse Pointe. I opened up the outboard down a long canal that was thickly wooded on each side. Green logs rolled against the bank in our wake and cranes and snow egrets and great blue herons lifted into the light and glided on extended wings out over the bay.

We passed acres of floating lilies and lotus flowers that had just gone into bloom, then crossed another bay that flowed into a willow swamp and anchored the outboard off a stand of flooded cypress and tupelo gums and watched our wake slide between the trunks that were as gray as elephant hide.

Clete sat on a swivel chair close to the bow, his porkpie hat low on his eyes, his blue denim shirt damp with sweat between the shoulder blades. He flipped his casting rod with his wrist and sent his treble-hooked balsa-wood lure arching through the air.

'How's it going with you and Passion?' I asked.

'Very solid, big mon,' he replied, turning the handle on his spinning reel, the lure zigzagging through the water toward the boat.

I took a cold can of beer from the ice chest and touched the back of his arm with it. He took it from my hand without turning around. I opened a Dr Pepper and drank it and watched the breeze blow through the cypress, ruffling the leaves like green lace.

'Why don't you say what's on your mind?' Clete said.

'I went through the transcript of Letty Labiche's trial. Both Letty and

Passion testified that Passion was auditioning at a Lake Charles nightclub for a record company scout the night Vachel Carmouche got it.'

''Cause that's where she was,' Clete said.

'They always performed together. Why would she audition by herself?'

Clete retrieved his lure and idly shook the water off it, rattling the two treble hooks against the tip of the rod.

'What are you trying to do, Streak? Drag Passion into it? What's to be gained?'

'I think both sisters are lying about what happened that night. What's that suggest to you? Letty is already on death row. She has nothing to lose.'

'The state's executioner got chopped into sausage links and somebody's going to pay for it. You remember the Ricky Ray Rector case up in Arkansas? The guy had been lobotomized. He looked like black mush poured inside a prison jumpsuit. But he'd killed a cop. Clinton refused to commute the sentence. Rector told the warden he wanted to save out his pecan pie on his last meal so he could eat it after he was executed. Clinton's president, Rector's fertilizer. I bet nobody in Little Rock gave up their regular hump the night he got it, either.'

Clete lit a Lucky Strike and set his Zippo on the top of his tackle box and blew smoke out across his cupped hand.

'I thought you quit those,' I said.

'I did. For some reason I just started again. Dave, it's grim shit. Passion says her sister's scared of the dark, scared of being alone, scared of her own dreams. I came out here to get away from listening about it. So how about lightening up?'

He lay his rod across his thighs and stuck his hand behind him into the crushed ice for another beer, his face painted with the sun's dying red light, his eyes avoiding mine.

According to his obituary, Robert Mitchum, when released from jail after serving time for marijuana possession, was asked what it was like inside the slams.

He replied, 'Not bad. Kind of like Palm Springs without the riffraff.'

It's gone downhill since.

Unless you're a black kid hustling rock and unlucky enough to get nailed under the Three Strikes and You're Out law, your chances of doing serious time are remote.

Who are all these people in the jails?

Meltdowns of every stripe, pipeheads and intravenous junkies who use public institutions to clean their systems out so they can re-addict, recidivists looking for the womb, armed robbers willing to risk ten years for a sixty-dollar score at a 7-Eleven.

Also the twenty-three-hour lockdown crowd: sadists, serial killers, necrophiliacs, sex predators, and people who defy classification, what we used to call the criminally insane, those whose deeds are so dark their specifics are only hinted at in news accounts.

I could have interviewed the jigger named Steve Andropolis on Friday, the same day that Don Ritter did. But what was the point? At best Ritter was a self-serving bumbler who would try to control the interview for his own purposes, probably buy into Andropolis' manipulations, and taint any possibility of obtaining legitimate information from him. Moreover, Ritter was investigating a homicide and had a legal reach that I did not.

So I waited over the weekend and drove to Morgan City on Monday.

Just in time to see Andropolis' body being wheeled out of the jail on a gurney by two paramedics.

'What happened?' I asked the jailer.

' "What happened?" he asks,' the jailer replied, as though a third party were in the room. He was a huge, head-shaved, granite-jawed man whose oversized pale blue suit looked like it was tailored from cardboard.

'I got people hanging out the windows. I got escapees going through air ducts. I got prisoners walking out the door with "time served," when they're not the guys supposed to be walking out the door,' he said.

He took a breath and picked up his cigar from his ashtray, then set it back down and cracked his knuckles like walnuts.

'I locked Andropolis in with eleven other prisoners. The cell's supposed to hold five. There's three bikers in that cell the devil wouldn't let scrub his toilet. There's a kid who puts broken glass in pet bowls. One guy shoots up speedballs with malt liquor. Those are the normal ones. You ask what happened? Somebody broke his thorax. The rest of them watched while he suffocated. Got any other questions?'

He scratched a kitchen match across the wood surface of his desk and relit his cigar, staring through the flame at my face.

The truth was I didn't care how Andropolis had died or even if he was dead. He was evil. He had been a jigger on hit teams, a supplier of guns to assassins, a man who, like a pimp or an eel attached to the side of a shark, thrived parasitically on both the suffering and darkness of others.

The following day Connie Deshotel called me at my office.

'I'm at my camp on the lake. Would you like to meet me here?' she said.

'What for?'

'I have a tape. A copy of Don Ritter's interview with Andropolis.'

'Ritter and Andropolis are a waste of time.'

'It's about your mother. Andropolis was there when she died. Listen to the details on the tape. If he's lying you'll know ... Would you rather not do this, Dave? Tell me now.'

12

That evening Clete and I drove to a boat landing outside Loreauville and put my outboard in the water and headed down the long, treelined canal into Lake Fausse Pointe. A sun shower peppered the lake, then the wind dropped and the air became still and birds rose out of the cypress and willows and gum trees against a bloodred sky.

The alligators sleeping on the banks were slick with mud and looked like they were sculpted out of black and green stone. The back of my neck felt hot, as though it had been burned by the sun, and my mouth was dry for no reason that I could explain, the way it used to be when I woke up with a whiskey hangover. Clete cut the engine and let the outboard float on its wake through a stand of cypress toward a levee and a tin-roofed stilt house that was shadowed by live oaks that must have been over a hundred years old.

'I'd shit-can this broad now. She's jerking your chain, Streak,' he said.

'What's she got to gain?'

'She was with NOPD in the old days. She's tight with that greasebag Ritter. You don't let Victor Charles get inside your wire.'

'What am I supposed to do, refuse to hear her tape?'

'Maybe I ought to shut up on this one,' he replied, and speared the paddle down through the hyacinths, pushing us in a cloud of mud onto the bank.

I walked up the slope of the levee, under the mossy overhang of the live oaks, and climbed the steps to the stilt house's elevated gallery. She met me at the door, dressed in a pair of platform sandals and designer jeans and a yellow pullover that hung on the points of her breasts. She held a spoon and a round, open container of yellow ice cream in her hands.

She looked past me down the slope to the water.

'Where's Bootsie?' she said.

'I figured this was business, Ms Deshotel.'

'Would you please call me "Connie"? . . . Is that Clete Purcel down there?'

'Yep.'

'Has he been house-trained?' she said, raising up on her tiptoes to see him better.

'Beg your pardon?' I said.

'He's unzippering himself in my philodendron.'

I followed her into her house. It was cheerful inside, filled with potted plants and bright surfaces to catch the sparse light through the trees. In the kitchen she spooned ice cream into the blender and added pitted cherries and bitters and orange slices and a cup of brandy. She flipped on the switch, smiling at me.

'I can't stay long, Connie,' I said.

'You have to try this.'

'I don't drink.'

'It's a dessert.'

'I'd like to hear the tape, please.'

'Boy, you *are* a pill,' she replied. Then her face seemed to grow with concern, almost as though it were manufactured for the moment. 'What's on that tape probably won't be pleasant for you to hear. I thought I'd make it a little easier somehow.'

She took a battery-powered tape player out of a drawer and placed it on the kitchen table and snapped down the play button with her thumb, her eyes watching my face as the recorded voices of Don Ritter and the dead jigger Steve Andropolis came through the speaker.

I stood by the screen window and gazed out at the lake while Andropolis described my mother's last hours and the hooker and pimp scam that brought about her death.

I wanted to shut out the words, live inside the wind in the trees and the light ruffling the lake's surface, listen to the hollow thunking of a pirogue rocking against a wood piling, or just watch Clete's broad back and thick arms and boyish expression as he flipped a lure with his spinning rod out into the dusk and retrieved it back toward the bank.

But even though he had been a parasite, an adverb and never a noun, Andropolis had proved in death his evil was sufficient to wound from beyond the grave.

'The guys who whacked her weren't cops. They were off-duty security guards or something. She had this dude named Mack with her. He told everybody he was a bouree dealer but he was her pimp. Him and Robicheaux's mother, if that's what she was, just worked the wrong two guys,' Andropolis' voice said.

As through a sepia-tinted lens I saw wind gusting on a dirt road that lay like a trench inside a sea of sugarcane. Black clouds roiled in the sky; a red and white neon Jax sign swung on a metal pole in front of a dance hall. Behind the dance hall was a row of cabins that resembled ancient slave quarters, and each tiny gallery was lit with a blue bulb. In slow motion I saw my mother, her body obese with beer fat, lead a drunk man from the back of the dance hall to a cabin door. He wore a polished brass badge on his shirt pocket, and she kissed him under the light, once, twice, working her hand down to his loins when he momentarily wavered.

Then they were inside the cabin, the security guard naked now, mounted between her legs, rearing on his stiffened arms, buckling her body into the stained mattress, bouncing the iron bed frame against the planked wall. A freight train loaded with refined sugar from the mill roared past the window.

Just as the security guard reached orgasm, his lips twisting back on his teeth like a monkey's, the door to the cabin drifted back on its hinges and

Mack stepped inside and clicked on the light switch, his narrow, mustached face bright with purpose. He wore pointed boots and striped pants and a two-tone sports coat and cocked fedora like a horse trainer might. He slipped a small, nickel-plated revolver out of his belt and pointed it to the side, away from the startled couple in the center of the bed.

'You just waiting tables, you?' he said to my mother.

'Look, bud. This is cash and carry. Nothing personal,' the security guard said, rolling to one side now, pulling the sheet over his genitalia, removing himself from the line of fire.

'You ain't seen that band on her finger? You didn't know you was milking t'rew another man's fence?' Mack said.

'Hey, don't point that at me. Hey, there ain't no problem here. I just got paid. It's in my wallet. Take it.'

'I'll t'ink about it, me. Get down on your knees.'

'Don't do this, man.'

'I was in the bat'room. I splashed on my boots. Right there on the toe. I want that spot to shine ... No, you use your tongue, you.'

Then Mack leaned over and pressed the barrel of the revolver into the sweat-soaked hair of the naked man while the man cleaned Mack's boot and his bladder broke in a shower on the floor.

Connie Deshotel pushed the off button on the tape player.

'It looks like a variation of the Murphy scam gone bad,' she said. 'The security guard came back with his friend and got even.'

'It's bullshit,' I said.

'Why?' She set two bowls of her ice cream and brandy dessert on the table.

'Andropolis originally told me the killers were cops, not security guards. Andropolis worked for the Giacanos. Anything he knew had to come from them. We're talking about dirty cops.'

'This is from another tape. The security guard *was* a Giacano, a distant cousin, but a Giacano. He was killed in a car accident about ten years ago. He worked for a security service in Algiers about the time your mother supposedly died.'

Far across the lake, the sun was just a red ember among the trees. 'I tell you what, Ms Deshotel,' I said, turning from the screen.

'*Connie*,' she said, smiling with her eyes.

Then her mouth parted and her face drained when she heard my words.

I walked down the incline through the shadows and stepped into the outboard and cranked the engine. Clete climbed in, rocking the boat from side to side as I turned us around without waiting for him to sit down.

'What happened in there?' he asked.

I reached into the ice chest and lifted out a can of Budweiser and tossed it to him, then opened up the throttle.

It was almost dark when we entered the canal that led to the boat landing. The air was heated, the sky crisscrossed with birds, dense with the distant smell that rain makes in a dry sugarcane field. I ran the boat up onto the ramp and cut the engine and tilted the propeller out of the water and flung our life vests up onto the bank and lifted the ice chest up by the handles and waded through the shallows.

'You gonna tell me?' Clete said.

'What?'

'How it went in there.' His face was round and softly focused, an alcoholic shine in his eyes.

'I told her if Don Ritter ever repeats those lies about my mother, I'm going to jam that tape up his ass with a chain saw.'

'Gee, I wonder if she got your meaning,' he said, then clasped his huge hand around the back of my neck, his breath welling into my face like a layer of malt. 'We're going to find out who hurt your mother, Streak. But you're no executioner. When those guys go down, it's not going to be on your conscience. My old podjo had better not try to go against me on this one,' he said, his fingers tightening into my neck.

The next morning I woke before dawn to the sounds of rain and a boat engine on the bayou. I fixed a cup of coffee and a bowl of Grape-Nuts and ate breakfast at the kitchen table, then put on my raincoat and hat and walked down to the bait shop in the grayness of the morning to help Batist open up.

'Dave, I seen a man wit' a boat trailer by the ramp when I drove up,' Batist said. 'I got out of my truck and he started to walk toward me, then he turned around and drove off. Later a boat gone on by the shop. I t'ink it was him.'

'Who was he?' I asked.

'I ain't seen him befo'. It was like he t'ought I was somebody else. Maybe he was looking for you, huh?'

'Why's this guy so important, Batist?'

'My eyes ain't that good no more. But there was somet'ing shiny on his dashboard. Like chrome. Like a pistol, maybe.'

I turned on the string of lights over the dock and looked out the screen window at the rain denting the bayou and the mist blowing out of the cypress and willow trees in the swamp. Then I saw one of my rental boats that had broken loose from its chain floating sideways past the window.

'I'll go for it,' Batist said behind me.

'I'm already wet,' I said.

I unlocked an outboard by the concrete ramp and headed downstream. When I went around the bend, I saw the loose boat tangled in an island of hyacinths close-in to a stand of flooded cypress.

But I wasn't alone.

An outboard roared to life behind me, and the green-painted aluminum bow came out of a cut in the swamp and turned into my wake.

The man in the stern was tall, dark-haired, his skin pale, his jeans and T-shirt soaked. He wore a straw hat, with a black ribbon tied around the crown, and his face was beaded with water. He cut his engine and floated up onto the pad of hyacinths, his bow inches from the side of my boat.

He placed both of his palms on his thighs and looked at me and waited, his features flat, as though expecting a response to a question.

'That's an interesting shotgun you have on the seat,' I said.

'A Remington twelve. It's modified a little bit,' he replied.

'When you saw them off at the pump, they're illegal,' I said, and grinned at him. I caught the painter on the boat that had broken loose and began tying it to the stern of my outboard.

'You know who I am?' he asked. His eyes were a dark blue, the color of ink. He took a bandanna from his back pocket and wiped his face with it, then glanced upward at the grayness in the sky and the water dripping out of the canopy.

'We don't hear a Kentucky accent around here very often,' I said.

'Somebody shot at me yesterday. Outside New Orleans.'

'Why tell me?'

'You made them think I was gonna turn them in. That's a rotten thing to do, sir.'

'I hear you killed people for the wise guys out on the coast. You had problems a long time before you came to Louisiana, Johnny.'

His eyes narrowed at my use of his name. His mouth was effeminate and did not seem to go with his wide shoulders and heavy upper arms. He picked at his fingernails and looked at nothing, his lips pursing before he spoke again.

'This is a pretty place. I'd like to live somewhere like this. This guy who got killed in Santa Barbara? He raped a fourteen-year-old girl at an amusement park in Tennessee. She almost bled to death. The judge gave him two years probation. What would you do if you were her father?'

'You were just helping out the family?'

'I've tried to treat you with respect, Mr Robicheaux. I heard you're not a bad guy for a roach.'

'You came here with a sawed-off shotgun.'

'It's not for you.'

'Who were the other people you did?'

The rain had slackened, then it stopped altogether and the water dripping out of trees was loud on the bayou's surface. He removed his straw hat and stared reflectively into the cypress and willows and air vines, his eyes full of light that seemed to have no origin.

'A greaseball's wife found out her husband was gonna have her popped. By a degenerate who specialized in women. So the wife brought in an out-of-state guy to blow up her husband's shit. The degenerate could have walked away, but some guys just got to try. Nobody in Pacific Palisades is losing sleep.'

'Who paid you to do Zipper Clum and Little Face Dautrieve?'

'The money was at a drop. All I know is they tried to pop me yesterday. So maybe that puts me and you on the same team.'

'Wrong.'

'Yeah?'

'Yeah.'

His eyes seemed to go out of focus, as though he were refusing to recognize the insult that hung in the air. He pulled at his T-shirt, lifting the wetness of the cloth off his skin.

'You gonna try to take me down?' he asked.

'You're the man with the gun,' I replied, grinning again.

'It's not loaded.'

'I'm not going to find out,' I said.

He lifted the cut-down shotgun off the seat and lay it across his thighs, then worked his boat alongside my engine. He ripped out the gas line and tossed it like a severed snake into the cat-tails.

'I wish you hadn't done that,' I said.

'I don't lie, sir. Not like some I've met.' He pumped open the shotgun and inserted his thumb in the empty chamber. Then he removed a Ziploc bag with three shells in it from his back pocket and began fitting them into the magazine. 'I dropped my gun in the water and got my other shells wet. That's why it was empty.'

'You said "not like some." You calling me a liar?' I said.

'You spread rumors I was a snitch. I was in the Flat Top at Raiford. I never gave anybody up.'

'Listen, Johnny, you backed out on the Little Face Dautrieve contract. You're still on this side of the line.'

'What are you talking about?'

'Don't pretend you don't understand. Look at me.'

'I don't like people talking to me like that, Mr Robicheaux. Let go of my boat.'

I looked hard into his face. His eyes were dark, his cheeks pooled with shadow, like a death mask, his mouth compressed into a small flower. I shoved his boat out into the current.

'You got it, kid,' I said.

He cranked the engine and roared down the bayou, glancing back at me once, the bow of his boat swerving wildly to avoid hitting a nutria that was swimming toward the bank.

13

Later that morning I called the prison psychologist at Raiford in Florida, a social worker in Letcher County, Kentucky, and a high school counselor in Detroit. By quitting time I had received at least three dozen fax sheets concerning Johnny Remeta.

That afternoon Clete Purcel sat next to me on a wood bench at the end of the dock and read through the file I had put together on Remeta.

'He's got a 160 I.Q. and he's a button man?' Clete said.

'No early indications of violence, either. Not until he got out of Raiford.'

'You're saying he got spread-eagled in the shower a few times and decided to get even?'

'I'm just saying he's probably not a sociopath.'

Clete closed the manila folder and handed it back to me. The wind ruffled and popped the canvas awning over our heads.

'Who cares what he is? He was on your turf. I'd put one through his kneecap if he comes back again,' Clete said.

I didn't reply. I felt Clete's eyes on the side of my face.

'The guy's of no value to you. He doesn't know who hired him,' Clete said. 'Splash this psychological stuff in the bowl.'

'The social worker told me the kid's father was a drunk. She thinks the old man sold the kid a couple of times for booze.'

Clete was already shaking his head with exasperation before I finished the sentence.

'He looked Zipper Clum in the eyes while he drilled a round through his forehead. This is the kind of guy the air force trains to launch nuclear weapons,' he said.

He stood up and gripped his hands on the dock railing. The back of his neck was red, his big arms swollen with energy.

'I'm pissed off at myself. I shouldn't have helped you fire this guy up,' he said.

'How's Passion?' I asked, changing the subject.

'Waiting for me to pick her up.' He let out his breath. 'I've got baling wire wrapped around my head. I can't think straight.'

'What's wrong?' I said.

'I'm going to drive her to the women's prison tomorrow to visit her sister.'

'You feel like you're involving yourself with the other side?'

'Something like that. I always figured most people on death row had it coming. You watch Larry King last night? He had some shock-jock on there laughing about executing a woman in Texas. The same guy who made fun of Clinton at a banquet. These are America's heroes.'

He went inside the bait shop and came back out with a sixteen-ounce can of beer wrapped in a paper towel. He took two long drinks out of the can, tilting his head back, swallowing until the can was almost empty. He blew out his breath and the heat and tension went out of his face.

'Dave, I dreamed about the Death House at Angola. Except it wasn't Letty Labiche being taken there. It was Passion. Why would I have a dream like that?' he said, squeezing his thumb and forefinger on his temples.

But I was to hear Letty Labiche's name more than once that day.

Cora Gable had volunteered her chauffeur, Micah, to deliver a thousand-name petition on behalf of Letty to the governor's mansion. After he had picked up several friends of Cora's in New Orleans, driven them to the capitol at Baton Rouge, and dropped them off again in New Orleans, he ate dinner by himself in a cafe by the river, on the other side of the Huey Long Bridge, then headed down a dusky two-lane road into Lafourche Parish.

He passed through a small settlement, then entered a long stretch of empty road surrounded by sugarcane fields. A white car closed behind him; a man in the passenger's seat glanced back over his shoulder and clapped a battery-powered flashing red light on the roof.

The cops looked like off-duty narcs or perhaps SWAT members. They were thick-bodied and vascular, young, unshaved, clad in jeans and sneakers and dark-colored T-shirts, their arms ridged with hair, handcuffs looped through the backs of their belts.

They walked up on each side of the limo. Micah's windows were down now, and he heard the Velcro strap peeling loose on the holster of the man approaching the passenger door.

'Could I see your driver's license, please?' the man at Micah's window said. He wore pilot's sunglasses and seemed bored, looking away at the sunset over the cane fields, his palm extended as he waited for Micah to pull his license from his wallet.

'What's the problem?'

The man in sunglasses looked at the photo on the license, then at Micah's face.

'You see what it says over your picture? "Don't drink and drive . . . Don't litter Louisiana," ' he said. 'Every driver's license in Louisiana has that on it. We're trying to keep drunks off the road and the highways clean. You threw a beer can out the window back there.'

'No, I didn't.'

'Step out of the car, please.'

'You guys are from New Orleans. You don't have authority here,' Micah said.

'Walk around the far side of the car, please, and we'll discuss that with you.'

They braced him against the roof, kicked his ankles apart, ran their hands up and down his legs, and pulled his pockets inside out, spilling his change and wallet onto the shale.

A car passed with its lights on. The two cops watched it disappear between the cane fields. Then one of them swung a baton into the back of Micah's thigh, crumpling it as though the tendon had been cut in half. He fell to one knee, his fingers trying to find purchase against the side of the limo.

The second blow was ineffective, across his shoulders, but the third was whipped with two hands into his tailbone, driving a red shard of pain into his bowels. Micah rolled in the dirt, shuttering, trying to control his sphincter muscle.

The cop who had taken his license dropped it like a playing card into his face, then kicked him in the kidney.

'You got a sheet in New Mexico, Micah. Go back there. Don't make us find you again,' he said.

'I didn't do anything,' he said.

The cop with the baton leaned over and inserted the round, wooden end into Micah's mouth, pushing hard, until Micah gagged and choked on his own blood.

'What's that? Say again?' the cop said, bending down solicitously toward Micah's deformed face.

Clete called me the next afternoon and asked me to meet him in Armand's on Main Street. It was cool and dark inside, and Clete sat at the antique, mirrored bar, a julep glass in his hand, an electric fan blowing across his face.

But there was nothing cool or relaxed about his demeanor. His tropical shirt was damp against his skin, his face flushed as though he had a fever. One foot was propped on the runner of the barstool; his knee kept jiggling.

'What is it, Clete?'

'I don't know. I probably shouldn't have called you. Maybe I should just drive up the stock price on Jack Daniel's by three or four points.'

'I got a call from Cora Gable. A couple of NOPD goons beat up her driver. She says they scared him so bad he won't press charges.'

'Jim Gable wants him out of town?'

'The driver had just delivered a petition for Letty to Belmont Pugh. Maybe the message is for Cora.'

'What's Gable's interest in Letty Labiche?'

'I don't know. You going to tell me why you called me down here?'

The affair had started casually enough. Clete had gone to her house at evening time and had found her working in back, carrying buckets of water in both hands from the house faucet to her garden.

'Where's your hose?' he asked.

'The boy who cuts the grass ran the lawn mower over it,' she replied.

They carried the water together, sloshing it on their clothes, pouring it along the rows of watermelons and strawberries, the sky aflame behind them. Her face was hot with her work, her dress blowing loosely on her body as she stooped over in the row. He walked back to the house and filled a glass of water for her and carried it to her in the garden.

She watched his face over the top of the glass as she drank. Her skin was dusty, the tops of her breasts golden and filmed with perspiration in the dying light. She lifted her hair off her neck and pulled it on top of her head.

He touched the roundness of her upper arm with his fingertips.

'You're a strong woman,' he said.

'Overweight.'

'Not to me,' he replied.

She kept brushing her hair back from the corner of her mouth, not speaking, letting her eyes meet his as though she knew his thoughts.

'I drink too much. I lost my badge in a bad shooting. I did security for Sally Dio in Reno,' he said.

'I don't care.'

She tilted up her face and looked sideways with her eyes, the wind blowing her hair back from her face.

'My ex said she could have done better at the Humane Society,' he said.

'What somebody else say got nothing to do wit' me.'

'You smell like strawberries.'

'That's 'cause we standing in them, Clete.'

She pushed the soft curve of her sandal across the hardness of his shoe.

They went upstairs to the third story of the house and made love in an oversized brass bed that was surrounded by three electric fans. She came before he did, then mounted him and came a second time, her hands caressing his face simultaneously. Later she lay close to him and traced his body with her fingertips, touching his sex as though it were a source of power, in a way that almost embarrassed him and made him look at her quizzically.

She wanted to hear stories about the Marine Corps and Vietnam, about his pouring a container of liquid soap down a hood's mouth in the men's room of the Greyhound bus depot, about growing up in the Irish Channel, how he smashed a woman's greenhouse with rocks after he found out her invitation for ice cream had been an act of charity she extended at her back door to raggedy street children.

'I'm a professional screwup, Passion. That's not humility, it's fact. Dave's the guy with the history,' he said.

She pulled him against her and kissed his chest.

He stayed away for two days, then returned to her house at sunrise, his heart beating with anticipation before she opened the door. She made love with him as though her need were insatiable, her thighs fastened hard around him, the small cry she made in his ear like a moment of exorcism.

Two weeks later he sat in her kitchen, a blue and white coffeepot by his empty plate, while Passion rinsed a steak tray under the faucet.

He ran his nails through his hair.

'I think you're looking for an answer in a guy who doesn't have any,' he said.

When she didn't reply, he smiled wanly. 'I'm lucky to have a P.I. license,

Passion. New Orleans cops cross the street rather than talk to me. I've had the kind of jobs people do when they're turned down by the foreign legion.'

She stood behind him, kneading his shoulders with her large hands, her breasts touching the back of his head.

'I have to go to the doctor in the morning. Then I want to visit my sister,' she said.

Clete drank out of his julep and stirred the ice in the bottom of the glass.

'She told me all the details about what Carmouche did to her and Letty. Somebody should dig that guy up and chain-drag the corpse through Baton Rouge,' he said. Then he seemed to look at a thought inside his head and his face went out of focus. 'Passion would let him exhaust himself on her so he'd go easier on her sister.'

'Get this stuff out of your mind, Clete.'

'You think she's playing me?'

'I don't know.'

'Give me another julep,' he said to the bartender.

Bootsie was waiting for me in the parking lot after work.

'How about I buy you dinner, big boy?' she said.

'What's going on?'

'I just like to see if I can pick up a cop once in a while.'

We drove to Lerosier, across from the Shadows, and ate in the back room. Behind us was a courtyard full of roses and bamboo, and in the shade mint grew between the bricks.

'Something happen today?' I said.

'Two messages on the machine from Connie Deshotel. I'm not sure I like other women calling you up.'

'She probably has my number mixed up with her Orkin man's.'

'She says she's sorry she offended you. What's she talking about?'

'This vice cop, Ritter, taped an interview with a perpetrator by the name of Steve Andropolis. The tape contained a bunch of lies about my mother.'

Bootsie put a small piece of food in her mouth and chewed it slowly, the light hardening in her eyes.

'Why would she do that?' she said.

'Ask her.'

'Count on it,' she said.

I started to reply, then looked at her face and thought better of it.

But Connie Deshotel was a willful and determined woman and was not easily discouraged from revising a situation that was somehow detrimental to her interests.

The next evening Belmont Pugh's black Chrysler, followed by a caravan of political sycophants and revelers, parked by the boat ramp. They got out and stood in the road, blinking at the summer light in the sky, the dust from their cars drifting over them. All of them had been drinking, except apparently Belmont. While his friends wandered down toward the bait shop for food and beer, Belmont walked up the slope, among the oaks, where I was raking leaves, his face composed and somber, his pinstripe suit and gray Stetson checkered with broken sunlight.

'Why won't you accept that woman's apology?' he asked.

'You're talking about Connie Deshotel?'

'She didn't mean to cast an aspersion on your mother. She thought she was doing her job. Give her a little credit, son.'

'All right, I accept her apology. Make sure you tell her that for me, will you? She actually got the governor of the state to drive out here and deliver a message for her?'

He removed his hat and wiped the liner out with a handkerchief. His back was straight, his profile etched against the glare off the bayou. His hair had grown out on his neck, and it gave him a distinguished, rustic look. For some reason he reminded me of the idealistic young man I had known years ago, the one who daily did a good deed and learned a new word from his thesaurus.

'You're a hard man, Dave. I wish I had your toughness. I wouldn't be fretting my mind from morning to night about that woman on death row,' he said.

I rested the rake and popped my palms on the handle's end. It was cool in the shade and the wind was blowing the tree limbs above our heads.

'I remember when a guy offered you ten dollars to take a math test for him, Belmont. You really needed the money. But you chased him out of your room,' I said.

'The cafeteria didn't serve on weekends. You and me could make a can of Vienna sausage and a jar of peanut butter and a box of crackers go from Friday noon to Sunday night,' he said.

'I've witnessed two executions. I wish I hadn't. You put your hand in one and you're never the same,' I said.

'A long time ago my daddy said I was gonna be either a preacher or a drunk and womanizer. I wake up in the morning and have no idea of who I am. Don't lecture at me, son.' His voice was husky, his tone subdued in a way that wasn't like Belmont.

I looked beyond him, out on the dock, where his friends were drinking can beer under the canvas awning. One of them was a small, sun-browned, mustached man with no chin and an oiled pate and the snubbed nose of a hawk.

'That's Sookie Motrie out there. I hear he's the money behind video poker at the tracks,' I said.

'It's all a trade-off. People want money for schools but don't like taxes. I say use the devil's money against him. So a guy like Sookie gets to be a player.'

When I didn't reply, he said, 'A lot of folks think Earl K. Long was just an ignorant redneck. But Earl did good things people don't know about. A whole bunch of Negro women graduated from a new nursing program and found out right quick they couldn't get jobs nowhere. So Earl hears about it and says he wants a tour of the state hospital. He pumps hands all over the building, sticks his head in operating rooms, flushes toilets, then gets all the hospital's administrators in one room and locks the door.

'He says, "I just seen a shameful spectacle here. Y'all got white nurses hand-waiting on nigra patients, carrying out their bedpans and I don't know what all, and I ain't gonna stand for it. You either hire nigra nurses in those wards or every damn one of you is gonna be out of a job."

'The next week the state hospital had two dozen black nurses on staff.'

'Makes a good story,' I said.

'Stories are all the human race has got, Dave. You just got to find the one you like and stay with it,' he replied.

'Are you going to execute Letty Labiche?'

He replaced his hat on his head and walked down the slope to rejoin his entourage, jiggling his hands in the air like a minstrel man.

14

Farther to the south of us, in the working-class community of Grand Bois, a young attorney, two years out of law school, filed suit on behalf of the local residents against a large oil corporation. The locals were by and large Cajuns and Houma Indians, uneducated, semi-skilled, poor, without political power, and bewildered by the legal apparatus, the perfect community to target as the open-pit depository of oil sludge trucked in from a petroleum treatment plant in Alabama.

Company officials didn't argue with the contention the pits contained benzene, hydrogen sulfide, and arsenic. They didn't have to. Years ago, during a time of gas shortages, the U.S. Congress had granted the oil industry blanket exemptions from the regulations that govern most toxic wastes. Secondly, the state of Louisiana does not define oil waste as hazardous material.

The state, the oil corporation, and the community of Grand Bois were now in court, and Connie Deshotel's office was taking depositions from the people in Grand Bois who claimed their children were afflicted with vertigo, red eyes, skin rashes, and diarrhea that was so severe they had to keep buckets in their automobiles.

Two of those Grand Bois families had moved to New Iberia and were now living up on the bayou road, not far from Passion Labiche's nightclub. On Monday Helen Soileau was assigned to drive Connie Deshotel and her assistant out to their homes.

Later she told me of Connie Deshotel's bizarre behavior, although she could offer no explanation as to its cause.

It had rained hard that morning, then the sun had become a white orb in the center of a windless sky, evaporating the water out of the fields, creating a superheated dome of humidity that made you feel like ants were crawling inside your clothes.

The air-conditioning unit in the cruiser began clanking, then gasped once and gave out. Connie Deshotel had removed her white suit coat and folded it on her lap, trying to keep her composure while her male assistant talked without stop in the backseat. Her armpits were ringed with sweat and a hostile light was growing in her eyes.

Her assistant paused a moment in his monologue, then cracked a mint between his molars and began again.

'Why don't the people of Grand Bois move to a place where there's no oil industry? Get jobs as whalers in Japan. Could it be they've done scut work all their lives in the oil industry and couldn't fix ice water without a diagram?' he said.

He took the silence in the cruiser as indication his point was not understood.

'The Houma Indians have a problem with oil waste. But they want to build casinos and addict their own people to gambling. I think the whole bunch is ripe for a hydrogen bomb,' he said.

'I don't want to add to your irritability, Malcolm, but would you please shut up?' Connie said.

'Y'all want something cool to drink?' Helen asked.

'Yes, please,' Connie said.

They pulled into Passion's nightclub just as a storm cloud covered the sun and the landscape dropped into shadow. Inside, electric fans vibrated on the four corners of the dance floor, and an ancient air-conditioning unit inserted in a sawed-out hole in the back wall blew a stream of refrigerated coolness across the bar.

Connie sat on a barstool and closed her eyes in the wind stream.

Helen whistled through the door that gave onto the café side of the building.

'Hey, Passion, you've got some customers in here,' she called.

Connie's eyes opened and she turned her blank face on Helen.

'Letty Labiche's sister owns this place. You know her?' Helen said.

'No.'

'From the way you looked, I thought you recognized the name or something.'

'Yes, I did recognize the name. That doesn't mean I know her,' Connie said.

'Yes, ma'am,' Helen said.

'I'd like to leave now,' Connie said.

'I thought you wanted a cold drink.'

'I just wanted to get out of the heat a few minutes. I'm fine now. We should make at least one other stop today,' Connie said.

'Too late,' her assistant, Malcolm, said, grinning from behind the bar. He opened two ice-cold bottles of Coca-Cola and set them in front of Helen and Connie just as Passion walked in from the café and tilted her head at the presence of the man behind her bar.

'Could I hep y'all?' she asked.

'Sorry, miss. I'm so dry I'm a fire hazard. I left the money on the register,' Malcolm said. He opened a long-neck bottle of beer for himself and stepped back from the foam as it slid over the neck.

Passion rang up the purchase, her back to them. 'Sorry I couldn't get over here to wait on y'all,' she said.

Connie's face looked stricken. She stared helplessly at the back of Passion's head, as though an element from a nightmare had just forced its way inexorably into her waking day.

Passion turned and placed a quarter and two dimes in front of the male assistant. Then her eyes fell on Connie's.

'You all right, ma'am?' she asked.

'Yes. Why do you ask?' Connie said.

'On days like this the tar on the road melts. You look like you got dehydrated. I got some aspirin.'

'Thank you. I don't need any.'

Passion started to turn away, then a look of vague recognition swam into her face.

'I seen you somewhere before, ma'am?' she asked.

'Perhaps. I'm the attorney general.'

'No, I seen you in an old photograph. Or somebody sure do look like you. You got nice features. They don't change with time,' Passion said.

'I'm sure that's a compliment, but I don't know what you're talking about.'

'It's gonna come. Y'all visiting New Iberia?' Passion asked.

Connie rose from her chair and extended her hand across the bar.

'It was very nice meeting you,' she said, even though they had not exchanged names or been introduced by a third party.

She walked out to the cruiser, her chin tilted upward, her face bloodless. The wind raked the branches of a live-oak tree against the side of the club and another rain shower burst from the heavens, clattering like marbles on the tin roof.

'I'm going to finish my beer. Who plays that piano?' Malcolm said.

Button man or not, Johnny Remeta obviously didn't fall easily into a predictable category.

The off-duty New Orleans cop who worked security at the historical museum on Jackson Square watched a lithe young man in shades and knife-creased khakis and half-topped boots and a form-fitting ribbed T-shirt with the sleeves rolled over the shoulders cross from the Café du Monde and walk through the park, past a string band playing in front of Pirates Alley, wrap his chewing gum in a piece of foil and drop it in a waste can, comb his hair and enter the museum's doorway.

Where had the off-duty cop seen that face?

A mug shot passed around at roll call?

No, he was imagining things. The mug shot was of a guy who was wanted in a shooting off Magazine. Yeah, the hit on Zipper Clum. A white shooter, which meant it was probably a contract job, somebody the Giacanos hired to wipe out an obnoxious black pimp. Contract shooters didn't wander around in museums under a cop's nose. Besides, this kid looked like he just got out of high school.

'You visiting from out of town?' the cop asked.

The young man still wore his shades and was looking at a battle-rent Confederate flag that was pressed under glass.

'No, I live here. I'm an artist,' he replied. He did not turn his head when he spoke.

'You come here often?'

'About every three days.' He removed his shades and looked the cop full in the face, grinning now. 'Something wrong?'

'Yeah, my feet hurt,' the cop said.

But later the cop was still bothered. He followed the young man across Jackson Square to Decatur, took down the license number of his pickup truck, and called it in.

One block away, a police cruiser fell in behind the pickup truck. Just as the uniformed cop behind the wheel was about to hit his flasher, the pickup truck turned back into the Quarter on Bienville and drove the short two-block distance to the police station at Royal and Conti.

The young man in shades parked his truck and went inside.

The cop in the cruiser kept going, shaking his head disgustedly at the cavalier misuse of his time.

Inside the police station, the young man gazed idly at Wanted posters on a corkboard, then asked the desk sergeant for directions to the battlefield at Chalmette.

The desk sergeant watched the young man walk out of the door of the station and get in his truck and drive down Conti toward the river. Then the sergeant was out the door himself, his arms waving in the air at two motorcycle cops who were coming up the walk.

'The guy in the black pickup! You can still get him!' he yelled.

Wrong.

Johnny Remeta cut across the Mississippi bridge onto the West Bank, caught Highway 90, wove five miles through residential neighborhoods and strip malls, and dumped the pickup in St Charles Parish and boosted an Oldsmobile out of a used-car lot.

He took back roads through Chacahoula and Amelia, crossed the wide sweep of the Atchafalaya at Morgan City, and hot-wired an ancient Volkswagen bus at the casino on the Chettimanchi Indian Reservation.

He created a one-man grand-auto crime wave across southwestern Louisiana, driving off idling automobiles from a Jiffy Lube and a daiquiri take-out window, blowing out tires and engines, lighting up emergency dispatcher screens in six parishes.

He almost eluded the army of state police and sheriff's deputies that was crisscrossing Highway 90, virtually colliding into one another. He swung onto a side road in St Mary Parish, floored the souped-up stock-car racer he had stolen out of a mechanic's shed, scoured a balloon of dust out of a dirt road for two miles through sugarcane fields that shielded the car from view, then swung back onto 90, a half mile beyond a police barricade, and looked down the long corridor of oaks and pines that led into New Iberia.

He shifted down, turned across a stone bridge over the bayou, arching a crick out of his neck, knotting his T-shirt in his hand, wiping the sweat off his face with it.

He'd outrun them all. He filled his lungs with air. The smoke from meat fires drifted through the oaks on people's lawns; the evening sky glowed like a purple rose. Now, to dump this car and find a rooming house where he could watch a lot of television for a few days. Man, it was good to be alive.

That's when the First Assembly of God church bus hit him broadside, springing his doors, and propelled him through the air like a stone, right through a canebrake into Bayou Teche.

He sat on a steel bunk in the holding cell, barefoot, his khakis and T-shirt splattered with mud, a bandage wrapped around his head. He pulled a thin strand of bamboo leaf from his hair and watched it tumble in a shaft of light to the cement floor.

The sheriff and I looked at him through the bars.

'Why didn't you get out of New Orleans when you had the chance?' I asked.

'It's a free country,' he replied.

'Not when you kill people,' I said.

'I'll ask you a better question. Why didn't you stay where you were?' the sheriff said.

Johnny Remeta's eyes lifted into the sheriff's face, then they emptied of any perception or thought. He looked at the wall, stifling a yawn.

'Get him processed. I want those detectives from New Orleans to have him out of here by noon tomorrow,' the sheriff said, and walked down the corridor and banged the heavy door behind him.

'What's his problem?' Remeta said.

'Our space is full up with local wise guys. We don't need imports. Why'd you come to New Iberia?'

'A guy looks for friends where he can.'

'I'm not your friend. You were hanging around New Orleans to pop the guys who took a shot at you, weren't you?'

'You blame me?'

'You know who they are?'

'No. That's why I hung around.'

I looked at him a long time. He dropped his eyes to the floor.

'You told the cop at the museum you were an artist,' I said.

'I paint ceramics. I've done a mess of them.'

'Good luck, kid. I think you're going to need it,' I said, and started to go.

He rose from the bunk and stood at the bars. His face was no more than three inches from mine.

'I've got money put away for a lawyer. I can beat the beef on Zipper Clum,' he said.

'So?'

'I have a feeling my kite's going down before I ever see that lawyer.'

His breath was like the stale odor of dead flowers.

His grief was his own, I told myself as I went home later that evening.

But I couldn't rest. Zipper Clum's dying statement, taped on the boom box in the lawn-mower shop off Magazine, said Johnny Remeta was the trail back to my mother's death.

I ate a late supper with Bootsie on the picnic table in the backyard and told her about Johnny Remeta's fears. I expected her to take issue with my concerns, which I seemed to bring home as a matter of course from my job. After I stopped talking, she was pensive, one tooth biting into her bottom lip.

'I think Remeta's right. Zipper Clum was killed because of what he knew about your mother's death. Now Connie Deshotel has taken a special interest in you. She called again, by the way.'

'What about?'

'She said she wanted to tell you Clete Purcel's license problems have been straightened out. How nice of her to call us rather than him.'

'Forget her.'

'I'd like to. Dave, I didn't tell you everything about my relationship with Jim Gable. He's perverse. Oh, not with me. Just in things he said, in his manner, the way he'd stand in his undershorts in front of the mirror and comb his hair, the cruelty that was threaded through his remarks.'

The blood had risen in her face, and her eyes were shiny with embarrassment.

'You didn't know what he was like, Boots.'

'It doesn't help. I think about him and want to wash my body with peroxide.'

'I'm going to help Batist close up, then we'll go for some ice cream,' I said.

I walked down to the bait shop and called Dana Magelli, my NOPD friend, at his home and got the unlisted number for Jim Gable's condo in New Orleans.

'Why are you messing with Gable?' Magelli asked.

'Cleaning up some paperwork, interdepartmental cooperation, that sort of thing.'

'Gable leaves shit prints on everything he touches. Stay away from him. It's a matter of time till somebody scrambles his eggs.'

'It's not soon enough.'

I punched in Jim Gable's number. I could hear opera music playing in the background when he answered the phone.

'Y'all are picking up Johnny Remeta tomorrow,' I said.

'Who is this?' he asked.

'Dave Robicheaux. Remeta thinks somebody might want to blow up his shit.'

'Hey, we owe you a big thanks on this one. You made the ID through that home invasion in Loreauville, didn't you?'

'He'd better arrive in New Orleans without any scratches on the freight.'

'You're talking to the wrong man, my friend. Don Ritter's in charge of that case.'

'Let me raise another subject. I understand you've made some remarks about my wife.'

I could hear ice cubes rattle in a glass, as though he had just sipped from it and replaced it on a table.

'I don't know where you heard that, but it's not true. I have the greatest respect for your wife,' he said.

I stared out the bait shop window. The flood lamps were on and the bayou was yellow and netted with torn strands of hyacinths, the air luminescent with insects. My temples were pounding. I felt like a jealous high school boy who had just challenged a rival in a locker room, only to learn that his own words were his worst enemy.

'Maybe we can take up the subject another time. On a more physical level,' I said.

I thought I heard the voice of a young woman giggling in the background, then the tinkle of ice in the glass again.

'I've got to run. Get a good night's sleep. I don't think you mean what you say. Anyway, I don't hold grudges,' Gable said.

The woman laughed again just before he hung up.

But the two New Orleans detectives who were assigned to take Johnny Remeta back to their jurisdiction, Don Ritter and a man named Burgoyne, didn't show up in the morning. In fact, they didn't arrive at the department until almost 5 p.m.

I stayed late until the last of the paperwork was done. Ritter bent over my desk and signed his name on a custody form attached to a clipboard, then bounced the ballpoint pen on my desk blotter.

'Thanks for your help, Robicheaux. We won't forget it,' he said.

'You taking the four-lane through Morgan City?' I said.

'No, I-10 through Baton Rouge,' Burgoyne, the other detective, said.

'The southern route is straight through now. You can be in New Orleans in two hours and fifteen minutes,' I said.

'The department uses prescribed routes for all transportation of prisoners. This one happens to go through Baton Rouge,' Burgoyne said. He grinned and chewed his gum.

He was young, unshaved, muscular, his arms padded with hair. He wore a faded black T-shirt and running shoes and Levi's with his handcuffs pulled through the back of his belt. He wore his shield on a cord around his neck, and a snub-nosed .38 in a clip-on holster on his belt.

'We've had Remeta in a holding cell since this morning. He didn't eat yet,' I said.

'We'll feed him at the jail. I'll ask him to drop you a card and tell you about it,' Burgoyne said, his eyes merry, his gum snapping in his jaw.

Ten minutes later I watched Ritter and Burgoyne lead Johnny Remeta, in waist and leg chains, to the back of a white Plymouth and lock him to a D-ring anchored on the floor. When they pulled out of the parking lot, Remeta stared out the side window into my face.

I went back inside the building, the residue of a burned-out, bad day like a visceral presence on my skin.

Why had they waited until quitting time to pick up Remeta? Why were they adamant about returning to New Orleans through Baton Rouge, which was the long way back? I was bothered also by the detective named Burgoyne. His clothes and looks and manner reminded me of the description that

Micah, Cora Gable's chauffeur, had given of one of the cops who had beaten and terrorized him.

I signed out a cruiser, hit the flasher, and headed for the four-lane that led to Lafayette and Interstate 10 East.

It was almost sunset when I crossed Henderson Swamp on the causeway. There was no wind, and the miles of water on each side of the road were bloodred, absolutely still, the moss in the dead cypress gray and motionless against the trunks. I stayed in the passing lane, the blue, white, and red glow of the flasher rippling across the pavement and cement railings in the dying light.

Then I was on the bridge above the Atchafalaya River, rising above its wide breadth and swirling current and the deep green stands of gum trees along its banks. Only then did I realize the white Plymouth was behind me, off the highway, in the rest area on the west side of the river.

I'd blown it. I couldn't remember the distance to the next turnaround that would allow me to double back and recross the river. I pulled to the shoulder, put the cruiser in reverse, and backed over the bridge to the rest area exit while two tractor-trailers swerved around me into the passing lane.

The rest area was parklike, green and freshly mowed and watered, with picnic tables and clean rest rooms, and a fine view of the river from the levee.

But the Plymouth was not by the rest rooms. It was parked not far from the levee and a stand of trees, in a glade, its doors open, its parking lights on.

I entered the access road and clicked off the flasher and parked behind a truck and saw Ritter and Burgoyne walking from the Plymouth to the men's room. Burgoyne went inside while Ritter smoked a cigarette and watched the Plymouth. Then Burgoyne came back outside and both of them sat at a picnic table, smoking, a thermos of coffee set between them. They watched the Plymouth and the T-shirted, waist-chained form of Johnny Remeta in the backseat.

I thought they would finish their coffee, unlock Remeta from the D-ring, and walk him to the men's room. The sodium lamps came on overhead and still they made no move toward the Plymouth.

Instead, Ritter went to a candy machine. He peeled off the wrapper on a candy bar and dropped the wrapper on the ground and strolled out toward the parking lot and used a pay phone.

The wind started to blow off the river, then I heard a solitary *pop*, like a firecracker, in a clump of trees by the levee.

Johnny Remeta pitched forward in the seat, his shoulders curled down toward the floor, his chained wrists jerking at the D-ring. There were three more reports inside the trees; now I could see a muzzle flash or light reflecting off a telescopic lens, and I heard the rounds biting into metal, blowing glass out the back of the car.

I pulled my .45 and ran toward the picnic table where Burgoyne still sat, his cigarette burning on the edge of the wood, his hands motionless in front of him. Ritter was nowhere in sight. The few travelers in the rest area had either taken cover or flattened themselves on the lawn.

I screwed the .45 into Burgoyne's spine.

'You set him up, you shitbag,' I said, and hoisted him up by his T-shirt.
'What are you doing?'

'Walk in front of me. You're going to stop it. You touch your piece and I'll blow your liver out on the grass.'

I knotted my fist in the back of his belt, pushing him ahead of me, into the mauve-colored twilight and the smell of cut grass and the wind that was filled with newspaper and dust and raindrops that stung like hail. I tried to see over his shoulder into the clump of trees by the levee, but the limbs were churning, the leaves rising into the air, and the light had washed out of the sky into a thin band on the earth's rim.

'I'm not part of this, Robicheaux. You got it all wrong,' Burgoyne said.
'Shut up. Get your cuff key out. Throw it to Remeta.'

We were on the lee side of the Plymouth now and Burgoyne's face had gone white. He thumbed his key out of his watch pocket and threw it inside the backseat. He tried to turn his head so he could see my face.

'Let me go, man. I'll give you whatever you want,' he said.

The shooter in the trees let off two more rounds. One whanged off the door jamb and the second round seemed to go long. But I heard a hollow *throp*, just like someone casually plopping a watermelon with his fingers. Burgoyne's head slammed against mine and his knees collapsed under him. My hand was still hooked inside his belt, and his weight took me down with him.

I was kneeling in the grass now, behind the shelter of the car, the events of the last few seconds out of sequence in my head. Johnny Remeta was working furiously to unlock his hands and ankles from his chains. His eyes were riveted on me, a look of revulsion on his face.

'What's the matter with you?' I said.

'The guy's brains are in your hair, man.'

The shooter opened up again, firing indiscriminately, burning the whole magazine.

'Get out of here,' I said.

'What?'

'The keys are in the ignition. When I put down masking fire, you get out of here.'

I didn't wait for him to answer. I crawled to the front of the car, then extended one hand out beyond the fender and began firing the .45 into the clump of trees. The sparks flew into the darkness and the recoil snapped my wrist four inches up in the air with each shot. I fired eight rounds in a row, the brass casings flicking past my eyes, until the breech locked open. Then I released the empty magazine and shoved in a fresh one.

The Plymouth's engine roared to life and the back tires spun in reverse on the wet grass. Johnny Remeta whipped the car around in the opposite direction, shifted into low, and floored the accelerator across the glade toward the entrance to the highway.

A full minute must have passed; there was no sound except a boat engine starting up on the river and the whir of tires on the bridge. The people by the rest rooms rose to their feet and stood like figures in a trance under the smoky glow of the sodium lamps. I pulled off my shirt, my hands trembling, and wiped my hair and face with it. Then I vomited into the grass. The detective named Burgoyne lay on his side, his head on one arm, his jaws locked open, his eyes looking vacuously into space, as though a terrible revelation about his life had just been whispered in his ear.

15

The sheriff paced back and forth in his office, reading from the folded-back front page of the *Baton Rouge Morning Advocate*. While he paced and read, he kept touching one eyebrow with a fingernail and widening his eyes, as though denying himself the luxury of an emotion that would turn his face crimson.

The story was a long one, of the kind written by a journalist who has learned the advantages of professional credulity over skepticism:

> HENDERSON – In what authorities believe was an attempted gangland assassination gone awry, a New Orleans city police officer was killed and a murder suspect escaped custody by stealing an unmarked police vehicle and driving it through a hail of gunfire.
>
> Dead upon arrival at Our Lady of Lourdes Hospital in Lafayette was Detective Sergeant James F. Burgoyne. Burgoyne and an Iberia Parish Sheriff's Department detective, David Robicheaux, tried to save the life of the intended victim, John Remeta, a suspect in a New Orleans homicide, investigators on the scene said.
>
> The shooting took place in an I-10 rest area close by the Atchafalaya River. Remeta was being transported in chains from New Iberia to New Orleans.
>
> Both officers advanced across an open field into sniper fire while Remeta huddled on the backseat of the unmarked police vehicle. When the officers freed Remeta of his handcuffs, Remeta escaped in the confusion and a bullet meant for him struck Burgoyne in the head, according to the crime scene investigator.
>
> Authorities believe Remeta has ties to organized crime and that a contract was placed on his life. A second New Orleans police officer, Lieutenant Don Ritter, is credited with coming to the assistance of Robicheaux and Burgoyne, putting himself in the line of fire.
>
> A St Martin Parish deputy sheriff on the scene said the behavior of all three officers was the bravest he had seen in his twenty years of police experience.

And on and on.

The sheriff tossed the newspaper on his desk and continued pacing, twisting the stem of his pipe in and out of the bowl.

Then he picked up a fax of the scene investigator's report and reread it and let it drift from his hand on top of the newspaper.

'The dead cop, what's his name, Burgoyne? He still had his piece in his holster. How do you explain that?' the sheriff said.

'Ask the scene investigator.'

'I'm asking you.'

'I'm not sure you want to know.' I looked at a spot on the wall.

'Ritter impressed me as a self-serving asswipe. He had a sudden conversion and ran into incoming fire to help you out?'

'I never saw Ritter. Not until the state police were coming down the ramp.'

'You'd better tell me what happened out there.'

'I made Burgoyne walk in front of me and give Remeta his cuff key. If Remeta hadn't taken off in the unmarked vehicle, the shooter would have nailed us both.'

The sheriff ran one hand through his hair. 'I don't believe this,' he said.

'Ritter fabricated the story to cover himself. I didn't contradict him. If I had, I would have been in custody myself.'

'Did you hold a gun on Burgoyne?'

'Yes.'

'You got a cop killed, Dave.'

'They had that kid staked out like a goat under a tree stand.'

The sheriff was breathing hard through his nostrils. His face was dark, his candy-striped snap-button shirt tight across his chest.

'I can't quite describe how angry this makes me,' he said.

'You wanted the truth.'

'You're damn right I do. Stay right there.'

He went out the door and down the corridor, then came back five minutes later, his blood pressure glowing in his face, the lines around his eyes like white thread.

'I've got Don Ritter and an IAD man in New Orleans on the line,' he said, and hit the button on his conference phone.

'What are you doing, skipper?' I said.

He held up his hand for me to be quiet. 'Ritter?' he said, standing erect in the middle of the office.

'What can I do for you, Sheriff?' Ritter's voice said through the speaker.

'Listen and keep your mouth shut. You set up a prisoner from my jail to be murdered and you almost got one of my people killed. You set foot in my parish again and I'm going to find a way to bury your sorry ass on Angola Farm. In the meantime, you'd better pray I don't get my hands on you . . . Is that IAD man still there?'

There was a pause, then a second voice said through the speaker, 'Yes, sir, I'm right here.'

'If the media want to buy that pig flop you people put out about y'all cleaning up your act, that's their business. But you either get to the bottom of this or I'm going to put an open letter on the Internet and notify every law enforcement agency in the country of the kind of bullshit you pass off as police work. By the way, spell your full name for me,' the sheriff said.

After the sheriff hung up, his throat was blotched with color.

'Hypertension is going to put me in a box,' he said.

'I wish it had worked out different. I never got a clear shot.'

He drank a glass of water and took a deep breath, then his eyes settled on my face.

'Burgoyne's brains splattered on you?' he said.

'Yes.'

'It happened to me in Korea. The guy was a prisoner I was taking back to the rear. I used to get up in the middle of the night and take showers and wash my hair and swim in the ocean and all kinds of crazy stuff. What's the lesson? Better him than me.'

His hand rested on the end of my shoulder and he kept massaging it like a baseball coach working a stiff place out of his pitcher's arm.

That night a fisherman on Calcasieu Lake, over by the Texas border, saw a man park a white automobile by the water's edge and start to walk away. Then the man looked back at the car as though he had forgotten something, or as though he'd had an argument with someone and could not quite bear to leave the other party with the last word. The man gathered an armload of creek wood and dry weeds and yellowed newspaper and sifted it through the windows on the seats, his face averted from the dust. He brushed his hands and shirt clean and took an emergency flare from the glove box and popped it alight. Then he methodically fired the inside of the car and stepped back from his work just before flames curled out over the roof. He tossed the flare hissing into the lake and walked down the road.

The next morning, which was Friday, the car was identified as the one stolen from NOPD by Johnny Remeta.

But he had dumped it over on the Texas border, I told myself. Which meant he was probably fleeing Louisiana and did not want to add a federal beef for interstate transportation of stolen property to the charges already pending against him.

Good. I was sick of Johnny Remeta.

I tried to forget that he had a 160 I.Q. That he was just the kind of perp who would burn a stolen car on the state line to let people think he was gone.

The call came at noon.

'Why'd you do that out there in that glade? I mean, walk into all that shooting and cut me loose?' he said.

'It's none of your business why I do anything,' I replied.

'I never saw anybody do anything like that.'

'You're an escaped felon. I'm a police officer. Don't get the wrong idea, Johnny.'

'I called to say thank you. You don't want my thanks, it's on you. But we got a mutual interest, Mr Robicheaux.'

'No, we don't. Get that out of your head. You come around here again and you're going to be back in custody.'

'You want the guys who killed your mother. That's the word on the street. You think they're the same guys who're trying to pop me.'

While he was talking I was waving my hand at Helen Soileau out in the hall, pointing at the phone so she would start a trace on the call.

'I met Jimmy Figorelli when I first got to New Orleans. He said if I wanted some work, I should rent a post office box and leave the box number for somebody named M.G. at a café across from the open-air market on Decatur. I wrote the box number down on a piece of paper and put it in an envelope and wrote M.G. on the outside and gave it to a black lady behind the register at the café. When I was going out, she said, "Maggie only eats here on the weekend. I'll give it to her then, okay?" '

'I'm writing all this down. You've got to go slower,' I said.

'Good try.'

Change the subject, I thought.

'What was the front money?' I asked.

'I didn't say I got any front money. Sir, I didn't say anything that indicates I committed a crime.'

'Did you burn the car to make us think you'd blown the state?'

'I started thinking about those cops leaving me chained up while a sniper tried to cut all my motors. That's what they call it. They use a hollow point or a steel-claw bullet to core a plug out of your head. If the target is armed, his motors shut down and all his muscles die . . . Anyway, their car got burned. They can buy a new one . . . Say, forget about waving to that woman cop to trace this call. I'm on a cell phone.'

He broke the connection.

I dropped the receiver on the desk blotter and went to the window.

The parking lot was full of cars and noon-hour traffic was backed up on the streets from a passing freight train. Then the caboose of the train clicked down the track, the red-and-white-striped mechanical guard rose into the air, and the traffic flowed out of the side streets and the parking lot, the white sun reflecting blindingly off the windows like the swimming, mismatched eyes of the mythological Argus.

I went into Helen's office.

'He was outside?' she said.

'He had to be.'

'He knows the drill. He was guessing. Every one of these morons wants us to think he's a criminal genius.'

'He knew I waved to a "woman cop." '

'You put out an APB?'

'Yeah. No luck.'

She put a stick of gum in her mouth and chewed it while she read the notes on my legal pad. Her hair was bright yellow and waved and molded into place with chemical spray.

'The go-between on the hit is somebody with the initials M.G.?' she said.

'First name Maggie,' I said.

Our eyes locked on each other's.

'Maggie Glick? I thought Maggie Glick was doing fifteen in St Gabriel,' Helen said.

'Let's take a ride to New Orleans Monday morning.'

She stood a ballpoint pen upside down on its cap and studied it.

'I've got a lot of work in my basket, Dave. I think right now this guy is NOPD's headache.'

I nodded and went back out in the hall and closed her door softly behind me.

She followed me into my office.

'I know I said I'd help, but this stuff is starting to eat you up,' she said.

'What stuff?'

'About your mother. Sometimes you just have to let the bad guys drown in their own shit.'

'You're probably right,' I said.

Ten minutes before 5 p.m. she opened the door to my office and leaned inside.

'Did you see the B&E report on Passion Labiche's house?' she asked.

'No.'

'I didn't know about it, either, not till a few minutes ago. Somebody came through a screen and tore her house up but didn't take anything except a box of old photos.'

'Photos?'

'Remember I told you about Passion saying she'd seen Connie Deshotel's face in an old photo?'

'Yeah, but Passion and Connie Deshotel just don't connect for me,' I said.

'You still want to go to the Big Sleazy?'

'With you, always,' I said.

'Hey, bwana?'

'What?'

'Connie Deshotel's dirty.'

The next morning, Saturday, I drove out to Passion Labiche's house. She unlatched the front door and asked me to follow her into the kitchen, where she was canning tomatoes. She lifted a boiling cauldron off the stove with hot pads, pouring into the preserve jars on the drainboard while the steam rose into her face. She had placed a spoon into each of the jars to prevent the glass from cracking, but one of them suddenly popped and stewed tomatoes burst in a pattern like a broken artery on her arm and the front of her dress.

She dropped the cauldron into the sink, her face bright with pain.

'You okay?' I said.

'Sure,' she said, wiping at her arm and dress with a dishrag.

She continued to wash her arm and scrub at her dress, rubbing the stain deeper into the fabric, spreading a huge damp area under her breasts.

'I have to change. Fix yourself something, or do whatever you feel like,' she said, her face sweating, her eyes dilated.

She ran up the stairs. When she came back down she had washed her face and tied her hair up on her head and put on a yellow dress. She cleaned off the drainboard with the heavy-breathing, self-enforced detachment of someone who might have just stepped back from a car wreck.

'I went over the breaking-and-entering report on your house. The intruder took nothing but a box of photos?' I said.

'That's all I'm missing so far. I wouldn't have known they were gone, except some shoes fell down from the shelf,' she said.

'You told Connie Deshotel you'd seen her in an old photo. Is there any reason she wouldn't want you to have a photograph of her?'

'It was probably kids. Who cares? Why you spending time on this, anyway? None of this got anything to do with my sister.'

'Was there a picture of Connie in the box that was stolen?'

'I don't know and I don't care. You stop bothering me with this.' She rubbed butter on the place where she had scalded herself with stewed tomatoes.

'Why'd that stain on your dress disturb you, Passion?'

She looked out the window at her garden and barn and the pecan trees down by the bayou, the skin twitching at the corner of her mouth.

'You better go about your business, Dave. I don't make good company some days. Funny how a policeman gives the grief to the person he can get his hands on, huh?' she said.

Monday morning Helen and I took an unmarked car to New Orleans and parked behind the old U.S. Mint on the river and cut through the open-air market on Decatur. The pavilion was crowded with people, and farther up the street a Dixieland band was playing in a courtyard and a man was selling snowballs from an umbrella-shaded cart on the sidewalk. We crossed Decatur to the café where Johnny Remeta had dropped off the number of his post office box.

It was not a place for the conventional tourist, particularly not someone with a history of coronary or vascular trouble. It had screen doors, electric fans instead of air-conditioning, an interior that looked painted with fingernail polish, and cuisine that featured sausage, bacon, cob corn glistening with butter, deep-fried pork chops, greens cooked in ham fat, potatoes floating in grease, and mounds of scrambled eggs that lay in bubbling heaps on a grill that probably hadn't been scraped clean since World War II.

'Does Maggie Glick come in here?' I asked the black woman who sat behind the counter, fanning herself with a magazine.

'Who want to know, darlin'?' she said.

I opened my shield.

'She eat breakfast here on the weekend,' the woman said.

'Do you remember somebody leaving a note for her a while back, one with the initials M.G. on the envelope?' I said.

'Could be. Don't remember.'

'I think it's a good time to focus on your memory skills,' Helen said.

The black woman kept flapping the magazine in her face. Her hair was threaded with gray and it rose and fell in the current of warm air generated by the magazine. She did not look at us when she spoke again.

'You see, Maggie comes over here to eat breakfast on the weekend 'cause she don't like the place where she lives or the work she do. When she was a li'l girl, she belonged to the same church as me over in Algiers. I still remember the li'l girl. Every time Maggie comes in here, I still remember that same li'l girl, I surely do. That enough for you, ma'am?'

We drove across the river into Algiers and parked on a narrow street lined with ancient buildings that looked like impacted teeth. The foundations had settled and the upper stories leaned into the sidewalks, the rooftops tipping downward against the light like the brim of a man's fedora. The hotels were walk-ups with stained sacks of garbage propped by the entrances, the taverns joyless, dark places where fortified wine was sold by the glass and where a person, if he truly wanted to slip loose his moorings, could create for himself the most violent denouement imaginable with a casual flick of the eyes at the bikers rubbing talcum into their pool cues.

But the real business on this street was to provide a sanctuary that precluded comparisons, in the same way that prisons provide a safe place for recidivists for whom setting time in abeyance is not a punishment but an end. The mulatto and black girls inside Maggie Glick's bar rejected no one. No behavior was too shameful, no level of physical or hygienic impairment unacceptable at the door. The Christmas tinsel and wreaths and paper bells wrapped with gold and silver foil stayed up year round. Inside Maggie Glick's, every day was New Year's morning, sunless, refrigerated, the red neon clock indicating either the a.m. or the p.m., as you wished, the future as meaningless and unthreatening as the past.

Maggie's father had been a Lithuanian peddler who sold shoestrings from door to door and her mother a washerwoman in an Algiers brothel. The tops of Maggie's gold breasts were tattooed with roses and her hair was the same shiny black as the satin blouse she wore with her flesh-tight jeans and purple heels. She was lean and hard-edged, and like most longtime prostitutes, withdrawn, solipsistic, bored with others and with what she did, and curiously asexual in her manner and behavior, particularly around johns.

Maggie sat at the far corner of the bar, a cup of tea on a napkin in front of her. She glanced at me, then at Helen, her eyes neutral, then picked up her cup and blew on her tea.

'You don't have to show me your badge. I know who you are,' she said.

'I thought you were in St Gabriel,' I said.

'Those cops who got fired or went to jail themselves? One of them was the narc who planted crystal in my apartment. He's in Seagoville, I'm outside. Everybody feeling good about the system now.'

'The word is you set up the drop for the contract on Zipper Clum. When'd you start fronting points for button men?' I said.

'Johnny Remeta told you that?'

'How do you know about Johnny Remeta?' Helen asked.

' 'Cause I read y'all had him in y'all's jail. 'Cause everybody on the street knows he did Zipper Clum. 'Cause he used to come in here. The boy has some serious sexual problems. But who want to go into details about that kind of thing?'

'That's so good of you,' Helen said, stepping close-in to the elbow of the bar, her forearm pressed flat on the wood. 'Is there something wrong about the words we use you don't understand? We're talking about conspiracy to commit murder for hire. There's a woman on death row right now. Would you like to join her there?'

Maggie picked up her cup again and drank from it. She watched her bartender break open a roll of quarters and spill the coins into the drawer of the cash register, then watched a man redeem a marker by counting out a stack of one-dollar bills one at a time on the bar. A young black woman sitting next to a white man in a suit quietly picked up her purse and went out the front door. Maggie Glick looked at the clock on the wall.

'The lady at the café across from the French Market said you used to go to her church when you were a little girl,' I said.

Maggie Glick's eyes cut sideways at me, her lips parting slightly.

'You're not a killer, Maggie. But somebody used you to set up a hit. I think the person who used you may have been involved in the murder of my mother,' I said.

Her eyes stayed fixed on mine, clouding, her brow wrinkling for the first time.

'Your mother?' she said.

'Two cops killed her. Zipper Clum was going to dime them. You're a smart lady. Put the rest of it together,' I said.

Her eyes shifted off mine and looked straight ahead into the gloom, the red glow of the neon tubing on the wall clock reflecting on the tops of her breasts. She tried to keep her face empty of expression, but I saw her throat swallow slightly, as though a piece of dry popcorn were caught in it. Her chest rose briefly against her blouse, then the moment passed and her face turned to stone and the slashes of color died in her cheeks. She raised her cup again, balancing it between the fingers of both hands, so that it partially concealed her mouth and made her next statement an unintelligible whisper.

'What?' I said.

'Get out of here. Don't you be talking about the church I went to, either. What you know about how other people grew up? You used to come in here drunk, but you don't remember it. Now you think you got the right to wipe your feet on my life?' she said.

She wheeled the top of her barstool around and walked toward the fire exit in back, her long legs wobbling slightly on her heels.

Perhaps it was my imagination, but I thought I saw a flash of wetness in the side of her eye.

That night Bootsie and I went to a movie in New Iberia, then bought ice cream on the way home and ate it on the redwood table under the mimosa tree in back. Clouds tumbled across the moon and my neighbor's cane field was green and channeled with wind.

'You look tired,' she said.

'I can't see through this stuff,' I said.

'About your mother?'

'All the roads lead back to prostitution of some kind: Zipper Clum, Little Face Dautrieve, this woman Maggie Glick, the story the jigger told about my mother working a scam with Mack—'

'It's the world they live in, Dave – prostitution, drugs, stealing, it's all part of the same web.' She looked at my expression and squeezed the top of my hand. 'I don't mean your mother.'

'No, it's not coincidence. Jim Gable—' I hesitated when I used his name, then looked her evenly in the eyes and went ahead. 'Gable and this vice cop Ritter are mixed up with hookers. Passion and Letty Labiche's parents were procurers. Connie Deshotel wet her pants when she thought Passion recognized her. Somehow it's all tied in together. I just don't know how.'

'Your mother wasn't a prostitute. Don't ever let anyone tell you that.'

'You're my buddy, Boots.'

She picked up the dishes to take them inside, then stopped and set them down again and stood behind me. Her fingers touched my hair and neck, then she bent over me and slipped her hands down my chest and pressed her body against me, her stomach and thighs flattening into my back, her mouth on my ear.

Later, in bed, she lay against me. Her fingertips traced the shrapnel scars that were like a spray of raised arrowheads on my hip. She turned her head and looked at the limbs of the oaks and pecan trees moving against the sky and the shadows the moon made in the yard.

'We have a wonderful family,' she said.

'We do,' I replied.

That's when the phone rang. I went into the kitchen to answer it.

It was an intern at Iberia General. 'An ambulance brought in a man named Clete Purcel. A gun fell out of his clothes,' he said.

'He's a P.I. He has a license to carry it. What happened to him?'

'Maybe you'd better come down.'

Clete had many enemies. Outside of the Mob, which bore him a special grudge, the worst were his ex-colleagues inside the New Orleans Police Department.

He had gone down to Cocodrie for the weekend, on Terrebonne Bay, where he still kept a rented cabin and a small boat. On Saturday morning he went south into the Gulf until the coast was only a low, green line on the horizon, then he floated with the tide and fished in the swells for white trout, baking shirtless under the sun all day, consuming one can of beer after another, his whole body glistening like an oiled ham.

At sunset, when he headed for shore, the crushed ice in his cooler was layered with trout, his empty beer cans floated in the bilge, and the flying fish leaping out of the crests of waves and the raindrops that dented the swells were the perfect end to a fine day.

He winched his boat onto his trailer and put on his tropical shirt, but his skin was stiff with sunburn and dried salt, and he was sure the only remedy for his discomfort was a foot-long chili dog and a six-pack of Dixie to go.

The 911 Club was built out of cinder blocks and plywood on a sandy flat by the side of the road. It was owned by an ex-Jefferson Parish deputy sheriff who supposedly welcomed everyone at his bar, but most of his clientele, particularly on weekends, was made up of police officers, male and female, or those who wished to imitate them.

A gathering of sports trappers was taking place at the bar and in the parking lot when Clete came down the road. The trappers wore olive-green T-shirts, dog tags, camouflage pants they tucked inside combat boots, goatees that bristled on the chin. They automatically crushed their aluminum cans in their hands after draining them, lit their cigarettes with Bic lighters, sucking in on the flame with the satisfaction of dragons breathing smoke, touching their genitalia when they laughed.

But Clete didn't care about the trappers. He saw at least four men and two women, white and black, he knew from the Second and Third districts in New Orleans. They crossed the parking lot and went inside the double screen doors. They were carrying open cans of beer and laughing, the way people would at a private party.

Just go on up the road, Clete thought.

He did. For a hundred yards. But if he didn't buy beer and something to eat at the 911 Club, he would have to drive two miles farther up the road.

There was a difference between caution and driving two extra miles because you were afraid of the people you used to work with.

He made a U-turn and pulled his Cadillac and boat trailer onto the oyster shells of the 911 parking lot and went in the side door.

Don Ritter was at the bar, peeling a hard-boiled egg while he told a story to the men around him.

'The Kit Carsons were VC who'd gone over to our side,' he said. 'This one little sawed-off dude, we called him "Bottles" because of his glasses, he kept saying, "Boss, you leave me behind, VC gonna make it real hard."

'So I told him, "I'd like to help you, little buddy, but you haven't showed us a lot. Let's face it. Your ville's VC. Those are your relatives, right? A lot of people might question your loyalties."

'He goes, "Time running out, boss. Americans going home. Bottles gonna be in the shitter." I go, "Wish I could help. But you know how it is. You got to bring us something we can use." '

Both of Ritter's elbows were propped on the bar while he picked tiny pieces of eggshell off his egg, grinning at the backs of his fingers.

'So what'd he bring you?' another man said.

'Can you believe this? He and his brother-in-law stole a slick from the ARVN and loaded it with these fifty-gallon drums of gasoline. They taped frags to the tops of the drums and flew over their own ville and burned it to the ground. He comes to me and says, "Ville gone, boss. That good enough?" '

Ritter started laughing. He laughed so hard tears coursed down his cheeks and a violent cough hacked in his chest. He held a paper napkin to his mouth, then began laughing and coughing again.

The cops and trappers standing around Ritter waited.

'What happened to Bottles?' another man asked.

'You got me. I was on the Freedom Bird the next week . . . Oh, he probably did all right,' Ritter said, wiping his eyes, lifting his glass to his mouth.

Clete ordered a chili dog and a draft and went to the men's room. Ritter's eyes followed him, then the eyes of the other men turned and followed him, too.

When Clete came back out, the jukebox was playing and someone was racking pool balls. At first he wasn't sure about the references he was now hearing in the story Ritter was telling his friends.

'His wife was a muff-diver. That's not exaggeration. My wife knew her. She dumped him for another dyke and went off to a Buddhist monastery in Colorado. Can you dig it? The guy comes home and thinks he's finally nailed her in the sack with the milkman and she's getting it on with another broad?' Ritter said.

They're shitheads. Walk away from it, Clete thought.

But the bartender had just set Clete's foot-long chili dog, smothered with melted cheese and chopped onions, in front of him and was now drawing a schooner of beer for him. So Clete hunched over his plate and ate with a spoon, his porkpie hat tilted over his forehead, and tried to ignore Ritter and his friends, whose conversation had already moved on to another subject.

When he had finished eating and had drained the last of his beer, he started to get up from the stool and leave. But he paused, like a man who can't make up his mind to get on the bus, then sat back down, his skin crawling with dried salt under his shirt. What was it he had to set straight? The lie that still hung in the air about his ex-wife? That was part of it. But the real problem was that Ritter could ridicule and sneer with impunity because he knew Clete was chained by denial to his past and would always be an object of contempt in the eyes of other cops.

'My ex left me because I was a drunk and I took juice and I popped a bucket of shit in Witness Protection,' Clete said. 'She wasn't a dyke, either. She just had the poor judgment to hang with your wife. The one who gave head to a couple of rookies at that party behind Mambo Joe's.'

They caught him in the parking lot, as he was opening his car door, Ritter and one of the trappers and an unshaved man who wore canvas pants and rubber boots and firehouse suspenders on his bare torso.

The man in suspenders hit Clete in the back of the head with brass knuckles, then hooked him above the eye. As Clete bounced off the side of the Cadillac and crashed onto the shells, he saw the man in suspenders step away and Ritter take a long cylindrical object from him and pull a leather loop around his wrist.

'You think you're still a cop because you throw pimps off a roof? In Camden guys who look like you drive Frito trucks. Here's payback for that crack about my wife. How you like it, skell?' Ritter said.

16

'He used a baton on you?' I said.

'Mostly on the shins,' Clete said. He lay propped up in the hospital bed. There was a neat row of black stitches above his right eye and another one inside a shaved place in the back of his head.

'How'd you get out of it?'

'Some other cops stopped it.' He took a sip from a glass of ice water. His green eyes roved around the room and avoided mine and showed no emotion. He pulled one knee up under the sheet and his face flinched.

'This happened on Saturday. Where have you been since then?' I said.

'Laid up. A lot of Valium, too much booze. I ran off the road tonight. The state trooper let me slide.'

'You weren't laid up. You were hunting those guys, weren't you?'

'The one in canvas pants and suspenders, the dude who gave Ritter the baton? He was buds with that plainclothes, Burgoyne. I bet they were the two guys who beat the shit out of Cora Gable's chauffeur. By the way, I called the chauffeur and shared my thoughts.'

'Don't do this, Clete.'

'It's only rock 'n' roll.'

'They're going to put you in a box one day.'

'Ritter called me a skell.'

Tuesday morning the sheriff came into my office.

'I need you to help me with some P.R.,' he said.

'On what?'

'It's a favor to the mayor. We can't have an ongoing war with the city of New Orleans. She and I are having lunch with some people to try and establish a little goodwill. You want to meet us at Lerosier?'

'Bootsie's meeting me in the park.'

'Bring her along.'

'Who are these people we're having lunch with?'

'P.R. types, who else? Come on, Dave, give me a hand here.'

Bootsie picked me up at noon and we drove down East Main and parked up from the Shadows and crossed the street and walked under the canopy of oaks toward the restaurant, which had been created out of a rambling nineteenth-century home with a wide gallery and ventilated green shutters.

I saw the sheriff's cruiser parked in front of the restaurant, and, farther down, a white limousine with charcoal-tinted windows. I put my hand on Bootsie's arm.

'That's Cora Gable's limo,' I said.

She slowed her walk for just a moment, glancing at the flowers in the beds along the edge of the cement.

'I just wish I could get my hydrangeas to bloom like that,' she said.

We walked up the steps and into a foyer that served as a waiting area. I could see our newly elected woman mayor and the sheriff and three men in business suits and Cora Gable at a table in a banquet room. At the head of the table, his face obscured by the angle of the door, sat a man in a blue blazer, with French cuffs and a heavy gold watch on his wrist.

'I have to go into the ladies' room a minute,' Bootsie said.

A moment later I looked through the glass in the front door and saw Micah, the chauffeur, come up the walk and sit in a wicker chair at the far end of the gallery and light a cigarette.

I went back outside and stood by the arm of his chair. He smoked with his face averted and showed no recognition of my presence. Even though his forehead was freckled with perspiration, he did not remove his black coat or loosen his tie or unbutton his starched collar.

'Miss Cora said you won't press charges against the two NOPD cops who worked you over,' I said.

'I'm not sure *who* they were. Waste of time, anyway,' he replied, and tipped his ashes into his cupped palm.

'Why?'

He moved his neck slightly, so that the skin brushed like sandpaper against the stiff edges of his collar.

'I got a sheet,' he said.

'People with records sue the system all the time. It's a way of life around here.'

'New Orleans cops have murdered their own snitches. They've committed robberies and murdered the witnesses to the robberies. Go work your joint somewhere else,' he said, and leaned over the railing and raked the ashes off his palm.

'You afraid of Gable?' I asked.

He brushed at the ashes that had blown back on his black clothes. Sweat leaked out of his hair; the right side of his face glistened like a broken strawberry cake.

I went back inside just as Bootsie was emerging from the ladies' room. We walked through the tables in the main dining area to the banquet room in back where Jim Gable stood at the head of the table, pouring white wine into his wife's glass.

'Jim says y'all know each other,' the sheriff said to me.

'We sure do,' I said.

'Bootsie's an old acquaintance, too. From when she lived in New Orleans,' Gable said, the corners of his eyes threading with lines.

'You look overheated, Dave. Take off your coat. We're not formal here,' the mayor said. She was an attractive and gentle and intelligent woman, and her manners were sincere and not political. But the way she smiled pleasantly at Jim Gable while he poured wine into her glass made me wonder in awe at the willingness of good people to suspend all their self-protective instincts and accept the worst members of the human race into their midst.

There was something obscene about his manner that I couldn't translate into words. His mouth constricted to a slight pucker when he lifted the neck of the wine bottle from the mayor's glass. He removed a rose that was floating in a silver center bowl and shook the water from it and placed it by her plate, his feigned boyishness an insult to a mature woman's intelligence. During the luncheon conversation his tongue often lolled on his teeth, as though he were about to speak; then his eyes would smile with an unspoken, mischievous thought and he would remain silent while his listener tried to guess at what had been left unsaid.

With regularity his eyes came back to Bootsie, examining her profile, her clothes, a morsel of food she was about to place on her lips.

When he realized I was looking at him, his face became suffused with an avuncular warmth, like an old friend of the family sharing a mutual affection.

'Y'all are fine people, Dave,' he said.

Just before coffee was served, he tinked his glass with a spoon.

'Ms Mayor and Sheriff, let me state the business side of our visit real quickly,' he said. 'Our people are looking into that mess on the Atchafalaya. Obviously some procedures weren't followed. That's our fault and not y'all's. We just want y'all to know we're doing everything possible to get to the bottom of what happened . . . Dave, you want to say something?'

'No,' I said.

'Sure?' he said.

'I don't have anything to say, Gable.'

'Friends don't call each other by their last names,' he said.

'I apologize,' I said.

He smiled and turned his attention away from the rest of the table. 'You lift, don't you? I've always wanted to get into that,' he said to me.

'I haven't had much time. I'm still tied up with that Little Face Dautrieve investigation. Remember Little Face? A black hooker who worked for Zipper Clum?' I said.

'No bells are going off,' he said.

'We hope to have all of you to a lawn party as soon as the weather cools,' Cora Gable said. 'It's been frightfully hot this summer, hasn't it?'

But Gable wasn't listening to his wife. His arm rested on top of the tablecloth and his eyes were fixed indolently on mine. His nails were clipped and pink on his small fingers.

'I understand Clete Purcel had trouble with some off-duty cops. Is that what's bothering you, Dave?' he said.

I looked at my watch and didn't answer. Gable lit a thin black cigar with a gold lighter and put the lighter in his shirt pocket.

'What a character,' he said, without identifying his reference. 'You and Purcel must have made quite a pair.'

'Please don't smoke at the table,' Bootsie said.

Gable looked straight ahead in the silence, a smile frozen on his mouth. He rotated the burning tip of his cigar in the ashtray until it was out, and picked up his wineglass and drank from it, his hand not quite hiding the flush of color in his neck.

From behind the caked makeup on her face, Cora Gable watched her husband's discomfort the way a hawk on a telephone wire might watch a rabbit snared in a fence.

After lunch, as our group moved through the dining room and out onto the gallery and front walk, the sheriff hung back and gripped my arm.

'What the hell was going on in there?' he whispered.

'I guess I never told you about my relationship with Jim Gable,' I said.

'You treated him like something cleaned out of a drainpipe,' he said.

'Go on?' I said.

But Jim Gable was not the kind of man who simply went away after being publicly corrected and humiliated. While Micah was helping Cora Gable into the back of the limo, Gable stopped me and Bootsie as we were about to walk back to our car.

'It was really good to see y'all,' he said.

'You'll see more of me, Jim. I guarantee it,' I said, and once again started toward our car.

'You look wonderful, Boots,' he said, and took her hand in his. When he released it, he let his fingers touch her wrist and trail like water down the inside of her palm. To make sure there was no mistaking the insult, he rubbed his thumb across her knuckles.

Suddenly I was standing inches from his face. The sheriff was out in the street and had just opened the driver's door of his cruiser and was now staring across the roof at us.

'Is there something wrong, Dave?' Gable asked.

'Would you like to have a chat over in the alley?' I said.

'You're a lot of fun,' he said, and touched my arm good-naturedly. 'Twenty-five years on the job and you spend your time chasing down pimps and whores and talking about it in front of your new mayor.' He shook the humor out of his face and lit another cigar and clicked his lighter shut. 'It's all right to smoke out here, isn't it?'

I went back to the office and spent most of the afternoon doing paperwork. But I kept thinking about Jim Gable. In A.A. we talk about putting principles before personalities. I kept repeating the admonition over and over to myself. Each time I did I saw Gable's fingers sliding across my wife's palm.

When the phone rang I hoped it was he.

'I thought I'd check in,' the voice of Johnny Remeta said.

'You have a thinking disorder. You don't check in with me. You have no connection with my life.'

'You know a New Orleans cop named Axel?'

'No.'

'When I was chained up in that car, that cop Burgoyne, the one who got smoked? He kept telling that other cop not to worry, that Axel was gonna be on time. He said, "No fuss, no muss. Axel's an artist." '

'What's that supposed to mean?'

'I found out Burgoyne partnered with a guy named Axel. He's a sharpshooter, the guy they use for, what do they call it, a barricaded suspect. He's got two or three kills.'

'Maggie Glick says you used to come to her bar.'

'I never heard of her. I don't even drink. Does everybody down here lie?'

'Don't call here again unless you want to surrender yourself. Do you understand that? Repeat my words back to me.'

'You saved my life. I owe you. It's a matter of honor, Mr Robicheaux. You got a cell phone in case I can't reach you at home?'

After I'd hung up on him I punched in Clete's apartment number.

'You know anybody named Axel?' I asked.

'Yeah, Axel Jennings. He's Don Ritter's buddy, the one who hit me in the back of the head with a set of brass knuckles.'

'Johnny Remeta just called me again. Maybe Jennings is the shooter who did Burgoyne by mistake.'

'I've got some plans about this guy Jennings. Worry about Remeta. He's got you mixed up with his father or something.'

'What do you mean you've got plans for Jennings?' I asked.

'How about I take y'all to dinner tonight? Dave, Remeta's a head case. Ritter and Axel Jennings are wind-ups. Don't lose the distinction.'

17

A storm had moved into the Gulf and the morning broke gray and cool and shrouded with mist, then it began to rain. I glanced out my office window and saw Passion Labiche get out of a car and step over the flooded curb and run up the front walk of the courthouse. Her hair and skin were shiny with water when she knocked on my office glass. Under her right arm she carried a scrapbook or photo album wrapped in a cellophane bag.

'You want to dry off?' I asked.

'I'm sorry for the way I talked to you at my house. I have days I don't feel too good,' she said.

'It's all right. How about some coffee?'

She shook her head. 'I found that picture of Ms Deshotel. The one I told her about when she came to my club. It was in the attic. My parents kept all the pictures of the places they lived and visited.'

She sat down in front of my desk and took a handkerchief from her purse and touched at her face.

'Why'd you decide to bring it in?' I asked.

' 'Cause you axed about it. 'Cause you been good to us.'

Passion turned the stiff pages of the album to a large black-and-white photo taken in a nightclub. The bar mirror was hung with Santa sleighs and reindeer and Styrofoam snowballs, and a group of five people, including Passion's parents, sat on stools looking back at the camera, their drinks balanced on their knees, their faces glowing with the occasion.

Someone had inked 'Christmas, 1967' in the corner of the photo, but there was no mistaking Connie Deshotel. She was one of those women whose facial features change little with time and are defined by their natural loveliness rather than by age or youth. She wore a black, sequined evening dress with straps and a corsage, and her champagne glass was empty and tilted at an angle in her hand. She was smiling, but, unlike the others, at someone outside the picture.

'Why should this picture be important to anybody?' Passion asked.

'Your folks were in the life. Connie Deshotel is attorney general.'

'They owned three or four dance halls. All kinds of people came in there. The governor, Earl K. Long, used to go in there.'

'Can I keep the photo?'

She popped the glued edges loose from the backing and handed it to me.

Her consciousness of its content, or any importance it might have, seemed to be already lost by the time I had taken it from her hand.

'My sister's got only one lawyer working on her case now. He's twenty-five years old,' she said.

'I think you helped Letty kill Vachel Carmouche. I don't think you're going to get anywhere until that fact is flopping around on the table,' I said.

She stared back at me with the transfixed expression of an animal caught in a truck's headlights.

She literally ran from the building.

I hated my own words.

I grew up in the South Louisiana of the 1940s and '50s. I remember the slot and racehorse machines, their chromium and electric glitter among the potted palms in the old Frederic Hotel on Main Street, and the cribs on each side of the train tracks that ran the length of Railroad Avenue. I collected for the newspaper on Saturday afternoons, and the prostitutes would be sitting on their galleries, smoking the new filter-tipped cigarettes and sometimes dipping draft beer out of a bucket a pimp would bring them from Broussard's Bar. They were unattractive and physically dissolute women, and they wore no makeup and their hair was uncombed and looked dirty. Sometimes they laughed like deranged people, a high, cackling sound that climbed emptily, without meaning, into the brassy sky.

None of them had Cajun accents, and I wondered where they came from. I wondered if they had ever gone to church, or if they had parents anywhere, or perhaps children. I saw a pimp strike one of them on the gallery once, the first time I had ever seen a man hit a woman. Her nose bled on her hand. Her pimp had oiled black hair and wore purple slacks that fitted him as tightly as a matador's pants.

'You got your money, kid?' he said to me.

'Yes, sir.'

'Better get on it, then,' he said.

I rode away on my bike. When I passed the crib again, she was sitting on a swing next to him, weeping into a red-spotted dish towel, while he consoled her with one arm around her shoulders.

I also remembered the gambling clubs in St Martin and St Landry parishes during the 1950s. Bartenders, bouncers, and blackjack dealers wore the badges of sheriff's deputies. No kid was ever turned away from the bar or a table. The women were brought in by the Giacanos in New Orleans and a Syrian family in Lafayette and worked out of air-conditioned trailers behind the clubs. The head of the state police who tried to enforce the law and shut down gambling and prostitution in Louisiana became the most hated man in the state.

Most of those same clubs stayed in business into the 1960s. Passion was right. People of every stripe visited them. Would Connie Deshotel need to hire someone to steal an old photograph showing her in the company of people whom she may have known in only a casual way?

I decided to find out.

'I'm sorry to bother you with a minor situation here,' I said when I got her on the phone.

'I'm happy you called, Dave,' she replied.

'There was a B&E at Passion Labiche's house. Somebody stole a box of photographs out of her closet.'

'Yes?'

'Passion says she'd told you about seeing you in an old photo she had. Is there any reason anybody would want to steal something like that? A political enemy, perhaps?'

'You got me.'

'I see. Anyway, I thought I'd ask. How you doin'?'

'Fine. Busy. All that sort of thing,' she said.

'By the way, the thief didn't get the photo. I have it here. It shows you with Passion's parents sometime around Christmas of 1967.'

'Could be. I don't know much about her family. Maybe I met them at one time. Dave, when my political enemies want to do me damage with pictures, they put them on dartboards. Say hello to Bootsie.'

The next afternoon Dana Magelli at NOPD returned a call I had placed earlier in the day.

'Can you pull the jacket of a cop named Axel Jennings?' I said.

'Why?'

'He and Don Ritter and another guy worked over Clete Purcel down by Cocodrie. I also think this Jennings character is a good guy to look at for the Burgoyne shooting.'

'Jennings shot his own partner on the Atchafalaya? You come up with some novel ideas, Dave.'

'Can you get his jacket?'

'I have it sitting in front of me. I was just going to call you about Purcel. Where is he?'

I had put my foot in it.

Axel Jennings lived uptown in the small yellow bungalow on Baronne in which he had grown up. It had a neat green yard, a stone porch, and an alleyway with palm trees that grew between the garages. The neighborhood was like neighborhoods had been during World War II, places where people cut the grass on Saturday evening and listened to the ball game on radios that sat in open windows. At least that's what his father had said.

Axel's father had flown with General Curtis LeMay on incendiary raids against Japanese targets between the dropping of atom bombs on Hiroshima and Nagasaki. LeMay's raids didn't do any good. It took a second atom bomb to vaporize another city to bring the war to an end. Most civilians, particularly these peace types, didn't know squat about what went on over there. That's what Axel's father had said.

Axel had three loves: firearms, model railroading, and the memory of his father, whose picture in uniform he kept on the mantel.

He was a member at a gun range in St Charles Parish, and almost every weekend he packed up his boxes of hand-loaded ammunition and his three favorite weapons – his .45 auto, a scoped '03 Springfield, and the civilian equivalent of the M-14 rifle – and fired them from under a wood shed at paper targets clipped to wires in front of a dirt embankment.

His father used to say marksmanship was simply the coordination of angles with the beat of your heart and the rise and fall of your lungs. The bullet's behavior was mathematically predictable and was governed by no rules other than physical principles. You simply had to make the weapon an extension of blood and sinew and thought so that the squeeze of your finger created a geometric certainty for your target.

It was all about control and order.

The same way with life, his father had said. People didn't respect authority anymore. You had to find a leader, a man you could respect, and put your faith in him, just as he placed his faith in you. His father called it a reciprocity of personal honor.

Axel's sunporch and guest room were covered with electric trains. The tracks ran across floors and tables and sections of plywood screwed down on sawhorses. The tracks wound through papier-mâché mountains and tiny forests, past water towers and freight depots and miniature communities; there were toy brakemen and gandy walkers along the tracks and switches that diverted locomotives past each other at the last possible moment, and warning bells and flashing lights at the crossings.

When Axel cranked up all his trains at once, the smells of warm metal and oil and overheated electrical circuits reminded him of the clean acrid smell of gunpowder at the range.

Two kills with a department-issue M-16, a third kill shared with Burgoyne.

He thought he might feel bad about the first barricaded suspect he popped.

He didn't. The guy had every opportunity to come out of the building. Instead, he turned on the gas jets and was going to take his child out with him. Just as the guy was about to light the match, Axel, in a prone position on a rooftop, sucked in his breath, exhaled slowly, and drilled a round through a glass pane and nailed him through both temples.

You believed in what you did. You trusted the man you took orders from. And you didn't look back. That's what his father had said.

It must have been grand to be around during World War II. Working people made good money and for fun went bowling and played shuffleboard in a tavern and didn't snort lines off toilet tanks; you walked a girl home from a café without gangbangers yelling at her from a car; blacks lived in their own part of town. Kids collected old newspapers and coat hangers and automobile tires and hauled them on their wagons down to the firehouse for the war effort. The enemy was overseas. Not in the streets of your own city.

Axel's occasional girlfriend, a barmaid named Cherry Butera, said he'd been depressed since Jimmy Burgoyne was killed in that shooting on the Atchafalaya. He'd taken a couple of vacation days, and he and the girlfriend had driven down to Grand Isle. A storm was tearing up the Gulf and the sky had turned green and the surf was wild and yellow with churning sand.

'There's a Nazi sub out there. The Coast Guard sunk it with planes in '42,' he said. 'I wish I'd been alive back then.'

'What for?' she asked.

'I would have been there. I would have been part of all that,' he replied.

They drove back to New Orleans in the rain and drank beer in a small pizza joint two blocks from his house. Banana trees thrashed against the side of the building, and the shadows from the neon signs in the windows cascaded like water down Axel's face.

'Somebody's following me,' he said.

'You're blaming yourself because you weren't there when Jimmy was killed,' his girlfriend said.

He looked at her a moment, then his eyes disconnected from hers and looked at nothing. He peeled the gold and green label off his beer bottle and rolled it into tiny balls.

'I saw somebody outside my window. He was behind us on the road tonight,' he said.

'The road was empty, hon. The bad guys are afraid of you. Everybody knows that.'

'I wish Jimmy was here. I wish he wasn't dead,' he said.

At 11 p.m. they went out the back of the café and walked down the alley toward his car. Rain blew in a vortex from a streetlight out by the sidewalk, and the palm trees between the garages filled with wind and raked against the wood walls.

The man waiting in the shadows wore a wide hat and a black raincoat with the collar up. The piece of lumber he held in his hands was thick and square and probably three feet long. Leaves clung wetly to his shoulders and hat, so that he looked like an extension of the hedge when he stepped into the alley. He swung the piece of lumber with both hands, as he would a baseball bat, into Axel's face.

Axel crashed backwards into a row of garbage cans, his forehead veined with blood and water. Then the man in the wide hat leaned over and drove the piece of lumber into Axel's throat and the side of his head.

The man stood erect, water sluicing off his hat brim, his face a dark oval against the streetlight at the end of the alley.

'Haul freight, unless you want the same,' he said to the woman.

She turned and ran, twisting her face back toward the hatted man, her flats splashing through puddles that were iridescent with engine oil. The hatted man tossed the piece of lumber in the hedge, then picked up a whiskey bottle and broke it against the side of a garage.

He stooped over Axel's body, the streetlight glinting on the jagged shell of the bottle, his extended arm probing downward into the darkness, soundlessly, like a man doing a deed he had conceived in private and now performed without heat or surprise.

'It'd take a real sonofabitch to do something like that, Dave,' Magelli said.

'It wasn't Clete.'

'How do you know?'

'Check out Jim Gable's chauffeur. He's an ex-carnival man named Micah. His face is disfigured.'

'Why don't you let Purcel cover his own ass for a change?'

'Jennings is a rogue cop. He brought this down on himself. Lay off of Clete,' I said.

'Tell it to Jennings. The doctor had the mirrors taken out of his hospital room.'

18

A week passed, and I didn't hear anything more from Dana Magelli. The night Jennings had been attacked Clete was picking up a bail skip for Wee Willie Bimstine and Nig Rosewater in Baton Rouge, which didn't mean he couldn't have attacked Jennings after he dumped the skip in Willie and Nig's office. But Clete Purcel had boundaries, even though they were a little arbitrary, and they didn't include mutilating a half-conscious man who was already on the ground.

I wanted to empty my head and caseload and go to Key West with Bootsie and Alafair and fish for three weeks. I was tired of other people's problems, of breaking up domestic arguments, of hosing vomit out of a cruiser, of washing spittle off my face, of cutting slack to junkies because they had the virus, only later to have one try to bite me when I cuffed him.

I was tired of seeing the despair in the faces of black parents when I told them their children had overdosed on meth or heroin or had been gunned down in a robbery. Or vainly trying to reassure a store owner of his self-worth after he had been forced at gunpoint to kneel and beg for his life. Nor did I ever again want to look into the faces of women who had been raped, sodomized, burned with cigarettes, and beaten with fists, every ounce of dignity and self-respect they once possessed systematically ripped out of their bodies.

If you meet longtime street cops who don't drink or use, they're usually either in twelve-step programs or brain-dead or they have criminal propensities themselves.

But each time I cleared my head and tried to concentrate on all the potential that every day could bring – the sun showers that blew in from the Gulf, Bootsie's meeting me for lunch at Victor's or in the park, the long summer evenings and the way the light climbed high into the sky at sunset, picking up Alafair at night at the City Library and going for ice cream with her high school creative writing group – my mind returned again and again to thoughts about my mother's fate, the pleas for help she must have uttered, and the fact her killers were still out there.

But it was more than my mother's death that obsessed me. Long ago I had accepted the loss of my natal family and my childhood and the innocence of the Cajun world I had been born into. You treat loss just like death. It visits everyone and you don't let it prevail in your life.

What I felt now was not loss but theft and violation. My mother's memory, the sad respect I had always felt for her, had been stolen from me. Now the tape-recorded lie left behind by a dead jigger in the Morgan City jail, that my mother was a whore and a thief, had become part of a file at the New Orleans Police Department and I had no way to change it.

'Something on your mind?' Helen Soileau said in my office.

'No, not really,' I replied.

She stood at the window and rubbed the back of her neck and looked out at the street.

'Connie Deshotel just kind of disappeared? Being photographed with a couple of procurers didn't rattle her?' she said.

'Not that I could tell,' I said, tilting back in my chair.

'She was in her office. All her power was right there at her fingertips. Don't let her fool you, Dave. That broad's got you in her bombsights.'

But it was Friday afternoon and I didn't want to think any more about Connie Deshotel. I signed out of the office, bought a loaf of French bread at the market, and drove down the dirt road toward my house, the sun flashing like pieces of hammered brass in the oak limbs overhead.

Alafair and Bootsie and I ate dinner at the kitchen table. Outside the window, the evening sky was piled high with rain clouds, and columns of sunlight shone through the clouds on my neighbor's sugarcane. Alafair ate with her book bag by her foot. In it she kept her short stories and notebooks and felt pens and a handbook on script writing. By her elbow was a thick trade paperback with a black-and-white photo of a log cabin on the cover.

'What are you reading?' I asked.

'*Night Comes to the Cumberland.* It's by a lawyer named Harry Caudill. It's a history of the southern mountains,' she said.

'For your creative writing group?' I asked.

'No, a boy at the library said I should read it. It's the best book ever written about the people of Appalachia,' she replied.

'You're going to read your new story tonight?' I said.

'Yeah,' she said, smiling. 'By the way, I might get a ride home tonight.'

'With whom?' Bootsie said.

'This boy.'

'Which boy?' I asked.

'The one who told me about *Night Comes to the Cumberland.*'

'That nails it down,' I said.

'Dave, I *am* sixteen now . . . Why are you making that face?'

'No reason. Sorry,' I said.

'I mean, lighten up,' she said.

'You bet,' I said, looking straight ahead.

A few minutes later Alafair got into the car with Bootsie to ride into town. Under the trees the sunlight was red on the ground, and I could smell humus and the wet, dense warm odor of the swamp and schooled-up fish on the wind.

'No riding home with boys we don't know, Alafair. We got a deal?' I said.

'No,' she said.

'Alf?' I said.

'You have to stop talking to me like I'm a child. Until you do, I'm just not going to say anything.'

Behind Alafair's angle of vision Bootsie shook her head at me, then she said, 'I'll be back in a little while, Dave,' and I watched them drive down the road toward New Iberia.

I don't know how good a father I was, but I had learned that when your daughter is between the ages of thirteen and seventeen, you will never win an argument with her, and if you fall back on anger and recrimination and coercion to prevail over her, you will come to loathe your triumph and the weakness it disguises and you will not easily find forgiveness for it in either her or yourself.

I read the newspaper on the gallery, then the dusk gathered inside the trees and the leaves on the ground darkened and became indistinct and a car passed on the road with its headlights on. I saw Batist walk out of the bait shop and scoop the hot ashes out of the barbecue into a bucket and fling them in a spray of burning embers onto the bayou's surface.

I went inside and lay down on the couch with the newspaper over my face and fell asleep. In my dream I saw the sculpted, leafless branches of a tree on an alkali plain, and in the distance purple hills and piñon and cedar trees and cactus and rain bleeding like smoke out of the clouds. Then a flock of colored birds descended on the hardened and gnarled surfaces of the barren tree, and green tendrils began to grow from the tree's skin and wind about its branches, and young leaves and flowers unfolded with the sudden crispness of tissue paper from the ends of the twigs, so that the tree looked like a man raising a floral tribute toward the sky.

But a carrion bird descended into the tree, its talons and beak flecked with its work, its feathers shining, its eyes like perfectly round drops of black ink that had dried on brass. It extended its wings and cawed loudly, white insects crawling across its feathers, its breath filling the air with a scrofulous presence that enveloped the tree and the tropical birds in it like a moist net.

I sat up on the couch and the newspaper across my face cascaded to the floor. I closed and opened my eyes and tried to shake the dream out of my mind, although I had no idea what it meant. I heard Bootsie's car outside and a moment later she opened the front screen and came inside.

'I fell asleep,' I said, the room still not in focus.

'You okay?' she said.

'Yeah, sure.' I went into the bathroom and washed my face and combed my hair. When I came back out Bootsie was in the kitchen.

'I had a terrible dream,' I said.

'About what?'

'I don't know. Is Alf all right?'

'She's at the library. She promised me she'd call or get a ride from somebody we know.'

I took two glasses out of the cabinet over the drainboard and filled them from a pitcher of tea in the icebox.

'Why wouldn't she tell me who this boy is?' I asked.

'The one who recommended the book about the Appalachians?'

'Yes.'

'Because she's sixteen. Dave, don't see a plot in everything. The kid she's talking about is studying to be an artist.'

'Say again?'

'Alafair said he's a painter. He paints ceramics. Does that sound like Jack the Ripper to you?'

I stared stupidly at Bootsie, and in my mind's eye I saw the humped black shape of the carrion bird in the midst of the flowering tree.

I dialed 911 and got the city dispatcher, then I was out the back door and in the truck, roaring backwards in the driveway, the rear end fishtailing in a plume of dust out on the road. The dust drifted out onto the glare of the electric lights over the dock, glowing as brightly as powdered alkali under the moon.

I came down East Main, under the oaks that arched over the street, and pulled into the City Library. The outside flood lamps were on and the oak trees on the lawn were filled with white light and shadows that moved with the wind, and next to the parking lot I could see a wall of green bamboo and the stone grotto that contained a statue of Jesus' mother.

A city police cruiser was parked under a tree by the grotto, and an overweight, redheaded cop, his cap at an angle on his brow, leaned against the fender, smoking a cigarette. He was a retired marine NCO nicknamed Top, although he had been a cook in the corps and never a first sergeant.

'I've already been inside, Dave. Your daughter's with a bunch of kids upstairs. I don't see anything unusual going on here,' he said.

'You didn't see a tall kid, wide shoulders, dark hair, real white skin, maybe wearing glasses with black frames?'

'How old?'

'It's hard to tell his age. He doesn't always look the same.'

He took the cigarette out of his mouth, and, without extinguishing it, tossed it in a flower bed.

'That's what I need. To be hunting down Plastic Man,' he said.

We entered the building and walked through a large reading area, then went up the stairs. I saw Alafair sitting with five or six other high school kids around a table in a side room. I stood just outside the door until she noticed me. Her concentration kept going from me to the creative writing teacher, a black writer-in-residence at USL in Lafayette who volunteered his time at the library. Alafair got up from the table and came to the door, her eyes shining.

'*Dave . . . ,*' she said, the word almost twisting as it came out of her mouth.

'The kid who paints ceramics? Is he here tonight?' I said.

She squeezed her eyes shut, as though in pain, and opened them again. 'I knew that was it.'

'Alf, this guy isn't what you think he is. He's a killer for hire. He's the guy who escaped custody in the shoot-out on the Atchafalaya.'

632

'No, you're wrong. His name's Jack O'Roarke. He's not a criminal. He paints beautiful things. He showed me photographs of the things he's done.'

'That's the guy. O'Roarke was his father's name. Where is he?'

A fan oscillated behind her head; her eyes were moist and dark inside the skein of hair that blew around her face.

'It's a mistake of some kind. He's an artist. He's a gentle person. Jack wouldn't hurt anybody,' she said.

'Alf, come with me,' I said, and put my hand on her forearm, my fingers closing around the skin, harder than I meant to.

'No, I'm not going anywhere with you. You're humiliating me.'

I could see the veins in her forearm bunched like blue string under the skin, and I released her and realized my hand was shaking now.

'I'm sorry,' I said.

'Everybody's looking at us. Just go,' she said, her voice lowered, as though she could trap her words in the space between the two of us.

'He's here, isn't he?'

'I'll never forgive you for this.'

'Alafair, I'm a police officer. I was almost killed because of this man.'

She squeezed her eyes shut again and I saw the tears well out of her eyelids and shine on her lashes. Then inadvertently she glanced beyond me.

'The rest room?' I said.

But she wouldn't answer.

I waited until the area around the door of the men's room was clear, then I slipped my .45 from its clip-on holster under my coat, holding it close against my thigh, and went inside.

No one was at the urinals or lavatories. I pushed open each of the stall doors, standing back as they swung emptily against the partitions. I put the .45 back in my holster and went outside and motioned to the city cop to follow me. I saw Alafair looking at me, hollow-eyed, from across the room.

We went back down to the first floor and I described Johnny Remeta to the librarian at the circulation desk. She removed the glasses from her face and let them hang from a velvet ribbon around her neck and gazed thoughtfully into space.

'Did he have on a straw hat?' she asked.

'Maybe ... I don't know,' I said.

'He walked past me a few minutes ago. I think he's in the historical collection. That room in the back,' she said, and pointed past the book stacks.

I walked between the stacks, the city cop behind me, to a gray metal door inset with a small rectangle of reinforced glass. I tried to look through the glass at the entirety of the room but I saw only bookshelves and an austere desk lighted by a reading lamp. I pulled my .45 and held it down against my thigh, then shoved open the door and stepped inside.

The side window was open and a straw hat, with a black ribbon around the crown, lay brim-down on the floor. A bound collection of Civil War-era photographs lay open on the narrow desk. The photographs on the two exposed pages showed the bodies of Confederate and Union dead at Dunker Church and the Bloody Angle.

'This place is like a meat locker,' the city cop said.

I looked out the window into the summer night, into the sounds of crickets and frogs on the bayou and the easy creak of wind in the oak trees. But the air inside the room was like the vapor from dry ice.

'You believe in the angel of death, Top?' I said.

'Yeah, I knew her well. My ex-wife. Or maybe she was the Antichrist. I've never been sure,' he replied.

I climbed through the window and dropped onto the lawn. I walked out on the street, then through the parking lot and down to the bayou. I heard the horns on a tugboat in the distance, then the drawbridge at Burke Street clanking heavily into the air. There was no sign of Johnny Remeta. The sky had cleared and was as black as velvet and bursting with stars, like thousands of eyes looking down at me from all points on the compass.

Later, when we drove home, Alafair sat on the far side of the truck's seat, staring out the window, her anger or regret or humiliation or whatever emotion she possessed neutralized by fatigue and set in abeyance for the next day.

'You want to talk with Bootsie?' I said.

'No. You're just the way you are, Dave. You're not going to change.'

'Which way is that?' I said, and tried to smile in the darkness.

'I don't want to talk about it.'

After I pulled into the drive and cut the engine, she got out and walked to the front yard and went into the house through the living room so she wouldn't have to see me again that night.

'What's going on, Dave?' Bootsie said in the kitchen.

'It was Remeta. I tried to take him down in the library. He got away.'

The phone rang. I heard Alafair walking toward the extension that was in the hallway by her room. I picked up the receiver off the wall hook in the kitchen, my heart beating.

'Hello?' I said.

'You came after me like I was a germ,' Remeta said.

'How'd you get this number?' I said.

'What do you care? I got it.'

'You stay the fuck away from my daughter,' I said.

'What's with you? Don't talk to me like that.'

My temples were hammering, the inside of my shirt cold with sweat, my breath sour as it bounced off the receiver.

'So far I've got nothing against you personally. Drag your crazy bullshit into my family life, you'll wish you were still somebody's hump back in Raiford.'

I could hear his breath on the phone, almost a palpable physical presence, like an emery cloth brushing across the receiver.

When he spoke again, his voice was not the same. It came out of a barrel, dipped in blackness, the youthful face dissolving in my mind's eye.

His words were slow and deliberate, as though he were picking them one by one out of a cardboard box. 'You're not a smart man, after all, Mr Robicheaux. But I got an obligation to you. That makes you . . . a lucky man. Word of caution, sir. Don't mess with my head,' he said.

There was a click in his throat, then an exhalation of breath like a damp match flaring to life.

19

A week and a half went by and I heard nothing else from Johnny Remeta or about Axel Jennings or Micah the chauffeur or Jim and Cora Gable, and I began to feel that perhaps they would simply disappear from my life.

But my conclusions were about as wise as those of a man floating down a wide, flat stream on a balmy day, when the mind does not want to listen to the growing sounds of water cascading over a falls just beyond a wooded bend.

'You ought to go easy on the flak juice, hon,' Cherry Butera said to him.

Axel Jennings sat at the kitchen table in an undershirt and camouflage pants and house slippers without socks, a bottle of tequila and a sliced lime on a saucer in front of him. He poured into a jigger and knocked it back and licked salt from between his thumb and index finger and sucked on the lime. His shoulders were as dark as mahogany, hard and knobbed along the ridges, the skin taut and warm and smooth and sprinkled with sun freckles. He wasn't a handsome man, not in the ordinary sense, but he had beautiful skin and she loved to touch it and to feel that she was pressing his power and hardness inside her when she spread her fingers across his shoulders and ran them down to the small of his back.

The barmaids she worked with said she could do a lot better. They said Axel had a violent history. They should talk. Their boyfriends hit them, hung paper and cadged drinks at the bar, and usually had somebody on the side. He killed those guys in the line of duty; that's what cops got paid to do. Besides, he didn't talk about that part of his life, and the people he hurt deserved it. Nobody came on to her or treated her disrespectfully when she was with Axel.

But it had sure gone south since Jimmy Burgoyne got killed out by the Atchafalaya. Axel brooded all the time, like he was responsible for Jimmy getting killed. Now there was even a worse problem, and she didn't have an answer for it, either.

'Drinking don't hurt anything,' he said. 'A man decides how much he takes out of the bottle. Then he puts the cork in it. He controls the situation. That's what my dad said.'

He had taken off his bandages and lain out in the backyard in his Jockey undershorts with a wet washcloth rolled across his eyes and talked for a half hour on his remote phone to another cop. When he came in he started up all his electric trains and poured himself a drink and didn't replace his bandages. The collective hum of the electric trains made the house reverberate like an enormous sewing machine.

'Maybe I'd better be getting home. I mean, so's you can rest,' she said.

'Come over here,' he said.

He extended his hand toward her, waiting for her to take it and sit on his lap. She placed her fingers in his, but remained standing, her vision fixed so his face did not come into focus.

'The doctor says you got to take care of yourself,' she said.

'You got a problem with this, Cherry?' he said, lifting one finger toward his face.

'No, baby,' she said.

He released her hand and watched two calico kittens out the window. The kittens raced after each other in a flower bed, their fur a patchwork of color among the elephant ears.

'Why'd you bag out on me?' he said, his eyes still concentrated out the window.

'Bag out on you?'

'In the alley. When the perp told you to boogie, you hoofed it big-time.'

'I called 911. I got help.'

'You didn't scream. That's what women always do when they're at risk. You didn't do that, Cherry.'

'You think I was in on it?'

'You knew you were safe as long as you didn't scream. It's funny how fast people can add up the score when they're scared.'

She stood motionless for a long moment, her mind back in the alley now, inside the vortex of rain. She saw herself running through the rain puddles that were rainbowed with engine oil, her windpipe constricted, her breasts bouncing shamelessly in her blouse, and she knew what he said was true, and that an even greater, uglier truth was about to surface in her mind, that she was glad it had happened to him and not her.

The house was hot, full of morning sun trapped between the glass and the freshly painted yellowed walls. The electric trains coursing down the tracks, emerging from tunnels, clicking across the switches, seemed to amplify in her head. She made herself look directly into Axel's face. The jaws and chin line and brow looked like they had been disassembled and then rejoined and sealed together like the sunken and uneven pieces of an earthen pot.

He touched the point of a canine tooth and looked at the spittle on the ball of his finger, just the way he once did right before he hurt a man in a bar. She saw the network of red lines on his face transferred to hers and she wanted to weep.

'I'll leave, Axel. I mean, if that's what you want,' she said, and folded her arms suddenly across her chest, gripping her elbows as though she were cold.

He closed and opened his hand and watched the veins pump with blood in his forearm. Then he picked an apple out of a bowl of fruit and began peeling off the skin with a paring knife, watching it curl like a red and white wood shaving over his thumbnail.

'I'm gonna have a lot of money. I think I'm going to South America and start up a business. You can come,' he said.

'Sure, baby,' she said, and she realized she was trembling inside.

'So you go home and think about it. Get in touch with your inner self. Then come back tomorrow and let me know ... You want to use the bathroom before you go? You look like maybe you're gonna have an accident.'

Clete had sublet his apartment from a couple who wanted it back, evidently after the manager had called them in Florida and told them Clete sometimes parked the Cadillac in front with bail skips handcuffed to a D-ring in the backseat while he showered and changed clothes or fixed lunch in the apartment. One of the skips yelled out the window for fifteen minutes, announcing to the whole neighborhood that he had to use the bathroom.

On Saturday afternoon Bootsie went to visit her sister in Lafayette and Alafair and I helped Clete move to a tan stucco cottage in a 1930s motor court down Bayou Teche. The motor court was hemmed in by live-oak and banana and palm trees, and toward evening working-class people cooked on barbecue grills outside the cottages. The sunlight off the bayou glowed through the tunnel of trees like the amber radiance of whiskey held up against firelight.

After we finished unloading Clete's things from my truck, Clete and I tore up the packing cartons and stuffed them in a trash barrel while Alafair put away his kitchen utensils inside.

'I'm gonna get us some po' boys,' he said.

'We'd better go,' I said.

'Y'all got to eat. Relax, big mon. Cletus is in charge,' he said, then got in his Cadillac and bounced out the drive onto East Main before I could argue.

Alafair walked out of the cottage and looked in both directions. She wore blue-jeans shorts that were rolled high up on her thighs, and a Clorox-stained lavender T-shirt that seemed to hang off the tips of her breasts. A man playing a guitar in front of the cottage next door let his gaze wander over the backs of her legs. I stared at him and he looked away.

'Where's Clete?' she asked.

'He went for some food.'

She made a pout with her mouth and blew her breath out her nose. 'I have a date, Dave.'

'With whom?'

'It's somebody I go to school with. He doesn't have two heads. He's very safe. In fact, he's gay. How's that?'

'I wouldn't have it any other way, Alf.'

'My name's Alafair. If you don't want to call me that, why didn't you give me another name?'

'Take the truck. I can get a ride with Clete,' I said.

She raised her chin and tapped her foot and put her hands on her hips and looked at the barbecue smoke drifting in the trees. 'It's not that big a deal,' she said.

I shook my head and walked out to the street and waited for Clete. He turned into the motor court, cut his engine, then walked back to the entrance and looked up East Main.

'What is it?' I asked.

'I'd swear somebody was watching me with binoculars from the Winn-Dixie parking lot,' he said.

'Who?'

'You got me. I circled around to get a look and he'd taken off.'

'Have you messed with Ritter or this guy Jennings again?' I said.

'I figure Jennings already got his. I'll catch up with Ritter down the road.' We walked back to the cottage, but he kept glancing over his shoulder.

'Alafair, take the truck on home, would you?' I said.

'Just stop telling me what to do, please,' she said.

Clete raised his eyebrows and glanced upward at the mockingbirds in the trees as though he'd suddenly developed an interest in ornithology.

'Y'all want to eat on that table by the water?' he said, and lifted a sack of po' boys and a six-pack of Dr Pepper out of the Cadillac, an unlit Lucky Strike hanging from his mouth. He waited until Alafair was out of earshot, put the cigarette behind his ear, and said, 'Tell me, Streak, if I quit the juice and start going to meetings, can I enjoy the kind of serenity you do?'

While we ate at a table among a cluster of pine trees, a tall, sinewy man in a small red Japanese station wagon drove farther south of town, crossed a drawbridge, then followed the road back up the Teche to a grassy slope directly opposite the motor court.

He pulled his car down the slope and parked by a canebrake and walked down to the water's edge with a fishing rod and a bait bucket and a folding canvas chair that he flopped open and sat upon.

An elderly black man who had caught no fish was walking up the slope to the road. He glanced into the tall man's face, then looked away quickly, hiding the shock he hoped had not registered in his own face.

The tall man seemed disconcerted, vaguely irritated or angry that someone had looked at him. He gazed at his bobber floating among the lily pads, his back to the black man, and said, as though speaking to the bayou, 'You have any luck?'

'Not a bit. Water too high,' the black man said.

The tall man nodded and said nothing more, and the black man gained the road and walked toward the distant outline of the house where he lived.

It was dusk now. Across the bayou, Clete Purcel lighted a chemically treated candle that repelled mosquitoes. The fisherman sitting on the canvas stool watched through a pair of opera glasses from the edge of the canebrake as our faces glowed like pieces of yellow parchment in the candlelight.

He went back to his station wagon and opened the front and back doors on the driver's side, creating a kind of blind that shielded him from view. He removed a rifle wrapped in a blanket from the floor and carried it down to the bayou and lay it in the grass at his feet.

It was all about breathing and heartbeat, locking down on the target, remembering the weapon is your friend, an extension of angles and lines whose intersection your mind created. That's what his father had said.

He began to feel the old excitement pumping inside him and he had to refrain from beating his fists together. It was too good, a trio of faces bent around a candle flame, an alcove of shadow surrounding their heads. It wasn't just a hit now, but the perfect challenge, to drill a clean shot into the target, snip all his wires, and leave the people around him intact, with stunned, disbelieving looks on their faces and a sudden jellylike presence on the skin they were afraid to touch.

The beauty of it was they'd never hear the shot. While people ran in circles and screamed and crawled under tables and hid behind parked cars, he would recover his brass and get back in his station wagon and drive away. People talking on trash TV about using politics and sex for power and control? Forget it.

The Bobbsey Twins from Homicide. What a joke. A drunk and a pile of whale sperm with a P.I. license. He bit down softly on his lower lip in anticipation of the moments to come.

Then, for just a second, he saw Jimmy Burgoyne's brains exploding in that gig gone bad on the Atchafalaya and he had to squeeze his eyes shut until the image disappeared from his mind.

It was starting to sprinkle. The bayou was suddenly dotted with rain rings and the bream started popping the surface among the hyacinths. He opened his eyes as though awakening from sleep and took a deep breath and resolved to order more flowers for Jimmy's grave, to send another card to the family, to continue making those incremental gestures that temporarily lifted the guilt for Jimmy's death from his soul.

Then anger bloomed in his chest like an old friend, cleansing his mind of all his self-accusatory thoughts.

Show time, boys and girls.

He flipped back the blanket that was folded around the M-1A rifle, the semiauto civilian equivalent of the old M-14. It was a far better piece than any of the other modified military weapons, silenced and scoped, deadly accurate, rapid-firing, the twenty-round magazine packed tight with soft-nosed .308s. He worked the blanket out from under the rifle and draped it over his head like a tent. Then he gathered up the weight of the rifle, knelt on one knee, and fitted the stock against his shoulder and cheek.

A man's head swam into the lens of his telescopic sight, and Axel's mouth opened wetly against the stock, almost like his lips were pressing at a twisted angle into a woman's throat. He exhaled slowly and tightened his finger inside the trigger guard. This one's for Jimmy and me, both, he thought.

'I heard you were queer bait with Vice before NOPD let you start blowing heads,' a voice said behind him.

Axel jerked around, the blanket sliding off his head and shoulders, and stared into the face of a kid who looked like a 1950s greaser. Where had he seen that face before? On a composite? The kid smiled briefly, as though he were about to introduce himself, then shot Axel with a .22 Ruger automatic between the eyes. The kid watched Axel tumble into the cane, then nudged Axel's head to one side with his shoe and leaned over and fired a second round into his ear and a third into his temple.

The splatter hit the barrel of his pistol and he used the blanket to wipe it off.

When the shots went off, the elderly black man had been walking back down the bank to look for a pocketknife he had lost. He stood stark still, his heart racing, and watched the young dark-haired man with white skin, who only a moment ago had seemed like a fellow taking a stroll, straighten up from his work and mount the slope, a pistol hanging from his hand.

The black man thought he should run, but his feet would not move. He was going to say, 'White people fightin' ain't my bidness,' but he never got the chance.

'How's it goin', cappie?' the young man said, and passed him by, shaking a pair of black-framed glasses loose from their case and slipping them on his face.

The black man watched him wrap his pistol in a paper bag and cross the road and toss the pistol on his car seat and drive away, his turn indicator clicking to warn oncoming traffic of his presence.

20

The night was absolutely black when Alafair and I got home two hours later. In the dash light her face was drawn, her eyes filled with questions that she didn't have adequate words for. And I was both depressed and angry with myself for having taken her to Clete's when I knew Axel Jennings might be coming after him.

I pulled into the drive and parked next to the gallery.

'I've got to help Batist close up. I'll see you in the house, okay?' I said.

But she didn't move. The light on the gallery shone through the trees and made shadows inside the truck. She stared at nothing, her eyes almost luminous in their solitary concern.

'You sure it was Johnny?' she said.

'That old black fellow picked out his photo from five others,' I replied.

'He shot point-blank in the man's ear? It wasn't self-defense or something?'

'It was an execution, Alafair.'

'But you said it saved Clete's life.'

'Remeta thought he owed me a debt and I guess this is how he paid it.'

'Then he's not all bad, Dave.'

'When people kill other people, they find a flag of some kind to do it under. But their motivation is always the same. They enjoy it.'

'I don't believe that about Johnny.'

She got out of the truck and walked across the yard to the front door. But she paused before she went inside and looked back at me, as though seeking approval or just the knowledge that I did not condemn her for her humanity.

'Alf?' I said.

She opened the screen and went inside.

I walked down to the dock and helped Batist total up the receipts and hose the dried fish blood and cut-bait off the dock.

Clete Purcel's Cadillac came down the road, bouncing through the rain puddles. Then Clete pulled up at an angle across the cement boat ramp and cut the engine and got out and left the door open. He walked toward me with a can of beer in one hand and a pint bottle wrapped in a brown bag in the other. Under the string of electric lights his face was oily and distorted, his mouth unnaturally red.

'I can't believe I let that asswipe get behind us,' he said.

'I love you, Cletus, but you're not using my shop to get drunk in tonight,' I said.

'I've got local leper status now?'

'Your skin's crawling because a shithead had you in his crosshairs. Booze only tattoos the fear into your sleep. You know that.'

'You're pissed off because you think I put your daughter at risk.'

'You didn't have anything to do with it.'

I used the pressure nozzle on the hose to blow the dock and railing clean. When I released the handle I could hear the water draining between the boards into the darkness below. Clete stood silently and waited, his booze in each hand, the hurt barely concealed in his face.

'Let me hold that for you,' I said, and eased the pint bottle from his hand.

'What do you think you're doing?' he said.

'I've got a couple of steaks in the cooler. You're going to eat one and I'm going to eat the other,' I said.

'I don't get to vote about my own life?' he asked.

'I'll do it for you.'

I lit the gas stove inside the bait shop, seasoned the T-bone steaks, and lay them on the grill. Clete sat at the counter and drank from his beer and watched me. He kept touching at his forehead, as though an insect were on his skin.

'What's with this kid Remeta?' he asked, forcing his concentration on a subject other than his self-perceived failure.

'You were right the first time. He's nuts.'

'He was putting moves on Alafair?'

'Who knows?'

The phone on the counter rang. I picked it up impatiently, waiting once again to hear the voice of Johnny Remeta. But it was the sheriff.

'I thought this shouldn't wait till tomorrow,' he said. 'Levy and Badeaux tore apart Axel Jennings' station wagon. There was fourteen thousand dollars in new bills hidden in the trunk. He also had a passport and an Iberia Parish map with an inked line from I-10 to just about where your house is.'

'My house?' I said.

'Your picture and an article about the shoot-out on the Atchafalaya were in a newspaper on the floor. He'd drawn a circle around your head. Purcel wasn't the target.'

I could feel the heat and moisture trapped between my palm and the phone receiver. A drop of sweat ran from my armpit down my side.

Clete lowered his beer can from his mouth and looked curiously at my expression.

Later I lay in the dark next to Bootsie, the window fan blowing across us, and tried to put together the events of the day. A rogue cop doing a hit for hire on another police officer? It happened sometimes, but usually the victim was dirty and shared a corrupt enterprise with the shooter. Who would be behind it, anyway? Jim Gable was obnoxious and, in my view, a sexual degenerate, but why would he want me killed?

The contract could have been put out by a perpetrator with a grudge, but most perpetrators thought of cops, prosecutors, and judges as functionaries of the system who were not personally to blame for their grief; their real anger was usually directed at fall partners who sold them out and defense attorneys who pled them into double-digit sentences.

The only other person with whom I was currently having trouble was Connie Deshotel. The attorney general putting a whack on a cop?

But all the syllogisms I ran through my head were only a means of avoiding a nightmarish image that I couldn't shake from my mind. I saw Alafair seated next to me at the plank table, petting a cat in the glow of the candle Clete had just lighted. Then, in my imagination, I saw a muzzle flash across the bayou, a brief tongue of yellow flame against the bamboo, and an instant later I heard the sound a soft-nosed round makes when it strikes bone and I knew I had just entered a landscape of remorse and sorrow from which there is no exit.

I picked up my pillow and went into Alafair's room. She wore a cotton nightgown and was sleeping on her stomach, her face turned toward the wall, her black hair fanned out on the pillow. The moon had broken out of the clouds, and I could see the screen hanging ajar and Tripod curled in a ball on Alafair's rump. He raised his nose and sniffed at the air, then yawned and went back to sleep.

I lay down on the floor, on top of Alafair's Navaho rug, and put my pillow under my head. Her shelves were lined with books, stuffed animals, and framed photographs and certificates of membership in Madrigals and Girls State and the school honor society. Inside a trunk I had made from restored cypress wood were all her possessions we had saved over the years: a Baby Orca T-shirt, red tennis shoes embossed with the words 'Left' and 'Right' on the appropriate shoe, a Donald Duck cap with a quacking bill, her Curious George and Baby Squanto Indian books, a brown, cloth Sodality scapular, the mystery stories she wrote in elementary school, with titles like 'The Case of the Hungry Caterpillar,' 'The Worm That Lost Its Wiggle,' and, most chilling of all, 'The Roller Rink Murders.'

Outside, the wind lifted the moss in the trees and I drifted off to sleep.

It was around 3 a.m. when I heard her stir in bed. I opened my eyes and looked up into her face, which hung over the side of the mattress.

'Why are you sleeping down there?' she whispered.

'I felt like it.'

'You thought something was going to happen to me?'

'Of course not.'

She made a solitary clicking sound with her tongue, then got out of bed and went out to the hall closet and came back and popped a sheet open and spread it across me.

'You are so crazy sometimes,' she said, and got back in bed, folding Tripod in the crook of her arm. She leaned over the side of the bed again and said, 'Dave?'

'Yes?'

'I love you.'

I placed my arm across my eyes so she wouldn't see the water welling up in them.

The next morning was Sunday and Bootsie, Alafair, and I went to Mass together. After we returned home I went down to the dock and helped Batist in the bait shop. It was unusually cool, a fine day for going after bream and goggle-eye perch with popping bugs, and we had rented most of our boats. It showered just after lunch, and a number of fishermen came in and drank beer and ate links and chicken at our spool tables under the awning. But regardless of the balmy weather and the cheerful mood out on the dock, I knew it wouldn't be long before Johnny Remeta came back into our lives.

The call came at mid-afternoon.

'I figure we're square,' he said.

'You got it,' I said.

He was silent a moment. I picked up an empty Coke can and looked at the label on it, trying to slow my thoughts and avoid the anger that was always my undoing.

'When you came after me in the library? How far were you willing to go?' he said.

'That would have been up to you, Johnny.'

'Gives me a bad feeling, Mr Robicheaux.'

'That's the way it is, I guess.'

Again he was silent. Then he said. 'Those things you said to me on the phone that night? My father talked to me like that.'

'I can't give you the help you need, partner. But no matter how you cut it, you have to stay away from us. I'm saying this with all respect.'

'It's over when I get the people who shot at me.'

'That's between you and others. We're not involved.'

'You thought maybe I had an improper attitude toward Alafair?'

Hearing him use her name made my breath come hard in my throat.

'I'm off the clock. I'm also off the phone. Have a good life, Johnny,' I said, and gently replaced the receiver in the cradle.

I stared at the phone like it was a live snake, waiting for him to call back. I rang up a sale, served a customer an order of boudin on a paper plate, and scrubbed down the counter with a wet rag, the tension in my ears crackling with a sound like crushed cellophane.

When the phone did ring, it was Bootsie, asking me to bring a quart of milk from the cooler up to the house.

Johnny Remeta may have been temporarily out of the way, but Connie Deshotel's possible involvement with Axel Jennings was not.

In Vietnam I knew a self-declared Buddhist and quasi-psychotic warrant officer who would fly a Huey into places the devil wouldn't go. He used to say, 'The way to keep your house safe from tigers is to return the tiger to its owner's house.'

I got Connie Deshotel's address from our local state representative, then drove to Baton Rouge late Sunday afternoon. She lived off Dalrymple, in the lake district north of the LSU campus, in a gabled two-story white house with azaleas and willows and blooming crepe myrtle in the yard. Her Sunday paper still lay on the front porch, wrapped tightly in a plastic rain bag.

I didn't try to call before I arrived. Even if she wasn't home, I felt my business card in her mailbox would indicate, if indeed she was the money behind Axel Jennings, that her intentions were known, and another visit from one of her emissaries would lead right back to her door.

I lifted the brass door knocker and heard chimes deep inside the house. But no one came to the door. I dropped my card through the mail slot and was headed back down the walk when I heard the spring of a diving board and a loud splash from the rear of the house.

I walked though a side yard under a long trellis that was wrapped with trumpet vine. I opened the gate into the backyard and saw Connie Deshotel in a purple two-piece bathing suit, mounting the tile steps at the shallow end of her swimming pool.

She picked a towel off a sun chair and shook out her hair, then dried her face and neck and blotted the towel on her thighs and the backs of her legs. She placed her feet inside her sandals and poured a Bloody Mary from a pitcher into a red-streaked glass with a stick of celery blossoming out of the ice.

I started to speak, then realized she had seen me out of the corner of her eye.

'Did you bring Bootsie with you this time?' she asked.

'No, it's still all business,' I replied.

'Well,' she said, touching the towel to her forehead, her chin raised, as though taking pause with an unacceptable intrusion rather than allowing herself to be undone by it. 'What is it that's of such great concern to us this Sunday afternoon?'

'Can I sit down?'

'Please do. Yes, indeed,' she said.

She sat across from me at a glass-topped table under an umbrella that was made from wide, multicolored strips of tin.

'Friday the sheriff and I were talking about an interesting attribute everyone of our generation seems to share,' I said.

'Oh?' she said, her interest wandering out into the yard.

'What were you doing when you heard John Kennedy had been shot?'

'I was coming out of gym class. Some girls were crying in the hallway.'

'See?' I said, smiling. 'Everybody remembers that exact moment in his or her life. They never hesitate when they're asked.'

'What's the point?'

'It's that photo taken of you with the parents of the Labiche girls. It troubles the heck out of me. Here, I brought it along,' I said, and removed a manila envelope from the pocket of my coat.

But before I could pull the photo out, she leaned forward and took both of my hands in hers, pressing down hard with her thumbs, her eyes fastened on mine.

'Dave, give this up. You're a good man. But you've developed a fixation about something that means absolutely nothing,' she said.

I took my hands from hers and slipped the photo out of the envelope and lay it flat on the table.

'You remember being with the Labiches?' I asked.

'No, I don't.'

'See, up here in the corner, someone wrote, "Christmas, 1967." So here you are in a nightclub, back in the civil rights era, in an evening dress, with a corsage on, at Christmastime, with a notorious mulatto couple who pimped for a living, and you have no memory of it. Does that seem strange to you?'

She picked up a big leather bag with drawstrings on it from the flagstones and dug a package of cigarettes and a gold lighter out of it and set them on the tabletop.

'I really don't have anything more to say on the matter. Would you like a Diet Coke or lemonade or decaffeinated coffee or ice water or whatever it is you drink?'

'In '67 you hadn't been out of the police academy too long. Does it make sense that a young cop could be around the Labiches, perhaps on Christmas Eve, and not remember it? Look me in the face and tell me that.'

'Do me a great favor, Dave. Go home to your wife. Sell worms to your friends. Play mind games with your sheriff. Just . . . go.'

'There's a bad dude by the name of Johnny Remeta running loose. In case you haven't heard, he's the same perp who cut Axel Jennings' kite string. He's got an iron bolt through his head and thinks he's my guardian angel. I wouldn't want Remeta on my case. You get my drift, Connie?'

She didn't answer. Instead, a strange transformation seemed to take place in her. She rose from her chair, an unlit cigarette dangling between her fingers, a gold lighter in her other hand, and studied the shadows that the banana trees and palm fronds created on her brick wall. Her face was bladed with the glare of the late afternoon sun reflecting off the pool; her eyes were narrow and hard, her lips crimped on the end of her unlit cigarette as she clicked her lighter several times without the flint igniting a flame. Her skin looked coarse and grained, like that of a countrywoman or someone who had stepped into a cold wind.

I replaced the photo in the envelope and put it in my pocket and walked across the flagstones toward the gate. I turned around and looked back at her once more before I entered the side yard.

The gold lighter. It was an archaic type, thin and lightweight, with strips of veined, dark leather inset in the casement and a horizontal lever the smoker snapped downward on top and a tiny cap that automatically retracted from the flame.

It was the same type of stylish gold lighter that Jim Gable used to light his cigars.

She got her cigarette lit and blew her smoke at an upward angle, her sandaled feet slightly spread, one hand on her hip, a private thought buried in her eyes.

21

Monday morning Little Face Dautrieve came to see me at my office. She wore a dark dress with green flowers printed on it, and a hibiscus in her hair, and hose and lavender pumps.

'You going somewhere special today?' I said.

'Yeah, you driving me and you to New Orleans,' she replied.

'Is that right?'

'The reason I call you "Sad Man" ain't 'cause of the way you look. It's 'cause you let Zipper Clum play you for a fool,' she said.

'Say again?'

'Zipper liked to make other people hate themselves. That's how he got people like me to work for him. That and the rock he give me.'

'You're not making a whole lot of sense, Little Face.'

'You never axed me how I got in the life. It was t'rew my auntie in New Orleans. She knowed Zipper. I visited my auntie this weekend. She say Zipper tole you a bunch of lies about your mother.'

I signed out a cruiser, and Little Face and I took the four-lane through Morgan City to New Orleans. The sugarcane was high and thickly clustered and pale green in the fields, and the cruiser was buffeting in the wind off the Gulf.

'Why are you doing this?' I asked.

'I seen the story in the paper. People trying to shoot at you and Fat Man. He doin' all right?'

'Sure.'

'Tell Fat Man I been going to meetings,' she said, her face pointed straight ahead to hide whatever emotion was in it.

'You still don't trust me enough to tell me how Vachel Carmouche died?'

'A lawman get killed in Lou'sana, somebody gonna pay. It don't matter who. Give them peckerwoods a chance, they'll strap another one down wit' her. Tell me I be wrong, Sad Man.'

The aunt lived on St Andrew, in a white shotgun house, between the streetcar line and the Mississippi River levee. She had been a prostitute thirty years ago, but her skin was smooth, unwrinkled, like yellow tallow, her gray-streaked hair combed out on her shoulders, her turquoise eyes and red mouth still seductive. At least until she opened her mouth to speak and you saw her bad teeth and the gums that were black and eaten with snuff.

She sat on the stuffed couch in her small living room, her hands clasped just below her knees to prevent the floor fan from puffing up her dress. From outside I could hear the streetcars grinding up and down the tracks on St Charles.

'You knew Mae Guillory?' I asked.

'I worked in a club in Lafourche Parish. Down on Purple Cane Road, almost to the salt water,' she said.

I repeated my question. The aunt, whose name was Caledonia Patout, looked at Little Face.

'Robicheaux been good to me, Callie,' Little Face said, her eyes avoiding mine, as though she had broken a self-imposed rule.

'The club was still for white people then. I worked out of the cribs in back. That's how I knew Mae Guillory,' Caledonia said.

'My mother worked out of the cribs?' I said, and coughed slightly in my palm, as though I had a mild cold or allergy.

'No, your mother wasn't no working girl. Zipper just putting some glass inside you. You seen that burn like a big ringworm on his cheek? Cops done that. Mae Guillory waited tables and hepped at the bar and cooked sometimes. She tole me she'd come there twenty years before with a man deal bouree. The bouree man got TB and died. So she just work there on and off. The rest of the time she work places around Morgan City and Thibodaux.'

'What happened to her, Caledonia?'

This is what she told me.

It was 1967, way down in the fall, hurricane weather. The sky turned green at evening and the air was palpable with the heavy, wet smell of seaweed laden with fish eggs and Portuguese men-of-war whose air sacs had popped and dried in a crusty web on the beach; it was weather that smelled of a storm-swollen tide surging over the barrier islands, bursting in geysers against jetties and sand spits.

The old owner of the nightclub had died and left his property to his half brother, a reckless, irreverent slaughterhouse butcher by the name of Ladrine Theriot. Ladrine had always wanted to be a professional cook, and he remodeled the kitchen of the club and began to serve gumbos and chicken and dirty rice dinners. He loved to cook; he loved women, and, like my father, he loved to fight with anyone foolish enough to accept his challenge.

For Mae Guillory, Ladrine had walked right out of her past. But, unlike my father, Ladrine wasn't an alcoholic.

Mae was working at the bar the night the two police officers drove an unmarked vehicle to the back door and cut their lights and walked out of the darkness in rain slickers and hats. Through the door she could see Ladrine in an undershirt and apron, butchering a hog with a cleaver on top of an enormous wood block, chopping through ribs and vertebrae, his arms and shoulders curlicued with black hair that was flecked with tiny pieces of pink meat. She did not see the faces of the officers, only their shadows, which fell across the butcher block, but she clearly heard the conversation between one officer and Ladrine.

'Tell them dagos in New Orleans I ain't buying from them no more. One man tole me the rubber he got out of the machine got holes in it. Their beer's flat and the jukebox full of rock 'n' roll. Them people in New Orleans ain't got no Cajun music?' Ladrine said.

'You want to use another distributor, that's fine.'

Ladrine began paring the rinds off a stack of chops, his long, honed knife flicking the gray dissected pieces of fat sideways into a garbage barrel.

'There's another t'ing,' he said. 'I'm closing up them cribs, me. Don't be sending no more girls down here, no.'

His knife paused over the meat and he raised his eyes to make his point.

'That not a problem, Ladrine,' the officer said. 'But your brother owed the people in New Orleans forty-three hundred dollars and change. The debt comes with the club. What they call the vig, the points, the interest, is running, tick-tock, tick-tock, all day, all night. I'd pay it if I was you.'

'Oh, you need your money? Go to the graveyard. My brother's got a bunch of gold teet' in his mout'. You can have them. He don't mind,' Ladrine said.

He resumed his work, his knife going *chop, chop, snick, snick* against the wood.

Two nights later they were back. A storm had made landfall immediately to the south, the tidal surge warping and twisting boat docks, rippling the loose planks like piano keys, and the cane in the fields was white with lightning, slashing back and forth as though the wind were blowing from four directions at once.

The two police officers ran out of the rain into the dryness of the kitchen, and one of them loosened the bulb in the light socket that hung over the butcher block, dropping the kitchen into darkness.

The nightclub was almost deserted. Mae stood behind the bar on the duckboards and stared at the kitchen door, her pulse jumping in her neck. 'Callie and me need you to hep out here, Ladrine,' she said.

'He's all right. Go about your business,' one of the police officers said. 'You can fix us some coffee, if you want. Set it on the chair by the door. I'll get it.'

'Ladrine ain't caused no trouble,' Mae said.

'He's a good boy. He's going to stay a good boy,' the officer said. 'That's right, isn't it, Ladrine?'

'Stay out of it, Mae,' Callie whispered in her ear.

Mae could hear them talking now from inside the darkness, the lightning in the fields trembling like candle flame on their bodies. Ladrine was uncharacteristically subdued, perhaps even cowered by what he was being told, his shape like that of a haystack in the gloom.

'It's nothing personal. Debts have to be paid. We respect you. But you got to respect us,' the officer said.

The officer picked up the demitasse of coffee and the saucer and spoon and sugar cube that Mae had set on the chair for him. He stood in the doorway and sipped from it, his back to Mae, his small hands extended out of the black folds of his slicker. His nails were clean, and his face looked rosy and handsome when the light played on it.

'Them Giacanos pretty rough, huh?' Ladrine said.

'I wouldn't know. I stay on their good side,' the officer said.

'I'll t'ink about it, me,' Ladrine said.

'I knew you'd say that,' the officer said, and placed his hand on Ladrine's arm, then set down his empty cup and saucer and went out the door with his partner in a swirl of rain and wind.

'You okay, Ladrine? They ain't hurt you, huh?' Mae asked.

'Ain't nothing wrong with me,' he replied, his face bloodless.

The storm passed, but another was on its way. The next morning was dismal. The sky was the color of cardboard, the fields flooded, the dirt road like a long wet, yellow scar through the cane, and moccasins as thick as Mae's arms crawled from the ditches and bumped under her tires when she drove to work. She mopped floors and hauled trash to the rusted metal barrels in back until 10 a.m., when she saw Ladrine drive a pickup into the parking lot with a hydraulic lift in the rear. He got out, slammed the door of the cab, and thumped a hand truck up the wood steps into the bar.

Later, from in back, she heard him laboring with a heavy object, then she heard the hydraulic lift whining and his pickup truck driving away.

He returned at noontime and opened the cash register and counted out several bills and pieces of silver on the bar. As an afterthought he went back to the register drawer and removed an additional ten-dollar bill and added it to the stack on the bar.

'I got to let you go, Mae,' he said.

'What you fixing to do?' she said.

He broke a raw egg in an RC cola and drank it.

'I ain't done nothing,' he said.

'You a big fool don't have nobody to look after him. I ain't going nowhere,' she said.

He grinned at her, the corner of his mouth smeared with egg yoke, and she was reminded in that moment of a husband whose recklessness and courage and irresponsibility made him both the bane and natural victim of his enemies.

Ladrine opened the New Orleans telephone directory and thumbed through the white pages to the listings that began with the letter 'G'.

He reached under the bar and picked up the telephone and set it down heavily in front of him and dialed a number.

'How you doin', suh? This is Ladrine Theriot. I t'ought it over. I called my cousin in the legislature and tole him what you gangsters been doin' down here in Lafourche Parish. He said that ain't no surprise, 'cause ain't none of you ever worked in your life, and if you ain't pimping, you stealing from each other. By the way, if you want your jukebox back, it's floating down the bayou. If you hurry, you can catch it before it goes into the Gulf. T'anks. Good-bye.'

He hung up the phone and looked at it a moment, then closed his register drawer quietly and stared at the rain driving against the windows and the red and white Jax beer sign clanking on its chains, his eyes glazed over with thoughts he didn't share.

'Ladrine, Ladrine, what you gone and done?' Mae said.

Mae lived twenty miles up the state highway in a cabin she rented in the quarters of a corporation farm. The cabins were all exactly alike, tin-roofed, paintless, stained by the soot that blew from stubble fires in winter, narrow as matchboxes, with small galleries in front and privies in back. Once a week the 'rolling store,' an old school bus outfitted with shelves and packed with canned goods, brooms, overalls, work boots, pith helmets, straw hats, patent medicine, women's dresses, guitar strings, refrigerated milk and lunch meat, .22 caliber and twelve-gauge ammunition, quart jars of peanut butter and loaves of bread, rattled its way up and down the highway and braked with a screech and a clanking of gears in the quarters. People came out of their cabins and bought what they needed for the week, and sometimes with great excitement received a special order – perhaps a plastic guitar, a first communion suit, a cigarette rolling machine – from New Orleans or Memphis.

It was Saturday and Mae had bought a sequined comb to put in her hair from the rolling store, then had bathed in the iron tub and powdered her body and dressed in her best underthings, tying a string around her hips so her slip wouldn't show, the way Negro women did. She put on her purple suit and heels, drawing her stomach in as she stood sideways in front of her bedroom mirror while Callie sat watching her.

'You t'ink I'm too fat?' she asked, pressing her hand flatly against her stomach.

'What you got in your mind ain't gonna happen,' Callie said.

'Ladrine gonna take me to the movie in Morgan City. That's all we doin'.'

'He got in the dagos' face, Mae.'

'You hung around, ain't you?'

'Zipper Clum got a new sit'ation for me in New Orleans. White man want what I got, he gonna pay for it,' Callie said.

'Maybe me and Ladrine are gonna run off.'

'What are you telling yourself? He growed up here. Coon-asses don't go nowhere. You gonna die, woman.'

Mae turned from the mirror and looked at Callie, her face empty, the words of self-assurance she wanted to speak dead on her lips.

Ladrine did not come for her that afternoon. She waited until almost dark, then drove to the club in her ancient Ford and was told by the bartender that Ladrine had left a note for her. It was written on lined paper torn from a notebook and folded in a small square, and the bartender held it between two fingers and handed it to her and went back to washing silverware. She spread the sheet of paper on the bar and looked down at it emptily, as though by concentrating on the swirls and slashes of Ladrine's calligraphy she could extrapolate meaning from the words she had never learned to read.

'I don't got my glasses, me. Can you make out what it says?' she said.

The bartender dried his hands again and picked up the sheet of paper and held it under the light. '"Dear Mae, I'm taking my boat out. Don't come back to the club no more. Sorry I couldn't call but you don't have no phone. Love, Ladrine,"' the bartender read, and handed the sheet of paper back to her.

The bartender's wrists were deep in the sink now, and she could see only his shining pate when he spoke again.

'I'd listen to him, Mae,' he said.

'Somet'ing's happened?'

'Some men from New Orleans was here. Know the way us little people get by? What you see, what you hear, you do this wit',' he said, and made a twisting motion with his fingers in front of his lips, as though turning a key in a lock.

'You tole them where Ladrine was at?'

'I ain't in this,' he said, and walked down the duckboards to the opposite end of the bar.

She drove in the rain to Ladrine's boat shed on the bayou. A pale yellow cusp of western sun hung on the horizon, then died, and the fields were suddenly dark. But a light attached to a pole over the shed was burning brightly, illuminating four or five cars that were parked in a semi-circle around the shed, like arrows pointed at a target.

The state highway was no more than fifty yards away, and cars and trucks were passing on it with regularity. Inside the warmth and dryness of those trucks and cars were ordinary people, just like her. They weren't criminals. They knew their only friends were their own kind. The ones who were lucky had jobs in the mill and hence were paid the minimum wage of one dollar and twenty-five cents an hour. The others worked for virtually nothing in the cane fields. But the highway was a tunnel of rain and darkness, and whatever happened out there by the bayou had nothing to do with those inside the tunnel. Their ability to see was selective, the fate of a friend and neighbor never registering on the periphery of their vision. That was the detail she would not be able to forget.

The planks in the board road that led to the boat shed were splintered and broken and half underwater, and Mae's car started to stall out when her front wheels sank into a flooded depression and steam hissed off her engine block. She put her car in reverse and backed up toward the highway, then cut the engine and lights and got out and walked down the incline, still dressed in her purple suit, the rain sliding like glass across the cone of light that shone down from the pole above the shed.

She could see them through the slats in the shed and the back door that yawed open above a mud-streaked wood pallet: Ladrine and two men in suits and two police officers in black slickers, the same officers who had tried to extort money from Ladrine; and a local constable, a big, overweight man who wore blue jeans, a cowboy hat, and a khaki shirt with an American flag sewn on the sleeve.

Ladrine had on strap overalls without a shirt or shoes, and his bare shoulders glowed like ivory in the damp air. He was shaking his head and arguing, when he seemed to look beyond the circle of heads around him and see Mae out in the darkness.

Then he called out, 'I ain't gonna talk to y'all no more. I'm going home. I'm gonna fix dinner. I'm gonna call up my grandkids. I'm gonna work in my garden tomorrow. I'm gonna do all them t'ings.'

He began to retreat in the opposite direction, inching backwards along the catwalk, stepping quickly out of the shed's far side into the darkness, then running along the mud bank, his bare feet slapping like flapjacks along the water's edge.

Someone turned on a large flashlight, and one of the raincoated police officers squatted in a shooter's position under the shed, the arms extended in a two-handed grip, and fired twice with a nickel-plated revolver.

Ladrine's head jerked upward, then he toppled forward, his left hand twisted palm-outward in the center of his back, as though he had pulled a muscle while running.

The group of five under the shed walked out into the rain, the flashlight's beam growing in circumference as they neared Ladrine. He had gone into convulsions, his wrists shaking uncontrollably, as though electricity were coursing through his body.

The shooter fired a third time, and Ladrine's chest seemed to deflate, almost like a balloon, his chin tilting back, his mouth parting, as though he wanted to drink the sky.

The other raincoated officer leaned over with a handkerchief-wrapped pistol in his hand and placed it in Ladrine's palm and wrapped Ladrine's fingers around the grips and steel frame and inside the trigger guard. The officer motioned for the others to step back, then depressed the trigger and fired a solitary round into the bayou just as a bolt of lightning struck in a sugarcane field on the opposite side of the highway.

That's when they saw her running for her car.

She drove twenty miles up the highway, in the storm, her car shaking in the wind. They had not tried to follow her, but her heart continued to pound in her chest, her breath catching spasmodically in her throat as though she had been crying. The quarters where she lived loomed up out of the green-black thrashing of the cane in the fields, and she saw lights in two of the cabins. She wanted to pull off the road, pack her suitcase and few belongings and retrieve the seventy dollars she kept hidden in the binder of a scrapbook, then try to make it to New Orleans or Morgan City.

But there was no telephone in the quarters and no guarantee the people who had shot Ladrine would not show up before she could get back on the road again.

She drove on in the rain, even though she had only three dollars in her purse and less than a quarter tank of gasoline. She would stop in the next filling station on the highway and use all her money to buy gasoline. If necessary she could sleep in the car and go without food, but every ounce of fuel she put in the tank bought distance between her and the people who had killed Ladrine.

Then she rounded a curve and realized all her decisions and plans and attempts at control were the stuff of vanity. Either high winds or a tornado had knocked down telephone and power poles as far as she could see, and they lay solidly in her path, extending like footbridges across the asphalt and the rain-swollen ditches.

She drove back to the quarters and sat on the side of her bed the rest of the night. Perhaps the next day the highway would be cleared and she could drive to Morgan City and tell someone what she had seen. If she could just stay awake and not be undone by her fear and the sounds of the wind that were like fists thumping against the walls and doors of her cabin.

The morning broke cold and gray, and in her half-sleep she heard trucks out on the highway. When she looked through the window she saw people in the trucks, with furniture, mattresses, house pets, and farm animals in back.

She stripped the clothes off the hangers in the closet and stuffed them in her suitcase, pushed her dress shoes in the corners of the suitcase, pulled the seventy dollars from the binder of the scrapbook and lay it on top of her clothes. She hefted up the suitcase and ran outside into the dirt yard, her car keys already in her hand.

She stopped and stared stupidly at her car. It was tilted sideways on the frame. The right front and back tires were crushed down on the steel rims, the air stems cut in half.

An hour later a black man drove her down a dirt road through a cane field toward a weathered shack with a dead pecan tree in the yard. He wore a flannel shirt and canvas coat, and had tied down the leather cap on his head with a long strip of muslin.

'That's where you want to go?' he asked.

'Yes. Can you wait so I can make sure she's home?' Mae said.

'You didn't tell me it was Callie Patout. Ma'am, she work up at the nightclub. In the cribs.'

'I'll give you an extra half dollar if you wait. Then fifty cents more if you got to take me back.'

'Ladrine Theriot got killed shooting it out wit' a constable. I ain't having no truck with that kind of stuff. Look, smoke's coming out of the chimney. See? Ain't nothing to worry about.'

Then she was standing alone in front of the shack, watching the black man's pickup disappear down the dirt road between the cane fields, the enormous gray bowl of sky above her head.

Callie sat on a wooden footstool by the fireplace, a cup of coffee between her fingers, and would not look at her.

'What I'm suppose to do? I ain't got a car,' she said. 'You the only one, Callie.'

'There's trucks up on the state road. There's people going by all the time.'

'I stand out there, they gonna get me.'

Callie pushed her hands inside her sleeves and stared into the fire.

'This white folks' trouble, Mae. Ain't right to be dragging colored peoples in it.'

'Where I'm gonna go, huh?'

'Just ain't right. What I got that can hep? I ain't even got a job. Ain't none of it my doing,' Callie said.

Mae stood a long time in the silence, watching the firelight flicker on Callie's averted face, embarrassed at the shame and cowardice that seemed to be both her legacy and that of everyone she touched.

Mae left the shack and began walking down the dirt road. She heard the door of the cabin open behind her.

'Zipper Clum suppose to pick me up this afternoon or tomorrow morning and take me to New Orleans. Where's your suitcase at?'

'My place.'

'You should have taken it, Mae. They would have thought you was gone.'

They waited through the afternoon for Zipper Clum, but no vehicles came down the road. The day seemed to have passed without either a sunrise or a sunset, marked only by wind and a grayness that blew like smoke out of the wetlands. But that evening the temperature dropped, sucking the moisture out of the air, fringing the mud puddles with ice that looked like badgers' teeth, and a green-gold light began to rim the horizon.

Mae and Callie ate soda crackers and Vienna sausage out of cans in front of the fireplace, then Callie wiped her hands on a rag and put on a man's suit coat over her sweater and went outside to the privy. When she came back her face and eyes looked burned by the wind.

'Their car's coming, Mae. Lord God, they coming,' she said.

Mae turned and looked through the window, then rose slowly from her chair, the glow of the firelight receding from her body like warmth being withdrawn from her life. She shut her eyes and pressed a wadded handkerchief to her mouth, swallowing, her brow lined with thought or prayer or perhaps self-pity and grief that was of such a level she no longer had to contend with or blame herself for it.

'Get under the bed, you. Don't come out, neither. No matter what you hear out there. This all started when I run off with Mack. The ending ain't gonna change,' she said.

A four-door car that was gray with mud came up the road and stopped in front, and two police officers got out and stood in the dirt yard, not stepping up on the small gallery and knocking or even calling out, but simply reaching back into the car and blowing the horn, as though they would be demeaned by indicating that the home of a mulatto required the same respect and protocol as that of a white person.

Mae straightened the purple suit she still wore and stepped outside, the skin of her face tightening in the cold, her ears filling with the sounds of seagulls that turned in circles above the sugarcane.

'Where's Callie?' the taller of the two officers said.

'She gone to Morgan City with a colored man. She ain't coming back,' Mae answered.

'Would you step out here, please? Don't be afraid,' the officer said.

'People call me Mae Guillory. But my married name is Robicheaux,' she said.

'We know that, ma'am. You saw something we think you don't understand. We want to explain what happened there on the bayou,' he said.

She ran her tongue over her lips to speak, then said nothing, her desire to respect herself as great as her desire to live, her pulse so thunderous she thought a vein would burst in her throat.

'Ladrine Theriot tried to kill a constable. So the constable had to shoot him. It was the constable. You saw it, didn't you?' the officer said. Then he began to speak very slowly, his eyes lingering on hers with each word, waiting for the moment of assent that had not come. 'The constable shot Ladrine Theriot. That's what you saw. There was no mistake about what happened . . . Okay?'

She stepped off the tiny gallery into the yard, as though she were in a dream, not making conscious choices now, stepping into the green light that seemed to radiate out of the fields into the sky.

'Ladrine was a good man. He wasn't like his brother, no. He done right by people. Y'all killed him,' she said.

'Yeah. Because we had to . . . Isn't that right?' he said.

'My name's Mae Robicheaux. My boy fought in Vietnam. My husband was Big Aldous Robicheaux. Nobody in the oil field mess with Big Aldous.'

'We'll take you to where Ladrine died and explain how it happened. Get in the car, ma'am.'

'I know what y'all gonna do. I ain't afraid of y'all no more. My boy gonna find you. You gonna see, you. You gonna run and hide when you see my boy.'

'You are one ignorant bitch, aren't you?' the officer said, and knocked her to the ground.

He unbuttoned his raincoat and exposed his holstered gun. He placed his fists on his hips, his jaw flexing, his raincoat flapping in the wind. Then a decision worked its way into his eyes, and he exhaled air through his nose, like a man resigning himself to a world that he both disdained and served.

'Help me with this,' he said to the other officer.

Mae's face was white and round when the two officers leaned out of the greenness of the evening, out of the creaking and wheeling of land-blown gulls, and fitted their hands on her with the mercy of giant crabs.

22

The next day the Lafourche Parish Sheriff's Department faxed me all their file material on the shooting death of Ladrine Theriot in 1967. The crime scene report was filled with misspellings and elliptical sentences but gave the shooter's name as one Bobby Cale, a part-time constable, barroom bouncer, and collector for a finance agency.

I called the sheriff in Lafourche.

'The shooter wasn't the constable,' I said.

'Says who?' he replied.

'A woman by the name of Mae Guillory saw it happen.'

'You wired up about something?'

When I didn't reply, he said, 'Look, I read that file. The constable tried to serve a bench warrant on Ladrine Theriot and Theriot pulled a gun. Why would the constable take responsibility for a shooting he didn't do?'

'Because he was told to. Two other cops were there. They put a throw-down on the body.'

'I couldn't tell you. I was ten years old when all this happened. You guys running short of open cases in New Iberia?'

'Where's Bobby Cale now?'

'If you're up to it, I'll give you directions to his place. Or you can get them from the Department of Health and Hospitals.'

'What do you mean "if I'm up to it"?'

'Maybe his sins are what got a fence post kicked up his ass. Check it out. Ask yourself if you'd like to trade places with him,' the Lafourche Parish sheriff said.

I drove my pickup truck to Morgan City, then down deep into Terrebonne Parish, toward the Gulf, almost to Point au Fer. The sky was gray and roiling with clouds and I could smell salt spray on the wind. I went down a dirt road full of sinkholes, between thickly canopied woods that were hung with air vines, dotted with palmettos, and drifting with gray leaves. The road ended at a sunless, tin-roofed cypress cabin that was streaked black with rainwater. A man sat in a chair on the front porch, his stomach popping out of his shirt like a crushed white cake, a guitar laid flat on his lap.

When I got out of the truck, the man leaned forward and picked up a straw hat from the porch swing and fitted it low on his head. In the shade his skin had the bloodless discoloration that an albino's might if he bathed in blue ink. He wore steel picks on the fingers of his right hand and the sawed-off, machine-buffed neck of a glass bottle on the index finger of his left. He slid the bottle neck up and down the strings of the guitar and sang, 'I'm going where the water tastes like cherry wine, 'cause the Georgia water tastes like turpentine.'

A mulatto or Indian woman who was shaped like a duck, with Hottentot buttocks and elephantine legs, was hanging wash in back. She turned and looked at me with the flat stare of a frying pan, then spit in the weeds and walked heavily to the privy and went inside and closed the door behind her by fitting a hand through a hole in a board.

'She ain't rude. She's just blind. Preacher tole me once everybody's got somebody,' the man on the porch said. He picked up a burning cigarette from the porch railing and raised it to his mouth. His hand was withered, the fingers crimped together like the dried paw of an animal.

'You Bobby Cale?' I asked.

He pushed his hat up on his forehead and lifted his face, turning it at a slight angle, as though to feel the breeze.

'I look like I might be somebody else?' he said.

'No, sir.'

'I was in Carville fifteen years. That was back in the days when people like me was walled off from the rest of y'all. I run off and lived in Nevada. Wandered in the desert and ate grasshoppers and didn't take my meds and convinced myself I was John the Baptizer come back in modern times. I scared the hell out of people who turned up the wrong dirt road.'

I started to open my badge.

'I know who you are. I know why you're here, too. It won't do you no good,' he said.

'You didn't shoot Ladrine Theriot,' I said.

'The paperwork says otherwise.'

'The two other cops there had on uniforms. They wore black slickers. They made you take their heat because they were from another parish and out of their jurisdiction.'

He threw his cigarette out into the yard and looked into space. His nose was eaten away, the skin of his face drawn back on the bone, the cheeks creased with lines like whiskers on a cat.

'You know a whole lot for a man wasn't there,' he said.

'There was a witness. She used the name Mae Guillory,' I said.

'Everybody's got at least one night in his life that he wants to carry on a shovel to a deep hole in a woods and bury under a ton of dirt. Then for good measure burn the woods down on top of it. I wish I was a drunkard and could just get up and say I probably dreamed it all. I don't remember no witness.'

'The two other cops killed her. Except a hooker saw them do it.'

His eyes held on me for a long time. They were green, uncomplicated, and still seemed to belong inside the round, redneck face of an overweight constable from thirty years ago.

'You got an honest-to-God witness can hold them over the fire?' he said, his eyes lingering on mine.

'She never knew their names. She didn't see their faces well, either.'

The moment went out of his eyes. 'This world's briers and brambles, ain't it?' he said.

'You a churchgoin' man, Mr Cale?'

'Not no more.'

'Why not get square and start over? People won't be hard on you.'

'They killed Mae Guillory? I always thought she just run off,' he said, an unexpected note of sadness in his voice.

I didn't reply. His eyes were hooded, his down-turned nose like the ragged beak of a bird. He pressed the bottle neck down on the frets of the guitar and drew his steel picks across the strings. But his concentration was elsewhere, and his picks made a discordant sound like a fist striking piano keys.

'I had a wife and a little boy once. Owned a house and a truck and had money left over at the end of the month. That's all gone now,' he said.

'Mae Guillory was my mother, Mr Cale. Neither she nor I will rest until the bill's paid.'

He set his guitar in the swing and placed his hat crown-down next to it and pulled the bottle neck and steel picks off his fingers and dropped them tinkling inside the hat.

'The old woman and me is going to eat some lima bean soup. You can stay if you want. But we're done talking on this particular subject,' he said.

'Those cops are still out there, aren't they?' I said.

'Good-bye, sir. Before you judge me, you might be thankful you got what you got,' he said, and went inside the darkness of the cabin and let the screen slam behind him.

Members in the fellowship of Alcoholics Anonymous maintain that alcohol is but the symptom of the disease. It sounds self-serving. It's not.

That night I sat at the counter in the bait shop and watched Clete Purcel use only one thumb to unscrew the cap from a pint bottle of whiskey, then pour two inches into a glass mug and crack open a Dixie for a chaser. He was talking about fishing, or a vacation in Hawaii, or his time in the corps, I don't remember. The beer bottle was dark green, running with moisture, the whiskey in the mug brownish gold, like autumn light trapped inside a hardwood forest.

The air outside was humid and thick with winged insects, and strings of smoke rose from the flood lamps. I opened a can of Dr Pepper but didn't drink it. My hand was crimped tightly around the can, my head buzzing with a sound like a downed wire in a rain puddle.

Clete tilted the glass mug to his mouth and drank the whiskey out of the bottom, then chased it with the beer and wiped his mouth on his palm. His eyes settled on mine, then went away from me and came back.

'Your head's back in that story the black hooker told you,' he said.

'My mother said her name was Mae Robicheaux,' I said.

'What?'

'Before she died, she said her name was Robicheaux. She took back her married name.'

'I'm going to use your own argument against you, Dave. The sonsofbitches who killed your mother are pure evil. Don't let them keep hurting you.'

'I'm going to find out who they are and hunt them down and kill them.'

He screwed the cap back on his whiskey bottle and wrapped the bottle in a paper bag, then drank from his beer and rose from the counter stool and worked the whiskey bottle into his side pocket.

'What are you doing?' I asked.

'Going back to the motel. Leaving you with your family. Taking my booze out of here.'

'That's not the problem.'

'It's not the main one, but you'd like it to be. See you tomorrow, Streak,' he said.

He put on his porkpie hat and went out the door, then I heard his Cadillac start up and roll heavily down the dirt road.

I chained up the rental boats for the night and was turning off the lights when Clete's Cadillac came back down the road and parked at the cement boat ramp. He met me at the end of the dock with a tinfoil container of microwave popcorn in his hand.

'I hate watching TV in a motel room by myself,' he said, and laid his big arm across my shoulders and walked with me up the slope to the house.

Early the next morning I put all the crime scene photos from the Vachel Carmouche homicide in an envelope and drove out to his deserted house on Bayou Teche. I pushed open the back door and once more entered the heated smell of the house. Purple martins, probably from the chimney, were flying blindly against the walls and windows, splattering their droppings on the floors and counters. I swatted them away from my face with a newspaper and closed off the kitchen to isolate the birds in the rest of the house.

Why was I even there? I asked myself. I had no idea what I was looking for.

I squatted down and touched a brownish flake of blood on the linoleum with my ballpoint pen. It crumbled into tiny particles, and I wiped my pen with a piece of Kleenex, then put my pen away and blotted the perspiration off my forehead with my sleeve.

All I wanted to do was get back outside in the wind, under the shade of a tree, out of the smell that Vachel Carmouche seemed to have bled into the woodwork when he died. Maybe I had to stop thinking of Passion and Letty Labiche as victims. I tried to tell myself that sometimes it took more courage to step away from the grief of another than to participate in it.

I felt a puff of cool air rise from the floor and I looked down through a crack in the linoleum, through a rotted plank, at a pool of water under the house with purple martins fluttering their wings in it. Then I realized the birds inside the house had not come from the chimney. But it wasn't the birds that caught my attention. One of the cinder-block pilings was orange with rust that had leaked from a crossbeam onto the stone.

I went back outside and lay flat on my stomach and crawled under the house. Three feet beyond the rear wall, wedged between the crossbeam and the cinder-block piling, was a one-handed weed sickle. I pried it loose and crawled back into the sunlight. The short wood handle was intact, but the half-moon blade had rusted into lace.

I slipped the sickle handle-first into a Ziploc bag and knocked on Passion's door.

'This is the instrument that slung blood on the ceiling and walls. Letty hit him with the mattock and you used this,' I said when Passion came to the door.

'It look like a piece of junk to me,' she said.

'I came out here because I feel an obligation to your sister. But I don't have time for any more of y'all's bullshit. I'm going to bust Little Face Dautrieve as a material witness and make her life miserable. She'll stay in jail until she tells me what happened and in the meantime Social Services will take her baby. Is that how you want it to play out?'

'You seen the paper today?' she asked.

'No.'

'The Supreme Court won't hear any more of Letty's appeals. Unless Belmont Pugh commute her sentence, she's gonna die. You want to know what happened? I'm gonna tell you. Then you can carry it down to your office and do whatever you want to wit' it.'

Her face was wan, her eyes unfocused inside the gloom of the house, as though she didn't recognize the words she had just spoken. But suddenly I felt my victory was about to become ashes in my mouth. She studied my face through the screen, then pushed open the door and waited for me to come inside.

Eight years ago Passion and Letty looked out their side window in dismay at the return of their neighbor, Vachel Carmouche. In their minds he had been assigned to their past, to a world of dreams and aberrant memories that dissipated with time and had no application in their adult lives. Now they watched him blow his gallery clean of birds' nests with a pressure hose while crushing the tiny eggs under his rubber boots; they watched him pry the plywood covering from his windows, hoe out a vegetable patch, and drink lemonade in the shade, a small sip at a time, like a man who was stintful even with his own pleasure, his starched and pressed gray work clothes and gray cloth cap unstained by sweat, as though the rigidity that characterized his life allowed him to control the secretion in his glands.

They left the house and went grocery shopping, hoping somehow he would be gone when they returned and a rental sign would be standing in the yard. Instead, they saw him moving his belongings into the house, ignoring Passion and Letty as though they were not there. They saw him split open a ripe watermelon and ease chunks of it off a knife blade into his mouth, his face suffused with a self-contained sensual glow. In the evening shadows they saw him scythe weeds out of his front yard and fire a barbecue pit and impale a pork roast on its rotisserie; they saw him pack rock salt and ice into a hand-crank ice cream maker, then give a quarter to a twelve-year-old black girl to turn the crank for him. They saw him press the coin into her palm and fold his fingers over her fist and smile down at her, her upraised eyes only inches from his gleaming cowboy belt buckle and the flatness of his stomach and the dry heat that emanated from his clothes.

Letty went into the yard with a paper sack and walked among the trees in front, picking up scraps of paper that had blown off the road. She waited until Carmouche went into his house, then called the little girl over.

'What are you doing around here?' she asked.

'Visiting my auntie up the road,' Little Face replied.

'Go back home. Stay away from that white man.'

'My auntie left me here. She rent from Mr Vachel.'

Letty squatted down and looked directly into Little Face's eyes.

'Has he touched you? Put his hand somewhere he shouldn't?' she said.

'No, ma'am. He ain't like that.'

'You listen to me –' Letty began, squeezing the girl's arm. Then she looked past Little Face's head at the silhouette of Vachel Carmouche, who stood in the drive now, leaves swirling around his shoes, the early moon like a pink wafer in the sky behind him.

He pinched the brim of his cloth cap with two fingers.

'Been a long time. You grown into a handsome woman, Miss Letty,' he said.

'Why'd you come back?' she said.

'A lot of building going on. A man with electrical knowledge can make a good deal of money right now.'

'You get your goddamn feet off my property,' she said.

'You might be righteous now. But you and your sister were always switching your rear ends around when you wanted something.'

'I can't tell you how much I hate you,' Letty said, rising to her feet.

'What you hate are your own sins. Think back, Letty. Remember how you'd turn somersaults on the lawn, grinning and giggling at me? You were thirteen years old when you did that. Now you reprimand me and blaspheme God's name in front of a child.'

Carmouche put his hand in Little Face's and led her back onto his property. The white streaks of cornstarch that had been ironed into his gray clothes recalled an image out of Letty's memory that made her shut her eyes.

Letty worked in the back yard, raking the winter thatch out of her garden, thrusting a spade deep into the black soil, taking a strange pleasure when the blade crushed a slug or cut through the body of a night crawler. Her flannel shirt became heavy with sweat and she flung the spade on the ground and went inside the house and showered with hot water until her skin was as red and grained as old brick.

'We'll try to do something about him tomorrow,' Passion said.

'Do what?' Letty said, tying the belt around her terry-cloth robe.

'Call Social Services. Tell them about the little girl.'

'Maybe they'll hep her like they hepped us, huh?'

'What else you want to do, kill him?' Passion said.

'I wish. I really wish.'

Passion walked over to her sister and put her arms around her. She could smell a fragrance of strawberries in her hair.

'It's gonna be all right. We can make him move away. We're grown now. He cain't hurt us anymore,' she said.

'I want him to pay.'

Passion held her sister against her, stroking her back, feeling her sister's breath on her neck. Through the second-story window she could see down into Vachel Carmouche's backyard. Her face tingled and a bilious taste rose into her mouth.

'What is it?' Letty said, stepping back and looking at her sister's expression. Then she turned around and looked down into Vachel Carmouche's yard.

He had set Little Face on his knee and was feeding ice cream to her with a spoon. Each time he placed the spoon between her lips he smoothed back her hair, then wiped the drippings from the corners of her mouth with the backs of his fingers. He kissed her forehead and filled another spoonful of ice cream and placed a fresh strawberry on it. She opened her mouth like a bird, but he withdrew the spoon quickly, offering and withdrawing it again and again, and finally putting it into her mouth and lifting the spoon handle up so as not to drop any of the melted ice cream on her chin.

Letty charged barefoot down the stairs, tearing the sole of one foot on an exposed nailhead. She found a pair of work shoes in the downstairs closet and leaned against the wall with one arm and pulled them on.

'He used to keep a shotgun,' Passion said.

'He put his hand on it, I'll shove it up his ass. You coming or not?' Letty said.

They went out the back door, into the twilight, into the smell of spring and cut grass and newly turned dirt and night-blooming flowers opening in the cool of the evening. They crossed into Vachel Carmouche's property, expecting to see him on his back porch with the little girl, expecting to confront and verbally lacerate him for a deed he had committed out in the open, upon the person of a third victim, a deed he could not possibly deny, as though Passion's and Letty's knowledge of their own molestation had long ago lost its viability and had to be corroborated by the suffering of another in order to make it believable.

But Carmouche was nowhere in sight. The little girl sat on the back step, coloring in a crayon book.

'What did he do to you, honey?' Letty said.

'Ain't done nothing. He gone inside to eat his dinner,' the girl replied.

'Did he touch you?' Passion said.

The little girl did not look back at them. A bright silver dime was on the step by her shoe.

'Mr Vachel gonna take me up to the video store to get some cartoons,' she said.

'You come home wit' us. We'll call your auntie,' Letty said.

'She at work. I ain't suppose to go nowhere except Mr Vachel's.'

Letty mounted the steps and shoved open the back door. Carmouche was sitting at the kitchen table, his back erect, his whole posture as rectangular as his chair, a fork poised in front of his mouth. He laid the fork down and picked up a glass of yellow wine.

'I'd appreciate it if you'd show some respect toward my home,' he said.

'You sonofabitch,' she said, and stepped inside the room. When she did, the belt around her waist came loose and her terry-cloth robe fell open on her body.

Carmouche's eyes moved over her breasts and stomach and thighs. He sipped from his wine and pushed back his chair and crossed his legs.

'Some say love's the other side of hate. You're a beautiful woman, Letty. An older man can bring a woman pleasure a younger man cain't,' he said, his voice growing more hoarse with each word.

He rose from his chair and approached her, his eyes liquid and warm under the bare electric light. She clutched her robe with one hand and stepped backwards, then felt her work shoe come down on the iron head of the mattock that was propped against the wall, knocking the handle into her back.

She reached behind her and picked the mattock up with both hands, her robe falling open again, and swung it into his face.

His nose broke and slung a string of blood across his shoulder. He stared at her in disbelief and she hit him again, this time directly in his overbite, breaking his upper teeth at the gums. His face quivered as though he had been electrically shocked, then the thousands of tiny wrinkles in his face flattened with rage and he attacked her with his fists.

He swung wildly, like a girl, but he was strong and driven by his pain and the disfigurement she had already done his face and she knew it was only a matter of time until he wrested the mattock from her.

His hands locked on the handle, his nose draining blood across his mouth, his broken teeth like ragged pieces of ceramic in his gums. She closed her eyes against the stench of his breath.

Passion picked up the weed sickle from the porch step and came through the door and drove the curved point into Carmouche's back, pushing with the heel of her hand against the dull side of the blade. His mouth fell open and his chin jutted upward like a man who had been garroted. He fell backwards, stumbling, reaching behind him with one hand as though he could insert a thumb in the hole that was stealing the air from his lung.

He collapsed on one knee, his eyes suddenly luminous, like a man kneeling inside a cave filled with specters whose existence he had long ago forgotten.

Letty hit him again and again with the mattock while Passion shut the back door so the little girl could not see inside the house. Letty's robe and work shoes and arms and thighs were splattered with Carmouche's blood, but her violence and anger found no satiation, and a muted, impotent cry came from between her teeth each time she swung the mattock.

Passion put her hand on her sister's shoulder and moved her away from Carmouche's body.

'What? What is it?' Letty said, as though awakening from a trance.

Passion didn't reply. Instead, she lifted the sickle above her head and looked into Carmouche's eyes.

'Don't ... please,' he said, his hand fluttering toward his cowboy belt buckle.

Then Passion's arm came down and Letty pressed both her forearms against her ears so she would not hear the sound that came from his throat.

23

I went home instead of returning to the office. I sat at one of the spool tables on the dock, the Cinzano umbrella popping in the breeze above my head, and looked at the blue jays flying in and out of the cypress and willow trees. I watched the clouds marble the swamp with shadow and light, and the wind from the Gulf straightening the moss on the dead snags. I stayed there a long time, although I didn't look at my watch, like a person who has strayed unknowingly into the showing of a pornographic film and would like to rinse himself of a new and unwanted awareness about human behavior.

The story of Carmouche's death was repellent. I wished I had not heard it, and I wished I did not have to make decisions about it.

I walked up to the house and told Bootsie of my morning with Passion Labiche.

She didn't say anything for perhaps a full minute. She got up from the kitchen table and stood at the sink and looked into the yard.

'What are you going to do?' she asked, her back to me.

'Nothing she told me can help her sister.'

'You have the sickle in the truck?'

'I put it back under the house.'

I went to the stove and poured a cup of coffee. She turned around and followed me with her eyes.

'You're going across a line, Dave,' she said.

'I virtually coerced a confession out of her. I don't know if Carmouche deserved to die the way he did, but I know the girls didn't deserve what happened to them.'

She walked to the stove and slipped her hand down my forearm and hooked her fingers under my palm.

'You know what I would do?' she said.

'What?' I said, turning to look at her.

'Start the day over. You set out to help Passion and Letty. Why bring them more harm? If Letty were tried today, she might go free. You want to enable a process that's already ignored the injury done to two innocent children?'

Bootsie was forever the loyal friend and knew what to say in order to make me feel better. But the real problem was one that went beyond suppression of non-exculpatory evidence in a crime of eight years ago. I was tired of daily convincing myself that what I did for a living made a difference.

I fixed a ham and onion sandwich for myself and ate it on the picnic table in the backyard. A few minutes later Bootsie came outside and sat down across from me, a small cardboard box in her hand.

'I hate to hit you with this right now, but this came in the morning mail. Alafair left it on her bed. I shouldn't have read the letter, but I did when I saw the name at the bottom,' she said.

The box was packed with tissue paper and contained a six-inch-high ceramic vase that was painted with miniature climbing roses and a Confederate soldier and a woman in a hoop dress holding each other's hands in an arbor of live oaks. The detail and the contrast of gray and red and green were beautiful inside the glazed finish.

The letter, handwritten on expensive stationery and folded in a neat square, read:

Dear Alafair,

I hope you don't think too badly of me by this time. Your father cares for you and wants to protect you, so I don't hold his feelings toward me against him. This is the vase I was working on. I tried to make the girl look like you. What do you think? You can't see the face of the Confederate soldier. I'll let you imagine who he is.

I wish I could have lived in a time like the soldier and the girl on the vase did. People back then were decent and had honor and looked after each other.

You're one of the best people I ever met. If you ever need me, I promise I will be there for you. Nobody will ever make me break that promise.

Your devoted friend from the library,
Johnny

'Where is she?' I asked.

'At the swimming pool.' Bootsie watched my face. 'What are you thinking?'

'That boy is definitely not a listener.'

I went back to the office and placed another call to the psychologist at the Florida State Penitentiary in Raiford. It wasn't long before I knew I was talking to one of those condescending, incompetent bureaucrats whose sole purpose is to hold on to their jobs and hide their paucity of credentials.

'You're asking me if he has obsessions?' the psychologist said.

'In a word, yeah.'

'We don't have an adequate vocabulary to describe what some of these people have.'

'You don't have to convince me of that,' I said.

'He was a suspect in a killing here. A gasoline bomb thrown inside another inmate's cell. Your man was probably raped. You were faxed everything we have. I don't know what else to tell you about him.'

'Wait a minute. You didn't know him?'

'No. I thought you all understood that. Dr Louvas worked with O'Roarke, or Remeta, as you call him. Dr Louvas is at Marion now.'

'Excuse me for seeming impatient, but why didn't you tell me that?'

'You didn't ask. Is there anything else?'

I called the federal lockup at Marion, Illinois, and got Dr Louvas on the phone. His was a different cut from his colleague in Florida.

'Yeah, I remember Johnny well. Actually I liked him. I wouldn't suggest having him over for dinner, though,' he said.

'How's that?'

'He has two or three personalities. Oh, I don't mean he suffers dissociation, or any of that *Three Faces of Eve* stuff. He has an abiding sense of anger that he refuses to deal with. If he'd gotten help earlier, he might have turned out to be a writer or artist instead of a candidate for a lobotomy.'

'Because he was raped in prison?'

'His father would take him to a blind pig on skid row. That's what they call after-hours places in Detroit. According to Johnny, a couple of pedophiles would use him while the old man got drunk on their tab. Family values hadn't made a big splash in the Detroit area yet.'

'So he's hung up over his father?'

'You got it all wrong, Mr Robicheaux. He doesn't blame the father for what happened to him. He thinks the mother betrayed him. He's never gotten over what he perceives as her failure.'

'He's making overtures to my daughter.'

There was no response.

'Are you there?' I asked.

'You're asking me to tell you his future? My bet is Johnny will do himself in one day. But he'll probably take others with him,' the psychologist said.

The next morning I drove to Baton Rouge and went to Connie Deshotel's office. The secretary told me Connie used her lunch hour on Thursdays to play racquetball at a nearby club.

The club was dazzling white, surrounded with palm trees that were planted in white gravel; the swimming pool in back was an electric blue under the noon sun. Inside the building, I looked down through a viewing glass onto the hardwood floor of a racquetball court and watched Connie take apart her male opponent. She wore tennis shoes with green tubes of compressed air molded into the rubber soles, a pleated tennis skirt, and a sleeveless yellow jersey that was ringed under the neck and arms with sweat. Her tanned calves hardened with muscle when she bent to make a kill shot.

Her opponent, a tall, graying, athletic man, gave it up, shook hands good-naturedly, and left. She bounced the rubber ball once, served the ball to herself off the wall, then fired it into a low ricochet that sent it arching over her head, as though she were involved in a private celebration of her victory. Her eyes followed the ball's trajectory until they met mine. Then her face tightened, and she pushed her hair out of her eyes and left the court through a door in the back wall, slamming it behind her.

I went down the stairs and intercepted her in the lounge area.

'I have some information about my mother's death,' I said.

'Not here.'

'You're not going to put me off, Connie.'

'What is it?'

I gestured at a table.

'I'm leaving here in two minutes. But I'll make you a promise. You follow me anywhere again and I'll have you arrested,' she said.

'I have a witness.'

'To what?'

'My mother's murder. Two cops in uniform did it. In front of a cabin a few miles off Purple Cane Road in Lafourche Parish. One of them called her an ignorant bitch before he knocked her down.'

Her eyes stared into mine, unblinking, her lashes like black wire. Then they broke and she looked at nothing and pulled the dampness of her jersey off the tops of her breasts.

'Bring your witness forward,' she said.

'Nope.'

'Why not?'

'I think the individual would end up dead,' I said.

'You don't want to indicate the person's gender to me? I'm the attorney general of the state. What's the matter with you?'

'You trust Don Ritter. I don't. I think he tried to have both me and Johnny Remeta killed.'

She motioned at a black waiter in a white jacket. He nodded and began pouring a club soda into a glass of ice for her. She touched the sweat off her eyes with a towel and hung the towel around her neck.

'I'll say it again. My office is at your disposal. But a lot of this sounds like paranoia and conspiratorial obsession,' she said.

'The cops were NOPD.'

'How do you know this?'

'They killed a Lafourche Parish nightclub owner named Ladrine Theriot and made a local constable take the weight. They weren't backwoods coon-asses, either. They were enforcers and bagmen for the Giacanos. So if they weren't New Orleans cops, where did they come from?'

She took the club soda from the waiter's hand and drank it half-empty. The heat seemed to go out of her face but not her eyes.

'You have a larger agenda, Dave. I think it has something to do with me,' she said.

'Not me. By the way, you play a mean game of racquetball for a woman who smokes.'

'How kind.'

'The other day I noticed your gold and leather cigarette lighter. Did Jim Gable give you that? Y'all must be pretty tight.'

She got up from the table with her club soda in her hand.

'My apologies to Bootsie for saying this, but you're the most annoying person I've ever met,' she said, and walked toward the dressing room, her pleated skirt swishing across the tops of her thighs.

'You *read* my mail?' Alafair said. It was evening, the sun deep down in the trees now, and she was grooming Tex, her Appaloosa, in the railed lot by his shed. She stared at me across his back.

'The letter was lying on your bed. Bootsie saw Johnny's name on it. It was inadvertent,' I replied.

'You didn't have the right to read it.'

'Maybe not. Maybe you know what you're doing. But I believe he's a dangerous man.'

'Not the Johnny O'Roarke I know.'

'You always stood up for your friends, Alafair. But this guy is not a friend. The prison psychologist said he's a sick man who will probably die by his own hand and take other people with him.'

'Bullshit, bullshit, bullshit.'

'How about it on the language?'

'You admit he saved our lives, but you run him down and take his head apart, a person you don't know anything about, then you tell me to watch my language. I just don't expect crap like that from my father.'

'Has he tried to see you?'

'I'm not going to tell you. It's none of your business.'

'Remeta's a meltdown, Alf.'

'Don't call me that stupid name! God!' she said, and threw down the brush she had been using on Tex and stormed inside the house.

That night I dreamed about a sugar harvest in the late fall and mule-drawn wagons loaded with cane moving through the fog toward the mill. The dirt road was frozen hard and littered with stalks of sugarcane, and the fog rolled out of the unharvested cane on each side of the road like colorless cotton candy and coated the mules' and drivers' backs with moisture. Up ahead the tin outline of the mill loomed against the grayness of the sky, and inside I could hear the sounds of boilers overheating and iron machines that pulverized the cane into pulp. Immediately behind the mill a stubble fire burned in a field, creeping in serpentine red lines through the mist.

The dream filled me with a fear I could not explain. But I knew, with a terrible sense of urgency, I could not allow myself to go farther down the road, into the mill and the grinding sounds of its machinery and the fire and curds of yellow smoke that rose from the field beyond.

The scene changed, and I was on board my cabin cruiser at dawn, on West Cote Blanche Bay, and the fogbank was heavy and cold on the skin, sliding with the tide into the coastline. To the north I could see Avery Island, like two green humps in the mist, as smooth and firm-looking as a woman's breasts. The waves burst in strings of foam against the white sleekness of the bow, and I could smell the salt spray inside my head and bait fish in a bucket and the speckled trout that arched out of the waves and left circles like rain rings in the stillness of the swells.

When I woke I went into the kitchen and sat in the dark, my loins aching and my palms tingling on my thighs. I held a damp hand towel to my eyes and tried to think but couldn't. Even though I was awake now, I did not want to look at the meaning behind the dreams. I went back to bed and felt

Bootsie stir, then touch my chest and turn on her hip and mold her body against me.

She was already wet when I entered her, and she widened her thighs and hooked her feet loosely inside my legs, slipping one hand down to the small of my back while she moved in a slow, circular fashion under me, as she always did when she wanted to preserve the moment for both of us as long as she could.

But I felt the heat rise in me, like fire climbing upward along a hard, bare surface, then my mouth opened involuntarily and I closed my eyes and pressed my face between her breasts.

I sat on the edge of the bed, depleted, my face in shadow, one hand still covering the tops of Bootsie's fingers, ashamed that I had used my wife to hide from the violent act I knew my alcoholic mind was planning.

24

Early Sunday morning I heard a car with a blown muffler pull into the drive and continue to the back of the house before the driver cut the engine. I slipped on my khakis and went into the kitchen and looked into the backyard and saw Clete Purcel sitting alone at the redwood picnic table, his Marine Corps utility cap on his head. He had a take-out cup of coffee between his hands, and he kept looking over his shoulder at the dirt road.

I went outside and eased the screen shut so as not to wake Bootsie and Alafair.

'What are you doing?' I asked.

He looked sideways, then pulled on his nose and let his breath out.

'I went after Ritter. Nobody's been by?'

'No.'

'The shit went through the fan.'

'I don't want to know about it.'

'I was trying to help. You got somebody else willing to cover your back on a daily basis?'

He looked miserable. He rubbed his face, then knocked over his paper cup and spilled coffee on his hands.

'Tell me,' I said.

'Ritter had dials on this stripper, Janet Gish. She'd been washing stolen money at the Indian casinos for some Jersey wise guys. Ritter nailed the wise guys but he left her out of the bust. The deal was she had to come across for him at least once a month. Guess what? Janet developed the hots for Ritter, can you believe it? So he knew he had a good thing and he played along with her and said he was going to marry her as soon as he could dump his wife. In the meantime he was bopping Janet every Friday afternoon at a motel on Airline.

'Last week she's in the supermarket and who does she see? Ritter and his old lady. Ritter looks right through Janet and studies these cans of beans on the shelf like he's never seen one before. But what's Ritter supposed to do? she asks herself. Introduce her? Except she's in the next aisle now and she hears Ritter's old lady say, "Did you see that? She's got jugs like gallon milk bottles. With tattoos yet. You didn't notice?"

'Ritter says, "I was never attracted to Elsie the Cow types." They both thought that was a real laugh.

'Janet decides it's payback time. She's got a bond on a soliciting charge with Nig and Wee Willie and she calls me up and asks if I can get the DA to cut her loose on the soliciting beef if she gives up Ritter. I told her that was a possibility but the DA would probably make her take the weight on the money laundering deal and maybe there was a better way to spike Ritter's cannon.

'I got her to call up Ritter's old lady at midnight and tell her she was sorry Don didn't introduce the two of them at the supermarket because they probably have a lot in common. Then Janet goes into detail about Ritter's sex habits and says it's too bad Ritter uses the same old tired line with all his broads, namely that his wife is a drag at home and an embarrassment at departmental social functions and he's shit-canning her as soon as he can make sure all the bills and charge accounts are under her name.

'It took about ten minutes for Ritter to come tearing across the bridge to Janet's place on the West Bank. She dead-bolted the back door on him and he got a ball peen hammer out of his convertible and started smashing the glass out of the door and trying to get his hand on the lock. That's when I clocked him with the bird bath.'

'You hit him with a cement bird bath?' I said.

'Hear me out, okay? Janet's brother owns this car wash behind the apartment. Ritter's half out of it, so I put him in the passenger seat of his convertible and hooked him up to the door handle with his cuffs and drove him up to the car wash entrance.

'I go, "Don, you're a dirty cop. Now's the time to rinse your sins, start over again, try keeping your flopper in your pants for a change. You set up that gig on the Atchafalaya and almost got my podjo, Dave, killed, didn't you?"

'He goes, "No matter how this comes out, you're still a skell, Purcel."

'So I drove his convertible onto the conveyor and pushed all the buttons for the super clean and hot wax job. The pressure hoses came on and those big brushes dipped down inside the car and were scouring Ritter into the seats. I shut it down and gave him another chance, but he started yelling and blowing the horn, so I turned everything back on and stalled the conveyor and left him there with the steam blowing out both ends of the building.'

'You're telling me Ritter's still in there?' I said.

'Yes and no.' His mouth was cone-shaped when he breathed through it. 'I had my hands full. Janet was getting hysterical and breaking things and throwing her clothes in a suitcase. Then I heard two popping sounds, like firecrackers in the rain. I went back to the car wash but there wasn't anybody around. Except Ritter floating face-down in all that soap and wax. He'd taken one in the ear and one through the mouth.'

I got up from the table and looked out at my neighbor's field and at the fog rising out of the coulee, my back turned to Clete so he couldn't see my face.

When I turned around again Clete's eyes were jittering with light, his lips moving uncertainly, like a drunk coming off a bender when he doesn't know whether he should laugh or not at what he has done.

674

Then his eyes fixed on mine and his expression went flat and he said, as though by explanation, 'This one went south on me.'

'Yeah, I guess it did, Clete.'

'That's all you're going to say?'

'Come inside. I'll fix you something to eat,' I said as I walked past him toward the house.

'Streak? . . . Damn it, don't give me that look.'

But I went through the kitchen into the bath and brushed my teeth and put cold water on my face and tried not to think the thoughts I was thinking or take my anger out on a friend who had put himself in harm's way on my account. But I believed Ritter'd had knowledge about my mother's death and now it was gone.

I dried my face and went back into the kitchen.

'You want me to boogie?' Clete said.

'Get the skillet out of the cabinet, then call Nig and Wee Willie and tell them you'll need a bond,' I said as I took a carton of eggs and a slab of bacon from the icebox.

After we ate breakfast, Bootsie, Alafair, and I went to Mass. When we got back, Clete was down at the dock, sitting at a spool table under an umbrella, reading the newspaper. From a distance he looked like a relaxed and content man enjoying the fine day, but I knew better. Clete had no doubt about the gravity of his actions. Once again his recklessness had empowered his enemies and he now hung by a spider's thread over the maw of the system.

Television programs treat the legal process as an intelligent and orderly series of events that eventually punishes the guilty and exonerates the innocent. The reality is otherwise. The day you get involved with the law is the day you lose all control over your life. What is dismissed by the uninitiated as 'a night in jail' means sitting for an indeterminable amount of time in a holding cell, with a drain hole in the floor, looking at hand-soiled walls scrawled with pictures of genitalia, listening to other inmates yell incoherently down the corridors while cops yell back and clang their batons on the bars.

You ask permission to use a toilet. When you run out of cigarettes or matches, you beg them off a screw through the bars. Your *persona*, your identity, and all the social courtesy you take for granted are removed from your existence like the skin being pulled off a banana. When you look through a window onto the street, you realize you do not register on the periphery of what are called free people. Your best hope of getting back outside lies with a bondsman who secretes Vitalis through his pores or a twenty-four-hour Yellow Pages lawyer who wears zircon rings on his fingers and keeps a breath mint on his tongue. We're only talking about day one.

That afternoon I finally got Dana Magelli on the phone.

'Clete says the entry wounds look like they came from a .22 or .25,' I said.

'Thank him for his feedback on that.'

'He didn't do it, Dana. It was a professional hit. I think we're talking about Johnny Remeta.'

'Except Purcel has a way of stringing elephant shit behind him everywhere he goes.'

'You want me to bring him in?'

'Take a guess.'

'We'll be there in three hours.'

There was a long silence and I knew Magelli's basic decency was having its way with him.

'IAD has been looking at Ritter for a month. Tell Purcel to come in and give a statement. Then get him out of town,' he said.

'Pardon?'

'Janet Gish confirms his story. We don't need zoo creatures muddying up the water right now. You hearing me?'

'You're looking at some other cops?'

He ignored my question. 'I mean it about Purcel. He's not just a pain in the ass. In my view he's one cut above the clientele in Angola. He mixes in our business again, I'll turn the key on him myself,' Magelli said.

I replaced the receiver in the phone cradle on top of the counter in the bait shop. Through the screen window I could see Clete at a spool table, watching an outboard pass on the bayou, his face divided by sunlight and shadow. I walked outside the bait shop and looked down at him.

'That was Dana Magelli. You're going to skate,' I said.

He beamed at me, and I realized all the lessons he should have learned had just blown away in the breeze.

The next day NOPD matched the .25 caliber rounds taken from Don Ritter's body to the .25 caliber round that was fired into Zipper Clum's forehead.

That night Alafair went with friends to the McDonald's on East Main. She came home later than we expected her and gave no explanation. I followed her into her bedroom. Tripod was outside the screen on the windowsill, but she had made no effort to let him in. The light was off in the room and Alafair's face was covered with shadow.

'What happened tonight?' I asked.

'Whenever I tell you the truth about something, it makes you mad.'

'I've shown bad judgment, Alafair. I'm just not a good learner sometimes.'

'I saw Johnny. I took a ride with him.'

I ran my hand along the side of my head. I could feel a tightening in my veins, as though I had a hat on. I took a breath before I spoke.

'With Remeta?' I said.

'Yes.'

'He's wanted in another shooting. An execution at point-blank range in a car wash.'

'I told him I couldn't see him again. I'm going to sleep now, Dave. I don't want to talk about Johnny anymore,' she said.

She sat on the edge of her bed and waited for me to go out of the room. On the shelf above her bedstead I could see the painted ceramic vase Remeta had given to her, the Confederate soldier and his antebellum girlfriend glowing in the moonlight.

The call came at four in the morning.

'You told your daughter not to see me again?' the voice asked.

'Not in so many words,' I replied.

'That was a chickenshit thing to do.'

'You're too old for her, Johnny.'

'People can't be friends because they're apart in years? Run your lies on somebody else.'

'Your problems began long before we met. Don't take them out on us.'

'What do you know about my problems?'

'I talked with the prison psychologist.'

'I'm starting to construct a new image of you, Mr Robicheaux. It's not a good one.'

I didn't reply. The skin of my face felt flaccid and full of needles. Then, to change the subject, I said, 'You should have lost the .25 you used on Zipper Clum. NOPD has made you for the Ritter hit.'

'Ritter gave up your mother's killers, Mr Robicheaux. I was gonna give you their names. Maybe even cap them for you. But you act like I'm the stink on shit. Now I say fuck you,' he said, and hung up.

At 9 a.m. I sat in the sheriff's office and watched the sheriff core out the inside of his pipe with a pen knife.

'So you got to see the other side of Johnny Remeta?' he said, and dropped the black build-up of ash off his knife blade into the waste basket.

'He pumped Ritter for information, then blew out his light,' I said.

'This guy is making us look like a collection of web-toed hicks, Dave. He comes and goes when he feels like it. He takes your daughter for rides. He murders a police officer and calls you up in the middle of the night and tells you about it. Forgive me for what I'm about to say next.'

'Sir?'

'Do you want this guy out on the ground? It seems you and he and Purcel have the same enemies.'

'I don't think that's a cool speculation to make, Sheriff.'

'Let me put it this way. The next time I hear this guy's name, it had better be in conjunction with either his arrest or death. I don't want one of my detectives telling me about his phone conversations with a psychopath or his family's involvement with same. Are we clear?'

'There're pipe ashes on your boot,' I said, and left the room.

Ten minutes later I received a phone call from a woman who did not identify herself but just started talking as though I already knew who she was. She had a heavy Cajun accent and her voice was knotted with anger and dismay and a need to injure.

'I t'ought you'd like to know what you done. Not that it makes no difference to somebody who t'inks he got the right to twist a sick man up wit' his words,' she said.

'Who is this?' I asked.

677

But she kept wading in. 'You was a lot smarter than him, you. You know how to put t'oughts in somebody's head, make him full of guilt, fix it so he cain't go nowhere in his head except t'rew one door. So it ain't enough leprosy eat him up and turn his hands to nutria feet. Man like you got to come along and push him and push him and push him till he so full of misery he gonna do what you want.'

Then I remembered the duck-shaped blind woman who had been hanging wash behind the cabin of Bobby Cale, the ex-constable, down by Point au Fer.

'Did something happen to Bobby?' I said.

She couldn't answer. She started weeping into the phone.

'Ma'am, tell me what it is,' I said.

'I smelled it on the wind. Out in the persimmon trees. He was gone t'ree days, then I found him and touched him and he swung in my hands, light as bird shell. You done this, suh. Don't be telling yourself you innocent, no. 'Cause you ain't.'

The side of my head felt numb after I hung up, as though a dirty revelation about myself had just been whispered in my ear. But I wasn't sure if my sense of regret was over the possibility that I was a contributing factor in the suicide of Bobby Cale or the fact I had just lost my only tangible lead back to my mother's killers.

25

The Shrimp Festival was held each year at the end of summer down by the bay. On Friday, when the day cooled and the summer light filled the evening sky, shrimp boats festooned with pennants and flags blew their horns in the canal and a cleric blessed the fleet while thousands wandered up and down a carnival midway, drinking from beer cups and eating shrimp off paper plates. College students, the working classes, and politicians from all over the state took part. Inside the cacophony of calliopes and the popping of .22 rifles in the shooting galleries and the happy shrieks that cascaded down from a Ferris wheel, the celebrants took on the characteristics of figures in a Brueghel painting, any intimations about mortality they may have possessed now lost in the balm of the season.

Belmont Pugh was there, and Jim Gable and his wife, and by the Tilt-a-Whirl I saw Connie Deshotel in an evening dress, carrying a pair of silver shoes in one hand, her other on her escort's arm for balance, her cleavage deep with shadow.

But the figure who caught my eye was outside the circle of noise and light that rose into the sky from the midway. Micah, Cora Gable's chauffeur, sat beside the Gables' limo on a folding canvas stool, tossing pieces of dirt at a beer can, his jaws slack, like a man who doesn't care what others think of his appearance or state of mind. A rolled comic book protruded from the side pocket of his black coat.

I left Bootsie at the drink pavilion and walked into the parking area and stood no more than three feet in front of him. He raised his eyes, then tinked a dirt clod against the beer can, his face indifferent.

'Looks like you're in the dumps, partner,' I said.

He flexed his mouth, as though working a bit of food out of his gums. 'I'm finishing out my last week,' he replied.

'You're not working for Ms Gable anymore?'

'She thinks I sassed her. It was a misunderstanding. But I guess it helped her husband.'

'Sassed her?'

'We were passing all these shacks where the sugarcane workers used to live. Ms Perez says to herself, "The glory that was Rome."'

'So I say, "It sure wasn't any glory, was it?"'

'She says, "Beg your pardon?"'

'I say, "Rich man got the poor whites to fight with the coloreds so the whole bunch would work for near nothing while the rich man got richer." It got real quiet in the car.'

'Sounds like you got your hand on it, Micah,' I said.

'Tell me about it,' he said resentfully. 'I looked in the rearview mirror and her face was tight as paper, like it had got slapped. She says, "This land belonged to my family. So I suggest you keep your own counsel."'

He removed the comic book from his pocket and tapped it in his palm, his anger seeming to rise and fall, as though it could not find an acceptable target.

'Doesn't seem like that's enough to get a person fired,' I said.

'Gable's been acting good to her lately. I think she's gonna let him have the money to build that racetrack out in New Mexico. I had to be a smart ass at the wrong time and give him what he needed to get me canned.'

'You cut up Axel Jennings, Micah?'

He opened his comic book and flopped the pages back on his knee, thinking, his deformed face like a melted candied apple in the glow from the midway.

'You're always trying to get another inch, aren't you? I'll give you something better to chew on,' he said. 'You know a woman named Maggie Glick, runs a bar full of colored whores in Algiers? It was Jim Gable got her out of prison. Gable's got a whole network of whores and dope peddlers working for him. That's the man gonna be head of your state police, Mr Robicheaux. Play your cards right and there might be a little pissant job in it for you somewhere.'

He smiled at the corner of his mouth, a glint in his good eye.

'Some people enjoy the role of victim. Maybe you've found what you were looking for, after all,' I said, and walked away, wondering if I, too, possessed a potential for cruelty I had chosen not to recognize.

When I returned to the pavilion I realized I had made a mistake. Belmont Pugh had cornered Connie Deshotel and Bootsie and there was no easy way of getting away from the situation. Belmont had launched into one of his oratorical performances, guffawing, gesturing at the air like Huey Long, slinging shrimp tails out into the darkness, the damp rawness of his body reaching out like a fist. He squeezed Connie with one arm while his wife, a black-haired woman with recessed dark eyes and a neck like a hog, looked on sternly, as though her disapproval of Belmont's behavior somehow removed her from all the machinations and carnival vulgarity that had placed her and her husband in the governor's mansion.

Sookie Motrie stood at Belmont's elbow, dressed in the two-tone boots and clothes of a horse tout at a western track, his salt-and-pepper mustache clipped and trim, his snubbed, hawk nose moving about like a weather vane. For years he had been an ambulance chaser in Baton Rouge and had self-published a detective novel that he tried to unload on every movie representative who visited the area. But he had found his true level as well as success when he became a lobbyist for Vegas and Chicago gambling interests.

Even though he had been indicted twice on RICO charges, no door in the state legislature or at any of the regulatory agencies was closed to him.

He laughed when Belmont did and listened attentively to Belmont's coarse jokes, but still managed to watch everyone passing by and to shake the hand, even if quickly, of anyone he deemed important.

Jim and Cora Gable stood at the makeshift plank bar that sold mint juleps in plastic cups for three dollars. He wore a pale pink shirt and dark tie with roses on it and a white sports coat, his face glowing with the perfection of the evening. No, that's too simple. I had to hand it to Gable. He exuded the confidence and self-satisfaction of those who know that real power lies in not having to demonstrate its possession. Every gesture, every mannerism, was like an extension of his will and his ability to charm, a statement about a meticulous personality that allowed no exception to its own rules. He walked toward Belmont's circle and lifted a sprig of mint from his drink and shook the drops from the leaves, bending slightly so as not to spot his shoes.

Cora Gable started to raise her hand, her lipsticked mouth twisting with alarm, like someone left behind unexpectedly at a bus stop. But almost on cue, as though Gable were privy to all the unconscious anxieties that drove her life, he turned and said, 'I'll be just a minute, sweetheart. Order another julep.'

Belmont asked Connie if she knew Jim Gable.

'I'm not sure. Maybe we met years ago,' she replied.

'How do you do, Miss Connie? It's good to see you,' Gable said.

They did not look directly at each other again; they even stepped backwards at the same time, like people who have nothing in common.

I stared at the two of them, as though the moment had been caught inside a cropped photograph whose meaning lay outside the borders of the camera's lens. Both Gable and Connie had come up through the ranks at NOPD back in the late 1960s. How could they have no specific memory of each other?

Then Connie Deshotel lit a cigarette, as though she were distracted by thoughts that would not come together in her mind. But she did not have the lighter I had seen her use by her swimming pool, the one that was identical to the thin leather and gold lighter owned by Jim Gable.

His face split with his gap-toothed smile.

'It's the Davester,' he said.

'I was just talking with your chauffeur about your friendship with Maggie Glick,' I said.

'*Maggie*, my favorite madam,' he said.

'You got her out of prison?' I said.

'Right again, Davester. A wrong narc planted crystal on her. It's a new day in the department. Too bad you're not with us anymore,' he replied.

It started to rain, thudding on top of the tents, misting on the neon and the strings of electric lights over the rides. A barman dropped a tarp on one side of the drink pavilion, and the air was sweet and cool in the dryness of the enclosure and I could smell the draft beer and whiskey and mint and sweet syrup and melted ice in the plastic cups along the bar.

'Remember me, Dave?' Sookie Motrie said, and put out his hand. After my hand was firmly inside his, he locked down on my fingers and winked and said, 'When I used to write bonds for Wee Willie Bimstine, I went to see you in the lockup once. I think you were doing extra-curricular research. Back in your days of wine and roses.'

I took my hand from his and looked out into the rain, then said to Bootsie, 'I promised Alf we'd be back early. I'll get the car and swing around behind the pavilion.'

I didn't wait for her to answer. I walked into the rain, out beyond the noise of the revelers in the tents and the rides whose buckets and gondolas spun and dipped emptily under the electric lights.

You just walk away. It's easy, I thought. You don't provoke, you don't engage. You keep it simple and your adversaries never have power over you.

I started Bootsie's car and drove through the mud toward the drink pavilion. Cora Gable had disappeared, but Jim Gable was at the plank bar, standing just behind Bootsie.

I kept working my 12-Step Program inside my head, the way a long-distance ocean swimmer breathes with a concentrated effort to ensure he does not swallow water out of a wave and drown. I told myself I did not have to live as I once did. I did not have to re-create the violent moments that used to come aborning like a sulfurous match flaring off a thumbnail.

Through the rain and the beating of the windshield wipers I saw Jim Gable standing so close behind Bootsie that his shadow seemed to envelop her body. She was dabbing with a napkin at a spot on the plank bar where she had spilled a drink and was evidently not aware of his closeness, or the way his loins hovered just behind her buttocks, the glaze that was on his face.

I stopped the car and stepped out into the rain, the car door yawing behind me.

Gable's nostrils were dilated as he breathed in the smell of Bootsie's shampoo, the perfume behind her ears, the soap from her bath, the heat off her skin, the hint of her sex in her underthings. I could see the cloth of his slacks tightening across his loins.

Then I was running out of the rain toward him. I hit him so hard spittle and blood flew from his mouth onto a woman's blouse four feet away. I drove my fist into his kidney, a blow that made his back arch as though his spine had been broken, then I hooked him with a left below the eye and drove a right cross into his jaw that knocked him across a folding table.

A man I didn't know grabbed my arm, and a big uniformed policeman crashed into me from the other side, wrestling with both of his big meaty hands to get his arms around me and smother me against his girth. But even while the two men tried to pull me off of Gable, I kicked him in the side of the head and kicked at him once more and missed his face and shattered his watch on the cement.

I fell over a chair and stared stupidly at the faces looking down at me, like a derelict who has collapsed on a sidewalk and must witness from the cement the pity and revulsion he inspires in his fellowman. Bootsie was between me and Gable now, her face incredulous. A wet cigarette butt clung to my cheek like a mashed cockroach. I could smell whiskey and beer in my clothes and Gable's blood on my knuckles and I swore I could taste whiskey surging out of my stomach into my throat, like an old friend who has come back in a time of need.

Through the sweat and water that dripped out of my hair I saw the governor and people from the crowd lifting Jim Gable to his feet. He was smiling at me, his teeth like pink tombstones in his mouth.

26

My hands still hurt the next morning. I ran cold water over them in the kitchen sink, then drank coffee out on the picnic table in the blueness of the dawn and tried not to think about last night. I walked along the coulee that traversed the back of our property and looked at the periwinkles along the bank, the caladiums and elephant ears beaded with moisture, the willows swelling in the breeze. I wanted to stay in that spot forever and not go into the department on Monday morning, not look at the early edition of the *Daily Iberian*, not deal with the people who would speak politely to me on a sidewalk or in a courthouse corridor, then whisper to one another after they thought I was out of earshot.

I walked back up toward the house just as the sun rose behind the cypress trees and seemed to flatten like fire inside the swamp. The back of the house was still deep in shadow, but I could see a white envelope taped to Alafair's screen. I pulled it loose and looked at her name written across the front in a flowing calligraphy. The flap was glued, with tiny felt-pen marks that transected both the flap and the body of the envelope so the dried glue could not be broken without the addressee knowing it.

I opened my pocket knife and slit the envelope all the way across the top and removed the folded sheet of stationery inside.

I went down to the bait shop and called Wally, our 275-pound dispatcher at the department, and told him I was taking a vacation day on Monday and not coming in.

'You axed the old man?' he said.

'I have a feeling he'll get in touch,' I said.

'Hey, Dave, if I pass the detectives exam, can I hang around wit' y'all, solve big cases, mop the shrimp tails off the floor with New Orleans cops?'

But as I went back on the dock, I wasn't thinking about Wally's sardonic humor or my eventual encounter with the sheriff. I sat at a spool table and read again the letter that was written with the symmetry and baroque curlicues of a self-absorbed artist or what a psychologist would simply call a megalomaniac.

It read:

Dear Alafair,
 I had a harsh conversation with your father. But he has tried to destroy

our friendship and has also been asking people about my private life, about things that are none of his business.

At first I could not believe your words when you said you couldn't see me again. Did you really mean that? I would never betray you. Would you do that to me? I already know what the answer is.

Remember all our secret meeting places? Just be at any one of them and I'll find you. You're the best person I've ever known, Alafair. We're like the soldier and the girl on the vase. Even though they lived long ago and have probably moldered in the grave, they're still alive inside the arbor on the vase. Death can be beautiful, just like art, and once you're inside either of them, you stay young forever and your love never dies.

See you soon.

> As ever, your loyal friend,
> Johnny

I walked up the slope to the house and went into the bedroom with the letter and showed it to Bootsie.

'My God,' she said.

'I'm at a loss on this one.'

'Where is she?'

'Still asleep. I'd like to—'

'What?' Bootsie said. She was still in her nightgown, propped on one elbow.

'Nothing,' I said.

She sat up and took both my hands in hers. 'We can't solve all our problems with violence. Remeta's a sick person,' she said.

'It sounds like we're talking about last night instead of Remeta.'

She lay back down on the pillow, then turned her head and looked out the window at the pecan and oak trees in the yard, as though fearing that whatever she said next would be wrong.

'You know why I don't believe in capital punishment?' she said. 'It empowers the people we execute. We allow them to remake us in their image.'

'Gable's a degenerate. You didn't see him. I hope I ruptured his spleen.'

'I can't take this shit. I can't, I can't, I can't,' she said, and sat on the side of the bed, her back stiff with anger.

I found Clete that afternoon, drinking beer, half in the bag, in a St Martinville bar. The bar had lath walls and a high, stamped ceiling, and because it was raining outside, someone had opened the back door to let in the cool air, and I could see the rain dripping on a banana tree that grew by a brick wall. A group of bikers and their girlfriends were shooting pool in back, yelling each time one of them made a difficult shot, slamming the butts of their cues on the floor.

'Passion tell you I was here?' Clete said. His lap and the area around his stool were littered with popcorn.

'Yeah. Y'all on the outs?'

'She's wrapped up in her own head all the time. I'm tired of guessing at what's going on. I mean who needs it, right?'

'If I wanted to have somebody capped, who would I call?'

'A couple of the asswipes at that pool table would do it for a hand job.'

'I'm serious.'

'The major talent is still out of Miami. You're actually talking about having somebody smoked? You must have had a bad day, Streak.'

'It's getting worse, too.'

'What's that mean?'

'Nothing. I want to throw a steel net over Johnny Remeta. Most button men know each other.'

'I already tried. A stone killer in Little Havana, a guy who goes back to the days of Johnny Roselli? He hung up on me as soon as I mentioned Remeta's name. What's Remeta done now?'

'He's got a death wish. I think he wants to take Alafair with him.'

Clete's face was flushed and he wiped the heat and oil out of his eyes with a paper napkin. The pool players yelled at another extraordinary shot.

'How about putting it under a glass bell, Jack?' Clete said to them, then looked back at me, a half smile on his face, his eyes slightly out of focus. 'Say all that again?'

'I'll catch you another time, Cletus.'

He removed a slip of paper from his shirt pocket and stared at it.

'What's scareoderm mean? I couldn't find it in the dictionary,' he said.

'I don't know. Why?'

'I took Passion to the doctor yesterday. I heard the nurses talking about her. I wrote that word down.'

'You mean scleroderma?' I asked.

'That's it. That's what she has. What is it?'

His mouth was parted expectantly, his green eyes bleary with alcohol, while he waited for me to reply.

It continued to rain through the afternoon into the night. Little Face Dautrieve put her baby to bed in his crib and watched television until midnight in the front room of her cabin in the Loreauville Quarters. Then she undressed and put on a pajama top and lay down on top of her bed under the fan and listened to the rain on the tin roof. The wind was blowing hard against the slat walls and she knew the storm would be a long one. The occasional headlights on the state road looked like spiderwebs flaring on the windowpane.

From the edges of sleep she heard a raw scraping sound, like a rat clawing inside the walls. When she raised her head from the pillow, she saw the dead bolt on the back door rotating in its socket, then sliding free of the door frame.

The man other people called Johnny Remeta stepped into the room, water sliding off his hat and black raincoat, a metal nail file glinting in his right hand.

'I t'ought you was my auntie. She fixing to be here any minute,' Little Face said.

'Long drive from Lake Charles. Because that's where she moved to.'

Remeta sat down in a chair next to the bed and leaned forward on his hands, his hatted profile in silhouette against the lightning that leaped above the trees on the bayou.

'Can I take off my things? They're wet,' he said.

'We ain't got nothing you want, Rain Man. My baby's got the kroop. I melted Vicks in hot water. That's how come the room smell like it do. You stay here, you get sick.'

He removed his hat and set it crown-down on the floor, then pulled his raincoat off his shoulders and let it hang wet-side out on the back of the chair. His eyes settled on her face and mouth and she saw his throat swallow. She pulled the sheet up to her stomach.

'I ain't in that life no more,' she said.

He opened and closed his hands on top of his thighs, his veins cording under the skin.

'You've been with white men?' he asked.

'Down South the color line never got drawn when it come to the bedroom.'

Then he said something that was lost in the thunder or the thickness that caused his words to bind in his throat.

'I cain't hear you,' she said.

'What difference does one more make?'

'I ain't want your money. I ain't want you, Rain Man. You got to go back where you come from.'

'Don't talk to me like that,' he said.

The rain clattered on the roof and sluiced down over the windows. Little Face could feel her heart beating inside the thinness of her pajama top. The elastic of her nylon panties cut into her skin, but she knew she should not move in order to make herself more comfortable, although she could not explain why she knew this.

Remeta's breath came out in a ragged exhalation before he spoke.

'I've used a trick to scare people so I wouldn't have to hurt them. I'll show you,' he said.

He slipped a blue-black snub-nosed revolver from a holster that was attached to his ankle with a Velcro strap. He flipped the cylinder out of the frame and ejected all six rounds into his palm. They were thick and brass-cased and seemed too large for the size of the revolver. He inserted one back into a chamber and spun the cylinder, then flipped the cylinder back into the frame without looking at where the loaded chamber had landed.

'Ever read about Doc Holliday? His edge was everybody knew he didn't care if he lived or died. So I do this sometimes and it makes people dump in their drawers,' Remeta said.

He cocked the revolver, pressed the barrel against the side of his head, and pulled the trigger.

'See, your face jumped. Just like it was you instead of me about to take the bullet. But I can tell by the weight where the round is,' he said.

She pushed herself up on her hands so her back was against the headboard. She thought she was going to lose control of her bladder. She looked at her baby in the crib and at the glow of a television set inside the cabin of a neighbor who worked nights and at her plastic welfare charge card on the table and next to it the thirteen dollars she had to make last until the end of the week and at the cheap clothes that hung on hangers in her closet. She breathed the funk that rose from her armpits and a soapy odor that either came from her bedclothes or her pajama top, and her breasts seemed to hang like an old woman's dugs from her skeleton. Her stomach had stretch marks on it and felt flaccid and like a water-filled balloon at the same time, and she realized she owned absolutely nothing of value in this world, not even in her own person, nor could she call upon one friend or resource, to bargain for her and her baby's life, that if she was lucky the world would simply take what it needed from her and leave a piece of something behind.

'I ain't gonna fight you no more, Rain Man. I'm just a nigger.'

She pulled the sheet off her and sat on the side of the bed, her feet not quite touching the floor, her eyes downcast.

'You shouldn't use racial words like that. It's what whites have taught you people to do. To feel bad about yourself,' he said, and sat beside her. He moved his arm around her waist but did not look at her. Instead, his lips moved silently, as though he were talking to other people in the room.

'You coming apart, Rain Man?' she said.

'You couldn't guess at what's in my head, girl.'

She unfastened his belt and unbuttoned the top of his trousers and pulled his zipper partway down. She placed one hand inside his underwear and looked into his eyes. They were black, then suddenly apprehensive in the flashes of light through the window, as though he were watching his own behavior from outside himself and was not sure which person he was.

Her hand moved mechanically, as though it were disconnected from her. She watched the side of his face.

She took her hand away and let it rest by his thigh.

'It ain't me you want,' she said.

'Yes, it is.'

'The one you want is the one you cain't have.'

He got up from the bed and stood in front of her, his legs slightly spread, his unbuttoned trousers exposing the top of his Jockey underwear. His stomach was as flat as a swimmer's, smooth as tallow in the flashes of lightning through the window.

'Take off your clothes,' he said.

'Won't do no good, Rain Man. Can kill me and my baby, both. But it ain't gonna get you no satisfaction.'

He made a sound that she could not interpret, like someone who knew his anger must always be called upon in increments and never allowed to have complete expression.

He tucked in his shirt and worked the zipper up on his trousers and fastened the button at the top and began buckling his belt. But his fingers started shaking and he could not line up the hole in the leather with the metal tongue in the buckle.

She reached out to help him. That's when his fist exploded on the side of her face.

She found Bootsie and me that Sunday evening at Jefferson Island while we were eating supper in the restaurant by the lake, the sun glowing through the oak trees and Spanish moss. I watched her come up the winding walkway through the flower gardens and groups of tourists, her diapered baby mounted on her arm, her blue-jeans shorts rolled up high on her thighs, her face bruised like an overripe eggplant.

She marched into the restaurant and stopped in front of our table.

'Somebody shit in that white boy's brain. It ain't me done it, either. You better get him out of our lives, Sad Man. I mean now. 'Cause he come back around, I got me a gun now and I'm gonna blow his fucking head off,' she said.

I walked outside with her into the gardens and we sat down on a scrolled-iron bench. Through the restaurant windows I could see Bootsie by herself at our table, staring out at the lake, her coffee cold and her dessert uneaten.

'Did you file a report at the department?' I asked.

'They was real hepful. Man kept looking down my top to make sure Johnny Remeta wasn't hiding there.'

'I doubt Remeta will bother you again.'

'Where Fat Man at?'

'Why?' I asked.

''Cause he ain't like you. 'Cause he don't fool hisself. 'Cause people mess wit' him only once.'

'Remeta might try to kill my daughter, Little Face. I'm sorry about what happened to you. But I'm tired of your anger,' I said.

I left her on the bench with her baby. When I went back inside the restaurant, Bootsie was gone.

The sheriff was at the bait shop before dawn Monday morning, but he did not come inside the building right away. He propped his hands on the dock railing and stared across the bayou at the cypress trees inside the fog. In his cowboy boots and pinstripe suit and Stetson hat, he looked like a cattleman who had just watched his whole herd run off by dry lightning. He took off his hat and walked through the cone of light over the screen door and entered the shop.

'You gave Jim Gable concussion Friday night. Now you take a vacation day and don't even have the courtesy to call me?' he said.

'Johnny Remeta is stalking my daughter and leaving notes at my house. I don't care what happens with Gable,' I replied.

'Everything's personal with you, Dave. You use the department the way a prizefighter uses a rosin box. You're an employee of the parish. Which means

I'm your supervisor, not a guy who follows you around with a dustpan and whisk broom. I don't like coming out here to explain that.'

'Did Gable press charges?'

'No.'

'Then it's a private matter.'

'As of this moment you're on suspension.'

'That's the breaks.'

'That casual, huh?'

'How'd you like Remeta creeping your place?'

'Do what you're thinking and I've got your cell already waiting for you.'

'I didn't call you because I can't prove what Gable was doing behind my wife's person in that pavilion. It would only bring her embarrassment.'

'Behind her person? What the hell does that mean?'

'End of conversation.'

'You're right. It does no good to talk to you. I wish I hadn't come here,' he said. He tapped his Stetson against his leg and walked out into the mist, his mouth a tight seam.

I worked with Batist at the dock all day, then drove to the Winn-Dixie in town, filled the back of the pickup with soda pop and loaded the ice chest with lunch meat for the bait shop cooler. Right down the street was the ancient motel where Clete was living. I had not seen him since Saturday afternoon, when I had left him bleary-eyed and alone with a scrap of paper in his hand that could have been torn from the Doomsday Book.

I pulled into the motel entrance and drove under the canopy of oaks to the stucco cottage he rented at the end of the row. Leaves were drifting out of the oak branches overhead and he was dusting the exterior of his Cadillac with a rag, flicking the leaves off the finish as though no others would drop out of the tree, the hair on his bare shoulders glowing like a blond ape's in a column of sunlight.

'What's the haps, Streak?' he said without looking up from his work.

'You doing all right?' I said.

'I used the medical dictionary at the city library. From what it says, that stuff's like going to hell without dying.'

'There're treatments.'

'The victims look like they're wrapped in sheets of plastic?'

'How's Passion?'

'She doesn't talk about it. At least not to me.' His voice was without tone or inflection. 'It's true, you tore up Jim Gable at the Shrimp Festival?'

'I guess I have to lose it about every six months to remind myself I'm still a drunk.'

'Save the dish rinse. You didn't lose it. He took it from you.'

'What?'

'Gable never does anything without a reason. You're trying to bring him down. Now nobody will believe anything you say about him.'

I stared at him. I felt like the confidence game mark who realizes his gullibility has no bottom. Clete threw his dust rag through the open front window of the Cadillac onto the front seat and walked over to my truck.

'You're just like me, Streak. You never left the free-fire zone. You think aspirin and meetings and cold showers are going to clean out your head. What you want is God's permission to paint the trees with the bad guys. That won't happen, big mon,' he said.

'I'm sorry about Passion.'

'Life's a bitch and then you die,' he replied.

27

Bed Check Charley still visited me in my dreams, crawling on his stomach through the rice fields, his black pajamas twisted like liquid silk on his dehydrated body. He used a French bolt-action rifle with iron sights, and Japanese potato mashers that he whacked on a banyan root, igniting the impact fuze prematurely, before he flung one into our midst. But even though his ordnance was antiquated, Bed Check was punctual and did his job well. We used him in our day as we would a clock.

We were almost disappointed when a stray gunship caught him under a full moon, running across a rice paddy, and arbitrarily took him out.

A predictable enemy is a valuable one.

I knew Remeta would be back. And I knew where he would come from.

He returned three nights after the sheriff put me on departmental suspension.

I heard the outboard deep in the swamp, then the engine went dead. I slipped on my khakis and shoes and lifted the AR-15 from under the bed and went outside and crossed the lawn. The trees were dripping with night damp, and I could barely see the bait shop in the fog.

But I could hear a boat paddle dipping into the water, knocking against a cypress root, scudding softly against the worn gunnel of a pirogue.

I walked down the concrete boat ramp into the water and stepped under the dock and waited. The bayou was moving northward, rising with the tide, and I saw a dead nutria in the current with a bluepoint crab hooked onto its side.

It was airless under the dock, the water warm inside my clothes, and I could smell dead fish among the pilings. Then the breeze came up and I saw the fog roll like puffs of cotton on the bayou's surface and the bow of a pirogue emerge out of the swamp twenty yards down from the bait shop.

I had inserted a thirty-round magazine in the rifle. The bow of the pirogue moved into the bayou and now I could see the outline of a kneeling man, drawing the paddle through the water in silent J-strokes. Farther down the bayou, at the four corners, the owner of the general store had left on a porch light, and the man in the pirogue was now lighted from behind, his features distorting like a figure moving about under the phosphorescent glow of a pistol flare.

I steadied the rifle against a piling and sighted along the barrel, no longer seeing a silhouette but in my mind's eye a human face, one with teeth, a hinged jawbone, an eye glinting in profile, a skull with skin stretched over its bladed surfaces.

A line of sweat ran through my eyebrow. You just squeeze off and not think about it, I told myself. How many times did you do it before, to people you didn't even know? You just step across the line into E-major rock 'n' roll and the concerns of conscience quickly disappear in the adrenaline rush of letting off one round after another. The only reality becomes the muzzle flashes in the darkness, the clean smell of smokeless powder, the deadness in the ears that allows you to disconnect from the crumpling figure in the distance.

But I hadn't yet actually seen the face of Johnny Remeta.

I clicked on the electric switch mounted on the dock piling. Suddenly the bayou was flooded with light.

'You must get mighty tired if you stay out here in the mosquitoes every night,' he said. He was grinning, his face bathed with white light, his mouth strangely discolored in the brilliance of the flood lamps, as though it were painted with purple lipstick.

I could feel my finger tightening inside the trigger guard.

'You're a pisspot, Johnny,' I said.

'I've heard it all before, Mr Robicheaux. My father said my mother would have gotten rid of me when I was in the womb but she didn't want to waste a coat hanger,' he replied.

Then he opened his palms, as though accepting grace from above, his head tilted, taking my measure.

'Use your left hand and drop your weapon overboard,' I said.

'I don't have one.'

I waded out from under the dock so he could see me.

'You're under arrest. Pull the pirogue into shore,' I said.

'You couldn't pop me, could you?'

I could hear myself breathing and feel the oil and moisture on my finger inside the trigger guard. He stood up in the pirogue, balancing himself, his hands extended outward. He stared at the muzzle of the rifle, his lips pursed, waiting.

'So long, Mr Robicheaux. Tell Alafair I said hello.'

He hit the water in a long, flat dive, his weight flipping the pirogue over. With two strokes he was inside the cypress trees, running across sand spits and through the sloughs, cobwebs and air vines swinging behind him.

I was trembling all over, as though I had malaria. My head thundered and my palms were wet on the plastic stock of the rifle. I leaned over and vomited into the water.

I walked up the boat ramp, then onto the dock, and pulled off my T-shirt and sat down on the planks and pulled my knees up in front of me and rested my face on top of them.

I stayed there until the sun rose, then got up and slung the AR-15 muzzle-down on my shoulder and walked up the slope through the trees with the knowledge I had deliberately set out to murder another human being and had simultaneously failed as both assassin and police officer.

28

That afternoon I got a call from Wally, our departmental comedian.

'Enjoying your days off?' he asked.

'I'm cleaning the grease trap right now. Come on over.'

'I got a little problem. I'd like to finish my shift without being taken out of here in a box. My systolic is 190. I don't need race riots. I don't need black people shouting into the phone at me. I don't need no white lesbian crazy woman firing up a mob over on Hopkins.'

'You're talking about Helen Soileau?'

'I knew you could think it out. Way to go, Dave.'

I drove into town, then over to the west side to Hopkins Street, which, along with Railroad, used to comprise New Iberia's red-light district. Helen Soileau had just handcuffed two black kids, about age fifteen, through the cap chain on a fire hydrant.

I parked the pickup in front of a liquor store and walked through the crowd that had formed on the sidewalk and the lawn of two houses. Helen was bent over at the waist, her hands on her hips, venting her spleen at the two kids sitting on the cement. A city cop in a uniform was looking nervously up and down the street.

Helen raised up and stared at me, her face still heated. Her slacks were torn at the thigh and mud was smeared on her white shirt. 'What are you doing here?' she said.

'I just happened by. What'd these guys do?'

'Not much. One shot a BB into a passing car and hit a six-week-old baby. This other little fuck put an M-80 under an old woman's bedroom floor.'

'I think we need to turn the butane down.'

'They're going to tell me where that BB gun is or stay here till they have to eat the paint on that hydrant. You hear that, you little pukes?'

'Walk over here with me, Helen,' I said.

'You got no business telling me what to do,' she replied.

'I can't argue with that. But we're on city turf. Let them handle it.'

She lifted her face into mine. Her eyes were blazing, her thick arms pumped.

'I'd like to punch you out, Dave. All the skipper needs is an apology and you're back on the clock,' she said.

'So let the city guy do his job and take the kids down.'

'Yeah, I give a shit,' she said, and bent over and unlocked the handcuffs on the boys' wrists, then cuffed them again and walked them to the city cruiser and shoved them inside and slammed the door behind them. Then she walked back to me and said, 'Buy me coffee, Pops.'

I expected one of Helen's harangues, but I was wrong. We went to the McDonald's on East Main and sat by the window. The sky had turned green and the wind was blowing the oaks on the street, and leaves were rising out of the crown of the trees high in the air.

'I was in Lafayette this morning. You know that tattoo and fortune-telling place right off the four-lane?' she said.

'An old cypress cabin with beads and colored lights hanging all over the gallery?'

'I saw Passion Labiche go in there. That girl bothers me.'

'How?'

'Vachel Carmouche was a shithead and everybody knew it. That whole trial sucked. I get pissed off every time somebody tells me Carmouche was a lawman . . . Why the face?'

'I found evidence she didn't do it by herself.'

'You're telling me Passion helped her?'

'Yeah, I am.'

'Big revelation,' Helen said. 'What else is bothering you today?'

'I set up an ambush on Johnny Remeta last night.'

'You did what?'

'I was going to flush his grits. I couldn't pull the trigger.'

She cleaned up our mess from the table and walked to the trash basket and stuffed it inside and came back to the table.

'This is a noisy place full of teenagers and echoes and cooks yelling and I couldn't quite make out what you were saying. See you around, bwana,' she said.

She walked out to her cruiser and drove away.

I slept that night with the remote phone under the bed. It rang just after 11 p.m. I picked it up and went into the kitchen before I clicked it on.

'You're in it for the long haul,' I said without waiting for him to speak.

'I figured you wrong last night. I thought honor required I tell you that, Mr Robicheaux.'

'Honor?'

'I said you didn't have in it you to drop the hammer on me. I know who popped your mother. That's why you let me live.'

'You're not even close, partner.'

I could hear him breathing on the mouth of the receiver. 'We're alike. I've seen it in your eyes,' he said.

'I always thought my mother betrayed me, Johnny. But I learned to forgive her. I did that so I don't have to be a drunk anymore.'

'You saying something about my mother now?'

'You're smart. Read Chaucer's story about the three guys who set out to find Death and slay him once and for all. They found him, all right. But things didn't work out as they expected.'

'Let me tell you what real revenge is. I'm gonna shake down the people who did your mother, then I'm gonna leave the country and have them killed by somebody else. But you'll never know for sure who they were.'

'Pull on your own pud, Johnny. This stuff is a real drag,' I said, and clicked off the phone. Then I walked through the house and pulled the phone connections from all the wall jacks.

The sheriff lived up Bayou Teche in a yellow and gray frame house with a wide gallery, set back under huge cedar and oak trees. When I drove out there Saturday afternoon, he was trimming back the climbing roses in his flower bed while his grandchildren played in the side yard. He wore a tattered straw hat to protect his head from the thorns, and his stomach hung heavily over his belt. In his home setting, clipping flowers and placing them gingerly in a bowl of water, his clothes stained with fungicide and house paint, the sheriff looked much older than he did at the department and nothing like a law officer.

I sat down on the front steps and picked up some pieces of bark from a bag of mulch and flicked them out into the grass.

'I made an ass out of myself when I attacked Jim Gable. I also brought shame on the department. I want to apologize,' I said.

'You got to rein it in, Dave.'

'I believe you.'

'Five-day suspension without pay, effective last Monday. A letter of reprimand in your jacket. Is that fair?'

'There's something else I have to tell you,' I said. 'Passion Labiche told me she helped her sister kill Vachel Carmouche.' I waited for him to speak but he didn't. 'Number two, I had the chance to plant one in Johnny Remeta's cauliflower and didn't do it.'

He paused in his work but his face showed no expression.

'You froze?' he asked.

'I had him set up. I was going to cut all his motors.'

A mosquito buzzed at his face and he rubbed his cheek with the back of his wrist.

'I'm going to retire soon. I'm glad you told me what you did.'

'Sir?'

'I'd like you to be my successor,' he said.

'Come again?'

'What are you going to do with Passion's confession?' he asked, ignoring my incredulity.

'It'll be dismissed as an eleventh-hour attempt to stop Letty's execution,' I said.

'Maybe that's just what it is. You think of that? Where's Remeta now?'

'He inasmuch told me my mother's killers are the same people who tried to have him killed on the Atchafalaya. He says he's going to extort them, then hire a button man to take them out.'

'You actually had that guy locked down in your sights? Then didn't say anything about it till today?'

'That's it, more or less.'

He locked the clasp on his clippers and dropped them in his pants pocket and looked at his grandchildren playing.

'Remeta is going to take you to your mother's killers, isn't he?' he said.

'That wasn't the reason, Sheriff.'

'Yeah, I know,' he said, scratching inside his shirt. 'Yeah—' But he didn't bother to continue, as though he were weary of contending with the self-serving machinations of others.

I ate an early dinner with Bootsie, then drove to New Orleans through Morgan City. The evening light still reached high into the dome of sky overhead when I parked my pickup truck down the block from Maggie Glick's bar across the river in Algiers. The street was busy with the type of people whose Saturday nights were spent in a facsimile of the places their fellow countrymen enjoyed: elderly pensioners who ate in decrepit diners that served a free glass of domestic wine with the special; young white couples without geographical origins or means of support who lived in walk-ups with no air-conditioning and strolled the sidewalks with no apparent destination; and the men whose thoughts made them wake each morning with a longing that seldom found satiation.

I walked down the alley and entered Maggie Glick's through the back door. It was crowded and dark and unbearably frigid inside. She was behind the bar, fixing a drink in a Collins glass, talking to a white man in a business suit. She had woven glass Mardi Gras beads into her hair and she wore a white knit blouse that exposed the roses tattooed on the tops of her breasts. The man did not sit but stood and grinned while she talked, his back stiff, his eyes drifting down the bar to a mulatto girl who could not have been older than eighteen.

His eyes met mine and he fiddled with a college or fraternity ring of some kind on his finger and turned his face away, as though he had heard a sudden noise outside, and walked down to the far end of the bar, then glanced back at me again and went out the door.

'My competition send you 'round?' Maggie asked.

'Johnny Remeta says he was never in here. He says you were lying,' I said.

'You a sober, thinking man now. Let me ax you a question. Why would I lie and tell you a man like that was a customer? 'Cause it gonna be good for my bidness?'

'That's why I believe you.'

'Do say?'

'Where can I find him?' I asked.

'He *used* to come in here. He don't now. Man shop for the trade in here got to be functional, know what I mean?'

'No.'

'That boy get off with a gun. And it ain't in his pants. Here, drink a free soda. I'll bag it to go.'

'Jim Gable sprung you from St Gabriel, Maggie?'

'I got sprung 'cause I was innocent. Have a good night, darlin',' she said, and turned her back to me, lighting a cigarette. Her hair was jet black, her skin as golden as a coin in the flare of light.

I walked toward the front of the building and was about to push open the door onto the street when I saw a muscular blond man in a pale blue suit with white piping on the lapels at the corner of the bar. His hair was clipped and combed neatly on the side of his head, one eye like a small marble inside the nodulous skin growth on the right side of his face.

'I thought maybe you'd gone back to New Mexico, Micah,' I said.

He had a long-neck bottle of beer and a shot glass in front of him, and he sipped from the shot, then drank a small amount of beer afterwards, like a man who loves a vice so dearly he fears his appetite for it will one day force him to give it up.

'The heavyweight champion of the Shrimp Festival,' he said.

I sat down next to him and took a peanut out of a plastic bowl on the bar and cracked the shell and put the nut in my mouth.

'You ever see a guy by the name of Johnny Remeta in here?' I asked.

'What would you give to find out?'

'Not much.'

He lifted the shot glass again and tipped it into his mouth.

'I might buy half of a carnival. What do you think of that?' he said.

'Maybe you can give me a job. I got bumped from the department after I punched out Jim Gable.'

He watched an overweight, topless girl in heels and a sequined G-string walk out on a tiny stage behind the bar.

'Miss Cora give you a severance package?' I said.

'The smart man squeezes the man who milks the cow. That don't mean anything to you. But maybe one day it will,' he said.

'Really?' I said.

'You're an ignorant man.'

'You're probably right,' I said, and slapped him on the back and caused him to spill his drink on his wrist.

I went outside and walked down to the old docks and pilings on the waterfront. It was dark now, and rain was falling on the river and I could see the nightglow of New Orleans on the far bank and, to the south, green trees flattening in the wind and the brown swirl of the current as it flowed around a wide bend toward the Gulf of Mexico.

Somewhere down on that southern horizon my father's rig had blown out and he had hooked his safety belt onto the Geronimo wire and bailed off the top of the derrick into the darkness. His bones and hard hat and steel-toed boots were still out there, shifting in the tidal currents, and I truly believed that in one way or another his brave spirit was out there as well.

The cops who had murdered my mother had rolled her body into a bayou, as contemptuous of her in death as they were of her in life. But eventually her body must have drifted southward into the salt water, and now I wanted to believe she and Big Al were together under the long, green roll of the Gulf, all their inadequacies washed away, their souls just beginning the journey they could not take together on earth.

The rain was blowing hard in the streets when I walked back to my truck, and the neon above the bars looked like blue and red smoke in the mist. I heard men fighting in a pool room and I thought of Big Aldous Robicheaux and Mae Guillory and the innocence of a world in which inarticulate people could not tell one another adequately of either their pain or the yearnings of their hearts.

29

That night I dreamed of roses. I saw the sheriff trimming them in his garden and I saw them tattooed on Maggie Glick's breasts. I saw them painted in miniature on the vase Johnny Remeta had given Alafair. I also saw the rose with green leaves that was tattooed on the neck of Letty Labiche.

But just as I woke and was momentarily between all the bright corridors of sleep and the grayness of the dawn, the flowers disappeared from the dream and I saw a collection of Civil War photographs on a library table, the pages flipping in the wind that blew through the open window.

I wanted to dismiss the dream and its confused images, but it lingered with me through the day. And maybe because the change of the season was at hand, I could almost hear a clock ticking for a sexually abused woman waiting to die in St Gabriel Prison.

On Monday morning I was out at the firing range with Helen Soileau. I watched her empty her nine-millimeter at a paper target, her ear protectors clamped on her head. When the breech locked open, she pulled off her ear protectors and slipped a fresh magazine into the butt of her automatic and replaced it in her holster and began picking up her brass.

'You're dead-on this morning,' I said.

'I'm glad somebody is.'

'Excuse me?'

'You're off-planet. I have to say everything twice to you before you hear me,' she said, chewing gum.

'Where'd you see Passion Labiche?'

'I told you. Going into that fortune-telling and tattoo place in Lafayette.'

'What for?'

'Ask her.'

'You brought up the subject, Helen.'

'Yeah. And I dropped it. Two days ago,' she said.

I went back to the office and called Dana Magelli at NOPD.

'I've got a lead for you,' I said.

'I see. You're doing general oversight on our cases now?' he replied.

'Hear me out, Dana. Johnny Remeta told me he was going to squeeze the people who killed my mother.'

'Are you kidding me? You're in personal contact with an escaped felon who's murdered two police officers?'

'Saturday night I was in Maggie Glick's bar over in Algiers. I ran into Jim Gable's ex-chauffeur, a guy named Micah something or another. He said he was going to come into some money by squeezing the man who was milking the cow.'

'What?'

'Those were his words. I think he was saying Remeta is shaking down Jim Gable.'

'You're saying Jim Gable killed your mother?' he said.

'Remeta forced Don Ritter to give up the names of my mother's killers before he executed him. At least that's what he says.'

'What am I supposed to do with information like this? I can't believe I'm having this conversation,' Magelli said.

'Put Micah under surveillance.'

'Shake loose three or four detectives and follow a guy around who has no last name? This sounds like something Purcel thought up, maybe to get even with the department.'

'I'm serious, Dana.'

'No, you're obsessed. You're a good guy. I love you. But you're stone nuts. That's not a joke. Stay out of town.'

The next day I drove to the City Library and found the collection of Civil War-era photographs that Johnny Remeta had been looking at just before he jumped out of the reading room window. I used the index, then flipped to the grainy black-and-white pictures taken at the Bloody Angle and Dunker Church.

The images in the pictures told me nothing new about Remeta. He was simply a necromancer with broken glass in his head trying to find a historical context for the rage and pain his mother had bequeathed him. But if that was true, why had the image of the book, its pages turning in the wind, disturbed me in my dream?

Because I hadn't considered he was looking at something else in the collection, not just at the photos of Union and Confederate dead at Sharpsburg and Spotsylvania?

I flipped back two pages and was suddenly looking at a photograph of a two-story, narrow, columned house, surrounded by a piked iron fence. The picture had been taken in 1864, in uptown New Orleans, after the Union occupation of the city by General Butler.

According to the historical notes opposite the photograph, the house was owned by a young woman, believed to be a southern spy, who hid her lover, an escaped Confederate prisoner of war, from General Butler's soldiers. The soldier was badly wounded, and when she discovered her own arrest was imminent, the two of them drank poison and died upstairs in a tester bed.

I went back to the department and called Dana Magelli at NOPD again.

'We haven't found Remeta because he hides in plain sight,' I said.

'I knew it was going to be that kind of day.'

'Give it a rest, Dana. When he had a cop on his tail in the Quarter, he parked his truck and went inside the police station. How many perps have that kind of cool?'

'Give me a street address and we'll swing by.'

'He's imbued with this notion he's a Confederate hero of some kind and my daughter is his girlfriend. He was reading an account in our library about two lovers who committed suicide during the Civil War in a home on Camp Street.'

'That doesn't mean he's living in New Orleans.'

'You have something better to offer?'

'Every cop in the city has a mug shot of this guy. What else can we do?'

'Pull Jim Gable's personnel records for me.'

'Forget it.'

'Why?'

'We'll handle our own people. Am I communicating here? Gable is none of your business.'

That's what you think, I thought as I lowered the receiver into the phone cradle.

I worked late that evening, then drove home along the bayou road in the dusk. I could smell chrysanthemums and a smell like gas on the wind and see fireflies lighting in the gloom of the swamp. The house had already fallen into shadow when I turned into the drive and the television set was on in the living room, the sounds of canned laughter rising and falling in the air like an insult to the listener's credulity. I tried not to think about the evening that awaited Bootsie and me as soon as I entered the house, hours of unrelieved tension, formality that hid our mutual anger, physical aversion, and periods of silence that were louder than a scream.

I saw Batist chopping up hog meat on a butcher table he had set up by the coulee. He had taken off his shirt and put on a gray apron, and I could see the veins cord in his shoulder each time he raised the cleaver in the air. Behind him, the sky was still blue and the evening star was out and the moon rising, and his head was framed against the light like a glistening cannonball.

'Sold thirty-five lunches today. We run out of poke chops,' he said.

A cardboard box by his foot contained the hog's head and loops of blue entrails.

'You doin' all right?' I asked.

'Weather's funny. The wind's hard out of the west. I seen t'ings glowing in the swamp last night. My wife use to say that was the *loupgarou*.'

'It's swamp gas igniting or ball lightning, podna. You know that. Forget about werewolves.'

'I run my trot line this morning. Had a big yellow mudcat on it. When I slit it open there was a snake in its stomach.'

'I'll see you later,' I said.

'When the *loupgarou* come, somebody gonna die. Old folks use to burn blood to run it back in the trees.'

'Thanks for putting up the meat, Batist,' I said, and went inside the house.

Bootsie sat at the kitchen table reading from two sheets of lined paper. She wore blue jeans and loafers and a denim shirt with the sleeves cut away at the shoulders; wisps of her hair had fallen loose from her barrette and hung on the back of her neck. Her fingers were pressed to her temples while she read.

'Is that from Remeta?' I said.

'No. I went to an Al-Anon meeting today. Judy Theriot, my sponsor, was there. She said I had a problem with anger.'

'She did?' I said, my voice neutral.

'She made me do a Fourth Step and write out an inventory. Now that I've read it again I'd like to wad it up and throw it away.'

I went to the icebox and took out a pitcher of iced tea and poured a glass at the sink. I raised the glass to my mouth, then lowered it and set it back on the drainboard.

'Would you care for one?' I asked.

'You want to know what's in my inventory?' Bootsie asked.

'I'm a little bit afraid of what's coming.'

'My first statement has to do with absolute rage.'

'That's understandable.'

'Hold your water, Streak, before I get charged up again. Judy made me write out a list of all the things you did that angered me. It's quite long.'

I looked out the window at Batist chopping meat on the wood table by the coulee. He had started a trash fire of leaves, and the smoke was blowing into my neighbor's cane field. I could feel my scalp tightening as I waited for Bootsie to recite her written complaint, and I wanted to be outside, in the wind, in the autumnal smell of smoldering leaves, away from the words that would force me to look again at the on-going insanity of my behavior.

Then, rather than wait for her to speak again and quietly accept criticism, I took the easier, softer way and tried to pre-empt it. 'You don't have to tell me. It's the violence. Nobody should have to live around it. I drag it home with me like an animal on a chain,' I said.

'Judy made me look at something I didn't want to see. I was often angry when you were protective of someone else. You beat up Gable because you thought he was treating me disrespectfully in public. Then I lectured you about your violent feelings toward Remeta.'

'You weren't wrong,' I said.

'What?'

'I set Remeta up the other night. I was going to dust him and take him out of Alafair's life.'

She was quiet a long time, staring into space, her cheeks spotted with color. Her mouth was parted slightly and I kept waiting for her to speak.

'Boots?' I said.

'You were actually going to kill him?'

'Yes.'

I could see the anger climbing into her face. 'In front of our home, just blow him away?' she said.

'I couldn't do it. So he'll be back. We can count on it.'

I could hear the wall clock in the silence. Her face was covered with shadow and I couldn't see her expression. I waited a moment longer, then rinsed out my glass and dried it and put it in the cupboard and went out on the front gallery. The screen opened behind me.

'He's coming back?' she said.

I didn't answer.

'I wish you had killed him. That's what I really feel. I wish Johnny Remeta was dead. If he comes around Alafair again, I'll do it myself. Get either in or out of the game, Streak,' she said.

'Your sponsor would call that rigorous honesty,' I said.

She tried to hold the anger in her face, then mashed her foot on top of mine.

The bedroom was filled with shadows and the curtains twisted and popped in the wind when Bootsie sat on my thighs and lowered her hand, then raised herself and placed me inside her. A few minutes later her mouth opened silently and her eyes became unfocused, her hair hanging in her face, and she began to say something that broke and dissolved in her throat; then I felt myself joining her, my hands slipping off her breasts onto her back, and in my mind's eye I saw a waterfall cascading over pink rocks and a marbled boulder tearing loose from its moorings, rolling heavily, faster and faster in the current, its weight pressing deeply into the soft pebbly bottom of the stream.

She kissed me and cupped her hand on my forehead as though she were checking to see if I had a fever, then pushed my hair up on my head.

'Alafair will be home soon. Let's take her to dinner at the Patio. We can afford an extra night out, can't we?' she said.

'Sure.'

I watched her as she put on her panties and bra; her back was firm with muscle, her skin as free of wrinkles as a young woman's. She was reaching for her shirt on the chair when an odor like scorched hair and burning garbage struck her face.

'Good Lord, what is that?' she said.

I put on my khakis and the two of us went into the kitchen and looked through the window into the backyard. The sun had dropped below the horizon, but the light had not gone out of the sky, and the full moon hung like a sliver of partially melted ice above my neighbor's cane. Batist flung a bucket filled with hog's blood onto the trash fire, and a cloud of black smoke with fire inside it billowed up into the wind and drifted back against the house.

'What's Batist doing? Has he lost his mind?' Bootsie said.

I rubbed the small of her back, my fingers touching the line of elastic across the top of her panties.

'It's a primitive form of sacrifice. He believes he saw the *loupgarou* in the swamp,' I said.

'Sacrifice?'

'It keeps the monster back in the trees.'

'You thinking about Letty Labiche?'

'About all of us, I guess,' I said.

30

The next day was Wednesday. I don't know why, but I woke with a sense of loss and emptiness I hadn't experienced in many years. It was like the feelings I had as a child that I could never explain to priests or nuns or any other adults who tried to help me. But when that strange chemical presence would have its way with my heart, like weevil worms that had invaded my blood, I was convinced the world had become a gray, desolate place without purpose, with no source of heat other than a perpetual winter sun.

I walked down through the mist in the trees to the road and took the newspaper out of the metal cylinder and opened it on the kitchen table.

The lead story had a three-column headline that read: 'Governor Sets Execution for Labiche.'

Unless Belmont Pugh commuted her sentence, Letty had exactly three weeks to live.

I drove to the department in the rain and talked to the sheriff, then went to the prosecutor's office.

The district attorney was out of town and would be gone for a week, and the ADA I caught was Barbara Shanahan, sometimes known as Battering Ram Shanahan. She was over six-feet tall and had freckles and wore her light red hair cut short and wore a blue suit with white hose. She worked hard and was a good prosecutor, and I had always wanted to like her. But she seldom smiled and she went about her job with the abrasiveness of a carpenter building coffins with a nail gun.

'Passion Labiche has confessed she participated in the murder of Vachel Carmouche?' she said.

'Yes.'

'Where is it?' she asked.

'Where's what?'

'The statement, the tape, whatever.'

'I didn't take a formal statement from her.'

'So what is it you want from us?' she asked.

'I'm apprising you of the situation.'

'It sounds like you're getting your chain jerked.'

'The weed sickle she used is still under the house.'

'I think you should get out of law enforcement. Become a public defender. Then you can clean up after these people on a regular basis. Talk to the DA when he gets back. He's going to tell you the right person is going to be injected three weeks from now. I suggest you learn to live with it,' she said.

It was still raining outside, and through the window I could see the old crypts in St Peter's Cemetery and the rain dancing on top of the bricks and plaster.

'Passion was telling the truth,' I said.

'Good. Make the case and we'll indict for capital murder. Anything else you want?' she replied, and began sticking files in a cabinet, her back to me.

But Barbara Shanahan surprised me. And so did Connie Deshotel, who rang my phone just before 5 p.m.

'Your ADA called me. She says you have new evidence in the Carmouche case,' she said.

'Both sisters killed him,' I said.

'You know this for a fact?'

'Yes.'

'Put something together. I'll take it to the governor.'

'Why are you doing this?' I asked.

'Because I'm the attorney general of Louisiana. Because I don't want to overlook mitigating circumstances in a capital conviction.'

'I want to offer Passion Labiche immunity,' I said.

'That's between you and the prosecutor's office.'

'Belmont thinks he's going to be a vice-presidential candidate. He's not going to be easy to move.'

'Tell me about it,' she said.

After she hung up I put on my coat to leave the office. Through the window I could see rain and leaves blowing in the cemetery. Helen Soileau opened my office door and leaned inside.

'Give me a ride, boss man?'

'Sure. Why would Connie Deshotel want to help Letty Labiche?'

'Simple. She's humanitarian and is always willing to risk her ass for a cop killer,' Helen said.

'Right,' I said.

In the morning I drove out to Passion Labiche's house, but she wasn't home. I drove up the road, along the bayou, to her nightclub outside St Martinville and saw her pickup truck parked by the back door under a dripping tree. She was unloading groceries from the bed and carrying them, two sacks at a time, through a puddle of water into the small kitchen in back. She wore baggy strap overalls and a gray T-shirt and a red bandanna tied around her neck. Her feet were wet up to her ankles.

'Need a hand?' I asked.

'I got it. What you want, Dave?' she said.

I followed her through the screen door into the kitchen.

'I talked to the attorney general. She wants to take your statement about Carmouche's death to the governor,' I said.

'What statement?'

'Excuse me?'

'I said what statement you talking about?'

She put a huge gumbo pot on the gas range and split open a bag of okra on the drainboard and began rinsing the okra under hot water and rubbing it smooth with a dish towel. Her hair looked oily and unwashed and I could smell a sour odor in her clothes.

'If you want immunity, we have to wait till the DA comes back from Washington,' I said.

'I got scleroderma. He can give immunity from that?'

'I'm telling you what's available.'

'It don't matter what I do. They gonna kill my sister. Your friends, the attorney general and Belmont Pugh? I wish it was them gonna be strapped down on that table. I wish they could know what it feels like to sit in a cage and wait for people to tape a needle on your arm and steal the breath out of your chest. You don't die easy on that table, no. You strangle to death.' She raised one arm from her work, her back still to me, and wiped at the corner of her face. 'It's over, Dave. Don't be bothering me and Letty again.'

When I drove back to the office, the sugarcane in the fields waving against the grayness of the sky, I kept thinking of Passion's words. Was it just a matter of her peculiar use of the second person, or had she described the execution as though she were speaking of her own fate, not Letty's?

The following Monday I received a call from Dana Magelli in New Orleans.

'I'm patched in on Camp Street. We got a "911 shots-fired" a half hour ago. The neighbors say a blond guy drove up in a Honda, went inside, then suddenly *pow, pow,* and the Honda drives back off. We showed the neighbors Remeta's picture. They say he looks like the guy who's been living upstairs.'

'Somebody hit Remeta?'

'I'm not sure,' Magelli said.

'You haven't gone into the house?'

'It's burning. There's another problem, too. Gunfire's coming from the upstairs window. Whoever's in there is going down with the ship.'

Helen and I checked out a cruiser, hit the flasher, and took the four-lane through Morgan City into New Orleans. We made it in less than two hours. We came off I-10 onto St Charles Avenue, passed Lee Circle, and headed uptown toward the Garden District. When we turned onto Camp, the street was sealed off with emergency vehicles and plumes of black smoke were still rising from the scorched brick shell and cratered roof of the building I had seen in the historical photograph.

Magelli stood behind an NOPD cruiser, looking at the destroyed building, his face flinching slightly when a live round popped inside the heat.

'You nail him?' Helen said.

'We never saw him,' Magelli said.

'You couldn't get anybody into the first floor?' I asked.

'We kept within our perimeter. We've got nobody down. Is that all right with you?' he said.

'You bet,' I replied.

The defensiveness went out of his face.

'We've heard ammunition popping for two hours. How many were in a weapon is anybody's guess. At least two rounds hit a fire truck. Another one went through a neighbor's window,' he said.

The wind changed, and he turned his head and cleared his throat slightly and spit in the gutter.

'Well, you know what's inside. You want to take a look?' he said.

'I guess we won't have ribs for lunch today,' Helen said.

Magelli, two cops in uniform, and Helen and I went through the piked gate and started up the stairs to the second story, our weapons drawn. But the top of the stairs was partially blocked by a pile of burned laths and plaster. A raincoated fireman pushed his way past us and cleared a walkway, then kicked the door loose from the jamb.

The smell inside did not fit in time and place; instead, I thought of a village across the seas and I heard ducks quacking in terror and the grinding sounds of steel tracks on an armored vehicle.

The fire had probably started on or near the gas stove, and the entirety of the kitchen looked like a room carved out of soft coal. The canned goods in the pantry had superheated, and exploded glass from preserve or jelly jars had embedded like teeth in the walls. Portions of the roof had collapsed into the living room, half covering a desk by a front window. On the floor, among hundreds of brass shell casings and shards of broken window glass and a network of incinerated rug fibers, were the remains of two bolt-action rifles, their magazines filled with melted lead, and a .45 and a nine-millimeter pistol, the slides blown back and jammed open.

We neared the front windows, and a fireman gagged behind his face shield. I pressed my handkerchief to my mouth and nose and thought of water buffalo and grass huts and rice in wicker baskets and penned hogs and the kerosene-like smell of a flame arching into a ville from a vehicle we called zippo tracks and another smell that was like the sweet, sickening stench a rendering plant makes. The fireman used the point of his ax to drag a pile of drenched debris off a desk, and the stench rose from the desk well as palpably and thick as a cloud of insects.

'Sorry for the remark outside,' Helen said, her eyes deliberately unfocused as she looked down at the shape curled inside the well.

'Is that Remeta?' Magelli asked.

There was little left of the dead man's features. The head was hairless, the skin burned black. His forearms were pressed against his ears, as though the flames had contained a sound he did not want to hear. The tissue around his right eye looked like a scorched and shriveled biscuit.

'He was a geek. I was wrong about him,' I said.

Magelli raised his eyes to mine, not understanding.

'It's Micah, Jim Gable's chauffeur. He used to be a carnival geek. He told me people paid to see the deformity on his face so they wouldn't have to look at the ugliness inside themselves.'

'So?' Magelli said.

'He was a carnie man. He knew better than to shake down a man like Remeta. He was sent here to kill him,' I said.

'You're saying Gable hired him?' Magelli said.

'A cop who had a whole family capped? Not a chance. I can't believe I was a meter maid here,' Helen said.

31

The next morning I called Clete's motel but no one answered. I tried again later and a woman picked up the phone.

'Passion?' I said.

'What you want?'

'Where's Clete?'

'Asleep. Leave him alone.'

'How about a little show of manners?' I said.

'I'll tell him you called. Right now he needs his rest,' she said, and hung up.

That evening I drove to the motel. It had been hot all day, and the sky was purple and red in the west and it had just started to rain. When Clete opened the door his clothes looked like they had been slept in and I could smell alcohol deep down in his lungs.

'What's up, Streak?' he said.

'Did Passion tell you I called?'

'She must have forgot.'

He closed the door behind me. The room was dark and in disarray. A red bandanna, like the one I had seen Passion wear around her neck, was on the nightstand. He took an open can of beer out of the icebox and drank the can empty and dropped it in a trash basket.

'Jim Gable's chauffeur tried to hit Remeta. Remeta put one in him and then set his own apartment on fire,' I said. I looked at the side of his face, his gaze that was focused on nothing. 'Clete?'

'Remeta wanted everybody to think the chauffeur was him?'

'Or to buy time till he could find Gable and cook his hash.'

'Gable set up the hit, huh?'

'That's my guess.'

He turned on the tap in the sink and washed his face with his hands. 'I'm out of hooch. I've got to get a drink,' he said.

'I thought you were breaking it off with Passion.'

'She's all alone. Her sister's going to be executed. She's got an incurable disease. What am I supposed to say? You were a good punch but hit the road?'

Then he started opening and closing cabinets, rooting in his suitcase, reopening the icebox, even though he already knew there was no more booze in the cottage.

'Passion wants me to go with her to Letty's execution. She got Letty to put my name on the list,' he said. 'You ever see the Stake in Saigon? I'm not up to this bullshit.'

He waved one meaty hand in the air, as though warning away an imaginary adversary. I sat down on the side of his bed and waited for his anger to pass. Then my gaze alighted on one of the pillows by the headboard.

'Who was bleeding?' I asked.

'Go home, Dave. Let me alone for a while. I'll be all right. I promise,' he said, and leaned heavily on the sink, his back swelling with breath like a beached whale's.

The next day I got another call from Connie Deshotel.

'I wasn't able to make any headway with Belmont,' she said.

'I see.'

'He's caught between his own inclinations and what his constituency wants. It's not easy for him,' she said.

'His inclinations? I'll float that by Letty Labiche if I get a chance.'

'I tried to help. I don't know what else you want.'

'Where's Belmont now?'

'I wouldn't know. Try his office. But I'm out of this. You understand? Frankly, I just don't want any more of your rudeness,' she said.

'What's your relationship with Jim Gable, Connie?' I said.

But the connection had already gone dead.

Connie Deshotel had said she didn't know Belmont Pugh's whereabouts. But today was Wednesday, and I knew where to find him. When Belmont had been a traveling preacher and broom salesman, he had made a regular midweek stop at a slat-board fundamentalist church outside the little settlement of Lottie, in the middle of the Atchafalaya Basin. The congregation had paid thirty-five dollars for every sermon Belmont gave, and today, either out of gratitude or the aura of humility his continued presence at the church brought him, Belmont was still a regular at Wednesday night meetings.

That evening I drove up through Opelousas and took Highway 190 toward Baton Rouge, then turned down a shale road and crossed a railroad track and went deeper into the Basin, past a community of small houses with rusted screens, to a church building with a blue neon cross on the roof.

The congregation had laid out dinner on plank tables by a grove of cedar trees. Among the cluster of pickup trucks and 1970s gas-guzzlers I saw Belmont's black Chrysler, a patina of gray mud on the fenders.

The windows were down in the Chrysler, and when I walked past it I could see a bored state trooper behind the wheel and a woman in back who was smoking a cigarette. She looked like she had been reconstructed in Dr Frankenstein's laboratory, with silicone implants, a face tuck, chemically dyed skin, and industrial-strength perfume. She blew her nose on a Kleenex and dropped it out the window on the grass.

Belmont's mouth was full of food, his Stetson pushed back on his head so that the ends of his hair were mashed against his forehead like a little boy's.

'You're not gonna punch nobody out, are you, son?' he said.

'I need to talk with you about Letty Labiche.'

'I knew it.'

'She's got two weeks.'

'You don't need to remind me of that. I got people marching with signs in front of the capitol. I got Italians calling me from the Vatican.'

'You don't want this on your conscience, Belmont.'

He tossed a chicken bone over his shoulder and got up from the table. 'Walk with me,' he said.

We went into the grove of cedars; the sky was purple now and filled with the drone of locusts. There was grease on his hands, and he kept opening and closing them and looking at the shine the grease made on his skin.

'I'll be right by the phone the night the death warrant is read. I get new evidence or hear from the federal court, I'll stop it. Otherwise, it goes forward,' he said.

'It's wrong. You know it.'

'I'm the governor. Not a judge. Not a jury. I didn't have a damn thing to do with that trial. It's on y'all's self, right down there in Iberia Parish. You quit carrying your guilt up to Baton Rouge and throwing it on my doorstep, you hear?'

He turned away from me and let out his breath. The curls on the back of his neck moved like chicken feathers in the breeze. In the distance his black Chrysler was painted with a red light against the western sun. Someone inside the church turned on the neon cross.

'Who's the lady in the car?' I asked.

'She's a missionary, as in "missionary position." I'm a sinner. I don't hide it. You stop climbing my back, Dave.'

'Connie Deshotel warned me.'

'What?'

'She said she didn't get anywhere with you. I don't know why I thought I could.'

'It's Connie Deshotel been telling me Letty Labiche takes the needle or I go back to selling brooms and bathroom disinfectant. Where in God's name do you get your information, son?'

He walked back to the picnic and stopped by a water spigot. He turned it on and washed his hands, scrubbing them in the spray as though an obscene presence had worked its way into the grain of his skin. Then he pulled at least three feet of paper towel off a roll and wiped his hands and forearms and mouth and wadded up the paper and bounced it off the side of a trash barrel. His Stetson hat had turned a soft blue in the glow of the neon cross on the church.

Saturday afternoon Dana Magelli walked into my bait shop, carrying a tackle box and a spinning rod. His blue jeans and tennis shoes looked like they had just come out of the box.

'Got any boats for rent?' he asked.

'Take your pick,' I said.

He pulled a soda out of the cooler and wiped the melted ice off the can and put a dollar on the counter and sat down on a stool. A customer was dipping shiners with a net out of the aerated tank in back and dropping them in a shiner bucket. Dana waited until the customer had finished and gone outside, then he said, 'You and Purcel haven't been running a game on Jim Gable, have you?'

'What game?'

'He says he found glass in his soup at a restaurant. He says people are following him. He says he saw what he believes was a scoped rifle in a window.'

'Gee, that's too bad.'

'Evidently he's got a fuckpad with an unlisted number. One of his broads is getting calls that scare her shitless.'

'You think Clete and I are behind this?'

'Purcel's an animal. He's capable of anything. Last night somebody blew out Gable's car window with double-ought bucks and missed his head by about two inches.'

'It's Remeta.'

'You're not involved? I have your word?'

'I'm not involved, Dana.'

'You all right?' he said.

'Why?'

'Because you don't look it.'

'Must be the weather.'

He gazed at the sunlight and shadows on the bamboo and the willows bending in the breeze off the Gulf.

'You must have a funny metabolism,' he said.

I had given my word to Dana that I was not involved in the harassing of Jim Gable or the shotgun attack upon him. I had said nothing about future possibilities.

Early Sunday morning I drove to Lafourche Parish and headed south through the cane fields toward the Gulf. The wind was blowing hard and the sky had turned black and I could feel the barometer dropping. I drove down Purple Cane Road, past the general store and the dance hall where my mother used to work, while raindrops as big as marbles broke against my windshield. In the distance I could see the three-story, coffee-colored stucco house where Jim and Cora Gable lived, the palm trees blowing above the roof.

But no one came to the door. I waited in my truck until almost noon under a sky sealed with clouds that looked like black ink floating inside an inverted bowl. I don't know what I expected to do or to find, but I knew that my mother's murderers would never be apprehended by my simply letting the system move forward of its own accord. The temperature must have dropped fifteen degrees and through the window I could smell speckled trout schooling up in the bay and the cool, wet odor of dust blowing out of the cane, and when I shut my eyes I was a little boy again, driving down Purple Cane Road with my mother and the bouree man named Mack, wondering what had happened to my father, Big Aldous, and our home on the bayou south of New Iberia.

Then the front door opened and Cora Gable looked out at my truck, her face as white and threaded with lines as old plaster, her scalp showing when the wind blew her hair. I got out of the truck and walked toward her. Her mouth was bright red in the gloom, and she tried to smile, but the conflict in her face made me think of a guitar string wound so tightly on its peg that it seems to tremble with its own tension.

'Oh, Mr Robicheaux,' she said.

'Is Jim home?'

'Sir, this upsets me. You attacked my husband. Now you're here.'

'I think your husband is responsible for Micah's death, Miss Cora.'

'Micah went back to New Mexico. Jim gave him money to go. What are you telling me?'

'May I come in?'

'No, you may not. Jim said you'd do something like this. I think I have some things of your mother's. Wasn't her name Guillory? They were in a shed. Maybe you should take them and go.'

'You have belongings of my mother?'

'Yes, I think I do.' Her face became disconcerted, wrapped in conflicting thoughts, as though she were simultaneously asking and answering questions inside her own head. 'I don't know where they are right now. I can't be responsible for other people's things.'

I stepped closer to the door. The rain was slanting out of the sky, running off the tiles on the roof, clicking on the banks of philodendron and caladium that lined the brick walkway.

'Go away before I call the police,' she said, and closed the heavy door with both hands and shot the bolt inside.

I drove back up the dirt road. Just as I reached the general store, I felt my left front tire go down on the rim. I pulled into the store's parking lot and got the jack, lug wrench, a pair of cloth gloves, and the spare out of the back and squatted down by the front fender and began spinning the nuts off the flat. I heard a car pull in next to me and someone walk toward the entrance of the store, then pause.

'Lo and behold, it's the Davester,' a man's voice said.

I looked up into the grinning face of Jim Gable. He wore a tweed sports coat and tan slacks and shined loafers and a pink shirt with a silver horse monogrammed on the pocket. There was only a yellow discoloration around one eye and the corner of his mouth from the blows he had taken at the Shrimp Festival.

He looked up at the gallery where an old man in overalls and a little boy sat on a wood bench, drinking soda pop and cracking peanuts.

'That's a mean-looking lug wrench in your hand. You're not in a volatile mood, are you?' he said.

'Not in the least, Jim.'

'Don't get up. I suspect you've already bothered my wife. I'll get the feedback from her later,' he said.

He walked past me, on up the steps and across the gallery, through the screen door and into the store. He shook hands with people, then opened the screen again in a gentlemanly fashion to let an elderly lady enter. I fitted the spare onto the axle and tightened down the wheel nuts and lowered the jack, then went inside the store.

Gable sat at a table with a checkerboard painted on top of it, drinking from a paper cup filled with coffee. The inside of the store smelled like cheese and lunch meat and microwave boudin and the green sawdust that was scattered on the floor. I turned a chair around and sat down facing Gable.

He grinned at me as he had outside, but his eyes wouldn't hold on mine.

'Remeta missed you with double-ought bucks? Maybe he's slipping. I'd hate to have him on my case,' I said.

He pulled at his collar and looked sideways out the window at the abandoned nightclub next door and the old Jax beer sign swinging on its chains.

'You don't have any idea of what's going on, do you?' he said.

'I don't have to. Time and Remeta are on my side.'

A family dressed in Sunday clothes came in, folding umbrellas, blowing and laughing at the rain.

'I've pulled your sheet. You have a violent, alcoholic history. You've spent a whole career discrediting yourself,' he said.

I stared directly into Gable's eyes.

'I know you murdered my mother. I know the words she spoke just before you and your partner killed her. "My name's Mae Robicheaux. My boy fought in Vietnam. My husband was Big Aldous Robicheaux." I'm going to smoke you myself or be there when you ride the needle, Jim,' I said.

He kept his eyes on mine now, so he would not have to look at the people who were staring at us from the grocery counter.

'I'm going to walk out of here now. These are my neighbors. You're not going to do anything. I'm carrying a weapon, but my hands are on the table. Everyone can see that,' he said.

'I promised Boots I wouldn't repeat my old behavior. I'm usually pretty good about keeping my word, Jim, but I'm just human. Also, I want you to understand the nature of our relationship and to form an idea of what will probably happen whenever we meet. So, in that spirit—' I said, and balled up my fist inside my cloth glove and leaned across the table and hooked him in the eye and knocked him into a stack of canned vegetables.

32

Wednesday evening Alafair was eating at an outdoor table at the McDonald's on East Main when a red car pulled into the parking lot and a young man wearing a freshly pressed white shirt and starched khakis and sunglasses and a straw hat got out and walked toward her.

He stood in front of her, the fingers of one hand touching the tabletop, his face expressionless behind his sunglasses.

'Can I sit down?' he asked.

'You shouldn't be here, Johnny. People are looking for you,' she replied.

'That's nothing new.' He glanced over his shoulder at a Cherokee filled with high school kids in the parking lot. They were listening to white rap music that beat like a fist on the walls of the restaurant. He sat down at the table. 'Take a ride with me.'

'Dave says you beat up a black woman in the Loreauville Quarters. For no reason,' she said.

'I'm sorry about that. I got strange stuff that goes off in my head sometime. I told the woman that. That's the way it flushes sometime.'

The rap music from the Cherokee increased in intensity. He turned irritably and glared at the kids inside the vehicle. One of them threw a box of trash out on the pavement. Alafair looked at Remeta's hands. For some reason they weren't like those of an artist any longer. They were knobbed with bone and they curled spasmodically into fists, as though he wanted to crush something inside them. He turned back to her and stared at her expression.

'You got something on your mind?' he asked.

'Your arms are sunburned,' she said.

'I was out on Lake Fausse Pointe. It's full of herons and cranes and flooded cypress. It's beautiful.'

'I have to go now.'

'No,' he said, and placed his hand across her wrist. He leaned toward her, his mouth parting to speak, but the kids in the Cherokee had turned up their stereo even louder and he looked at them again over his shoulder. A pop can flew out of the Cherokee's window and clattered across the pavement.

'Wait here a minute,' Remeta said, and got up from the table.

He walked to the Cherokee and picked up all the Styrofoam cups and hamburger containers and dirty napkins that had been thrown on the pavement and stood with them at the driver's window.

'Turn off the radio,' he said.

The high school kid behind the wheel stopped talking to the others in the vehicle and looked dumbly at Remeta, then began turning down the dial on the stereo until the sound bled away into silence.

'You guys are seriously pissing me off,' Remeta said, pushing the trash through the window. 'The next time I see you throwing garbage on the ground, I'm going to kick the shit out of you. And if I hear that rap music again, I'm going to tear your stereo out of the dashboard and shove it up your ass. Now get out of here.'

The driver started the Cherokee, grinding the starter, and bounced out onto the street, while his passengers looked back white-faced at Remeta.

He sat back down at the table, his eyes following the Cherokee down the street.

'That was mean,' she said.

'They deserve worse.'

'I'm going to the library now.'

'I'll drive you there. We can meet later.'

'No.'

'I had to shoot that guy. The one in the fire in New Orleans. He was sent to kill me.'

'Don't tell me about it. It's disgusting.'

There were shards of color in his cheeks and throat.

'I can't believe you're talking to me like that. Who did this to us, Alafair?' he said.

'You did. Go away, Johnny.'

She could not see his eyes through his dark glasses, but his head protruded on his neck toward her, and his breath seemed to reach out and touch her cheek like a dirty finger.

Then he drew his hand back off the table, his skin squeaking on the surface.

'The vase I gave you? I want you to break it. You're not one of the people in that painting anymore, Alafair,' he said.

He got up from his seat and stared down at her, his silhouette motionless against the late sun. She could see her reflection in his glasses. She looked small and diminished, her image distorted, as though it were she who was morally impaired and not he.

After a long moment, as though he had reviewed his judgment, he said, 'You're just a little traitor. That's all you ever were.'

She waited until he had driven out of the parking lot, then went to the pay phone and dialed 911.

Two days later Wally, the dispatcher, buzzed my office phone.

'There's a guy out here says he's Goldie Bierbaum from New Orleans,' he said.

'Send him back.'

'Didn't he fight Cleveland Williams?'

'Goldie fought everybody.'

A minute later I saw Goldie at my door. Even though he was almost seventy, his chest was still flat-plated, his muscular thighs wider than his waist. Before he had opened his saloon on Magazine back in the 1960s, he had fought in three weight divisions and had been a contender in two.

Goldie sat down and put a gumball in his mouth and offered the remaining one in his palm to me.

'Not right now,' I said.

'That button man you were looking for, the one who did Zipper Clum, you still after him?' he asked. His few strands of hair were coated with gel and looked like copper wire stretched across his scalp.

'Yeah, he's a real headache,' I said.

'I hear he's been living on Camp Street. He boosts cars all over the neighborhood, like the Garden District is the Hertz company.'

'Thanks, anyway, Goldie. That place burned down last week. Our man has moved on.'

'You're kidding?'

'Why didn't you report him to NOPD?'

'I don't have a good history with those guys.'

'Tell me, you remember a cop named Jim Gable, from back in the sixties?'

'Sure. He was a bum.'

'In what way?'

'He did scut work for the Giacanos.'

'You positive about that?'

'Hey, Dave, I got into Didoni Giacano for ten large. The vig was four hundred a week. You know how it works. The principal don't ever go down. I was late a couple of times and Gable came by and picked it up. He'd leave the woman in the cruiser and drink a cup of coffee in back and talk about the weather like we were old friends. But he was a bum.'

'What woman?'

'She was a rookie. Maybe she didn't know what was going on. She's big shit in Baton Rouge. You know, what's-her-name, Deshotel, she's the attorney general now.'

That same evening Jim Gable told his wife he was going to cut his losses, take early retirement, and move the two of them to New Mexico. Dana Magelli had actually sicced IAD on him. Could you believe it? Two plainclothes picked him up in the mayor's office and grilled him down at the district like a perp. A pair of polyester desk pilots who smelled like hair oil and made grade by jamming up other cops.

'What's your association with Maggie Glick?' one of them asked.

'I don't have one.'

'That's not what she says.'

'Let me give you guys a short history lesson,' Gable said. 'This used to be a good city. We knew who and where everybody was. People say they don't like vice. What they mean is they don't like it uncontrolled. We'd tell the dagos somebody was out of line and they'd throw him off a roof. Muggers got their noses broken with a blackjack. The whores didn't spread clap through the tourist trade. That's the way the old days were, boys. Go back to Dana Magelli and tell him to open a fruit stand.'

Jim Gable stood in his den, surrounded by his collection of ordnance, and drank from a glass of whiskey and ice. He opened a mahogany humidor and took a plump cigar from it and gingerly bit off the tip and lit it.

He could probably get around the IAD investigation. He was too high up in the department, too long term, and he knew too many secrets about the misdeeds of others to be a sacrificial offering now. When a police department got hosed, a few street cops and midlevel functionaries took the heat and did the time, if any indeed was ever forthcoming.

The real problem was this guy Johnny Remeta. How did he, Jim Gable, get mixed up with a psychopath, particularly one who could boost cars all over the state, smoke two police officers, and walk through walls as though he were invisible?

He didn't like to think about Remeta. Perps and lowlifes were predictable as a class. Most of them were dumb and did everything in their power to get caught. They sought authority in their lives and attention from father figures and were too stupid to know it. Remeta was different. He brought both intelligence and genuine psychosis to his work, a combination that made Gable swallow unconsciously when he thought about it.

He picked up the jar containing the head of a Viet Cong from the table and set it on the mantel in front of the mirror. The head wobbled slightly in the yellow fluid and nudged against the glass, the slitted eyes staring up at Gable. It gave him a sense of comfort to be able to pick up the jar and move it wherever he wanted, although he wasn't sure why. He looked out the window at the fall colors in the trees and the glitter of the sunset on the bay, and he wanted to wedge a revolver in the mouth of Johnny Remeta and blow the back of his head off.

His mood was broken by the sound of his wife dropping something in the bedroom.

'Dear, would you come in, please? I can't bend over to get my cane,' she called.

He went into her bedroom and picked it up for her, then had to help her out of bed. She had not dressed that day and was still in her nightgown, and she smelled like Vicks VapoRub and sour milk. Her hand clung to his wrist after she was on her feet and in her slippers.

'Let's have dinner out on the terrace. It's such a lovely evening. I'll order from the restaurant and have them bring it down,' she said.

'That'll be fine, Cora.'

'Would you do a favor for me?' she asked, smiling wistfully. She wore no makeup, but there were gin roses in her cheeks and a merry light in her eyes. He nodded, then shivered at the prospect of what she might ask.

'Would you rub my feet? They ache terribly when the season changes,' she said.

But he knew what that meant. At first it would be her feet, then her back and neck, and at some point she would touch him on the cheek and let her fingers trail down his sternum and come to rest on his thigh. A visceral sensation washed through him and made his scalp tighten against the bone.

'I'm going through the accounts now. Can I fix you another drink and join you later on the terrace?' he said.

That was smart, he thought. She couldn't expect him to perform romantically on the terrace.

But when he looked at her face, the pinched mouth, the eyes that were suddenly masked, he knew she had seen through him.

'I'll call the restaurant now. But do fix me a drink, and bring my medicine from the cabinet, would you, please? I hate to be a bother. I am a bother, aren't I?' she said.

He hated the tone in her voice. She was the cloying victim and martyr now, a role she was a master at. Her entire personality was a snake pit of neurotic aberrations. He never knew which one was going to slither out on the floor.

He took a bottle of vodka out of the icebox and placed it on a silver tray with a Gibson glass and a jar of tiny pearl onions and a demitasse spoon and set the tray out on the terrace. In the distance he could see a boat with a red sail disappearing over the horizon, and he wanted to be on the boat, the salt breeze in his face, a new life waiting for him somewhere in the Caribbean.

He just had to be patient. Every quart of gin or vodka she drank was like lighting a Chinese firecracker in her heart. She probably had over nine million in her portfolio at Piper, Jaffray. Even after he paid the tax on the capital gains, he could begin construction on his quarter horse track in New Mexico and still be able to live on a ranch in the high desert country and keep a cabin cruiser on the Texas coast.

Not bad for a working-class kid who actually walked a night beat in the Irish Channel.

He went back into the den and picked up his whiskey and ice and sipped from it. Through the window he heard Cora on the remote phone, calling the restaurant for a delivery. He just didn't know if he could bear another evening at home with her. He pulled open a side drawer on his cherrywood desk and removed an address book and thumbed through the names inside. He had entered only the initials beside the telephone numbers of the Mexican, Puerto Rican, and black girls who one way or another had come under his sway. There were over three dozen sets of initials in the book.

Some might consider him profligate, he thought. But so what? Long ago he had learned that most people admired the pagan virtues rather than the Christian ones, particularly in their leaders, no matter what they said. Libido and power and success and creativity were interchangeable characteristics of the human personality. Ask any woman whether she preferred a lover who radiated a quiet sense of power and confidence or one who was self-effacing and pliant. If he was lucky, Cora would drink herself unconscious and he could make a call and meet a woman at a motel in Grand Isle. Why not? He could be back in three hours.

But the quickening of his heart already told him why not.

In his mind's eye he saw himself on an empty stretch of highway, in the dark, the walls of sugarcane twelve feet high on each side of him. Then a tire went flat or a fan belt broke, and while he was jacking up the car or staring down at a steaming radiator a car pulled in behind him, the high beams on, but the driver remained behind the wheel, faceless, letting him burn with apprehension in the headlights' glare.

A film of perspiration had formed on his forehead and he drank from his whiskey. But the ice had melted and the whiskey tasted as though it had been aged inside oily wood. Why was his heart beating so rapidly? Was he a coward, afraid to go down the road because of this kid Remeta?

No. He was just using his judgment. Remeta was a cop killer. The odds were good that if cornered Remeta would never make the jail. All Jim Gable had to do was wait.

He was hungry. He washed his face and hands and combed his hair in the bathroom mirror and went into the kitchen and opened the icebox. It was virtually empty. He pulled back the sliding door on the terrace and went outside. She lay supine on a reclining chair, her face rosy with vodka, her teeth yellow in the waning light.

'Hungry, dear?' she said.

'Yes.'

'You've always been a hungry little boy, haven't you?'

'I'd appreciate it if you wouldn't talk to me like that, Cora.'

'Well, your dinner will be here shortly. You'll see.'

'Thank you,' he said, and went back inside and slid the glass door shut.

How long had her mother lived? Ninety-six years? Good God! Maybe not even a quart of booze a day could kill genes like that. What a horrible thought. No, he was not going to have thoughts like that.

To hell with Johnny Remeta, he told himself. He called the beeper number of a woman in New Orleans, and a half hour later she called him back. Her nickname was Safety Pin Sue, a mindless, totally dependent addict who took a narcissistic pleasure in her own self-destruction.

'Meet me in Grand Isle tonight,' he said.

'For you, Jim, anywhere, anytime,' she said, her voice warm with crack.

That was more like it, he thought.

He tonged fresh ice into his drink and gazed out the high window at the darkening greenness of the land, the gold light trapped on the bay's horizon, the sailboat that had turned around and was tacking for home. He raised his drink in salute to the evening.

That's when he heard a vehicle under the porte cochere. He opened the middle drawer of his desk and removed a blue-black .38 revolver and let it hang loosely from his hand.

The house puffed with wind when Cora opened the side door onto the drive.

'That smells delicious. Bring it into the kitchen, would you? My purse is on the table,' Cora's voice said.

Jim Gable replaced the revolver in the drawer and closed it and finished his drink. The wind was picking up, and a red leaf tore loose from a maple

722

and plastered itself against the window. For some reason the leaf, its symmetrical perfection arbitrarily terminated by a gust of cold air, made Jim Gable brood upon an old prospect that he had tried to bury on the edges of his consciousness for many years. Was it just mortality? No, it was the darkness that lay beyond it and the possibilities the darkness contained.

Don't have those thoughts. They're the products of old wives' tales, he told himself, and turned to the mirror above the mantel and started to comb his hair, then realized he had just combed it.

He heard Cora's stoppered cane scudding softly on the floor behind him.

'This is my husband,' she said. 'Jim, this is the young man who delivered our dinner. I can't find my checkbook. Do you have some cash?'

Gable looked into the mirror and saw his own startled expression and the floating head of the Vietnamese soldier and the reflected face of Johnny Remeta, like three friends gathered together for a photograph. The teeth of the dead Vietnamese were exposed at the corner of his mouth, as though he were trying to smile.

33

On the following Tuesday the early edition of the *Daily Iberian* said Letty Labiche had been moved from St Gabriel Prison to the Death House at Angola. Belmont Pugh held what he said was his 'last TV news conference on the matter' on the steps of the capitol building. He used a passive voice and told reporters 'the death warrant has been signed and will be carried out tomorrow at midnight. It's out of my hands. But I'll be waiting by the telephone up to the last second.' He turned his face into the sunrise and presented a solemn profile to the camera.

Helen and I went to lunch together and were walking back from the parking lot to the department when a deputy in uniform passed us.

'The old man's looking for you,' he said.

'What's up?'

'Nothing much. Your man Purcel is trying to destroy St Martinville. They use animal darts on people?' he replied.

Inside, I stopped by my mailbox. It was filled with pink message slips. Three of them were from the St Martin Parish Sheriff's Department. Two others were from Dana Magelli. Another simply stated, in capital letters, 'SEE ME!' The sheriff's initials were at the bottom. I walked down to his office and opened the door.

'What's going on?' I asked.

'I don't quite know where to start. Where's your beeper?'

'Wally sat on it. That's not a joke.'

'Dana Magelli called. Remeta got into Jim Gable's house, locked the wife in the garage, and kidnapped Gable.'

'Too bad. What's the deal with Purcel?'

'I knew you'd be torn up over Gable.'

'Come on, skipper. What's Clete done?'

'He's in a bar in St Martinville. Three bikers are already in the hospital.' I started to speak, but he held his hand up. 'He broke a pool cue across a city cop's face. It's not the barroom follies anymore, Dave. He might get his light blown out. Everybody around here, including me, is sick of this guy.'

Helen Soileau and I drove the nine miles to St Martinville in under ten minutes. The square by the old French church and the Evangeline Oak was filled with emergency vehicles, and the feeder streets were blocked to keep out traffic. We parked the cruiser a hundred feet from the bar where Clete was barricaded and walked up to a black police lieutenant with a thin mustache who stood with a bullhorn behind the open door of his vehicle. The windows of the bar were shattered, and the wall above one of them was scorched black and dripping with fire retardant.

I fanned the reek of tear gas out of my face.

'The shell hit the windowsill and started a fire. You're friends with this character?' the lieutenant said.

'Yeah. He's generally harmless,' I said.

'Oh, I can see that,' the lieutenant said. His name was Picard and he was a Vietnam veteran who had gone away to school on the GI Bill and earned a degree in criminal justice. 'I've got an officer in the hospital. The inside of that bar is totally destroyed. He beat those bikers till they cried and got down on their knees. You either get your friend out of there, and I mean in cuffs, or we cool him out.'

'I think we're overreacting to the situation, Loot,' I said.

'Are you hearing anything I say? He has the bartender's shotgun,' Picard replied.

'Bullshit,' Helen said, and pulled the bullhorn from Picard's hand. 'Hey, Clete. It's Helen Soileau. Dave and I are coming in,' she said into the horn, its echo resonating under the bar's colonnade. Then she threw the horn back into Picard's hands.

We pushed open the front door and went inside. Chairs and tables were broken; glass littered the floor; the liquor bottles on the counter behind the bar had been smashed into jagged shells. In one corner, by the pool table, was the unconscious form of a head-shaved and tattooed man dressed in jeans and a leather vest with no shirt underneath.

Clete sat at the end of the bar, grinning, his scalp bleeding on his face, his slacks and tropical shirt stained with tobacco juice and talc, a can of Budweiser by his fingers. A twenty-gauge, single-load shotgun rested against the inside of his thigh, the barrel pointed toward his chest.

'Is there a safety on that thing?' I asked.

'I haven't checked,' he replied.

'What the hell's the matter with you?' Helen said, glass snapping under her shoes.

'It's just been that kind of morning,' he said.

'We need to hook you up,' I said.

'Bad idea, Streak.'

'Beats being dead. That's the itinerary outside,' Helen said.

He touched the corner of his mouth with the ball of one finger and looked at the wet spot on his skin. His eyes were lighted, his cheeks filled with color.

'The cop I took down with the cue? He tried to rip my head off with a baton,' he said.

Helen removed her handcuffs from the leather case on her belt, her eyes never leaving Clete's, and threw them on the bar.

'Hook yourself up, handsome,' she said.

'Nope,' he said, and smiled at her with his eyes and lifted his beer can to his mouth.

I stepped beyond Clete's angle of vision and made a motion with my head toward the front of the building. Helen walked with me across the broken glass until we were at the door. Clete salted his beer can, the shotgun still resting between his legs, as though the events taking place around him had no application in his life.

'When you hear it start, come running. Tell the locals we swarm him. If one of them draws a weapon, I'm going to stuff it sideways down his throat,' I said.

I walked behind the bar, across the duckboards, and opened a bottle of carbonated water and sat down next to Clete. I glanced at the biker who lay unconscious in the corner.

'You didn't kill him, did you?' I said.

'They were eating reds in the john. It was like beating up on cripples. I don't see the big deal here,' Clete said.

'The big deal is I think you want to go to jail. You're trying to fix it so you won't get bail, either.'

There was a self-amused light in his face. 'Save the psychobabble for meetings,' he said.

'You'll be in lockup. Which means no trip up to the Death House tomorrow night.'

He lowered his head and combed his hair back with his nails.

'I've already been. This weekend. I took Passion. Letty got to have a dinner with some of her relatives,' he said.

The whites of his eyes looked yellow, as though he had jaundice. I waited for him to go on. He picked up his beer can, but it was empty.

'I need some whiskey,' he said.

'Get it yourself.'

He got up and tripped, stumbling with the shotgun against the stool. Unconsciously he started to hand me the gun, then he grinned sleepily and took it with him behind the bar.

'Up on the top shelf. You broke everything down below,' I said.

He dragged a chair onto the duckboards. When he mounted the chair, he propped the shotgun against a tin sink. I leaned over the bar and grabbed the barrel and jerked the shotgun up over the sink. He looked down curiously at me.

'What do you think you're doing, Dave?' he asked.

I broke open the breech, pulled out the twenty-gauge shell, and tossed the shotgun out the front door onto the sidewalk.

Helen came through the door with one city cop and two sheriff's deputies. I went over the top of the bar just as Clete was climbing down from the chair and locked my arms around his rib cage. I could smell the sweat and beer in his clothes and the oily heat in his skin and the blood in his hair. I wrestled with him the length of the duckboards, then we both fell to the floor and the others swarmed over him. Even drunk and dissipated, his strength was enormous. Helen kept her knee across the back of his neck, while the rest of us bent his arms into the center of his back. But I had the feeling that, had he chosen, he could have shaken all five of us off him like an elephant in musth.

Twenty minutes later I sat with him in a holding cell at the city police station. His shirt was ripped down the back, and one shoe was gone, but he looked strangely serene.

Then I said, 'It's not just the execution, is it?'

'No,' he said.

'What is it?'

'I'm a drunk. I have malarial dreams. I still get night visits from a mamasan I killed by accident. What's a guy with my record know about anything?' he answered.

I woke before dawn on Wednesday, the last scheduled day of Letty Labiche's life, and walked down the slope through the trees to help Batist open up the shop. A Lincoln was parked by the boat ramp in the fog, its doors locked.

'Whose car is that up there?' I asked Batist.

'It was here when I come to work,' he said.

I unchained our rental boats and hosed down the dock and started the fire in the barbecue pit. The sunlight broke through the trees and turned the Lincoln the color of an overly ripe plum. Water had begun streaming from the trunk. I touched the water, which felt like it had come from a refrigerator, and smelled my hand. At 8 a.m. I called the department and asked Helen Soileau to run the tag.

She called back ten minutes later.

'It was stolen out of a parking lot in Metairie two days ago,' she said.

'Get ahold of the locksmith, would you, and ask the sheriff if he'd mind coming out to my house,' I said.

'Has this got something to do with Remeta?' she asked.

The sun was hot and bright by the time the sheriff and the locksmith and a tow truck got to the dock. The sheriff and I stood at the trunk of the Lincoln while the locksmith worked on it. Then the sheriff blew his nose and turned his face into the wind.

'I hope we'll be laughing about a string of bigmouth bass,' he said.

The locksmith popped the hatch but didn't raise it.

'Y'all be my guests,' he said, and walked toward his vehicle.

I flipped the hatch up in the air.

Jim Gable rested on his hip inside a clear-plastic wardrobe bag that was pooled at the bottom with water and pieces of melting ice the size of dimes. His ankles and arms were pulled behind him, laced to a strand of piano wire that was looped around his throat. He had inhaled the bag into his mouth, so that he looked like a guppy trying to breathe air at the top of an aquarium.

'Why'd Remeta leave him here?' the sheriff asked.

'To show me up.'

'Gable was one of the cops who killed your mother?'

'He told me I didn't know what was going on. He knew Johnny had cut a deal with somebody.'

'With who?'

When I didn't reply, the sheriff said, 'What a day. A molested and raped girl is going to be executed, and it takes a psychopath to get rid of a bad cop. Does any of that make sense to you?'

I slammed the hatch on the trunk.

'Yeah, if you think of the planet as a big blue mental asylum,' I said.

34

As a police officer I had learned years ago a basic truth about all aberrant people: They're predictable. Their nemesis is not a lack of intelligence or creativity. Like the moth that wishes to live inside flame, the obsession that drives them is never satiated, the revenge against the world never adequate.

Johnny Remeta called the office at two o'clock that afternoon.

'How'd you like your boy?' he asked.

'You've killed three cops, Johnny. I don't think you're going to make the jail.'

'They all had it coming. Tell me I'm wrong.'

'You've been set up, kid.'

After a beat, he said, 'Alafair wants to be a screen writer. Tell her to write better lines for you.'

'You cut a deal. You thought you were going to pop Gable and have it all,' I said.

'Good try,' he said. But the confidence had slipped in his voice.

'Yeah? The same person who sent you to kill Gable gave orders to the Louisiana State Police to shoot you on sight. There are two Texas Rangers sitting outside my office right now. Why is that? you ask yourself. Because you whacked a couple of people in Houston, and these two Rangers are mean-spirited peckerwoods who can't wait to blow up your shit. You wonder why your mother dumped you? It's no mystery. You're a born loser, kid.'

'You listen—' he said, his voice starting to shake.

'Think I'm lying? Ask yourself how I know all this stuff. I'm just not that smart.'

He began to curse and threaten me, but the transmission was breaking up and his voice sounded like that of a man trying to shout down an electric storm.

I hung up the receiver and looked out the glass partition in my office at the empty corridor, then began filling out some of the endless paperwork that found its way to my basket on an hourly basis.

I tried to keep my head empty the rest of the afternoon, or to occupy myself with any task that kept my mind off the fate of Letty Labiche or the razor wire I had deliberately wrapped around Johnny Remeta's soul. I called the jail in St Martinville and was told Clete Purcel had thrown his food tray in a hack's face and had been moved into an isolation cell.

'Has he been arraigned yet?' I asked.

'Arraigned?' the deputy said. 'We had to Mace and cuff and leg-chain him to do a body search. You want this prick? We'll transfer him to Iberia Prison.'

At 4:30 I went outside and walked through St Peter's Cemetery. My head was thundering, the veins tightening in my scalp. The sky was like a bronze bowl, and dark, broad-winged birds that made no sound drifted across it. I wanted this day to be over; I wanted to look at the rain-worn grave markers of Eighth and Eighteenth Louisiana Infantry who had fought at Shiloh Church; I wanted to stay in a vacuum until Letty Labiche was executed; I wanted to slay my conscience.

I went back into the department and called Connie Deshotel's office in Baton Rouge.

'She's taken a few vacation days, Mr Robicheaux. What with the demonstrations and all outside,' the secretary said.

'Is she at Lake Fausse Pointe?'

'I'm sorry. I'm not at liberty to say,' the secretary replied.

'Will you call her for me and ask her to call me?'

There was a long pause.

'Her phone is out of order. I've reported it to the telephone company,' the secretary said.

'How long has it been out of order?'

'I don't know. I don't understand why you're asking me these questions. Is this an emergency?'

I thought about it, then said, 'Thanks for your time.'

I walked down to Helen Soileau's office and opened her door without knocking. She looked up from her paperwork at my face. She was chewing gum and her eyes were bright and focused with a caffeinated intensity on mine. Then one finger pointed at an empty chair by the side of her desk.

A few minutes later she said, 'Go through that again. How'd you know Remeta was working for Connie Deshotel?'

'The last time Alafair saw him he was sunburned. He said he'd been out on Lake Fausse Pointe. That's where Connie's camp is. Connie was Jim Gable's partner at NOPD back in the sixties. When Remeta tried to shake her down, she got him to hit Gable.'

'How?'

'He's a basket case. He's always looking for the womb.'

'You sure of all this, Dave?'

'No. But Johnny went crazy when I convinced him he'd been betrayed.'

'So you set Connie up?' Before I could reply, she picked up a ballpoint and drew lines on a piece of paper and said, 'You'll never prove she was one of the cops who killed your mother.'

'That's true.'

'Maybe we should just let things play out,' she said. Her eyes drifted back on mine.

I looked out the window. The sky was the color of brass and smoke, and the wind was gusting in the streets.

'A storm is coming in. I have to get out on the lake,' I said.

Helen remained seated in her chair.

'You didn't do Gable. You want to nail Connie Deshotel yourself,' she said.

'The other side always deals the play. You coming or not?'

'Let me be honest with you, bwana. I had a bad night last night. I couldn't get Letty Labiche out of my mind. I guess it's because I was molested myself. So lose the attitude.'

Wally, the dispatcher, stopped us on the way out of the office. He had a pink memo slip in his hand.

'You wasn't in your office. I was fixing to put this in your pigeonhole,' he said to me.

'What is it?'

'A cop in St Martinville said Clete Purcel wants to talk to you. It's suppose to be important,' Wally said.

'I'll take care of it later,' I said.

Wally shrugged and let the memo slip float from his fingers into my box.

Helen and I towed a department outboard on the back of my truck to Loreauville, a few miles up the Teche, then drove through the sugarcane fields to the landing at Lake Fausse Pointe. The wind was blowing hard now, and I could see waves capping out on the lake and red leaves rising in the air against a golden sun.

Helen laced on a life preserver and sat down in the bow of the boat, and I handed her a department-issue cut-down twelve-gauge pump loaded with double-ought buckshot. She kept studying my face, as though she were taking the measure of a man she didn't know.

'You've got to tell me, Dave,' she said.

'What?' I smiled good-naturedly.

'Don't shine me on.'

'If Remeta's there, we call in backup and take him down.'

'That's it?'

'She's the attorney general of Louisiana. What do you think I'm going to do, kill her in cold blood?'

'I know you, Dave. You figure out ways to make things happen.'

'Really?' I said.

'Let's get something straight. I don't like that snooty cunt. I said she was dirty from the get-go. But don't jerk me around.'

I started to say something, then let it go and started the engine. We headed down the canal bordered by cypress and willow and gum trees, then entered the vast lily-dotted expanse of the lake itself.

It was a strange evening. In the east and south the sky was like a black ink wash, but the clouds overhead were suffused with a sulfurous yellow light. In the distance I could see the grassy slope of the levee and the live oaks that shadowed Connie Deshotel's stilt house and the waves from the lake sliding up into the grass and the wildflowers at the foot of her property. An outboard was tied to her dock, straining against its painter, knocking against one of the pilings. Helen sat hunched forward, the barrel of her shotgun tilted away from the spray of water off the bow.

I cut the engine and we drifted on our wake into the shallows, then I speared the bottom with the boat paddle and the hull snugged onto the bank.

The lights were on inside the house and I could hear music playing on a radio. A shadow crossed a screen window. Helen stepped out into the shallows and waded out to the moored boat and placed her hand on the engine's housing.

'It's still warm,' she said, walking toward me, the twelve-gauge in both hands. She studied the house, the skin twitching slightly below her left eye.

'You want to call for backup?' I asked.

'It doesn't feel right,' she said.

'You call it, Helen.'

She thought about it. 'Fuck it,' she said, and pumped a round into the chamber, then inserted a replacement round into the magazine with her thumb.

But she was wired. She had killed three perpetrators on the job, all three of them in situations in which she had unexpectedly walked into hostile fire.

We walked up the slope in the shadows of the live oaks. The air was cool and tannic with the autumnal smell of flooded woods, the windows of the house gold with the western light. I took out my .45 and we mounted the steps and stood on each side of the door.

'Iberia Sheriff's Department, Ms Deshotel. Please step out on the gallery,' I said.

There was no response. I could hear shower water running in the back. I pulled open the screen, and Helen and I stepped inside, crossed the small living room, and looked in the kitchen and on the back porch. Then Helen moved into the hallway and the back bedroom. I saw her stop and lift the shotgun barrel so that it was pointed toward the ceiling.

'You better come in here, Dave. Watch where you step,' she said.

Johnny Remeta lay on top of a white throw rug in his Jockey undershorts, his chest, one cheek, and his arm peppered with five entry wounds. A cut-down Remington twelve-gauge was propped in the corner. It was the same pump shotgun he had been carrying when he first visited my dock. He had not gone down all at once. The blood splatter was on the walls, the floor, and the bed sheets, and he had torn one of the curtains on the doors that gave onto a roofed deck.

The doors were open and I could see a redwood table on the deck, and on top of it a green bottle of wine, a platter of sandwiches, a package of filter-tipped cigarettes, Connie's gold-and-leather-encased lighter, and a big box of kitchen matches with a Glock automatic lying across it. The spent shell casings from the Glock were aluminum reloads and glinted on the deck like fat silver teeth.

I heard a faucet squeak in the bathroom, then the sound of the shower water died inside the stall. Helen pushed open the bathroom door and I saw her eyes go up and down the form of someone inside.

'Put a robe on and get out here, ma'am,' she said.

'Don't worry. I heard you long before you started banging around inside. Call in the report for me, please. My phone's out of order,' Connie Deshotel's voice said.

Helen picked up a pink robe off the toilet tank and flung it at Connie. 'Get your ass out here, ma'am,' she said.

A moment later Connie emerged into the bedroom, flattening her hair back wetly on her head with a hairbrush. She wore no makeup, but her face was calm, dispassionate, ruddy from her warm shower.

'I don't know if I can prove this, Dave, but I think you sent this man after me,' she said.

'You talked Remeta into the sack, then wasted him,' I said.

'He tried to rape me, you idiot. I got my gun out of my bag and shot him through the door. Otherwise I'd be dead.' Then she said 'God!' between her teeth, and started to walk past us, as though we were only incidental elements in her day. Her slippers tracked Remeta's blood across the floor.

Helen pushed her in the chest with her fingers. 'You're tainting a crime scene. You don't do anything until we tell you,' she said.

'Touch my person again and you'll be charged with battery,' Connie said. '*What?*'

'I'm the chief law officer of Louisiana. Does that register with you at all? A psychopath tried to rape and sodomize me. Do you think I'm going to let you come in here and treat me like a perpetrator? Now, get out of my way.'

Helen's face was bright with anger, a lump of cartilage flexing against her jaw. But no words came out of her mouth.

'Are you deaf as well as stupid? I told you to get out of my way,' Connie said.

Helen held the shotgun at port arms and shoved Connie through the side door onto the deck. 'Sit in that chair, you prissy bitch,' she said, and snipped a cuff on Connie's left wrist and hooked the other end to the handle on a huge earthen pot that was planted with bougainvillea.

'Are you placing me under arrest? I hope you are, because I'm going to ensure you live in penury the rest of your life,' Connie said.

'No, I'm restricting you from a crime scene. You want my job, you can have it,' Helen said.

I could hear lightning popping in the swamp and raindrops striking the tin roof. Helen began punching in numbers on her cell phone, then she hit the phone against the wall.

'I can't get through. I'm going out front,' she said.

I followed her into the living room.

'Take it easy,' I said.

'She's gonna walk.'

'There's no statute of limitations on homicide. We'll get her sooner or later.'

'That's not enough. When they blow somebody apart and take a shower and then get in your face, it's not enough. It's not nearly enough,' she said.

I put my hand on her arm, but she stepped away from me. 'Just let me do my job. Not everybody in this world is a member of the walking wounded,' she said, and flipped the shotgun's barrel up on her shoulder and pushed open the screen door and went out on the front porch, punching in numbers on her cell phone with her thumb.

I went back through the bedroom onto the deck. Connie Deshotel was gazing into the distance, at a heron, perhaps, or at her plans for her future or perhaps at nothing.

'When you and Jim Gable killed my mother, she took back her married name,' I said.

'Excuse me?' Connie said.

'Right before she died she told you her name was Mae Robicheaux. Y'all took her life, Connie, but she took back her soul. She had the kind of courage you and Jim Gable couldn't dream about.'

'If you want to charge me with a crime, that's your prerogative. Otherwise, please shut up.'

'You ever think about what lies beyond the grave?'

'Yes. Worms. Will you unlock this handcuff and keep that ridiculous woman away from me?'

I looked at her eyes, the sun-bleached tips of her wet hair, the healthy glow of her skin. There was no dark aura surrounding the head, no tuberous growth wrapping its tentacles around the spirit, no guilty attempt to avoid the indictment in my stare. She was one of those who could rise early and rested in the morning, fix tea and buttered toast, and light the ovens in Dachau.

I gave it up. I couldn't look at her face any more. Connie Deshotel's eyes had once contained the reflected image of my mother dying on a strip of frozen ground between fields of sugarcane that creaked with ice, whose clattering in the wind was probably the last sound my mother ever heard. Whatever Connie had done or seen that winter day long ago meant nothing to her, and when I looked into the moral vacuity of her eyes I wanted to kill her.

I turned my back to her and leaned on the deck railing and looked out at the rain falling on the lake. Out of the corner of my eye I saw her shake a cigarette out of her pack and place it in her mouth. Then she picked up her cigarette lighter, the one probably given her by Jim Gable, and snapped it dryly several times. She replaced it on the table and leaned forward, her redwood chair creaking under her, and reached for the box of kitchen matches on which rested the Glock automatic she had used to murder Johnny Remeta.

Simultaneously I heard Helen Soileau say, 'Hey, Dave, the St Martin sheriff's office is trying to patch into you. Clete's going cra—'

That was as far as she got. When she reached the door she saw Connie Deshotel's hand lift the Glock to get to the box of kitchen matches.

Connie's unlit filter-tipped cigarette was still hanging from her mouth when Helen blew most of her head off.

Epilogue

Johnny Remeta took the fall for Connie Deshotel's death. It wasn't hard to arrange. In fact, Johnny had made it easy. His cut-down Remington was already loaded with double-ought bucks. I fired one round out into the trees, slipped the shotgun under his chest, and let the coroner and the state police and the sheriff's deputies from St Martin Parish come to their own conclusions.

It was dishonest, certainly, but I don't think it was dishonorable. In fact, it probably saved Helen Soileau's career. Besides, the print and electronic media loved the story we had created for them, and who could be so unkind as to disabuse them of their romantic fantasies? Connie Deshotel was much more likable as a blue-collar heroine in death than the self-serving political functionary she had been in life.

My own role in her death was not one I cared to think about. I wondered why I didn't unlock Connie's handcuff and allow her to walk outside, away from the crime scene, away from any other confrontations with Helen. There was no evidence to disprove her claim that Remeta had tried to assault her. In fact, I believed at the time, as I do now, that she may have told the truth.

Was it natural to turn my back on my mother's murderer, knowing a pistol lay within ten inches of her grasp? Or was I deliberately incautious? Age has brought me few gifts, but one of them has been a degree of humility, at least a sufficient amount so that I no longer feel compelled to take my own inventory and I can surrender that terrible burden to my Higher Power.

It was late when the paramedics and the coroner and the parish deputies and the state troopers finally wrapped up their work at Connie Deshotel's camp on Lake Fausse Point. The sun was below the horizon in the west, and a green aura from the wooded rim of the swamp rose into the sky. I could hear alligators flopping and nutrias screaming back in the flooded trees, and when the moon came up the bass starting hitting the insects in the center of the lake, chaining the lake's surface with water rings.

I had forgotten all about the call from the St Martin Parish Sheriff's Department. I used Helen's cell phone and got a night deputy at the jail on the line.

'Somebody called earlier. A problem with Clete Purcel,' I said.

'Sonofabitch is spreading chaos all over the lockdown unit. You either quiet him down or he's gonna have an accident with a baseball bat.'

'Put him on,' I said.

'Are you nuts?'

'How'd you like him to do six months with you guys?' I asked.

There was a brief pause. 'Hang on,' the deputy replied.

A few moments later I heard a cell door open and the tinkle of waist or leg chains.

'Hello?' Clete said hoarsely.

'You going to tell me what it is now?' I said.

'When I took Passion up to Angola last weekend? For the dinner with Letty and their relatives? She was wearing a raincoat and that bandanna around her neck. There were two gunbulls outside and a matron inside, but nobody with a lot of smarts. Letty and Passion were going in and out of the john. You get my drift?'

'What are you telling me, Clete?'

'On the way back home Passion was like somebody I didn't know. Weirded out. Crying. Looking out the side window into the dark. I told her I'd be there when Letty went to the table. She said she wasn't going back up to the Death House. Just like that. No explanation.'

I could hear him breathing against the phone, his chains tinkling.

'I think they've both made their choice. I think it's time to leave it alone,' I said.

'You've got to give me a better answer than that,' he said.

But I didn't have a better answer. I heard Clete drop the receiver and let it swing on its cord against the wall. Then someone gathered it up and replaced it in the cradle.

It started to rain again after I got home. I listened to no radio or television that night, and at ten minutes after midnight I put on my raincoat and hat and walked down to the bait shop and turned on the string of lights over the dock and the flood lamps that shone on the bayou and every light in every corner of the shop. I fixed coffee and mopped down the floors and cut and trimmed bread for sandwiches and said my rosary on my fingers and listened to the rain beating on the roof until it became the only sound in my head. Then I realized I was not listening to rain anymore but to hail that bounced and smoked on the dock and melted into white string on the flood lamps, and I wanted to stay forever inside the lighted, cool brilliance of the dock and bait shop, and to keep Bootsie and Alafair there with me and let the rest of the world continue in its fashion, its cities and commerce and inhumanity trapped between morning and the blackness of the trees.

But it was I who would not let the world alone. The next day I drove out to the Labiche home and was told by a tall, high-yellow mulatto I had never seen before that Passion was at the nightclub, preparing to open up. He wore a mustache and tasseled, two-tone shoes and dark blue zoot pants with a white stitch in them and a black cowboy snap-button shirt with red flowers on it and a planter's straw hat cocked at an angle on his head.

'How's she feeling?' I said.

'Ax her,' he said.

'Excuse me, but who are you?'

'What do you care, Jack?' he said, and closed the door in my face.

Passion's pickup truck was the only vehicle in the nightclub's parking lot. I went in the side door and saw a woman at the antique piano by the back wall. She was totally absorbed in her music and was not aware that anyone else was in the building. Her powerful arms lifted and expanded in silhouette as she rolled her fingers up and down the yellowed keys. I couldn't identify the piece she was playing, but the style was unmistakable. It was Albert Ammons, Jerry Lee Lewis, and Moon Mulligan; it was out of the barrelhouse South of fifty years ago; it was Memphis and Texas R&B that could break your heart.

The woman at the piano stool wore jeans and an LSU T-shirt. A streak of gold sunlight fell across her neck like a sword, and on her neck was a tattooed red rose inside a cluster of green leaves.

She finished her song, then seemed to realize someone was standing behind her. She stayed very still, her hair lifting on her neck in the breeze from the fan, then closed the top on the piano keys.

'You want something?' she said, without turning around.

'No. Not really,' I replied.

'You figured it out?'

'Like Clete Purcel says, "What do I know?"'

'You think bad of me?'

'No.'

'My sister was brave. A lot braver than me,' she said.

'The dude at your house looks like he's in the life.'

'It's a life, ain't it?'

'I never heard anybody do "Pine Top's Boogie" as well as you. Don't sell yourself short, kiddo,' I said, and squeezed her on the shoulder and walked outside into the sunlight.

This story has only a brief postscript, and it's not a very dramatic one. Yesterday a package wrapped in white butcher paper arrived in the mail. In it were an old scrapbook with a water-faded purple binder and an envelope taped across the binder's surface. The letter read as follows:

Dear Mr Robicheaux,

Enclosed please find an item that evidently belonged to your mother. When the quarters were torn down, a number of such personal belongings were placed in a storage shed by my father, who was kind and thoughtful toward his workers, white and Negro alike, regardless of what his detractors have written about him.

It is not my responsibility to hold on to the discarded memorabilia of people to whom it obviously did not have great import. Frankly, you have proved a great disappointment. You besmirched my husband's name, and it would not surprise me that you are responsible for the rumor that I deliberately admitted a murderer to my home in order to rid myself of my husband. I understand you invested much of your life in drunkenness. Perhaps you should seek help.

Sincerely,
Cora Gable

I flipped through the pages of the scrapbook, stiff with photos and postcards and ticket stubs and sealed locks of hair and pressed flowers that had been glued in place with brush and jar. There was a wedding photo of her and Big Aldous taken in front of the brick cathedral in Abbeville; a menu from the restaurant in the old Jung Hotel in New Orleans, where she and Big Al had their honeymoon; a newspaper article from the *Daily Iberian* about my return from Vietnam; another article about my graduating from the New Orleans Police Academy.

The next ten pages, the only ones remaining in the book, were filled with articles from both the *Times-Picayune* and the *Daily Iberian* about my career. Inside the back of the binder she had pasted a newspaper photograph of me in uniform, leaning on a cane, and below it a photo of me taken in third grade at the Catholic elementary school. She had created a frame around the two pictures by gluing strips of pink ribbon along the borders of the binder.

My mother had been virtually illiterate and was probably not sure of the content of many of the articles she had saved. Nor was she able to make annotations in her scrapbook to indicate what the articles meant to her. But I knew who my mother was. She had said it to her killers before she died. Her name was Mae Robicheaux. And I was her son.